"YOU'RE NO SCHOOLGIRL. LOOK AT ME."

Mystere complied to his demand, her eyes wary even in the dimness.

He took her face in both his hands. If the lights had been up, she would have struggled, but no one could see them in the darkness, half-hidden behind thick velvet curtains.

"Please, Mr. Belloch—"

"Rafe. My name is Rafe."

A surge of unwanted emotion caught in her throat. In truth she shouldn't have desired his hands on her face, or the intimacy of using his first name, but the notion of both moved her. And she didn't know why. She didn't even want to know why because it might prove her more vulnerable than she ever thought possible.

"Please, Rafe," she nearly begged. "I'm not the one for you to pursue. Your fascination may even prove dangerous to us both. Believe me, I can't bring anything good to you—"

"You bring to me a kind of truth I've rarely seen in this crowd. I can't help it if I'm drawn to it."

"There is no truth. None," she whispered, her voice harsh with strange, unshed tears.

"You're wrong," he whispered back harshly before his lips crushed hers.

<u>BOOK YOUR PLACE ON OUR WEBSITE</u> <u>AND MAKE THE</u> <u>READING CONNECTION!</u>

We've created a customized website just for our very special readers, where you can get the inside scoop on everything that's going on with Zebra, Pinnacle and Kensington books.

When you come online, you'll have the exciting opportunity to:

- View covers of upcoming books

- Read sample chapters

- Learn about our future publishing schedule (listed by publication month *and author*)

- Find out when your favorite authors will be visiting a city near you

- Search for and order backlist books from our online catalog

- Check out author bios and background information

- Send e-mail to your favorite authors

- Meet the Kensington staff online

- Join us in weekly chats with authors, readers and other guests

- Get writing guidelines

- AND MUCH MORE!

Visit our website at
http://www.kensingtonbooks.com

Moonlight Becomes Her

Meagan McKinney

ZEBRA BOOKS
KENSINGTON PUBLISHING CORP.
http://www.kensingtonbooks.com

To Jude Nicholas Foret—
An Officer and a Gentleman

No other thought . . .

Prologue

September 1881

Rafael Belloch pushed the leather curtain aside as his carriage rolled past City Hall. He thrust his head outside and called up to the driver, "Cut over to Baxter Street."

"But that's Five Points, sir. And dark's coming on."

"Correct on both counts. Now please cut over."

"It's full of rough customers, sir. The cradle of gangs and all that."

"I don't give a tinker's damn. Cut over."

"As you will, sir."

The driver sounded his yard-of-tin to warn other traffic. Then he slapped the reins across the team's glossy rumps, and the japanned coach veered around the next corner.

Rafe left the curtain pulled back and wearily relaxed into the quilted satin seat, watching day bleed into night. A nascent moon had risen over the Upper Bay. From here he could glimpse the shadowy mass where the Manhattan tower of the still uncompleted bridge thrust itself boldly above the skyline over the East River. Its hanging maze of wire cables made a spidery outline against the darkling sky.

The editorials confidently predicted the unwieldy structure would collapse under its own weight any day now. But out west, he had watched his own engineers and workers blast train tunnels through "impenetrable" mountains of sheer granite. The bridge would stand. He would bet on it.

Anything men could dream seemed possible to achieve these days. Some believed the heady age had finally reached the useful limits of all knowledge. But Rafe scorned their smug blindness. Men could blast mountains, build towers to pierce the sky, but they couldn't keep a child from going begging in the dark alleys of Baxter Street. Progress was good for the bank account, but of no avail to the soul—or to the hardened heart of a man who lived mainly for vengeance.

The fast clip-clop of cabriolets and calashes faded behind him as his carriage left the well-maintained streets and blue-stone sidewalks for the crumbling pavements of the slums. For a few moments, before the raucous bray of Five Points enveloped him, it was almost peaceful. So quiet and still he even heard the evening Angelus from St. Patrick's.

By day Baxter Street was no stranger to "respectable" men. Its Lower East Side location made it ideal for many City Hall officials. A man could visit his tobacconist and his whore in one convenient trip, for often they were in the same building.

Rafe knew the area had improved somewhat from the no-torious era when rival gangs publicly broke each other's skulls. Charles Dickens himself had refused to enter its realm without an escort. But that was thirty years ago. A church mission now occupied the once dangerous Old Brewery. Nonetheless, most New Yorkers still avoided Five Points as though it were the mouth of hell, especially after dark. Which was precisely why he insisted on going there time and again—he, an exalted Patriarch of the Four Hundred, Mrs. Astor's elect. The Fifth Avenue Brahmins, as he scornfully called them.

Them? Us, he corrected himself. *Us.*

A drive through Five Points was just the antidote whenever he caught himself becoming complacent. The luxury and status of his newfound wealth was an easy bath in which to sink. He needed the vinegar of poverty to remind him: His role was revenge; revenge upon the very people who embraced him now. The same wretched rich who had caused his family ruin and shame. The same amoral persons who would have cast him to Five Points as a child and never looked back.

Outside, lurid shadows flickered in the gaslights; wooden houses rolled past, rotting and unpainted, interspersed with a few tall brick tenements. Sympathy warred with disgust within him as he glimpsed tramps and bummers, beggars and thieves, murderers, harlots, madmen, grifters. And everywhere the "street arabs," abandoned and orphaned children fending for themselves, competing with the stray dogs for a dry place to sleep.

Wall Street needs one more exchange, he thought. *A squalor exchange.* It was one of the city's most abundant commodities.

Abruptly, the carriage lurched to a stop. A moment later it was in motion again. Just off the Five Points, which was formed by three intersecting streets, was a confusing warren of dark, seedy alleys, home to the gin shops and demimonde rarely acknowledged except in the penny papers. Without warning, the carriage suddenly veered into one of these alleys and stopped again, so abruptly the tug chains rattled.

Rafe had been tossed off the seat in the violent turn. He thrust his head outside. "Wilson, damnit, what in blazes—?"

Before he could finish his question, a slim, well-formed feminine hand shot toward the window and pushed a damp pad under his nose. Rafe managed to avert his face, but not before he breathed in the stench of chloroform. It did not render him unconscious, but had the momentary effect of a stunning blow.

He sprawled back onto the seat, senses reeling. Everything seemed to be a ringing confusion of sounds he could not quite identify. Then someone jerked the door open.

"Climb out, Jack, and do it in one puffin' hurry or I'll shoot an air shaft through you."

Still unsteady, fighting down nausea, Rafe alighted on wobbly feet in the dusty, trash-littered alley. In the gathering twilight he could just make out a big man wearing a sturdy hopsack coat and dirty sailcloth trousers tucked into peg boots. An old dragoon pistol was clutched in his right hand.

Rafe glanced over his own left shoulder and saw a second man up on the box, holding a huge knife to Wilson's throat. Someone thrust a lantern up into Rafe's face, nearly blinding him.

"Look at these fine feathers," the man in the alley exclaimed, feeling the material of Rafe's greatcoat. "Our cornucopia runneth over, darling."

Darling, Rafe quickly realized, was the one holding the lantern—the same woman who had gassed him. A black domino mask obscured half her face, and a scarf of magenta silk sewn with beads restrained her thick dark hair. She wore a patched brown wool skirt and a dingy green velvet jacket that outlined the generous swell of her bosom.

She studied him right back with cool, glistening eyes that peered from behind the black domino like two chips of ice. He might have thought her heart was just as cold except for the unexpected emotion he saw in them. In the startling blue depths was a wounded, reproachful expression that seemed to have nothing to do with him, and everything to do with the world.

It told him she wasn't a completely hardened character. Not yet.

His stare brought a faint smile that lifted one corner of her mouth. The blue eyes flashed but looked away as if she were uncomfortable.

"Surely you recognize him?" she scoffed to her companion, her voice shocking in its refinement. "It's Rafael

Belloch himself. The mountain mover, they call him. He builds tunnels and trestles for the Kansas-Pacific. Or used to, for I hear he's become an owner now."

"God's trousers! You're right, it's Belloch."

The robber up on the box snorted. "Sure, and this is Jay Gould up here."

"It's Belloch, damn you," insisted the large man who held Rafe with the dragoon pistol. "His picture was just in the *Herald*. There, look! Look at the harnesses—plated in gold."

"Of course it's Belloch," the woman's velvet voice affirmed. "His handsome face is not one a woman is likely to forget."

The very next moment, however, her words took on a mocking edge. "You're a long way from Fifth Avenue, Mr. Mountain Mover."

"Perhaps," Rafe replied. His head had cleared, and his fascination for her was quickly melting into outrage. "But I wager the three of you aren't very far from the Ludlow Street jail."

"If we need your opinion," snarled the man standing next to her, his face twisted with coarse insolence, "we'll beat it out of you. Hand over your wallet and watch. And *don't* try any of your fancy parlor tricks here."

Rafe withdrew the pigskin wallet from his inside coat pocket, then the gold watch and chain from his fob pocket and handed them over.

"Your coat, too, Baron," the woman added, her cold, bewitching eyes warming with merriment.

"Baron?" he repeated scornfully as he shrugged out of his greatcoat. "Have I acquired a title now?"

"Yes. You rank high among the peerage of the robber barons."

"If I'm the robber, then perhaps you three should raise your hands, not I."

"He's just whistling past the graveyard," scoffed the man on the box. "Just covering his milk-livered fear."

"Oh, he's not afraid," the woman answered, watching his face closely in the lantern light. "Mr. Belloch is neither timid nor fearful. That sneer on his face right now is not war paint. He's thinking how he'd love to thrash all three of us." She released a wicked, lilting laugh.

"Madam, you read thoughts—do you also interpret spirit knockings and tea leaves? Surely a woman of your obvious beauty and refinement can find a higher station in life than coarse thievery?"

The expression in her eyes darkened. The wounded child he had seen before in her eyes skittered away and hid, as if she was used to cloaking herself in shadows.

Right then Rafe knew one thing: this woman didn't like being reminded she had been born to better things. It was a sore point and most likely a great cause of the wounded expression she sometimes let slip into view.

"This, Mr. Belloch," she assured him coldly, draping his coat over her arm as though it were a blanket of roses, "is much more profitable than going blind doing piecework in a garment factory."

"You're a good one to talk, Belloch," sneered the man on the box, his voice caustic as acid as he tightened the knife on Wilson's throat. "You railroad toffs would steal the coppers from a dead man's eyes. At least we rob our victims honest-like, face-to-face. Your ilk hide on Wall Street and let the banks do your dirty work."

Rafe clamped his teeth rather than retort. He had no illusions about the two men's willingness to kill him. Instead he concentrated on studying the raffish beauty's face. He committed every pleasing feature—those he could see, at least—to memory. Her fine brow, the comely lines of her nose, and the sweet, luscious curve of her lips. He *would* find her again. The unmasking would be a pleasure.

But perhaps he stared too hard. For suddenly the ice appeared in her eyes once more. Wickedly, she said, "Don't stop with the coat, Mr. Belloch. Take the rest of your clothing off, too. It'll all bring a fine penny or two at the rag merchant."

"The rest . . . ? But surely to God you cannot be serious?"

Rafe winced when the muzzle of the dragoon pistol pressed hard into his sternum. "You heard the lady. Peel 'em."

"It's for my hope chest," she informed him, laughing seductively.

He bit back his rage. Tightly, he said, "Bethink yourself my puppetmaster?"

"I *am* thinking, Mr. Belloch. You are clearly a proud and dangerous man. But no man is dangerous when he is naked."

"Is that theory or experience speaking?"

She looked away again. "I want to be sure the first place you go is home. Now disrobe."

"I'll need a bootjack," he insisted sullenly. "These boots are new and they're tight—"

"Plague take him!" the man up on the box burst out. "I'm shooting the bastard."

"No!" She spun around toward the speaker with the grace of a ballerina standing on her pointes. "No shooting!"

She turned toward Rafe again. Closer, he got a better look at her. For a few seconds her eyes were illuminated in the warm light—eyes that became the perfect blue of forget-me-nots.

So she was not all cold. Not all wicked.

"Strip quickly, sir, or I'll change my mind about the shooting." Her words were almost a plea.

Malice heated his blood, but Rafe complied. First he handed over his waistcoat, vest, and shirt of finespun linen. She was not at all bashful about keeping plenty of light on him.

"Who'd have known. The bloke's got muscles as hard as sacked salt," the man atop the carriage said.

Her gaze almost reluctantly wandered along Rafe's sloping pectorals. "I see why you're such a favorite with Mrs. Astor. Quickly, Mr. Belloch, boots and trousers."

The boots were a struggle, and he almost toppled over as he wrenched them off. The thief brandishing the pistol snatched them from his hands. "We ain't good enough to lace these boots, but by Saint Barbara we're good enough to steal 'em."

When the woman had his trousers, Rafe demanded boldly, "Underdrawers, too?"

Despite his angry contempt, her blunt answer caught him flat-footed.

"By all means," she told him. "The preamble has been pleasing, indeed. Don't disappoint me now."

Her faint smile goaded him again.

He hesitated.

"H'ar now!" protested her companion on the box, jumping down. "Never mind his damn skivvies, you little wanton. I'll not be sent to Blackwell's just so you can ogle this fancy man. Let's dust."

The two men pulled her along with them like the hooligan she was. Rafe watched as her sweetly shaped lips curved in another secret smile. She laughed full outright at her fun.

Even as the trio of robbers faded deeper into the murky alley, her taunting voice called out, "I'll always be wondering, Mr. Belloch."

His anger did not abate nor his humiliation. She had just thrown down the gauntlet, and suddenly his will clenched like a fist.

"Then, go ahead and wonder, you impertinent little wench," he muttered to himself.

Let imagination increase her appetite. It certainly would his.

For by all things holy, whatever she was secretly wondering about, Rafe swore she *would* one day find out.

Chapter 1

June 1883

"Ladies and gentlemen," Paul Rillieux announced in a cultivated, resonant voice that showed no sign of his advanced age. "Among our number there exist some who possess the gift—as yet shrouded in mystery—of making contact with powers beyond our physical realm. They are sometimes known as 'sensitives.' I myself stake no claim to such a title. However, I do dabble somewhat in the mystic arts. Knowing of my interest, Mrs. Astor has asked me to provide a brief demonstration of telepathic mentalism, the well-documented ability to harvest the thoughts of others from the ether—that gaseous element which permeates our atmosphere."

An orchestra on a dais at one end of the gallery had been playing waltzes and operatic scores. But the musicians now surrendered their stage to the wealthy old inventor, explorer, and reputed clairvoyant.

"We all know," Rillieux added with a rueful grin, "that a request from Mrs. Astor carries the force of a government draft notice. So here I am, reporting for duty."

He bowed in the direction of a neatly coiffed matron with a waterfall of diamonds at her neck. She nodded graciously, and at this permission to reward his wit, delayed laughter bubbled through the decorated gallery and surrounding gardens.

Only a year earlier, District One in lower Manhattan was the first to be supplied with electricity from the new power plant on Pearl Street. Now, even in the Maitland mansion of lower Fifth Avenue, incandescent lamps glowed, steady and unwavering, from brass-and-crystal five-light sconces. These were cast in the shape of putti, grinning little cherubs, each sconce separated by large verdant tapestries.

"Mind is psyche," Rillieux yammered on, "but there is also pneuma, the soul or etheric double. Seldom are the two in harmony. The conscious mind may ponder what's for dinner while the soul secretly frets about some promise left broken or dream unfulfilled."

Poised and confident, courtly and gaunt, Rillieux surveyed the illustrious gathering before him, one hand resting on his slender rattan walking stick. Besides Caroline Schermerhorn Astor, his audience included Alice Vanderbilt; an émigré French nobleman, the Comte de Chartrain; debutante Antonia Butler, in line to inherit a fortune that rivaled that of the Vanderbilts'; and the evening's host, real estate mandarin Jared Maitland.

Mrs. Astor's presence proved that her rigid exclusivity had lately been attacked, then finally worn down, by the sheer numbers of new millionaires. Especially those from out west, who possessed fewer manners but much more money than even her snobbery could continue to ignore. Indeed, thanks to all this new money, a radical new notion had recently emerged and begun to take root: if you know exactly how much money you're worth, then you can't be truly rich. Relentless, uncountable quantity was replacing inherited quality.

"Someone among us," Rillieux announced abruptly, "recently dreamt about a dearly beloved pet she lost some years ago. Now she secretly grieves anew. And someone else is trying gamely to be impressed by this evening's glitter, but in reality he's preoccupied by mundane thoughts of buying prime real estate on . . . why yes, on West Fifty-fourth Street."

An excited murmur broke out among a group of women standing near the dais.

"Why, Thelma says she dreamt of her Scottish terrier Jip only two nights ago," Lydia Hotchkiss, resplendent in chartreuse satin, called out. "And this is the first time she's mentioned it."

A male voice chimed in. "I wasn't aware I was actually thinking about it, but I admit I have lately been contemplating some land on West Fifty-fourth."

The speaker was attorney Albert Gage, whose Wall Street firm represented half of the city's nouveau riche as well as many in the old aristocracy.

"You were not *consciously* thinking about it, Mr. Gage," Rillieux corrected him.

For a moment Rillieux's gaze paused on a petite young woman who sat by herself on a laurel-pattern cast-iron bench, demurely watching. He made the slightest of nods, and a minute later she began slowly circulating among the distracted guests.

"Here's something else," Rillieux called out, his seamed face capturing the attention of everyone except the lady coursing through the crowds like a puma on the hunt. "Someone among us feels greatly irritated at . . ." He beamed a manufactured smile. "Why yes, at an upstart reporter for the *New York Herald*. . . ."

Perhaps twenty minutes after it began, Paul Rillieux's impressive demonstration concluded to an enthusiastic round of applause.

Even those who were not convinced, Mystere told herself,

looked highly entertained. Popularity was assured when your champion was Mrs. Astor. Or destroyed if your name went into her bad book.

Mystere carried a misted glass of lemonade and a small fan of white lace as she slowly made her way back toward the cast-iron bench, weaving through a formidable maze of financiers and steel magnates, oil tycoons and railroad barons.

Only one of them, however, caused her any real concern. Although she kept her gaze shyly discreet, and like a proper young miss didn't once take a full look at the man, she was nonetheless aware of him watching her from his solitary vantage point. She could not make out his face but knew that he wore a dark suit of worsted wool, eschewing the elegant swallow tails of the Old Guard.

Brushing off her premonitions, she slipped, unnoticed, past Philip Armour, the millionaire meat packer from Chicago. He was holding forth for a group of his fellow merchants.

"The best property is taken now," he assured them, "and even if we do eventually force Brooklyn kicking and screaming into our civic ambit, the only way to grow is *up*. As Chicago is already doing. With ships passing through the Narrows at a record pace, we have no other choice."

Even Mystere, whose life was remote from the money fever gripping much of the city, knew it was Wall Street that had bankrolled the Union during the American Civil War. And now it was Wall Street reaping the astronomical capital gains of the long post war boom. By her headline-grabbing attendance at the Vanderbilt ball in March, Mrs. Astor had placed her rare imprimatur on these new "pick-and-shovel millionaires" she once condemned.

And the rest of the old aristocracy had dutifully followed her lead. Mystere noticed that Old New Yorkers, too, had turned out in force, radiating their sober, proper, Knickerbocker reassurance. However, old prejudices died slowly, and this group pointedly avoided Armour and anyone else who violated strict social punctillo by discussing commerce at evening gatherings. Mrs. Astor's core elite did not deny vulgarity, but they insisted on keeping it in its proper place. "Commerce is useful," as she once confided to Mystere, "but then so is a sewer."

Mystere had nearly reclaimed her bench when she felt a hand grip her right elbow.

"Miss Rillieux," a pallid and stout man of indeterminate middle age greeted her. "You look quite smashing this evening, young lady. I haven't seen you since the Vanderbilt ball."

"Thank you, Mr. Pollard. Yes, I'm afraid I've been quite the stay-at-home lately. Mrs. Astor coaxed me out this evening."

"Good for her. Although one can hardly blame a recluse these days," Abbot Pollard carped. "Why, we're being pre-empted on all sides. Have you *seen* the Upper East and Upper West sides lately? It's a regular blight of row houses and tenements. And the park? God help us, it's all hod carriers and shop girls crowding it now, coming in streetcars and that smelly, smoky, noisy El. One must go clear across the Harlem River for a peaceful carriage ride anymore. It's disgraceful, but there's Tammany politics for you."

Abbot was notorious for his snobbish tirades. Mystere gave him a tolerant smile. "The park was not built exclusively for the rich," she reminded him gently. "It was intended to be the city's drawing room, remember?"

"That's quite noble, my dear. You're still young and innocent, so I forgive you. But I, for one, do not allow any person into my drawing room who requires the services of a lice comb."

She was about to reply when a strong, masculine voice interceded from behind her.

"That's narrow-minded and cruel, Abbot. I have seen many a shop girl who is gracious, intelligent, and beautiful. Where is your spirit of noblesse oblige, sir?"

A slow, dreadful chill crept down her spine. Mystere turned around to meet the teal eyes of Rafael Belloch. The tight-lipped smile he gave her seemed to cost him an effort. His chestnut hair was cut unfashionably short and combed straight back from a strong brow and a fine Romanesque nose.

"Noblesse oblige," Pollard fired back, "has produced filthy wallows like the Fourth Ward and populist demagogues like Tom Foley, who bait the Irish and the Italians against us. The unwashed mobs nearly burned this city down in 'sixty-three. Next time perhaps they'll succeed thanks to all this new 'enlightenment' you champion."

Pollard stomped off, florid-faced with irritation. Mystere noticed, however, that Belloch hadn't really listened to the older man. He had only made his goading remarks to shoo Pollard off. Now his eyes took Mystere's measure with frank interest.

Her stomach knotted. She had managed to avoid the man since her introduction into society, but now here he was. Rafe Belloch. The notorious robber baron himself, with the gaze that probed too intently; with words that held all the softness of a razor.

"This crowd despises Tammany," he remarked. "But who else bothers to build hospitals and orphanages for the poor?"

"I shouldn't be too hasty, Mr. Belloch, in praising orphanages."

Mystere instantly regretted speaking up in a moment of unguarded feeling. But the words had spurted out before she could stop them. Feeling trapped by his stare, she added in a much lighter tone, "Mr. Pollard is just a harmless old sobersides. Did you enjoy my uncle's demonstration?"

The stare never wavered. "It was clever and entertaining, to be sure. And despite all the financial wizards in attendance, I don't think anyone has guessed his secret yet."

For a few seconds his unsettling words hung in the air between them, menacing and accusing. As his gaze seemed to probe her very soul, Mystere was gripped with panic. All the voices surrounding them, along with the soaring strains of a Strauss waltz, suddenly became grating noises screeching in her ears.

He knows, she thought in numb confusion. The awful moment of public exposure had come.

However, she had learned the art of dissembling from a true master. She gave him a demure little Mona Lisa smile. "Guessed my uncle's secret, Mr. Belloch? I'm afraid I fail to take your meaning."

"Why, it's quite simple. It is startling, Miss Rillieux, how much one can learn about any household by simply sending a servant to search through a parked carriage. Or even better, does your uncle find his information merely by passing some idle moments with a talkative upstairs maid, perhaps inducing her to read a private journal?"

Relief made her smile, and her confidence surged. Belloch only meant the little secret, not the Big One.

"I suppose that's possible," she allowed without much interest. "I don't profess any great belief in the occult. I look on my uncle's demonstrations as harmless entertainment. No doubt he has his little tricks."

"Of course. Encouraged by Mrs. Astor herself. Speaking of whom . . ."

He pointed with his chin—the great matron was even now aimed straight toward them. And of course her favorite minion, Ward McCallister, hovered at his carefully fixed distance like a moon orbiting its planet. Officially her social director, he was also less officially a matchmaker.

"Good evening, Mystere," Caroline greeted her with a genuine show of affection, bussing the younger woman's cheek. "You've been far too shy lately. You need not live in the shadow of your uncle's greatness. Don't forget that 'coming out' means precisely that. You're a debutante, not a cloistered nun."

Caroline turned to Belloch. "As for you, Rafe, *really*. You know perfectly well that one does not call a count 'monsieur.' One addresses him as *le comte*. I'm afraid poor Emile is terribly miffed."

Rafe bowed his head. "I'm truly mortified at the depth of my own ignorance, Caroline. Thank you for edifying me. I shall study to be deserving."

"You're scandalous," she assured him, raising a perfectly manicured hand to touch his cheek for a moment. "Mortified? You couldn't care less. And I am so smitten with you, you handsome brute, that I can't even be properly annoyed. Sensing my weakness, you abuse it."

Despite her bantering tone, Caroline sent him a low-lidded smile that went well beyond mere flirting, at least as Mystere understood the rules. Caroline turned to her again.

"Keep your guard up around this one, my dear," she confided. "New Orleans could not have prepared you for his species of male. Rafe is a jaded idealist, and your youth and naivete excite him. He's a man used to getting what he wants. And by the most direct path."

Caroline and Ward glided off, and Mystere hoped Belloch might follow them. However, he continued to stand close by, watching her from half-accusing, half-speculative eyes.

"Isn't this amusing?" he demanded, indicating the gathering with a wave of his hand. "The dryasdusts and the parvenus, all together under Caroline's newly expanded umbrella. And which are you, Miss Rillieux? Day coach or Pullman?"

"For one who scowls and makes acerbic remarks," she informed him, "you were certainly tame just now with Caroline."

"Of course. One does not visit Rome and insult the Pope."

She laughed even as she wondered: what did he want from her? Surely he did not recognize her. She looked very different from two years before. If anything, with her figure bound and strapped to appear younger, she had dropped an age instead of gaining one. Her education complete, her mentor Paul Rillieux had finally allowed her to earn her way out of her dirty, wretched rags. Her garb now was the most innocent blue satin gown Charles Frederick Worth could produce.

He couldn't recognize her, but oh, did she remember him, standing nearly naked in the alley in Five Points, rage and promise of vengeance hard on his face. He had been a spectacular sight, and she awoke from many a nightmare with his face etched in her mind like a photograph on albumen.

She glanced at him to reassure herself. It did no good. She swore he kept changing his position slightly, as if to study her from several angles.

She still knew little more about him than she had from the newspaper articles two years ago. He was a Patriarch of the Four Hundred. But whereas she and Paul Rillieux belonged only by special declaration of Mrs. Astor, Belloch could claim tradition of birth. There were vague rumors about some tragedy, although some preferred the word scandal. Perhaps so, for he was known to have many acquaintances but few friends. He had amassed a dizzying fortune in railroad ventures, lived part of each year at his magnificent estate in Virginia's hunt country, and owned a private steam yacht as luxurious as a small ocean liner. His yacht enabled him to take up local residence on Staten Island, deliberately snubbing Manhattan.

And, of course, he was an eminently eligible bachelor—which explained why, even now, Miss Antonia Butler was watching him like a cat on a rat.

"Miss Rillieux," he said, abruptly cutting into her thoughts, "what do you think about all this business with the Lady Moonlight?"

She did not miss a beat. "I confess I've given it scant attention. But it seems to have become a nine days' wonder in the press."

"Of course. After all, our thief is getting the best of the Four Hundred. Making all of us look like fools while robbing us in the very midst of our soirees. When she actually relieved Caroline of her best diamond bracelet, the Lady Moonlight's infamy was assured."

His probing eyes sent a message she couldn't decipher.

"It's a foolish name for her, if the thief is even really a woman," she opined. Her tone was polite but slightly bored.

"She's 'ethereal as a moonbeam, as elusive as a jungle cat,'" he quoted the papers, and they both laughed. Still, however, his greenish blue eyes seemed to be reading every detail of her face.

"She's also been described," Belloch added, "as a Valkyrie of a woman, huge and powerful. No match for a mere mortal man. But the only witnesses admit they glimpsed her only from behind in the shadows. And I suspect the press has seized on the Amazon angle to sensationalize the case. I'm of the opinion she is petite and extremely dexterous rather than big and strong."

"You seem quite immersed in the matter."

"I have a great interest, Miss Rillieux, in the methods and techniques of the society thief."

"Really? How amusing."

"Yes, isn't it?"

He moved even closer until she could feel his breath on her face, moist and warm and sweet from the brandy he had drunk earlier. The panic returned, and for a moment she feared a devastating exposure right here and now. Her legs felt watery and weak, and she wanted to sit down. But his intense gaze held her in place with the authority of a gun muzzle.

"You see, Miss Rillieux, the cleverest of thieves operate as teams or even vast syndicates." His eyes narrowed. "I shouldn't be at all surprised to learn that our infamous Lady Moonlight was once a common street thief, roaming with a band of coarse grifters. They stick together, these types, always prefering the safety of diversions to cover their activi-

ties. Perhaps she has even struck again this very night—
while your uncle held us all in thrall."

She looked at him, ready to confront him with denial
even though she longed to run away.

But she didn't expect to see the handsome grin on his
face as he stared back.

"There it is again," he nearly whispered, his expression
rapt. "That look—so full of reproach—so full of old wounds.
What does a young debutante from New Orleans have to
look wounded about?"

She turned away, choosing instead to focus on the ball-
goers, but the parfait colors of satin ball gowns began to
swirl in her vision as if washed in tears. Freezing up, she admonished herself not to be afraid. He had nothing on her. He
was only speculating. As she had told herself a thousand
times, she would do what she had to do to survive. For she
had endured this long in order to keep alive the hope she
would one day find her brother Bram. And when she did
that, he would take her away from all the filth and lies. He
would see that she was safe again, and all would be fine once
more.

Then all the thievery, all the fear, would have been worth
it.

The realization quelled her panic in a heartbeat.

"I can't imagine what you're talking about, Mr. Belloch.
All this nonsense about syndicates and old wounds. I think
you must have had too much brandy." She released a small
laugh.

"How is it I've missed you during all these soirees? Tonight is the first night I've really looked at you, Miss
Rillieux. I don't know how you've managed to stay out of
my path at these functions, but now that I've seen you, I
can't help but think you look familiar." The intent, mocking
gaze raked down her figure. "Admittedly there are differ-
ences. The woman I recall was certainly more . . . robust,

shall we say? She was not the pallid little mouse you appear to be, but that would be in keeping with my theory of diversions, would it not?"

"And no doubt," she taunted him with confident scorn, "my uncle is part of this wicked syndicate?"

"Perhaps," he answered with another wire-tight smile. "And perhaps you are the Lady Moonlight."

His tone left open the possibility that he was joking. But those dark eyes told another story altogether.

She felt a cold hand grip her heart, and her pulse leaped into her throat. Before she could reply, however, a startled cry rose above the music and the hum of conversation.

"Oh! My brooch! Someone has stolen my brooch!"

Chapter 2

Mrs. John Robert Pendergast of Grammercy Park clutched her neck as if garroted. At first, as news of the latest theft spread like grass fire through the assembly, everyone was at sixes and sevens. There seemed less concern for the missing brooch, Mystere noticed, than excitement about possibly spotting the exotic "Lady Moonlight."

"Well, Mr. Belloch," she forced out in a light tone, "it would appear that your clairvoyant powers rival my uncle's. You predicted this only moments ago."

Belloch folded his arms over his chest, watching her with all the alertness of a lion in the brush. "So I did. And to think I almost couldn't bring myself to attend tonight."

To avoid his probing gaze, she feigned an interest in monitoring the nearby commotion. Mrs. Pendergast, a stricken look on her face, continued clutching the high neck of her dress, open at the throat where the brooch was missing.

"Surely you must have dropped it?" Thelma Richards asked her. "*How* could anyone possibly have removed it without your knowing? Literally from under your nose!"

"How, indeed?" Belloch whispered, still watching Mystere. "Unless our Lady Moonlight is a true artist at her craft."

"Aren't you drawing some hasty conclusions, sir?" she challenged him without flinching. "A theft has not yet been established much less the gender of the thief."

She had begun to edge away from him with hopes of losing him in the commotion, but Belloch had other plans for her. Taking her by one arm, his grip firm and utterly merciless, he guided her closer to the hubbub around the victim.

It so happened that Chief of Detectives Thomas F. Byrnes was in attendance. He was a great favorite with the Four Hundred, for he had established the strictly enforced "dead line" north of Fulton Street that kept criminal predators out of the financial district. After a brief, confused search of the grounds and gallery floor by servants turned up nothing, he approached the distraught woman.

"What type of brooch, Mrs. Pendergast?"

"Why . . . a yellow-gold flower brooch, Inspector. There were five oval opals and twenty-two round rubies."

"Quite valuable, I take it?"

The matron paled. "Quite."

"Good luck to you, Inspector," Belloch called out through the crowd, though his gaze still lingered on Mystere. "You might have better results trying to hold back the ocean with a broom. It appears that our Lady Moonlight has struck again from within our very midst. Perhaps a thorough search of all our female guests would be in order?"

His tone was jesting, and a few men chuckled at his mild ribaldry while some of the ladies took obvious offense.

"That might prove most pleasant, Mr. Belloch," Byrnes admitted. "But also most unpolitic. I'd be demoted to a beat on South Street."

Antonia Butler caught Belloch's attention and smiled at him—showing too many teeth, Mystere criticized silently. She and Antonia had both come out this season, though, as Rillieux planned, Antonia was allowed to make the greater stir. Her father had originally made his fortune in Canton,

Ohio, manufacturing carbon dioxide for the soda pop industry. But like Rockefeller, Carnegie, Armour, and so many others, he had moved to New York to put his fortune to work.

Mystere watched Antonia excuse herself from the group around her and cross toward her and Belloch. Thankfully, she felt Belloch's hand drop from her arm. In the crowd no one had noticed Belloch's manhandling of her.

Antonia looked quite fetching, Mystere had to admit, in a pinch-waisted sateen gown with black-velvet trim. Certainly it flattered her figure quite frankly, whereas Mystere's prim dress, while of high quality and an excellent complement to her opalescent complexion, had been selected to make her look more the girl than the woman.

The heiress was beautiful, Mystere allowed, but in the stiff way of a fine porcelain piece. In her ungracious mind, she thought Antonia radiated all the elan of a sleepwalker. And what little animation she possessed was mainly school-girl spite. She was purse proud and enjoyed parading her purchases in a way that suggested some early brushes with want. Worse than that, she had always treated mousey little Mystere as a sort of charity mascot for the rich and famous.

"Good evening, Mystere," Antonia greeted her with patronizing politeness. "Your uncle's little show just now was quite amusing. I didn't realize there was such theatrical talent in your family."

That was another Antonia trait—disparaging words delivered in a sweet tone. Everyone knew theater people were a socially degraded lot. Anger touched Mystere for a brief moment. But Antonia had already turned her toothy smile toward Rafe, and Mystere found herself grateful to the girl for her diversion.

"Mr. Belloch, you gentlemen have us ladies at a distinct disadvantage. We must languish at home while your sex is free to circulate at will. You might send up your card now and then, you know."

"Miss Butler, the prospect is daunting. The one time I did screw up my courage to visit, you were surrounded by a galaxy of hopeful admirers."

"Why, Mr. Belloch! So timid—and yet, you are the man who moves mountains."

Antonia's eyes flicked dismissively toward Mystere as she added, "I thought you were one to relish a challenge, Mr. Belloch, not the assured victory?"

"I do, Miss Butler, so long as some profit is likely on my investment."

His innuendo was a bit crude and direct, in Mystere's opinion, but Antonia did not appear offended. Still including Mystere in her gaze, she replied, "My father assures me that no one can hope to gain without taking great risks. I hope your success in commerce has not made you . . . too easily complacent in your personal affairs?"

Clearly pleased with herself, Antonia bid them both good evening and returned to her friends.

"There may, indeed, be a galaxy of men around her," Mystere commented in a neutral tone. "But it's quite clear *your* orbit has top priority."

"Oh, I may eventually play with her," he replied with scant interest.

"Are you playing with me, too? Is that what you've been doing? Amusing yourself?"

"Yes, but different women, different games, Miss Rillieux. Tell me something. I'm told that your uncle is a great favorite of Mrs. Astor's?"

His self-satisfied voice irked her, and she replied curtly. "She's been quite kind. We haven't been in New York long, as you know."

He greeted her answer with a rude bark of laughter. "At least two years, according to my count."

" 'Different women, different games,' " she coolly tossed back at him. "I do think you have me mistaken for someone else."

He ignored her words, his eyes narrowing again in speculation. "Caroline tells me your uncle went wide upon the world in his youth?"

"He has traveled extensively, yes. However, that was before I went to live with him in New Orleans."

"Ahh, that's right. After your parents were taken by . . . cholera, was it?"

"Yellow fever. It's a terrible problem in New Orleans. There was a particularly bad outbreak in 'seventy-one."

By now Mrs. Pendergast and Inspector Byrnes had withdrawn to the parlor to complete a more detailed report. Mystere gazed around until she caught old Rillieux's eye. He was seated at a marble pedestal table with Alice and Alva Vanderbilt. He nodded in her direction, and Mystere began to edge away from Belloch. But again the railroad plutocrat detained her with a grip like a steel trap.

"Yes, New Orleans is a charming city," he pushed on despite her evident desire to leave. "But the area is afflicted with a wretched climate. I was down there once on business. Do they still burn Beast Butler in effigy?"

"Who?"

"Who?" His face clouded. "Surely you're being ironic?"

Mystere fought off her distress, trying to place the familiar name. Then she remembered Rillieux's coaching. "Oh, of course. You mean Ben Butler, the Union general who occupied New Orleans during the war."

"Yes. But I'm surprised a New Orleans native wouldn't know that right off. As I understand it, he's the most hated man in the city's history. He practically accused every lady in New Orleans of being a harlot."

"I have little memory of the war, sir. You forget my tender age. I just made my debut," she reminded him.

"Miss Rillieux, time does *not* heal all wounds. I was down there only five years ago. He was still reviled by one and all."

Mystere's uneasiness over all the questions gave way to

sheer indignation at his bulldog tenacity. With a spirited wrench, she freed her arm from his grip.

"You've made your point that I must be a stupid creature, Mr. Belloch. Now, if the insults are through, I hope you'll excuse me."

Obviously he wasn't done with her, but she had had her fill of him. She turned quickly away before he could detain her again. If he even tried, she was prepared to cry for help. It would cause a scandal, but she could not let him get the upper hand. There was too much danger in him.

"Stupid is not the adjective I have in mind for you," his voice taunted behind her.

Without turning around, she stiffened her spine and left him to his mocking laughter.

As their carriage rolled past the great stone gateposts of the Maitland mansion, Paul Rillieux inserted a pinch of snuff behind his upper lip. Then he snapped his silver snuff box shut and said to Mystere, "Well now, my dear. Let me examine our latest sparkler."

She lifted her left forearm a few inches. The frilled cuff on the embroidered undersleeve of her dress was visible beneath the ermine lappet of the sleeve. A strategically located drawstring pocket had been sewn between them, obscured by the voluminous folds. After years of literal sleight of hand practice under Rillieux's exacting tutelage, she could remove and hide an item of jewelry so effortlessly even someone watching her closely saw nothing but a woman absentmindedly adjusting one sleeve.

She took out the brooch and handed it across to Rillieux.

He thumb scratched a lucifer, and the flaring glow of the match reflected brilliant points of color from the beautiful, richly jeweled piece.

"Superb craftsmanship," he pronounced in a reverent tone.

"Mystere, I've had some brilliant protégés in my time. Your talent, however, is unsurpassed."

"Talent," she repeated, bitterness edging into her tone, "applies to painting or poetry or acting, not to stealing."

"Wrong. But at any rate, we do not 'steal.' I've told you that before. We arrogate. There's a vital difference. Stealing is low, vulgar, and common. You remember it well with your background, don't you, love? I plucked you from Five Points myself."

He gave a self-satisfied grin. "No, indeed. Stealing is a shameful, sneaky act by those who snivel when captured. Arrogation, in contrast, is refined, high-minded, and bold. It is seizure of property with no regard whatsoever for moral justifications. What the Romans called *pecca fortiter*, sinning boldly. How do you think the Four Hundred got so rich? By arrogating unto themselves that which they desired, that's how."

The match went out, and Rillieux dropped the "sparkler" into his coat pocket. "Speaking of the Four Hundred," he added, "what was Belloch saying to you? It certainly didn't look like polite small talk."

"He's suspicious of me. Even before the Lady Moonlight. It was the robbery at Five Points—he remembers me."

"Nonsense. That was two years ago. Has he accused you of anything?"

"Not in so many words, but—"

"Come now, my dear, you know how excitable you can be. You're building a pimple into a peak. You were masked at Five Points. Besides, you appear even younger now with, ahh, your womanly figure restrained."

"Yes, he perhaps thinks me seventeen and not the twenty I am. But that has him confused, not fooled. You should have heard him pressing me about New Orleans. And about you. He nearly tripped me up with a question about Beast Butler. Thank God I read the books you gave me and recalled him in the nick of time."

"Belloch had better keep his nose out of the pie. Simply avoid him."

"I'll try, but what if he won't avoid me?"

"He'll learn to, or he'll end up like the curious cat."

"What does that mean?" she demanded, a thread of alarm in her voice.

"Nothing that concerns you. Don't worry overly much about Belloch. He's an odd one. There's a rumor he's not quite right in his upper story. Some embarrassment involving his parents and their loss of fortune."

"He seemed quite lucid to me, odd or not."

The carriage crossed Broadway at Madison Square, the hotel district. The Ladies' Mile sprawled from Twenty-third Street south to Fourteenth Street, the world's unsurpassed shopping district. The Marble Palace, Lord & Taylor, and the other huge department stores were mostly dark and silent now. Only Delmonico's Restaurant and a few of the specialty shops were still open for business.

"Paul?" she said, her voice tentative now. "The brooch—will it bring a good price?"

"I expect so. That's up to Helzer, you know. Why do you mention it?" If a voice could frown, his did now. Mystere never asked such questions.

"I . . . that is, I only wonder if I might possibly have a larger share?"

"Whatever for? Do I stint you? Don't forget I must run a household for all of us. You have a fine home, good clothes, pocket money, liberal use of a carriage and driver." He wagged a warning finger at her. "My dear, you *must* stop playing ducks and drakes with your money."

For a moment his lecturing tone made her face heat with anger. Despite her fear of Belloch, right now she shared his apparent disdain for the Four Hundred. If they were so superior and discerning, why could a callow fraud like Rillieux so easily fool them with good tailoring and a Continental flair?

Perhaps her stony silence warned him. His voice lowered

an octave, menace in his tone. "Mystere, there's one thing I will *not* tolerate and that is a Judas kiss. In our little group it is all for one and one for all. No one holds out on the others. Is that clearly understood?"

For a moment, with the darkness as her cloak, she felt tears sting her eyes and throat. "Yes," she managed.

But Rillieux, who knew her moods to a hair, shifted to a sympathetic tone. "Mystere, have you forgotten the orphanage I took you out of?"

Forgotten? Never would she be that fortunate. The freezing nights, the severe punishments, and there had been little to eat except panada twice a day—a sort of bread soup with some pieces of turnip floating in it. But thanks to Rillieux, she had left as an eight-year-old child and learned to thieve her way to the ripe old age of twenty. She had started as an alley thief and alongside Rillieux had worked her way into the highest ranks. She had shed the old suffering life as completely as a snake sloughs its old skin. But not, however, the memory of it or the fear of returning.

"No," she told him with feeling, "I haven't forgotten. And I'm grateful. You've been good to me."

She slid the curtain aside and glanced outside. Manhattan was still only partially electrified, and gas lamps lined the street. A rising moon lit the spire of Trinity Church to a silver patina.

Rillieux's voice, still kind, sliced into her thoughts. "It's Bram, isn't it? You still miss him. You still think of your brother."

"He's twenty-six now," she mused, more to herself than Rillieux. "If he's still alive, he's the only family I have left."

"Wrong, dear. *We* are a family. All of us. I, you, Baylis, Evan, Rose, now even little Hush when he's ready. Concentrate on what you have, not what you've lost. Bram's been missing for twelve years. Frankly, those unfortunate enough to be shanghaied don't usually last too long. He'll not likely turn up."

Her eyes trembled, and again she felt the saline sting of tears. He was probably right, but she would not give up her secret, costly search to locate her brother. Hope was her waking dream, the only thing that kept her going.

Their carriage rolled under the El just as a late commuter train steamed overhead, and Mystere heard Baylis, up on the box driving the team, curse when soot rained down on him. Again, in flashes between the steel support beams, she caught sight of the pale moon. Despite her remark to Belloch about how silly the name Lady Moonlight was, she knew it was in fact eerily apt. And not because of that foolish "ethereal as a moonbeam" business, either.

The first time Lady Moonlight had gained press attention was after the grand, citywide gala surrounding the opening of the Brooklyn Bridge last March. That evening, New York and Brooklyn had staged a spectacular fireworks show the likes of which the world had never seen before. For hours the night sky over the East River had blazed with brilliant colors. Everyone, rich and poor alike, had gathered outdoors to witness it.

Then, only moments after the last Roman candles blazed out, a stunning full moon had emerged from dark clouds and bathed the new bridge in an otherworldly luminous aura. The natural light show had entranced viewers even more than the fireworks—and it was then that Mystere, honed by twelve years in training under Rillieux, had removed Caroline Astor's bracelet.

Thus the Lady Moonlight instantly seized the public imagination and became a heroine to the less fortunate. Soon there was even a certain cachet to becoming one of her victims. After all, to be robbed by the Lady Moonlight was to be designated an elite—she never robbed the middle class, did she? Watching for her, speculating on her identity or next victim—all of it lent the rather dry lives of the upper crust a bit of titillation.

Again Rillieux's voice scattered her thoughts.

"Take this," he told her, pressing some folded bank notes into her hand. "Perhaps I can scrape up a bit more money for you now and then. But you must promise me you *won't* waste it searching for Bram."

Waste it . . . no, she thought, it would be wasted if it went for more gowns or perfumes. But the search for Bram was as vital to her as the breath in her nostrils. So her reply was at least a half truth.

"I won't waste it," she promised. "I really won't."

Chapter 3

Once Caroline Astor had fallen under the spell of Paul Rillieux's glib erudition and Old World charm, his acceptance was complete. No one even dreamed of investigating the claim that his wealth derived from French baronial land holdings. Thus, with no further references required, he had secured a roomy brownstone mansion near Great Jones Street and Lafayette Place, one of the most sought-after locations in Manhattan.

Mystere had been assigned an entire upstairs wing as her private quarters. She was awake early on the morning after the Astor soiree, for she had an appointment at mid-morning in Central Park.

She performed a hurried toilette and dusted her face lightly with powder. Then came a tedious daily ritual: wearing only pantalets, she stood before a sterling silver and green-velvet dressing mirror, carefully binding her chest with strips of linen. The procedure was cumbersome and uncomfortable, but Rillieux had insisted.

"We want a pretty debutante, not a beautiful woman," he had instructed her. "We want men to look at you and think 'Well, perhaps in a few years, but not now.' We want them to dismiss you and look somewhere else while you separate them from their possessions."

She finished wrapping the linen and donned a silk chemise. Then she crossed to a tall satinwood wardrobe and selected a black cambric dress. It was frumpy and stodgy, but that was precisely what she wanted for this meeting. After she dressed she drew her mahogany-colored hair back into a neat coil on her nape.

Quite drab and dreary, she approved, examining her appearance in the mirror. To check the final touch, she put on a widow's bonnet with a veil. Yes, that should do it—a poor widow could travel alone, unharassed. And covered by the veil, no one of the Four Hundred would likely recognize her at her assignation in the park.

A sudden knock at the door of her dressing room made her start. "Mystere? Are you awake?" called a woman's voice.

Hastily she took off the bonnet and stuffed it in her wicker tote—just in time—the door clicked open, and a woman of about thirty years of age, with her fiery red hair in curl papers under a mobcap, thrust her head into the room.

"Up and dressed already, la! I'm just up myself."

"Good morning, Rose."

Rose O'Reilly gave the black dress a skeptical glance. She had coarse-grained skin in a careworn face old before its time. "You've lost your pretty feathers in that raggedy dress."

Mystere ignored that. "Is Paul up yet?"

"Yes, he's with Hush in the downstairs parlor. Lesson time, you know."

"All right. I'll be down presently."

Rose started to shut the door, then hesitated. "By the way, it's all over the papers this morning."

"What—oh. You must mean Mrs. Pendergast's brooch."

"It's all the buzz. Evan says even the milkman went on

and on about it. The police are vowing to catch the thief, Mystere. They're even forming a special team just to trap the Lady Moonlight. I told Paul he's paring the cheese mighty close to the rind, but he told me shush, he knows what he's up to. I sure to God hope so, or it'll go hard for all of us."

Having said her piece, Rose departed. But her warning words left Mystere feeling anxious and uneasy. Especially when she recalled Rafe Belloch and his dark, accusing eyes probing her last night. Paul dismissed him as "odd," but she sensed the dangerous, suppressed tension in him. The man was a caged tiger just waiting for some fool to open the door.

Nonetheless the risk was worth it. None of the others, not even the resourceful Hush, who was an astounding pickpocket despite his youth, were producing "sparklers" to match the hauls of the Lady Moonlight. They could not, for they were deprived of her easy access to the very wealthy. And the more she brought in, the more her share—or so Rillieux had promised. Money she desperately needed.

She unlocked the top drawer of a Louis XVI gilt bronze writing desk and took out a small birchwood box. The tattered and torn letter she carefully removed and unfolded had been written on foolscap, now dog-eared and faded from age, handling, and exposure. She chastised herself for handling it yet again, but there were times when she had to or else she might quit believing her struggle was worth it.

The most legible part was the printed letterhead, a split image of half an eagle joined to a man's arm holding up a dagger. The date below the letterhead was also clear, April 12, 1863. But the neat handwriting itself had nearly faded, and grew progressively dimmer as her gaze fell down the page.

Dear Brendan,

I pray God this letter and enclosed bank draft find you and your family well. I know how terrible things are in Dublin these days. Believe me, it was hard here in New York, too, when I first arrived.

However, I have prospered beyond my wildest expectations. I know your health is poor lately, but if at all possible, I urge you to bring your family here to New York City. Rest assured I have the means to make sure you will be well set up. Life here is turbulent and confusing, especially as we await the outcome of this terrible war. However, a man willing to roll up his sleeves will find ample chance to better himself and his children.

Speaking of that, also rest assured that whether or not you make it over here, you, Maureen, Bram, and Mystere have been provided for in my will. I could never have made it to America without your help. The money you gave me, at great hardship to you and your family, paid my way over. God bless you and answer my prayer that soon all of us may be united once again.

She could not read the final paragraph, however, which had faded too much. And try as she might she could not decipher the almost completely faded signature. At some point water had smeared the ink even before it faded. She had once taken it to a restorer of antique manuscripts, who tried without success to clarify the signature with tincture of mercury and zinc.

Nor did she even have a name to begin the search with, for she had never known—or had long forgotten—her last name. Brendan, her father, had died even before her mother received this letter, and Mystere had been only two when consumption took her mother, too. One of Maureen's final acts had been to place her and eight-year-old Bram on a ship bound for America.

Mystere carefully folded the letter and put it away. Memory amazed and frustrated her: It could run through a person's entire life in the time it took to tie a shoe. Yet it could also fail to answer the most fundamental questions about one's existence. She had no memory of her life in Ireland, only this letter and the things Bram had told her. And one thing he had insisted, over and over, was how their mother told him he and Mystere had rights to a great fortune.

Downstairs, the tall case clock in the hallway chimed the quarter hour and jolted her back to the present. She gave herself one final glance in the mirror and clutched the wicker tote that held her veil.

"Today," she said hopefully to her reflection. "Today Lorenzo will have something for me."

"Remember, lad," Rillieux's sonorous voice leaked through the hand-carved teakwood doors of the parlor, which stood ajar, "an excellent moment to exploit is during the first critical seconds when two acquaintances meet on the street. That moment when their eyes lock and they decide to acknowledge each other with the rituals of greeting."

Mystere peeked through the open doors into a sumptuously appointed room illuminated by gilt brass astral lamps, recently electrified. The even lighting accentuated a Persian Hamadan carpet of rose, blue, and green on a black background. Rillieux sat in a carved walnut armchair, gesturing with his walking stick like a conductor with a baton. And young Hush, the only name they knew him by, had perched on a cushioned footrest, literally at the feet of the master.

"The greeting ritual," Rillieux lectured on, "is one that requires complete focus of attention for a few seconds. I once even relieved a gentleman of his portmanteau during just such an opportunity. But timing is everything, along with lightning speed and flawless movements. *The readiness is all,* Hush. That and absolute confidence, for you are an artist at your craft."

"An artist, sir?"

"Of course. Thievery—which I call arrogation—is a

complex and beautiful art when done correctly. It should never involve threats, violence, or bloodshed. I absolutely abhor these Plug Uglies and Roach Guards who intimidate, injure, even kill their victims. Why would you kill a breeder of more rich men? Just as a good farmer treats his fertile dirt with respect, *we* must cherish those whom we separate from their costly baubles."

"Really, Paul," Mystere teased as she stepped into the parlor, "the boy is only twelve years old. You sound like Plato lecturing his disciples."

Hush scrambled politely to his feet when she entered, flashing the sadly disjointed smile that had instantly captured her heart when she first met him. The orphan worked as a rat catcher and lived in a basement hovel in Little Italy on the southern end of Mulberry Street. His trousers made of leftover Union blue shoddy were held up with a leather belt three sizes too big for him; his shirt was of wool, and it was clear by its dirty and patched appearance that the boy wore the shirt summer and winter.

Rillieux was in a good mood this morning and greeted Mystere with a smile. "Only twelve, yes, and just look at these. He is not just a disciple but a prodigy."

He pointed to the loot heaped up on a nearby marquetry tea table. Besides several billfolds, Hush's latest haul included a gold Italian rope bracelet and a pair of sapphire and diamond drop earrings.

"The lad has remarkable talent," Rillieux gloated. "I haven't seen his like since you, Mystere. What he's learned in the alley will graduate him to the Four Hundred, I tell you. Pickpocket hands that could easily master the piano or the surgical knife. The gold, by the way, is twenty-four karat."

She kept her face impassive, but his smug good mood about the child's deliberate corruption filled her with anger. Rillieux had a reputation as a world-traveled scholar. In truth, however, his "genius" was nothing but a near-photographic memory. This served two useful purposes: By dint of memorizing facts alone he could pose as broadly learned, and even more useful, he never forgot the location of any item of value.

"Did someone die?" he added, giving her somber black dress a puzzle-headed look.

"I think she looks beautiful, sir," Hush spoke up boldly. "Like a lady in some famous painting."

"We know you're smitten, lad. No one can blame you. She is a tonic to the eyes even in black. Will you be requiring the carriage today, Mystere?"

She had to be careful. It was part of the reason she wore the black dress. Widows out alone were usually left to their grief, while other young women out in the city alone, at best might be mistaken for prostitutes. And she was going into the city alone.

Certainly the carriage could take her, but she knew Rillieux had his private reasons for being so generous with the carriage. If Baylis drove her, he would dutifully report her actions to Rillieux. All of the servants, including Rose, were extremely loyal to him. After all, he had taken them away from places like Rag Picker's Row and Bandits' Roost, and given them a good place to live and some security in their heretofore desperate lives. Baylis genuinely liked her, and she him, but she had learned he would not keep any secret from Paul.

"I think the omnibus will do for me," she told him. "I plan to do some shopping on Broadway, and you know how congested it gets. Poor Baylis hates all that jockeying about for position."

"Well, at least call for a carriage. The Four Hundred do not ride on omnibuses."

"Good," she replied lightly. "Then none of them will be there to see me. I enjoy riding the omnibus."

Rillieux frowned, forming spiderwebs of squint lines at the corners of his eyes. "As you will, my dear. But make sure you're home by three P.M. We've been invited to a poetry reading at the Vernons'. Sylvia Rohr will be there—I've had my eye on a little trinket of hers."

"I'll be back in time," she promised, hiding her resentment.

On the face of it she had a highly desirable social calendar. Besides the numerous—endless, she corrected herself—balls, soirees, and high teas were the excursions to museums, operas, the theater, and lyceums. Yet despite it all she was in a state of unutterable loneliness. She was among people but not *of* them—she was there only to steal.

Hush followed her out of the parlor and through the main salon into the front vestibule. "Mystere?" he said behind her as she reached for the glass knob of the front door.

"Hmm?" She turned, her thoughts elsewhere, to look down into his dark, intelligent gaze.

"When will I be allowed to live here with you . . . uhh, I mean with the rest of you?"

She smiled, though his words gave her a stab. "Quite soon now, I think. However, that's up to Paul."

As was his habit, he shook his thick shock of dark hair out of his eyes. "Mr. Rillieux . . . he likes me, don't he? He thinks I do good work, right?"

Mystere believed that if she looked at faces very carefully, she could not only see what a person was, but what he would become. And she liked what she saw in Hush's face. Behind the grime and the scars and the tough veneer of a street arab, she saw an honest heart and a genuine depth of character.

"Hush," she replied, "he's quite satisfied, yes. Don't worry on that score. But you do understand, don't you, that no one is forced to . . . to become a thief?"

"Forced? I like it. It sure beats the hell out of crawling under houses to poison rats."

"I know. But remember, even while you do what Paul

tells you, you can also pursue something you like even better. Something more honorable. Teach yourself a useful trade—can you read?"

He shook his head. "But I can cipher some."

"Well then, I'll teach you how to read. For a bright boy like you, it will be easy to learn. We'll start next time you come."

His face brightened at the prospect. She turned toward the door, but again his voice arrested her. "Mystere?"

"Yes?"

He sent a quick glance over his shoulder, making sure Rillieux hadn't left the parlor. "Are you . . . you know, forced?"

She searched his face. "You've guessed, haven't you? About the Lady Moonlight?"

He nodded.

"You *are* bright. Don't let on to Paul that you know."

"But are you? Forced to do it?"

Something about the curious glance he gave her reminded her of the way Rafael Belloch had looked at her last night, as if sounding the very depths of her soul.

She started to attempt a reply, then caught sight of the brass-and-glass mantel clock: already past ten A.M.

"We'll talk later," she told him, giving him a quick kiss on the cheek. "Just know this: Fancy words like 'arrogation' don't change a thing. Stealing may seem easy and profitable, but no matter how good one becomes at it, it is still a sin and a crime."

"Not when *you* do it," he insisted, his tone brooking no debate.

Paul isn't the only one corrupting him, she thought with a sinking feeling as she let herself out. Despite what he had just said, she was completely unable to meet his eye or utter a word of denial.

Chapter 4

No omnibus served Lafayette Place, but Mystere could walk a few blocks to catch an express car pulled by a huge dray horse. It took her directly to the park entrance at Fifth Avenue and Fifty-ninth Street.

Despite her nervous anticipation about what she might learn at her meeting with Lorenzo Perkins, she enjoyed the long, slow ride. It was a fine day, bright with unclouded sunshine while a steady breeze from the north kept the heat bearable. True, one could happen to glance south of Washington Square, where there was always that pall of dense, dark smoke floating above lower Manhattan—the factory district, choked with everything from chemical plants to tanneries—but Mystere simply accepted it as a fish accepts water, for she had grown up with the city, watching it push farther and farther north until the only rural part of Manhattan left was the upper end. There farm animals still grazed even as sidewalks were being laid out and gas lines installed around them. She had read recently that the last squatters and subsistence farmers were being chased out around Seventy-eighth and Seventy-ninth streets. Even the farm fields of Harlem were now being surveyed for housing lots.

The remarkable progress was evident all around her, especially overhead where a thick, tangled web of telephone and electrical wires blotted out the sky in some places.

She was about to enter the park when a handsome, loden green carriage rolled by on the opposite side of the avenue. The glittering gold harness rig caught her attention, and too late she realized who owned the coach. Before she could turn away, she found herself trapped under the almost physical force of Rafe Belloch's stare.

She dared not duck into the park as if hiding from him. So she simply let him scrutinize her at will, hoping her veil would protect her. From a sidewalk filled with prospects, he selected her to watch with minute attention. Despite her apprehension she couldn't help but notice how the window seemed to frame him like a painting, a portrait of a strong-browed, dark-eyed, dangerous young nobleman.

I have a great interest, Miss Rillieux, in the methods and techniques of the society thief.

Then, mercifully, he was past her, and she had safely entered the park.

She and Lorenzo Perkins had agreed to meet behind the *Angel of the Waters* at the Bethesda Terrace north of the lake. But, as usual, he was late. She found an empty stone bench that gave her a good view of the crowded plaza and sat down to wait. Water brawled from the bronze feet of the *Angel*, cascading down the tiers of the fountain.

Only sheer desperation to find out about her brother could have induced her to hire a former Pinkerton man. First she had exhausted every possible means. Interviews with Irish immigrants from her old neighborhood in Dublin, research at the university library—she even regularly lighted a candle to Saint Jude, the patron saint of all lost causes. Secretly, of course, for she was a devout Catholic awash in ruling-elite Protestants and attended Trinity Church with Paul.

But eventually she decided that God helped those who

helped themselves. So she had also, at great expense and risk, engaged Perkins's services. So far, however, he had turned up little of any real use, only vague, unsubstantiated bits of information.

Thus ruminating, she didn't even notice Lorenzo until he sat down beside her. "What's with the widow's weeds?" he greeted her.

"Just a bit of prudence. Were you able to find out anything?"

Perkins looked at her with small, dull eyes like a turtle. He was somewhere in his thirties, she guessed, his teeth badly neglected. He was foolishly vain about his waxed mustache, which he carefully pointed every now and then with thumb and forefinger—perhaps to detract from his teeth, though it only pulled her eyes to his mouth even more often.

"I've been asking around on the quiet about that ship I mentioned to you, the *Sir Francis Drake.*"

"And . . . ?"

He shrugged, watching the motley flow of humanity all around them. Children in white linen were watched by nannies in blue serge. Mixed among them were the street arabs, the children like Hush who wore rags and lived virtually on the street. But even they were children and couldn't resist the sight of pennies in a fountain and the hurdy-gurdy man.

"Every lead just turns into a dead end," he told her. "This kind of search takes time. But I am closing in on your brother's whereabouts. I feel it in my bones."

"Yes, but that's precisely what you told me last time, Mr. Perkins. You've learned *nothing* since then?"

"What could you possibly know about the detective business? You must understand something—all's grist that comes to my mill. It must be sorted through at great pains. I'm getting there, I tell you, but you must be patient."

"But you've absolutely nothing to report in two weeks? What have you been doing?"

"I don't live in your pocket, you know. I have several other cases I'm working on."

"Yes, you told me. Debt skippers, I believe you said."

"Among other things," he assured her, his tone defensive.

A storm of anger began to rise inside her, but for Bram's sake she quelled it. Her attitude toward Perkins was forged of distaste and forbearance, for he was her only hope—yet, a forlorn hope. However, detectives were not so easily acquired, and she was not eager to search out another who might prove even worse.

"If he did sail aboard the *Drake,*" she pressed on, "wouldn't there be some record? Ship's log or something?"

"That's one nut I haven't cracked yet."

Among many others, she thought bitterly.

"I mean to look into it," he added, seeing the anger in her eyes and firmed lips.

In the distance factory steam whistles blew the lunch call. Mystere remained in a moody silence, watching a sudden, stiff breeze wrinkle the surface of the lake. The boaters were all forced to grab their hats.

But the water jogged her memory, and her inside eye saw Bram's abduction happening all over again.

It was only a few weeks after Rillieux had rescued her and Bram from the Jersey Street Orphanage. She had been eight at the time, Bram fourteen. One day, while they were wandering around Manhattan seeking victims to rob as Rillieux had instructed them, a dark carriage had suddenly pulled up beside them.

Four men dressed like ordinary seamen had grabbed Bram and thrust him into the carriage, evidently impressing him for duty on a ship. The carriage had then sped away, leaving her helpless, devastated, and bereft of family.

Bram had haunted her ever since. His disappearance was as if her very arm had been cut off. She was tormented by visions of what had happened to her only relative, the beautiful boy with the platinum blond hair so different from hers and eyes the exact green color of Ireland's dewy fields. Sometimes she wondered if the person who wrote the letter had found Bram. She tried to picture him living in a fine house, beloved and cherished—a man now of twenty-six, perhaps even with a family of his own. But if so, why would he have deserted her—or did he think she was dead?

"Once, when I was twelve," she told Perkins, breaking the long silence, "I thought I saw Bram. He was up in the rigging of a ship that was sailing from the docks on South Street. The same hair and eyes. But I was too late to board the ship."

"A packet ship?"

She nodded. "Square-rigged," she added, for she had done some reading about ships after that.

"Did you notice the name of the ship?"

"No, I . . . I was too upset to think of it at the time."

"Upset" was a vast understatement. She had called out Bram's name over and over, yet those magnificent emerald eyes had merely stared at her as she ran along the docks screaming, no recognition in his cold, blank stare.

Lorenzo watched her from a sullen deadpan. She had noticed that he rarely smiled, and when he did it was a scornful smirk that suggested a lack of ironic subtlety. He gave her one of those smirks now.

"It's not wise to stack your conclusions higher than your evidence. He may indeed be alive. But it's also possible he's buried in a nameless grave in Potter's Field by now. Or locked up in the penitentiary on Blackwell's Island."

"If it's the latter," she pointed out, "couldn't you find out? The prisoners' names must be recorded somewhere."

Shrewdness seeped into his eyes. "I can make some inquiries, yes. But as they say: An empty hand is no lure for a hawk."

Nor for a rook, she thought bitterly. Out loud she only said, "More money already?"

"It's not for me; it's to bribe the right officials."

Frustration sharpened her tone. "But, Mr. Perkins, I gave you one hundred dollars only two weeks ago."

He forced out a fluming sigh. "Yes, well, you needn't get your nose out of joint. I'm afraid I find myself temporarily in straitened circumstances. My wife has been feeling poorly of late and requires much medical attention."

"Yes, you mentioned that last time we met." *When you reeked of liquor,* she thought. She suddenly remembered Hush, and it occurred to her: She could find out how Lorenzo was spending his time—and her money.

But for right now she only opened her purse and took out the money Paul had given her last night.

"This is all I have right now. Fifty dollars."

"It'll help," he assured her, tucking the folded bills into his fob pocket.

"When do you think you might know something?"

He shrugged one shoulder. "What's after what's next? Ask me something easy. I told you before I'm getting closer."

She had noticed he always got flip with her once he pocketed her money. By now her anger at him had driven her past the point of discretion. Rather than risk a nasty, pointless fight, she abruptly stood up.

"Since it's needless to keep meeting regularly, will you please call me if anything turns up? Our number is in the telephone directory."

He stood up, too, his turtle eyes studying her clothing again. "Under Rillieux, right?"

"Yes."

"It's a small directory," he said, still watching her. "Few people can afford telephones. I see your name in the society columns, you and your uncle. So I'm naturally curious. Why do you keep it on the quiet that you've hired me? And if you know you're a Rillieux, why don't you also know your own brother's last name?"

The question had come up before. But she had not told

him about the letter at home in its birchwood box. Bram had sworn her to secrecy about that, claiming only the right people should see the letter. However, he had been abducted before he could find those right people.

"I'm not aware," she replied archly, "that *I'm* the subject of your inquiries."

His little smirk-smile was back. "It might make my job easier if you were honest with me."

"I'm as honest as I need to be," she assured him. "I hope you are, too."

With that she turned and walked away, her hopes thoroughly dashed and a sharp pang of despair in her heart.

Chapter 5

Mystere had no appetite, but she felt slightly dizzy as she exited the park onto Fifth Avenue. Remembering that she had left home without eating breakfast, she stopped at a tea shop and ordered a light lunch.

She returned to the house shortly after two P.M. After a quick but relaxing hot bath in her quarters, she changed into a royal blue silk taffeta dress. Like most of her dresses, it had a high bodice and was cut to downplay her womanly figure.

She found Rillieux downstairs in the parlor with Rose, Evan, and Baylis gathered around him. Hush had gone.

"Baylis will take Mystere and me to the Vernons'," Rillieux was saying as she came into the room. "But he'll have ample time to drive back here and pick up Evan. I've culled the newspapers to determine who has gone abroad for the summer."

He handed Evan a sheet of paper and an odd-looking key Mystere recognized as a *passe-partout*, or master key. He made them himself in a lead ladle. Known simply as bar keys on the street, they included as many as four standard bits found in domestic locks of the day.

"Here are the addresses. Some will have left servants staying on the premise, some not. So use caution. Remember: only cash, good jewelry and time pieces, and good silver service. That's all Helzer wants at the present time."

"Not even good furs?" Baylis asked. Only in his twenties, he had a hard little face like a terrier and wore a derby hat with a grouse feather in the band. He had no beard except a line of hair between the chin and the neck—called a Newgate fringe because it covered the spot where a rope was placed in a hanging.

Rillieux shook his sleek white head. "Presently no. He has trouble disposing of them quickly."

"Helzer's getting mighty picky these days," Evan complained in his barrel-chested voice. At first glance the man who served as the Rillieux's "butler" appeared hulking and simian. But further study revealed a big, powerful man who was strikingly quick and coordinated for his size. A "cauliflower" left ear attested to many fights in his youth. Mystere knew that he and Baylis both still carried their knuckle dusters from the old days at Five Points—loops of heavy, shaped brass that fit over the knuckles in a fight.

"Yes, well, it can't be helped," Rillieux explained. "This new chief of detectives, Inspector Byrnes—he's brought in new methods that put pressure on our fences."

He turned his attention to Mystere, who had joined Rose on the carved rosewood sofa.

"You look quite charming, dear. An improvement over the rag you donned earlier. Did your shopping go well?" The old con's searching look told her he still suspected her story.

"Quite well," she lied, not backing down from his scrutiny. After all, she had learned the art of lying from him. "But mightn't I beg off from the poetry reading this afternoon?"

"Why? I thought you liked poetry. Don't you feel well?"

"I do enjoy it, and I'm not ill. Just a bit people weary, is all. It's been a hectic social calendar lately."

All that was true. She was tired. She hadn't slept well last night, and today's fruitless meeting with Lorenzo had drained her. She would love to spend a quiet afternoon in her quarters just reading and thinking.

"Buck up, Mystere. It wears on me, too. But remember, membership in the Four Hundred confers obligations as well as privileges. One of those obligations is to be a highly social creature."

There it was again, she fretted—the "kind choke hold" as she called Rillieux's grip on her. He had given her so much, but he required a great deal, too. Yet, he rarely made demands, for he could easily coerce her with kindness. And if kindness didn't work, then there was always the "other Rillieux" to go to work on her. That man was no gentleman of the Four Hundred. Paul Rillieux's dark side was in keeping with the liar and the fraud that he was. Deep inside him was a hard, cruel spirit that showed itself infrequently because he did believe one got more flies with honey. She had seen that man only once when she had refused to lift a brooch from a matron who was rumored to be on the verge of bankruptcy. Before the ball, Rillieux had entered her bedroom and beat her with his silver-and-ebony walking stick. And even when the stick broke under the strain of the lashing, he continued, his face frozen in hard, earnest contempt.

She had hardly been able to move at the ball, let alone dance with her beaux. He had been careful not to touch her face, so the bruises were well covered, and he gallantly attributed her new-found reluctance to dance as shyness. Despite her soreness and pain, she got him the brooch. But the memory of the episode was worked into her mind like a brand.

She and the others let Rillieux rule with his kind choke hold, for the other choke hold was much worse.

"I'll go to the poetry reading if you like," she said, quietly resigned to it. "But I can't guarantee I'll be able to take anything."

Rillieux nodded. "Mainly I just want both of us to get familiar with the place this visit. Trust me, we'll be invited back. If you see a target of opportunity, of course, then seize it. But you might be too busy keeping Carrie Astor entertained."

Mystere groaned. "You mean she's back from boarding school in England?"

"Yes, and she'll be with her mother this afternoon. Caroline wants you to be kind to her. The girl's very reserved, but evidently she's quite taken with you, Mystere."

"She does fancy Mystere," chimed in Rose, who had seen the two women together. "But she ain't 'reserved,' Paul—she's a reg'lar dimwit."

Old Rillieux snorted. "Of course she is, but she's also an Astor. Every blemish is a beauty mark when it's on the rich. But nothing has assured our own success with Caroline as much as her daughter's affection for Mystere."

He's right about that, Mystere thought. Proof that Mrs. Astor favored her could be found in the matron's sincere words, which never took on a cutting edge when directed at her or old Rillieux. Usually the only compliments Caroline gave were left-handed, always managing to insult even as she flattered. "Now *that's* a magnificent gown," she might bestow on some dowager, her tone implying that it was high time she finally dressed smartly.

"I'll be nice to Carrie," Mystere promised. "She's boring, but at least she isn't a horrid snob. But Rafael Belloch may show up, too. He's known for appreciating poetry. And if he's there, he'll keep a close eye on me. I still say he's trouble, Paul."

Rillieux's sharp, foxy face eased into a knowing grin. "Oh, he's watching you, all right. But has it ever occurred to you, dear heart, that it isn't *suspicion* that motivates his interest?"

Baylis, Evan, and Rose exchanged covert glances, all three of them joining Rillieux in a knowing grin.

"Mystere thinks them linen wraps make her a little Miss Pink Cheeks," Baylis said.

"They do," Rillieux insisted. "But that's my point. Some men don't *want* to wait for a girl to become a woman—they desire the girl and her innocence. It excites them, makes them want—"

"I take your meaning," she cut him off abruptly, flushing at his words. "But I assure you that none of his remarks suggest that sort of thing."

"What sort of thing?" Evan teased, and the rest all laughed.

"Words," Rillieux informed her, "were given to us to disguise our true thoughts. Belloch isn't trying to arrest you; he's interested in seducing you. Perhaps we could even coerce him into marrying you. It could prove a quite profitable union, Mystere."

"Especially," Evan chimed in, "when the groom dies tragically, leaving you everything he owns."

She felt her pulse speed up as heat flooded her cheeks. She directed her words at Rillieux. "Earlier today you told Hush thievery should never involve violence or bloodshed. Are you abandoning your credo?"

He frowned at Evan. "Of course not. That kind of talk is just more of Evan's air pudding. Now stir your stumps, Baylis, and hitch the team. We must get a move on."

Fifth Avenue's once middle-class brownstones had become Manhattan's Palatial Row, stretching north for miles. Nothing in the world rivaled it for sheer ostentation, especially the Vanderbilt chateau at the corner of Fifth Avenue and Fifty-second Street, built of imported marble at a staggering cost of three million dollars.

The Vernon mansion was located on the lower end of the avenue. While not so lavish as some, it was nonetheless a stately granite structure built in the style of a medieval cathedral—the ideal setting, Rafe Belloch told himself, to enjoy some good poetry, if, indeed, any were to be had today.

His sense of anticipation only sharpened when he was escorted into the huge second-floor library with its magnificent vaulted ceiling. Mahogany bookcases filled with leather-bound volumes were separated by paintings in gold scrollwork frames—privately owned master-pieces that occasionally graced the walls of the Louvre and Saint Sophia, for the Vernons were collectors of European paintings.

Tea was served in fine and rare Russian porcelain. For those desiring something stronger than tea, bottles of wine and liquor crowded a carved mahogany sideboard manned by a dapper bartender with neatly pomaded hair. Rafe had ordered a Scotch and soda almost the moment he arrived. Now, as usual at such gatherings, he stood off by himself, watching the crowd as he pretended to study an enormous floor globe on a walnut pedestal base.

As was the custom, Caroline Astor reigned over everything with matriarchal reserve. She shared a white brocade sofa at the front of the room with her daughter Carrie. But the sofa might as well have been a throne—every arrival, Rafe included, first paid obeisance to Mrs. Astor and Carrie before greeting the hosts.

He had met Carrie the last time she came home from school. The girl was maddening to talk to, for she floundered from notion to notion like a parrot among shiny objects. And while not precisely unattractive, she had a soft, lopsided mouth that irritated him.

Seeing the two women together made him grin inwardly at the ironies of life among the Brahmins. Everyone knew that Caroline had mentored him from the first moment he had returned to New York with his new fortune—despite his dark history, known to all in the Four Hundred, it was Caroline who made sure he was included in every social occasion.

She seemed quite fond of him—too fond, some whispered. The matron of hyphenated New-York society would not lightly take on a lover, he knew. But if she ever did, he would bet his whole fortune she would make a play for him, Rafe Belloch. And he was eagerly waiting for the day Mrs. Astor let her heart get the better of her. Either for herself or for the vicarious thrill through her daughter, she would one day let down her guard with him. And it would cause her own social ruin. *Damn her,* he thought, *damn her and her kind to hell anyway.*

He felt the old anger rising inside him like a tight bubble. Those assembled here today had no idea what a ferocious grudge he harbored against them. His impeccable family lineage, and his massive railroad fortune, easily qualified him as a Patriarch. But their social aspirations were all a shallow, pathetic game to him. Twenty years earlier his own parents had been caught in the social noose that had only tightened under the reign of Caroline Astor and her court. The Belloch family background was unassailable, their fortune—when intact—had been old and immense.

But then his father, in one tragic moment of bad business judgment and unlucky timing, lost virtually everything in risky foreign bond investments. Two days later, on Rafe's fourteenth birthday, he locked himself in his study and shot himself. His mother died in a tenement bed right in front of him only a few years later, a lonely and broken woman, her "society friends" having turned their backs on her.

The pain and despair he saw during his drives through Five Points was not so far away from the life he once knew. And he would see the best of them—Mrs. Astor herself—take a taste of it if he could.

He consented to play Patriarch only as a form of dark ironic revenge. They were the architects of his family's demise, and he swore by all things holy that he would wreak havoc. He would crush their precious hierarchy; he would soil their debutantes and toss out their queen. The upper crust would crumble with a nasty public scandal—or even two. He despised the effete elite with their mordant wit and snobbish gossip. The women were bloodless harpies, the men soft-handed barbers' clerks.

"Ease off, old son," he cautioned himself, for he felt anger and alcohol making him reckless.

Again he searched the room, cataloging the familiar faces of the enemy.

There was that pompous, arrogant ass Abbot Pollard, a fancy foulard tucked into his shirt and making him look like an aging, bandy-legged dandy. And Antonia Butler's fetching amber brown eyes occasionally peeked at him over her palmetto fan, letting him know his advances were welcome. He smiled right back, anticipating the trouble in store for her.

Different women, different games.

And the one he gamed for now had blue eyes the frosty color of a moonbeam.

Lady Moonlight was feasting on the fools more quickly than even he could, and a begrudging admiration had formed inside of him for her. He had no real proof Mystere Rillieux was the notorious jewel thief, nor even the young bandit who had made him strip in the alley off Baxter Street.

But if eyes were the windows of the soul, then he had peered into that soul once before.

Mystere Rillieux's eyes were the same eyes that had haunted him for two years. No matter how many trips he and Wilson had taken to Five Points, the masked girl had never crossed their path again. But then, wholly unexpectedly, she had appeared to him, pale and girlishly straight, dressed in an innocent's gown. In his heart and soul he burned with the conviction that he had found her.

Different women, different games.

If he was truthful with himself, he knew he wanted her if only for the secret chase of unmasking her. He wanted her for the vengeful gratification of disarming her. And in the darkest part of his soul he knew he wanted her for the sweet sexual thrill of her surrender.

The reproach in her eyes, her wounded expression—those were things he would deal with afterward. He was a man first, and he hungered for conquest. Of the prey of his choosing.

But, as the poetry reading progressed, it appeared the Rillieux might not attend. Rafe couldn't escape a sting of disappointment. If there was one among them he ached to toy with, it was that beauty.

Then, only a few minutes into the reading, he saw Mystere enter the library on her uncle's arm.

Her glance touched him and quickly slid away.

His instincts raged, and his suspicions fired anew. He had noticed something else about the girl. She seldom smiled, but when she did it was a restive smile, the smile of a woman who knew too many secrets.

Staring at her, he watched her uncle seat her. Though it was not warm, she fanned herself with a small white lace fan. Her delicate shoulders were tense and knotted, and he wondered if it was their late arrival that had her on edge.

But then she made the fatal error of meeting his gaze.

Her hesitancy, her worry, sent an electricity through him that could have lit the whole of Manhattan for a week. And then he knew: She was the Lady Moonlight, and she was his back alley assailant. And she would be his whether she knew it or not.

It's about time, he decided, surveying the room full of rigid matrons and pompous buffoons, *that I make some inquiries about the supposed Creole miss from New Orleans.* He eyed Rillieux. *And that "uncle" of hers, they could both do with a little digging.*

A dark, derisive smile graced his lips. He ached for Mystere to turn and look at him again, but she sat as rigid as the matrons, seemingly transfixed by the reading, holding her secrets as close as stolen jewels.

Chapter 6

David Cyril Oakes, the much ballyhooed poet championed by Mrs. Astor, turned out to be a pop-eyed, wild-haired, white-bearded old man straight out of Genesis. A visiting professor at Columbia College, the Welshman's dark and gloomy meditations about death and dying, as well as his pompous worship of the pastoral life, struck Mystere as cloying and sickly sweet—just like the overpowering odor of the creamy gardenias Emma Vernon had chosen to decorate the library.

But predictably, those who were bored stiff feigned interest as good breeding required. The room erupted in loud applause when Oakes had finally dragged to a groaning, despondent conclusion with a verse called "Ode to a Mortuary."

"The man's dull as ditch water," Abbot Pollard muttered in Mystere's ear even as he clapped with enthusiastic vigor. "The ass waggeth his ears, and another society poet is born. 'Death, thou dusky demon.' What tripe! Pope and Dryden must be turning in their graves."

"He's certainly dour," she agreed. But even as she smiled at the perpetually displeased Pollard, she felt Rafe Belloch's glacial gaze like a cold hand on her neck.

An alarm went off inside her.

He's watching me, she decided. *Waiting for me to make the wrong move.*

Meantime, Pollard had got going on one of his favorite tirades: the decline and fall of New York's superior caste.

"It's a real disgrace how Caroline's head has been turned by all this new money. J. P. Morgan is the only one in that scrabbling, grasping crowd I truly respect. He, at least, appreciates rules and controls. These nouveaux riches are bent on seizing power and ousting the genteel aristocracy. But perhaps blood will win out—you may not know this, my dear, but the very first John Jacob Astor was an absolute savage of a man, ill-mannered and unclean in his habits."

"Mr. Pollard," she chided, still watching Rafe from the corner of her eye, "you sound as pessimistic as our gloomy old poet."

"Nonsense, *ma chere.* You are too young to remember Black Friday, caused by our greedy robber barons. But certainly Caroline remembers it. Or ought to, for pity's sake."

"I remember the Panic of 'seventy-three," she assured him.

"Yes, well, both resulted from railroad men and their criminal recklessness. Now suddenly all is forgiven them."

He aimed a spiteful glance at Belloch, and she wondered if there was something personal to Rafe's lone-wolf attitude toward the rest of the Four Hundred.

Pollard loved to grandstand, and his bold insults soon attracted a circle of listeners around them.

Mystere saw Belloch edge nearer. She hoped to latch on to Carrie, but the younger Astor was presently chatting with Paul and the poet. Oakes appeared to be showing them drawings or photographs, and Carrie had gone whey-faced.

"I've noticed something else," Pollard nattered on in his nasal baritone and affected pronunciation. "As Caroline's attitude toward the newly rich has altered, so has her view of the poor. She will soon jump on the bandwagon and blame the wealthy for their plight. Why, much of Oakes's sweet-lavender asininity just now was an elegy to the unwashed. What's next? Shall we invite Celts and Negroes to our next ice cream party?"

"Tell us, old roadster," Rafe's powerful voice spoke up behind Abbot. "Do you ever take time to smell what you shovel?"

Pollard didn't even bother to turn around. "I have never handled a shovel in my life, Mr. Belloch, and never will."

"Yes, believe me, it's shown in your physique."

Mystere was forced to cough to cover her sudden laughter. A few others smiled, while some frowned at Belloch's unseemly aggression.

"No doubt," Pollard responded with casual malice, "your own unfortunate childhood poverty has left you with a bias, Mr. Belloch. However, the Reverend Conwell is absolutely right. The poor have made their own beds; now they can damn well sleep in them. There are, indeed, 'acres of diamonds' for all with the will and courage to harvest them."

Belloch kept his hard gaze fixed on Mystere even as he directed his remarks at Pollard. "I might feel more impressed," he pointed out, "if I didn't know that your own fortune is inherited. What diamonds have you ever harvested?"

"Not one, I'm proud to report. Self-made men bore me. As usual you have the truth hind side foremost. Raw greed, sir, is no substitute for superior birth and breeding."

"Yes," Belloch said, his voice so quiet now Mystere had to strain to hear him. "I know all about your superior ways."

Mystere knew from Rillieux's schooling that Belloch was violating strict code by going on the offensive and "making speeches," although Pollard well deserved it. But again, she suspected Rafe spoke up more from some personal strategy than deep emotional conviction.

Just as his manner had done last night, his attack sent Pollard and the others packing. She looked up and realized Rafe had her all to himself. She wondered if it had not been his goal all along.

His intense dark eyes raked over her, frank and disdainful at once. But she refused to be intimidated. She had decided to take the offensive herself lest this dangerous man gain power over her.

"Well, you can certainly be belligerent, Mr. Belloch," she taunted him. "No one can accuse you of being a play-the-crowd man."

"Truckling to people of rank is fine, Miss Rillieux, if your only goal is to be a fawning lapdog like Ward McCallister."

"You have farther reaching goals, I take it?"

Those impertinent dark eyes seared into her. "Oh, indeed. There's no limit on my . . . desires."

Or my thirst for destruction, his tone seemed to add.

Despite her newfound resolve, his double entendre made her blush. "I'm curious, Mr. Belloch. Clearly you are a man of some passion. Also rich and, I might add, quite pleasing to the feminine eye."

He gave a gallant half bow to acknowledge the compliment.

"So why on earth is a good catch like yourself still off the hook? Is it us women you despise or just marriage?"

"Neither, Miss Rillieux, although I confess that marriage holds little appeal for me. While I do not find it totally inconceivable, in my case it must be, as they say, a *pisaller,* the last resort."

"The last resort for what?"

A smile tightened his lips. "Has this child a nurse? Does her mother know she's out?"

Again she felt his smug, goading, self-satisfied voice grate on her nerves. In his own way he was as egocentric as Pollard. But where Pollard was a harmless crank, this man was as dangerous as unstable nitro. She had no hard proof for her conviction, but she was convinced nonetheless.

"Perhaps," she suggested, pretending to study the gathering, "you had better inform Antonia Butler of your instinctive aversion to wedlock. She hasn't kept her eyes off you since I've been here."

"You noticed that, have you? Well, *I'll* not warn her. The eagle has no pity for the lambs."

She baited him with her smile. "Caroline Astor is no lamb. And her 'lapdog,' as you call Ward, has made some noise lately about a possible match between you and Carrie."

"So that's two women, so far, you've conferred on me. Are you assembling a harem for me?"

"Why not? *Eagles* take what they want anyway, right? Perhaps I'll make it three by adding Caroline herself. She so enjoys touching your cheek."

His eyebrows arched, and his mouth set itself in a hard smile. "This is interesting."

"What is?"

He gave a harsh bark of laughter. "You, that's what. It would seem that our helpless little kitten has discovered her claws since last night."

"Even kittens fight back when they are being bullied."

"Bullied? Come now, that's much too harsh."

Even as he spoke, however, his actions belied his words, for he had taken her arm in his iron grip. Full-length windows stood open to admit the breeze. He "escorted" her through the nearest one onto a scrolled-iron balcony. Then he stood between her and the window, blocking her escape.

"I don't wish to be out here," she informed him, biting off each word in anger.

"No? Then jump. It's only two floors. Perhaps your *innocence* will save you."

"Mr. Belloch, seriously, Caroline asked me to spend time with Carrie, and I—"

"Carrie's busy with your uncle. He charms all the ladies, I've noticed. Did you happen to see this morning's *New York World*?"

"No," she retorted coldly. "I barely manage to read the *Times*."

His probing eyes forced her to break eye contact. "They have a very colorful story today about the theft of the Pendergast brooch. Indeed, the writer seems quite enamored of our Lady Moonlight. Sees her as a class warrior punishing the rich."

"As I said last night, Mr. Belloch, no one has even proved the thief is a woman. But frankly I don't care either way. I don't share your apparent obsession with common thieves. Now, if you will excuse me. . . ."

She tried to duck around him, but he was too quick. For a moment he detained her with both hands almost circling her waist. At the unexpected contact, she felt a current jolt through her, taking the strength from her legs. She strained to break free, but he held her back with effortless ease. His strength, she realized, was impressive—and daunting.

She met his gaze. A smoldering emotion touched the color of his eyes. He looked down at his hands, and a wry smile twisted the corner of his mouth. "If I weren't a gentleman," he whispered in her ear, "I might move my hands a few inches higher and test a theory of mine."

Alarm made her heart race. An uninvited, tingling warmth spread low through her stomach. She stared up at him. His gaze held hers. Her breathing grew faster and uneven.

"Please, Mr. Belloch, this is most improper," she whispered, almost pleading with him.

He leaned closer. So close she felt his breath caress her temple.

"You needn't fear me," he said, his voice a low rumble. "We're alike, you and I. We both prey upon the Four Hundred—"

"I don't know what you're talking about," she interrupted, struggling with his hold to be free.

"You don't, eh?" He chuckled, and his grip became a manacle. Slowly his hand rose up her corset. Slowly, as if he was relishing his greed and his suspicions. And his lust.

She grabbed his hand and gave him a poisonous stare. Paul had alluded to some trinket that belonged to Sylvia Rohr. But not only would there be no theft today, Mystere would be fortunate to get away with her disguise still a secret.

"If you don't remove your hands this instant," she threatened him, "I swear I'll scream for my uncle."

He released her, but he still blocked her passage.

Unable to face his mocking, accusing eyes, she turned and went to the balcony railing. The light of late afternoon had begun to take on the mellow richness just before sunset. A pair of silky English setters were playing in the garden below. She watched them while she got her breathing under control.

"It's not common thieves who interest me, Miss Rillieux," he said behind her. "As I told you last night, I'm fascinated by the society thief."

"Yes, and you also hinted that my uncle and I are part of some theft ring. If you have evidence, then why not go to the police with it and stop harassing me?"

"I don't have a shred of evidence. But almost two years ago I was robbed by a gang at Five Points. One of them was a woman. A beautiful woman who looked very much like you. Except that she was . . . hmm, shall we say fuller in her figure than you appear to be."

"Oh? Do you expect me to disrobe for you to prove my innocence?"

"Actually, yes. You see, the woman who robbed me also made *me* strip naked. Turnabout is fair play."

"Well, you'll have to go on being suspicious of me, for I assure you I shan't strip for you."

He laughed, though it was mirthless. His voice deepened, coarsened, and some animal part of her thrilled at the sexual urgency in his tone even as it frightened her.

"All I need to do," he reminded her, "is toss chivalry to the wind. I can reach out *right now* and see if those French wineglasses are really the full, succulent fruits I suspect they are."

"Do it," she flung at him, meeting his stare and matching wills with him. "Prove that Abbot Pollard is right about you and your kind."

"By God I will," he almost whispered, stepping closer.

"Mystere!" chimed a female voice from the open window behind him. "I wondered where you were hiding. Or have I interrupted plans for an elopement?"

For once in her life Mystere was overjoyed to see Carrie Astor. She rushed forward, sweeping quickly around Belloch. "Carrie, it's good to see you again. Oh, Mr. Belloch and I were merely discussing a point of anatomy in Greek statuary. How *are* you, Carrie?"

She took the new arrival by the arm and started back inside.

"You won't believe it," Carrie confided in a shocked tone, "but Mr. Oakes is showing photographs of cadavers. I was very nearly sick. The man is . . . rather queer."

"Miss Rillieux?"

Mystere looked back over her shoulder. "Yes, Mr. Belloch?"

"I'll always be wondering," Rafe said in a taunting voice, repeating her own words from that night at Five Points.

A sick dread engulfed her. He knew. He knew, and he was going to be ruthless until he could be certain.

She flushed, and he laughed outright. And despite her bravado, it was she who first lowered her eyes and turned away.

Chapter 7

Hush's first reading lesson took place in the same parlor where Rillieux and his unique retinue of thieves had met the day before. Mystere sat in the master's favorite carved walnut chair while her dirty-faced pupil straddled a three-legged stool close beside her.

The lad was smart, she already knew, but also undisciplined and unused to concentration—except for an amazing focus of attention when it came to learning thievery from old Rillieux, a master educator. So she contented herself, this first lesson, with making him memorize the letters *A* through *L*. This he mastered in mere minutes. Then she showed him how to sound out the letters while he copied them from a hornbook she had purchased for him.

"Now listen and follow my finger while I read aloud," she instructed him. "Notice how the letters sound. Especially those you've learned today."

She read slowly from *Leslie's Illustrated Weekly* a breezy little piece about the recently opened Brooklyn Bridge. Hush followed along closely, as if the pleasure of being so near to Mystere was easily worth the pain of scholarship.

"There," she announced, closing the magazine and laying

it aside on the coffee table. "That's enough for your first lesson. That wasn't so awful, now, was it?"

"Hunh-uh. You sure got a nice voice, Mystere. I really like hearing you read."

She smiled and tousled his wild dark hair. "Thank you, charmer. Would you like some more lemonade?"

"It's mighty nice of you and all, but see—lemonade is sorter for women and kids."

She bit her lower lip to keep from smiling at his serious manner. "Oh? I see . . . so what beverage do you think might be more appropriate for a young gentleman such as yourself?"

"I like a drink called Humpty Dumpty," he boasted like an old hand.

"I've not heard of it. Is it good?"

"*I'll* tell the world! It's ale boiled with brandy. Everyone in my tenement drinks it."

Mystere looked scandalized. "You are too young for spirits."

"Aww, Hookey Walker," Hush protested. He also scowled as if he hated nothing more than when she treated him like a child. "I'm too old for lemonade is what you mean."

"All right, that's fair enough. I'll serve you coffee or tea from now on."

"With a sup of whiskey in it?"

She wagged a finger at him. "Those who drink whiskey will think whiskey."

"Huh! And them as drink lemonade will think lemonade," he retorted.

That earned him an admiring laugh, and he smiled proudly, happy to have pleased her. She was about to remonstrate further when the heavy teakwood doors parted and Rose hurried inside. She wore her usual mobcap and crisp muslin apron, her red hair done in two thick plaits.

"Just a warning," she told them in a voice barely above a

whisper. "Stand by for a blast. Paul's home from his club, and he's in an awful wax."

"Why?" Mystere demanded.

"You know how Evan and Baylis were sent foraging yesterday, among the homes of those vacationing this summer?"

Mystere nodded. "During the gathering at the Vernons', you mean?"

"Uh-hunh. Paul's alibi is fine, and yours, too, of course. But somebody botched it. They picked a house they thought was shut up tight for the season. Cleaned it out of clocks and silver and the Lord knows what all. But turned out a maid is staying there; she was only out shopping."

Mystere paled. "You don't mean they were caught?"

"No, they got out in time. But the robbery was discovered immediately and reported. Worse yet, the carriage was parked close by, and Paul's afraid that maid glommed it as she returned home. He's so angry he actually struck Baylis. I saw it myself. Oops, here they come now, saints preserve us."

Rose escaped even as Rillieux's anger-sharpened voice sounded out in the vestibule. *"Now* see what your carelessness has cost? Helzer will rook us now. A lot of money down the drainpipe, that's what it is."

"Why am *I* being pilloried?" the voice of Baylis howled indignantly. "It was this whoreson shirker who swore the place was empty."

"H'ar now!" Evan thundered. "Don't lay it at *my* door, chowderhead. I'm a mild man until I'm pushed; then I become a hellcat unleashed."

"Shut your infernal mouths, both of you!" Rillieux bellowed with amazing force for his age and physical frailty. "You're *both* a pair of bumbling idiots. My fault, though, for thinking you were exceptional men."

"We done what we was told," Baylis protested.

"Yes? Well then, it was done damned slapdash, was it not?"

All three men had paused in front of the partially open doors.

"Is the swag hidden in the coach house?" Rillieux asked a few moments later, his voice calmer.

"Sure," Evan affirmed. "That was the plan."

"Well, now the plan is changing. Take everything to Helzer immediately. We'll have to accept a lower price for rushing him. I have a paid informant among the police, a district roundsman. He tells me this investigation is being pursued vigorously. That maid may have seen our blasted carriage. Get rid of the swag. And just in case one of Byrnes's men comes nosing about, have some cock-and-bull story ready to explain why you were parked over on Riverside Drive without me or Mystere."

Mystere heard Evan and Baylis leaving. Moments later Rillieux stepped into the parlor. He showed no sign of his incensed mood from just moments ago.

"Here's my two prize pupils," he greeted them, crossing the parlor with the assistance of his cane. He bent to kiss Mystere's cheek. She smelled the cloying sweetness of his lilac cologne.

"Mystere's learning me to read," Hush bragged.

" 'Teaching' me," she corrected him.

Rillieux hardly seemed to digest any of it. "That's good, every man should be a reader," he said absently. The web of lines at the corners of his sloe eyes deepened as he studied Mystere closely, lost in some line of speculation.

"I noticed how Belloch herded you off to himself yesterday," he told her. "But judging from both your faces, he certainly wasn't making love to you. You were quite chilly toward him, evidently?"

"I was rather . . . crisp with him, yes."

Rillieux smiled at her word choice. "Fueling the flames,

dear heart, fueling the flames. I still say this chap Belloch has a sweet tooth for nymphs."

Mystere sent him a warning glance, for Hush could hear every word and she didn't like such talk in front of him. Not that he didn't hear far worse in the streets, she reminded herself.

"It's not what you think, Paul, I'm sure of it. I think he's . . . guessed some things about us. Or perhaps 'intuited' is a better word."

"Nonsense. But even if you are right, that contingency can be dealt with."

"Whatever you mean by that, perhaps you are rating him too low? He strikes me as a dangerous and capable man."

Rillieux gave a snort of contempt. "Indeed? Dangerous and capable? And yet he strips bare naked *at Five Points* on the command of a mere chit of a girl? Oh, terror has me by the throat, Mystere! God save us from this nude *Ubermensch.*"

"Paul," she chastised him, glancing quickly at Hush.

"Oh, the boy's no baby; let him hear us. Actually, Mystere, you may have a point about Belloch, my teasing notwithstanding. I quizzed Caroline about him. She used the word 'harum-scarum' to describe him. She seemed to like that idea, too."

"What's that word mean?" Hush inquired.

"Reckless and unpredictable," Rillieux explained. He glanced at Mystere. "From now on I will take him a bit more seriously."

So will I, she vowed to herself. Several times, since yesterday afternoon, she had reflected on how close things had come out there all alone with him on the balcony. A mere move upward of his hands . . . Of course, she dared not stop stealing now that he was suspicious—that would only egg him on to persecute her even more.

The danger of discovery, however, was not her only fear involving him. How many times, since yesterday, had she indignantly denied the arousal his grip on her waist had fired within her? The strong, overpowering grip of those well-formed hands had stirred a pulsing loin warmth that left her weak and breathless, entertaining mental images that shamed her in their torrid frankness.

But she *had* to curb such thoughts. Not only because they were unseemly, but because they lured her into letting down her guard. And there was not a man yet born who could do that. She was a virgin still, and planned to stay one. Forever.

Indeed, sometimes a deep, dark loneliness engulfed her, but she knew her worth to Rillieux lay not only in her "art," but also in her untainted beauty. He often spoke of making brilliant matches for her. It couldn't be done for a girl who was not an innocent. If Rillieux ever found her with a man, if he ever found her taken, she didn't know what he would do. Kill her perhaps. The idea was not out of the question. She knew his brutality firsthand. While she had never known him to kill, she had never seen him that angry either. He might sacrifice her to get at Rafe Belloch's wealth, but she wasn't available for mere love and marriage. Until she broke from him, she was his property, and Rillieux would see her dead before his goods were spoiled. She would have to run from Rillieux, and from his care. Her only two sorry choices then would be to sell herself at South Street for a bottle of whiskey or endure the rest of her life sewing shirts in a sweatshop. Neither was endurable, so she would never take the risk. Never. She would remain hungry and lonely. And alive.

Her thoughts returned to Belloch. *You were in an emotionally charged mood,* she argued even now as if defending herself to Rillieux's tribunal. *You were keyed up and tense from his prying questions—certainly it* must *be that. No decent woman would desire such a conceited, devious man as he.*

While all of these thoughts whirled through her mind, Rillieux had turned to Hush again. "Well, b'hoy, we'll soon have you living here as our new footman. Did you bring anything for the family kitty today?"

"Not yet, sir, for I spent the morning trapping rats in a concert saloon on the Bowery. Also, as you taught me, I am avoiding the park for a few days so my face is not so familiar to the roundsmen. That purse I brought you on Sunday came from there."

"That's the lad—always be cautious and crafty."

"But now the bridge is open, I can easy cross over to Prospect Park. It's chock-full of rich toffs just like our park is."

"Good, good, have at it. Just remember, don't ever discuss what you do with anyone but us. Success in this game means keeping your mouth shut. And remember we're a family here, all for one and one for all. No one"—here his glance shifted to include Mystere—"may skim off anything. I will fairly distribute our collective wealth."

"Fairly," she realized, was his call. Just as "the family kitty" was merely Paul's term for "my own pocket." She had noticed something else about Rillieux: he assured the rest they were only pretending to be his servants, but in fact they were servants, servants trained to spy, steal, and gather information. She refused to treat them as menials except in public, but he had no problem with it.

Rillieux turned and started out of the parlor.

"Sir?" Hush called behind him. "You forgot something."

Rillieux turned back around. Mystere's jaw fell open in astonishment when she saw the pingrain leather billfold that Hush held out to him.

"Well, I'm a New Amsterdam Dutchman," Rillieux said, stunned by the youth's boldness. "You cheeky little rapscallion."

An eyeblink later, however, and the old man's eyes puckered in satisfaction, and he beamed with pride and greed. "Outfoxing the old fox, eh? *That's* the ticket, tadpole.

Always keep an eye to the main chance. You're a credit to your dam—whoever she was," he added as he took his wallet back and discreetly counted the money.

Then he glanced at Mystere. "I've had only one other pupil show such immense promise, Hush. But she's left my wallet alone—so far."

It made Mystere nearly ill to see the gratitude evident in the boy's eyes. Poor Hush was fairly starved for some sense of pride in himself, and only look at the kind of praise Paul supplied for it.

After Rillieux had gone, she asked Hush, "Do you remember what I said last time you were here? About doing something *you* want to do, not just what others tell you?"

He nodded.

"Well, it doesn't really matter if someone older orders you to steal. There's an old saying: 'Those who hold a candle for the devil share his guilt.'"

"Is that what we do, Mystere? Me 'n' you—hold a candle for the devil?"

"Yes. And the crime of it isn't all. Sometimes, when you are good at what others tell you to do, you can give up your freedom just trying to please them. They become rich and powerful from your risks and skills. They are free to exercise choices while you are owned by them."

Hush, who could only see such abstractions in terms of his own life, said, "Do you mean . . . I should steal for myself?"

"I'm not sure what I mean," she confessed helplessly. She worried lest, in trying to lift the boy's morals too high, she might set him at odds with Paul's temper. For no matter how kind Rillieux might, at times, appear to be, she knew he could inflict some intense cruelties, especially on those who proved disloyal after he had placed trust in them.

But secretly she had another answer for Hush: *Yes. If you must steal, then do it for yourself, not for a master.* Tough talk.

If she ever hoped to find Bram, she would have to stop talking tough and *be* tough.

Such thinking inevitably reminded her it wasn't just Paul about whom she had to worry. There was also Lorenzo Perkins. She felt a tumult of fresh misery sweep over her. How could she ever locate her brother so long as she could not trust the very man she had hired to find him? Yet, neither did she have the strength of will to dismiss him without proof. He had, after all, come up with some bits of information such as the name of the *Sir Francis Drake*, the ship aboard which Bram might once have sailed.

She made up her mind to do what, until now, she had only contemplated.

"Hush?"

"What?"

She took out her reticule and removed a five-dollar bill. "This is yours," she told him, "if you'll do a favor for me."

He took the bill and stared at it. "Jaysus! But you don't have to pay me, Mystere."

"Never mind, take it, but don't let Paul see it. Do you know Amos Street?"

"Sure. The dispens'ry is there. Where they give medicine free to the poor."

She nodded. "At the corner of Amos and Greenwich is a druggist's shop. You can tell it by the wooden mortar and pestle out on the curb. There's a man and his wife living in the flat above the shop. The man is tall and thin, always wears a rather shabby suit and vest, and has a silly waxed mustache that looks drawn on. I need to know something about how he spends his time. Are you willing to follow him, off and on, over a few days?"

Hush grinned. " 'At'll be fun."

"Good. But you *must* be careful. Don't let him know what's up. Promise?"

"Cross my heart," he promised.

A few minutes later she saw Hush off at the front door, then lingered a moment in the vestibule, as still as the marble letter stand near the door, her thoughts again returning to yesterday, the balcony, and Rafe Belloch.

What a crying shame, she told herself, that such a well-knit and handsome man could be so dangerous to her. Rafe Belloch struck her as a brutal enemy, and she vowed to avoid him by any and all means—never mind her electric response to his touch.

Perhaps, after all, she was wrong about his interest in her. Perhaps he was only sufficiently interested to be cruel, but no more. She hoped so. But some inner self doubted that he was merely toying with her. She feared he was like a young boy who had trapped a fly—her—and now he meant to pull its wings right off and watch it die.

Chapter 8

Unlike Manhattan, Staten Island had so far escaped the frenetic pace of urban progress. It still appeared cutoff and quiet, a rural respite of wooded lots and narrow lanes, wide verandas and rush-bottom chairs. Its population of fewer than fifty thousand was dwarfed by almost two million just across the Upper Bay. Here there were no tar-papered squatters' shacks such as those dotting upper Manhattan, and the only shapes thrusting up into the sky were a few modest steeples topped by weathercocks.

Rafe Belloch liked the sense of being isolated, yet conveniently adjacent to the vital nerve center of the Wall Street financial district. He maintained a suite at the Astor House, its location across from City Hall Park convenient for occasions when business or social obligations demanded he stay near his Manhattan offices. But whenever he could, he literally retreated to Garden Cove, his seventeenth-century country estate on Staten Island's Bay Street. When the ferry didn't suit his mood, there was always his private steam yacht in a nearby slip. The three-man crew lived aboardship, ready to sail at a moment's notice.

At the same time that Mystere was teaching Hush the front half of the English alphabet, Rafe was in his study at

Garden Cove dictating letters to his correspondence secretary, Sam Farrell.

"In summation, gentlemen, I'm convinced the timing of events is propitious to our interest. The consolidation of our Midwest short-line railroads into one centrally managed corporation will greatly enhance service as well as profits. I direct that consolidation be put to a binding vote at the next regular meeting of the board of directors. Cordially yours, etcetera."

Rafe watched Sam's face closely, curious to gauge his response to this latest bombshell. Farrell often startled people at first meeting, for his snaggly-toothed grin was at odds with the deep-sunken eyes like a pair of wounds. Rafe had often thought that Sam's face blended the mask of tragedy and the mask of comedy into one disconcerting visage.

But right now that visage gave the boss no clues to his reaction.

"Can't you hear them howling already?" Rafe prompted. "And see my caricature in the editorial cartoons with octopus tentacles and a pirate's eyepatch?"

"Of course, it's predictable from that crowd of hyenas. Wear it as a badge of honor, sir. Joseph Pulitzer's ink-slinging, calamity-howling hacks can rip away at the railroad enterprise and robber barons all they like. The fact is there's been a booming bull market for twenty years now except for the scare in seventy-three. And it's chiefly thanks to the railroads. As for consolidation—the New York Short Line proves the wisdom of that, in spades. The Commodore did not abandon his beloved steamships for some pipe dream."

"Wear their scorn as a badge of honor, eh? That's good, Sam, I'll remember that."

Because much railroad work was dangerous, it had always been Rafe's company policy to hire and retrain injured blue-collar workers for clerical positions. But Sam Farrell—who had suffered a crushed right hip while dropping a coupling pin into place between two coal cars—had required little training. After reading glowing reports from his field manager in Ohio, Rafe had personally interviewed Sam and then immediately transferred him to New York with a hefty new salary.

In the years since, Sam had mastered law on his own time, passed the New York Bar, and now also served as chief legal advisor for Belloch Enterprises. It had been his steady hand on the tiller when Rafe steered the rocky course from railroad builder to investor-owner. Through all the changes Sam remained a blunt, simple, fiercely loyal man with an amazingly resourceful mind.

"I'll post the letters this afternoon," Sam told him. "Yesterday you said there was something else you needed me to do? Some inquiry to New Orleans, I believe you said?"

"Ahh, that's right."

Rafe began pacing his study, Sam's question having jolted his thoughts back to Mystere Rillieux. His study doubled as a commercial office, an odd function for a wainscoted room enhanced with Georgian carvings. The Cornelius and Baker gas chandeliers were hung to the ceiling with ropes of dangling brass serpents. The light was further augmented by old seven-arm candelabrums. A Sultanabad carpet and Gothic armchairs struck some visitors as stately and imposing, others as simply cold and tasteless. For his part, Rafe liked it all just fine and agreed heartily with those who thought he lacked refinement.

Mystere Rillieux . . . He mused, again thinking of how his hands had felt with her tiny waist in his grip. And she had not needed the corset, for he had proved that to his own satisfaction. She was petite, beautiful, and harbored some major secret suggested by her very name. And by the Lord Harry, she possessed the most striking blue eyes he had ever looked into.

But damn her beguiling bones, for it was *she* who had humiliated him at Five Points, he was almost certain now. She was a fine actress, but he felt that something within her was at war with evil and almost *wanted* to be exposed. As if . . . as if she were some kind of noblewoman trying to masquerade in criminal costume.

"I'd like you to contact Stephen Breaux's law offices on Canal Street in New Orleans," he told his secretary. "You'll find the address in the files. I once worked with them on a contract to haul cotton. He's a good man and very discreet. Have his people make some inquiries concerning a Mr. Paul Rillieux and his grandniece, Mystere, who claim to be from New Orleans."

Sam, taking notes in a flip-back pad, knew something about discretion himself. "Precisely what type of inquiries?" he pressed. "Financial information, legal records . . . personal matters?"

Rafe's expressive lips firmed in a cynical grin. "I see you're thinking like an attorney. Nothing for use as leverage. No. I think . . ."

His voice trailed off as he considered the matter. He crossed to his favorite thinking spot in the entire house, a casement window facing northeast across the Narrows.

His housekeeper always kept the blinds shut at this time of day so the sun couldn't fade the rugs. He tugged them open just in time to watch as a huge foreign steamship with three stacks cleared the Narrows and hove to for the docks at the Battery, passengers crowding the taffrail for their first good view of Manhattan. Those in first and second class would get a quick look-over and be on their way; those in steerage would be detained for processing and medical examinations at nearby Castle Garden.

But Rafe's inner eye saw only Mystere's flawless opalescent skin, smooth as some elegant lotion. He had thought more than once about sliding his hands and lips over that skin, feeling her pent-up need quiver to his touch. . . .

But no. He forced himself not to be distracted from the real issue of her true identity. There were light-skinned

Creoles, all right. He knew that. However, how many of them from New Orleans didn't know who Beast Butler was the very moment his name was uttered? Damnit, first he must expose this woman to sate his own curiosity. Then he might see about seducing her.

"Chiefly," he finally answered Sam, "I'd like to verify their identities as well as their addresses over the past years, their general social standing. Get something about the old man's character. Frankly, Sam, I suspect they're both superbly clever grifters and thieves working as a team."

It was Sam's habit to scour every daily paper in the area. He was quick to see where this was headed. "Holy Hannah! The Lady Moonlight . . . you think she's Mystere Rillieux?"

"I suspect so, yes, but keep that to yourself. Do you know of her? Mystere, I mean?"

"Only through the columns. Her uncle receives plenty of ink since he's one of Caroline Astor's acolytes."

Rafe nodded, still gazing outside. From his spot in the window he had an excellent view of the terraced garden that surrounded the house on three sides. It was teeming with a bright confusion of colors, more of his undisciplined taste: China roses, narrow-leaved asphodels with yellow flowers, brilliant poinciana bushes and marigold beds. Rising up out of the center of this floral profusion was a patinaed bronze figure of Victory holding upraised laurel wreaths. In a paddock behind the garden, a pretty sorrel horse with four white socks was enjoying a lazy roll in the grass.

"Yes," Rafe resumed, "Paul Rillieux has made quite a splash in the 'best' circles."

Indeed, there was an irony in this situation that had begun to please Rafe immensely. For whoever the Lady Moonlight really was, she was in one bizarre sense his ally. Regarding the Four Hundred, she was a pox on *all* their houses. Cleverly sailing under false colors, she stole gems from the rich. He, in contrast, meant to steal their hearts and reputations. He would ruin Carrie Astor, and by ruining the queen's most valued possession, he would take Mrs. Astor and her iron-clad position in society down with her.

Then there would be no more Four Hundred to follow her and mince about. The lot of them would suffer the humiliation of realizing they prayed to a tin idol. New York society would be finished. So let the Lady Moonlight relieve them of their trinkets. He, in fact, had plans to be the greater villain.

Such thinking, however, dredged up the anger seething just beneath his calm surface. Again he gazed at the bronze figure of Victory. Seeing it always steeled his resolve and gave him solace and strength. It made him understand something his father had somehow momentarily forgotten: A man must always see things through to the end; that was the real victory—to endure and prevail.

Never, if he lived a century, would Rafe ever forget the curt final message his father had left the world: *I am too ashamed to live a moment longer. Please forgive my weakness.*

Not one member of that group Abbot Pollard called "the elect" had turned out for John Belloch's funeral. The fact was quite conspicuous inasmuch as the successful investor had helped many of them prosper and even carried a few of them with quiet loans during the hard times.

It had killed Rafe's mother to be left a pariah, pitied and scorned by those who had once valued her company and sought her out. But her end had come more slowly, a lingering death by the self-inflicted torture of social shame. . . .

Rafe had watched it, seen what it was as it destroyed her, yet been unable to utter a word that might have prevented it.

But no more. No more.

For Sam, who glanced up from his blotter just then, the jut-jawed anger on his employer's face was all too familiar. Sam had guessed something few others even suspected: Rafael Belloch was that saddest of modern creatures, infinitely successful yet infinitely disappointed.

"Well then," Sam finally said, snapping Rafe back to the present. "Shall I send a telegraph or a letter?"

"It's not urgent, so use the mail. Tell you the truth, I'd like a little time to keep an eye on her—on them, I mean," he corrected himself quickly. "It's rather amusing, actually. What do I care if she picks clean the bones of Dame Astor's fawning lick-spittles?" He laughed. "Mainly, you understand, it's personal. You see, Sam, I'm very nearly convinced that Mystere is not *just* the Lady Moonlight. I think it was she and her gang of cutthroats who robbed me a couple years back."

Sam gaped. "You don't mean—the pert skirt who left you nearly naked at Five Points?"

"Yes, damn her. And don't worry about dragging the police into this, all right? I've some questions of my own before the police have at her."

Sam looked innocent as a parson. "The police? They're a heavy-handed lot of bunglers. I'd say you're far more likely than they to fit the punishment to the crime—pardon me the liberty of saying it, sir."

"No pardon needed, but I appreciate your good manners, Sam. Yes, you're right," he promised. "Our haughty little bandit will eat a good helping of what she dished out, count upon it."

"I believe you," Sam replied. "Then again, if she's who you think, I suspect you've got a bit of a road to travel just yet. She might prove your match."

Rafe snorted, and his dark eyes glittered with anticipation of the challenge.

Chapter 9

"**M**y dear," Paul Rillieux said in the magisterial tone he had lately picked up from Mrs. Astor, "tonight you will see the sparkler of all sparklers, one that belongs under a bell jar, not on a finger. Caroline telephoned me today with the details. Antonia's newest play-pretty is a twenty-four-karat gold ring with a huge Indian emerald set in the center and eighteen radial-cut diamonds."

"She always prefers understatement," Mystere replied drily, although Rillieux hardly seemed to notice.

Through the uncovered carriage window she looked out on a pleasant stretch of Riverside Drive overlooking the Hudson. It was a cloudy night, and dark moon shadows prowled the river and the distant New Jersey shore. The restless, shape-changing shadows seemed to match her mood.

"Of course, you won't take the ring," Rillieux nattered on. "You will simply admire it along with everyone else—for the time being. The fate of that ring will be sealed at some later date, when less publicity surrounds it. Tonight, while everyone waits for Lady Moonlight to take the obvious bait, she will instead relieve Sylvia Rohr of a most charming sapphire-and-diamond brooch. Pin, my dear, not a clasp, so it's tuck and slide as we've practiced. I know her habits well by now, and I think she's due to wear it again."

Dr. Charles Sanford and his wife Catherine (nee Logan of the Boston real-estate clan) gave their Summer Solstice Ball every season, and it had quickly earned a reputation as bland and predictable, yet entirely unavoidable. Sanford had some remote connection to the British peerage, while his wife's fortune ensured their membership on Mrs. Astor's short list. Caroline herself would be there, and so it would follow that all the other Chosen would make an appearance.

"Do you really suppose," Mystere asked idly as she watched the well-illuminated Sanford mansion draw nearer, "that Antonia has actually planned it all out with the police?"

"Mystere, I do not depend on suppositions when it comes to such matters, you ought to know that by now. It's not just Antonia Butler—the entire scheme has Caroline's blessing, too. You must remember, the Lady Moonlight may be titillating the many, but most of the stately matrons are losing patience. This thief is flouting them, making a mockery of them. That's why Antonia plans to make it obvious when she removes the ring and places it in her handbag."

"I don't doubt your information, Paul. It's just hard to believe Caroline would actually permit that all the women present would be searched."

"Only in recognition of the ring's extraordinary value. The emerald is huge and can be cut up quickly into several fine stones. Don't forget the genius of the compromise Caroline worked out with Inspector Byrnes: Each lady must volunteer to be searched, and needless to say, only police matrons will be allowed to verify compliance. Caroline knows that once she herself submits, the rest of the women will, too."

"Why are you so confident the same search will not take place when Sylvia's brooch is missed?"

He snorted. "I forget sometimes that you really *are* still

young, Mystere. First of all Sylvia's family, while old money, has lost status over the years as railroads have cut into shipping. The Butlers, in contrast, are at their social zenith. Also, the brooch, while a lovely little prize, will fetch only one-quarter of that ring's value. Byrnes depends on the goodwill of the Four Hundred for his popularity—neither he nor Caroline will go forward with a search for anything less than that ring, count upon it."

Rillieux paused to take a pinch of snuff. "However, in the unlikely event that a search does go forward, you are an unequaled expert at sleight-of-hand, my dear. Merely deposit the brooch somewhere safe, preferably outside, where we can send one of our lads to retrieve it later. If we lose it? So, we lose it. Other baubles will await in the future, that ring among them."

A strong, sudden spurt of cool breeze blew in from the river and tickled Mystere's cheek. This section of the Upper West Side, Morningside Heights, was an acceptable if not exclusive area of Manhattan, still a bit barren and open but with the city's mass hunkering nearby and rapidly closing in around it. There was talk of soon building an academic grove out where the insane asylum was, for lately New Yorkers had begun to notice they lacked a high culture to match their high wealth.

They were only three long blocks from the Sanford residence now. The three-story mansion of gray masonry had an impersonal, functional design more appropriate to the financial district. Night's dark cloak masked the dull outside, but inside, Mystere knew from several visits, all was sumptuously appointed. Besides, the dance was actually being held in the adjoining gallery, which had been temporarily expanded with a sturdy dance pavilion that jutted right out over the Hudson. Because of the stiff winds, the ladies had been advised to wear gowns with weighted hems.

Rillieux's voice cut into her thoughts. "Mystere? You know that Belloch may attend? He's been quite the bon vivant lately. And everyone has noticed his disinclination to mingle—except when you're around."

The very mention of his name caused a curious, ambivalent kind of dread inside her. On the one hand, she feared Belloch's prying eyes and his prying questions. On the other, he stirred illicit feelings of pleasure and excitement she had never before felt—nor even suspected existed.

"What of it?" she replied carefully.

"If you must know, you and he have become a speculated about 'item' in the gossip columns. Or so Caroline reports. She doesn't read them, but Ward does. In fact, I suspect he even writes some of them since they're so preposterous."

Alarm quickened her pulse. "What kind of item would anyone write about Rafe and me?"

"That's still up in the air, of course. No one is publishing the banns, believe me. Caroline is offended by it. I thought perhaps she had her own Carrie in mind for Belloch—if not herself by the way she looks at him—but she punctured that balloon the moment I floated it. She doesn't want talk, and to quell it, she might be rather inclined to push Antonia Butler as her new choice for him."

"From what I've seen," Mystere said, "Mrs. Astor has very personal reasons for making sure Belloch does not pursue Carrie."

Rillieux sniffed, amused. "My, you *have* grown up lately. You've been quite observant, dear heart, and quite discerning. I share your suspicion—there is a naughty gleam in that woman's eye when she looks at Rafe. However, I doubt she would do anything so bohemian as take on a lover. At any rate it hardly matters. I think Belloch has made it clear lately he prefers his women almost scandalously young and innocent."

"You misunderstand his interest," she insisted again. "The man is not flirting—he's persecuting me."

"Perhaps he is digging at you a bit. But that's the way of

some young men—he has the sardonic wit, as we say. For all
your skills and talents, don't forget you've known little about
men *as lovers."*

The unmitigated gall of reminding me, she fumed silently.
The smug tone was back in his voice, and again she had a
glimmer of suspicion about Paul's ultimate motives for making her a rich widow. Nor had she forgotten Evan's remark
about a tragic accident befalling Rafe after she married him.

She tried to convince herself she was being foolish. Evan
said plenty of careless, sinister-sounding things that meant
nothing. Rillieux was a thief and confidence man, yes, but no
murderer. At least not yet. . . .

But there was the coldness in his eyes when displeased or
disappointed. She knew by all her experience on the street
that he had murder in him somewhere; the fear of what he
could do was part of the choke hold. A man who methodically trained children to steal was not above furthering his career of crime. She could enumerate Rillieux's good points all
she liked—the shackles he had placed on her, though kind,
were nonetheless ironclad and binding. She was not free. And
she might never be free.

The tug of a forbidden lure pulled on her. To be her own
woman was to be awakened from a nightmare that had endured since she was a child and Rillieux had snatched her
from the orphanage. Antonia's new ring beckoned her like
bread to the starving.

*The gem is huge and could be cut up quickly into several
fine stones.*

But no . . . first she must see what Hush had to tell her
about Lorenzo Perkins. *It's one thing to want to be free,* she
told herself; *it's another altogether to be foolish.* Life on the
street was hard. She knew it too well. Rillieux was a devil,
but he was the devil she knew. Besides, in her station, she
had money to pursue Bram. She had to wait to see if the tree
bore fruit before she cut it down. Lorenzo Perkins was worth
the indenture if he was at least making some effort to find

Bram where she could not. But it was another game entirely if she found out he was simply a thief.

Simply another *thief, you mean,* her conscience pricked her.

"Paul?" she burst out suddenly, motivated by guilt and some nameless but very real fear.

"Yes?" The new caution in his tone showed that he was instantly alerted by her voice.

"All this nonsense in the gossip columns—is it wise to call attention to myself while the press is also looking for the Lady Moonlight? I . . . all the attention, it frightens me. Can't we let it all die down, try something else? Perhaps not tonight. Not now."

Mystere rarely expressed such apprehensions, and Rillieux responded with alacrity. By now they were only a half block from the Sanfords', approaching at a trot. Rillieux slid back his window panel.

"Baylis!" he called out. "Walk the team in, we need a moment."

He reached across the space between their facing seats and took both of her hands in his. "Mystere, *look* at me."

She didn't want to; she just wanted to get out of the carriage and walk for hours, alone with her thoughts. But there was no resisting years of established habit between them. Although there was no electricity this far north yet, flickering gaslights gave off enough illumination to make out his sharp facial features and the mesmeric intensity of his eyes.

"Breathe deeply and slowly," he commanded her. "Not from the lungs but even deeper, lower. Slow and steady, that's our girl."

As his will mastered her own, she felt a calm confidence replace the giddy lightness of her limbs.

"I *trained* you to shine under the most brilliant lights, remember? Finishing school in London, a tour of the Continent, ballet lessons under the incomparable Mademoiselle Dupree. You are not some base thief pretending to culture, you are an *artiste*. Like any *artiste,* you fear the attention, the challenge. But you also thrive on the very things you fear. You turn your fear into your greatest triumph."

"Yes," she answered, rallying somewhat. "You're right. I'm . . . I'm sorry."

"Nonsense, you needn't apologize for being high-strung; it's in your fam—"

He caught himself. "It's your nature," he amended. "And remember something else, Mystere. For you and me, there is no middle way out. In one sense we are astride a tsunami, and we must ride it until it crashes. Or more precisely: until the moment *just before* it crashes, when we must escape."

"And if we miss our moment—what then?"

"Hah! What do you think, m'love? They'll give me the gibbet. As for you—even Caroline Astor couldn't get them to hang a woman. You will be 'reformed' in a women's penitentiary by wiry, horse-faced old virgins who stink of rejection and failure—and hate you for being everything they are not."

He patted her cheek fondly. "But we *won't* miss our moment, for timing is all, and timing is my great skill."

Mystere began to hope, early on, that Rafe Belloch might not show up. She saw no sign of him inside the house, where the Sanfords, and Mrs. Astor, and a few others had set up a reception line for the guests; nor anywhere outside among the invitees scattered between the gallery and the adjacent pavilion, at the near end of which an orchestra was tuning up.

Already the Vanderbilt sisters, Alva and Alice, formed the nucleus of a large gathering inside the porticoed gallery, socializing rather than pairing off for the dancing. Even three months after the widely reported Vanderbilt ball, the penny papers were still abuzz with articles about the costume Alice had worn. She had come as "Electric Light" in an astonishing gown of white satin aglitter with diamonds—real diamonds for a one-occasion gown.

As usual after the initial reception, the men joined the more seasoned old guard outside for cigars and politics. The matriarch herself, Mrs. Astor, regal in a flowing summer-weight cape with a sealskin collar, claimed Paul Rillieux's company.

"You," she told Mystere, taking her off alone for a moment, "are the picture of innocence, and I for one judge the picture genuine. Remember that when others throw a shadow over your name."

"Has someone done so?"

Caroline looked closely into the younger woman's face, then shook her head in wonder. "Most likely, or will soon. But never mind it, Mystere. The public has its insatiable thirst to know all the 'inside' details about the rich, you see. And publishing scoundrels like J. Gordon Bennett are eager to provide those details, even if it means informants who tell outright lies and slander us by name."

They moved a few steps, and Ward McCallister followed them like a ship's wake, always the same discreet distance—not close enough to eavesdrop, but ready to hand should his mistress need a date written down or some new occasion "gotten up" as Caroline called setting the social agenda. His sycophantic face and manners irritated some, but influenced others around her to a more ceremonial conduct. This visible loyalty made him more valuable than his menial services.

"You just enjoy yourself, dear," Caroline urged her. "Go mingle, let your youth take over and never mind those of us who have learned to sneer at everything. You have your life before you, and you are beautiful and men want you. I envy you, Mystere. But remember that scandals are easily kindled and nearly impossible to extinguish. You have no mother to advise you, poor thing, but I share Carrie's genuine affection for you. That is why I mention such things to you, dear girl."

With those startling words, she joined Paul again and left

Mystere to her own devices. Nearby, a second large gathering had formed around Antonia Butler, mainly women paying homage to her new ring. Mystere did not hesitate, but moved forward to merge with the admirers, knowing she mustn't make herself conspicuous through aloofness.

"Mystere! How absolutely wonderful to see you again," Antonia gushed in the minor-key tone she reserved for those who did not quite rate her full enthusiasm. "You look quite lovely tonight. And well protected from any sudden chill."

This last remark was barbed and elicited a few hidden smiles, for it was an obvious slap at Mystere's wardrobe. Current evening fashions for ladies bared much of the back and shoulders, although decollete necklines were less daring than in the risque 'sixties and 'seventies. Mystere, however, as usual had worn a gown with a high bodice that hooked almost completely up the back, exposing only her delicate collarbones. Antonia, of course, assumed she dressed this way to cover her immature lack of feminine shape.

"Your new ring is gorgeous," Mystere forced herself to say in a sweet tone. She was genuinely impressed, however, by the size and purity of the emerald. For a moment, as the stone glimmered in the light from the Chinese lanterns, she was even caught in déjà vu. Again, as if the vision was embodied in the deep green center of the emerald, she saw a sailor's emerald eyes watching her, lifeless as the stone. They were Bram's eyes. And many a night she had awakened from a dream where she was again running down the docks after the departing ship, screaming Bram's name to the man who knew no recognition.

"Yes, it's quite nice, isn't it?" Antonia responded, already bored with Mrs. Astor's charity mutt. "It is frightfully heavy, though. Would you like to try it on?"

"Oh, might I?"

Antonia got it off with some slight difficulty. Both women were startled when the heavy, glittering ring proved to be a perfect fit on Mystere's finger.

"It might have been made for you," Antonia conceded, the sarcasm momentarily deserting her voice—the ring was not just a perfect fit; it was simply beautiful against Mystere's skin.

Suddenly aware how a dozen people were staring at her, Mystere slid the ring off and handed it back. "Nonsense, Antonia, it clashes with my eyes. It's perfect on you."

Mystere edged away and began chatting with Thelma Richards and Sylvia Rohr, who was, indeed, wearing the very brooch Paul lusted for. Thelma was still in a snit over the congestion, earlier that day, at the corner of Broadway and Fulton.

"Traffic was absolutely frozen for over an hour," she lamented. "A dray wagon had broken an axle, and barrels were tumbling everywhere. I do wish they would restrict commercial vehicles in the upper wards."

While Mystere nodded sympathetically, she searched everywhere for Rafe Belloch under the pretense of idly surveying the crowd.

Safe for now, she decided when she failed to spot him. However, Abbot Pollard was upon the little trio before she could think about Rafe any further.

"Ladies," he greeted them all, lifting each one's right hand with a gallant flourish and touching his dry lips to it. "What's this I see—no Lydia tonight?"

He pinched in his lips like some little schoolyard prissy who knew a secret. "And thereby hangs a tale, but *I* shan't tell it."

He didn't need to, Mystere knew, because everyone listed in the Manhattan Telephone Directory already knew about the latest scandal involving one of their own. It was a fait accompli that Mrs. Astor was the central figure in the best society of Old New York—the fixed pole around whom all the glittering stars rotated. But yesterday that comfortable universe had been shaken when one of the stars plunged from its orbit forever.

Lydia Hotchkiss, wife of a city magistrate, had been apprehended in an act of genteel kleptomania, as it was delicately called in some quarters. She was caught at Tiffany's trying to drop a locket case into her purse. Normally such crimes by the well-heeled were kept quietly hushed up.

Unfortunately for Lydia and the rest of the Four Hundred, class chivalry was dead at the *Sun*. An enterprising crime reporter bribed a store detective, and the matter quickly got noised about. Within hours Lydia's ruin was complete.

"Just think," cut in a strong, familiar voice behind Mystere. "If Lydia's genteel thievery has caused her such utter social ruin, how shall we treat our Lady Moonlight when *she's* finally . . . exposed?"

Chapter 10

Mystere spun graciously around, nodding a cool greeting to the late arriver. She felt heat leap into her cheeks as the rest, following Rafe Belloch's lead, all gazed at her, waiting for the reply.

"I'm sure I couldn't say, Mr. Belloch. Nor, unlike you, do I care overly much what happens to thieves," she replied coolly.

He threw back his head and laughed, strong white teeth flashing in the soft halo light of hundreds of translucent lanterns. Tonight, Rafe had shown up in swallowtails and a fancy frilled shirt. Women's gazes turned in his direction and lingered. The chestnut brown hair was combed straight back, revealing the strong angles of his brow. His teal gaze, more green than blue in the light, taunted her.

"Yes, I've noticed your apparent apathy about our infamous lady," he said, "but think of the excitement, the amusement—why it's better than Barnum's museum. One little slip, and our legendary thief winds up in a filthy holding cell at the Tombs."

"You have an odd idea of amusement," she demurred.

"Nonsense, you're turning into a humorless old stuffed shirt like Abbot here. I find the Lady Moonlight's activities quite diverting. Certainly more exciting than some pathetic larceny at Tiffany's."

Pollard, never one to suffer a slight in silence, pandered to the rest, deliberately avoiding Rafe's intimidating eyes: "There's no accounting for taste, ladies. It's the same with these 'progressive' poets and historians winning favor lately: the *bad smell* of an age is what they choose to remember it by."

However, the clash of stags was cut short by the sudden arrival of Mrs. Astor at the periphery of their group.

"Rafe, you've a stone for a heart," she accused, offering her hand to be kissed. "You slipped past me deliberately and positively crushed me."

Rafe assumed a contrite look, lifted her hand to his lips, then made a point of holding it as he replied with sly gallantry: "Perhaps, Caroline, I did so only to see if you'd even notice?"

"Oh? And are you experimenting on Antonia, too? She is quite miffed at you, sir, though the dear holds it in well. You may toy roughly with us old married women; we deserve what we get. But our belles have certain rights."

She paused to look at Mystere. "This lass is quite lovely, and no one can fault your interest in her company. But shall the rest merely wither on the vine?"

Mystere watched her as she again touched Rafe's smooth-shaven face with her fingertips, stroking it lightly.

"As to married women or virgin belles," Rafe assured Caroline, "maiden or matron, *no* woman should ever feel neglected."

His obvious innuendo struck Mystere as scandalous and crude, but Caroline only smiled mysteriously as she turned to speak with Thelma and Sylvia.

Mystere turned to Rafe. "It's all a glass-bead game to you, Mr. Belloch, isn't it? Utterly insignificant, like killing a fly."

His eyebrows tented in surprise. "What is?"

"Women. Antonia, Caroline—I. Any of us."

"Perhaps, but after all, glass beads should not be disparaged. They purchased Mana-hata from the savages."

She longed to put him in his place, but before she could respond, she realized that Caroline had not joined their little group merely to flirt with Rafe. Mystere watched her turn to Abbot Pollard and assume a steely-eyed look that could have frightened a Hussar.

"You, sir," she bit off coldly, no trace of humor in her voice, "are in my bad books."

This was not banter, but a literal statement of excommunication, and Pollard knew it. Pale by nature, he now went so alabaster he looked chemically preserved. "My dear woman, whatever for?"

"Crimes so vile, Abbot, that your usual blandishments and cunning wit will not save you. I shan't drag it all up now. It's sufficient to note that you've been making some rude remarks lately about me and some of those I happen to admire."

"Why, if it's that poet you mean, Oakes, we all deprecate at times; it's—"

"Do *not* interrupt me, sir," she nearly snarled, and Mystere saw a fierce, tyrannical power in Mrs Astor's eyes that chilled her blood. It cowed Pollard, too.

"Your rapier wit," she added, "is famous and often admirable. But when it skewers me continually, Abbot, it is misdirected."

Pollard opened his mouth to plead his case. But Caroline turned away and moved back to her group, leaving him to stare foolishly at the rest.

"Oh, well, *sic transit gloria mundi* and all that," he japed, putting a brave face on his ruin.

"If it's Latin you crave, old roadster," Rafe goaded him, "how about *persona non grata?*"

Refusing to buckle under the crushing rebuke, Abbot remained true to form. With an audience watching him expectantly, he piped up with spiteful gusto: "If it's rudeness you people abhor, why not pray someone of taste will finally hold sway in City Hall? Will someone here make a stand and prevent the vulgar monstrosity they want to erect on Bedloe's Island? I implore you. It's bad enough the rabble in France want to foist their populist dogma upon us. But why on earth would we help pay for it? Mark my words—that hideous statue will come to be a laughingstock among future generations. They'll show better taste and demand it come down."

"As usual, Abbot," Rafe dismissed him absently, eyes watching Mystere, "you're jabbering pompous nonsense. My God, gentlemen, has someone died?"

This last remark was directed loudly toward the orchestra. Earlier, shortly after Mystere arrived, they had gotten everyone's blood stirring with the rousing strains of the "Triumphal March" from Verdi's *Aida*. But at some point Abbot had collared the conductor, and now a gloomy, ponderous movement Mystere did not recognize, or like, filled the night with an incessant groan like dying elephants.

"It's not a railroad work song," Pollard jibed, "so you wouldn't recognize it, Rafe. It's from *Ring of the Nibelung* by Wagner. I thought it appropriate tonight as the master has only recently passed from us."

"He could have taken his infernal racket with him," Rafe muttered, strolling purposefully toward the conductor's dais. Mystere saw him slip some folded banknotes to the conductor, who seemed relieved by the request, judging from his new animation as the orchestra struck up three beats to the measure and broke into a lively waltz.

With no one yet dancing, she felt a jolt of alarm when Belloch returned and took her firmly by one arm. "May I have the honor?"

"I'd rather not, I . . . Mr. Belloch!"

But her protest meant nothing to him. His left hand fit itself to the small of her back, and he literally swept her out onto the empty outdoor pavilion.

She saw right away that he meant to intimidate her with his strength and skill, for it quickly became clear that Rafe Belloch was an excellent—if somewhat possessive—dancer. However, no matter how violently he flung her into a spin, she managed to turn it into a graceful pirouette, twirling back into his arms with perfect timing.

A raft of clouds floated away from the moon, and suddenly the surface of the Hudson behind the pavilion became a million glittering pinpoints of diamond light. For the first time that evening, the listless gossip writers spying from behind the iron palings out front began scratching furious notes.

"My compliments, Miss Rillieux," Rafe murmured against her hair, genuinely impressed. "I've been told that I lead too forcefully, yet you make me look meek."

She ignored him. Four gliding steps, his powerful thrust, and her perfect balance bringing her thrusting right back into him like a fencer.

"You always seem to be laughing up your sleeve," she accused.

"I'd rather take a look behind your chemise," he riposted, laughing when two splotches of color stained her cheeks.

Step, thrust, pirouette, and thrust again back at him. "You're also very quick with such improper evasions."

"Evade, parry, and *thrust*," he replied, twirling her out at arm's length, and yet again some invisible counterweight within her brought Mystere spinning back into his arms with such graceful precision that spontaneous applause erupted around them.

Soon nearly everyone—including the journalists outside—had noticed how superbly Rafe Belloch and Mystere Rillieux were gliding and turning with such effortless artistry. Many even assumed it was planned deliberately to enliven another garden-variety ball.

By now their dancing had inspired a few other couples out onto the pavilion. The first to join them were the new-money crowd, New Yorkers now but few by birth. But then, just as she had publicly blessed the Vanderbilts last March, Mrs. Astor deigned to dance among them, Ward McAllister giving her ever-present escort.

"You're quite accomplished at everything you do, aren't you?" Belloch probed strangely, this time with no sarcastic intent.

Brought up short at the end of the dance, Mystere gave him a small, gracious curtsey. "I'd hardly say everything," she said in dismissal.

His gaze was merciless, giving her no place to run. "Well, of course I imagine there are many things you still haven't tried yet."

"Many, perhaps, but I mean to do some of them, sir."

He laughed, still holding her hands so she couldn't escape. "Oh, that's capital. You tossed the 'sir' in just perfect. Young and innocent, aren't you, the debutante come forth like a sweet new flower. Well, just remember—as to the things you haven't done yet, but mean to . . . Thoughts need never submit to a master. No one can be arrested for one's own private mental images."

"I've figured all that out without your telling me."

His eyes lowered to her modest chest. "Of course you have, but it excites me to talk about such things with you."

She tried to pull free, but he restrained her, still studying her in the soft light.

"Yes," he said with newfound conviction, looking closely into her vivid blue eyes. He held a hand to the lower half of her face as if mimicking a domino. Then he stared, a triumphant smile growing on his hard mouth. "It was you. Indeed, the light was dim that night, but it was you. If I stripped you naked right now . . ."

The band struck up another waltz. He swept her around . . . three, four, pirouette and back. . . .

"What night?" she countered as if he had said nothing else.

But he only laughed again, a caustic bark, at her show of perplexity.

"You're a capable actress," he admitted, "but something deep within you cannot fully embrace deception as can your loving uncle."

Harder he led through the gliding steps, not guiding but forcing, and by now both of them were breathing like Thoroughbreds breaking out of the second turn. Soon his violence even commanded the musicians, who unconsciously picked up the tempo to match him.

Mystere gave thanks that other couples had joined them, for their presence seemed to rein him in somewhat. But she knew perfectly well what he meant by "that night," and he had unnerved her enough that she gave up any idea of stealing Sylvia Rohr's brooch. It would be too risky with his eagle eyes on her.

It wasn't just him, either. There lingered over everything and everyone a sense of dramatic expectation. It was cheap and sensational; few spoke of it directly. But in truth almost everyone present tonight had been poring through the smutty dailies produced by Printing House Row, hungry for more details about this celebrated thief who was all the rage even in the British and European papers.

But now, she thought, *right now* while they were dancing, Rafe did not expect her to make such a move. She must try something, just to prove her defiance, for obviously he now assumed he could strike terror into the Lady Moonlight by his mere presence.

For a moment, however, after her decision to steal, fear hammered at her temples. But Rillieux's lessons had taught her well. When she made her move, it was precisely executed and over in an eye blink.

Rafe had sent her twirling yet again at arm's length, a sweeping flourish that spun her right past Garrett Teasdale and his wife Eugenia. For a fractional second Mystere's trained eyes focused on the heavy gold pin in Rafe's black silk cravat; then she diverted him by looking at Garrett with smiling eyes. Garrett nodded in greeting, and Rafe's gaze followed.

With a swift whisper of a movement, her outflung hand brushed him, and the pin was gone. Tuck and slip, just like she was going to do to Silvia Rohr's brooch. In one continuous, fluid motion she stuck it safely inside her chignon, the entire gesture looking like nothing more than an absent pat to her hair.

Her empty hand came back to join Rafe's, and the theft was accomplished. She knew Rillieux would howl about the pin's scant value. But instinct told her the Lady Moonlight had to strike, had to shake Rafe's confidence that he was in control, or all was lost.

Sudden relief at her bold success altered her mood. For a few enchanted, heady moments, as the violins rose and he swept her along above the sparkling ribbon of water, she felt the power and masculine strength in him, the incredible agility that matched his pleasing face and form. In that timeless moment of enhancement, she felt, too, the thrill of life's promise, the sense that her own existence was a story still unfolding, felt her youth and her woman's hunger to be completed.

Then his breath was warm and moist on her cheek, intimate like a lover's, and he pressed closer until she swore she could sense the forbidden swell of his gender.

He had begun guiding her away from the other dancers with a purpose. In the shadows beyond the edge of the pavilion, he suddenly swept her into a nearly hidden gazebo.

"No," she protested when he crushed her to him, "what are you—?"

The protest was smothered on her lips by his almost bruising kiss. For a few moments her traitorous body responded instantly, her passion rising to equal his. Then, with a violent effort, she broke free of his embrace.

"*Stop* it," she flung at him. "Are you insane? People saw us come in here."

"This time I'll stop," he husked, his voice altered by his lust. "But as I just said, thoughts need not submit to a master. *I'll be wondering.*"

She pushed past him, face flaming when she saw all the heads turned in their direction.

Only moments before, she had felt transported to the very heavens. Now she came tumbling down to earth. Suddenly all of it, as she gazed round at the people and the pavilion, seemed falsely bright and artificial, like painted flats at the rear of a stage.

"That's twice you've said that to me," she managed to whisper, as if to herself.

"Yes, but only because you once said it to me," he taunted behind her in a voice for her ears only.

She turned to look at him one last time.

In his eyes was the promise of damnation. He gestured to his empty black cravat where his gold stickpin used to be. He had known all along that she took it. "And that will be your undoing, Lady Moonlight."

Chapter 11

Even before full sunrise the streets of lower Manhattan began to writhe with people and conveyances, all jockeying and jostling for position. Hush started watching the flat on Amos Street shortly after seven A.M. Just after eight A.M., by the bells of St. Paul's, a plump woman in a faded calico dress emerged from the private street entrance, on the ground floor right around the corner from the pharmacy. She walked across the brick street to a bakery, returning with a loaf of bread wrapped in wax paper.

The next two hours dragged by for Hush, as slowly as the preaching he had to endure before he could eat the free supper at the Methodist Mission. He occupied a good vantage point on the roof of a three-story warehouse across the street. By now he knew the Lower East Side so well that he could travel through much of it atop the buildings, avoiding the traffic, police, and gangs prowling below.

A steady stream of customers entered the pharmacy, emerging with mineral waters, salts, and patent medicines of every sort. The church bells gave ten peals, and still he saw no sign of the man Mystere had asked him to spy on. It wasn't Sunday, so why hadn't the man gone off to work? The area was no slum, but neither was it Rich Man's Row.

Bored and hungry, Hush climbed down the rickety back steps and hoofed it to Cherry Street. There he bought an apple and a wedge of suet pudding.

His appetite slaked for now, the twelve-year-old noticed a well-dressed elderly woman waiting at the corner for her hansom. A huge crushed-velvet bag dangled from her right arm. He noted the brass clasp with a studied eye, recognizing it as a type he could work with just one thumb.

He glanced around to make sure no roundsmen were nearby. Then he fished a jet earring out of his pocket—Rillieux had taught him to employ diversions when possible—and dropped it onto the sidewalk to the woman's left.

" 'Scuze me, ma'am," he piped up. "Did you drop your earring?"

He pointed at it, and her curious eyes followed his finger. The few seconds she spent studying the earring were more than ample for him to fish the Italian leather billfold from her purse and drop it behind the baggy front of his shirt.

"Why—no, it's not mine, young man, but thank you for mentioning it."

"Oh, well, finder's keepers," he said as he scooped up the earring and hurried off.

As taught, he would not steal in this neighborhood again for a few weeks. And he would not even look at the billfold's contents—it would go straight to Rillieux and the family kitty. The family . . . *his* family if he went by all the rules.

He returned to his post atop the warehouse. Again boredom quickly set in; but all he had to do was think about soon living in the same house with Mystere, and that funny knot was back in his stomach. She was right out of the top drawer, all right, even if she did practically admit she was the Lady Moonlight. He was determined to do good work for her. *Cripes,* he thought—after imagining her velvet voice and ivory skin—*I'd sneak into hell with a pocketful of firecrackers if she asked me to.*

Just past noon his patient loyalty was rewarded. A big,

swarthy, mutton-chopped man with hairy hands and a splay-footed walk stopped at the door and banged the brass knocker. He was let inside, emerging a few minutes later with the man Mystere had described.

Hush scrambled down to the street and caught up with them as they aimed toward the unceasing racket and activity on Broadway. Dogging them from a few yards behind, he quickly recognized the big one from his odd walk—he was called Sparky, and he was one of the regular loafers who hung around the South Street docks, pitching pennies until laborers were called to unload a cargo ship. When he had worked long enough to finance his next drunken rout, he was a loafer again. The cycle went round and round.

Hush followed them across Broadway, no mean feat in the lethal traffic. Even a veteran like him had to leap at the last moment to avoid being run over by a buggy with its top up.

At first he thought the two men were headed for the Bowery, only three blocks east of Broadway, with its less-fashionable array of disportments. Instead, the pair aimed for the strip of concert saloons on lower Broadway.

Now and then Hush heard a glissando of piano notes growing louder as they approached. The two men ducked past the slatted batwings of a saloon, and Hush paused outside to study the sign with gilded wooden letters hanging over the entrance. For practice he sounded out the letters Mystere had taught him, and to his proud surprise he knew all of them except the last: "A . . . l . . . i . . . b . . . i . . . B . . . a . . . urr," he guessed for the last sound. The Alibi Bar. Cripes, thanks to Mystere he could already read a little.

The variety show did not start until later, so the toughs hired to sit inside the doors, brandishing billy clubs, were not yet on duty. Hush slipped inside the dim, smoky interior; it exhaled an odor of sweat, beer, and tobacco. He spotted the two men at an S-shaped mahogany bar, each with one foot up on the rail while Sparky talked and gestured. Hush knew he would be chased out, but he headed back toward them anyway.

Sawdust covered much of the floor, and unshaven men with cigarettes stuck to their lips played billiards and darts. Hush cast a longing glance at a huge joint of meat on the free-lunch counter. But it was only for those who purchased cocktails costing fifty cents and better.

"Two ales, Jimbo!" Sparky called to the bartender. "And draw 'em nappy."

So far no one seemed to notice the boy with shabby cloth trousers gone out at the knees. He edged in closer to the two men. Sparky's bray was easy to hear.

"I'm telling you, Lorenzo, we can make a fortune in Little Italy and never break a sweat. Just collect our fee on each rental. My hand to God, trained monkeys rent as high as thirty dollars a month. Add four dollars rent for the street organs, and Easy is the street we'll live on, b'hoy. All you need to get in the operation on equal shares is a thousand dollars. Can you raise the money?"

"Hold off a bit, Sparky—I'm damned if I'll train any filthy monkeys—"

"Shoo, *we* don't train 'em, slick; we pay some eye-tye brats a few bits a day to do it. We don't have to go near the damned monkeys; we'd just be the owners. Why, it's money for old rope. You're a fool if you don't buy in."

Both men had quickly finished their first huge schooners of beer. Sparky signaled for two more. Hush watched Lorenzo place his elbows carefully to avoid beer slops on the bar, evidently mulling Sparky's offer. He kept patting his mustache with three fingers as if afraid it might fall off.

"I may indeed be interested," he finally replied. "As to the money I must pay—that's no piddling amount."

"Nor no piddlin' profits, anh?"

"Perhaps, but at any rate I only have some of the money. I still need to raise about four hundred."

"Are you in the way of raising it quicklike? Nick has other takers lined up if we don't want it."

"I may be at that," Lorenzo replied, nodding. "I have a very wealthy client these days. You see, she——"

"All right, just so you get it. But remember, by the street of by and by you'll arrive at the house of never. We must move quickly, you and me."

Even as Lorenzo got drunker, Hush noticed, his voice held one flat pitch, rarely varying. He also liked to drink at Freeman's Quay—here came their third beer, and again Sparky paid for it. Odd, considering it was Lorenzo wearing the suit and vest. Unless Sparky was working a con on him. Sure, and Mystere was that "very wealthy client" Lorenzo had in mind.

By now the bartender had spotted Hush and thumbed him toward the door. But it wasn't long before the two men came outside, shook hands, and parted. Sparky headed back toward the waterfront while Lorenzo cut over only as far as lower Fifth Avenue.

Hush was surprised when he turned in under the Arch and entered Washington Square. He headed toward the northeast corner of the square, and at first Hush was sure he would enter the marble-fronted administration building of New York University.

Instead, Lorenzo aimed for a row of pleasant brick-and-masonry flats just behind the university. He tugged the bellpull at number 17 Washington Street and was admitted by a slim, smiling young woman who wore her dark hair loose and flowing.

Hush took a turn around the square, wary of a roundsman lingering under the Arch. One block west of the square, a group of young girls, having met their morning quota, emerged from a huge brick shirtwaist factory. While the cop was distracted calling out flirtatious exchanges with one of them, Hush ducked into the narrow strip of garden between number 17 and the next building.

He stopped at the first window he came to, where a gap in the curtains allowed him to see through the lace curtain. He glimpsed fleur-de-lis wallpaper, needlepoint tapestries, and tall glass-fronted cabinets filled with glazed porcelain figures. But the room appeared empty of people.

He slipped back to the next window. Here the curtains were tightly drawn. But he carefully pressed one ear flat against the glass. The noises he heard inside were familiar; he had learned them long ago from living in crowded tenements. Lorenzo's wife lived on Amos Street, all right, but obviously he kept a whore in Washington Square, too. And Hush had a pretty good idea, by now, just whose money was paying for her.

Much as he hated to, he decided it was time to go see Mystere.

"You ask me, all he's doing for your money is washing bricks," Hush informed Mystere almost the very moment his second reading lesson had concluded. She had insisted on the lesson first, suspecting the lad's report might upset her. "And he wants still more for some scheme to rent out monkeys and organs."

"I never said anything about paying him money," she pointed out, though neither did she bother denying it.

"Well, he's just sittin' on his pratt when he ain't drinking or visiting his wh—his sporting gal. And his pal Sparky, he ain't worth a rap. Ask anybody 'at knows him—all you'll get from the likes of him is short measure for a long price."

Hush held the McGuffey's primer Mystere had given him today. Both of them had taken their usual places in the downstairs parlor. Mystere was glad she had insisted on the lesson first—Hush's report, while in no way shocking, quickly scuttled her hopes for a good mood.

"You say he's quite the drinker?" she clarified.

"Huh! He don't just sip it down—he drinks it like he's a pipe through the floor."

Yes, she thought, *I know that pipe—the same one that's been draining off my money for months now.*

"Did you see the wife?"

He nodded. "She went to the bakery."

"Walked?"

"Sure, it was only across the street."

"She didn't look ill to you?"

"Naw. Fat and healthy."

Hush watched worry mold her face. He obviously wanted to say something to make her feel better. So he told her about sounding out the letters on the Alibi's sign and how he had guessed the *r* by himself. It did coax a brief smile from her.

"Good for you," she told him absently. "You must practice whenever you can."

Her thoughts, at the moment, had gotten into a confused moil. She was still trying to understand the events of last night at the Sanford ball. Then Hush had arrived with this latest confirmation of her fears. Clearly certain events were coming to a head, but she felt swept up by them, washed along, when she wanted desperately to somehow gain control.

There was some hopeful news, at least. As she had prayed for, Belloch had kept his mouth shut about the cravat pin she took last night, and there was no new spate of Lady Moonlight stories in today's papers—at least, not in the *Sun,* the *World,* the *Herald,* or the *Independent,* which Baylis had purchased as usual for old Rillieux's ritual morning perusal, along with the more respectable *Times.*

Unfortunately, some of the gap in Lady Moonlight fare was being filled with more speculative gossip about her and Rafe Belloch. The *Herald*'s wildly popular gossip maven, Lance Streeter, asked provocatively, "Exactly what transpired inside that gazebo? Will this *pas de deux* lead to wedding bells or ruinous scandal? A lady's innocence may well be intact, yet suddenly at issue."

If that was not painful enough for her, Streeter, so powerful he often sniped at Mrs. Astor by name, had even launched a new sidebar column titled "Inside the Gazebo." He promised it "will take you, the curious reader, inside the private love nests of the wealthy and famous."

She had started to walk Hush toward the front vestibule when Rillieux suddenly pushed open the teakwood doors of the parlor, blocking their exit. His face was choleric with anger, and she instantly saw why: the monthly bills were clutched in his left hand. Paying accounts always left him in a pettish mood.

"Young woman," he greeted her without preamble, "I am fed up with your extravagances, do you mark me? All the cash I give you, yet *still* you charge on my name? From now on you must cut your coat according to your cloth."

He was not one to brook interruptions when he was in a rage, so Mystere only submitted meekly, letting him rant it out. He had maintained a stone-faced silence last night when she had given him the gold pin instead of Sylvia's brooch as he had expected. Now, however, he erupted, revealing the darker, more threatening side of his personality.

"Do you think the cream you poured on your strawberries this morning delivered itself free for your enjoyment? This lad"—he nodded toward Hush—"will need new footman's liveries when he joins us, complete with our family crest embossed on them. Do you have any idea what it costs to outfit Baylis as our coachman, to maintain the expense of a team and carriage? Or to keep a roughhouser like Evan in good suits and linen?"

You pay none of them any salary, you old piker, she wanted to fling at him.

"Your little gewgaw from last night," he raged on. "At face value, why yes, the pin's worth a few dollars. From Helzer, however, it will at best fetch perhaps forty."

Rillieux paused, leaning more heavily on his rattan cane, as if she were becoming, literally, an intolerable burden.

Hush chose that moment to try and lift the master's mood. He presented the wallet he had stolen earlier while spying for Mystere. It had the unforeseen affect, however, of feeding into Rillieux's tirade.

"There, you see?" he demanded of Mystere, sliding an impressive sheaf of banknotes from the wallet. "Thank God the boy has taken up your slack, Mystere, or we'd've been dunned out of our home by now. And do you understand what a dunning notice means for us? It means complete public exposure of our artfully constructed facade."

"You're right," she conceded. "But I promise to do better at the opera this Saturday."

"That's the gait," he approved.

He had forgotten all about Mrs. Astor's annual opera party, and Mystere's contrite tone seemed to temper his spleen somewhat. But it wasn't just a chance to throw a bone to Paul—once again it was an opportunity to ease the pressure on Lady Moonlight, for the suspect pool at the opera house would be much larger. And certainly all the ladies could not be searched.

Though somewhat appeased, Rillieux hadn't yet finished his admonitions. He slid the bills into his vest pocket and tucked the cane under one arm, all so that one fist could beat the palm of his other hand to underscore his points.

"Mystere, I mention the danger of public exposure because, ironically, *that* is the fear making you so timid of late. You've been educated too well, I'm afraid, in the ways of the upper crust. Now I think your fear is the shame it will bring you even more than the punishment."

"Perhaps," she admitted, but nothing more.

"Of course, but in our walk of life such conventional morality must be set aside now and then. Do not mistake my patience for indulgence. Nor is your gender fair excuse to go puny. Rose is not only a good maid, but she keeps a sharp ear and eye on the daily doings hereabouts, and still brings home some prizes now and then. You must earn your keep in this family as does everyone else."

She was forced to bite her lower lip until she tasted blood. His words angered her. *Earn her keep?* In the past three months alone she had brought in at least five thousand dollars for the household, no Vanderbilt allowance, perhaps, but a good sum at a time when workingmen kept families alive somehow on three hundred dollars a year.

Some of that loot, of course, never made it into the family kitty. Most of the stolen goods were kept hidden out in the coach house until they were taken to Helzer's front operation, a giant salvage yard down on Water Street. That way Evan or Baylis would be the scapegoats if it was discovered.

But Rillieux had quietly been skimming off cash and a few items of very special value, locking all of it in a safe in his bedroom. She had glimpsed the contents by accident only once. They included a beautiful diamond tiara she had stolen this spring, among the Lady Moonlight's first coups.

"You must stop fretting about the right and wrong of your actions," he concluded in a kinder tone. "Is it *right* for the fox to seize the chick? I assure you, where money is involved there can be no hypocrisy. You're succumbing to a humbug morality. *Sin bravely,* for then you will get away with it."

A canny gleam seeped into his eyes. "Apropos brave sins—what *did* happen inside that gazebo, dear heart?"

She flushed to the roots of her hair. It pleased a chuckle out of Rillieux.

"There, there, never mind," he soothed as if she were a child. "Your color speaks volumes. At any rate, those few moments, and your dancing, have insured a memorable Sanford ball this year."

His eyes narrowed as they focused on her, accusing. His voice hardened. "But don't think I don't consider what's going on. I see how Rafe Belloch may be the perfect way out for you."

"Way out?" she repeated, his meaning escaping her.

"Of course. You act like you've grown sick of thieving. You admit you're worried about a devastating exposure. Marry Rafe and you'll never have another money worry except how to spend it all before you die."

"Never minding, of course," she interjected hotly, "the fact that he is too conceited to ever submit to the sacrament of marriage. Or that I find him an arrogant beast."

Rillieux's lips formed a crude wolf grin, revealing his gold crowns. "Can you look at me and say he doesn't make your blood hot?"

This time she had to turn away, he shamed her so.

"Oh, don't overdo the ingenue," he snapped impatiently. "You'll not be trapped in any marriage. When you tire of his . . . conjugal attentions, Rafe will have an accident. You'd have nothing to do with it."

She stifled her first impulse to argue this point, trying another tack. "You fail to understand him, Paul. Even if I agreed to such a plan, even if by some incredible series of events, he proposed to me and I accepted—he is no old man careless of his wallet. He would be a fearsome adversary if violence confronted him, I'm sure of it. The man is dangerous."

"Humph. Trust me, *any* man becomes a pussycat once his blood is hot for a particular woman. I have seen how he looks at you, practically licking his lips at the flat-chested little nymph—"

"Paul, that's enough." She frowned at such improper talk in front of the boy. But Rillieux only chuckled again, tousled Hush's wild mop of dark hair, and went upstairs to his quarters.

"What does 'dunning' mean?" was Hush's only question before Mystere let him out of the house.

He knew he was woefully ignorant, but even a blockhead

understood that men who courted real ladies like Mystere must know their letters. And even write poetry and such gimcracks to impress the fair sex, he thought, for they were a deep-feeling lot; he could see it in Mystere's expressive face as Mr. Rillieux raked her over the coals. *I must never,* he vowed solemnly to himself, *let a lady see my rat pail when it is filled brimming.*

"I'll tell you what it means at our next lesson," she promised. "I'll show you how to use the dictionary."

One important task remained. After Hush left she went into the little telephone niche midway down the hall and lifted the handset from its wall-mounted cradle. She turned the magneto crank, ringing up a hello girl, and nearly yelling into the receiver, asked for a connection with a bicycle-messenger service located near Fourteenth Street and Sixth Avenue.

A tinny, faraway voice that could have been either gender answered, and she dictated a brief message for Lorenzo, telling him she would be waiting at the usual place tomorrow at one P.M. She hung up, heart racing, for she sensed she had reached a critical juncture in her life.

She wasn't sure what she was going to tell Perkins—or what he might do. But if she ever hoped to find Bram, she had to become her own woman in a hurry; she was sure of that much, at least. As Paul's chilling remarks about Belloch had revealed, she must also put out the flames, his *and* hers. Not only was Rafe a threat, but he was *threatened*. No matter how much he infuriated and frightened her, she would not even entertain the idea of violence against his person.

If only she could be strong enough, tomorrow she would begin to take control of her own destiny.

Chapter 12

"Awake already?" Rose called from the bedroom doorway, breakfast bell in hand. Mystere, eyes open wide but her attention obviously inward, was clearly visible through the hyacinth blue French silk hangings of her four-post canopy bed.

"Since well before sunrise," she confessed, "but still lying here like a slug-a-bed."

"Well, perhaps you should humor His Nibs and join him for breakfast this morning," Rose suggested tactfully, adding, "I heard him hollering at you yesterday in the parlor. Mother Mary, he rattled the shutters!"

"Perhaps I should join him," Mystere agreed, throwing back the counterpane.

She had not been loafing, however, so much as paralyzed by worry. Her newfound resolve of yesterday had somehow weakened during the nearly sleepless night. The thought of what lay ahead—today with Lorenzo, and beyond with Paul, with Rafe Belloch—made her want to burrow under the bed linens and never come back out.

"Rose?"

"Hmm?"

Mystere's gaze went to the writing desk beside the east

window. But she fought down the urge to handle the letter yet again—she had nearly worn it out. *Reading it again,* she lectured herself, *will reveal no secrets.* Yet, there was a secret—she knew that as surely as she was alive. And no matter what, she would, she *must* learn that secret. Because somehow it was linked to Bram's disappearance.

"Yes?" Rose reminded her gently, used to Mystere's dark moods.

"Do you think of Ireland much?"

The question did not seem to surprise Rose. Even though she was not from Dublin, as Mystere was, but from the farm country bordering the Irish Sea, she seemed to understand Mystere's curiosity. Because Rose was older and had remained in Ireland longer, Mystere often plied her with questions. Indeed, the young woman's thirst to know about her homeland, and her family roots, was insatiable. All her reading, the endless questioning of Irish expatriates . . . Mystere had even gone to the American Museum every single day while Barnum's elaborate scale model of Dublin had been on display.

"I do think of my family some, but I still say I don't miss the place much. I was born in 'fifty-three during the midst of the crop failures, although the very worst of it was over."

Mystere had a shadowed, faraway look in her eyes. "So many died in the famine that killer hunger seems to be our only national identity." She retreated farther into her black thoughts. She herself was Irish. Enduring the open contempt the predominately Protestant Four Hundred heaped on the Irish, and of course Catholics, was one of the most difficult aspects of her deception.

She rose, shrugged into a dressing gown, and crossed to the satinwood wardrobe. Whatever she chose to wear, first would come the tiresome, undignified ordeal with the linen wraps.

"At least you have *some* memories, good or bad," she pointed out. "I think that's better than none at all."

"No doubt. I remember that things were still bleak in the countryside by the time I came over in 'sixty-three—no prospects for the young, which is why my parents sent me. I went straight to the Five Points, where I had an uncle. But he had died of cholera. That's another reason they hate us so much here, you know—there's no denying the cholera some of us brought over."

"If so, it was mostly Irish who died of it."

"Yes, may Uncle Liam rest in peace. Mystere, the Five Points is still a rough place now, but in 'sixty-three? It was corruption and death for children, especially them as had no family. If Paul hadn't taken me in, I'd've copped it sure as the Lord made Moses."

Rose did not say this with intention to make her feel guilty, Mystere realized. But her remark was a goading reminder of Mystere's rebellious plans. Rillieux had rescued her and Bram, too, and now only look how ungrateful she was.

But within, her bold new self spoke up in vigorous defense of individual liberty, and Bram was the very reason she needed her freedom, needed also to get rid of that bloodsucking leech Lorenzo Perkins. She was "arrogating" thousands each year for Rillieux—why, she could live decently and still finance a thorough search for Bram, for their roots, too, if she could only keep some of that money herself.

Money . . . without willing it, she suddenly thought of Antonia's pure emerald, of that soft, dewy green shade exactly like Bram's eyes. She wasn't overly superstitious, but couldn't help wondering if that ring was meant to spur her will. It was a mere show trinket to Antonia, but for Mystere could mean the independence to continue her all-important search.

"Try to hurry," Rose reminded her softly just before she backed out and shut the door. "It always cheers him when you have breakfast together. He is so fond of you."

"He's fond of all of us," Mystere conceded. "Perhaps that's our problem."

Rose started to respond, then abandoned the effort and hid behind her careful housemaid's face.

"Rose?" Mystere managed just before the door closed.

The mobcapped head and twin red plaits came back around the door. "Yes?"

"I . . . I mean, it's not *my* idea that Paul and I should live so finely and be waited upon." Mystere knew all about the cramped cubbyholes in the attic that were provided for servants, stifling in summer, unheated in winter. And they took every meal in the servants' dining room in the basement. Rillieux insisted on it, claiming the ruse was vital to their deception.

"Push all that right out of your head," Rose deprecated. "My room is dry and clean and has a lock on the door. We all eat well, and Paul does not begrudge us time off. Though he occasionally thumps the boys, they're used to it and would not respect him if he didn't." Her eyes clouded, as if she was thinking of the incident when Mystere had gotten her beating. "He's never hit me," she offered, as if it was some kind of excuse. "Besides all that—you have no special privileges that you have not earned dearly. The risks you take . . . la! Worry about your own lot, poor thing, for he's become quite dependent upon . . . well, never mind, I'm running on. I pray for you, Mystere, and feel no envy or resentment, none at all."

Mystere joined Rillieux for a pleasant breakfast in the solarium, and he was on his best behavior after the abusive remarks he had made yesterday. He did, however, make a pointed remark about having his kid gloves and silk topper cleaned for Mrs. Astor's upcoming opera party—and thus, holding her to her promise that she would make up for the paltry take at the Sanford ball.

He did not question her story, however, that she would be spending much of the day at the park and then Macy's reading room, for she often wiled away an hour or two there after a trip to the park. Nor did he offer the carriage since he required it himself.

Despite her new resolve to economize, however, Mystere flagged down a hansom cab the moment she was out of sight of their brownstone.

"How much for a trip to Brooklyn, then back across to Central Park—say a couple hours or a bit more?"

"Set rate, ma'am," he lied without a blink. "One dollar an hour."

The price was dear, based on his quick assessment of her fine cotton linen skirt and side-lacing silk boots. But today she could spend recklessly.

"All right," she agreed without haggling, and he handed her in without relinquishing his seat at the rear.

Long before the bridge had opened, Mystere had begun taking trips on her own to Brooklyn when she had something important weighing on her mind. The quiet residential city was a relaxing, calm, reflective place compared to the teeming behemoth just across the river. There were five ferry lines back then, though she had almost always taken the Wall Street ferry.

Now, of course, the bridge made the trip faster and offered a spectacular view, especially for the pedestrians dawdling up on the elevated promenade: a busy confusion of steamships and barges and the sturdy cargo packets of the Black Ball line far below them, with smaller skiffs and sailing boats flitting among them like water bugs.

But though Mystere's eyes registered all of it, all she could really dwell on were Rafe Belloch's cruel, fascinating eyes, all she could think of, his violent, passionate mouth igniting her body like a flambeau.

"Where to now, lady?" The driver's voice slapped her rudely back to awareness, and she saw with a little start that the gothic arch of the Brooklyn tower of the bridge was passing.

"Take a turn through Prospect Park," she directed him.

Ashamed by the . . . warmth of her prurient thoughts, Mystere resolved all over again *not* to let a few wanton moments of unseemly sexual ardor be her undoing, socially or emotionally. Not for a king's ransom would she surrender physically to such a conceited, arrogant man. His behavior toward Caroline and Antonia proved the wisdom of avoiding him as did the way he had practically . . . why, practically shanghaied her into that gazebo to force himself on her with the manners of a common gardener's boy. . . .

Abruptly she became aware that the cabman was peering at her through the small opening between the covered vehicle and his seat, peering at her with his face squinched up anxiously.

"Pardon me?" she managed, suddenly disoriented for she had lost all track of time.

"I said are you all right, lady? That's twice now I've asked where you wish to go next. We've been around the park twice."

"Oh, I'm sorry. I'm fine, I just—"

"Look, are you *sure* you can cover the fare?" he challenged, his tone skeptical. "For aught I know, you escaped from Bellevue and stole them fancy clothes."

"Here's three dollars now to calm you." She handed the bills through the opening. "What time is it, please?"

"Nearly eleven."

Her heartrate slowed, for it was not so late as she had feared. But she *must* stop thinking of Rafe Belloch and concentrate on the immediate problem of Lorenzo Perkins.

"Take High Street for a bit," she decided.

They left the park and headed north, following the pleasant, tree-lined parkway through blocks of comfortable rowhouses. Land was cheaper here, and the less-affluent could afford decent homes, yet be proximate to their work in Manhattan.

But Perkins, *Perkins,* she forced herself to stay focused.

She had an unsettling feeling that canceling his services would be neither quick nor cheap. All his prying questions about her and Rillieux . . . all this time she had pinned her hopes on him, and for what? Less than mince pie. Perhaps it would even turn out worse than a waste of time and money.

Again Mystere thought of her letter at home, its strange, intriguing letterhead—her forlorn hope of locating Bram, perhaps even of inheriting a great fortune. But she could not stake her rightful claim unless she at least found out her family name. Bram had told her so much, but not that—*why* not that?

Now, blood prickling her nape, she recalled what Rillieux had almost said that night in the carriage, on the way to the Sanford ball: *It's in your family.* She had thought it was just a mistake, a simple slip of the tongue. She had no idea why he almost said it. But suddenly she wondered if he knew something he wasn't telling her. And if that was the case, the sheer irony of it would almost drive her mad. Here she had been secretly searching the world for information on Bram, and the information may have been at home all along. Withheld for reasons she knew would not prove good.

Again the driver's voice startled her like a cold touch. "Quite a view, eh, lady? I've a cousin means to build near here before long. A ward boss," he added proudly. "You'll find no hominy on *his* plate, I'll warrant."

He had reined in his horse atop the airy bluff, overlooking the East River, that gave High Street its name. The view was a breathtaking panorama in the late-morning spun-gold sunshine.

She gazed across the crowded river and saw boys playing under the Manhattan tower of the bridge, insect-size from where she stood as were the day laborers rolling heavy barrels of fish across the docks.

She could see the proud spire of Trinity Church, the eight-story Equitable Building on lower Broadway, the massive spans of the bridge . . . all of it heaven-grasping grandeur and wealth. But she could also see the crazily leaning tenement buildings crowding the waterfront of the East River, each one so poorly built that it leaned against its neighbors for its main support. No longer just the Lower East Side, either—the slum blight now covered much of the east and west shores of Manhattan, human beings "packed in like maggots in cheese" as one shocked reformer had described the population density of Manhattan's tenements.

However, it wasn't reform on her mind now; she didn't have the capacity for good works beneath Rillieux's heavy thumb. But seeing all of that darker side of the metropolis, she was suddenly numbed by the old insecurities and fears. For in reality, much less than a half mile separated her from horrid squalor.

A horrid squalor she knew like the back of her hand.

Unless she somehow became dependent on no one but herself, the threat of poverty would continue to hang over her. She was only one man's whim away from disaster at any moment, one glaring headline from becoming one of those desperate women she saw everywhere: shabby-genteel creatures fallen on hard times, proud but destitute, scrabbling to attach themselves to the wealthy in some menial capacity.

But *no,* she mustn't let the destructive fear engulf her; she must be strong for herself and Bram. Even today she could visualize the big brass plaque that she, Bram, and the other children had been required to read every night before prayers at the orphanage, the pithy wisdom of Cornelius Vanderbilt: *Let others do what I have done and they need not be around here begging.*

All right then, she decided, *from here on out I'll be tough and iron-willed like the Commodore.*

"Driver," she called up, "please take me to the Bethesda Fountain now."

* * *

"It's the devil's own work," Lorenzo began his report—perhaps the only part of it, she thought, that would be true. "These last few days I've been going at it hammer and tongs from sunrise to dark."

That was a bald-faced lie and she knew it. His dull little turtle eyes peered out at the boaters on the lake, avoiding her scrutiny. His usual sullen, apathetic mood was replaced by an urgency she hadn't figured out yet—though she remembered Hush's report that Lorenzo and Sparky were cooking up some scheme that required money.

However, before she could even accuse him of lying, he pressed on with precipitate haste, as if sensing why she had asked to meet him. "But I think all my efforts might have paid off," he vouchsafed. Despite her determination to end this, Mystere had to let herself take this much bait, just in case.

"And . . . ?" she encouraged him.

"It's this fellow out on Blackwell's, you see, a guard at the penitentiary. He *may* have had your brother locked up in his cell bay some time back."

"He 'may' have? Doesn't he know?"

Perkins expelled the long, fluming sigh of a patient, put-upon man. "Of course he knows. But you've no idea," he assured her, "how greedy and rough and cunning these prison screws are. Oh, they're a sweet bunch, all right."

"I see. You require more money, is that it?"

He spread both hands in a gesture of helplessness. "It's not for me but to oil their tongues."

For a few moments, literally sickened by his lying face, she turned her eyes to the magnificent bronze figure of the angel rising triumphantly from the water. Right now the statue gave her great solace, for she believed that despite Lorenzo Perkins and all she had suffered, this was the same angel who had guided her here to New York to fulfill her destiny. And she *would* fulfill it.

"Mr. Perkins," she told him in a voice of unwavering resolve, tinged by anger, "you have *not* been working on my case at all these past few days and you know it."

The little eyes blinked rapidly from a face gone blank with surprise. Caught flat-footed, he fell back on his favorite tiresome maxim. "Never stack your conclusions higher than your evidence."

"Well, how's this for evidence? You spent the better part of yesterday at home, as well as drinking beer with a pal on Broadway and then visiting a . . . female friend at Washington Square."

His jaw went slack.

For such a dishonest man, she thought, he was a poor liar.

"That's barmy," he protested. "I took some time off yesterday, sure. She who pays the piper calls the tune, I agree. But the piper decides what key to play it in."

That was actually quite clever, for him, she thought. "It's not just yesterday," she insisted. "You've been nowhere near Blackwell's Island recently."

Actually she couldn't prove that, but it must have been true because he offered no denial. He simply glowered at her as if his foul mood meant more than her grievance. When she refused to be cowed, he demanded as if he had a right to know, "Who says so?"

"It really doesn't matter, Mr. Perkins. The report is reliable, and I'm terminating your services, for I mean to find my brother on my own."

"Balls. You'll make cheese out of chalk first."

"Perhaps, but that's my plan."

She gathered her skirt and made as if to rise from the bench. But his sullen, menacing tone stopped her.

"It's Belloch, ain't it?"

"I beg your pardon?"

"Beg a cat's tail," he snarled, his coarseness surfacing under this pressure. "I've had my stomach full of you acting so fine haired and la-de-da. My wife reads them tattletale columns; she's told me all about you and your fancy man."

"Would that be your ill wife, Mr. Perkins, or your secret one?"

He ignored that, or pretended to. She watched him rapidly turning this new problem back and forth in his mind, studying its facets, looking for the angle he needed.

"It's Belloch," he repeated with bulldog tenacity, having seized something he refused to let go. *"That's* why you're giving me the boot. You've got your claw into him, and you don't want him finding out all the skeletons in your closet. Now you've cooked up these false accusations to fire me."

"That's utter nonsense, I—"

"You must understand, *Miss Rillieux,"* he cut her off, dark innuendo seeping into his tone, "that I've come to depend on your reg'lar payments. We have what the law calls a spoken contract."

"Mr. Perkins, that's preposterous. You are not on permanent remittance; I hired you for a specific service that you have not even remotely performed. Furthermore, I paid you generously and certainly owe you no more money."

With that she again started to rise, her nexus to the boorish lout permanently severed in her mind.

Obviously, however, he had a different view of it.

"You'll pay me," he snarled, "or I'm going to Belloch."

Alarm tightened her throat, but the warmth of anger made her cheeks feel as if they were swelling. "And telling him what?" she challenged.

Here his certainty crumbled somewhat, but it did not crack completely. Nor did his spiteful belligerence. "It's my profession to find out that sort of thing," he assured her. "Call yourself Rillieux, do you, but don't even know your own brother's hind name? P'r'aps I'll just see about this fancy-dan uncle of yours, too."

His threat shot chills into her extremities, and she only hoped he was as inept in other matters as he had been with her case. For a long moment she felt the despair of those who wonder if the game is even worth the candle. So many impediments, so many traps and obstacles such as this dull, grasping man who threatened her now.

Just then, however, her eye latched on one man among the flow of humanity crossing the terrace. He strolled slowly among the throng, leafing through a copy of *Leslie's Illustrated Weekly*. She focused on the bold type of a full-page advertisement on the last page: WHAT ABOUT BUB 'N' SIS?

Seeing the familiar words at that very moment, hot tears instantly filmed her eyes. The popular phrase "bub 'n' sis," was used by everyone from politicians to advertisers. "What about bub 'n' sis?" had come to mean "Say! Let's not forget the children." Bub 'n' sis were synonymous with hearth and home. And even though it was just silly commercialism, seeing the phrase now pinched her throat shut and trapped the sob trying to get out of her.

"Here now," Perkins ventured awkwardly, misreading her reaction and feeling guilty at having frightened her too severely. "No one wants to harm you, Miss Rillieux, I—"

"Never mind, Mr. Perkins," she cut him off in a peremptory tone, rising from the cast-iron bench. "I consider my arrangement with you terminated. Should you choose to carry out your absurd threat of blackmail, only remember that adultery is a felony and carries with it a prison sentence."

"You've not heard the last of me!" he shouted behind her. "Damn your threats, we have a contract, and by God you'll pay one way or the other!"

Chapter 13

Even the weather seemed to come under Mrs. Astor's wide circle of influence. The Saturday evening designated for her annual opera party turned out storybook perfect, with a sky full of dazzling stars and a gentle, warm, caressing breeze. But Mystere wondered when her enchantment would be shocked out of her by Rafe Belloch's prediction that she and Paul would soon be officially exposed as frauds and criminals.

"Man alive!" Baylis exclaimed when he caught sight of her emerging, on Rillieux's arm, from the brownstone. The carriage waited in the crushed-marble cul-de-sac. "You'd make a gelding feel like a stud, girl."

"Baylis," Rillieux snapped in an undertone, "stop that tomcat talk in front of the boy; you'll ruin him for his job."

"What, mooncalf there?" Baylis jeered. He meant Hush, who stood near the open door of the carriage, uncomfortable but proud in his stiff new scarlet-and-gold livery and visored cap. The sight of Mystere in her silver satin gown with hand-sewn crystals swagged over her hips, emerging from the house like a sudden vision, had arrested him in the act of holding the door open wider.

"Hush!" Irritation raised Rillieux's voice to a shrill. "You're a footman now, not a love-struck puppy. Keep your eyes in your head and stand at the ready beside the door. As we approach, you look to be sure the step is down and secure. Then you simply hand us in. That's all. Do not gawk like a bumpkin nor speak unless spoken to by one of us."

"Yessir!"

The lad hastened to open the door and swing down the step for them, somehow disciplining himself not to gaze at Mystere in the flickering glow of the gas yard lights.

Baylis stood nearby with his hands in his pockets, watching all of them and shaking his head in amusement. Rillieux frowned at the coachman's slovenly appearance.

"If you must wear that ridiculous neck beard," he snapped, "can't you at least trim it?"

Baylis proudly combed his Newgate fringe with his fingers. "Nix on that, boss. I endure enough of this highhanded carrying on. It's royalty in Europe, the Astors in America, and the same damned story—all the land for a few great lords. A poor man might at least have dominion over his own damned beard."

"I don't give a hang about your politics," Rillieux grumped as he settled into the carriage, careful of his creases. "We're *robbing* the great lords, you blockhead. Isn't that enough revenge for you?"

"Yes," Baylis ventured just before Hush shut the door and climbed onto the high seat. "Others rob them, however, while you prate about among them and damn well seem to like it."

"Insolent dog," Rillieux muttered as Baylis took his whip from the socket and lashed the team into motion.

"I don't blame Baylis. You *do* enjoy passing yourself off as one of the Four Hundred. It's gone to your head that Mrs. Astor's latched on to you, and you talk to Baylis and the others as if they were actually your servants."

She rarely challenged him like this. He frowned so deeply his silver-white eyebrows touched. In the shadowy illumination of the streetlights his face looked thin and sharp-nosed, younger and vaguely menacing. But he surprised her by only saying mildly, "If youth but knew and age could do."

He studied her in silence for perhaps thirty seconds. "Mystere, Baylis clings to his pathetic politics because it offers castles in the sky to poor, ignorant men who are less than drops of piss in a cesspool, to put it bluntly. But one cannot inhabit castles in the sky, do you at least see that much?"

She still said nothing to all this. As if sensing her turmoiled mood, Rillieux became even more patient.

"As to your constant harping lately about treating the rest as servants—only think a moment. I *must* run a tight ship. What happens the moment one of them slips up in front of the wrong person and somebody twigs our game? A consummate actor takes on a role and *lives* it to be convincing."

"There you go again, comparing sneak thievery to an art."

"Young woman, what I've taught you is, indeed, art, and you are an artiste, deny it or no. Has it occurred to you how *minimal* I have kept our apparent household staff? Mystere, even merely middle-class households these days generally keep four to six servants. Households among the Four Hundred employ twice or three times that number. Mrs. Astor has tactfully overlooked our lack of a resident gardener and a parlormaid, but acquiring a footman was de rigueur."

"I suppose you're right," she surrendered a little, though grudgingly. "But you mentioned castles in the sky—our own house is built from cards and must eventually collapse."

"Dear heart, should a man stop eating forever because someday he might choke on a bone? Ours is no profession for those who worry about the disasters that *might* happen. You can wail that your best friend is dead, or you can declare with joy that *once he lived*. Both are equally true, yet how one chooses to see it divides life's happy from the wretched. Do you take my meaning?"

Strangely enough, she did. Sometimes he made great sense—she did see the truth of his observation. And thanks to his training she could discipline everything except her emotions, which refused to be curbed. Especially the emotion of fear, for she sincerely doubted that a positive attitude would ever turn Rafe Belloch into anything but what he was—a serious threat to anyone who crossed him.

"Let not your heart be troubled," Rillieux continued in his soothing, authoritative voice. His sloe eyes burned into her, powerful and compelling, and years of submission quickly brought her under his mesmeric spell. "Tonight you will take Sylvia Rohr's brooch. You will do it quickly and be out of her proximity before she even misses it. Right?"

She nodded. "Right."

"That's the girl. Just remember: Be sure that your eyes do not telegraph your movement or intention. Use some natural diversion as your cover. Be confident, fast and fluid, one single movement to take and conceal."

Again she nodded, obedient as ever, appearing to be the weak reed bent to his will.

But tonight she was stealing only to mollify Paul. Next time it would be Antonia Butler's fine emerald ring, and Mystere meant to keep the money, after selling it, for herself—for Bram.

Any gathering of Mrs. Astor's drew press attention. But tonight, Mystere quickly realized, the press scoundrels had turned out in throngs. To ogle the high-and-mighty in their finery, of course. What truly had them slavering, though, was the hope of more Lady Moonlight nonsense.

Even she, jaded by the false glitter of high society, was impressed by the roll call at tonight's event. Before their conveyance even reached the Astor Place Opera House, just off Broadway, they were engulfed in a crush of expensive carriages, surreys, calashes, and other vehicles forming a congested knot, all heading for the opera.

"H'ar now! Are you bolted to the damn pavement, Jack?" Baylis screamed at a driver just ahead of them. He added a string of curses, and Rillieux angrily thumped the carriage ceiling with his walking stick.

"Keep a civil tongue in your head, Baylis!" he called out.

Mystere, in contrast to Paul's irritability, had begun to feel a stirring of anticipation despite her dread of seeing Rafe Belloch again. A renowned company from Madrid was performing Bizet's *Carmen,* one of her favorite operas.

As they inched nearer to the opera house, Rillieux pulled a curtain aside.

"There's Inspector Byrnes," he said grimly. "He's entering by himself, but rest assured he will be prominent in the Astors' box."

"Watching for the Lady Moonlight," she remarked, feeling the irony of it. "And never once suspecting he's sharing a box with her."

She had naturally assumed she would be among the Astors' immediate party since Paul was. But now he cleared his throat, his gaze evasive.

"You'll not be with us, my dear, during the performance. I forgot to mention that."

"Why won't I be?"

"Well, I'm sure you've heard the Duke and Duchess of Granville are visiting the city with a large retinue. Many from Caroline's inner circle will be seated in adjacent boxes."

Excluding myself, of course, his smug tone added.

"And with whom will I be seated?" she demanded, suddenly suspicious.

"Oh, someone will claim you." He shrugged off the question. "Of that I have no doubt."

"Hmm," was all she said, although she suspected treachery was afoot.

However, they had finally gotten their turn at the curb, and too many sights and sounds, as well as a flurry of greetings, distracted her. Hush had leaped down to let them out, but he was edged aside by a dignified porter wearing gold-braided livery with the Astor crest.

The cream of the upper wards had turned out. In one sweeping glance, she spotted steel magnate Andrew Carnegie, several of the Vanderbilt clan, and Wall Street fixture George Templeton Strong. Speaking quietly and earnestly to Strong was Trevor Sheridan, whose sister Mara was now the Duchess of Granville. Sheridan was tall, broad-shouldered, and uncommonly handsome. He was an Irishman through and through, but the story was that he had succeeded in spite of his shunning. And then a great Knickerbocker beauty had fallen in love with him. He and Alana Van Alen Sheridan were considered one of the great love matches of the century. Whenever his wife was not at his side, there was an intense grimness to him. It was said of him that he hoarded his smiles like he hoarded his gold, but when Mrs. Sheridan appeared, the harshness rolled away. Anyone could see that he still had eyes only—and always—for her.

And there, about to enter the opera house, were Caroline and Carrie, Mrs. Astor looking every bit the regal matron in a foxskin cape. Antonia Butler milled nearby on the arm of some insipid little English count Mystere had once danced with and forgotten. He looked as though his chin had melted half away and seemed fearful of the beauty on his arm.

And there—there was Sylvia Rohr, and just as Paul predicted, she wore the beautiful shoulder brooch Mystere had promised to "arrogate" this very evening.

She glanced to her left, immediately challenged by the commanding teal gaze of Rafe Belloch. Many of the older men, Paul included, wore shiny silk top hats and wide trousers. Rafe, however, was hatless and wore the patent leather shoes and thin trouser legs currently in fashion with young captains of commerce.

"I knew you'd be here tonight," he said, masterfully walking to her and bowing to kiss her hand.

Her heart hammered in her chest. Fear was a metallic taste in her mouth. He was dangerous. He suspected too much about her. Now he toyed with her like a cat with a mouse. It was a good thing she was soon getting out of the game.

"How did you know I'd be here, Mr. Belloch? Have you learned the telepathic arts from my uncle?" Her voice was cool and assured, not revealing any of her fear.

"Nothing so occult, Miss Rillieux. It's quite predictable that a lady with your . . . interesting secret life would adore the character of Carmen."

"Oh, yes, excuse me. I'd forgotten that I am the Lady Moonlight," she said in a mocking little tone.

"Indeed. And after all, Carmen is a wily seductress who dupes all the men around her."

She boldly matched his stare. "I rather prefer the bullfighter who stabs her."

He took her arm in his before she could pull away. "He's my favorite also. I compliment your taste, madam, even as I ponder: Should I search this dangerous beauty for weapons before I share my box with her?"

"*Your* box?" She halted.

"Yes, it's all been arranged," he divulged, the issue apparently settled. Then his voice and his eyes softened. "By the way, you look quite beautiful this evening. As you always do."

Numbly she allowed him to escort her again, knowing they were being watched by all and sundry. Forcing a confident smile when she was anything but that, she said, "How kind of you, but I fear I'm just a brown house wren next to Antonia. I certainly can understand if you would prefer to accompany some other—"

"I would not prefer," he interrupted, brooking no discussion.

Her smile turned brittle. Coyly, she warned under her breath, "You're in danger of appearing gallant, Mr. Belloch."

His hand turned to steel on her arm. "I fear that impression may soon diminish."

The buzzing throng slowly made its way into the lobby with its Bergama runners and huge portrait of John Jacob Astor in a giltwood frame centered on one wall. Electric lamps with milky glass shades emitted a soft, pleasing light.

"I don't believe my eyes," Mystere remarked, determined to show that Rafe wasn't rattling her. "Look. It's Abbot, and he's escorting Caroline and Carrie. After just being excommunicated by her only three days ago."

"Oh, Abbot has tremendous influence with Mrs. Astor," Rafe assured her. "Don't forget, she heartily agrees with his vitriolic snobbery when it's not directed at her or her Chosen. What you see tonight is his public penance. He must meekly escort her and Carrie because opera bores the Astor males. They seem to want no part of it."

Mystere had to smile at the truism, for she had once known Astor to exclaim that all operas were female nonsense "except that one with that sly old rascal Figaro in it; now *that's* a capital show."

Rafe met her gaze again. "Caroline will put him through his facings. But remember, a family tree as old as Abbot's cannot easily be uprooted, even by Caroline. Never mind that he has squandered much of his fortune, that he's refused to wed and leave an heir."

Then, a rarity in Mystere's experience with him, Rafe lost his ironic mask, and pure malice glittered in his eyes. "The *only* mortal sin, to Caroline and her ilk, is poverty. Against that they will close ranks. As for Abbot, he will submit, for after all he is a Patriarch of the Four Hundred."

"As are you, Mr. Belloch."

"As is your uncle, Miss Rillieux."

His gaze was minatory and mocking all at once. But she refused to be cowed, holding his stare with bold defiance.

The faint shadow of a smile touched his lips. "Good, that's good. I see you've decided to fight. I like it when we fight."

"The way you made me fight at the Sanford ball, you mean? Forcing yourself on me like a drunken boor?"

"Ahh, that's been on your mind, has it, Lady Moonlight?"

"Here comes a woman who might not fight you off at all," she observed drily, neatly sidestepping his question. Antonia had left her insipid count to greet Rafe. She wore her beautiful emerald ring, and Mystere had to force herself not to stare at it covetously. *Soon,* she promised herself.

"Rafe Belloch, you heartless rogue," Antonia greeted the railroad plutocrat, flashing her excess enamel and virtually ignoring Mystere. "You do force us women to be shamefully forward, don't you?"

"You'll *have* to be forward with that British biscuit of yours," he replied with scarcely disguised cynicism. "But don't hurt him. He looks fragile."

"This was Caroline's iron hand—she keeps all of us away from you, especially Carrie. Does that hint at her thoughts? The shameless woman is saving you, Rafe, and who could blame her?"

What's truly shameless, Mystere thought, *is this brazen, unseemly talk.* But only look how Rafe was grinning, cunning as a wolf, and how Antonia made a wanton of herself in public.

However, Mystere missed the rest of the unseemly exchange, for Abbot had eased away from the Astor ladies to mutter in her ear.

"I've disliked that man"—his hostile eyes settled on Rafe—"from the day I met him. We shook hands, and God strike me down now if *his* wasn't callused. The man's as common as a ditchdigger. You deserve better, my dear. Watch him, for he's a scoundrel."

Alarm constricted her throat—so she and Rafe Belloch were, indeed, an item now. In one sense or another.

"Take care yourself," she replied lightly. "Caroline is looking daggers at you for leaving her side."

"The woman's like Satan with a sunburn," he agreed, already turning to head back. "But she's predictable, and I can play her like a piano." He gave a last glance at Rafe, who stared back, a ferociousness in his eyes.

"You, however," Abbot sniveled before fleeing, "are handling a mountain mover—quite volatile. Be very careful, or he'll have you blown to bits, too."

Chapter 14

"Glasses, miss?" inquired a polite usher, offering Mystere a dainty pair of pearl-and-gold-inlaid opera glasses as he led them to Rafe's private box.

"Oh, this young woman has excellent eyes," Rafe interceded, tucking a banknote into the man's hand and waving him off. "Especially for anything that sparkles."

Dread stabbed at her heart. Had she stupidly let him see her staring at Antonia's ring? Was she walking into the lion's den? Certainly it looked that way. She would have to have her whip and chair ready at all times.

"What can I do to convince you I'm not the dark and mysterious Lady Moonlight? After all, I thought we were to see the opera tonight, so must we ride this hobbyhorse all evening?" she asked wearily, gazing round the plush interior of the Astor Place. Romanesque arches and swagged boxes lured the eyes above, and from thence to steep tiers of velvet plush seating, all narrowing as they approached the proscenium-arch stage and the orchestra pit.

He smiled wolfishly. "But that's your lure, my love. I want to be seduced by such a siren. Yes, all evening and beyond. In the meantime, I would like my stickpin back whenever you should find it convenient."

She ignored him, glancing around the roomy opera box. "This could easily seat four more persons. Who will be joining us?"

"Not your make-believe uncle, certainly."

She ignored him again, and unfortunately found his hand on her back as he chivalrously seated her.

He taunted, "No, you're completely in my clutches this evening. But never mind that, artful dodger. I'm waiting to hear your protest, for I just called your uncle make-believe."

"I heard you, Mr. Belloch; it's just that I feel foolish encouraging your obsession. Do you have proof he's make-believe, or is proof unneccesary when you exalted Patriarchs make accusations?"

You. The word seemed to sting him like buckshot. His mouth firmed in anger. "Proof is on it's way," he told her bluntly. "A very capable employee of mine has begun some inquiries. Mail now moves fairly quickly up and down the Mississippi. I expect news from New Orleans any day now."

Despite her resolve to resist his bullying, the announcement made her face suddenly tingle. No doubt she paled, too, for he laughed. "I believe the ladies' press calls that a 'blanche.' "

"So what if I did blanche? How *should* I react when I learn that an obviously obsessed man is investigating my life?"

"What matters that to an innocent and untried flat-bosomed girl like yourself?"

She gave a look that knifed him. "Can't we at least leave my bosom out of this?"

He chuckled. "You've been trying to, haven't you? You've done some handy disguising, too, for as I recall you at Five Points, you had plenty to 'leave out.' "

"You are absolutely disgusting," she announced with cold, angry precision, pointedly ignoring him while she surveyed the assembled crowd below. Those not privileged enough to sit in the boxes included Thelma Richards, Dr.

and Mrs. Charles Sanford, Jared Maitland and his wife Constance, Garret and Eugenia Teasdale. . . .

She lost her concentration, aware that he continued to study her from a smug, knowing face that angered her.

"Tell me something," he requested. "Sam, that resourceful employee I mentioned to you, has already told me some things about you. Is it true you can handle a Thoroughbred as well as any man? I heard tell you learned to foxhunt at that fancy school Rillieux sent you to in Britain."

"Yes, I can ride very well, thank you, and that's no secret, Mr. Belloch."

"No wonder you handled me with such graceful contempt during our waltzes. You're obviously used to handling power."

He leaned across the narrow space between their gold-embroidered armchairs.

"But I'm no animal used to a bit and harness." He shocked her by stroking the fine hairs at her nape, his hand behind them where no one could view the impropriety. "The strumpet who robbed me at Five Points," he confided in a low tone, "was also quite graceful."

"Strumpet? So she was a prostitute also?" she asked stiffly, praying his hand would leave her nape, praying the ceaseless tingling that electrified from his fingers would refrain from running down her spine and heating her entire body.

"You tell me."

Mystere didn't move. Her thoughts stumbled over one another.

He's more suspicious than ever, she realized. *Why?* For a fleeting moment, she thought of Lorenzo Perkins and his veiled threats of blackmail when she had sacked him.

"It's a shame you never got to know her better," she rebuffed, running her own hand down the back of her neck, chasing him away. "Obviously you're quite smitten with her."

His eyes bored into her. "She was indeed comely. I liked her audacity, but she's sorely in need of a keeper."

"Because she bested you?" Her gaze met with his. She was a fool to show the audacity he had just lauded, but it was freeing and exhilarating at the same time. She was no mincing debutante to run at his every scowl. Her only true fears were of the law and Rillieux, both of whom were seated in the box with Mrs. Astor.

He tipped his head back and laughed. The strong—and, indeed, Pollard was right—callused hand again went to her nape. This time with a hangman's grip. "She bested me not once, but twice. I relish the moment when I get to show her who her master is."

His tone, suddenly harsh, made her resolve to speak with Paul as soon as possible. She *had* to make him understand the danger they faced, especially once Rafe heard from New Orleans. But would Paul listen? Even now she could glance to her right and see his sleek white head amidst those in the Astor box.

Then another possibility besides Lorenzo occurred to her. Paul had already made ominous remarks about "an accident" befalling Rafe Belloch. Would news of Rafe's inquiry to New Orleans cause Paul to exercise more caution, or would he instead have Evan and Baylis rough him up? No matter how reprehensible she found Rafe's talk and behavior, she refused to be a party to violence against him or anyone else.

"Your fascination in this matter is ill-advised, Mr. Belloch. I'm not the adventuress you imagine. I'm just having my first debut, hardly the kind of woman for a scandal, or a romance. So I must point out that your efforts are failing miserably."

The houselights winked out, and the opera began. But in the darkness Rafe was even more of a threat and a presence. He leaned close. So close she could feel his breath against her temple, his heavy, strong thigh against hers. Wretchedly, he stroked her cheek with all the intimacy of a lover.

"You're no schoolgirl. Look at me."

She complied to his demand, her eyes wary even in the dimness.

He took her face in both his hands. If the lights had been up, she would have struggled, but no one could see them in the darkness, half-hidden behind thick velvet curtains.

"Please, Mr. Belloch—"

"Rafe. My name is Rafe."

A surge of unwanted emotion caught in her throat. In truth she shouldn't have desired his hands on her face, or the intimacy of using his first name, but the notion of both moved her. And she didn't know why. She didn't even want to know why because it might prove her more vulnerable than she ever thought possible.

"Please, Rafe," she nearly begged. "I'm not the one for you to pursue. Your fascination may even prove dangerous to us both. Believe me, I can't bring anything good to you—"

"You bring to me a kind of truth I've rarely seen in this crowd. I can't help it if I'm drawn to it."

"There is no truth. None," she whispered, her voice harsh with strange, unshed tears.

"You're wrong," he whispered back harshly before his lips crushed hers.

The kiss was long and hard and wet. She wanted to scurry away, but the iron hold on her face was unrelenting. Slowly he coerced her rebellious mouth into surrender. The molten pink flesh of her lips parted; he gained free entry.

His tongue penetrated her with the thoroughness of a wine taster. Again and again he entered her, until her loins ached with emptiness. Shuddering, she fell against him, her breathing irregular and hard. Her heart pounding and yearning all at the same time.

"You played a ruffian's game at Five Points, Lady Moonlight," he said against her hair when they parted. "But that means you must honor ruffians' rules. You see, it's far better to kill a man and be done with it than to shame him and force him to revenge."

"You're either a madman or having me on," she whispered back. "I'm not sure which, but I warn you, this is dangerous. I'm not available for these games. They're dangerous, I tell you. Dangerous."

"It's you who are in danger, Mystere." His voice turned dark and rich. "I find myself wanting you. And I always get what I want."

She wanted to lower her head to her hands and weep. Moaning, she turned away from him. "You're a fool, then," she told him, thinking all the while of Rillieux and his murderous notions.

"I can assure you I've never been a fool for any woman, but never have I met a woman like you, Lady Moonlight. You steal men's jewels and their good sense."

A sob caught in her throat. Unable to speak, she placed her fingers to her mouth that still burned with his kiss. His ominous presence prevented her from enjoying the opera. Though the production was spectacular, the arias elaborate, the costumes, sets, and lighting lavish, she was too overwhelmed. Inside her, it was as if several productions were competing at once, none of them ever touching her distracted heart except the dark torment of his thigh against hers, his wicked torturous hand at her nape.

During the intermission Rafe made a point of dogging her like a shadow, as if daring her to steal something under his very nose. She was thinking about doing just that when Carrie Astor somehow made her way across the crowded lobby to briefly join them.

"Enjoying the show?" she greeted them.

Mystere, busy searching for Sylvia Rohr and her brooch, replied absently, "Yes, it's wonderful. I especially like the lead tenor."

"Is that right?" Rafe mocked her. "Well, I saw Colonel

Cody's new Wild West show last summer, and this production tonight is quite similar. It's all noise and spectacle. All they need are a few whooping savages."

His eyes narrowed suggestively. "Although that's not so bad—a few Indians would certainly prove *diverting,*" he finished on an emphatic note that subtly accused Mystere.

She couldn't prevent a sudden flush, for he was letting her know that he understood what she was up to. He laughed at her, and poor Carrie seemed confused.

"My mother asked me to remind you," she told them just before she left, "that she'll be hosting a late supper and cocktails at our house."

"Oh, the two of us will be there," Rafe assured her. He deliberately raised his voice, Mystere thought, so that a nearby gossip writer would overhear him.

With Rafe watching her like a prison guard, she had no opportunity to approach Sylvia. And by now his constant vigilance had stretched her nerves to the breaking point. Just before the lights dimmed to signal the end of intermission, Inspector Byrnes's gaze met hers.

His eyes only brushed lightly over her, moving on. But icy fingers touched her heart. Suddenly everyone seemed to be watching her from sly, caged eyes. And Rafe's words echoed menacingly in her thoughts: *Mail now moves fairly quickly up and down the Mississippi.*

Despite all that weighed on her mind, Mystere eventually found herself being momentarily transported by the drama unfolding below her on the stage—and especially by the music of the rousing "Toreador Song."

A powerful thumping of timpani, a plaintive crying of violins, and suddenly she saw herself again dancing out over the moonlit Hudson with Rafe. His forceful kiss burned anew on her lips. Again that strange sensation that all time had been suspended, and there was only this quivering effulgence of joy within her, her heart wildly pulsing *I want, I want*. This sense that her own life, too, was a dance unfolding moment by moment.

But then she glanced over at Rafe, and his alert, taunting eyes made her taste fear like a mouthful of corroded pennies. The orchestra slowed to a sleepy interlude, and he bent close to whisper in her ear.

"You've already stolen something, haven't you?"

"Of course," she lied in a whisper. "I'm the Lady Moonlight, remember? 'Elusive as a jungle cat.' "

"It's hidden on your person, but where?"

"Quiet, you two," came Caroline's hissing whisper from the adjacent box.

But Rafe only drew his lips even closer, until his hot breath tickled her ear. "Hidden where?" he repeated.

She shook her head and touched her lips, warning him to be quiet. Rafe only smiled at her and scooted his chair closer. She realized why when, gasping at the shock of touch, his right arm encircled her just above the waist.

"I asked politely," he muttered. "Now I'm searching."

"You wouldn't!" she protested, whispering harshly, grasping his right hand in her left and trying to break his grip on her right hip.

"Shh," he responded, touching his own lips in a mockery of her gesture only moments before.

In her effort to pry his hand loose she noticed the calluses again. Rafe Belloch had calluses to go with his muscles. His hand began to move around to her thigh, and despite her outrage she also felt that electric, erotic response to his intimate touch.

Her breathing quickened, deepened, and though she still placed heavy resistance against his hand, secretly she was almost willing to tolerate this new sensation, this fiery stirring of desire in a place now shamelessly close to his intrusive fingers.

But suddenly he surprised her by sliding his hand quickly

up across her stomach, stopping only a fractional inch from discovering her tightly bound chest.

In a panic, she began exerting more pressure to force his hand down.

Rafe was so amused he emitted a coughing chuckle. Caroline's face turned in their direction, and even the dim box lights showed the angry set of her features.

Again he pressed his lips against Mystere's ear, the touch thrilling and galling all at one time.

"Show me all your treasures, Lady Moonlight," his whisper goaded, his lips a silky caress to her ear that both thrilled and reviled. "Let's make a wager, little beauty. Allow me to move my hand just one inch higher. If my suspicion about you is wrong, I shall have purchased a virgin bride. If right, I'll have exposed a treacherous siren. What say you?"

The mail from New Orleans, she realized in a moment of breathless fear, was a remote threat, indeed, compared to the danger now. Her only chance was to resort to the deceptive skill Rillieux had instilled within her.

"As you will, sir," she whispered back, eyes boldly meeting his. "But a gentleman's word is his bond, and I take your wager at face value. If you are wrong, then I must insist you marry me for the sake of my honor. I believe the threat of marriage will stay your hand, Rafe Belloch."

Brave words.

However, her heart sat out the next few beats as her fate remained in doubt.

Their eyes held a mutual, unblinking stare. As if to verify her confidence, she removed her hand from his. Now nothing restrained him—one little flex, and he would settle the issue once and for all.

But for reasons she could not fathom—unless he was simply less cynical and debauched than he behaved—he suddenly removed the offending hand.

"Ahh, but it's the *suspense* that keeps life interesting," he surrendered. "As to that body of yours—the time is coming when I shall learn much more about it than I can in this opera box."

"You'll have better prospects with Antonia Butler. Much better prospects," she answered emphatically.

"Perhaps. But something tells me your body has a different opinion than your sanctimonious speech."

By now neither one of them was even pretending to watch the drama unfolding onstage, where Carmen had just escaped from jail by manipulating yet another man. They had begun by whispering, but Mystere's voice had risen with her anger. Mrs. Astor was again sending her a reproving glance. But Mystere couldn't resist one last thrust.

"Are you truly human, Mr. Belloch, or just a beast? Have you ever *loved* anyone?"

For a moment his face became clearly angry. And as she was finding out, with anger came danger. "That's good, coming from you. Shall I have the usher fetch us some water so you can baptize me?"

Before she could reply, however, Mrs. Astor suddenly entered their box.

"You two are spoiling the opera," she announced in her formidable tone. "Rafe, push your chair back where it belongs. I'll be sitting between the two of you for the rest of the performance. Now your names, too, are in my bad book."

Chapter 15

Rafe Belloch inhaled deeply, relaxed his body, and sighted carefully along the barrel of his .22 target pistol. Slowly he took up the trigger slack until the gun bucked in his fist.

He fired six times, emptying the weapon.

Sam Farrell peered through binoculars to study the target fifty yards downrange.

"Boss, you shoot that gun like you run your business," he reported. "Solidly in the black. Six bull's-eyes."

Rafe snapped open the loading gate of his custom-made Belgian pistol and thumbed brass-shell cartridges into the empty chambers. "My father taught me to shoot, Sam. He was a line officer during the War Between the States, you know."

"Yes, I do know," Sam replied as if reading information from a file card. "The 15th New York Rifles Regiment. He was wounded three times and won the Distinguished Service Medal for valor at Cold Harbor."

Rafe smiled. "You amaze me. Does anything slip past you?"

But a moment later the smile faded as he added, "A man stands tall in the teeth of enemy fire, then kills himself to avoid the shame of poverty. Makes you wonder, doesn't it, just what courage really is?"

"Killing an armed enemy is one thing; killing a chimera in the mind is another."

"Yes," Rafe agreed softly. "Good point. 'Kill me the chimera.' "

He thumbed the safety on and slid his weapon into a flap holster slung over one shoulder. His private shooting range was located on the northeast shore of Staten Island, shoehorned between the main grounds of Garden Cove and the Upper Bay.

"Had any breakfast yet?" Rafe asked his correspondence secretary.

Sam shook his head. "I spent most of the morning perusing the papers in my quarters."

"Ahh, good man. One of us has to read the damned things. Well, let's wrap our teeth around some food. Anything interesting in the news? Did our Lady Moonlight strike again?"

Both men had begun walking back to the house, following a graveled path through a magnificent flower garden. Long, narrow fingers of sunlight poked through the leaves of oak trees surrounding the garden. Rafe set a slow pace to accommodate Sam's ruined left hip, which caused him a pronounced limp.

"If she did, it wasn't mentioned," Sam replied from his usual deadpan. "But Lance Streeter's column in the *Herald* was . . . notable."

"Streeter? The wag who writes that Gazebo thing?"

" 'Inside the Gazebo,' yes. Only, this morning's installment is more like 'Inside the Opera Box.' "

Rafe chuckled. "I knew the gossip merchants were watching. Did Streeter lay it on thick?"

"Your name was repeated a dozen times, as was that of Mystere Rillieux."

Rafe smirked, bending down to pluck a white carnation. He poked its stem into a buttonhole of his jacket.

"Good," he replied with enthusiasm. "Was the word 'scandal' also used?"

"Implied only."

"Even better. The substance of real scandal, Sam, lies in what's left unsaid."

Despite Sam's careful control and blank expression, Rafe knew him well and sensed his silent disapproval.

"Well, old son, if you've something to say, I want to hear it. You're my trusted advisor—so advise me. You don't approve of this shameless public scandal business, do you?"

"My approval isn't the issue. Most prudent men avoid scandal; they don't deliberately court it."

"I see. After all, I have my lofty position to consider, right?"

Sam nodded. They had cleared the garden by now and were crossing a wide, immaculate lawn toward a white-painted house sprawled atop a low rise. Built in the 1790s by a Dutch merchant, its batten shutters and numerous French doors were flung open wide to admit the warm sunshine and gentle breeze.

"My business accomplishments are important to me," Rafe conceded. "And I fully understand, Sam, that the wrong publicity can damage a company's stock value. But in that event the mantle of leadership can be passed on. If I become too great a liability to Belloch Enterprises, I'm stepping down and you're taking over."

"I appreciate your trust, but I like my present job just fine."

Rafe smiled sympathetically but stuck to his guns. He had decided it was high time to rock Mrs. Astor's staid, comfortable world with a scandal the Fifth Avenue Brahmins would never forget. Exposing Paul and Mystere Rillieux was not his main priority—his investigation of them was for purely personal reasons, not public exposure. He meant to verify his belief that Mystere was both Lady Moonlight and the forward, acid-tongued wench who had robbed him at Five Points.

He would then get his revenge, but not by exposing her and her uncle. No, his greatest prize would be the public ruin of Caroline or Carrie Astor, and Carrie seemed an unlikely prospect for scandal. She was an inspid, shallow bore, though harmless and sweet in her own way, and he had little heart to hurt her. But Caroline was another matter. . . .

A floored breezeway led off the west wing to a comfortable breakfast nook. Just before the two men entered it, Rafe paused. He turned around and from this high-ground vantage point gazed across the bay past Governor's Island to crowded Manhattan.

"Baron Rothschild was right, Sam. The whole world *has* become a city. That thirteen-mile-long island will soon lose its last cows and chickens."

"But never its rats," Sam added, and both men laughed.

Rafe liked to converse freely at mealtimes, free of servants' prying ears, so breakfast waited, as usual, in covered chafing dishes on a sideboard. Each man helped himself, then sat at a wrought-iron table commanding a good view of ship traffic in the Narrows.

"Any word yet from New Orleans?" Rafe inquired.

Sam, busy spreading marmalade on a scone, shook his head. "It's only been five days since I posted the letter to Stephen Breaux's law offices. I predict we may hear something in about a week."

Rafe said nothing to that, for in his mind's eye he was back in his opera box with Mystere. *Why* hadn't he simply moved his hand one inch higher and proven to himself that she was hiding her full breasts under wraps of some kind? After all, his guess had by now become almost a certainty.

Perhaps, despite his deep cynicism, the Code Duello of the gentleman still governed his actions. Or perhaps he was foolishly falling in love with the little imposter, and he feared being right about her. He was willing to wound, and yet afraid to kill.

"Tell me, Sam—how could the devil's daughter be such an innocent-looking beauty?"

"I take it you mean Mystere Rillieux?"

Rafe nodded.

"What other form," Sam reasoned, *"should* the devil's daughter take? For she must, above all, beguile—the very essence of the infernal."

Again Rafe nodded, seeing the wisdom of that. But he warned himself: He must vigilantly battle his emotions. For he was a man on a mission, and Mystere was a threat to its success.

"Hush, clean your ears or cut your hair," Paul Rillieux snapped at the youth. "I've told you before *not* to hover near Mystere. When the footman is not attending to his carriage duties or running an errand, he waits in the main hall to answer the door or telephone. Now scoot."

"But, sir, I'm not hovering. Mystere said I could have a reading lesson this morn—"

"Glad you reminded me," Rillieux cut him off, aiming a disapproving glance across the parlor toward Mystere. "I want this reading-lesson foolishness to stop."

She stopped her coffee cup halfway to her lips and set it back in its scallop-rimmed saucer. "Why, Paul, that's unfair. You yourself said the boy should know how to read."

"Well, I was wrong. He'll simply get foolish ideas. Look what rubbish these radical pamphlets have stuffed into Baylis's and Evan's ignorant heads. *Scoot,* I said," he repeated, and Hush did.

"Really, Paul, he's not a dog," Mystere rebuked him.

"Oh, *bother* your do-good claptrap. He was a filthy street urchin before I gave him a home. I'm tired of your damned complaints."

"I don't understand why you're in such a foul mood. I got Sylvia's brooch for you, didn't I?"

The same brooch, she hadn't the courage to add, *which went into your private safe, not the family kitty.* She had managed to snatch it at the Astor residence, after the opera, waiting until Rafe had gone and striking during the hectic flurry of good-byes. The theft hadn't even made the morning papers, so most likely Sylvia hadn't noticed until she had arrived home, if then.

"My mood has nothing to do with that," he replied. "Don't you realize that you and Belloch nearly spoiled the opera for us. After all my hard work to penetrate Mrs. Astor's inner circle. You two were worse than schoolchildren, and Caroline was quite miffed at me on account of you."

"Paul, you're missing the important point. Caroline's anger isn't the real issue. I told you last night, Rafe Belloch is about to expose us. He told me he's written to New Orleans about us."

"I say that's all bluff. Why would he *tell* you anything about it before he'd received some kind of reply?"

"That's the kind of man he is—arrogant and cocksure."

Paul snorted. "Yes, I forgot you've had so much experience with men. But let's assume, for sake of argument, that he has, indeed, made some inquiry. You're telling me that your response is to avoid him from now on?"

"Yes, of course, he—"

"They always talk who never think. Use your head, you naive little fool. If you have a sliver in your finger, do you cut your arm off at the elbow?"

"That's a clever question, but I don't see how it's relevant."

He sighed impatiently. "Look, clearly the man is infatuated with you, burning to debauch you. If he *is* snooping into our past, then you had better be prepared to . . . appease him if trouble comes. You have the one thing that Rafe Belloch, with all his money, doesn't own and dearly desires."

Paul's bluntness was coarse, but she had to admit his logic made some sense. But could she "appease" Rafe in the sense Paul meant? She wasn't convinced that Belloch could be so easily controlled. Nor convinced she could be that debased.

He seemed to pluck that last thought from her mind. "Needs must when the devil drives," he assured her. "I'm only warning you what might be required assuming your fears are justified. Even if Belloch isn't bluffing, don't forget that I was careful to establish the legitimate existence of Paul Rillieux in New Orleans."

"Yes, but there's no record you had a niece there, no record of Mystere Rillieux."

"That's problematic," he conceded, his tone conveying the bored arrogance he had picked up from Mrs. Astor. "But only if a more in-depth investigation is pursued."

His voice seemed to hammer at her brain. Earlier Hush had gone out for the morning papers. Now Paul crossed the parlor toward her, holding out the *Herald*. She smelled the cloying stench of his lilac cologne.

"Read Lance Streeter's column," he told her, his tone less harsh.

"I did." A warm flush crept into her face as she remembered the opening sentence: *Every private box in the Astor House was crowded last night except that of a certain wealthy mover of mountains.*

"Well then," he admonished her, "use your head. Rafe Belloch is a powerful, important man. Yet look how willingly he lets himself become embroiled in juicy gossip so long as you're involved. That's not the behavior of a man engaged in a woman's destruction."

"You mustn't be so sure. He's not like other men."

"Of course not, he's wealthier than most."

"No," she protested, "I mean . . ."

But perforce she fell silent, at a loss for the right words to convince him a trap was closing around them. She would never make Paul understand because *she* didn't understand. Never in her life had any other man evoked this strange response of fear and desire all at once.

Out in the hallway the telephone shrilled. She heard Hush answer it. A moment later he thrust his head into the parlor. "Telephone for you, Mystere."

"Thank you. Who is it?"

"I dunno. I asked but he wouldn't say."

Mystere recognized Lorenzo Perkins's voice the moment he said hello.

"What is it, Mr. Perkins?" she asked with cold precision.

"Our business arrangement has been terminated."

"Not yet. I'm calling to let you know that five hundred dollars will buy my permanent silence."

"Silence about what, Mr. Perkins?"

"I'm thinking Rafe Belloch might be quite interested to learn that his fancy lady has been searching for a brother whose name she don't even know. A brother that was once shanghaied like a common mutt."

"Just as I'm sure your wife, Mr. Perkins, will be quite interested to learn about your visits to 17 Washington Street."

With that she hung the earpiece back in its cradle, heart hammering from this latest threat.

The noose was tightening, and no matter which way she turned disaster loomed just over the horizon. Worse, Paul was so taken with his newfound popularity that he felt falsely secure—dangerously underestimating Rafe and his intentions.

Five hundred dollars . . . a staggering sum even if she agreed to pay it. But she wouldn't.

What about bub 'n' sis?

Tears stung her eyes, and she tried desperately to renew the resolve, the confidence she had felt during that cab ride to Brooklyn a few days ago. She *would* become her own woman and use her new freedom to find Bram. Without him she was truly alone in the world, bereft of any real family.

But time was a bird, and the bird was on the wing. With a new sense of urgency she again resolved to steal Antonia Butler's emerald ring and, eventually, flee to another city, assume yet another identity. The main difficulty would be holding the ring back from Paul. She would have to fabricate a very clever plan.

Hush, watching her from the opposite end of the long central hallway, called out, "You okay, Mystere?"

Somehow she mustered a smile. "I'm fine," she lied.

She beckoned the lad closer with her finger. Lowering her voice so Paul wouldn't hear from the parlor, she added, "Later, bring your primer up to my quarters and we'll have that reading lesson."

Chapter 16

Mystere remained upstairs in her quarters on Tuesday morning, preparing for the impending disaster that Paul stubbornly denied was about to engulf them. With both Rafe Belloch and Lorenzo Perkins each mounting threats, she wanted to be prepared with an emergency escape plan in case of sudden crisis.

She readied a trunk, filling it with clothing and essential personal belongings such as the mysterious letter written long ago to her dying father. Leaving the city was not in her immediate plans because the search for Bram was still centered there. But there were some respectable ladies' boarding-houses on Centre Street. She could don widow's weeds again, and take a room under an alias. It wouldn't protect her indefinitely, but she might buy some time that way.

Her fall-back plan was far from perfect, but she tried to school herself in the belief that it would protect her. It wasn't just shame, social ruin, and prison she faced—exposure and capture meant the end of all, even the end of her dream to locate her brother.

She was just closing the leather trunk when Rose poked her head into the room.

"Telephone, Mystere. It's Mrs. Astor."

"Thank you. Oh, Rose?" she called just before the red-head shut the door.

Her mobcap-framed visage came poking back around the jamb. "Yes?"

Mystere hesitated, unsure what to say. She wanted to warn Rose and the other "servants" that trouble might be looming—serious trouble. But it would get back to Paul, and he would be livid.

"It'll keep," Mystere told her reluctantly.

On her way downstairs to the telephone she felt a little stirring of apprehension. While phone calls from the great lady were not exactly rare, she was still in Caroline's bad book over the disturbance at the opera on Saturday.

"Hello," she said in a loud voice.

"Good morning, dear," Mrs. Astor's distorted voice greeted her, rendered metallic and high-pitched by the phone mechanism. "Have you plans for later this morning?"

"I have none, but I believe Uncle Paul has an appointment with his dentist."

"Never mind Paul, it's you we wish to see."

Again Mystere felt an inner stirring of unease. "We? You and Carrie?"

"No, Carrie's taken the steamer up to West Point to visit her cousin Andrew. I mean Abbot and I, sweet love. We'd like you to accompany us to a lecture on Fourth Avenue. Afterward we'll all lunch at Delmonico's."

"I'm flattered you thought of me," Mystere assured her.

"Yes," Mrs. Astor replied, accepting that as her due. "But you might not like what we have to say."

It was Caroline's way to be brusque and cryptic. Nonetheless, her remark sent fear pulsing through Mystere's limbs. Had the trouble begun already?

"We'll go in my landau," Caroline added. "It's a gorgeous day to ride with the top down. We'll be by at half past ten."

Paul had come downstairs during the call. He watched

Mystere suspiciously as she hung up the earpiece. "Who was that?"

"Mrs. Astor."

"And she didn't ask for me?"

"She wanted me. She and Abbot are taking me to a lecture and then lunch."

"You alone? She doesn't want me along?"

Mystere shook her head, wondering if Paul was going to act like a jealous child. Instead, he unexpectedly smiled at the news. "Well, well. This is quite interesting. You are a charming young woman, Mystere, but Caroline isn't seeking out your youth or your charm. She has an ulterior motive for everything she does."

"Such as . . . ?"

"Rafe Belloch."

"Do you mean—she's still angry about last Satur—"

He silenced her with an impatient wave of his hand. "No, you goose. She's not your governess. I suspect she has matchmaking on her mind."

"That's preposterous," she told him sincerely. "And even if Caroline did have such intentions, it wouldn't matter. Rafe Belloch does not have matrimony in his plans. Caroline ought to know that better than anyone."

"Rafe clearly has *you* in his plans, my dear."

"Yes, but not for the reasons everyone thinks."

"Please don't start with all your alarmist theories again. Belloch may or may not be in love with you. But he *is* burning with lust for you, your modesty notwithstanding. Considering his fortune, lust is enough to build your hopes on. Caroline knows this and is doing you a great favor."

"Favor? Caroline? But you just said she always has an ulterior motive."

"Of course," Paul agreed. "And that motive is to protect Carrie from Rafe. I think she sees now that Belloch is the kind of man who's a fine catch—for someone *else's* daughter.

Caroline finds Rafe intriguing and attractive, but the mother in her also recognizes the man is dangerous."

She shook her head. "If matchmaking were on her mind, why would she warn me I might not like what she has to say?"

Paul started to reply. Just then, however, the front door opened, and Baylis and Evan entered the house, embroiled in an altercation.

"Teach your grandmother to suck eggs!" Baylis fumed. "I don't need you to tell me how to hitch a team!"

"Ease off, dunghill, or I swear I'll—"

"*Both* of you shut up," Paul snapped. "I won't have you carrying on inside the house like this! Mrs. Astor will be here shortly, mind yourselves. Evan, brush your jacket off; it's filthy with lint. You, Hush!"

The lad sat dutifully in a ladder-back chair near the front door. Now he leaped to his feet. "Yessir!"

"Get rid of that confounded pipe. Smoke in your room, not in front of guests. Look sharp when Mrs. Astor arrives."

"Yessir!"

"I'll go change," Mystere said, turning toward the spiral staircase.

Paul detained her with a hand on her arm. "You saw the invitation that arrived yesterday?"

She nodded. James and Lizet Addison were hosting a ball this coming weekend, and the guests of honor included the Duke and Duchess of Granville.

"Pretty sparklers galore," he gloated. "The ladies will wear their best jewels. You may even have a chance at Antonia's prize emerald. She often takes it off, I noticed, and carries it in a little beaded reticule."

"Yes," she agreed, taking care to meet his gaze frankly. She had Antonia's ring on her mind, all right, but that was one sparkler she had no plans to turn over to Paul.

But his perception, at times, was daunting. She wondered if a subtle clue in her face made him remind her, "I'm a mild man until pushed. No one in this family holds out on the others, understood?"

Then what about the private safe in your room? she wanted to shout at him. Instead, she only nodded obediently.

"Of course," she assured him. "Have I ever held out before?"

"Probably not," he conceded. "You're a good girl. But you're also highly notional, and I fear your impulses. Especially concerning your brother Bram."

"You've nothing to worry about."

"I hope not, sweet love, for your sake." His steady, menacing gaze sent a cool feather tickling down her spine. "Disloyalty to the family is one sin I cannot forgive."

"Careful of the dashboard, miss," Mrs. Astor's driver warned Mystere as he handed her up into the four-passenger landau. "I forgot to mention earlier that it's freshly blacked and may rub off."

"Why in God's name," Abbot carped, taking his spot in the seat facing Caroline and Mystere, "should any man bake his own bread and then write a poem about his pure digestion? That's just twaddle."

"I rather enjoyed Mrs. Hanchon's perspective," Caroline disputed. "She's been a Methodist missionary to the poor for nearly thirty years; she understands their mindset."

Mystere, too, had enjoyed the lecture on "Creating Self-reliance Among the Working Classes." However, Mrs. Hanchon had spoken about a worker's commune in New Hampshire. And it didn't take much to spring Abbot's hair-trigger contempt for "that sweet-lavender crowd who flock to utopias like flies to a molasses barrel."

"Abbot, you're incorrigible," Caroline admonished absently, her attention fixed on Mystere. "As Mrs. Hanchon advised—despise poverty, not the poor."

Was that a subtle innuendo? Mystere fretted. *Is she on to me?*

"My dear," Abbot told Caroline, "the rabble need to be kept down, not stirred up." This pronouncement was delivered while they passed Vanderbilt's Grand Central Depot at Forty-second Street and Fourth Avenue. Across the depot clock tower ran gigantic letters spelling out NEW YORK & HARLEM R.R. As the landau eased away from the curb, Abbot cast a sneering glance at the four-block-long depot building. His ire at the Four Hundred's acceptance of the nouveau riche Vanderbilt clan was legendary.

"What do *you* think, my dear?" Caroline turned to Mystere. "Can the poor be morally uplifted? Or are they simply depraved as Abbot insists?"

Again, in her apprehensive mood, Mystere feared that Caroline was somehow toying with her.

"I know of no evidence," she replied, "that moral depravity is the exclusive domain of the poor."

Mrs. Astor nodded. "Well put. Look at our own Lady Moonlight. All evidence suggests she is one of our own."

Mystere's heart suddenly began racing; her throat felt constricted. *They* are *on to me*, she despaired, trying to keep her fear out of her expression. It took great effort for her to meet Mrs. Astor's gaze. Yesterday's papers had created a great stirring and to-do over Sylvia Rohr's stolen brooch.

"Yes," she agreed. "Lady Moonlight is a good example that hits close to home."

"You're both pouring kerosene on a burning building," Abbot insisted. "Give the hoi polloi an inch and they'll seize an ell. Look what these filthy malcontents in the Fourth Ward are howling for now—a land tax on the rich to subsidize public transportation for the masses. It's gotten so that we can't even escape them anymore."

Even as Abbot launched his tirade, however, Mystere could see scores of slat-ribbed children on the sidewalks gaping at their landau. They stared with the vacant, glazed stare of hunger and chronic illness. She herself had once been one of them, and her heart ached to help them. But she would never be able to do them any good if she found herself returned to that abject hopelessness or in prison.

As they passed the massive arch at Washington Square she again thought of Rafe Belloch. All that power at his disposal, massed against only her ingenuity and quick wits. The prospects for her survival seemed daunting, indeed. Especially right now, with Mrs. Astor keeping her in suspense—she couldn't think what the powerful matron was going to tell her.

Delmonico's was located in the Ladies' Mile, towering department stores surrounding it like steep canyon walls. The maitre d' made a noisy fuss over Mrs. Astor and her party, escorting them to a roomy table covered with an ivory-lace cloth, aglitter with long-stemmed glasses and brilliant silver.

Mystere, her stomach nervously churning, ordered only artichoke salad and a bisque. After their waiter had departed with their order, bowing obsequiously to Mrs. Astor, the grand dame fixed her steely eyes on Mystere.

Here it comes, she thought, her heart in her throat.

"My dear," Mrs. Astor began with regal formality, "you are young and lack the advice of a knowledgeable female who has your best interests at heart. Your Uncle Paul is a dear, dear man who obviously loves you as a daughter. But he is *only* a man"—here her eyes cut to Abbot, a disparaging glance—"and he is incapable of understanding the finer points of, ahh, feminine decorum."

A great weight suddenly lifted from Mystere. She wasn't sure yet where this lecture was going. Clearly, however, it wasn't the crisis she had feared was coming.

"You must never forget," Caroline resumed, "how easily the word 'scandal' can attach itself to a woman. The very same actions which only increase a *man's* social standing can plunge a woman into ruin. Do you take my meaning?"

Mystere said, "I think so. You mean Rafe Belloch."

Caroline nodded. "The days of public respect for the wealthy are behind us, dear. There was a time when our private lives were never discussed. But John Gordon Bennett and his damnable *Herald* have changed all that. He has placed paid informants among our servants, even put his reporters in disguises to infiltrate our private gatherings."

"Thanks to that scoundrel," Abbot chimed in, "hounding the rich has become a veritable sport."

"And now that Lance Streeter has got hold of this . . . evident intrigue between you and Rafe," Caroline pressed on, "you *must* be cautious, dear. I admire Rafe greatly and recognize his appeal to our sex. But I fear he is a reckless bounder who flouts convention."

"You're gilding the lily," Abbot scoffed. "The man is base and utterly without honor."

"That's too harsh," Caroline objected. "He is an honorable man, but follows his own code of honor, not ours."

Abbot snorted. "By that reasoning, every convict on Blackwell's Island is honorable."

They fell silent as the waiter arrived and served their lunch on French Limoges porcelain, each piece with pale blue and floral borders. Every time the swinging doors of the kitchen burst open, Mystere glimpsed the restaurant's famous roasting range of brick and mortar with its beautiful copper canopy to channel smoke and smells into a flue in the chimney.

"At any rate," Mrs. Astor continued when they were alone again, "you must be more assertive with Rafe, my dear. Make it clear that *you* value your virtue even if he does not."

Before she could think of a reply, Abbot suddenly muttered, "Oh, *this* is delicious."

His ironic tone made it clear he wasn't praising his lunch. Mystere and Mrs. Astor followed his gaze, and suddenly Mystere felt herself flushing: Rafe Belloch had just been escorted into the dining room, Antonia Butler on his arm.

It took Mystere by surprise when she realized her first reaction was not fear, but jealousy. Nor did Caroline seem very pleased at the sight of Antonia gazing up at Rafe in clear admiration, laughing at something he had just said, flashing her excess of enamel in an otherwise beautiful face.

However, Mystere had no time to wonder at Caroline's puzzling response. Rafe had spotted them, and he and Antonia were aiming straight for their table.

"Sorry, old sock," Abbot greeted him, contempt clear in his tone. "Our table's too small to accommodate two more."

Caroline scowled at Abbot's boorish rudeness.

Abbot flushed, swallowing so hard his Adam's apple jumped visibly.

"Really, Abbot," Caroline objected, "you do exaggerate."

"Nonetheless, we can't join you. I've a room upstairs," Rafe bit out methodically.

Caroline Astor stared at Antonia. Everyone knew what the private rooms upstairs at Delmonico's were for. Very little of the culinary delights were appreciated once the doors closed.

Antonia, to cover her nervous fluster, began making small talk with Caroline while Abbot scowled at his plate. Mystere found Rafe's intense teal gaze upon her.

He stepped behind Mystere's chair and brought his lips close to her left ear.

"Lady Moonlight," he whispered.

Before he straightened up again, the hot, moist tip of his tongue briefly tickled her ear. The touch should have disgusted and enraged her; instead, a hot wave of response passed through her.

He bade Caroline good day, then took Antonia's arm again and steered her off to the staircase.

"Antonia and Rafe," Abbot said speculatively. "Well, perhaps the gossip columnists will leave you alone now, Mystere."

"I shouldn't read too much into what you're seeing,"

Caroline cautioned him. "Rafe Belloch is a complex man with a purpose, and the surface events do not reflect what he is really after."

The matron's eyes rested on Mystere as she added, "And one thing he's after, I'm beginning to suspect, is deliberate public scandal."

By now Mystere could trust her voice again. "But, Mrs. Astor, why would he do something so reckless and pointless?"

"Reckless, yes, for that's in his nature. His father had it, too, and it ruined him. But pointless? Perhaps not, to him."

Mystere wanted to ask what she meant about his father's ruining himself. But Abbot spoke up first.

"Belloch wants everyone to see him as the tortured idealist," he said in a voice sharp with scorn. "An idealist with a grudge to avenge."

Mystere turned immediately to Abbot. "What grudge?"

"Never mind, it's ancient history now," Caroline said dismissively. "Young lady, I need a promise from you."

"Yes?"

"This weekend, at the Addison ball—will you promise to be more circumspect with Rafe?"

Mystere felt heat flooding into her face. *"I?* It's not I who force myself on him."

"Dear, men are aggressive by nature, particularly American men. It is the woman's job to curb that aggression. You are young and still learning—"

"Unlike Antonia," Abbot cut in, "who is young and well-versed, evidently. *Look* at her, the little wanton—assenting to go upstairs with the man. In public."

"Cut me off again, Abbot," Mrs. Astor rebuked him with cold authority, "and your credit will be worthless in this city."

Abbot turned fish-belly white.

Again Mystere felt an unwelcome sting of jealousy—and

anger over the intimate liberties Rafe had taken. Now he was with a woman she absolutely detested.

Caroline turned to Mystere once more. "Promise me you'll nip this scandal in the bud, dear. I admire much about Rafe Belloch, but I will *not* stand idly by and let him ruin you, Mystere. Promise me you'll not let the Addison ball or yourself be ruined by scandal."

Even now, torn in several directions by conflicting emotions, Mystere felt the irony of Mrs. Astor's request. Caroline had evidently dismissed the threat of scandal from Lady Moonlight ruining the ball. Why was she so confident?

"Of course," she replied, meaning it sincerely. "I promise. I *will* avoid Rafe Belloch. And if he won't let me avoid him, I promise to discourage his advances in the strongest possible manner."

Chapter 17

On Friday morning Mystere finished packing her "escape trunk" as she had begun calling it. She was tucking fragrant sachets among the clothing when a knock sounded at the door of her dressing room.

"Just a moment," she called out, recognizing Paul's knock. "I'm still dressing."

Hurriedly she closed the leather trunk. With some effort she pushed it behind her dressing screen. She hurried to the connecting bedroom and shut the door behind her.

"Good morning," she greeted Paul, letting him in. "You're up early."

His dry lips brushed her cheek in a kiss. "So are you. What's this? Wearing that stodgy black dress again? Dear, we want you to look younger, not frumpy and bereaved."

"I like black," she lied. In fact she decided to wear widow's weeds again so she wouldn't be recognized when she went out to rent a room. The bonnet with its black lace veil was tucked into her wicker tote once more.

"To each her own," he said gallantly. But something in his tone and manner alerted her to trouble.

"What's the matter, Paul?"

"Now, now, calm yourself, my dear, it may be nothing at

all. Here, let's sit down, shall we? My bones are older than yours."

They settled into a pair of upholstered mahogany chairs.

"You know," he began, "that I have a paid informant among the city roundsmen?"

She nodded, her stomach suddenly in a nervous flutter.

"Well, evidently," Paul resumed, "that special police team—the one set up to apprehend Lady Moonlight—is planning a trap to catch her."

"A trap? How? I mean, what kind of trap?"

He shook his head. "Evidently they're holding their cards close to their vest. But something is definitely afoot. This past week Inspector Byrnes has been paying visits to Mrs. Astor and others in her circle. I fear they mean to spring their trap tomorrow night at the Addison ball."

Although this was bad news, it wasn't the killing blow she had feared—such as a full report from New Orleans, exposing her and Paul for the imposters they were.

"Unfortunately," he resumed, "our informant is not high enough in the constabulary to be privy to much useful information. Clearly, however, something is in the wind. Regretfully, I think it's best if Lady Moonlight goes into retirement—at least temporarily."

Mystere had no response, at first, as the irony of this latest development struck home. Such a suggestion would have been welcome had she not decided to keep the next sparkler for her own needs. And she had planned to retire Lady Moonlight tomorrow night assuming she managed to steal Antonia's emerald ring or something else of high value.

"What . . . what about the lost income?" she asked him. "Can we afford to retire her?"

"Afford it? Of course not! You've seen our monthly accounts. Rent alone costs a small fortune. And now that Hush lives here with us, his duties have cost us the sparklers and extra cash he used to bring in."

"So . . . what will we do?"

Paul's sharp fox face revealed nothing of his inner thinking. "Do? Well, in the short run, I suppose we can send Evan and Baylis out more often. It's vacation time, and many wealthy homes are only lightly guarded."

"You saw what happened last time," she reminded him. "A maid nearly caught them red-handed."

"Yes, well, I suppose Rose and Hush, too, can return to pickpocketing on the streets. I hesitate to take that risk, since they might be recognized as our servants. But the alternative is even worse."

"That's only for the short run," she reminded, watching him closely. "What about the long run? Will we have to resume highway robberies?"

He shook his silver head. "Of course not. At least—you won't need to *if* you pursue other, far safer and more lucrative avenues, armed only with your considerable charms."

Suspicion formed in her stomach like a cold ball of ice. "Other avenues such as . . . ?"

"Such as marrying Rafe Belloch," he replied with blunt candor.

She wanted to laugh outright, this was so preposterous and thick-headed. Instead, she only shook her head in negation, urgent to convince him how wrong he was to think this way.

"Paul, I've told you all along that Rafe Belloch is *not* marriage-minded."

"But he—"

"Yes, yes, I know, he's shown great . . . interest in me. You call it lust, and perhaps that's in the mix. But lust alone will not compel a man like him to the altar."

"All right then, but scandal might compel him where lust leaves off."

Heat crept up her neck and into her face. "I would rather rob a man at gunpoint."

"Mystere, where money is involved there can be no

hypocrisy, don't you see that? Do you think John Jacob Astor or Cornelius Vanderbilt acquired their fortunes through chivalry? Do you have any idea how many are killed in dangerous mines so that New York's upper-class women may sport gold and diamonds? And personally, I don't give a damn."

"Even if I could ensnare Rafe in scandal, even if I *wanted* to marry him, it wouldn't matter."

"And just why not?"

"For one thing, he is out to destroy me, not seduce me. Destroy us, Paul, you and me."

"If that's the case, why does he seek every opportunity to get his name paired with yours in the gossip rags? This isn't some foppish dandy in the theater world, where scandal only enhances one's reputation. Rafe is a solid man of empire! Why should he risk so much for mere ink in the penny papers?"

"I can't answer that, for I have no window into his soul—assuming he has one. But he is the very last man you should be trying to manipulate," she implored.

"He'll have to be the solution, Mystere."

Rillieux's ominous tone sent a prickle of alarm down her spine. She knew it well, always a prelude to trouble.

Early on Friday afternoon Mystere rented a small but reasonably clean room at 720 Centre Street, a neighborhood of shabby-genteel homes, most subdivided into apartments and rooms.

She used the name Lydia Powell, explaining that her husband had recently been killed in a steamboat explosion on the Hudson and she had sold their home in Brooklyn. The landlady seemed inclined, at first, to require letters of reference; however, a month's rent in advance, plus the young widow's wealthy appearance and manners, swayed her. She became even more genial when she learned that Mystere would not be taking meals with the other boarders, yet requested no discount.

With the key safely in her purse, and the boardinghouse a block behind her, she quickly removed the uncomfortable bonnet and veil and tucked them away. The day was warm and humid, and besides, she had no great fear of being recognized now.

But one unpleasant task remained. Paul had not been generous lately with her allowance, and she had just spent most of her ready cash to rent the room. So she had brought a few pieces of her own jewelry to be appraised. There was a reputable pawn broker in the heart of the commercial district; she knew of him through Paul. A legitimate jeweler, he discreetly bought some nice pieces from time to time.

It was the final irony. The Lady Moonlight pawning her very own jewels.

Trouble struck again on the morning of the Addison ball; only later, when it was too late to save herself, would Mystere realize the day's bad beginning was an omen she should have heeded. By now, however, sheer desperation and chronic worrying had skewed her judgment.

She had come downstairs early, for she meant to visit the Columbia College library in midtown Manhattan and spend a few hours doing some research on heraldry. She had recently read that they had a new collection of armorial insignias, and she hoped to track down the coat of arms, if that was what it was, that served as letterhead on that frustratingly incomplete letter to her father.

She could hear Hush's voice while she was still descending the staircase, rising in volume as if he were arguing with someone.

Another set-to with Evan or Baylis, she assumed at first, for neither of them liked the lad very much, considering him

Paul's spoiled brat. She hurried her step, meaning to quiet them before they woke Paul. But as she reached the central hallway, she heard a loud, boisterous voice she did not recognize.

"You'll shut your gob, you insolent pup, or I'll give you more than the rough side of my tongue! I said go get Miss Rillieux, and, mister, I mean *now!*"

"I will not," Hush insisted, standing his ground. "Not till you state your business."

"Why, you little cur, I'll—"

"Stop that, sir!" Mystere exclaimed, hurrying toward the two of them. "Leave the boy alone."

Hush had leaned one shoulder against the front door, doing his best to prevent the forced entry of a rough, unsavory-looking man she had never seen before. He was almost as burly as Evan, swarthy, with shaggy muttonchop whiskers the color of wet sand.

"Well now," the roughian greeted her belligerently, "here's the great lady her ownself, I'd wager. Be you Mystere Rillieux?"

"I am. Do I know you, sir?" she demanded.

Hush spoke up first. "This is Sparky, Mys—I mean, ma'am. You know—that one fellow I already told you about?"

For a moment she drew a complete blank. Then she remembered. "Oh, yes. Lorenzo Perkins's friend."

"More in the way of a business partner, miss, than a friend," Sparky corrected her.

"What do you mean by forcing your way into our home?" she asked, although she knew he must be here with blackmail on his mind.

"Now, lookahere, let's come down off our high horse, missy." Sparky, half-in, half-out of the house now, took her in with a leering glance. Despite his size and evident strength, he had unhealthy skin like yellowed ivory.

The elegant luxury of the interior seemed to intimidate

him somewhat, for he suddenly lost interest in hurling insults.

"Please state your business, sir," she told him, her voice firm but her knees feeling watery and weak with dread.

He slid a folded sheet of paper from the pocket of his frayed and stained work shirt, a cheap "reach-me-down" as the new ready-to-wear garments were often called.

"The thing of it is," he began, his voice brimming with swagger again, "I'm actually on my way to deliver this to a certain railroad toff known to both of us. Seems you two been mentioned in the rags quite a bit lately."

Without a word she moved up beside Hush to take the paper from Sparky. Then she moved off a few paces and unfolded the sheet. The note was printed in black ink, carelessly blotted, and although the spelling and grammar were almost sound, the tone was both childish and pompous at once.

Dear Mr. Belloch,

I am a detective who happens to be in the way of knowing some inturesting facts about a certain young woman. Facts you might want to know. For instance, why is this woman searching for a brother whose name is different than her own? Why does she wear a disgise when she meets me in the park to pay me? And if she is so high-society, why would her brother be forced to sea as a commun sailor? If you desire more information, send a message to me at 21 Amos Street.

Yrs. truly,
L. Perkins

While she read it, Hush moved back closer to her.

"Sparky and that other man," he reminded her in a low voice, "are looking to get rich in Little Italy—remember, the monkeys and street organs?"

She nodded, folding the sheet back up. She could tell,

from the vague phrasing of the letter, that the two inept blackmailers actually knew very little about her—in fact, ironically, nothing she hadn't already disclosed voluntarily to Lorenzo. Unfortunately, given Rafe Belloch's obvious vendetta, the wealthy industrialist would pursue even a dubious lead to learn more about her.

"The five hunnert is to be paid in cash," Sparky stipulated. "You can pay me now or take it to Lorenzo at the Bethesda Fountain by five P.M. today. Elsewise this note gets delivered."

Obviously, Mystere lamented, her thoughts a confused riot, the threat to expose Lorenzo's adultery hadn't scared him. Although probably lying about ever being a detective, he was evidently smart enough to realize she would have to expose her own secrets to expose his crime—and that she had far more to lose than he did.

"This is just absurd," she told Sparky.

He snatched the note out of her hand. "A good joke, is it? Then, we'll share it with Belloch."

"I—that's a huge sum," she protested. "I don't have that kind of money."

"So you say." Sparky's fleshy face twisted into a smug smirk. "I know *b* from a bull's foot, missy."

He kept his head past the door far enough to take in the hallway's long Persian runner and the fancy marble letterstand behind the door. "Aww, come now, muffin. Why *look* how you live! This here's a reg'lar palace. We ask very little of you. The dog must be bad, indeed, that is not worth a bone."

"Five hundred dollars is hardly a bone," she retorted, panicked.

Hush didn't like any of this one bit, and he started to speak up. But Mystere silenced him with a hand on his shoulder. She had decided on a stalling tactic. If only she could hold them until she had Antonia's ring, then she could escape all these threats that were about to overwhelm her.

"I cannot possibly pay the total amount at once," she reiterated. "I'll send Hush to the fountain today with a payment."

"How much?" Sparky demanded.

"Fifty dollars."

"T'ain't near enough."

"You roll fish barrels all day long for *one* dollar," Hush jumped in, anger spiking his voice.

"Roll a cat's tail, you insolent pup," Sparky snapped.

"Fifty dollars," Mystere repeated. "With more to come."

"When?"

"Soon. As soon as I can raise more."

Sparky pretended to consider her offer. But she knew the prospect of fifty dollars had enticed him.

"Well—by five o'clock, then," he told her. "Cash money. And *no* parlor tricks, muffin, or we spill it all to Belloch."

"Spill *what?*" she challenged, staring straight into his bloodshot eyes.

"Hunh!" Her blunt demand called his bluff, and he promptly left. Even if the note was really all they had, however, she knew it could be plenty in the hands of Rafe Belloch, who could afford a bevy of detectives far more competent than Lorenzo.

She had managed to keep up a strong front until then. The moment Hush shut the door, however, she felt the full weight of her growing despair. Her legs suddenly began trembling.

"Mystere!" Hush exclaimed when she stumbled and almost fell, near the point of fainting. He took her arm and led her to an old-fashioned Sheraton chair near the telephone. "Can I get you something?"

The boy's face was pale with concern. She patted his cheek. "There's a decanter of brandy and some glasses in that corner cabinet in the parlor. Would you be a dear and pour me some? Just a little."

He nodded before hurrying into the parlor. How, she wondered glumly, had her life come to this sorry state of affairs? All she desired of this world seemed so straight-forward: to find her brother, and to find out who they were. Without Bram she was all alone in the wretched world, and without a surname she was deprived of any family history, left without any blood connection to the world around her.

But the forces arrayed to prevent her quest were more complex—brutally so, as this ruffian's visit just now had proved.

"Here you go, Mystere."

A solicitous Hush returned with brandy in a balloon glass. The stricken look on his face touched her heart. She set the glass on a stand beside her and gave him a big hug.

"I want you to remember what we've talked about," she told him. "A lad with a sound education can land an honest trade. One that makes him proud. You're a bright boy with a wonderful heart."

"What was in that letter he showed you?"

"Never mind that. Do you promise to keep up your education no matter what?"

He nodded.

"And promise me this. If . . . trouble comes to all of us, trouble with the police—I want you to tell the proper authorities the truth about how Paul gave you lessons in stealing."

"Trouble?" he repeated. "Is something gonna happen to us, Mystere?"

"Maybe, but whatever happens you just be truthful and respectful with the authorities, and you'll be all right. Promise me?"

Reluctantly he nodded. "What about you? Will *you* be all right?"

"I hope so," she replied honestly. "Do you know where the big fountain is in the park?"

"The angel?"

"Yes."

He nodded.

"Later today I'll give you some money to take to Mr.

Perkins, the man with the waxed mustache. The man you followed."

There went her research time, she thought despondently. Instead, she would now have to visit that pawn shop on Broadway and sell her favorite gold drop earrings set with large black pearls. They had already been appraised at fifty dollars.

"Them two got no right to treat you like this," Hush declared angrily.

"Never mind," she told him gently. "We'll be all right, both of us."

But her mind's eye saw Rafe Belloch's cruel, handsome face accusing her, and even the warming glow of the brandy could not quell the cold fear within her.

Chapter 18

Retired State Supreme Court Justice James Addison and his wife, Lizet, spent each winter at their villa in Mexico City, returning to Manhattan and their upper Sixth Avenue estate by late April. Their annual summer ball had evolved into a great favorite among Mrs. Astor's elect, in part because it had become de rigeur that visiting foreign dignitaries attend. New Yorkers, labeled money-grubbing boors in the haute circles of Paris and London, were anxious to show their cosmopolitan side.

Mystere welcomed all the stirring and to-do, for it drew press and public attention to something besides Lady Moonlight or Lance Streeter's gossip. Especially tonight, for the Duke and Duchess of Granville were in attendance— which added old money and ancient title to the mix.

Soon after Paul and Mystere arrived, they were briefly presented to the duke and duchess. The duke brimmed with irrepressible youth and energy while his attractive young wife's charm was more sedate but no less genuine. Mara Sheridan was a black-haired Irish-American beauty who may have shared her older brother Trevor's good looks, but she showed no sign of his notorious quick temper or his condemning glances.

Both seemed quite taken with Mystere, the duchess twice complimenting her sleeveless dress of creme de menthe silk. But Paul surprised Mystere by suddenly acting almost shy, taking her hand and pulling her away before she had finished speaking to the duchess.

"Mustn't dawdle, dear, there's a line behind us yet," he muttered.

"But, Paul! She asked me a question, and you jerked me away in midsentence. You were rude, and I saw it in her face."

"Oh, never mind her, I've something more important to show you."

As Paul and Mystere left the reception line, a footman escorting them into the gallery ballroom, Paul leaned closer to speak in her ear.

"Don't stare, but there's Inspector Byrnes over by the orchestra. There's a rumor that several of the 'servants' here tonight are actually his men. And notice all the pretty sparklers on display this evening. Some kind of trap has been laid, all right. Desperate though we are, better resist temptation this evening, my dear."

"Believe me, I will," she promised, and at that moment she almost meant it. But a quick glance around verified two reassuring facts: Rafe was not present and Antonia was—her emerald ring conspicuous.

Soon, however, Mystere's anxiety and wrought-up emotions gave a sinister meaning to every circumstance, even those that seemed favorable. Rafe's absence, for example. Had he finally heard something from New Orleans? If so, his absence might well be part of the trap Paul mentioned. Intentionally designed to make her bold. And that could mean the police already had her in mind as a suspect.

However, she had to balance the very real danger against her increasingly desperate plight. Paul's notion that Rafe could somehow be their financial salvation was absurd. Her only real alternatives were stark: either take Antonia's ring, or passively await exposure, capture, humiliation, and imprisonment.

She circulated among the glittering throng, trying to remain part of the background. Twice she danced, a waltz with lawyer George Templeton Strong, a longer quadrille with a stiff young naval cadet who flushed beet red when she coolly rejected his attempts at flirting. The last thing she wanted was a man on her elbow all evening.

Alone again, Mystere visited the cocktail bar and requested a glass of lemonade. Abbot Pollard, working on his third or fourth gin-rickey judging from his unsteady gait, suddenly appeared at her side.

"I spotted Lance Streeter among the throng of newspapermen outside," he greeted her. "Looks like you mean to disappoint him tonight, eh? Congratulations."

"Whatever for?"

"Why, on your ability to avoid that vulgar lout Rafe Belloch. Just as Caroline and I advised you. Good girl."

"Avoid him? That's not very difficult since he didn't come this evening."

Abbot gave a little snort. "No? Then that must be his twin brother dancing with Carrie right now."

Utterly confused, she followed the direction of Abbot's gaze. Suddenly, among the swirl of dancers, she spotted Rafe and Carrie.

Immediately alarm bells went off within her. It wasn't like her to not notice something like an arrival. Particularly when it involved a man who was fast becoming her nemesis. She was slipping. It wouldn't do for her to fall apart on this, her last night. Again she worried that it was all part of some clever trap.

"Did he just this moment arrive?" she asked Abbot.

"I couldn't tell you, love, nor could I care less. Just keep up the good work. Belloch's money be damned, the man should be selling mulberries on Apple Street. Oops, mixed my fruits."

However, as the night progressed, Mystere realized her promise to Mrs. Astor was moot, for it was Rafe who was doing the avoiding. All except for his probing eyes, which seemed to follow her relentlessly.

He had evidently attached himself to Carrie, dancing with her repeatedly despite the angry, accusing stares of Antonia Butler. Whatever mischief he was up to, Mrs. Astor clearly meant to disrupt it. After Rafe and Carrie had danced yet again, Caroline interceded. She paired Rafe with the duchess, Carrie with the duke, and both visitors seemed well pleased with their escorts.

Paul managed to detach himself from Caroline's group long enough to get Mystere alone for a moment.

"You just *have* to upset the cart, is that it?" he accused her in a low, urgent tone.

"What are you talking about?"

"Belloch, you little fool. Can't you see he's flirting with Carrie to make you jealous? Go talk to him."

"I will *not* approach him. Besides—your overseer, Mrs. Astor, has ordered me to avoid him."

"Fine," he muttered with quiet anger. "Send us to the almshouse—or worse."

"It's not I who squanders our household money on spurious investments to impress the wealthy."

"It's necessary to our deception," he riposted venomously, adding, "You young fool."

"You *old* one."

Paul composed his face for the crowd, then abruptly left. Mystere found a dimly lit corner where she could monitor everyone under the innocent guise of watching the dancers. She expected Rafe to escape the Duchess of Granville at any moment so he could torment Lady Moonlight anew.

But again he surprised her. Perhaps an hour and a half into the ball, she realized he had simply disappeared. In Rafe's case that was not really unusual, for he rarely stood on formalities when it came to departing a social function. However, Mrs. Astor, too, had clearly missed him, judging from the way she was scanning the entire gathering, her face puzzled.

Mystere didn't believe he had simply decided to quit tormenting her. Yet, if it was all part of a trap, she couldn't puzzle it out. With Rafe gone, no one seemed at all aware of her presence. It was reassuring to feel so anonymous.

Yet . . . wasn't it perhaps a bit *too* reassuring? she wondered. She could almost believe that the guests were watching her with caged eyes and slanted glances.

Nonsense, her mind commented. *Do you honestly think everyone present is conspiring to trap you? Perhaps even the duke and duchess are in on this grand scheme. Paul's right, you* are *a fool.*

In the midst of these conflicting thoughts, a neatly mustachioed face suddenly seemed to detach itself from the crowd and approach her.

"Are you all right, Miss Rillieux?" Inspector Byrnes inquired solicitously. "You look a bit pale."

For a moment her throat closed in fear. Then she realized: If she was the object of a police net, the lead detective would hardly approach her and comment like that, bringing attention to himself.

"I'm fine, Inspector. Thank you for asking, it's very kind of you. It's just a slight headache. I'll take a powder for it when I return home."

"Shall I bring you a spot of champagne? My wife often takes a glass against headaches; it seems to work well."

"Why yes, thank you, that might be just the tonic I need."

He went to fetch it, and she felt some of her old confidence returning like strength to a muscle. Again she told herself he would not approach her like this if she was under suspicion. He returned with her libation, and they made pleasant small talk for a few more minutes. Then, with the propriety required of a married gentleman talking to a single woman, he excused himself and left her alone again.

Thus bolstered, she turned her attention to Antonia and her dazzling ring. Mystere had found an excellent vantage point along the back wall of the gallery, obscured somewhat by an uncovered harp with gilt strings. Anyone watching her saw only the prosaic sight of a young woman idly plucking at the harp strings as she enjoyed the dancers.

In reality she was carefully studying the entire gathering while also following Antonia, who no longer served as the duke's escort.

Finally, the opportune moment seemed to arrive.

Antonia, perhaps miffed that Rafe had ignored her for Carrie, had been freely indulging in wine. Never one to play the wallflower, she was now flirting animatedly with the same young cadet Mystere had discouraged. His uniform, she surmised, might be lulling any policemen present into a false sense that Antonia's ring was safe for now—for certainly very few people even seemed to be eyeing her.

But opportunity alone was useless if Antonia decided to wear the ring all night long. Mystere was immensely talented, thanks to Rillieux's drilling, but even she could not remove a ring from a finger undetected—though she could sometimes remove a bracelet from a wrist. The ring, however, was heavy and uncomfortable, and in the past Antonia had always removed it at some point, sometimes several times in the course of an evening.

A few moments later she did just that, unconsciously slipping it off her finger and placing it in her small beaded handbag.

Mystere felt her heart pounding like fists on a drum. She had prepared for just this contingency, tucking a small pair of sewing scissors into her chatelaine before she left home.

As inconspicuously as possible, she began moving toward the engrossed couple even as her eyes ran quickly over the entire gallery, "judging the moment" as Paul called the final decision before a theft.

No one seemed aware of her. Apparently Caroline had convinced Paul to put on a little demonstration of "mentalism." Many who weren't dancing had congregated around him in a far corner, including a totally absorbed Inspector Byrnes.

Seize the moment, an inner voice urged her—the experienced voice of a master thief. Yet, even as she drew nearer to Antonia and the cadet, fears and doubts threatened to paralyze her will. Under the best of circumstances this would be a difficult theft. She would have to brush fairly close to Antonia and move with lightning speed, with absolutely no margin for clumsiness.

She was on the verge of changing her mind. But suddenly Bram's image filled her head, that golden-haired sailor she had cried out to years ago. Abruptly filled with new determination, she bore down on her target.

Now Rillieux's long years of excellent training took over. *Graceful and smooth, Mystere, like a ballerina executing a plié; swift and decisive like an eagle killing a hawk.*

She snapped open the clasp on her chatelaine so it would be ready. Timing her approach with great concentration, she waited until a moment when Antonia was absorbed in something she was telling the cadet. The beaded handbag was in her left hand, dangling behind the folds of her gown.

She made one deft, swift snip.

The ring was hers.

Girding herself for a sudden outcry that never came, Mystere made a straight but slow-paced beeline through the open side of the gallery. In mere moments she was on the side lawn of the Addison mansion, safe so far. Of course, her quick departure would be associated with the theft, but she meant to be in hiding by then.

Exposed to the wind, she realized the night had turned

surprisingly chilly for late June. A sudden, whipping gust sent a knife edge of cold cutting into her exposed skin and made her wish she had brought a cloak. She saw a footman standing under a gaslight and called to him.

"Yes, ma'am?" he replied, trotting over to her.

"Please summon a cab for me. I don't feel well and I'm leaving early."

"Right away, miss."

He hurried out toward the avenue. Mystere knew she still faced plenty of difficulties with Rillieux. The cry would go up at any moment, as soon as Antonia missed her ring. But with a bit more luck, she could return for her escape trunk, pay the cabbie to carry it down for her, and be in her new room on Centre Street before she had to face Paul.

In the midst of these thoughts, a shadowy form suddenly emerged from the nearby shrubbery. She thought it might be another footman, but suddenly she was staring at a policeman, his pistol outstretched toward her as she stood holding her own purse—and the damning evidence of Antonia's cut one.

"So this is our notorious little thief. Let me take a good look at you under the gaslight so I can tell Inspector Byrnes who you are." He pulled out of the shadows as she drew back.

A rush of panic filled her. Her ears pounded with the sound of her own blood seeping from her cheeks. She had been caught. Her worst nightmare was now going to come true.

"Come along here," he said, giving her a menacing wave of the gun. "Give me your name so I can take you to the inspector."

She took an instinctive step backward.

"Here now, no trickery. I never shot a lady before, but there's always the first time for everyth—Hey!"

A wild passion to survive gripped her. Blinded her. Irrationally, she picked up her skirt and took off like a wild mare running from a fire. She ran in the direction of the front and the carriages. Perhaps in her staccato thoughts she meant to find a cab. Perhaps Hush would be there and help hide her. She didn't know. All she did know was that she ran as if the devil was at her heels, and amid the deafening noise of her own heartbeat, she barely heard the policeman's whistle; nor did she hear the outcry within the ballroom when one lone report came from the policeman's revolver.

She had heard of shot dogs running for miles to find their masters, then dropping dead at their masters' feet. The burn in her upper arm was probably not life threatening, but the pain was excruciating. Still she ran, even shot like a dog. Even stumbling under the weight of the heavy mint-colored satin of her gown, she ran.

Until a strong pair of arms reached her in the darkness and pulled her inside a waiting carriage.

Wounded, her pale mint gown drenched in a widening ripple of scarlet, she struggled against her captor. Viselike, callused hands held her down against the button-tufted seat. Then his words told her the game was lost.

"Caught you, Lady Moonlight," Rafe Belloch gloated.

Chapter 19

At the sound of Rafe's voice, Mystere's heart sank like a stone.

"Let me go," she pleaded, making a futile effort to free herself from his grip. "Let me *go!*"

"I think not," he said drily, then knocked on the front wall of the carriage. They took off at a gallop.

He settled on the seat in front of her, eyeing her in the dim lantern light.

She scrambled to the door latch, but her ebbing strength couldn't get it released before he pushed her back on the seat once more.

"You're damned lucky a norther is blowing in from Canada," he told her. "The reporters have left. This little scene won't end up in the gossip rags. But of course, they'll have a bigger story, won't they?"

He waited for an answer, his silence taunting her.

She refused to even look at him.

A strong but gentle grip pulled back her hand from her wound. Tersely he examined it, then tied it with a handkerchief from his jacket pocket. "You're due for a pretty fine scar, Lady Moonlight, but I doubt you'll die. The bullet just grazed your arm."

Take **4 FREE** Books!

We created our convenient Home Subscription Service s
you'll be sure to have the hottest new romances deliver
each month right to your doorstep — usually before the
are available in book stores. Just to show you how
convenient Zebra Home Subscription Service is, we wou
like to send you 4 Kensington Choice Historical Romance
as a FREE gift. You receive a gift worth up to $23.96 —
absolutely FREE. You only pay for shipping and handli
There's no obligation to buy anything - ever!

Save Up To 30% On Home Delivery!

Accept your FREE gift and each month we'll deliver 4 bra
new titles as soon as they are published. They'll be your
to examine FREE for 10 days. Then if you decide to keep
the books, you'll pay the preferred subscriber's price. Tha
all 4 books for a savings of up to 30% off the cover price
Just add the cost of shipping and handling. Remember, y
are under no obligation to buy any of these books at any
time! If you are not delighted with them, simply return th
and owe nothing. But if you enjoy Kensington Choice
Historical Romances as much as we think you will, pay t
special preferred subscriber rate and save over $7.00 off
bookstore price!

We have 4 FREE BOOKS for you as your introduction to
KENSINGTON CHOICE!

To get your FREE BOOKS, worth up to $23.96, mail the card below or call TOLL-FREE 1-800-770-1963
Visit our website at www.kensingtonbooks.com.

IIIııılıılIIIıııılIIlıılııIıılıllıılııIıılııIIIııl

KENSINGTON CHOICE
Zebra Home Subscription Service, Inc.
P.O. Box 5214
Clifton NJ 07015-5214

PLACE
STAMP
HERE

He sat back on the opposite seat and studied her for several long, torturous moments. "So what did you steal?" he asked bluntly. "I'm guessing you somehow got hold of Antonia's emerald."

She said nothing. There was no point. So she balefully stared at him, one hand cluching her tied-up arm, the other Antonia's precious silk bag with the emerald.

His mouth twisted in a derisive smile. "You've really made a mess of things, Lady Moonlight, now, haven't you? I suspected you'd try something. I watched you all night. Imagine my surprise when I saw you outside with a gun being held on you. Now look at you. You're hurt and you're captured. Things couldn't get worse, could they?"

"Let me go," she demanded, summoning all her bravado.

"Let you go?" He abruptly stopped as if an idea occurred to him. "Tell you what, I'll give you the choice. Either come with me, to face God knows what, or we'll return to the ball and face *them*. Perhaps I'll announce that all ladies inventory their valuables. What say you? Make good your escape with me, or go with Inspector Byrnes and the fine gentleman who shot you?"

The monstrousness of his offer struck her full force. Her damning silence coaxed another laugh from him.

"Just as I thought."

She had begun to tremble, not from the chill or the pain in her arm, but rather from acute fear. There was nothing worse to face than the unknown, and with Rafe Belloch, there was no way to predict the outcome.

Studying her, he slowly took off his jacket and flung it over her shoulders.

"Now then," he said with smug satisfaction as he took hold of Antonia's bag, "hand me your prize."

Feeling utterly helpless and doomed, she watched him open the clasp of Antonia's purse and dump the contents into his lap. He opened one of the leather curtains, letting the lurid illumination from the gaslights on the street seep in.

There, nestled among a lace handkerchief and the small party favors that had been given to the women, lay the object of her desire: the astonishingly large emerald ring encircled by diamonds. Even in subdued lighting its translucent green glimmer was breathtaking.

"Well, look at that," Rafe muttered in an almost reverent hush.

He picked up the ring and studied it as if unable to comprehend a gem so huge and skillfully cut. Each perfect facet was clearly delineated.

His gaze lifted from the ring and bored into her. "So. Our little innocent has been a wayward all this time, just as I knew she was."

"If you were so sure of it, why do you now act so surprised?" she replied coldly.

"It's not surprise," he assured her. "Just a certain amazement. It's always impressive to see a theory become a fact. What were you planning to *do* with this stone? Purchase France?"

She opened her mouth to somehow defend herself, but suddenly the remark got stuck in her throat as a shock wave slammed into her. She couldn't believe what she was seeing.

A little cry escaped her throat. Her hand shot out.

"Oh, no you don't," Rafe taunted, pulling the emerald out of her reach.

But she wasn't after the emerald. Instead, she snatched up one of the party favors scattered from Antonia's purse—it was a silk-and-lace fan dotted with gold sequins.

Mystere had not even glanced at the fan when she put her own favor in her purse earlier that evening. But Antonia's had come partially open when it fell out into Rafe's lap. Now, unable to believe her eyes, she stared at the strange motif that had plagued her since her arrival in America.

Printed on each side of the fan was the split image of half an eagle and a man's arm holding up a dagger. The exact same motif that was embossed on the top of the letter that alluded to a will which included her and Bram—the very reason they had been sent to New York by their dying mother. Only this time another insignia was added just under the arm: a stag wrapped by laurel leaves.

"What . . . ?" She had to pause and swallow, for her voice had nearly deserted her. "What is this?" she demanded of him.

Rafe, eyes narrowed speculatively as he watched her, said solemnly, "Don't think to pretend madness; it won't work. You're about as calculating as a pair of crows, and this jibberish won't sway me—"

"No," she gasped, still transfixed upon the fan, "you don't understand, I know this—"

"Back to the subject at hand, baggage," he growled, ruthlessly tossing the emerald in his hand. "Not only are you the Lady Moonlight, but it *was* you who robbed me at Five Points. I want a confession. That's the first bill that's come due here."

A few moments ago she would have admitted it—and why not? Her plight seemed hopeless. But seeing the strange motif again, so unexpectedly, had filled her with new will to resist, to lie, to do *any*thing that might permit her to remain free to explore the unexpected revelation.

"I'm not the Lady Moonlight," she retorted. "I found Antonia's bag on the floor of the ballroom and went into the garden thinking she had gone there with the young soldier. Then the policeman frightened me by surprising me in the shadows, and when I turned to go back to the ballroom, he wounded me. So of course I ran. I was terrified."

His jaw dropped in astonishment at her brazen lies and accusations. "Oh, how could this be? You mean it's all been a terrible mistake?" he played along sarcastically.

"Yes," she whispered, weak from her still-bleeding wound. She distractedly opened the fan, and then studied it as if it were a sacred relic.

He stared at her, strange conflicting emotions riding across his hard face.

"What does this symbol mean?" she asked, her eyes earnest.

He leaned closer to study her face. "You aren't acting, are you? You really do want to know?"

"Please. Do you know what it means?"

He seemed somewhat nonplussed. "Look, you have more important problems than—"

"Please. Do you know?"

"The fans were given to the ladies by the Duchess of Granville, who as you surely know is visiting from London. That primary motif on the fan, I learned just this evening from Carrie, is from the shield of Connacht where the duchess has roots. The stag and laurels are from the Granville coat of arms. Why are you so taken with it?"

Instead of any sense of enlightenment, however, his reply left her feeling devastated and emotionally drained. Now she had been caught thieving, and for the first time in all her years of trying to find answers to the riddle of her past, the answers stumped her more than ever.

She and Bram were from Dublin, a city on the opposite side of Ireland from the province of Connacht. And they surely had no indication, in the letter from New York, that they might find their relations connected to London and the British peerage. The Duke and Duchess of Granville were in no way linked to two orphans trained in thievery—she could have laughed at the very idea. Rafe's answers only seemed as useless as her questions.

"Why are you so taken with it?" he repeated impatiently.

"I'm not," she finally replied in a hopeless, defeated tone. She slumped in her seat, discouraged and in pain, resigning herself to a terrible fate at the hands of Rafe Belloch.

"Are you taking me to the police?" she asked him, her voice dead.

"Since you so loudly protest your innocence, would that be a problem?"

It would be, she thought. In truth, however, she worried

more about Rillieux. He would kill her now that he knew she was working on her own. His wrath would be worse than anything the authorities might do. He might appear to be the kindly gentleman, but she knew for a fact the man had performed intense cruelties, especially to those who showed him disloyalty.

Belloch gave a harsh laugh. He held the ring up under her nose, forcing her to turn her head away like a child refusing its lunch.

"You professional thieves fight from instinct, don't you? Well, never mind the police, Lady Moonlight. I have no interest in letting an inept government settle my personal scores. Remember, it was me in that alley in Five Points. I've never forgotten it."

Alarm tightened her throat. "What do you plan on doing, then?"

"I have my own punishment in store for you. You are going to board my yacht in just a few minutes. Then I'm taking you to my house, where you will be subjected to the self-same humiliation *I* had to endure in the alley at Five Points."

Stunned, she nontheless managed to whisper, "What humiliation?"

"Still playing the innocent little cherub, eh? Well then, let me spell it out plain." His face turned hard, his words harsh. "I'm going to have that wound of yours treated. Then when you're good and well, I'll see you undress in front of me— stripped right on down to that lovely 'Creole' skin of yours. And then, if the whim takes me, I'll let you leave my house, but you'll leave with nothing more than I had on when you finally left me in the shadows."

Chapter 20

Traffic was almost nonexistent at the late hour, and Rafe's coachman let the horses out, their iron-shod hooves striking sparks on the cobblestones. Within minutes they had reached the silent, nearly deserted Battery. The night had turned chilly and gloomy, with a dank mist clinging to everything.

The day's last ferry to Staten Island had already docked until morning. But Rafe's steam yacht, the *Courageous Kate,* waited in a nearby slip, crew on standby and boilers at cruising pressure. A few other private yachts were moored nearby, including one belonging to the Astors.

Mystere, still numb with shock at Rafe's pronouncement of her punishment, was almost docile as he led her up the gangplank.

"A bit brisk tonight, eh, Skeels?" Rafe greeted a crewman waiting to secure the plank and cast off the mooring rope.

"Colder than a landlord's heart, sir. Your stove's been lit belowdecks," Skeels replied, his eyes raking quickly over Mystere in the flickering glow of a kerosene running light.

Mystere still shivered despite the added warmth of Rafe's jacket. She took heart at the mention of a warm stove. But as if seizing that thought from her mind, Rafe replied, "Thanks, but I think we two will tough it out on deck."

More of his deliberate cruelty, she thought, *for he sees I'm chilled. So is he, but he'll gladly suffer if it means more misery for me.*

But even her irritation at him could not long quell a growing nausea caused by fear. She didn't know how she would ever survive the night.

The crew hoisted anchor, and the yacht hove to, her bow pointed southwest for the brief trip across the Upper Bay to Staten Island. Keeping one hand firmly on her arm, Rafe guided her to the gunnel and leaned against it, watching her as they cut through the water.

"You're making a terrible mistake," she told him in a small, helpless voice, her teeth actually chattering a little from the brisk northern gusts.

He patted his shirt pocket, which now contained Antonia's ring. *"You* sent out the first soldier in this war," he reminded her, "when you robbed me at Five Points."

"Damn you, I did *not* rob you!"

"The cursing is a nice touch. Very ladylike," he assured her.

A sickening misery filled her as if she were a glass under a tap. Desperately, she tried another tack. "Even if I were in fact Lady Moonlight," she reasoned, "that wouldn't mean I robbed you at Five Points, would it?"

"We both know it was you who robbed me. And soon we'll prove it. As for your Lady Moonlight persona—I harbor no great grudge toward her. In fact, I've actually enjoyed watching her—you—rattle the Four Hundred." He stared at her, studying her, a cloaked expression on his face. "I suppose that explains my obsession with catching you . . . with having you."

The yacht eased past Governors Island and steamed steadily closer to Staten Island, where a few solitary shore lights winked like fireflies. Mystere felt the engines thrumming through the soles of her shoes. A deep, defeated sadness gripped her. Again she felt her joyous surprise at seeing the insignia from the shield of Connacht—and then her bitter despair that the answer to her quest answered nothing at all. Perhaps if Rafe hadn't been holding her so tightly, she might have leaped over the gunnel and ended it all.

For a moment the moon emerged from a scud of dark clouds, illuminating the bay in silvery light, and she witnessed a sight off the port bow that only sharpened her sorrow. Every two weeks, under the cloak of night, the Charity Commission's boat made the trip to Hart Island, a desolate spot in Long Island Sound where the city buried the poor in anonymous mass graves.

She glimpsed the boat now, loaded down with cheap coffins and steaming toward the mouth of the East River. Suddenly a chance remark Lorenzo Perkins had made about Bram echoed in her mind: *He may be buried in Potter's Field by now.*

She turned away from the sight, overcome.

"The death boat is a sad sight," Rafe remarked with a rare trace of sympathy in his voice.

"You don't know what it means to be poor and friendless," she bit out.

"I give as good as I get," he told her coldly. But then his voice changed. A strangely wistful note came to his words. "That night I kissed you in the gazebo—I was planning on giving more. I would have wanted to give you more had you—reciprocated."

She averted her face, refusing to even look at him. But that only egged him on to further torment. He took the hand off her arm and used it to cup her chin and force her to look at him.

"That's a full moon behind those clouds," he reminded her. "Widely known as a lunatic moon because of the widespread belief that the mind is affected by the phases of the moon—that the insane are literally 'moonstruck.' Tell me, Lady Moonlight, is that *your* defense? It might play well in court: 'The moon makes me do it, Your Honor, I just can't help it.' "

He laughed again, his eyes mocking her, and in that moment she was filled with a bottomless hatred for him.

"In court? I thought you weren't taking me to the authorities," she reminded him. "I thought this torment was a way of avoiding jail."

"If you continue on this wayward career, someone will see you go to jail. You thieving types are too clever by half and inevitably get caught. However, I plan to take this night and the next and the next to see that you reform."

She stared at him, sickened, speechless, and wondering if she had just made a bargain with the devil.

The *Courageous Kate* docked within easy walking distance of Rafe's house. From the shore of the island, the dark building hunkered atop its small rise in menacing profile, reminding Mystere of some ancient Rumanian castle in a gypsy folktale. The moon appeared briefly from a cloud bank, and she also glimpsed a coach house nearby, grown over with wisteria.

During their brief walk Rafe remained silent, and the clouded moonlight did not reveal his face. Her instincts raged, in spite of her growing despair, to protest her innocence to the last. But it was quite possible, however, that he had finally heard something—perhaps from New Orleans—that explained his total confidence in her guilt. She had no doubt she would know his thoughts soon.

They drew up at a stately fieldstone gatehouse topped with cast-iron pillars.

"Jimmy!" Rafe called out, and a moment later somebody uncovered a lantern only a few feet away. Mystere shrank back, intimidated by the massive gatekeeper of big-boned

Ulster stock who emerged from the gatehouse. She stared at the sidearm tucked into his belt.

"My male domestic staff are all armed, well-trained marksmen as am I. You're not the only one who hates me, Lady Moonlight," Rafe muttered as Jimmy unlocked the heavy gate and swung it open. "The pops and the Wobblies are also howling for my robber-baron hide."

She had no idea who the Wobblies were, but she had heard Abbot Pollard damning the pops—populists—plenty of times. Jimmy secured the gate behind them as Rafe, using merciless force now, literally dragged her up to the front entrance of the nearly dark house.

He tugged a bellpull beside the massive doors. Soon a woman in her middle years, dressed in crisp white linen, admitted them. Mystere took a quick glance behind her and saw a stately central hallway with an English oak tall-case clock. But the only light, barely adequate, came from a brass, six-candle chandelier.

"Gas is available out here now," Rafe explained, seeing her look of astonishment, "but I hate the smell of it and only use it in the study where I work. I'll wait for electricity."

He turned to the servant. "Good evening, Ruth. This is Miss Rillieux. She'll be visiting tonight."

"Ma'am." Ruth sent her employer a discreet, questioning glance. "Shall I ready up a room for her, sir?"

Rafe's lips parted in a wolf grin. "I think not. A *guest* deserves a room. But a criminal deserves a cell."

The woman was obviously startled at this news as if the last thing the young elegantly gowned woman seemed to be was criminal.

"She's had an accident, however," he added, removing his jacket from Mystere's shoulders. "Do you think one of your witch's unguents can cure it or should I send for a physician?"

The housekeeper Ruth studied the flesh wound after Rafe

untied the handkerchief. Confidently, she said, "I can tend to it, sir. No need to call the butcher."

Rafe laughed. "I'll let you take over from here, then, Ruth," he added. "Is Sam still awake?"

"Reading in his quarters, sir. I just took him in some cocoa."

Ruth cast a last, dubious glance at Mystere, then disappeared somewhere in the dark interior of the big house. Rafe, holding Mystere's wrist so tightly it ached, led her to a narrow, descending stairwell off a smaller hall that evidently led to the kitchen.

"Let me show you your eventual quarters," he mocked in a proper and polite tone, as if he were an innkeeper and she a guest. He borrowed a four-branch candlestick from the stand beside the stairwell door.

Holding the light out before them, he led his reluctant captive downstairs into a damp, gloomy chamber she could only call a dungeon. The light cast shape-changing shadows on walls of cold gray stone. Cobwebs clung everywhere, and she shuddered at the clammy tickle when one brushed her cheek.

"Watch out for rats, too," he warned her, grinning when she actually drew closer to him and his circle of light.

He stopped in front of an iron door with a covered judas hole. He thumbed the cover back.

"Peek inside," he invited her cheerfully. "There's a grate near the ceiling that lets moonlight in. Won't that be cozy for a nocturnal predator such as yourself?"

"You would not dare lock me up," she protested, covering her fear with boldness. "You have no authority whatsoever to do so."

"Oh, it won't be necessary if you cooperate. Otherwise you'll spend the rest of the night down here—some house-arrest time, so to speak, to examine your conscience. But if you fail to cooperate, you'll remain here much longer, 'authority' be damned." He chuckled and motioned to the judas hole. "Go ahead, look inside."

She lowered one eye to the hole and glimpsed a bare stone cell with only a thin rug braided out of shoddy scraps covering part of the rammed-earth floor. The "bed" was a narrow wooden shelf jutting out from one wall.

"I suppose you can guess what the bucket in the corner is for," he remarked, and she shuddered, looking quickly away.

"This place held rebel espionage agents during the war," he explained. "Female spies, mostly, sent here for . . . special interrogations, you might say. Perhaps not unlike what you're about to experience."

"You cannot do this," she spat at him in contempt, although fear still made her knees tremble like rain-soaked kittens.

"No?" he beckoned, leading her back toward the narrow stairwell. "Then, convince me otherwise. I'd much rather see you in silk sheets than in this low and dangerous dungeon."

Her spine tingled at the reference. "And what of mercy, Mr. Belloch?"

"I haven't informed the police about you, have I? Nor the press. That's mercy. Your . . . indiscretions remain our little secret."

"I see."

He grinned. "I'm not quite the mad lecher you think I am. Ah, here we are."

He flung open the oak-paneled doors of a magnificent drawing room with tall, narrow windows and woolen draperies. She glimpsed Jacobean-style carved furniture, carved rosewood bookcases lined with leather-bound volumes, and friezed walls displaying French watercolors from the early nineteenth century framed in gold scrollwork. A cozy fire crackled in a wide fireplace of Italian black marble. Its flames reflected in the polish of the floor and furniture, making them glow like rubescent embers.

"Cozy and warm," he remarked as he pulled her in, closing the doors behind them. "You'll feel better once Ruth has tended to your arm."

As if listening at the keyhole, the housekeeper appeared with bandages and a strong, volatile green ointment. After Mystere's arm was cleansed and dressed, Ruth poured her a warmed brandy. Mystere wanted to take it in two gulps but was afraid to do so might show her fear.

Ruth excused herself for the night. It was then that Mystere decided to begin her plea. Her voice had lost its proud formality. "So what exactly do you want from me? Is it a take of the loot you're after? Or is this just some game in which you want to be declared the winner?" She was completely honest now, her head swimming with fear, fatigue and warmed brandy. "If that's what you desire, know that I declare you the winner and let this Inquisition be over."

"*Inquisition*, is it?" He tossed back his head and mocked her with laughter. "No, Lady Moonlight, tonight I am not Rafe Belloch. Since you have accused me of being an inquisitor, tonight I am Tomás de Torquemada, First Inquisitor General."

He stepped behind a lift-top desk and raised the mahogany lid. She felt her blood run cold when he removed a sharp silver knife.

"As Inquisitor General," he announced, teal eyes pinning her to the spot, "I have learned that the cowl does not make the monk. So disrobe, my lady, and let me see how holy you are."

He crossed to where she stood, then moved around behind her. "I'm going to get you started. No need to hurt your arm all over again."

An involuntary shudder, very different than fear, moved through her as she felt his fingers unlooping the stays of her gown in back.

"From the outside it seems you don't wear—or need—a corset. But I think you are too modest in displaying your charms. Let's have a look, shall we?" He ran his warm, rough palm between the satin lacings and her bare skin. His fingers stopped at the linen bindings that held her bosom.

Deftly, he slipped the blade of the knife between the straining linen. She heard it rip like the tattering of a sail.

Her breasts bloomed forth, betraying her, spilling into the front of her innocent satin gown. She clutched her front with her one good hand, desperately trying to keep the gown up despite its unlacing.

He leaned down from behind, capturing her jaw with his hand and turning her head to look at him. The sudden glint in his dark eyes told her that any final doubts were now removed: he was sure he had nabbed his highwaywoman.

He was so close, she felt his breath like the devil's hot caress upon her temple. "So wicked, so deceiving. Confess now, my lady. Why do you do it?"

"I cannot tell you," she whispered, her eyes suddenly filling with helpless tears.

An unnamed expression crossed his face as he held her gaze. His mouth grew hard. "Does your 'dear' uncle make you do these things?"

She ripped her jaw from his grasp, the pain of her arm unmatched to the pain in her heart. "I will not tell you," she said coldly, convinced of Rillieux's wrath if she did.

His voice softened to a whisper. "A very thin line separates the madman from the hero."

"And which are you, sir?" Never one to weep, she shocked even herself at the unexpected tears that slipped silently down one cheek. She was at the cracking point.

He held up the knife to her eyes. It glistened in the orange fireglow. "Tonight I confess I'm not sure. I've never kidnapped a woman before. But then, I've met very few women who've managed to rob me—twice."

Straightening, he moved to the nearest windowsill and sat on it, watching her with the intensity of an unrequited lover.

"You may have the ring if you let me go. I can get you

more, too, if you like," she offered, her face proud and defiant, her eyes dark with unspeakable sadness.

"It was you who robbed me at Five Points. Was that some kind of training for the bigger thievery?"

She took a deep, wretched breath and confessed, "It was shameless the way I behaved that night. I never dreamt I'd see you again."

With his uncanny insight he goaded, " 'I'll always be wondering, Mr. Belloch.' "

Warmth flooded into her face. "If the only way to appease you is to see me suffer the same humiliation, then so be it. If only you'll let me go afterward." She whisked away the moisture still clinging to her lashes. Defiantly, she stood, shrugged the mint satin gown off her shoulders and let it fall in a puddle around her feet. The bindings scattered across the costly carpet. Only a whisper-light pink silk chemise and lacy pantaloons covered her nakedness.

Rafe nodded. His next remark proved he had a merciless memory for details: " 'The preamble has been pleasing, indeed. Don't disappoint me now.' "

Again, she was slapped by her very words to him on that shameful night in the alley. She hated him, but he had only spoken the cruel truth when he said *I give as good as I get*.

Her shame and hesitancy was clear. She wanted to cover herself with her hands and run from the room. The sheer chemise left nothing to the imagination. Even she could see her chilled nipples through the pale pink silk. Her heavy breasts belied any claim of childish innocence. She was a woman in full.

"Any more denials?" he whispered, his gaze clouded by dark hunger as he looked at her chest.

"It was I who robbed you," she confessed, neither her face nor her tone remorseful.

"You beguiling little wretch," he said, his gaze finally holding her own. "Our flat-chested chit of a girl proves to be a buxom woman after all. So continue. I swear I'll not stop until I'm satisfied."

The ambiguity of his last sentence terrified her, but defiant anger burned in her veins like hot acid.

"You've had payment enough. Now go to hell, Rafe Belloch!" She turned from him and hid her chest with her crossed arms. "I am a thief, not a prostitute," she informed him with cold, determined precision. "If you want me naked, you'll have to shoot me first. Since you plan to rape me anyway, I'd prefer the bullet."

"You shameless hypocrite. All this 'noble virtue' now—where does it go when you rob and steal, when you live a lie about who you really are?"

Her small shoulders trembled from fear and exhaustion, but her face was a calm mask of strength. "I don't live a lie. I know what I am," she said, her insides raw from the honesty of it. "But it's you, the Four Hundred, who lie. You pretend there is no vulgar poverty, no starving children. I'm like so many others of my kind, a product of the famine in Ireland. At the tender age of eight I was left on the streets of New York to fend for myself. Rillieux saved me from death and prostitution. He is, at heart, an evil man, but I'll be indebted to him forever for his salvation. And believe it or not, Rafe Belloch, I pay back my debts."

At her remarkable confession, the hardness in his eyes seemed to soften. A muscle bunched in his jaw as if he was contemplating something distasteful. "I've told you before, my lady, that you and I are alike. I have no love lost for the Four Hundred, though I may be counted among them. They are nothing but the pampered purveyors of hypocrisy. And I scorn them above all others."

"And yet you look through me now as if I were a pane of dirty glass," she said softly.

His gaze flicked down at her near nudity. By his expression, he almost seemed to chastise himself. Gently, he asked,

"Who are you, really? Is your name in fact Mystere Rillieux?"

"My name is Mystere, yes, but—but Rillieux is assumed."

"And the old man—he's no relation?"

She shook her head.

"So what *is* your last name?"

"I don't know. I've either never known, or have long since forgotten, my family name."

He shook his head as he stood up and crossed to his desk, putting the knife away. "You live up to the name Mystere." He turned to her. Almost begrudgingly, he tossed her a paisley cashmere lap blanket from a nearby chair. "Cover yourself, then, but bare more of your past."

She wrapped the lap blanket over her shoulders and clutched the ends to her chest. Slowly, she offered him her story, from her earliest memories in Dublin to the horrible years in the Jersey Street Orphanage, and on to losing Bram and her ignoble "rescue" at the hands of Paul Rillieux.

He asked constant questions, obviously looking for holes in her story. When she was through, he was silent for a very long time, just staring at her, studying her as if she were some kind of thing he had never laid eyes on before.

Slowly, he murmured, "You intrigued me from the first moment of your entry into society. The insignia in your letter—you may be placing too much store in it. But whoever wrote it could have been a domestic servant who purloined some of his employer's stationery—that's quite common. Also, printers often usurp armorial insignias without authority, for it is not illegal and makes their stationery more appealing to the masses. Remember, the Granvilles are an old, established family, and it is highly unlikely there would be any unknown claimants on their name."

His offhand remark crushed her hopes even more, for clearly he spoke with great authority and good sense. But she could hardly continue to stand, let alone gather her thoughts.

The night's ordeal had taken a harsh toll on her—she was trembling visibly, and not from cold.

"Come closer to the fire," he murmured, taking her by the hand. He sat her upon an ornately carved Jacobean daybed that flanked one side of the hearth, then took the place next to her.

"You know you can't continue being Lady Moonlight," he said. "It's too dangerous."

She released a bitter laugh. "You sound almost as if you care."

"I don't want to care, but you keep making me do so."

She met his gaze. "I took Antonia's ring so that I might be free of Rillieux. If I now must escape you—"

"You need not escape." His eyes warmed.

She shook her head. "Rillieux will demand marriage." She stared at him steadfastly. "And so will I," she whispered.

He tossed his head back and laughed.

Anger shot through her veins. "Is it so ridiculous, then?" He could hardly answer, he was laughing so.

She turned away from him. "You claim you hate the Four Hundred, but look at you; you're just as haughty as the rest of them. And why shouldn't you be? Though you spurn them—and perhaps with good reason—your upbringing was far superior to mine. Why, if you hadn't had the misfortune of your parents' deaths, you'd have no feeling whatsoever. You ought to be beaten soundly for not having turned out better considering all the privileges you've known."

"I have feeling," he said, his voice holding no mockery now.

She turned back to him, tears glistening in her eyes. "Then, show some."

"You want marriage—but what about love? Shouldn't that be a part of it?" he demanded.

"I've known little love in my life, but I believe I would recognize it. You're an arrogant beast, I admit." Her voice softened. "But there have been moments when I think I could love you."

He was deathly silent for several long moments. Finally he said, "You know, if this is some kind of new con, I have to say it's brilliant. It's almost working."

Disheartened, she shook her head, convinced she would never reach him.

"You need protection, Mystere. I would like to provide that."

"I can protect myself."

"Yes, your claws are sharp, but I daresay your heart is not." Slowly he lifted his hand to her chest and placed his palm over her fast-beating heart. "You talk of love, but I see very little of it in you."

"I can love," she vowed. "No one has taken that away from me."

"Then, show it," he whispered, his eyes holding hers.

She took a deep, wretched breath and gazed into the distance. It was against all her instincts to kiss him; it would only lead her down more treacherous paths. But suddenly the future looked so bleak, she wondered if she was a fool not to fall into his arms. Nothing awaited her but jail and loneliness. If she grabbed some happiness now, she would have some comfort in her memories. She knew he would never ask her to marry him; she knew also she could never be his mistress. But one night of love—it didn't seem so wrong with him near, and the fire warming them, and brandy inside her giving her courage. . . .

Her heart quickened. She turned her head toward him and met that infamous teal gaze. Slowly, she put out her hand and ran her soft palm down his beard-roughened cheek. She might have quit there had he not closed his eyes as if savoring the caress, had he not grabbed her hand and placed an achingly grateful kiss upon her sensitive palm.

Everything moved very quickly after that. It was as if

they were dancing a waltz that she knew even without lessons. Her shift and pantaloons slid to the thick carpet with the paisley lap blanket. His lips hungrily took each of her breasts, licking them, nibbling at them until the warmth between her legs became a fire.

He stood over her and unbuttoned his shirt.

With an almost drugged gaze, she watched him, instinctively covering herself with her hands. His chest was magnificent, hard and ridged with muscle, lightly sprinkled with dark hair. She longed for it to cover her and take away the chill.

He slid off his trousers and underdrawers. As she already knew, his legs were long and well-formed. In full regalia, he returned to the daybed, pulling away her arms from her body, silently forbidding her to hide from his view.

"I don't want to hurt you," he whispered, taking her lips in a deep soul kiss.

"Then, don't," she answered simply as he slid between her legs.

He filled her mouth with his tongue and thrust inside her. If there was any pain, she lost the sensation in his kiss and the sweet, exquisite fullness of him. Gently, he sucked on the white skin of her neck and coaxed her into following his rhythm. He thrust harder and harder, his greed for her increasing until it seemed to swallow them both.

The sensation drifted through her like a wave. It swelled and swelled until finally it peaked and broke over her. She moaned with pleasure, tears of joy squeezing from her eyes and mixing with their kiss. His pounding body brought her to another spasm of pleasure, this one sharp and drawn out, until he groaned and she felt him pour inside of her, sated and spent.

Panting, he fell on top of her and held her, his warmth and hardness comfort against the cold rainy night. Sleep seemed to tug at both of them, but she knew she wouldn't sleep. Her mind raced with the fear of the pain that she knew was to come.

It came much too quickly.

He stood and gathered his trousers, pulling them on.

Naked and cold on the daybed, she fumbled for her chemise and pantaloons, wondering how she had succumbed so quickly. Spots of blood from her maidenhead dotted her pantaloons, evidence of her surrender.

Dressed, he looked down upon her, studying her, gauging her. Hesitantly, he began, "I suggest a truce of sorts between us."

She said nothing; she merely stared at him, holding her raging emotions in check like the lap blanket around her shoulders.

"I'll contemplate sending you back to your uncle. In the meantime I'm sure Rillieux can dodge the scandal of your disappearance, especially if there is no evidence it was you who was shot by the policeman. I'll do my part by squelching the story of Antonia's missing ring. By the time I'm through, the policeman and Antonia will believe they imagined the entire night." He paused and stared hard at her. "But I must tell you one thing: You do need a protector, Mystere. Rillieux is only hungry for the riches you can steal for him. I, on the other hand, find myself hungry for something much more pleasurably provided."

By now, only inches separated them. He reached out and stroked the smooth skin of her cheek. The touch confused her, and strangely left her aching for more.

"I'm not a whore. I told you that," she said, her stare shadowed with misery.

"I know. The evidence is between your legs." He outlined her lips with one strong finger. "Besides, mistress is a much prettier word."

"But I won't—"

The finger silenced her. "Rillieux has obviously not kept you, but it's time someone does."

"You cannot do it," she whispered harshly, heartbroken. "Besides, Rillieux won't let me go easily."

He laughed. "You forget the old adage about beggars, love. But this time it's robbers who can't be choosers."

"If you force me, there will be no love between us."

He took her face in his large hands and studied her. "It will not be loveless, Mystere. No, it must be seduction. Nothing else will do for my mistress." He noticed her trembling again and dropped his hands. "But for now the first seduction is to see to your care. I'll have Ruth show you to your room, and she'll see to it that your wound bothers you no more."

"I cannot stay here—Rillieux will—"

"Shall I see to it he bothers you no more?"

Helpless and bewildered, she stared at him while he rung for his housekeeper. Desperate to save herself, she said, "Your offer is tempting, Mr. Belloch—"

"Rafe."

"R-Rafe—" she stammered, "but all my things are with Rillieux. I *must* return there. The letter is with him. It's all I have of my past, and I will not let it go. So I must refuse your offer, chooser or not, because as much as it would be nice to be protected and cared for, I know better than anyone else such things come at a cost."

"Hardly any cost at all," he tossed out, a wicked smile curving his hard lips.

"I shall give you the emerald. I'll do anything you want, but I cannot stay here—"

He only smiled and rolled Antonia's emerald between his hands. "You forget, love, that I already have the emerald."

"Yet there must be something else you want that I can get for you. Are none of Mrs. Astor's jewels temptation?"

Unexpectedly, he tossed her the emerald. "As you can see, my lady, I'm no pauper and do not have to steal to make my living." His eyes narrowed. An idea seemed to be eating at him. "However, I can make you this bargain: You stay here and heal your arm. If you still object to the role of mistress,

I may have a nice little job for you after all. There is one piece I covet which has long been out of reach."

"Tell me and I'll work for it this very night," she said desperately.

He grimaced a soft smile. "Your face is white from loss of blood; you're trembling from shock. I daresay you won't be doing anything tonight but taking Ruth's cures and sleeping."

With that the housekeeper knocked on the door and let herself in.

"N-no. I can't stay here," Mystere stammered, backing away from both of them.

"Ready the Venetian suite, Ruth."

The middle-aged woman nodded. Her frilled cap bobbed.

"No—" Mystere moaned. Weak and unsettled, her legs tangled in the tasseled points of the lap blanket. Before she could steady herself, she was in his arms, being carried up a handsome mahogany staircase.

"I cannot do this," she pleaded with nearly her last breath.

"I like the fight in you, my lady. Use it to heal, not to go against the one who cares for you."

"But you do not care for me," she nearly wept.

He placed her on a French bed in a glorious bedroom painted Venetian pink. Before he left, he swept away a lock of her dark hair and held her gaze for several long moments. "If you fear I do not care for you, do nothing to make that your fate. Now sleep and do as Ruth says."

"I'll do anything you want. Anything, but not—" Her words were drowned by a glass of laudanum. Her last memory was that of the kindly housekeeper fussing over her bedclothes, and the fierce stare of Rafe Belloch as he gave emphatic instructions to Ruth as to her care.

Chapter 21

There were horrifying moments when darkness seemed to crash over Mystere like a liquid shroud. In her drugged sleep, her body awash in heat, she tossed and turned in the satin sheets, moaning, pleading for mercy. Lost in shadow, she was unmindful of the cool cloth held to her brow; blinded to the strong, masculine hand that ministered.

But blessed daybreak arrived. Slowly, fluttering, her eyes opened to a golden shaft of sunbeam that fell across the coverlet. Her arm still throbbed in pain, but it was a dull ache, not the sharp, exquisite pain of the night before. She rose to a sitting position and looked around the unfamiliar room. The sun lit the Venetian velvet draperies until they flamed pink gold. On one Louis XVI bergere was her ruined mint green satin dress, its side drenched in ugly dried blood. On the other bergere was a man, his long legs stretched out before him, his arms held tightly across his chest. Rafe was fast asleep in his clothes. He still wore his trousers from the night before and had stripped down to only his fine batiste shirt.

Nervously, she assessed him. She was caged with the lion, and her options were few. Even if she could dress and sneak away, she still had to get back to Manhattan on her own. Her things were at Paul's, and he would not be pleased at her return. There seemed no way out.

His hand came up and rubbed his face. Teal eyes now stared at her.

"Sleeping Beauty awakes," he said, straightening in the chair. "How do you feel?"

Unsure and stammering, she said, "F-fine, but I-I'd like to go home."

"You have no home to return to." The statement was made like a death sentence. She had no real way to refute it.

He stood and stretched. His chest was visible through the thin batiste. The muscles she had come to know beneath her fingertips rippled; the fine sprinkling of black hair showed through the unbuttoned front. With his face still wearing sleep, he looked impossibly relaxed and handsome. Not at all like the demon who was bent on chasing her to her doom.

"If I'm to be held captive here, I should at the very least like to request that I get my things. My letter is still at Paul's house."

"You'll get whatever you desire," he answered gruffly. "But in good time. First I'd like a few days to see how biddable a mistress you prove to be."

She stared at him, silent, thinking.

He stared back, then laughed. "I see you're still plotting my demise." He walked to the bed. Taking both her arms, he held her down upon the mattress and said, "I assure you, I've never been kicked out of a woman's bed, and I don't plan on having you be the first one to do it."

She was nearly naked beneath the fine silk sheets. Her filmy blush-colored chemise provided no modesty at all. When he sat on the edge of the bed, his weight pulled away the sheet that covered her chest. Cold and vulnerable, her breasts seemed to entice his hand, but he restrained himself, brushing the tip of one hard nipple with his palm before he caressed her face.

"I can see you're not up to bedroom play yet, so come

downstairs with me. We'll eat and discuss our new"—he smiled—"our new 'alliance.' "

A knock came to the door. "Is the young lady up?" Ruth popped her head through the door. The housekeeper entered with a silver tray, apparently not even noticing the impropriety of the master of the house sitting on the edge of a guest's bed.

"I'll leave you to Ruth's good care. It's cold this morning, so we'll break our fast in front of the library fire." He stood and went to the door.

Mystere stared after him, helpless to fight, unable to surrender.

"This is already healing nicely," the kind housekeeper said as she unwrapped Mystere's arm. "It shouldn't leave too fierce a scar, I wager."

"I'll always be indebted. Thank you," Mystere murmured, her heart too heavy to utter anything more.

Two hot cups of coffee by the fire and Mystere felt herself begin to rally. As she faced off against Rafe, she realized escape of any kind was her only path to salvation. But the more she plotted in her head, the more his stares became pointed and intrusive. He would be a difficult predator to evade. She didn't delude herself.

"Come here," he finally said when they were through and Ruth removed the breakfast tray.

Warily, she stood up from her chair. She tightened the black silk tasseled cord that held together his robe. The black vicuna dressing gown was more than a foot too long for her, so she almost tripped on the hem.

When she stood in front of him, she watched in horror as his hands went to the silk cord.

"I could pull this away and then feast my eyes." He locked gazes with her. "But I would far prefer you undo the cord. I like you to be the one to come to me. To undress for me."

"I won't," she whispered harshly.

He nodded. His hands lowered to her hips and he dragged her down into his lap. "You won't because you so quickly forgot the rewards, my love." His mouth found hers. She wanted to struggle, to flee, but the warmth of his lips, the comforting strength of his unyielding chest, made her succumb.

The satin kiss deepened into velvet. His hot tongue thrust into her, branding her with possession. Without any manipulations on either side, the robe loosened. It parted at the top revealing the lush swell of her breasts. Worse, it parted between her legs, leaving invitation for a caress.

His hand stroked her. Masterfully.

Her breath froze in her chest.

A melting sensation seeped between her legs. Her breathing returned, this time quickened. She was grateful the robe hid the wickedness of his actions, for even she herself couldn't bear to see.

It was as if he was a spell caster and she the unwary victim. Paralyzed, she sat half-naked upon his lap, accepting his wicked caress like a purring kitten. The spell seemed complete as his finger sought her most holy spot, and she could think of nothing more than how empty she was there, and how she longed for him to fill it again.

"God in heaven!" came the voice from the door.

Drugged by their own loveplay, neither Rafe nor Mystere had heard the door open.

There, with jaws agape, stood Mrs. Astor and Ward, and a very upset housekeeper Ruth in their wake.

The master of control, Rafe made a concise effort to maintain Mystere's modesty. He closed up the parted robe and slowly allowed her to get to her feet. Joining her, he watched as Caroline entered the library, Ward like a sniffing dog behind her. Ruth moaned several apologies before he nodded her out the door.

The entire proceedings were a confused blur to Mystere. She snatched the shawl collar of the robe and clutched it to her neck, utterly mortified, praying she could wake up and find the last twenty-four hours nothing but a bad dream.

Rafe, however, recovered his aplomb quickly after the initial shock. A grim, cynical, tight-lipped smile divided his face, reminding Mystere of a soldier who had resigned himself to dying well for a lost cause.

"Caroline, Ward," he greeted them cordially. "Won't you take off your things?"

Mystere couldn't believe the audacity of his bad joke. Nor did it improve Caroline's mood. Her expression was as jaundiced as the mustard yellow taffeta of her dress.

"You callous, unprincipled scoundrel," she pronounced coldly. "You base seducer and defiler of innocence. You have led this lamb to the slaughter."

"Wait, Mrs. Astor," Mystere tried to protest, "you—"

"Be quiet, child," the matron cut her off with decisive finality. "I am not all that surprised by your lack of . . . self-control. Rafe is highly attractive, and you've had no motherly hand to guide you. I do not consider you the villain in this sordid drama. You have been beguiled by a master. But do *not* presume on my goodwill, for it has its limits."

Mrs. Astor turned her wrathful eyes toward Rafe again.

He spoke before she could. "Just curious, Caroline—why are you and Ward here? What could have inspired you to desert the noble rock of Manhattan and cross the bay so early on a cold morning? Just to see me," he added in a sly undertone, and she seemed on the verge of slapping him.

"Misplaced concern, that's what. You disappeared so suddenly last night, a rumor sprang up that you were taken ill. To think I went to all the bother of rousing our boat crew only to discover *this*. Have you anything to say for yourself?"

Here it comes, Mystere warned herself, trying hard to overcome the trembling weakness in her legs. *He's going to tell her everything, and I will be ruined.*

Instead of addressing himself to Mrs. Astor, however, Rafe's eyes cut to Ward, whose own eyes were absorbing the striking image of the scantily clad Mystere.

"Move toward the back wall, old sock," Rafe suggested, "and you'll have a much better view."

McAllister flushed and started to protest, but Caroline's voice overrode his.

"This is not a game," the iron-willed woman snapped. "There can be no way to prevent a scandal, Rafe, do you see that?"

"Sure there is," he gainsaid calmly. "You and Ward just keep your mouths shut."

Mrs. Astor was suddenly on her full dignity as she glowered at him. "I do not 'conspire' in shameful activities. You may think I am nothing but a snob; however you are wrong. I hold our strata of society to a high-minded code of conduct."

"A high-hatted code, you mean," he corrected her.

"This is not the time for your insolence. I can ruin you, Rafe, you know that. One word to the right man on Wall Street, and your company stock will be wrapping fish. Do you doubt I could do that?"

"Caroline," he confessed with weary candor, "I honestly believe your influence could make the sun rise in the west."

"Good, it seems that at least we understand each other. This is not just a scandal—it is a scandal that now includes me if I choose to keep it quiet. There has never been a mark against my name, and there never will be."

Mystere simply could not believe that Rafe was protecting her secret in the face of this threat to himself. Nor could she understand where all this was going. All was made horribly clear, however, when Mrs. Astor turned to her social director.

"Ward, what we have seen here never happened. Tonight I will compose a message that you will take to Reverend Lowell early in the morning. He is to immediately post the banns so that Mr. Belloch may marry Miss Rillieux and vanquish any rumors of scandal."

The room seemed to spin dizzily for a moment, and Mystere saw a gray pallor settle over Rafe's handsome features. She opened her mouth to protest, but she simply had no power of utterance. Caroline's pronouncement had literally stunned her.

"Those are my non-negotiable terms," the matron added resolutely. "Do you object, Rafe?"

"Of course I object."

"Yes, but will you comply?"

"If I don't, it will cost me a corporation, am I right?"

"Among other things. Do you doubt I'd do it?"

For the first time since she had arrived, a trace of anger hardened his tone. "Why should I? You and your ilk didn't hesitate to kill my father, did you?"

"My 'ilk,' Rafe, includes you," she rejoined without missing a beat. "As to your father, he dug his own grave. Just as you appear to be doing. Now come along, Ward, I have a splitting headache."

They left, not wasting a backward glance.

Rafe expelled a long sigh and wearily lowered himself into a Queen Anne mahogany armchair behind his desk. Uttering a little cry of despair, Mystere grabbed up the hem of the robe and made a dash for the doors. Rafe, however, surprised her with his quick athleticism, leaping up and grabbing her by the arm once more before she could escape.

"Damn you," he muttered, "you've cost me enough trouble. Now stay put a moment until I think this thing through."

"Rafe, please let me go! I promise I'll pay back every cent I stole from you, I—"

"Pipe down. Right now I've got bigger fish to fry. She means it; she will destroy my corporation. *I* could survive that blow—I'm diversified enough. But do you realize how many of my employees will be plunged into utter destitution? I have an obligation to them and their families, and I don't take it lightly. Besides, did you hear what she told McCallister to do?"

"She—she can't really force us to get married. I mean, she won't really post the banns once she settles down a bit. Remember how she vowed to ruin Abbot but didn't?"

Rafe laughed and shook his head. "In some ways, at least, you *are* still innocent, Lady M, and I confess it's charming. Forgiving Abbot was not a serious blow to her pride. Forgiving me would be."

"Why?"

"Why?" he repeated, anger spiking his tone. "Because she had no plans to make Abbot her illicit lover, you little simp."

Mystere stared at him in wide-eyed disbelief. "You mean she . . . and you? You can't possibly believe that of Caroline!"

"She's not the Virgin Mary, you know. Why in hell do you think she got on her high horse and gave me that lecture about her high-minded morals? It was guilt over what she wanted to do with me. And do you really believe she came out here to see if I was ill?"

"Ward was with her."

He snorted. "She trusts Ward absolutely; he's as loyal as the Swiss Guard. And I'll tell you quite frankly: Had I not begun wasting so much time on *you,* the seduction of Mrs. Astor would be a fait accompli by now. And known to all by my own efforts."

His smug, bragging tone made her bristle, as did the distasteful topic. "Well, I knew you were conceited. But *this* is preposterous. You heard her just now, boasting how there has never been a mark against her name."

"Caroline is talking about *being caught,* not about avoiding transgression. You see, I had it all worked out. I was just waiting for the day when Caroline Astor would succumb to her inner temptations. Now, thanks to you, that day will never come."

"But . . . but you clearly despise her. Why in God's name would you plot the seduction of a woman you—"

" 'The heart has its reasons,' " he cut her off, " 'which reason may never know.' "

"Your father," she said quietly. "That's why, isn't it? I heard what you said, and Abbot mentioned some 'grudge' of yours. What did she do to your father?"

"Nothing," he replied bitterly. "And that nothing was everything. But it's none of your damn business, never mind all that."

With a visible effort he shook off his anger and met his captive's eyes. He said, perhaps thinking out loud more than talking, "Well, today is Sunday; we may not have to wait long to see what Caroline's next play will be. Right now she holds all the cards."

He aimed a low-lidded gaze at her, and she paled slightly. "But I still have a proposition for you."

The sudden fear in her face made him laugh harshly. "Not that kind of proposition, you little coward, although I confess, after what I've seen of you this morning, it will be on my mind. No—I want you to do what you do best, Lady M. I want you to steal something for me. Steal it back, actually."

"I don't understand," she blurted out, numb and afraid.

"Think back to the middle of March and a soiree hosted by John and Joanna Strahan. It was shortly before the Vanderbilt ball, and before you had been dubbed Lady Moonlight by the press. You stole a diamond-and-sapphire tiara from a dizzy old matron named Louise Blackburn."

Mystere recalled it immediately, for it was one of the prizes she had glimpsed in Paul's wall safe.

"It wasn't stolen," she said very quietly. "It was arrogated."

"How's that?" he demanded, impatient at the interruption.

"Nothing. What about the tiara?" she inquired reluctantly, for even now—fully exposed as Lady Moonlight—it was unpleasant to acknowledge her crimes.

"It was my mother's, that's what. An item she prized dearly in her lifetime. It was auctioned off as part of our estate sale after she died, all the proceeds going to creditors. And I want it back."

"That's impossible."

"Too bad for you, then. Because I was planning to make you a very fair offer. Get that tiara for me, and I'll consider my score against you settled. No time down in the cell, and no more threats of exposing your crimes. Plus . . ."

He dipped one hand into his shirt pocket and retrieved Antonia's ring. It caught some light from the fireplace and glowed the radiant green color of sun-pierced seawater.

"This will be yours. The ring for the tiara."

Considering everything, Mystere thought, it was, indeed, a fair offer. The idea of stealing from Paul terrified her, but the trouble Rafe could stir up terrified her even more. Besides, even if he was bluffing about exposing her—she needed that ring.

"It will be very difficult," she finally replied. "Nor can I guarantee success. But I will try."

He nodded. "If I were you, I'd try very hard. I'm damned if I know why I protected you today by keeping my mouth shut." His voice turned dark and threatening. "Remember, all I need do is sit down with Caroline and explain this entire sordid mess. Once she learns who—and what—her 'lamb' truly is, you will find yourself in a world of suffering."

Chapter 22

As part of his elaborate masquerade, Paul Rillieux often attended Trinity Church on Sunday mornings along with many others in the Four Hundred, forcing Mystere to go with him. She knew he secretly delighted in the irony of a devout Catholic awash in Anglicans.

However, this Sunday he was in a terrible mood and skipped church in order to confront her about the events of the night before at the Addison ball. Unpleasant as that was, Mystere preferred Paul's bad temper to the possible shock of hearing Reverend Lowell publicly proclaim her engagement to Rafe Belloch. She could only hope against hope that Mrs. Astor, having calmed down, might rescind her drastic order. She would have perhaps gladly married Rafe if he had asked her, but to find herself chained to an unwilling groom, especially the lion Rafe was, seemed like an unimaginable nightmare.

"Have you seen the late edition newspapers, young lady?" Paul demanded the moment Mystere entered the parlor.

She looked pale and distracted, almost frail in her linen wrapper. Dark circles under her eyes testified to a bone-tired exhaustion.

"You know I only read the *Times*," she replied, taking a seat across the alabaster table from him and pouring herself some brandy from the decanter. "And they don't keep people like Lance Streeter on their staff, if that's what you mean."

"I'm not talking about gossip," he snapped. "And for your information, what I'm alluding to *is* mentioned in the *Times*. On page one, as it is with every other paper."

He shook the creases out of the *Herald*, his personal favorite, and began reading aloud: " 'Once again the elusive society thief known as Lady Moonlight has victimized the city's wealthy elite, striking sometime last night at the annual ball hosted by James and Lizet Addison. This time the mysterious purloiner of jewels has captured a true prize: a beautiful, one-of-a-kind emerald ring, its value undisclosed to the press, belonging to Miss Antonia Butler.' "

Paul closed the newspaper and cast it aside, glowering across the table at her. "Where is that ring?" he demanded. "It's one thing for you to whore all night for that bastard Belloch; it's another for you to provide for him."

Normally, Paul's wrath cowed and terrified her. However, the new crisis that she and Rafe both faced with Mrs. Astor tended to dwarf all else. Yet again she fretted, wondering if the vengeful matron would actually hold them to a forced marriage. If Rafe's back was to the wall, he would expose her; she had no doubt of it. Now she also faced the thorny problem of somehow getting into Paul's safe to retrieve the tiara for Rafe.

"I stole nothing last night," she informed him in a bold, bald-faced lie, feigning surprise at hearing the news. She added truthfully, *"I* don't have that ring."

Clearly Rillieux did not expect a denial. After a moment to collect himself, he went on in a chillingly quiet tone, "What have I told you, Mystere, about disloyalty to the family?"

"I don't like your tone," she snapped.

"Goddamnit, I don't give a hang *what* you don't like, you ungrateful little witch. If you didn't steal it, *why* did you disappear so suddenly?"

She stared into the dark depths of her coffee, saying nothing. She flinched when Paul smacked the tabletop so hard it rattled the cups.

"Why did you disappear?" he repeated. "And where did Belloch take you? You obviously did not return here until just an hour ago."

She met his eyes and played the one card she knew would calm him down. "Perhaps," she said quietly, "I have my own big plans for our prosperity."

For a moment her words only irritated him, and he was about to snap at her again. Then, abruptly, a look of enlightenment seized him.

"Do you mean marriage?" he asked.

She nodded, flushing slightly. "I . . . I went with Rafe to his home. There was talk of marriage."

As understanding set in, hope worked into Paul's seamed face, replacing the anger. "Well, I'm a Dutchman," he said in a tone of wonder. "But you weren't so foolish as to let him . . . ?"

She shook her head, genuinely embarrassed. Paul, if not quite completely mollified by this turn of events, had certainly calmed down.

"I see. Well . . . that *is* interesting. So you've taken to heart some of the things I've told you? But if you didn't take that ring, who did?"

He paused to reflect, pulling at the point of his chin. Mystere's unexpected news had put him in a much better mood.

"You know," he finally said, "it *is* quite possible that some clever, enterprising thief took advantage of the Lady Moonlight's publicity, knowing the crime would be attributed to her. There was the shot fired. The policeman thought he hit the mysterious woman."

He looked at Mystere and studied her in the linen wrapper. "But she couldn't have been you. You look too fit to have been shot." Then he actually smiled. "Well, I guess *we* don't have exclusive rights to rob the wealthy, eh? The ring will hardly matter if this new development between you and Rafe bears fruit—so to speak. I'm sorry, my dear, that I was so snappish with you. I should have known that a good, obedient girl like yourself would not let the family down."

"You needn't act as if our future is now secured," she demurred. "Rafe is still his own man."

"Well, yes . . . of course, of course. And I don't mean to be indelicate, Mystere, but what about . . . the bindings? How did you explain that part of it to him?"

She blushed again, dropping her gaze from his. But it was feigned to buy a little time. Rapidly her mind searched for a convincing lie.

"You *are* being indelicate, Paul. I told him . . . I said that I felt self-conscious about the . . . the fullness of my figure, that it bothers me to have others notice it. He must have believed me, for he teased me about it."

"Teased you, did he? Good, good." Paul's mood was getting better and better as the possible implications of all this began to register with him. "Have the two of you reached any, ahh, understanding? Is the relationship to continue?"

She had to be cautious here. She dared not say no in case Mrs. Astor had, indeed, announced the banns. Then again, if she had relented, Mystere did not want to build Paul's hopes too high—his wrath would truly be terrible once his hopes were dashed.

She opted for tactful ambiguity.

"The relationship will continue," she replied, "although on what footing, I'm not completely sure at this time."

"Well, that's certainly better than a poke in the eye with a sharp stick, eh? Tell me one more thing: How definite was he on the subject of marriage?"

The irony of this question almost coaxed a smile out of

her despite the problems weighing so heavily on her mind. "He was," she told him, again truthfully, "very definite."

"Hmm," was all he replied, but his ear-to-ear smile spoke volumes.

Rafe Belloch was not a religious man, and although his domestic staff received Sundays off, the Sabbath was merely another working day at Garden Cove for him and Sam Farrell. At nine A.M. both men met in Rafe's study-cum-office for their usual weekly conference.

"This arrived by late post yesterday," Sam informed him first thing. He handed his employer a letter postmarked New Orleans. "I looked for you, but Ruth told me you were to stay in town yesterday."

"Ah, finally. Our report from Stephen Breaux," Rafe said, using a solid gold letter opener shaped like a railroad spike to slit open the envelope. "It may prove a bit anticlimactic, Sam, after the dog-and-pony show that took place here last night. Still, I've been curious."

Rafe's gaze quickly fell over the cordial greeting from Breaux, then slowed as he reached the meat of the report.

We have unearthed no trace whatsoever that Paul Rillieux had a niece living with him, or any other relative for that matter. Nor do any city records record the name Mystere Rillieux. As for Paul Rillieux himself, he was quite active in what is known locally as the Lafayette Circle, i.e., the wealthy class who live "up-town" on the streetcar line from the Vieux Carré, the old French Quarter heart of New Orleans.

I never personally met him, but all reports indicate the man was quite popular with some of our leading citizens, and apparently pursued no profession. Reportedly he lived quite comfortably, though not lavishly, on income derived from land holdings in France.

However, after his departure (back to France, he claimed) an interesting development occurred.

A young man who once served as Rillieux's valet was caught stealing an expensive gold watch from a visitor to our city. When remanded to parish court for the offense, he claimed to have been trained in the art of theft by his former employer, Rillieux. He told an incredible tale (too incredible, in the judge's opinion, for it was dismissed out of hand) of a "master thief" who recruited denizens of Gallatin Alley, set them up as servants in his home, and lived well off the sale of their plunder.

Rafe glanced up at Sam after reading the letter, a smile pulling at his lips. He handed it to Sam, who quickly read it.

"So the old scoundrel is up to the same tricks," Rafe remarked. "Well, it's damning, all right. Especially as it concerns Paul Rillieux. In fact, this is all we need to turn his cake into dough. He'd spend the rest of his life in prison."

"I assume it could also go very hard for Mystere," Sam put in quietly.

Rafe nodded. "Yes, damn it. Perhaps harder than she deserves, which is why I won't go to the authorities. I see now that she most likely told me the truth last night. She claims Rillieux recruited her from an orphanage and trained her to steal just as you might train a yearling horse to pace."

"Consistent," Sam pointed out, "with his modus operandi in New Orleans."

"Yes, and that mitigates the girl's guilt somewhat. But no amount of pity makes me want to *marry* the charming little thief."

"Marry?" Sam repeated, a rare look of surprise widening his eyes.

"Yes, my reaction precisely."

Briefly Rafe outlined the situation in the drawing room that had culminated with Mrs. Astor's merciless ultimatum.

"No," Sam agreed when he had finished. "Pity is certainly the wrong motivation for wedlock. Assuming, of course, that's *all* you feel."

Sam seldom pushed into his employer's personal affairs; so seldom, in fact, that Rafe did not resent it now. Nonetheless, he sent Sam a sharp glance, eyes narrowed.

"Well, of course she's a beauty," Rafe conceded. "Especially when she isn't . . . shall we say, downplaying her full charms. But lust is no better reason to marry than pity."

Sam had a rare knack for using silence to great effect, and he did so now.

"You think I'm in love with her, is that it?" Rafe demanded.

"I have no idea. But there's more than lust and pity that's been causing you to be preoccupied with her these past weeks."

"I can't deny that," Rafe begrudged. "But don't forget, old son—there's also the small matter of Caroline's threat to the solvency of Belloch Enterprises."

"Would she follow through on that threat?"

"To quote you just now, I have no idea. If you're asking me if she's capable of following through, absolutely. The woman is solid iron."

He lapsed into silence, and the pleasing image of Mystere's near nakedness recurred unbidden to his mind. Lust might not justify a marriage, he reasoned, but neither could he deny its compelling allure—especially in her case. He had spent much of the past few weeks tossing sleepless in his bed, and it wasn't the threat of bankruptcy that kept him sweating into the sheets.

On the heels of this reaction, however, followed another: intense irritation at his own weakness. Why in God's name did he protect her secret from Caroline? It would bollix up all his plans if he *did* let himself fall in love with this treacherous little thief.

He could no longer deny that his frivolous adventure with

Mystere had distracted him from his primary goal: to make Caroline his greatest coup by embroiling her in a nasty scandal. Mystere had lost him that goal forever. There were still plenty of eligible socialites, of course, Antonia Butler included. He must not let himself get trapped in a marriage with some deceitful little beauty who, for all he knew, might poison him for his own fortune.

"In any event," Rafe finally resumed, "I won't be able to plan my next move until I find out if the banns have been announced. That news could come at any moment now. In the meantime . . ."

Rafe handed the letter back to Sam. "Type out a copy of this, would you? Then file away the original and mail the copy to Mystere Rillieux. You'll find her address in the Manhattan phone directory."

Just a bit of incentive, Rafe told himself, *to remind her I'm dead serious about getting that tiara.*

Chapter 23

L ess than an hour after church services ended at Trinity, the telephone in the hallway of the Rillieux residence suddenly shrilled. Mystere, busy in the parlor repairing the rickrack braiding on one of her gowns, started at the sound, pricking her finger with the needle.

She felt like the condemned who had just heard the executioner testing his scaffold. Mrs. Astor and Ward had escorted her back to Rillieux's as though she were a prisoner. Few words had been exchanged. The only admonition Caroline had given Paul was, "Do not let her out of your sight."

What Mrs. Astor wanted, Paul Rillieux was sure to do. Now he watched her from his leather chair, like a cat on a canary, waiting patiently for her to confess or explain. But so far, she had chosen to do neither. She still wanted her options open, and she didn't yet know when the other shoe was to fall.

But by the sound of the ringing in the hallway, the boot was coming down fast.

Even though Hush had the day off and wasn't present to answer the phone, Mystere made no move for it. She remained frozen in her chair. However, Baylis was just then in the hallway and picked up the phone. She heard the brief drone of his voice, the words indistinct at this distance. A moment later he poked his head inside the room.

"Telephone, Paul," he informed Rillieux, who was on the opposite side of the parlor from Mystere. "It's old lady Astor."

"*Mrs.* Astor," Paul corrected him with an angry frown. "Show some respect for your betters."

Baylis sneered while Paul, using his walking stick for support, rose from the chair and limped out of the room. When Rillieux was out of earshot, Baylis winked at Mystere from beneath the brim of his feathered derby.

"Hell, the old bag never bought *me* a beer," he told her in a low voice.

Mystere tried to smile politely at his poor joke, but she was suddenly overcome with a paralytic dread. *Please,* she prayed silently, *let it just be an invitation to a Sunday outing.*

It became clear the moment Paul returned, however, that her prayer had not been answered.

"Mystere, you little imp," he said from the doorway of the parlor, beaming fondly at her. "You kept your great secret all morning, didn't you? Letting me scold you as I did, shame on you!"

Baylis, about to exit through the front door, returned to the parlor. "What secret?" he demanded curiously.

"Baylis," Paul announced grandly, barely able to contain himself, "our little girl has trumped us all. Mrs. Astor called just now to congratulate me on Mystere's official engagement to Rafe Belloch."

"Well, by the Lord Harry! *The* Belloch? That rich toff we heisted at Five Points? The Mountain Mover himself?"

"The very man," Paul confirmed, still beaming proudly at his "little girl." "And to think I questioned her loyalty to the family. Will you forgive me, my dear?"

But Mystere hardly heard him. For a long moment the room seemed to be a rapidly spinning top, and she clutched the arms of the chair as if afraid she might be flung off.

"Belloch's a reg'lar Vanderbilt!" Baylis exclaimed.

"Not quite," Paul corrected him. "But without question he's one of the wealthiest men in the nation. And to think our girl is to be his wife."

"Our ship has finally come in," Baylis gloated. "Look at her, boss—the great lady. Ain't *she* silky satin? When's the wedding, hon?"

Mystere tried to speak, but it felt as if a hand was choking her throat.

"The poor thing's overcome at the thought of it," Paul effused. "The date's not been set yet, according to Caroline. But the sooner the better, I say." He winked at her, looking for all like Satan himself. "Just to let you know, Mystere, I reassured Mrs. Astor that I would not let you out of my sight, and I mean to stick to that promise. You've had way too much freedom for an unprotected debutante, and that's what's gotten you into this mess." Paul laughed. "We don't want the goose to fly the coop before she lays the golden egg, do we?"

Staring at him, Mystere knew the end had come. If she couldn't flee, she would be forced to marry Belloch for their profit. She couldn't predict how it would all end, but she saw a funeral much too soon into the marriage.

"When *this* kind of opportunity presents itself, best to strike while the iron is hot," Paul continued.

"Or while Belloch is," Baylis punned, and both men laughed coarsely.

Still numb, Mystere was suddenly desperate to be free of their barracks-room joviality. She gathered up her gown and somehow willed her legs to support her when she stood up.

"I . . . I think I'll work on this upstairs," she managed to say.

"Oh-*ho!*" Baylis teased. "See how it is? She's already too good for our company."

"Now, now," Paul admonished him. "You've embarrassed her. Don't be twitting her so much; the poor thing must be feeling overwhelmed right now. I certainly am, and I'll only be giving away the bride."

Both men stepped aside as she approached the doorway, beaming at her as if she had just saved Western civilization. She was halfway down the hall, aiming for the spiral staircase, when their excited voices from within the parlor arrested her.

Quickly and quietly she retraced her steps, stopping when she was close enough to the doors to make out what they were saying.

"Yes, well, no doubt," Baylis was pointing out, "Belloch plans to hang on tight to his fortune."

"Of course, wouldn't you? But you know, I've begun to think Mystere looks quite fetching in black."

"We must *all* go home to God someday," Baylis quipped, and both men laughed.

An icy finger touched her heart. She would have to protect Rafe. The words now only steeled her resolve to refuse his hand as resolutely as Rafe protested taking hers.

Choking back a sob of despair, she hurried toward the staircase.

Mystere had no idea how long she lay on her bed, crying into her pillows and repeating Bram's name over and over. Even now he was first in her thoughts, and she despaired of ever seeing him again. She could never hope to find him when one awful complication after another prevented her from even searching.

It struck her now, more forcefully than ever, how she had grown up the child of two extremes. One extreme was the overwhelming urge to solve the enigma that had become central to her existence, the enigma of her very identity—an urge literally self-centered; the other extreme was the collective memories of those early years, the hopeless existence on the streets and later at the orphanage—that part of her, in short, that was just the opposite of self-centered. The candid part of her that knew full well her existence mattered to no one, that she could be snuffed out in a heartbeat.

Gradually, however, her personal despair gave way to thoughts of Rafe.

Despite all his horrid words and behavior toward her these past weeks, she couldn't help a growing feeling of gratitude at the way he had borne the brunt of Mrs. Astor's wrath, all to protect her from exposure. Her gratitude made her wonder again about Rafe's "grudge," as Abbot called it. Rafe had flatly accused Mrs. Astor of killing his father—if that was even remotely true, it certainly helped explain Rafe's cynical attitude and harsh manner.

A sudden knock at her bedroom door startled her thoughts back to the present. "Mystere?" Rose's voice called to her.

She quickly sat up on the bed, using one corner of the counterpane to dry her tears. "Come in, Rose."

Rose, too, had Sundays free. However, she often insisted on working a few hours to keep the house tidy. She smiled affectionately at the younger woman as she stepped inside and crossed to the bed, sitting down beside Mystere and taking both of her hands in hers.

"I don't mean to butt in," she apologized, "but earlier I heard you crying. That seems a peculiar response to one of the most joyous days of your life."

Joyous. The word seemed to mock her, but Mystere stoically kept her feelings from her face.

"You've already heard?" she asked.

"Heard?" Rose laughed. Her bright red hair hung in thick

plaits. "Baylis is like a newsboy with it, hawking the word to everyone he sees. You'd think *he* was getting married."

A rogue tear spilled from Mystere's eye, but she kept her voice firm. "Yes, Paul acted the same way. But they—"

She caught herself in the nick of time, remembering that Rose was, after all, trained in loyalty to Paul. She would never intentionally hurt Mystere, and she could be counted on to keep some things secret from Paul and the others in the name of female camaraderie. But it would be indiscreet, and needlessly risky, to tell Rose she was *not* marrying Rafe Belloch come hell or high water.

"But they only see the gain for themselves," she amended.

"Yes," Rose agreed. "Frankly that's all they've ever seen in you—a source of profits. When in truth there is so much more to you."

Mystere embraced her for a long moment, hugging tightly. "*You* should talk. I'm afraid we're both in the same leaky boat."

"Yes, but before Paul we were drowning," Rose reminded her dutifully. "So a leaky boat is an improvement, I s'pose. Why are you crying, hon?"

Reluctantly, Mystere forced her mind back to more pressing matters—namely that tiara Rafe had demanded. She knew there would be the devil to pay once Paul missed it. But she couldn't expect to get out of her terrible predicament without some cost.

Nor did Rafe's apparent gallantry last night fool her into forgetting that he was a cynical, dangerous, unpredictable man. She must try to do his bidding—and after all, it *had* been his mother's possession. She could hardly fault him for wanting it. Rose, as their resident maid, knew more about Paul's secrets than anyone.

She decided to just be honest and throw herself on Rose's mercy.

"I'm in a nasty dilemma," she finally replied. "Rafe Belloch very much wants a silver tiara that I stole this past spring. You see, it was his mother's, and she's passed away now."

"But it will have been sold to Paul's fence by now," Rose pointed out. "Lord knows where it is."

"No, I think I saw it once in Paul's wall safe. You know how he holds back some things."

Rose nodded. "So you've tumbled to that fact, too? I thought only I knew."

"Yes. But you see, Rose, Rafe *truly* wants that tiara. He's told me that if I don't get it for him . . . well, suffice it to say things will go hard for me. Very hard."

"This from the man who is going to marry you?"

Mystere frowned, a sadness entering the depths of her forget-me-not eyes. "Rose, it's very complicated. You mustn't mention this to anyone, but—you see, Rafe didn't *ask* me to marry him. Mrs. Astor's forcing his hand under threat of financial ruin."

"Oh, good heart of God," Rose breathed. "So *that's* why you're crying, you poor thing."

"Yes. I know I'm asking a lot of you, but I'm in a terrible bind. Can you . . . do you know where Paul keeps the key to his safe?"

Rose paled slightly at what was being asked of her. Yet clearly her heart went out to Mystere, who had always treated her like a big sister, not a menial servant as did the others.

"You know he'll be in an awful wax, Mystere, when he misses it."

"Yes, and don't worry, I'll confess to it when he discovers it."

"It's not just the value—he'll be outraged that someone snooped into his safe. You've heard his speeches about loyalty."

Mystere nodded. "I know. But I'll have to count on his new good mood caused by the engagement announcement."

Rose brightened a little. "Yes, there's a point. He wants to keep on your good side now. Well . . . I think I know where he keeps one of the keys. Have you ever seen that old, battered Gladstone bag of his?"

"The green one with rusty brass clasps?"

"That's it. I once saw him take a key out of a little manila envelope he keeps in that bag. The bag itself, unless he's moved it, is somewhere under his bed."

Now that she was committed to helping, Rose was all business. She stood up, smoothing her cotton skirt. "This is a good time, dear. Evan and Baylis have gone to the tavern, and Hush is off God knows where. I left Paul writing letters in the parlor. I'll go back down and keep him occupied. Hurry now."

"*Thank* you, Rose," Mystere said, hugging her again.

"Hurry," Rose repeated, leaving the room.

Now that the moment to act was at hand, Mystere felt a nervous stirring in her stomach. She rushed out into the long hallway that led to the opposite upstairs wing, Paul's quarters.

She hesitated for a few moments outside the door to his bedroom, trying to hear any sounds above the surf-crashing roar of her pulse in her ears. The hinges creaked when she opened the door, and though no one else was even remotely close enough to hear it, she winced at the sound.

The large room was nearly dark, for Paul was a human bat and hated sunlight. Drapes made of heavy monk's cloth covered both windows. She switched on the newly installed electric light, revealing a walnut half-tester bed and a three-door carved walnut armoire with a beveled mirror on the center door. The old grifter was vain, despite his age—a second looking glass, a French Empire gilt bronze dressing mirror, was mounted on the lefthand wall.

She hurried to the bed, kneeled, and quickly spotted the battered old Gladstone bag. Mystere dragged it out and unsnapped the clasps, exposing a confusion of old letters, newspaper clippings, and photographs, mostly from his younger days in New Orleans. Almost immediately she found the small envelope Rose had mentioned—and there was, indeed, a brass key inside it.

The safe was located on the back wall behind a western landscape painted by Albert Bierstadt. With trembling hands she removed the framed painting and set it aside, admonishing herself to hurry. Despite her urgency to get out of there, however, she was startled into momentary immobility by the sight of the contents when she opened the iron door of the safe.

The tiara was there, all right, its pure silver offset by oval blue sapphires. She also saw a solid gold cameo brooch, a gold filigree cross encrusted with mine-cut diamonds, a pair of sapphire-and-diamond drop earrings, and other high-price sparklers as well as cash—more cash than she had time to count.

Mystere recognized items she had stolen as well as contributions from Hush and the others. She had just reached inside for the tiara when she heard Rose's voice out on the stairway, and her heart leaped into her throat.

"Yes, there will, indeed, be many preparations for the wedding. But Mystere and I will handle it easily, Paul, don't you worry."

Rose, her voice deliberately raised to warn Mystere that Paul was on his way up. A blind panic almost overtook her, but she forced herself to act without delay. Paul's lameness made him quite slow going up steps, so there was still a slim chance of escape. However, taking the tiara now was out of the question—not when he might well catch her in the hallway with it.

She slammed the safe shut, hung the painting again, returned the key to the bag and kicked it under the bed. She switched off the light and escaped from his room just in time, encountering Rose and Paul when she was safely out of range of Paul's door. It appeared that she had just left her own room.

"There's our wedding girl." The old con man beamed at her. "Has it finally sunk in that you're going to be one of the wealthiest women in America?"

"No," she managed to reply in a steady voice. "Right now it all still seems like a dream."

By the time Hush finally spotted Lorenzo Perkins exit his house on Amos Street, only a couple hours of daylight remained. The man's shadow was long and thin and sinister in the setting sun as he bore toward the saloons scattered throughout Tin Pan Alley, a busy block of Twenty-eighth Street between Broadway and Sixth Avenue, home of the music-publishing industry.

Hush was spying on his own initiative now, watching Sparky and Lorenzo whenever he could. For he was determined not to let these two double-poxed hounds ruin Mystere. So he had decided to find out what they were planning.

The Sunday shift ended at a nearby tannery, and the weary workers emerged into the dying light, looking like damned souls escaped from hell. They provided good cover as Hush moved up closer to his man, who abruptly ducked into a brick building with iron shutters—the C-note Bar, a favorite with local songwriters and performers.

Since Tammany politicians had managed to repeal the unpopular "blue laws," bars throughout the city were packed on the Sabbath. This tavern was of slightly better class than those on the Bowery—Hush spotted Currier and Ives prints lining the walls, and here and there hung a few wooden cages with starlings inside.

At first, in the crush of noisy men and thick pall of tobacco smoke, he couldn't see Lorenzo. Then he spotted him at a table near the back wall, huddled close with Sparky.

Luck was with Hush today. The interior was dark, and he managed to wedge himself behind a hogshead filled with ice, only a few feet from the two men. Despite the din of voices and a player piano, he could hear them clearly.

"Are you sure of it?" Sparky demanded.

"I swear it on the bones of my mother."

"Your mother is still alive, you blockhead."

"Right, and hasn't she bones? I'm telling you, my wife heard it in church this morning. The preacher himself announced it."

Sparky absently scraped the mud off his right boot on a chair rung. One of his suspender loops had come unbuttoned, and his britches sagged on that side.

"Then, by God," he said, "let's win the horse or lose the saddle. I'm *sick* of being poor as Job's turkey."

Sparky took the clay pipe from his mouth—the universal mark of the dirt-poor—and held it out over the table. "Never mind any stinking, flea-bit monkeys. I dream of smoking from meerschaum like the toffs do. And this wedding, b'hoy, is our big chance. We'll go straight to Belloch ourselves and make him hungry to know what we can tell him."

"Just hold your whist," Lorenzo warned. "We must use caution with him, for the man has a good think-piece on him."

"No misdoubting that. Stupid men don't get filthy rich, do they? But any man can be stupid where a woman he loves is involved."

From his cramped vantage point Hush had a good view of Lorenzo's dull little eyes and stiffly waxed mustache. The man took down half a schooner of beer in one sweeping-deep draught, backhanding the foam off his mustache.

"This is fate, Sparky. Our destiny. The wheel of fortune has finally turned round to *us.*"

"*Now* you're whistlin'!"

"You know, I've always wanted to be a ward boss. I've felt it in my bones that I'm bound for greatness. Even the wife thinks so; that's why she goes to the rich man's church even though she must stand at the back."

"That's the gait. T'hell with this penny-ante game, eh? Why bust our humps to squeeze fifty bucks out of the woman—Christ, Belloch's going to *marry* her. Now it's out in public, we can threaten him with ruination."

Hush felt a jolt of shock. Hookey Walker! Mystere getting married?

"We must somehow arrange a meeting with Belloch," Lorenzo said. "Make it clear his money will buy our silence."

Unfortunately Hush was privy to no more of their plans, for at that moment an employee hauled him out from his hiding place and soundly slapped his ears before tossing the boy outside. But he had heard enough to realize these men meant to cause Mystere great harm. Even the sting of jealousy, when he heard she was getting married, paled in comparison to his fear for her safety.

Hush ducked into a dark alley for a moment to remove the money from the wallet he had just stolen off the man who threw him out. Only three dollars, but it might help Mystere. He had decided to defy Rillieux by giving most of what he stole to her—she needed it more than the old man did.

He tossed the empty billfold onto a heap of garbage and headed home, trying to puzzle out a plan to help Mystere. He meant to act on his own now, for the poor girl had so much on her mind lately. He had seen her crying when she thought she was alone, and the sight pained him worse than any beating. So did the fine little worry lines that seemed to be forming around her mouth.

How anyone could want to hurt her was beyond him, for she was as sweet as she was beautiful. He loved it when she read to him, for her voice must be the sound made by angels' harps. When he gazed into her perfect blue eyes he felt all funny inside—as if he could conquer nations for her sake.

He wanted to marry her. Why couldn't he be as rich as Rafe Belloch so she would love him instead?

At the back of his mind, however, Sparky's words echoed like the threat of distant artillery: *I say let's win the horse or lose the saddle. This wedding, b'hoy, is our big chance.*

Chapter 24

On Tuesday morning Ward McCallister called the Rillieux residence to announce that Mrs. Astor was hosting an engagement party for Rafe and Mystere at the Astor residence the coming Saturday.

As usual, Mystere noticed in a flush of impotent irritation, there was no polite attempt to make sure that date was convenient for her. Caroline had simply issued marching orders, and everyone else must get into lockstep.

Lance Streeter, too, had complicated her life with a gushing column on Monday, most of it purple tripe devoted to "the match of the season." The phone had not finally stopped ringing until well into the evening as well-wishers called, raising a litany of clichéd congratulations that soon left her with a pounding headache.

Mystere felt the full irony of her situation. Not too long ago, during her last cab ride through Brooklyn, she had made a determined vow to "become her own woman." Now, only look—a highly public pseudoengagement, completely forced on her, that made her feel as if she was living in a glass cage, her every action visible from any angle. Under such conditions she had no more chance of finding Bram than she had of going to the moon.

As if she didn't have enough to contend with, she had still not managed to get the tiara out of Paul's safe. That goal acquired a new urgency with the arrival of the Tuesday afternoon post.

"Letter for you on the stand," Rose informed her when Mystere came downstairs around one P.M. "The return address is Staten Island," she added, and Mystere felt apprehension quicken her pulse. Where Rafe Belloch was concerned, no news was good news.

She took the neatly typed envelope from the marble stand and opened it with trembling fingers. The likewise neatly typed letter inside—marked "original on file"—needed no explanation. While it barely mentioned her, the letter from Stephen Breaux's law firm in New Orleans was potentially damning to Paul and his entire "family," herself included. She did not require a tutor to understand why Rafe had sent it.

Rose worked nearby as she read it, busy running a feather-duster over the hallway furnishings.

"Mystere! What is it!" she demanded, for the younger woman suddenly paled as if she had lost half her blood.

"That stupid tiara," she replied, close to tears of frustration. "Rafe is pressuring me to get it."

"You'll not likely have a chance to grab it today," Rose fretted. "Paul told me to cancel all his appointments today, for he's under the weather. He'll most likely lay abed all day."

Paul . . . Mystere tore the envelope and letter into bits and dropped them into the nearby litter can, shaking it to make sure they dropped out of sight. One reason he was happy as a clam about the engagement, of course, was that he expected Rafe's money to cover his bad investments. He would be terrifying in his rage against her if she ever jeopardized that. But even worse if he ever learned that Rafe had discovered the old thief's modus operandi.

It's the attention from Mrs. Astor, she reminded herself. *It's turned his head more than anything ever has, for it's not only certified approval of his worth, but top certification. So even more than poverty he fears exposure, for it will cost him his prize.* And that made him, age notwithstanding, dangerous.

Rafe was clearly a strong and capable man, and probably quite safe when at home at Garden Cove. But when he left Staten Island, he carelessly placed himself in danger of attack—as her own robbery of him two years earlier proved. Evan or Baylis would not hesitate to kill him on Paul's orders—she was sure of that. They would do it all wrong and quickly be caught, probably, but Rafe would be just as dead.

In the midst of her troubled thoughts, the telephone shrilled. Rose answered.

"Yessir," Mystere heard her tell the caller. "It happens she's right here beside me. One moment please."

She held the earpiece out toward Mystere. "For you. It's your fiancé."

Your fiancé. Those two little words struck her like quick slaps to the face.

"Yes?" she answered curtly.

"What's this?" His distorted voice still managed to convey sarcasm. "No 'good afternoon, darling' for your sweetest love?"

"What do you want?" she demanded impatiently.

"Ouch, what has made our girl so peevish? Have you perchance received the afternoon mail?"

"You know I have," she retorted coldly. "Must you play everything to the gallery?"

"Oh, put aside your lah-de-dah, Lady Moonlight—I've seen you naked, and—"

"Damn you!" she blurted, shocked that he was saying it over a party-line phone, and Rose gaped in astonishment. "Tell me why you called or I'll hang up this instant."

"All right," he complied, dropping the mincing voice. "Consider this phone call a follow-up to the letter. Have you got the tiara?"

"Not yet. I've not had a clear chance to get it. You said nothing, when we reached our little agreement, about any deadline."

"Well, now I am. If you don't place that tiara in my hands this very afternoon, I'll call your 'uncle' this evening and read Breaux's letter to him."

A muscle twitched in her throat. "Rafe! That's impossible, I can't—"

"*That* shocked the sass out of you, eh? Listen here, you are the most accomplished thief in this entire city, and that's saying a lot. Don't go crying how you can't get it."

"You don't understand, Paul is—"

"This afternoon," he repeated with merciless insistence. "I'm working in my suite at the Astor House Hotel between two and five P.M. Room 511."

"Rafe, please, I simply cannot—"

"You will or face the consequences. Sunday I kept my mouth shut about you to Caroline, though God knows why. Don't forget I can get free of this entire mess by going to see her and explaining everything."

"Then, why don't you?"

"Where's the fun in that? I confess to a certain perverse pleasure in having some laughs at everyone's expense."

"Including mine."

He said nothing. His lack of a taunt seemed to mean something, but what she couldn't tell. He finished with, "I'll look for you between two and five. Until then, *darling.*"

He hung up before she could plead further. In her anger and frustration she slammed the earpiece into the wall unit so hard that she made the bell ring for a moment.

"I heard your end of it," Rose apologized. "And I think I have a plan to help you."

"Anything," Mystere grasped desperately. "He's adamant."

"You know how Paul never refuses to come to the phone when called? Hush is out in the carriage house right now repairing harness. You'll go on up to your quarters and listen for the phone. I'll send Hush to the exchange and have him request our number of the hello girl. He can hang up once I've answered."

Mystere had forgotten about the nearby telephone exchange, where the general public could place local calls for the astronomical price of five cents.

"Yes, of course." She felt a nubbin of hope work its way into the core of her despair. "You'll call upstairs for Paul. He takes forever to get up and down the stairs."

Rose nodded, already fishing a nickel out of the household-expense drawer and heading for the front door. "I'll say it's . . . some woman named Sandra. He'll think the connection got broken. But be quick, hon. God help us all if he catches you in the act and figures out how we foxed him."

"Oh, *thank* you, Rosie," Mystere called as she started up the stairs. "And don't worry. This time I'll get it."

Rose's plan went off without a hitch. By the time Paul returned upstairs, swearing profusely about the needless climb, the diamond-and-sapphire tiara was safely tucked into Mystere's handbag. As soon as Paul shut his door again, she demanded Baylis take out the carriage for her to go out for a ride.

The brief ride to the Astor House, a massive structure of six stories and three hundred rooms located across the street from City Hall Park, gave her some welcome time to collect her thoughts a bit.

It was a gorgeous July afternoon, hot but with a steady, cooling breeze. However, the sunny streets and shimmering green park lawns were wasted on her today as she began to worry if Rafe would really give her Antonia's ring, as he had promised, in exchange for the tiara. He hadn't given her a chance to mention it before he had rudely hung up on her.

Rudely . . . that was the only way he seemed to know how to treat her. And by now it should have taught her to despise him. Instead, she caught herself remembering, with shameless frequency, the dangerous excitement of his kisses, the illicit fire in her loins, when his hands touched her in a way—and in places—that *should* have enraged her.

And for all his surface rudeness, she knew he, too, felt a powerful sensual attraction to her. Indeed, his rudeness might well be his masculine defense against admitting that attraction.

But lust, she lectured herself, was an animal response. How could she possibly sanction a lust devoid of affection? His constant cruelty toward her would obviate any possibility of her actually caring for him. As for Rafe—his rudeness was directed toward almost everyone, not just her. She feared that he was simply incapable of affection for anyone, his heart as hard and unbending as Caroline Astor's will to power.

Baylis's voice scattered her thoughts. "Here we are, madame," he taunted in a self-satisfied tone.

He reined in his horse in front of the gray masonry facade of the Astor House, leaping down to hand her out. She tried to tell him to stay with the carriage, but there was no getting rid of him. Ignoring the amused eyes of the liveried bellhops, she hurried across the lobby toward a bank of pneumatic elevators, Baylis glued to her side. The elevator boy took them up to the fifth floor, watching her with a knowing smile no doubt reserved for women without luggage. He made her wish she had taken the stairs.

Suddenly, at the prospect of entering Rafe's hotel suite, a fist seemed to clench in her chest. She told Baylis to wait outside, then took a deep breath to steady herself as she clapped the brass knocker on the door of room 511.

"It's open," Rafe's strong, commanding voice called from within, sounding a bit impatient at the interruption.

Her eyes rushed over the plush interior of the outer room, which he had managed to turn into a drab, cluttered, workaday office space. The textured walls were covered with a hodgepodge of charts and graphs and maps, and every available piece of furniture was piled high with notebooks and binders and thick reference manuals with scintillating titles such as *Subsurface Sedimentation in the Cumberland Valley*.

Rafe sat studying something at a wide, pecan-veneer desk dotted with deep gouges. He wore a pair of horn-rim reading glasses which he took off as she entered, tucking them into his shirt pocket. He stood up, making his action seem more pro forma than courteous, even as the usual cynical smile flitted over his lips like an ingrained reflex.

"Ahh, my lovely bride-to-be," he greeted her. "Come kiss me hello, darling."

She stoically ignored his sophomoric taunting. "I have the tiara," she announced in a cold, businesslike tone. "Do you have the ring here?"

He feigned puzzlement. "Our engagement ring, do you mean? Darling, I've hardly had time—"

"You know very well which ring I mean, Rafe. Do you have it here?"

Clearly enjoying himself, he perched on the edge of the desk. His eyes never once leaving her, he picked up an obsidian paperweight from the desk and began tossing it from one hand to the other.

"I have it," he assured her. Instead of pursuing that topic, however, he suddenly demanded, "I take it you already know there's to be an engagement party for us this weekend?"

She nodded. "What do you propose we do?"

"Do? What would any two people madly in love with each other do? We'll dress up and be gracious and smile into each other's eyes all night. What else can we do? After all, we're to be married."

"You can't be serious."

"What, about marrying you?" The amusement still laced through his voice. "Your beauty, grace, and intelligence are nothing to the matter when the only proven way to reform a hardened character like you is with the lash. And I would have no taste for beating my wife."

He pointed toward a door in the rear wall with his chin. "However, I *would* very much enjoy making you my mistress. That's the bedroom there—shall we skip the wedding and go directly to the honeymoon?"

Anger stung her like hot acid. "You're a cad."

His arrogant smile made her almost strike him, but she recovered her dignity in only moments. "I brought what you asked. Are you to keep your side of the bargain?"

His jaw tight, he snipped, "The moral high ground does not suit you, Lady M, so best to surrender it."

"I'll surrender nothing to you but my part of the bargain."

"No matter. As Caroline has already warned you: I get what I want, one way or another."

His gaze dropped from her face to the lace-trimmed bodice of her rose damask dress. "What's this? That flat-chested look of a *jeune fille* again?"

She felt herself blushing to the roots of her hair. "I can hardly develop a full bust overnight, can I?"

"Why not? It only took about two minutes on Saturday night. I assure you Ward McCallister will never look at you the same again. What about Caroline? Surely she noticed, too. What if she—"

"May we drop this subject?" she interrupted him sharply. "I came here to trade the tiara for the ring, not to endure your insufferable boorishness."

"All business, eh? All right, let me see it."

"First let me see the ring."

"Whence all this mistrust? I am a gentleman, a Patriarch of the Four Hundred. *You* are the common-born criminal who can't be trusted."

"Yes, I heard your 'gentlemanly' filth only a moment ago. First show me you have the ring."

He stood up again and slid open the wide top drawer of

the desk, producing the ring. But when she reached for it, he pulled it back from her.

"Restrain yourself, Lady Moonlight. First the tiara."

She hesitated, trying to read the intention in his face. Then she took the tiara from her purse and handed it to him. A sea change seemed to come over him, a new softness moving into his face for a few moments. Even his voice lost its scalpel edge.

"Yes, that's it, all right. I'd forgotten how pretty it is. No wonder my mother loved it best among all her possessions. She used to positively glow when she wore it."

His altered mood affected her own, and suddenly she felt less combative. The only time he seemed to lose his cynical shell was when he talked about his parents.

"What did you mean," she asked him in a quiet tone, "when you accused Caroline of . . . killing your father?"

Immediately she realized she had blundered. His face was instantly hard as granite again.

"They're both dead—no point in throwing salt into the wound."

He put the tiara in the drawer but kept Antonia's ring in his clenched fist.

"May I have the ring now?" she reminded him.

"But why, darling? The emerald is so big it's vulgar, even if I rather like the encircling diamonds."

Shock thrummed in her veins like a narcotic. Sputtering, she blurted out, "You promised!"

"You stole the tiara, after all. Twice, as a matter of fact."

"But I gave it to you, didn't I?"

"So what do you want, a gold medal from Congress?"

"No, I want the ring. It's not yours by law, either."

He gave her a long, hard stare. Something softened in his eyes—something almost like empathy—but the straight-seamed grin registered his point. "Yes. Yes, you're right. Technically speaking, I'm receiving stolen property, aren't I? I suppose that makes us accomplices. The Mountain

Mover and the Lady Moonlight—sounds like a strange new minstrel show, doesn't it?"

When he still made no move to give her the ring, sudden anger tightened her face. She lunged at him, grabbing his fist and trying to force it open. But it was like trying to pry open a rock. He made no attempt to stop her, merely laughing in great delight at her useless efforts.

The struggle had forced him back onto the desk, and suddenly she became aware that all of her weight was leaning tightly against him. She was breathing heavily from her exertion, and her face was only inches from his.

Their gazes locked, all struggle ceased, and she saw the mirth bleed from his eyes as some very different emotion took over his being. She could smell his masculine scent and feel the power and danger coursing through him. She could not deny the abrupt, pulsing desire low in her belly, but also the fear that left a bitter metallic taste in her throat.

She placed both fists against his broad chest and pushed herself back, turning away from him.

"You *promised,*" she repeated, so frustrated now that hot tears welled in her eyes. She thought of how Baylis was watching her like a prison guard, and of her rented room on Centre Street, the last possibility of her salvation. The ring was her last resort. Even if she could escape from this new trap of Caroline's, she could never hope to survive on her own without that ring.

Rafe watched a crystal teardrop gather on one of her eyelids, quiver for a moment like quicksilver, then splash zigzag down her cheek.

"Why is it so important?" he relented. With a grand gesture, he finally handed her the ring. "Will old Rillieux beat you if you don't give it to him?"

Mystere held the emerald in her palm, staring at it as if giving a silent prayer. She then tucked it into her purse and said, "He doesn't know I took it. I told you on Sunday, I need money to search for my brother."

"Yes, and I told you that no doubt you're wasting your time. If an impress gang grabbed him and forced him to sea that long ago, he'd stand little chance of being alive now."

"Fine. You've said it twice now. It's *my* time; I can waste it if I choose."

She made a movement toward the door, but he grabbed one wrist, detaining her.

"Are you still stealing for the old man?" he demanded.

"No."

"Yes you are."

"Why bother to ask me if you're simply going to call me a liar?"

"Liar? Well, if that offends you, allow me to phrase it more delicately: I would call your answer remote from the truth. After all, you obviously have a great talent for deceit."

She tried to pull her arm away. "You must be sure to search the place after I leave. Let *go* of me!"

He ignored her. His cynical veneer was back now in full force.

"No more of this damned stealing," he ordered her. His tone heightened ironically as he added, *"My* future wife must be pure as the driven snow."

For the moment she ceased struggling, his tasteless remark reminding her again of the terrible trap Caroline had set for them.

"Rafe, seriously—you seem to find this matrimonial charade highly amusing. But don't you realize the longer we pretend, the harder it will be to extract ourselves from it? And have you stopped to realize how Caroline will seek retribution when we cross her? You stand to lose more than I, for she's vowed to ruin you financially."

This time her words, and earnest tone, actually seemed to sink through to him. For a moment he looked serious but not quite so overbearing.

"We're in a dirty corner, all right," he conceded. "Both of us. I meant to teach you the lesson of your life, and damned if I didn't end up hoisted on my own petard. How appropriate," he added bitterly, "that a man in my business ends up *railroaded* to the gallows."

Despite her gratitude that he hadn't revealed her secret to Caroline, his comment made her bristle with sudden anger.

"Gallows?" she flung at him. "Gallows? It's I who face the true gallows. Marriage is nothing compared to that, and for your information I'd rather join a nunnery than marry you."

"Why? So you could steal all the crucifixes?"

"Rot in hell, you self-adulating tyrant!"

Again she turned toward the door, and again he detained her. The last thing she wanted to do right now was cry again, but she had been too emotionally keyed up these past few days. She felt the warmth of tears filling her eyes.

"There, there," he soothed in an even tone, "that's a tough old soldier."

It surprised both of them when she suddenly slapped him so hard it left a red imprint of her hand on his cheek.

Now the anger shifted to him, and she nearly quailed at sight of the sudden fury in his blue-green eyes.

"So you want to make it physical," he told her in a dangerously quiet voice. The next moment his strong hands cupped her face, and he crushed his lips to hers with almost bruising power, forcing her mouth open. Just as she had done that night in the gazebo, her body reacted hungrily to his demanding need. One of his hands slid down to the small of her back, pulling her against him, and for a long moment their two bodies seemed to meld into one.

She finally managed to pull away, every sense in her body acutely enhanced. It shamed her that she was practically panting. He wasn't holding her trapped now, and even though she had trouble meeting his eyes, neither did she escape to the door. It was as if the kiss had destroyed her will.

"What kind of con are you up to now?" he demanded harshly.

"None."

She placed the back of her hand on her burning lips and turned toward the door, but his voice arrested her. "It's understandable that I wouldn't want to marry a criminal. But satisfy my curiosity on one point. Why are *you* so opposed to marrying me? I think you actually mean it, yet just now when I kissed you, I think you felt something else for me entirely."

She looked back over her shoulder at him. "My rejection wounds your vanity, does it?"

"You stand to gain everything."

"Your modesty and humility included?"

He gave that a contemptuous little snort. "I'm an honest man. Why should I fake common virtues when I have none? Tell me—why do you so oppose this match?"

She might have told him the truth, because there was something frightfully dangerous about him, a kind of self-destructive, self-loathing recklessness that made being close to him feel as if she were balancing on a tightrope over boiling rapids. And only look how he played with human hearts like a boy pulling wings off flies for sport.

But even that truthful answer didn't completely explain her motivation. For she was compelled to protect him from Paul's treachery. She would not see him harmed from her actions. No matter what.

"Why not at least become my mistress?" he demanded when she turned silently away and placed her hand on the porcelain doorknob.

"Because, Mr. Belloch," she replied coolly just before she left his suite, "I personally find more honor in being a thief than a concubine. Nor would I ever feel comfortable enjoying the caresses of a man I so thoroughly despise."

Chapter 25

Because the thieves who masqueraded as Paul Rillieux's servants were not fairly compensated for their domestic servitude, Mystere had steadfastly insisted they must be allowed free time whenever their services were not immediately required. Rillieux carped about this constantly, complaining that such liberties jeopardized the illusion he had so artfully constructed. But on this one point Mystere had stubbornly put her foot down, and the old man grudgingly relented.

Thus it was that Hush found time, early on the Saturday afternoon of Mrs. Astor's party, to take the ferry from the Battery to Staten Island. He was free until six P.M., when he had to again don his monkey suit, as he called it, and be ready for the trip to the Astor residence.

He had used the new reading skills Mystere taught him to look up Rafe Belloch's name in the phone directory. There were two addresses listed for him, one at the Astor House Hotel and another on Staten Island. But when he went to the hotel, the desk clerk told him Belloch would not return there until Monday. So Hush decided to try the Bay Street address.

Only a few other passengers disembarked with him at the

wooden slip, mostly island residents returning from shopping trips or their jobs in the city. It was a hot, windless day, a few ragged tatters of cloud strung thinly across a sky as blue as a lagoon. Hush tramped along the crushed gravel of Bay Street, which followed the curving sea wall, south toward a huge white house that sat atop a low rise, offering a commanding view of the Upper Bay.

"Jiminy!" he said under his breath as he approached the impressive gate of fieldstone and wrought iron, its cast-iron pillars thrusting into the sky like artillery guns. He was even more impressed—and intimidated—by the huge gatekeeper who stepped out of the gatehouse to greet him.

The man smiled down at him in a friendly manner. But Hush could barely take his eyes off the ivory-grip pistol tucked into his belt.

"Hey there, lad," the giant greeted him in a thick Irish accent. "What's on your mind besides your hat? Be you lost?"

"No, sir. I've come to see Mr. Belloch, please."

"Oh, you have, eh? Is he expectin' you?"

"No, sir."

"Sonny, this ain't a penny arcade. Mr. Belloch is an important man. He generally sees visitors by appointment, y'unnerstan'."

"Yessir. But—but it's very important that I see him."

"Important, you say?" The giant mulled this for a few moments, watching the boy through the gate from amused, curious eyes.

"How old are you, tadpole?"

"Twelve, sir."

"And the nature of your visit?"

"It's . . . quite private, sir, no disrespect to you. I can only discuss it with Mr. Belloch himself."

By now the guard's curiosity seemed to overcome his hesitation. He glanced toward the house, and Hush followed his gaze. In a fenced-off paddock behind one corner of the house, he could see a distinguished-looking man in tan riding breeches and tall oxblood boots. He was currying a sorrel horse that was stripped down to the neck leather.

The gatekeeper turned around to pull a bell on the gatehouse door, getting the man's attention. Hush watched him hand the brush to a stable boy and stroll across the green, sloping lawn toward them, his step purposeful. He wore his chestnut hair short and swept straight back. In this better lighting, Hush liked the man's face even though he felt a little inner stab of jealousy—this was Rafael Belloch himself, the man Mystere was going to marry.

"What's up, Jimmy?" the man asked, nodding at the visitor as he drew up at the gate.

"This young fellow says he's come to see you on important business, Mr. Belloch. Says it can only be discussed privately with you."

By now Rafe's curiosity was piqued. He looked at Hush. "Private business, you say? What's your name, son?"

"I'm called Hush, sir."

"Hush." Rafe studied him a few moments in silence. "Hush, is it? Well, young Master Hush—what business could you have with me? Or have you come to dust my doublet?"

Hush grinned, embarrassed. "No, sir."

He glanced up uncertainly through the black wrought-iron bars at Jimmy. "It's about Mystere Rillieux, sir. Sorter privatelike."

Rafe's eyes narrowed in suspicion. "Mystere? Tell me straight-arrow now, did old man Rillieux send you here?" he demanded.

"No, sir. I've come on my own."

"Is that the truth?"

Hush placed his right hand over his heart. "God strike me down, sir, if it's not."

The solemn earnestness in the boy's pale face softened Rafe's features. "Let him come in, Jimmy."

When Hush had come inside the grounds, Rafe Belloch offered his hand and both of them shook.

"Well, sir," Rafe said in a brisk, businesslike manner. "Shall we go inside and discuss this man-to-man over coffee and cigars? Or perhaps you'd prefer brandy?"

Hush fell into step beside him, practically running to keep up with Rafe's long stride. "No, sir, coffee is fine."

"Then, coffee it shall be. I like a man who avoids spirits during the daytime. Show me a daylight drinker, sir, and I'll show you a man who does not take proper care of his family."

"Yessir," Hush said, feeling pleasantly overwhelmed by Rafe Belloch's reception. He was treating him like a man, not some snot-nosed brat. Hush had come prepared to dislike this man who was marrying Mystere; now, however, he could not blame her one bit for liking him.

A pleasant-looking older woman admitted them to the house, and Rafe requested that she bring them coffee in the library. When Rafe flung open the oak-paneled doors, Hush gaped in astonishment at the luxuriously appointed room.

"Have you read all them books, sir?" he asked, awed at the hundreds of leather-bound volumes with gold-embossed titles on their spines.

"Many of them, and I'm working through the rest. Some are pure drivel, but others are quite good. Do you read?"

"I've just started, sir. Mystere taught me."

"She did?"

"Yessir. Mystere says a man must be a reader to get on properly in this world."

"I heartily agree," Rafe approved, watching Hush from thoughtful eyes. "Do you have a mother and father?"

Hush shook his head. "I never knew my father. I'm told the white plague got Mother, sir. I don't hardly remember her, neither."

Rafe nodded. "When a man has lost his parents," he told Hush, his tone matter-of-fact, "he can sometimes feel alone even in a big city surrounded by people."

"Yessir. Have you? Lost your parents too, I mean?"

Rafe dropped into a mahogany armchair and waved Hush into another nearby.

"Yes," he replied. "And everything you see around you, Hush, I earned after their deaths and with no one's help. Don't ever think that being an orphan is a crippling strike against you, do you understand me? Ours is not a perfect nation by a long shot, but it *is* a land of opportunity for those who roll up their sleeves."

Hush nodded. "That's sorter like what Mystere tells me, too. Study hard and learn an honest trade instead of—"

He caught himself just in time, and Rafe gave him another thoughtful glance. Ruth saved Hush by arriving just then carrying a silver coffee service.

"How do you take your coffee, young Master Hush?" she inquired, beaming at the awestruck lad.

Unsure, he glanced over to see how Rafe had taken his. "Black, please," he replied.

"That's the lad," Rafe encouraged him. "They say the man who drinks black coffee will rule Ireland."

"I wouldn't care much for that job, sir," Hush replied with a straight face. "You see, I want to drive trains when I'm older."

Ruth and her employer exchanged discreet, mirthful glances. Then she left the room, and Rafe crossed to a nearby lift-top desk, returning with a box of cigars. He used a small silver cutter to snip the ends off two, handing one to Hush. Rafe struck a match to life and lit first his, then Hush's.

"Good Cuban hand-rolleds," he remarked between puffs. "I like a good cigar now and then."

Hush had smoked only a pipe in his time, but felt foolish admitting it. "Me, too," he fibbed just before a coughing fit silenced him.

"Don't inhale it," Rafe advised him casually, barely restraining a grin. "Now then, Hush—what is it you wish to discuss with me?"

"It's about Mystere, sir."

"Mm, you said that already. What about her? You don't mean to challenge me to a duel for her hand, do you?"

Hush's mouth fell open, and he almost lost his cigar. Then he saw Rafe grinning and smiled a little himself. But now that the moment was at hand, he found himself at a loss for words.

"It's just that . . . well, I mean . . . you see, sir, she's in deep soup. And I *won't* let anyone hurt her, Mr. Belloch, sir."

"Do you think I mean to hurt her?"

"Oh, no, sir. You're going to marry her, ain'tcha?"

Rafe took the cigar out of his mouth and studied it a moment, a thin, bitter smile touching his lips. Or did he just have smoke in his eyes? Hush wondered.

"So it would seem," Rafe finally replied. "Does she seem happy about that?"

Hush had trouble fibbing to people he liked. He was suddenly embarrassed and feigned interest in a world globe standing near his chair.

"Not like you'd expect, sir," he admitted. "She . . . cries all the time now."

"She does, eh?"

"Yessir, but only when she thinks no one is looking. And Mystere ain't no bawl baby. For a girl so pretty and sweet, she's a tough one."

Rafe pondered this a moment, his eyes going distant.

"Women are often difficult to fathom, Hush," he finally replied. "And their tears are seldom a clear clue to anything. But what do you mean about not letting anyone hurt her? *Is* someone hurting her?"

Hush nodded. "Yessir. Or trying to anyhow."

He paused, obviously reluctant to continue. Rafe guessed why.

"Just between me and you, Hush," he confided, "Mystere has already told me the truth."

"The . . . truth, sir?"

"Yes. About the old man, Rillieux, and how he sets up

school to teach youngsters to steal for him. He's taught her, and he's taught you, hasn't he?"

Hush remained perfectly still for perhaps ten seconds. Then he nodded.

"Yessir. You see, Mystere had no choice about it. Mr. Rillieux, he has this sorter . . . power. Power to make you do what he wants."

Rafe flicked his cigar ash into a ceramic ashtray. "I see. Is it the old man you mean when you say someone is trying to hurt her?"

"No, sir. It's two other men."

Feeling uninhibited now, Hush explained everything he knew about Lorenzo Perkins and his partner, Sparky.

"And now," he concluded, "they've decided to come see you, sir. They haven't beat me here, have they? I come quick as I could."

Rafe shook his head. "I'm not an easy man to catch during the week. They might have tried and missed me."

"They mean to get a lot of money from you, sir. And if you don't pay them, they mean to . . . humiliate you, I think is how they said it. You and Mystere."

"That's quite interesting. Just how do they mean to do this? What do they know—or think they know?"

Hush shrugged one shoulder. "I ain't sure, sir. Something about how Rillieux ain't really Mystere's name, how she's a big fake. They mean to go to the police and the newspapers if you don't pay them."

"I see. And so you've come to me on your own to warn me, is that it?"

"Yessir. I daren't say anything to Mystere, for she has so much on her mind now."

"Yes," Rafe muttered, pulling on his chin. "I suppose she must."

After a moment he shook off his pensive mood.

"Well then, Hush," he said in a brisk tone, smiling at his

visitor. "You and I are going to become partners. Would you like that?"

"Partners, sir?"

"Of course, for this woman is my fiancée. And it certainly appears to me that you have more than a casual regard for her or you wouldn't have come here like this."

"Oh, yessir. She's the specialest person I've ever knowed. I'd do anything for her."

"I see that. And I'll be counting on you to serve as her chief protector when I'm absent. Are you willing?"

Hush visibly swelled with pride and determination. "You bet! You can count on me, sir."

Rafe leaned over and patted the boy's shoulder. "I know I can, for you have the look of a stout fellow. Don't you worry. I'll be ready for this Lorenzo and—who?"

"Sparky, sir. A big, dumb galoot."

"Yes, this Sparky. I'll have a little welcome ready for them, and don't worry—I'll not mention your name."

Hush suddenly coughed again, turning a bit pale from the cigar. Rafe, covering a grin by averting his face, offered the box. "Care for another?"

"No thanks, sir. One is my limit."

"Ahh, a disciplined man, too. I like that. Well, I have some work to do, Hush, so I hope you'll excuse me. Have we covered everything to your satisfaction?"

"Oh, yessir."

"Good, good. How are you getting back to the city—by the ferry?"

Hush nodded.

"I take it sometimes, too, but it's a long wait on the weekends," Rafe pointed out. "I'll walk you down to the slip and have my crew take you across on the yacht."

Hush went wide-eyed with surprise. "You will?"

"Of course. You've done me a service, have you not? Turnabout is fair play. How'd you like to take the wheel?"

This time his boyish excitement made Hush forget to be formal. "Boy, would I! Man alive!"

Rafe laughed, enjoying his excitement. "One more thing, Hush," he said as the two of them started out of the drawing room. "Not a word to Mystere about this visit, eh? Mum's the word?"

"Mum's the word, sir."

"Good man. Remember we're partners now in looking after her. If we play our cards right, no one will hurt her."

As he was about to close the doors to the drawing room, Rafe thought of one last thing. "Hush, wait for me a few moments outside with Jimmy, will you? I'll be right out."

Rafe went back into the room and took a sheet of stationery from the desk. Dipping a steel nib into a pot of ink, he wrote only one sentence: *Get some relevant information on Lorenzo Perkins, who lives on Amos Street, and a dock laborer called Sparky, friend of Perkins.*

On his way out front to join Hush, Rafe gave the note to Ruth.

"See that Sam gets this tonight. And when you give it to him, tell him the sooner the better."

Sam would know full well what Rafe intended by "relevant information." And Sam also knew at least a dozen private detectives who had worked for Belloch Enterprises at one time or another. Rafe had learned long ago that any person was guilty of something if one looked closely enough. Let the two would-be blackmailers come—he would be ready for them.

Chapter 26

Dread lay heavy in her stomach as Mystere prepared for her first "engagement party."

Since Mrs. Astor herself was hosting it, Mystere knew full well that the night's gala would be only the first of many, for any marriage among the Four Hundred was always treated as an historical event ranking with the coronation of kings. How she could ever hope to maintain the deception was beyond her.

But she had pondered Rafe's motivation, his seeming eagerness to indulge this dangerous hypocrisy, and she had hit upon a suspicion that deeply troubled her. The first chance she had to get him alone, she meant to confront him about it.

Rafe might not care about the ultimate consequences of building false expectations, but *she* could hardly ignore them. Paul's new "affection" for her would turn ugly in a heartbeat once the engagement was broken off. And Evan and Baylis had suddenly become solicitous toward her in a manner that indicated they, too, had great expectations of personal gain. Baylis had even shaved off his ridiculous Newgate fringe, declaring it unworthy of a great lady's coachman.

Only Rose and Hush seemed to understand and sympathize with her latest dilemma. While drawing Mystere's dark coffee-colored hair into a chignon, late on Saturday afternoon, Rose offered some encouragement.

"Things may seem terrible now, hon, but you must not give up hope. When we brood, we create a picture of hell that fate may not have in store for us. Worry only about that which you can control, and let God handle the rest."

It was fine advice and did serve to cheer her mood considerably. So did Hush's whispered remark as he handed her into the carriage that evening.

"Don't you worry, Mystere, no one is going to hurt you on *our* watch."

The lad seemed so confident that she had to smile—her first in some time.

"Our?" she repeated. "Have you joined forces with a guardian angel?"

Hush only sent her a mysterious wink as he closed the door. It was but a brief ride to the Astor residence, located on upper Fifth Avenue.

"Remember, m'love," Paul said just before Baylis reined in the team out front, "you will be expected to join Rafe the moment you see him. This night is intended as a showcase for the two of you. Caroline told me she has even taken the unprecedented step of actually inviting newspaper people. Lance Streeter himself will be here, nibbling canapés alongside the Vanderbilts. No more of your caustic glances and cold shoulders—be radiant and submissive. This is theater, and the lights must come up, so to speak, the moment you and Rafe are together."

He took both her hands in his and leaned close, his sharp features sinister in the flickering gaslights from outside. "This tonight, why it's nothing. Your preparation and training will see you through it. The Lady Moonlight will soon be no more, and tonight you are under no pressure to steal sparklers under the noses of the rich. You are Mystere Rillieux, an accomplished Creole miss from New Orleans. Soon to become Mystere Belloch."

Except, she thought silently as Hush handed her out, *that Rafe knows precisely who—and what—I am. And being a man with secret, bitter, destructive motives, he might well turn Paul's "theater" into a farce, his "showcase" into a travesty.*

Hundreds of Chinese lanterns showed that many of the guests had already arrived, mingling in twos and threes in the lush gardens that wrapped the house on three sides. A servant led them along a slate pathway, setting a slow pace to accommodate Paul.

Despite Paul's reassurances just now, Mystere felt a nervous tickle in her chest like cobwebs brushing her heart. She mentally cataloged the guests she could recognize as she approached: Garret and Eugenia Teasdale, James and Lizet Addison, Sylvia Rohr, the Vernons, Antonia Butler with her parents, Dr. and Mrs. Sanford, and of course the Vanderbilt sisters, social fixtures who prized Mrs. Astor's invitations much more than did the male Vanderbilts.

"There's Trevor Sheridan and his sister," Paul remarked, visibly impressed that the Duchess of Granville had deigned to attend. "Caroline told me the duke, too, would have been here except that he is upstate on a hunting expedition."

The Duchess of Granville . . . Mystere thought again about the armorial insignia that she had so foolishly clung to for so many years. And for a few fleeting moments she wondered if somehow, despite the apparent absurdity of it, there *was* some kind of real link between the British peerage and two children of the Dublin slums. Or, more likely, at least some logical reason why someone would write to her family on stationery bearing the Connacht coat of arms.

However, she had no time to dwell on anything, for she had just spotted Rafe standing near the orchestra dais and talking animatedly to Mrs. Astor and Carrie.

"This way, miss," the servant said deferentially, surprising her by taking her hand and leading her up three marble steps that led to a broad, well-illuminated garden terrace.

As if on cue, Paul stepped aside for the moment. As she moved from shadow into light, Mystere realized this was deliberately choreographed by Caroline as the bride-to-be's grand entrance. The orchestra struck up a soft rendition of Liszt's "Beauty Triumphant." The hubbub of conversation and laughter abruptly abated, and men seemed to shed their slouches as she passed. She had chosen her finest gown, fulllength and sleeveless, of emerald green satin with a doubleribbon tie at the waist, no jewelry except a simple pair of pale moonstone earrings. Even Rafe seemed genuinely transfixed at first sight of her.

He stepped forward as she approached, gallantly bowing and touching his lips to her hand. "Darling, your loveliness puts the Vestal Virgins to shame," he greeted her, his eyes silently goading her.

"They were selected for their chasteness, not their beauty," she reminded him, poking right back.

"Better chased than chaste, eh? Besides, this maidenhead business is vastly overrated."

Outsparred again, she managed a cold, withdrawn smile as he took her arm in his and led her to Caroline and Carrie.

"Oh, Mystere, I'm so happy for *both* of you," Carrie effused with genuine sweetness, hugging her close. Unlike her astute and jaded mother, Mystere realized, Carrie accepted this engagement at face value, and her deluded gushing hurt almost as much as Rafe's secret cynicism.

Caroline bussed her cheek, a bit more reserved than usual but keeping up a good front. Rafe, however, had evidently decided to show Mrs. Astor that he was not entirely her puppet.

"How do you like Mystere's gown, Caroline?" he asked in a pointed tone. "Don't you agree it *brings out* something in her?"

He meant just the opposite, of course, for Mystere had again carefully bound her breasts. But if Mrs. Astor was at all curious about the girl's adjustable bustline, she had decided to keep any questions to herself—no difficult matter for a woman who dealt almost exclusively in appearance over substance.

Refusing to be baited, she sent Rafe a quelling stare. "Heel, Mr. Belloch," she muttered, "or I'll bring out *my* artillery. Do I make myself clear?"

"Implicitly," he surrendered.

Caroline turned away for a moment to speak with the orchestra leader. Rafe seized the opportunity and led Mystere away from the throng, bearing toward a cast-iron footbridge that arced across a lovely, lily-covered pond.

However, before he could get her alone, Abbot Pollard, emitting a reek of whiskey, suddenly ambushed them from behind a clump of oleander shrubbery.

"Permit me to congratulate the happy couple," he slurred in his nasal baritone and affected enunciation, the words obviously ringing a false note.

He leaned close to whisper in Mystere's ear, "But *entre nous,* my dear, the pearl is being cast to the swine."

"Say it out loud, Pollard, you drunken sot," Rafe snapped impatiently. "Or has Dutch courage replaced your spine?"

Abbot raised his sweat-beaded cocktail glass in a mock salute. "Oh, come now, Mr. Mountain Mover, you are a friend of the laboring man. Don't you realize that drink is the work of the cursing classes?"

"Abbot," Mystere admonished him gently, "you *are* drinking too heavily. And what are you doing hiding over here all by yourself?"

Again he raised his glass, this time pointing in Caroline's direction with it. "Blame that humorless shrew. She's miffed at me again. I merely referred to the Astor Place riots as 'Disastor Place,' and she did not appreciate my taking her name in vain."

This confession actually evoked a chuckle from Rafe. "An old joke, but quite brazen right in front of her," he admitted with grudging admiration. "Perhaps I've underrated you a bit, Abbot. *Just* a bit."

Rafe led Mystere toward the footbridge again.

"Well, as long as we're being mawkishly sentimental," Abbot called out behind them, "you two really do make a fine-looking couple even if Mystere does deserve far better."

Rafe led her out onto the footbridge. They suddenly found shadowed solitude amidst the many, with a wonderful view of everything and everyone. Now and then violins rose above the muted hum of the guests, and a few couples had begun waltzing on a wooden dance floor constructed in the middle of the terrace.

"We must give the gossip merchants some juicy items," Rafe remarked, all the time studying Mystere as if she were a curious museum exhibit.

"I noticed you looking at Caroline's ruby bracelet," he remarked, still watching her closely. "A fine addition to your trousseau, eh, Lady Moonlight?"

"Lady Moonlight is no more now that I have the emerald." She didn't look at him.

"Yes, the ring. Your price of freedom. How is the search for that brother of yours going—this missing brother of yours, Brad."

"Bram."

"Right, Bram. You said he's eight years older than you. Do you seriously expect me to believe *he* never mentioned your last name to you?"

"My mother made him promise not to divulge it to others. I think she made such a point of that, and he was afraid I, being younger, would tell someone if I knew it."

"All right, but why would your mother do such an odd thing?"

It surprised her to realize that Rafe seemed genuinely curious to know the same answers she herself had sought for so long. She was about to mention the letter to him again, but his next question interrupted her.

"How do I know all this lost-identity business is not just concocted to hide a shadow on your name?"

Although the question angered her, she realized again that his tone implied genuine curiosity, not just his usual bullying sarcasm.

"It's no concoction," she assured him. "Rather, my name *is* a shadow, and I'm trying to throw light on it."

He digested her answer in silence, leaning both forearms on the handrail of the bridge and watching the dancers.

He truly is a handsome man, she thought, studying his swept-back chestnut hair and the strong patrician nose. Perhaps his claim that Caroline had intended to seduce him was not so absurd after all.

Thinking about this, however, also reminded her of the question she had determined to ask him.

"Rafe?"

"Hmm?"

"Your decision last Sunday to play along with Caroline rather than expose me—at first I flattered myself that you chose to protect me. But I have another theory."

He glanced at her, eyebrows raised in bemused inquiry. "Then, by all means, expound it."

"I think you meant it when you said you feel obligated to protect your employees from deprivation. But I also think you *are* perhaps willing to risk financial ruin—that you're doing all this to somehow eventually humiliate Caroline."

"Oh? And why would I want to do that?"

"Because more than anything else, you want to hurt her, hurt her entire social class, in fact, for what you think they did to your parents."

Instantly she realized she had touched a raw nerve. His face tightened, jaw muscles bunching, and he turned to face her. The comingling of great hurt and great anger in his face made her deeply regret being so blunt.

"You fight your battles and I shall fight mine," he lashed out, his voice barely under control. "And 'think' hasn't got one damn thing to do with it. It was a bullet my father fired into his own brain, not my opinions. It was *grief and shame* that took my mother early from this world, not my thin-skinned perceptions. . . ."

But his voice broke as powerful emotions overwhelmed his careful defenses. Mystere felt as though a dagger had been thrust into her heart when she thought a tear escaped one of his eyes, but he turned away from her as if hiding his weakness.

Overcome, she clutched his arm. "Oh, Rafe, I'm so terribly sorry. I didn't know anything about—"

He wrenched his arm away. "That's right, you didn't know, so keep your shallow theorizing to yourself, do you hear me?"

For the first time since she had known him, his cold words did not anger her, so overcome was she by remorse. She wanted, more than anything, to find something that might comfort him. But their brief time alone had come to an end. With the worst possible timing, Carrie Astor now joined them on the bridge.

"Forgive the interruption, you two lovebirds," she greeted them with an apologetic smile. "But Mother has requested that the two of you come dance a waltz for us. She has even cleared everyone else off the floor. It's your own fault, you know, for being such stunning dancers at the Addison ball."

"Anything for dear Caroline," Rafe responded, his old self securely back in place. "Come along, Lady M," he added in a lower tone when Carrie was far enough ahead of them, leading the way off the bridge. "Let's give Lance Streeter something to gush about."

Aware of all the eyes watching her, Mystere carefully made sure that her face mirrored nothing of her heart-pounding fear. But as the orchestra struck up "The Blue Danube," and Rafe led her out onto the dance floor, she mentally prepared herself for a repeat of his aggressive performance at the Addisons', when he had tried to turn dance into physical combat.

Especially after his angry, emotional outburst just a few minutes ago, she feared even her rigorous years of training could not help her control his turbulence, which always seemed to need release in physical action. But how wrong she was tonight.

With perhaps half of Mrs. Astor's elect ringed about them, not to mention a dozen or so mesmerized gossip writers, Rafe became a new man in her arms. Rather than *force* her to the very limits of grace and balance, he encouraged and joined her.

They seemed to become one person in mind and movement, sweeping round the floor so effortlessly and flawlessly that no seam existed between the dancers and the dance— "as if," Lance Streeter would later write in rapturous prose, "perfection were no longer an illusion of the artist, and Michelangelo's great *David* suddenly breathed life with the rest of us."

Again and again the music rose in a powerful shout of brass and percussion, then settled into a silken whisper of strings and woodwinds, and to a transported Mystere, it seemed that her heart kept the tempo, not the conductor's hand. But as she gazed up into Rafe's eyes, which now looked back at her in a new tenderness, she had to force herself back to the solid ground of reality.

He is only playacting, her mind lectured. *Do not confuse appearance and reality where he is concerned; this is not the storybook romance you have always pictured for yourself. He is a cruel and dangerous man, and while there may be just causes for his cruelty,* you *must fear only the results of it.*

When the musicians had reached their final flourish, Rafe, still holding one of her hands, stepped back and bowed gallantly to her. The spellbound audience erupted in a cheering ovation that no one could ever have expected from such a normally staid and reserved group. Mrs. Astor herself, whom Lance Streeter once described as "possessing no more emotion than a stone lion," was forced to blink back tears of feeling.

"I confess," she whispered afterward to Mystere, "that I had second thoughts about my decision to compel this marriage. But no two persons were ever more intended for each other than you and Rafe."

Mystere somehow managed a smile to that, but each word was a nail in the coffin of her hopes. And Rafe, as if sensing that his little performance had only plunged her deeper into despair, was now truly enjoying his ironic game for the public's consumption. He was tender, attentive, gallant, never once leaving her side for the rest of the evening.

Nor was everyone present completely captivated by this "perfect romance." Even as Mystere watched, Antonia Butler stared in her direction and made some obviously barbed comment that caused the women around her to laugh. Antonia's venom made Mystere almost glad she had stolen her ring, which was now carefully hidden in the same box that held the letter to her father.

She was actually grateful for Antonia's animosity, for it burst the illusive bubble of this night and reminded her of the threats she must not underestimate. Threats such as Lorenzo Perkins and Sparky. They had not bothered her since her fifty-dollar payment, but why had they been so quiet lately? She doubted that their greed could be so easily appeased. They were planning something, and she mustn't let a few minutes of waltzing fool her into a false sense of security.

"Why so despondent, darling?" Rafe's voice startled her back to the present. "You look like you're being led to the guillotine. Is my girl unhappy about something?"

His sarcasm was back, and he had managed to lead her aside for a moment, a shimmering fountain hiding them from the others.

"The splendor of the moment won't last, and you know it as well as I," she whispered intimately to him. "We each must strike out upon our own path. The folly of this becomes ever more like a knife through the heart."

He suddenly brought both arms around her and pulled her close before she could prevent him. She felt his strength, the solid form that felt like a coiled spring about to release. It attracted, yet frightened her, and even as she felt the inner stirrings of sexual response, her mind recoiled from the sheer danger of him.

"All right, then," he said close to her ear, his breath moist and warm as the response within her, "let's change this statas quo you cannot abide. I meant what I told you at the hotel—I want you."

This time, however, she turned her face away when he tried to force a kiss on her.

"Why should I?" she shot back angrily. "So that once your passion is spent, you can shove me out of your bed and go back to your ledgers and maps as if you'd just finished a cup of tea? I've told you before that I have no desire to become your whore."

"Some would say that Lady Moonlight has already made a whore of her soul. Why not bring your body into harmony with it?"

"Perhaps that's true, but at least I *have* a soul, however tarnished. You have willingly banished yours and allowed an unreasoning hatred to take its place. Let me *go!*"

Rafe laughed harshly, easily forcing her even closer despite her best efforts to get free. "I keep seeing you as you looked that morning in my library," he said, his voice a low husk as desire tightened his throat. "And I feel my body on fire, a fire only you can quench."

"Gracious God, what's this?" exclaimed a mocking, slurred voice behind them. "Have I caught the lovebirds in flagrante delicto?"

Abbot, so drunk by now that he seemed to be walking on

sea legs, had come around behind the fountain. One hand held his latest cocktail glass; the other wagged a shame-on-you finger at them. "Naughty, naughty. I shall run and tell the Shrew, and you'll be forced to do pennance."

Reluctantly, cursing under his breath, Rafe was forced to let her go. Mystere quickly turned to Abbot, managing a smile for him. He had suddenly become her unlikely knight.

"I see you've raided Caroline's prize flower beds," she said lightly, for now there was a fresh chrysanthemum in Abbot's lapel. "Perhaps I shall tell on *you.*"

Taking one quick backward step to retain his shaky balance, Abbot lowered his nose to sniff the purloined flower.

"It covers the stink of all this new money," he confided, thick-tongued. "So many minks, so few manners. And Caroline actually *invited* them, the traitorous bitch. Lovebirds, I ask, 'If gold will rust, what then will iron do?' "

Rafe snorted but seemed quite amused at the spectacle of a drunken, disheveled Abbot Pollard acting as a lone crusader for New York's embattled Old Guard.

Mystere moved away from Rafe and took Abbot by the arm. "Come along, we're getting some coffee into you. You've always been a scratchy old grump, but now you're becoming downright mean."

"So what?" he slurred belligerently, although he allowed himself to be led. He looked at Rafe, who had come up on his other side to help support him. "Some men mellow with age. Others, like myself, harden and narrow. So? Who's to say which group is right? I ask you, Mr. Mountain Mover—who's to say?"

"Who, indeed?" Rafe replied, his invasive teal eyes leveled at Mystere—as was his next remark. "One man's 'unreasoning hatred' is often the next man's reason for being."

Chapter 27

"It's now or never, Sparky," Lorenzo Perkins announced, glancing nervously across Broadway toward the massive structure of the Astor House Hotel. "We played hell tracking him down; let's not botch it now."

He and Sparky occupied a wrought-iron bench in City Hall Park, killing the few minutes left before their eleven A.M. appointment with Rafe Belloch.

"Tell you the honest-to-Christ truth," Sparky replied, "I'd feel better about this if we had more to spill about the girl."

"You're not getting icy feet on me now, are you?"

"You fool, you know damn well I'd kiss the devil's ass if it meant a quick profit," Sparky assured his partner. "But you never shoulda made no appointment until we had more solid goods on his woman. *You're* the one alla time bragging how you was once a Pinkerton. I've heard that's just a lie; all you done was type up surveillance reports for them."

"You just don't grasp it, do you? The details ain't so important. It's the fear of what we *might* know or find out; that's what we have to plant inside Belloch's mind. We paint a picture for him, see? He's engaged to this woman; the last thing he'll want is any dirt coming out about her now. Am I right 'r not?"

"I s'pose you've got a point."

"All right, then." Lorenzo stood up, slapping the dust off his trousers. "Let's go. Just let me do the talking, and you watch how quick our boy Belloch reaches for his billfold."

Rafe, seated at his work-cluttered desk, watched his visitors from eyes as hard as gems. The two men stood just inside the open door of room 511, for Belloch had not even asked them to have a seat.

"No one asked either of you to stick your oar in my boat, gentlemen. Now that you have, please get to your point. I have a business to run."

"P'r'aps you should keep a more civil tongue in your head, Mr. Belloch," Lorenzo replied boldly. "We're the ones holding all the aces."

Rafe cast an amused glance toward Sam Farrell, who occupied a corner sofa at the rear of the room, idly scanning the *Times*.

"All right, then," Rafe countered. "Let's go with your metaphor. I call. Let's see these aces of yours."

"For starters, your fiancée is not who she claims to be," Lorenzo stated with melodramatic triumph.

"Who among us is? All the world's a stage, Mr. Perkins."

"This ain't philosophy I'm talking," he persisted stubbornly. "I'm telling you she *claims* her last name is Rillieux, but it ain't."

"No? Then, what is it?"

Lorenzo failed to respond quickly, evidently taken aback by the blunt, practical way Rafe posed his question.

"Well, it sure's hell ain't Rillieux," Sparky chimed in, sending a warning elbow into Perkins's side.

Rafe laughed, shaking his head. "I'm dubious, gentlemen, to say the least. You march in here boasting how you're 'in the know,' but frankly I think you have less than spider leavings. I ask you again: If Rillieux is not my fiancée's last name, what *is* her real name?"

"She don't know that fact herself," Lorenzo volunteered. "For I was hired to locate a brother of hers, and she admitted to me she didn't know his last name."

"Did you find the brother?" Rafe demanded.

"No," Lorenzo admitted.

"But got paid plenty for it, I'll wager."

Lorenzo ignored that. "What else could that mean except she don't know her own name?"

Rafe drummed his fingers impatiently on the desk. "Mere mental vapors, gentlemen. For your information she's told me all this already. Did you ever find out anything at all about this brother?"

"Some things," Lorenzo replied cryptically.

"Such as . . . ?"

Lorenzo's turtle eyes slanted away from Belloch's probing stare. "This. That."

Rafe laughed again, looking from one to the other. "I figured as much. You took the girl's money and lied about trying to find the brother. Simply exploited her love and concern to make an easy buck."

Neither man responded. Rafe slapped the desk. "Well, come on then, boys—*one* of you had better quit scowling at me and pull a rabbit from a hat."

"Listen, Belloch," Lorenzo protested, "I worked for your fiancée, and I'm saying it would've been obvious to a blind man she's hiding plenty of secrets about her past and who she is."

The two blackmailers were mostly engaged in stalling tactics. Nonetheless they did know just enough to perhaps cause Mystere some trouble somewhere down the line; Rafe could see that. That might interfere with his own plans. He looked at Sam and nodded once.

Sam, sighing as if bored, laid his newspaper aside and

produced a file folder from the leather briefcase leaning against his legs. He opened it and took out a hand-written letter.

"Mr. Perkins," he announced, "I have here a letter written by Miss Laura Driscoll of 17 Washington Street. Your mistress of nearly two years now by her own admission. You may examine the letter if you wish. No? Well, in summation, she agrees to testify in court how you have given her money that by your own admission, should have been used for an operation your wife requires. I think you know what a dim view the city courts take of adultery. You can expect a few years at hard labor on Blackwell's Island."

Rafe watched Perkins remove his derby to mop the sweat from his brow with a limp handkerchief. His heavily pomaded hair had a part down it straight as a pike.

"As for you, Sparky," Sam continued in an efficient drone, "your penchant for carnal knowledge of juveniles may not much interest the city courts, for your victims are, like you, from the dregs of society."

Sparky frowned, his big nose wrinkling at the bridge. "Careful, you little barber's clerk," the big man interrupted angrily. "I'll make you swallow back them insults."

Sam's right hand disappeared inside his suit jacket and reemerged cocking a .38-caliber derringer. Both of the visitors paled noticeably. Sam continued reading from his notes.

"But one of your favorite victims is a girl named Sissy Folam, only fourteen. And her brother is Terrance Folam, leader of the Five Points gang known as the Plug Uglies. Terrance is said to be a hard, ruthless man with only one soft spot in him, and that's for his kid sister. Tell us, Sparky— Terrance doesn't know yet what you've done to the girl, does he?"

A radical transformation had come over Sparky. His cocky beligerence had become cunning servility. "I . . . no, sir, I 'spect he don't, at that. And I'm after keeping things that way, for a fact I am."

Rafe looked at Lorenzo. "Is that how you see it, too, Perkins?"

Lorenzo gave a surly frown, but he also nodded.

"You two bungling fools should stick to the Bowery," Rafe advised, his tone bristling with impatience. "On Wall Street you're just chum among sharks."

He took a jade-inlaid teak box from his desk. "Nothing is owed to you by law or morality. But here's two hundred fifty dollars for each of you. I do this for my fiancée's sake, not my own, so you'll have no cause to victimize her in the future."

Rafe handed each man his share, forcing eye contact before letting go of it. "Now you'll have no claim to any grudge against her, neither of you, so leave her alone, I warn you. Mark me, men, for I keep my word: Every man who works for me is an armed marksman, as am I. Show your greedy faces here, at my Staten Island property, or at my office on Wall Street ever again, and you'll be arrested on sight. I have a witness here that you are blackmailers, a serious felony. You've both been warned, now good day."

When both men had hurried out, Rafe crossed to the door and shut it. Then he went into the bedroom, where he could lean out an open window and verify that Lorenzo and Sparky had emerged on the sidewalk below. He went back to the outer room and looked at Sam. "Think we adequately neutralized the risk?"

"No question. The charges we have against them are strong, and they both know it. You gave them enough money to quench any thirst for revenge. But not so much that you appear desperate to muzzle them. By the way—that 'chum among sharks' business almost got me up laughing. Scared them, though."

"I hope," Rafe said absently. "You know, Sam, I really was hoping to learn something from them. About the woman, I mean."

"I noticed that. I was, too, actually."

"See? See how she is? She does that to people, gets under their skin quick, but she doesn't try to—it just happens." Rafe put the box back in the drawer, then began pacing slowly between the desk and the bedroom door.

"Damnit anyway, Sam, but I'm letting her get *to* me."

"There's a bold theory," Sam remarked drily, and Rafe grinned quick, a brief apology for being so obvious.

"I understand now," he continued, "why the Roman generals considered women such a bad influence on the warrior. They give men too much to think about, and men with naked women on their minds do not boldly face death."

Rafe knew he was waxing dramatic, yet he truly resented Mystere for weakening his resolve of destruction in the interest of vengeance. To Caroline Astor and her cohorts, the deaths of John and Kathrine Belloch were not simply forbidden topics. In a sense they were less than that—utterly insignificant. So what if his father had kept many of them solvent during the sluggish days before the War of Rebellion? Not even one of them had shown up to give a decent man a decent burial.

When his mother died soon after, Caroline and a few others did send condolences. But her funeral, too, was an ostracized event, attended only by a few relatives. Those final slights had remained with Rafe all these years—cankering.

All right, then, a sickness, he admitted to himself. *Perhaps we are only as sick as our secrets.*

And that was probably the lure of Lady Moonlight, he thought with a dark smile. No one, it seemed, had more secrets than her.

"You're being too hard on yourself," Sam assured him as he packed everything back into his briefcase. "I've not met her yet, but from all indications the woman truly is remarkable. I think you've discovered that her captivating personality is not all an act."

"No, you're right, she really is a mystery, just like her

name. But this is one time when I'd rather handle the fact-finding myself, Sam."

Farrell flashed his snaggled grin. "I wasn't aware that I'd offered my services. I'm glad you feel that way about it, though."

"I believe most of her story, and no matter how lowly her beginnings in Dublin, there's no denying her accomplishments now. The woman is a superb dancer, and in one eye-blink she can leap from the subject of French laces to the battle acumen of Julius Caesar."

But never mind all that, he urged himself desperately. *You're foolishly making room in your one-track mind for her, and it's partly the fault of that boy, Hush. Unless the lad, too, is a cynical, first-rate actor, that visit on Saturday was genuine.* And the boy's notions about Mystere fit Rafe's unwilling view of her, too. Still, he mustn't dwell on her like this; he must defeat this unwanted attraction.

Because in cold, hard truth, *she* had become his best possible instrument of revenge. Sickness, unreasoning hatred—maybe so. But wasn't Caroline's pathetic, last-gasp aristocracy also sick in its own way? As Pasteur had proved, the best way to cure sickness was *with* sickness.

He suddenly stopped pacing and looked at Sam, who was patiently awaiting his employer's orders.

"At one moment, Sam, I think I've grasped everything. The next moment my insight is gone, like a fist when you open your hand. The truth about women, I fear, abides someplace where language can't quite reach it."

"A mystery," Sam summed up, smiling apologetically for the obvious pun.

Rafe nodded, his eyes clouded with conflicting ideas. He saw her again in the burnished gold candlelight of his drawing room, how the lines and form of her nakedness were so clear in that thin chemise. The dark, plum-colored circles where her nipples prodded the fabric, the dark and mysterious shadow between her legs . . . Suddenly his blood was pulsing in demanding, needful surges, and only reluctantly he picked up his own briefcase.

"Yes. Mystere," he finally replied. "Now let's find Wilson and head back to the offices. She's cost us enough time."

Mystere knew she was in trouble, and why, the moment Paul called for a family meeting after lunch on Wednesday.

The quarterly payment on his "sure investment" had recently come due, and she knew, without being told, that he had gone to his safe and discovered the tiara was missing. With Mystere, Rose, Evan, Baylis, and Hush all assembled in the downstairs parlor, he drew himself up in a fearfully pompous huff and announced, "There has been an intolerable invasion of my privacy."

Before he could even find his verbal stride, Mystere spoke up boldly: "It was I who invaded your privacy, Paul. I took the tiara. The rest of them had nothing to do with it."

She knew she was taking a dangerous chance. It was true that she was his meal ticket now, and Paul's greed made him a calculating man—but only to a point. He had become insufferably self-important since he had been absorbed into Caroline Astor's inner circle. He saw the entry into his safe as an absolute affront.

So his rage now was immediate and terrifying. His face went splotchy with choleric blood. He rose unsteadily from his chair and hovered in front of her, raising his cane as if to strike her.

"Paul!" Rose exclaimed. "No!"

Evan moved quickly for such a big man. With one hand he collared Hush, who was about to tackle old Rillieux; with the other he gently, respectfully stayed Rillieux's hand.

"Nix on that, boss," Baylis reminded him. "Hand that feeds us and all that."

The hint was clumsy, perhaps, but Rillieux was crafty

enough to heed it. This defiant young woman was his best hope of financial salvation, and he knew it.

But even as he calmed down, his petty tyranny only made Mystere all the more defiant.

"Paul, we're *all* sick and tired of your heavy-handed manner," she berated him. "You go too far in what you call 'loyalty.' "

"All of you?" he repeated, making it a demand as he looked round at the others. "Is this a rebellion, then?"

She, too, looked from one to the other, but even Rose and Hush glanced away, refusing to side against Paul.

"Baylis," she pleaded, "won't you at least be consistent? Every Thursday evening you attend the workers' free lectures. Where's that 'surplus labor value' talk you spout all day long?"

Baylis shrugged awkwardly. "Talk's cheap. I got no real kick, hon. Hell, it was a lucky night for me if I had a haystall to sleep in before Paul took me in. If not for him, the eye-ties would've gutted me by now."

"That's it." Evan nodded. "It ain't so bad, what we all got here. It ain't so bad at all, Mystere, and once we fit Belloch for a pine box—"

"That's enough," Paul interrupted hastily. "The rest of you can go now. I wish to speak with Mystere alone."

Having refused to support her courage, they were now slow in dispersing, as if to warn Paul against turning his temper on Mystere again. She was forced to accept it: Paul had given them, or so they viewed it, the only way they knew out of a miserable existence. Having tasted this new life, they were all justifiably frightened of returning to the old. She was on her own in resisting Paul's despotism. And she realized Rafe would almost surely be in danger if by some unlucky stroke of fortune or his sick will, this match between them actually resulted in marriage.

She couldn't be sure if Rafe would actually push things that far, even to satisfy his spite. But he might, and if it went that far *she* had to prevent marriage by disappearing. But it was going to be difficult to escape Paul's watchful eye. It was as if he knew she wanted flight. She could go nowhere without escort. Even the room on Centre Street, she now realized, would not prove the safe haven she had hoped. It might give her a few days at best—her disappearance would be a windfall for the daily papers, and even disguised she could not long maintain the fiction of Lydia Powell, bereaved young widow.

But if she hurried, she could sell the emerald ring and make arrangements to leave the city—perhaps by steamship to Europe, where it would be easier to get lost among the faces. She could give lessons in English, perhaps, or find some minor theatrical work.

When the others had filed out, Paul's cold, precise words nudged her back to the moment.

"Mystere, it's sufficient to tell you I cannot possibly countenance what you did. But at least you own up to taking the tiara. Will you also honestly tell me what you did with the money you got for it, for I assume it's sold by now?"

At least, she comforted herself, *he doesn't know the real reason I took it.* However, if Paul ever did find out somehow just how much Rafe knew about him, Paul's desperation would be unpredictable. Thus she must deflect his rage onto herself.

"I've used it to search for Bram," she lied in a clear, quiet voice.

Her answer didn't seem to surprise him, but he barely restrained his anger. "And have you found him?"

She shook her head. "Not even a trace of him."

"Did you also steal Antonia's ring for this purpose?"

"Someone else took it."

His questions answered, he allowed his rage to erupt. "I have repeatedly ordered you to give up this ridiculous search, have I not?"

"Yes, but why? Why does it anger you so inordinately that I search for my only blood relative?"

"You ask why? Mystere, have you gone insane? *Why?* Tell me, how much money has it cost me already?"

"Cost you? Only you?"

"All right, cost the family, I mean. Mystere, I trained you. I rescued you from that roach pit on Jersey Street and gave you all this. Not just table scraps, either! Look how you live here, privileged, with servants and—"

"Those servants include myself. Paul, even when you took me around the Continent, you had me stealing. Rose makes your bed and must still go out to pick pockets. It's our efforts that keep you in tailored clothing."

But her tone as she said this was almost mild, for a new suspicion had begun to poke at her. She didn't believe his implication that only the wasted money was behind his anger. She had begun to wonder if Paul had another reason why he didn't want her looking for Bram. Curiosity to know made her less eager to leave the city just yet.

"Paul, what is it you know about Bram that you won't tell me?"

"Nothing," he snapped. "Except that only a fool would waste good money searching for a man who's most likely long dead."

"You have proof Bram's dead?"

"Proof? We aren't talking about Jesus Christ here! Your brother no doubt became a common sailor. Especially if they're impressed into service, common seamen often die without record of the event."

She could say nothing to refute that, and Paul seemed eager to change the subject.

"Mystere," he began, his face grimly calm now, "with astute management and great personal hardship, I have managed to make the quarterly note on my—that is, the family's investment. Another payment comes due in November. In the interim, we have plenty of additional expenses. Especially now that you're engaged."

"Meaning . . . ?"

"Meaning it may prove necessary for Lady Moonlight to strike again."

Reflexively, she shook her head no.

"Better think a moment," he cajoled. "It's starting to look a little suspicious already."

"What is?"

"Why, the naked facts! The moment your engagement, to one of the wealthiest men in the city, is announced, no more Lady Moonlight. Even the stupid newspaper hacks can deduce a story from that."

Paul saw that his logic was at least making her think. His tone became even more ingratiating.

"Mystere, I saw the pained look on your face when Evan stupidly alluded to fitting Rafe for a coffin. You know how that big blowhard likes to shoot off his mouth; it's all that gutter bravado he grew up with."

But his sincere assurances did nothing to assuage her doubts. *You're lying,* she thought. *I've heard you and Evan gloating, and I know you mean to kill Rafe.*

"There would be no need whatsoever for violence," he continued, "if Rafe were generous and forthcoming with you, financially speaking. All you need do is catch him at a . . . close and personal moment. You know, mention how beastly the expenses are becoming, that sort of thing."

"And if he were not forthcoming?"

Paul shrugged, giving her a ruthless look that chilled her spine. "Needs must," was all he replied.

"Suppose it's not him," she challenged. "What if I refuse to cooperate?"

She had deliberately pushed him to confirm what she already feared.

"You don't have the option to refuse," he replied in a

voice entirely devoid of humanity. "You'll do what I tell you to do."

"But if I don't?"

"Then, I'll kill you myself," he declared unflinchingly. "I created you, and I can damn well destroy you."

Chapter 28

As he frequently did after using deadly threats against Mystere, Rillieux tried being affable and contrite during afternoon tea, but she merely retreated behind the distant, forced smile she had perfected over the years. Paul's most recent tantrum had left her feeling more than ever how *she* was the key to avoiding bloodshed or prosecution on either side. Despite her increasing fear of Paul, and her loathing for his "art of arrogation" as he called thievery, this was her family of sorts. Rose and Hush especially. She must do the best thing for them, too, not just herself and Rafe.

But she did not want to flee the city forever without first satisfying her latest doubts about Paul, for the conviction was growing within her that he was part of a conspiracy surrounding Bram's disappearance. An incident right after tea only increased her conviction.

The afternoon post had arrived during tea, and Hush had dutifully sorted it out on the letter stand in the hallway. Mystere's little pile held only a note from a former school friend now vacationing in Greece.

On the top of Paul's pile, however, she spied the familiar gold-embossed insignia of the Granville line, with Sheridan's arm-and-eagle joined to it. Paul picked up his mail without comment, turning toward the stairway.

"Aren't you going to open your mail?" she called out behind him. "Usually you can't wait and tear it open right here."

"I'm tired," he called back without turning around. She couldn't be sure if he was exaggerating his lameness for pity's sake, but he really did sound tired. She hated the twinge of sympathy she felt for him; after all, he was an old scoundrel who deserved his troubles.

Hush saw her getting her pongee parasol out of the umbrella stand. "Shall I hitch the team to the traces?" he asked, eager to be in her company.

"I'll not be using the carriage today," she told him, fondly tousling his thick shock of coal black hair. "But I still want to hear you read some Wilkie Collins for me. Perhaps later."

Hush glanced quickly toward the staircase and saw that Paul was only halfway upstairs, the spiral turn giving him an excellent view of everything below. He followed Mystere out onto the front steps and quickly tucked something into the pocket of her ivy silk dress.

She glanced down and saw an impressive wad of banknotes.

"Almost a hunnert bucks," he boasted before she could speak. "And Paul don't know I got it. It's all yours."

"Hush, I—"

She wanted very much to ask him to stop stealing for *any*one. But she couldn't be such a hypocrite, for if she could manage it under Baylis's constant watch, she herself would be all too happy to sell Antonia's ring. And she really did need Hush's gift, for disposal of the ring had become problematic. Some stolen items were always "hotter" than others, and word was out on the streets how the police especially wanted this thief. There was a rumored reward, too, which made it dangerous to even discuss the ring with potential buyers.

"You shouldn't worry about Sparky and Lorenzo no more, neither," he added.

"And why shouldn't I?"

"You just shouldn't, that's all," he eluded her. "You got enough on your mind, forget them."

"Hush, thank you for the money," she finally settled on saying, giving him a quick hug. "I only hope we both can stop being thieves," she whispered just before she let him go and Baylis appeared at her side.

She spotted Rafe's carriage almost immediately, parked tight to the slate curb of Great Jones Street, perhaps fifteen yards back from the stone-paved cul-de-sac of the Rillieux residence.

She turned around. "Did you know he was there?" she asked Hush, who still stood on the front stairs. A little flush of annoyance warmed her face when the boy only grinned and defiantly closed the door against her.

After her first hesitation, she gathered her skirt with her free hand and began walking briskly toward the carriage, anger tightening her face. She wondered how long Rafe had been lurking there, spying on her in broad daylight.

Under Wilson's bemused scrutiny, she marched straight up to Rafe's side of the carriage. "Why don't you just fit me with a collar and leash?" she demanded.

"Oh, I think you're already restrained enough," he managed, eyes hovering pointedly at the level of her subdued breasts. "Get in. Take a ride with me on this beautiful day like the good fiancée you are."

"I will not."

She started walking quickly along the bluestone sidewalk, using her parasol to block him from view. Wilson needed no orders; he unwrapped the reins and gave them a little snap, the team beginning to pace Mystere at a walk.

Rafe swung the door open and kicked the step down. "I said get in."

"And I said I will *not*. I'm not one of your employees; I needn't jump at your commands."

"Lofty, are we?" He seemed in no mood for her high-hatting manner. "Wilson, hard right," he shouted, and the well-trained coachman instantly veered them toward the sidewalk. Mystere hardly had time to react before Rafe leaped athletically out, carriage still rolling, and seized her under each elbow with his powerful hands.

He literally manhandled her inside and landed against her in the same seat.

"Get off me," she protested, pushing against him with little effect.

He laughed, enjoying her futility like a young boy with a bird trapped in his hand. "Pipe down. Will you cry rape next?"

"No, for that would only excite you. Please get *off* me!"

"Wilson," he called out past the open leather curtain. "Take the long way to the park."

"The park?" she echoed, her struggles ceasing for a moment. "Why not be honest about it and command him take us to your hotel?"

He laughed again, his face only inches from hers. Much of his body was pressed tightly against her, including some pressure that made her intimately aware of his gender.

"Because not even Wilson would believe I asked you to my hotel for your advice on an engineering problem."

Before she could say anything, his mouth took possession of hers.

She couldn't deny his need to use her in a quest for revenge, but his kiss also assured her of his lust to bed her. And for a few fatal moments, her own physical desire rose to match his, complicating her plight as the fire within her threatened to destroy all her plans.

"Why this again?" he demanded, breathing in ragged gasps, when she finally managed to turn her face away.

She suddenly moved over to the empty seat, trying to get her own breathing under control. From the window, she could see Baylis running to the front door to tell Rillieux she had been "kidnapped." If she had had Antonia's emerald and her letter on her, she would have taken just such an opportunity to disappear.

But timing, once more, was against her.

"Perhaps a prostitute might be more expedient," she clipped.

"Believe me," he assured her bitterly, spearing his fingers through his hair, "I would if I thought it would help me."

"Rafe?" she said after they had ridden in strained silence for perhaps two minutes.

"What?" He sounded vaguely annoyed, like a harried parent who needed a quiet moment to think.

"What kind of man is Trevor Sheridan?"

He narrowed his eyes as if to ask her something. Instead, he only replied absently, "The usual kind, I suppose, of his type—walks on two legs and never stops scheming. I don't know him that well, but one hears things from reliable sources."

"Things such as . . . ?"

He frowned harshly. "Look, he's too old for you, if it's seduction you have in mind. Also he is happily married to Alana Van Alen, a great wit and beauty. Nor is he any man to champion a calculating social climber, though it's been said was once one himself. Indeed, he has acquired a nickname among the social clubs, the Predator, so you'd also be a fool to rob him."

"Why is he called—"

But he raised a peremptory hand to silence her. He looked intensely curious all of a sudden. "If it's about that unsigned letter of yours, I warned you before not to spin grand ideas from little threads. What's got you all worked up about Sheridan?"

She said nothing at first, only studying his face closely as she decided whether or not to trust him.

"Is this some voodoo hex?" he complained irately, averting his gaze from her close scrutiny.

She made up her mind and told him about the letter that arrived today, how she had spotted the Granville-Sheridan crest and Paul's refusal to open it in front of her.

"I can tell you exactly what it is," he interposed, "for I received one also. No intrigue involved, it's just an invitation for a soiree this weekend at the Sheridan mansion, in honor of the duke and duchess. Rillieux surely knew it was coming, for he's tight as ticks with Mrs. Astor."

"Well, he certainly doesn't want me to know about it," she pointed out. "And he became almost violent earlier when I told him I'm still searching for Bram. When I pressed him to see if he knew anything about Bram's disappearance, he lied to me. I could tell."

She was silent perhaps another thirty seconds, brow furled with the effort of concentration.

"It's Evan," she said abruptly, thinking out loud.

"Evan who?"

"The man who serves as our butler. He's always been civil toward me, even kind. But I seem to remember him somehow from the days before Paul snatched us away from the orphanage. Remember seeing him briefly."

"Us? So Rillieux did take your brother, too?"

"Yes. One afternoon each week the orphans were sent out to beg for their keep. Paul caught us on a little alley off Lexington Street, I think it was. I forget where, exactly, but there were tenements on one side of the alley, restaurants and groceries on the other. I think it was he and Baylis who approached us. They were never violent; there was no force or threats. They bought us a fine restaurant meal, and treated our escape from the orphanage as a great adventure with our new 'family.' They all spoiled us terribly and seemed genuinely grieved when Bram was taken."

" 'Seemed' may be the operative word," Rafe tossed in with mild sarcasm. "Could you or your brother have inadvertently said something to suggest you had people with money here in America? Anything that could've gotten back to old Rillieux?"

"It's certainly possible, although we were both tight-lipped by habit; my mother saw to that. It's more likely someone could have seen the letter at some point. But Bram was always careful with it."

"Careful for a boy, sure. But there had to be times when it was left unguarded. By the way, I'd like to see this letter sometime myself."

Sudden alarm tingled her skin as she realized she was taking a dangerous risk with the one secret her dying mother swore her and her brother to protect. This man with her now proved that "close" did not always mean affectionate, and she was a fool to forget *he* might be one of the dangers her mother had foreseen. As for all his questions and apparent curiosity, he was a general collecting intelligence for a war, that's all, not someone concerned to help her.

"Anyhow," he added with brusque dismissal as the Astor House began to appear a few blocks ahead, just in glimmers through the trees, "you're almost surely reading too much into this supposed nexus to the house of Granville. All due respect to your mother, but she was leaving life feeling desperate to help her children survive. She—say, that's all right, then, stop that. I'll shut up."

She had surprised both of them when his description of her mother evoked sudden tears, just two, one clinging to the high promontory of each curved cheekbone.

"You women agitate for suffrage," he groused, "yet look how weepy and weak you are."

"This woman agitates for nothing," she declared in a rush of defensive anger and hurt. "Shall we casually discuss *your* mother's last moments? Or is her death more tragic because she was wealthier? Believe it or not, Rafe, a poor heart breaks as deeply as a rich one."

"She was poor when her heart broke, too, you forget." He

leaned closer to her side of the carriage and kissed her on the lips again, this time not so forceful but no less passionate. Again she felt the heart-racing, pulse-shaking demands of her physical desire for him.

"Here's the park," he urged in a strained whisper. "Shall I have Wilson rein in?"

"At least you're asking now," she said, grudging him a brief smile.

Chapter 29

A ll week long Mystere waited for Paul to mention the upcoming soiree at the Sheridan mansion, honoring the Duke and Duchess of Granville. However, he made no reference to it. He kept to his room often, complaining, "My damned *age* is what I've caught." Overall he was civil but distant with everyone. Even when he overheard Rafe calling on Thursday, arranging to stop by for Mystere on the night of the Sheridan affair, Paul still acted as if nothing were happening.

It made no sense to Mystere. By now Paul had become such a fixture at Caroline's side he was jokingly referred to as Ward the Elder. When he had still said nothing by Saturday morning, she decided to brooch the topic with him.

She found him seated at a little escritoire in the downstairs parlor, still in his robe.

"Paul?"

Slowly he looked up from whatever he was studying under an electric reading lamp. One corner of the bright light beam caught his face, revealing an ashen pallor that shocked her. He had been feeling poorly all week, and now she realized it wasn't just his usual hypochondria.

"You'll have to speak up, my dear. I've just taken quinine, and the damnable stuff makes my head ring."

"I just wondered if, assuming you feel better, you have plans to attend the Sheridan affair this evening? If so, you can ride with me and Rafe."

She had no idea if Rafe would tolerate that, but it didn't matter. She only wanted an excuse to gauge Paul's response. But instead of mentioning the soiree itself, he focused on Rafe.

"Mr. Rafael Belloch," he mused in a distracted tone. "And I always wondered why the man will barely nod to the uncle of his fiancée."

The answer worried her. She wondered how much he suspected of Rafe's knowledge. Cautiously she inquired, "What do you mean?"

"Never mind. No, I'm not going," he finally answered her. "Caroline has agreed to give my regrets."

"But . . . why didn't you at least tell me about the soiree?"

"Why? You found out, didn't you?"

His cryptic answer further convinced her he knew something he had been keeping to himself. But she couldn't find the courage to ask him about it directly. He was not a man, even old and frail, whom she cared to corner.

"But why don't you want me to go?" she persisted.

"Go, don't go, I don't care. But has it ever occurred to you that it might be wise to place more value on your presence by *removing* it once in a while?"

He gazed up at her where she stood just inside the open doors. "Especially after that impressive performance you and Rafe put on at Mrs. Astor's last weekend. By the bye— Antonia, I'm told by Caroline, immediately planted the nasty rumor that you and Rafe secretly rehearsed for that apparent moment of dance-floor spontaneity. But Lance Streeter, romantic ponce-man that he is, has led the charge against such vicious snipes. You are winning the Consul of Plebians, my dear. You should be pleased."

"Immeasureably," she replied with scant attention, for she was still trying to understand Paul's new reasoning. "Since when have you become so strategic about public appearances? Your usual approach is simply to go out each time you're invited. What's different now?"

"I'm not the issue, goose. I am an old man on tottering legs. Addicted to wealth and power."

"Especially power," she reminded him, though with a disarming smile.

"Of course. Just look at me. I've developed a sort of compensatory adaptation to my decreasing . . . potency, if you will. I admit it. I've become a vampire bat, flitting about and sucking blood where I can."

"Paul, I only meant—"

"But you," he pressed on, "are not a predatory old man, cursed with my limitations. And I see now that I've pushed you too far in the wrong direction. Do you want to become like the Vanderbilt sisters, so *grateful* that you never snub an invitation? I've always said look to the old sayings, for there is where you'll find God's truth. Familiarity does, indeed, breed contempt, while a certain aloofness inspires awe and respect."

It was a good argument, she realized, but suspicious nonetheless. None of this had concerned him one whit until the Sheridan invitation.

"I'm glad to see you're suddenly a student of 'God's truth,' " she finally replied, her submissive tone softening the irony of her words.

"I'm a criminal," he insisted brusquely, "not a heretic."

That he had actually called himself a criminal shocked her into thoughtful silence. She had observed Paul closely for many years now, and she knew his infrequent attacks of conscience usually accompanied his darker deeds.

"Have you and Rafe decided on a wedding date yet?" he abruptly demanded.

"*I* and Rafe? You grant me more powers than I possess."

"Nonsense. You *use* fewer powers than you possess, and I don't mean psychic. At any rate you'd better settle on a date, the sooner the better."

"Paul, you've been acting oddly for days. What's bothering you?"

"Where do past years go?" he countered evasively, struggling to his feet. "Excuse me, dear, but I'm off to take a nap."

She watched him make his way unsteadily out of the parlor. The tiara incident, she reflected, seemed to have been a turning point of sorts, perhaps triggering his fear that he was losing control of her. That might explain his remark about having the wedding as soon as possible.

But the rest of it, his atypical behavior about the Sheridan affair, and that odd remark about how Rafe would barely nod to him—she could fathom no reason for it.

While she mulled all these impressions, she absently started across the room to turn off the light Paul had forgotten. She was perhaps halfway to the escritoire when something caught the corner of her eye, something on the blotter reflecting a bright, almost accusatory white. With no clear view of it yet, she nonetheless realized that Paul had not forgotten the light—this was left for her to see.

She leaned closer, body trembling all over when she realized what lay there. All her fretting about others, and *she* had become her own worst enemy. She and her stupid, stupid carelessness. Those little, torn scraps of paper meticulously reassembled and pasted to a sheet of stationery had been fished from the bottom of the litter can in the hallway: the letter from Stephen Breaux's law offices.

In a heartbeat her legs felt hollow and weak, and she was forced to sit in the chair still warm from Paul's body.

"Mother Mary," she whispered, too stunned to even feel properly afraid.

"I swear this isn't hair; it's Persian silk," Rose praised, her tone as ebullient as her mood. She pulled a horn brush through the dark brown tresses, marveling at the mahogany hues where late-afternoon sunlight drenched Mystere's hair.

Mystere's eyes lifted to the vanity mirror for a moment, meeting Rose's as she smiled her thanks at the compliment. The older woman's good mood had actually begun two nights ago, when Rafe called and Rose took his message.

Rose knew her well by now and could guess Mystere's thinking at times.

"Oh, I know," she confessed as she deftly tied the hair and slipped a black net over it. "But life around here is usually quite unromantic. Now your gentleman's to be calling on us regularly, it's more exciting. More like a proper love story, it is."

A proper love story . . . The cruel hoax of those words blemished her smile, but Mystere had no heart to dampen Rose's spirits. "You seem to like Rafe Belloch," was all she said.

"He's dangerously good-looking," Rose giggled, "and they say his past is terribly romantic and sad."

"Why? What have you heard about him?"

"Well, there's . . . It's said how he was only a lad, perhaps the age of our Hush, when his father threw away the family fortune—some terrible gamble on the foreign banks, or some such. The old man, 'tis said, after being frightfully cut by Mrs. Astor's crowd, blew his own head off. He faced a prison term for his debts, and not one of them would loan him a cent. I s'pose he could not stomach the shame of it."

"Yes," Mystere said, amazed how the version spread by Dame Rumor got it all more-or-less accurately, assuming her own view of it was right.

"But we cannot lick old wounds forever," Rose pointed out, refusing to surrender her gay, hopeful mood. "I know everything seems so frightful and complicated to you, hon. But 'tis a long lane, indeed, that takes no turns."

Rose turned away and began humming to herself as she laid out Mystere's silk-and-lace gown for tonight, giving it a final inspection for flaws.

Mystere felt suddenly angry with herself. After all, if Rose could feel her spirits buoyed by the prospect of a marriage—"a *grand* marriage," she had called it—why was she herself immune to at least some share in Rose's hope? Perhaps playacting was all anyone ever really did anyway, so why not act happy?

"Honey, what are you thinking about?" Rose asked, crossing back to the mirror and standing beside her. "Don't let my silly whistling keep you from complaining if you'd like."

"Rose, I'm sorry, I don't mean to be so gloomy."

"I won't allow you to apologize," she insisted. "This time *I'm* the one gets to be sorry. It's been troubling me since Wednesday."

"What has?"

"The way you spoke up for us to Paul's face, and we all just stood there like clothes poles."

"You don't need—"

"I can't speak for the boys, mind you, but *I'm* proud of what you said, saints preserve you. But I was also afraid, Mystere. Not just for me, but for you also."

"Afraid to encourage me, you mean?"

"Yes. Sure, Paul's too old and frail to seem very dangerous. Except that Evan and Baylis prac'ly lick his hand. They'll do his bidding, Mystere, never mind how stupid and wrong it may turn out. You *must* think of that, and fix your thoughts on any way out of here. So what if it's really Mrs. Astor's doing—can marrying Rafe Belloch place you in worse danger than you face here?"

"I don't know," she replied honestly. "I wonder, sometimes, if 'choice' is a word invented by the devil to drive us mad."

"No, it was men he invented for that," Rose corrected her, and they both laughed. "When men cannot refute us with reason, they find other ways to enforce their wills."

"I'm not so sure it's only men, Rosie. Mrs. Astor plays by the same rules and always wins. May I ask you something?"

The sudden change in her tone caused a slight tensing of Rose's features. "Shame on you for asking my permission first."

"It's just that . . . it's about Evan. You mentioned once that he spent six months on a jailhouse work crew. Years ago?"

Rose nodded.

"Perhaps twelve years ago?"

Rose knew where this was headed; Mystere could read the uncertainty and fear in her eyes. But she also saw resolve in the set of Rose's jaw.

"Yes," she replied, adding in a firm voice, "about the same time you ran away from the orphanage."

"And he was already working for Paul, too?"

"Yes." This time Rose hesitated only a moment, then quickly blurted the fact she knew Mystere was driving at: "Evan's crew often hauled donated furniture to city orphanages. Paul had him on notice to keep his eye open for 'likely waifs' as Paul called them. I'm sure that's how he first learned of you and . . . well, you and your brother."

Furniture . . . Mystere now remembered where and when she had seen Evan's face for the first time. He was with several other unshaven convicts in striped clothing and knit caps who had carried new wooden bedsteads into the top floor of the Jersey Street Orphanage. The children had all been chased out into the common room . . . and Evan, especially after Paul's training, would surely have been watching for valuables of any kind. He could also read, and Bram had sometimes kept the letter hidden under his mattress cover.

She looked at Rose. "You've known for some time about the letter I have, haven't you?"

"Yes. Not right off, nor have I ever read it. But Baylis told me about it."

Mystere started to speak, but her voice failed her for a moment, and she was forced to start over. "Rosie, what about Bram? Did Paul and the boys arrange for him to be taken?"

Rose took both of Mystere's hands in hers. "Mystere, I would not lie about that if I knew the truth. But I just don't. It's not below them, of course, but I can't see what Paul would gain except perhaps a bit of money from an impress gang. However, we both know a sharp child is worth far more than a bit of money, at least to Paul."

Mystere believed her. She was silent a minute, trying to grasp the meaning of all this; however, Paul's ultimate motives eluded her.

"Rose, I don't understand, what is Paul's plan? What does he know that I don't? He's had the information for years, yet apparently done nothing with it."

"Baylis tells me more than Evan will, but he's said nothing to me about it even if he knows. But, hon, you already found that pasted-together letter, didn't you? The one Paul sifted from the litter can?"

Mystere nodded, feeling a tightening around her heart at the reminder.

Rose clucked. "La, girl, I wish I'd seen you do it. You *know* he pokes through the trash, don't you?"

"Yes, I . . . oh, it's just there's been so much on my mind, I got careless."

"You did, indeed, and like you I have no idea what Paul means to do about it. He may see that Rafe has kept quiet this long for your sake, and count on your marriage to protect him in the future."

"Yes, for no doubt he knows that copies of that letter could hang him if he harms Rafe. Unless Paul can arrange an 'accident' so convincing that Rafe's estate will not suspect him."

"It's all in a frightful boil," Rose admitted, "and I can't blame you for being afraid, Mystere. But if Paul is placing his hopes on this marriage, you have even more reason to. It may be your new dawn, hon. Place all your hopes on that thought."

Chapter 30

"Sheridan residence, Wilson," Rafe called out, handing Mystere into the carriage.

"That's lower Fifth?" Wilson called back.

"Yes. I forget the number, but you'll see the traffic."

"Right. Be there in jig time, sir!"

The conveyance started forward, and Rafe opened the leather curtains on both sides, letting in the dim illumination of the streetlights. He had taken the opposite seat instead of crowding her. He studied her for some moments in silence.

"Old Rillieux gave me a dirty look," he finally commented. "What's going through his head?"

"He knows that *you* know—about him, I mean. He found the letter from Stephen Breaux."

"Ahh . . . careless, were you? Is that why he chose not to go with us?"

"I'm not sure. I suspect he originally planned on staying home in hopes I would also. I think he doesn't want me too near Trevor Sheridan or the duke and duchess."

"Then, why didn't he avoid the Addison ball? They were all present."

"Yes, but he hustled me away from them. And that was before I started asking him questions."

"Well, I'm glad the old reprobate found Breaux's letter. Let him sweat a little. He's had it too damned easy at everyone else's expense."

"You shouldn't underestimate him. He is old and ailing, yes. But his mind never stops scheming. He represents a very real danger."

"To hell with him. Actually, that letter is perfect. It serves to warn him, yet doesn't involve the police, nor is there any direct threat."

"As *you* interpret the phrase."

"Never mind him. Tell me, how much did you get for Antonia's ring?"

Resentment at his blunt, demanding manner filled her. In fact she had decided to let the ring lose a bit of its notoriety before she approached Helzer, Paul's usual fence, in person. She dreaded the thought of visiting his salvage yard on Water Street, a terrible rough area. But she had met him once at their home, and he had been quite kind and urbane with her. He had survived in an illegal business for many years through greed and cunning and, above all, discretion—she might be able to deal with him.

"Nothing yet," she answered truthfully.

His taunting laugh only irritated her further. "So. You're finding out, eh, that a hungry dog must eat dirty pudding. You can't get even a tenth of its true value, can you?"

"Don't you have an empire to run? Why are you so preoccupied with the ring?"

"That's obvious and you know it. I half expect you to disappear once it's sold."

She glanced out her window, ignoring him. "Thus breaking your heart, I'm sure."

"Oh, I'd miss you for a day or two, I suppose. But my heart isn't the point. Your disappearance would humiliate me publicly; that's the big problem. All that speculation as to whom my fiancée has dumped me for . . . not to mention that you'll only get caught, anyway."

"That's hogwash and you know it," she accused, still refusing to look in his direction. "The true reason you fear my running away is the blow it would deliver to all your sick plans."

"You, of all people, lecture on sickness—a robber and thief whose very life is a lie? Those cloths wrapping your breasts right now, hiding charms that ought to be proudly revealed—no sickness there, eh?"

"No! It's wrong and it's illegal, what I do, but it's not sick. My end is survival, not revenge. But you—you are going to ruin both of us, aren't you? All just to break another useless arrow on Caroline's hide."

"Caroline's alone, do you mean? No, I'm out to destroy the rank, not the woman. There are Four Hundred in my sights, though I confess she is center of the target and will take the most direct hit. And you're wrong; I don't have any special plan to destroy you. But . . ."

"But to continue your metaphor," she finished when he paused, "often there are peripheral victims in any great battle."

By now she was watching him again.

He smiled at her cynical phrasing. "Well said," he praised. "Besides, you've apparently got me down for one nefarious deed. But I did not go to so much trouble to become a gossip-page celebrity for nought. Now I'm front stage, and perhaps I mean to chip away at the edifice of respectability, one crack at a time."

His words stung, for she took his meaning immediately. The dancing, the stolen kisses, all of it calculated to hook reporters and acquire a mouthpiece and an audience for his plans. That answered Paul's question as to why a "man of empire" was so eager to get his name in the papers.

And she was being used like everyone else.

"Yes," she retorted, injured feelings making her raise her voice a little, "that's how you'll do it at first, for what's the point of cruelty if one cannot prolong and enjoy it. But when you see your main chance, you'll seize it."

Only part of his face was visible to her at the moment, but

even in the shadow light she could see the anger that tightened his jawline.

"Leave all this thought reading to that charlatan 'uncle' of yours," he snapped. "My plans aren't spoken into my ear by a genie. I live my life as I go, like most."

"No. Despite all the opportunities of great wealth, you're simply a doomsday prophet, and your tale is doom from the opening. But your grand scheme of destruction will succeed only in your mind. You will topple the pyramids at Giza before you topple Mrs. Astor."

"And you? You who level *my* plans—what about your own quixotic quest for the Holy Grail? Not only a brother, who's no doubt a prince by now somewhere in Tahiti, but a fortune, too, if only she can find them. End of fairy tale."

His words struck like blows, both for their scorn and their accuracy. With great effort she fought back tears, knowing he would only mock her for a bawl baby.

"I said nothing about any fortune," she corrected him. "And I fail to see how my love for Bram compares to your overweening hatred."

After a moment's silence he relented a bit. "You've a point, I suppose. I don't blame you one bit for keeping up the search for Bram, especially given your cruel parody of a family with Rillieux's bunch. I'd want my real brother, too, even if he turned out to be Sheriff of Nottingham. But I advise you to gird for bad news after so many years."

This was an olive branch, of sorts, or at least a twig, she supposed. So she decided to extend one herself.

"You've talked to Perkins and Sparky on my behalf, haven't you?" she asked him. "Scared them away from me? You and Hush working together somehow?"

"I and Hush? Well, we did have a bit of conversation over a cigar, yes."

"A cig—you despise my uncle, but your own corruptions of youth don't matter much, I see."

"Corruption? That's harsh. I probably put him off stogies

for life. Tell me, am I 'corrupting' you with my seductions; is that the coy hint here? For if I am, then, by all means I will stop and desist. The choice is yours."

His demanding eyes would not let her off the hook. Despising him even as she surrendered, she replied in a snappish voice, "No, you're not corrupting me. I'm a woman and know what I'm about. But Hush is only twelve."

"That's old enough to keep his word, yet the little scamp told you anyway."

"He didn't actually tell me. But I guessed from his behavior and certain remarks. I . . . anyway, thank you, Rafe. For chasing off Lorenzo and Sparky, I mean."

"You needn't thank me. I just don't want those two bunglers in my way."

"You can't ever appear human, can you? You snap if someone looks at you too long or only tries to be cordial. What are you so afraid of?"

"Afraid of," he repeated irritably. "Death, disease, poverty, the usual gang. Have you become an alienist now, charting people's psyches?"

"Oh, Rafe, stop it! How can a man so successful and brilliant fail to see that revenge is not a good enough reason to live?"

"Damnit, I've told you before to spare me your pious, Brook Farm sermons. I'll live for whatever the hell I please. You ought to read some history some time, not just all these foolish, sentimental love stories you women devour like bon bons. *Revenge* is at the heart of human events, Lady M. Men like Alexander the Great and Genghis Khan placed it above all else."

"It's no use," she surrendered. "No one can win against you, for you know everything and you're always right."

"Just keep that in mind," he advised her, "and we'll get along fine."

* * *

They finished the journey in a strained silence, Mystere staring out the windows at the well-lit homes and superbly maintained lawns rolling past on either side. This stretch of Fifth Avenue, where the Sheridan mansion was located, had seen some flight of the rich lately as business interests were starting to squeeze in to capitalize on the prestigious address. But there were still plenty of grand mansions.

Rafe finally broke the silence, but only to be insulting.

"Look," he remarked, pointing out the window and up at the night sky. "A moon bright enough to make shadows. Are you succumbing?"

"In no sense of the word, Mr. Belloch," she assured him.

"You're daring me now. Daring me to *make* you succumb?"

"Here, do you mean? Along Fifth Avenue in a carriage?"

"It's done quite commonly in carriages."

"Quite commonly, indeed."

He laughed at her offended tone and manner. "Perhaps all that rocking on the braces only makes it—"

She tried to slap him, but he easily caught her wrist. Laughing to taunt her, he tugged her off balance from her seat and easily toppled her into his lap. Before she could even recover, his hungry mouth had opened hers, and his tongue was greedily exploring, teasing.

An unwilling moan escaped her, heat flared in her loins, and her anger at him became a resentful, aggressive passion matching his own and daring him to get hotter. Only Wilson's voice, commanding the team to slow, made her turn her face from his, gasping to find her breath.

"Still claim you're not succumbing?" he whispered, kissing her ear and giving it a little nibble that made her wish she was naked in his arms.

"Not of my own volition," she protested lamely as she struggled to her feet and sat down on the other side of the carriage.

"Blame it on the moon," he said innocently.

Wilson joined the queue of arriving conveyances before a high wall of alternating white and black marble blocks. Massive black-iron gates on the avenue side were now thrown open wide to reveal a well-lit house with a mansard roof. French doors were thrown open, and Mystere saw guests mingling throughout the first floor and attached gallery, groups and couples spilling out onto the front lawn. Her eyes sought Trevor Sheridan, always easy to spot because of his ever-present ebony and gold lion-ornamented walking stick. But she could locate neither him nor the duke and duchess.

Nervous expectation left her feeling short of breath. She made up her mind to finally end, if she could, this long uncertainty. She would ask Sheridan outright if he might have some knowledge of her family—or at least of anyone else in New York who might have sent letters bearing the Connacht motif to Dublin.

But Rafe had evidently anticipated her decision. As he handed her out and Wilson moved to join the line of parked vehicles, Mystere tugged Rafe's arm to halt them in front of the gates emblazoned with the familiar half eagle and arm holding a dagger.

He studied her transfixed, purposeful face. Suddenly he cursed under his breath. "You damned fool."

With a burst of strength she didn't even try to resist, he pulled her perhaps ten yards away from the paved drive to a little niche in the surrounding wall.

"Lady M, I'm afraid your wick is flickering. You don't just approach a man like Sheridan at a social function," he admonished in an urgent tone of voice, "and blurt out a damned-fool lot of questions about possible connections to the peerage."

"That's easy for you to—"

"For one thing," he silenced her with commanding anger, "he'll be surrounded by lick-spittles and toadies, at least one of whom is bribed regularly by the yellow press. Do you want all of your precious secrets told in lurid headlines? *All* of them?"

The urgency of his anger made her think about his questions. In a few moments it became clear that he was right; she was being a fool. Let one gossip writer get hold of even a hint, and it would all come out in shocking, newspaper-selling detail.

"Then, how?" she pleaded. "I *must* talk to him."

"Then, you're a bigger fool than God made you."

"Why?"

"Because Sheridan is a man well worth fearing, that's why. He's ruthless."

"He has no monopoly on that market, has he?"

Rafe gave her an impatient little shake. "Listen to me. Trevor Sheridan is best avoided like the plague. In any event, you must realize that claims of 'family ties' are common—and commonly proved false. You would begin with Sheridan's attorneys, not with him."

"Yes," she agreed after a moment. "That's how I'll do it, you're right."

As Rafe led her back toward the front gates, she noticed a streamer of sparks ahead about a block away, shooting up into the night sky. A group of men surrounded some sort of big bonfire built right in the avenue. They were surrounded, in turn, by a line of policemen wielding shotguns and clubs. She could hear a confused hubbub of shouted taunts and curses, the words indistinct at this distance.

"What's all that?" she asked Rafe.

"Some longshoremen who blame 'the bosses' for bloody union-busting tactics. Of course, their own unions are run by honest, peace-loving angels. Look sharp—here comes Her Nibs."

Caroline and Ward had paused near the gate, seeing the two of them approach from the shadows. Rafe glanced at McCallister, who in turn couldn't take his eyes off Mystere.

"Easy, Ward," Rafe laughed. "You're leering. Get control of yourself and save it for your wife."

Caroline, however, was in no mood to let Rafe take charge.

"Have you two discussed a date yet?" she queried Rafe without preamble.

"Alas, Caroline, in our heady delirium of joy we—"

"Everyone likes a June bride," she rode him down, "but that's nearly a year off. This coming September might do quite nicely, don't you think? The frightful heat will have broken, yet you can fit in a lovely honeymoon trip before winter."

Rafe was no longer in a joking mood, for there was no trace of suggestion in Caroline's tone.

"But . . . September," Mystere managed to protest weakly in the face of Rafe's continued silence. "It's . . . only month after next, so—so soon."

Caroline fixed unblinking eyes on her. "Have you two noticed one welcome by-product of your engagement? We now hear of something besides the Lady Moonlight."

Mystere lost all strength, and only Rafe's support kept her standing as she feared in a rush of pounding blood to her face, *Caroline knows. Somehow she has figured it out.*

The matron's eyes shifted to Rafe as she added, "It's been good for us."

There was a subtle but definite emphasis on the word *us*. As if she were warning Rafe to walk the straight and narrow for the sake of the Patriarchy, or face dire consequences.

"Come along, Ward," she added, and the two of them glided off, leaving Rafe and Mystere both impressed into silence. It was a full thirty seconds before Rafe broke it.

" 'The devil is sailing on a sinking ship, and the place where he reigns is called Doomed Domains.' I heard a preacher spout that once."

"Yes," Mystere agreed softly, studying his chiseled-coin profile in the shadowy gaslight. "But which devil must I fear?"

"'Our name is Legion,'" he assured her. "And you can't say you haven't been properly warned about us. Behave with good sense and be damned careful what you say to whom, Sheridan included. Caroline has just made it clear: We buy her silence by announcing a September wedding date. And so we shall cooperate."

"Until *you* decide not to, right?"

"Strong dogs dominate."

"And you're stronger than Caroline, is that it?"

"I—*damn* it," he muttered in annoyance as Abbot Pollard's bulk suddenly blocked their path just inside the gates.

At least he appears sober, Mystere thought.

His annoyed face confused her until he nodded in the direction of the noisy protestors. "Angry peasants with pitch-forks. And we permit them to vote, so in a sense they're right—America's troubles *are* all our fault. As generously as we bribe our elected officials, and they still betray us by kowtowing to these mudsills."

"Yes, yes, the public be damned and all that rot," Rafe snapped impatiently, brushing past Abbot and propelling Mystere with him. "Look, Abbot, hurry up and get drunk. You're more entertaining that way."

"Ahh, of course," Abbot called out behind them, loud enough for others to hear. "I've interrupted you in a 'heated moment.' You two strike me as shameless exhibitionists."

"Worthless old nancy," Rafe muttered. "I don't doubt he keeps a catamite somewhere."

The rest of the evening proved uneventful and anticlimactic to Mystere, who had arrived hoping she was on the verge of some critical revelation about her past. Instead, with Rafe refusing to give her any free leash, she ended up exchanging only brief, polite remarks with the duke and duchess, and speaking briefly to Alana Sheridan and not at all with her infamous husband Trevor. In fact, it might be easier to pet a wild bear—the Irishman had an intimidating, imposing manner and seemed little concerned with the banal exchanges of "socializing." In that respect, at least, he was like Rafe.

They left little over two hours after they had arrived. Mystere felt sore around the mouth from all her insincere smiling. However, the evening's pretending had produced an unintended—and very unwelcome—response within her. Rafe's attentions all evening in public, his little touches and compliments, the way he smiled into her eyes, his masculine solidity at her side—she was beginning to wonder if some of his acting might not be genuine affection.

When he had first intruded his way into her life, she had heard only his words. But by now his every tone of voice had taken on new meaning, every nuance of accent becoming crucial to her. That was all new, and she found herself, more and more, wondering, Was *he*, too, possibly losing the war with his own heart? She thought, sometimes, that he looked at her with something besides lust or cunning; thought, too, that he might have protected her from Caroline, and now from Sparky and Lorenzo, for kind reasons.

But *no*, she resolved anew as Rafe's carriage rolled off into the night, carrying her home, and she coldly resisted his physical advances. She must cling to cold logic, not to longing. She was vulnerable now, in her growing desperation, and had to remember that Rafe was probably the most serious danger of them all. She must pin her hopes on finding Bram and learning more about their family—and perhaps on somehow getting away from New York well before September.

You would begin with Sheridan's attorneys, not with him.

All right, then, she vowed. *They should be in their offices on Monday. So that's when I'll begin.*

Chapter 31

Monday morning dawned gloomy and sunless, a solid pewter sky threatening rain. In her nervous anticipation of Sheridan's attorneys, however, Mystere failed to plan for bad weather. She would soon bitterly regret that failure of foresight, among others even greater.

The Manhattan Phone Directory listed Trevor Sheridan's business address as a suite in the Commerce Building on Wall Street, and she could only hope that office included his attorneys. She spent much of the weekend rehearsing what she would say. Her situation was fraught with dangers, and she must carefully avoid revealing too much, which in turn would make it harder for her to elicit information.

Another problem was the danger of being recognized. She briefly considered telephoning, but decided it was too easy for them to hang up on a stranger. After considering the problem further, she found a solution that would alter her usual physical appearance without clumsy disguises. Since, in public, she almost always wore her long hair drawn back tightly in a chignon, she would let it down to cover the sides of her face before knotting it to her nape. And today she would not bind her chest. She knew from experience that if she wore the right dress, most men wouldn't waste much attention on her face anyway.

There was one brief item of business before she made her much-anticipated, much-dreaded visit to Wall Street. She wrote a brief note to Helzer, Paul's fence, requesting a meeting about "an object of unusually high quality." Then she went searching for Hush.

It was still early, not quite eight A.M., and Paul had not yet come down for his papers and coffee. Mystere found Hush out back in the carriage house, which was merely a stable with a few stalls knocked out. By arbitrary decree of Baylis, it was the lad's job to take care of the team, carriage, and tack.

"Good morning, Hush," she greeted him after angling between the open doors. "Are you too busy to do me a favor?"

He was kneeling beside a front wheel of the carriage, smearing grease on the hub. Hush gaped when he saw her, for she literally looked like a new woman. And the light garden dress of cream-color cotton—he had never seen her with her breasts unrestrained, she realized, and the sheer material only emphasized the change.

Slowly he put down the grease pail and stood up. "Mystere?"

She laughed. "Who else would I be?"

"Well, it's your voice, anyhow, that ain't changed."

His prolonged stare made her uncomfortable. "I have a face, too," she reminded him, and he flushed slightly, raising his glance.

She handed him the note, sealed in a blank envelope. "Would you please take this to Mr. Jerome Helzer at Helzer's Salvage Yard on Water Street? It must go to him personally. And then you must wait for his reply. It would be a great favor to me, Hush."

"Shoot, you can't ask *me* for favors," he scoffed, still sneaking peeks at her full bosom. "I'll go right now."

"*Thank* you. Here's some money for the omnibus. If Paul is cranky with you when you get back, just tell him . . . tell him I sent you out to drop off some shoes for repairing."

They both left the stable together, Hush banging the doors shut and securing the latch.

"Mystere?" he said before they headed their separate ways on Great Jones Street.

"Yes?"

"I won't ask where you're goin' nor nothing, but—you gonna be okay?"

"I'll be fine," she assured him even as another tickling spasm of nervous fear made her worry she might not be up to this visit. So much weighed on her mind, and she was so desperate to answer some vexing questions. And there was always the very real risk that her visit today would blow up in her face, exposing the tangled web of lies and deceptions for all to see.

Thus preoccupied, she commanded Baylis to get the carriage, hardly aware that the first great, splattering drops of rain were falling. When the downpour began in earnest she rued not grabbing an umbrella.

Her letter, at least, would remain safe inside her leather handbag.

During the ride to Wall Street she tried to make herself more presentable, but she shivered despite the morning's balmy temperature. It wasn't just the damp air that chilled her. The tightrope she had been walking for some time was becoming infinitely more dangerous. If her visit to the lawyers somehow became public, the results could be catastrophic. Paul, always unpredictable, was capable of any desperate act if he felt cornered. And Caroline, while perhaps more predictable, was just as dangerous in her own way.

The rain slacked off as the carriage turned east on Wall Street, bearing toward the river. But she could not shake the memory of Caroline's eyes, glinting like new, hard steel, as she seemed to reveal to Rafe and Mystere the chilling suspicion that *she*, too, had guessed the truth about Lady Moonlight's true identity.

How or why she had guessed was irrelevant now, although Mystere had a hunch it began with that shocking scene in Rafe's drawing room. Caroline must have put her considerable intelligence to the baffling puzzle of Mystere's chest bindings, and that clue would have led to others. Including Caroline's inevitable conclusion that Paul must be the mastermind of a great hoax.

With the wisdom born of ceaseless calculation, Caroline had so far revealed no outward sign of strain between herself and Paul. But Mystere knew that was just cosmetic to save the precious "respectability" of the Old Guard. Paul would, indeed, be "cut" socially, but probably not until after the September wedding Caroline was determined to force. This kind of scandal, since Mrs. Astor herself had championed the Rillieuxs, could stain her and the Four Hundred indelibly.

And that, Mystere told herself, was the greatest irony of all. For Rafe was planning to foment just such a scandal—planning, too, to lock horns with Caroline in a final death struggle—and it appeared that Caroline had begun to sense his true intentions.

"Commerce Building, Madame," Baylis taunted, wheels sending up a little swell of water as the conveyance pulled up at the curb.

She allowed him to disembark and help her to the curb. Becoming drenched, she turned to face the four-story office building with its lancet-arched windows and Gothic-style gargoyles.

Her legs refused, at first, to take that first marble step. She felt the annoyance of those on the busy sidewalk, forced to steer around her.

"For Bram," she whispered, and moments later, soaked and scared, she found strength to hurry up the steps.

"And what concern is it to you," demanded the stern-faced man who had finally come to the counter to talk with her, "whether or not Mr. Sheridan's lawyer is available?"

This man was around thirty, better dressed than the half dozen clerks in eyeshades and sleeve garters who were busy in the big central office behind the counter. Typewriters rang and banged all around her, and she had to raise her voice to be heard.

"Are you an attorney?" she inquired politely, for he had not even had the decency to introduce himself.

"That's none of your concern," he snapped, and she noticed how his vandyke beard made him look like a devil. "Just state your business here."

Her wet clothing felt even colder now, a clammy, chilling pressure that made it difficult to control her trembling. Now it was time to actually say it, and she felt utterly foolish.

"I'm trying to find out," she replied as bravely as she could with Baylis waiting across the room, out of earshot, "if perhaps Mr. Sheridan might have some knowledge about my family."

"Why? Do you think he's a public genealogist?"

"Of course not. But my famil—"

"And just which family might that be? Oh, but don't tell me," the clerk or whatever he was mocked, "you don't really *know* your surname, is that it?"

Heat leaped into her face. The man had deliberately raised his voice so those working nearby could overhear.

"Actually, that's . . . that's right," she managed.

"Yes, and what you'd *really* like to know," he continued, ruthless mirth glinting in his unblinking gray eyes, "is whether or not you're related to either Mr. Sheridan or his sister's Granville line?"

"Perhaps not related," she qualified, "but in some way linked. You see, I have a letter. . . ."

Before she could open her purse, however, the man exclaimed loudly, "Say, fellows! This one has a *letter.* Now that's a different matter, hey?"

Howls of derisive laughter momentarily replaced the typewriter noises. Her adversary stood behind the long wooden counter that kept visitors out of the working office. He banged open a drawer, then thumped a thick stack of correspondence down on the counter in front of her.

"We have perhaps fifty or so letters of our own right here," he retorted. "And these are only those we've collected. Care to add yours to the heap?"

He riffled quickly through the stack, and she felt her heart plummet when she realized at least half the letters were written under the Granville crest.

"Your confidence game is old," the man assured her harshly. "It's not just the house of Granville—every established family of the aristocracy is deluged with greedy, lazy claimants."

Only now did she become fully aware of the way he, and others in the office, were staring at her soaked form. She had been too preoccupied and nervous, at first, to think about the physical picture she must present. A thin dress, with only a chemise and slip beneath, all soaked clear through—and those bright, unshaded electric lights suspended from the ceiling cast a cruelly clear view of her . . . *much* of her, she realized as the men's eyes seemed to touch her like probing hands.

"I make no claims whatsoever," she insisted. "But if I might have just a brief appointment with—"

"Bother your appointment," the man cut her off impatiently. "I assure you that Mr. Sheridan wants nothing to do with your inquiries. Just because a man is wealthy, and his sister has married well, does not mean he's related to every gold digger who ever sailed to America in steerage class."

"She thought that fine figger would open doors," jeered a

clerk. "Deliberately came in here soaking wet, she did, to get us all het up. So I say let's take 'er back in the storeroom and show 'er *our* 'roots.' "

His filthy pun evoked a chorus of taunts and laughter.

"It's far easier to sponge off the rich than to earn your way; that's how so many of you comely young wenches think," the man assured her. "Now get the hell out of here before I have you arrested."

Crushed, she hadn't even had a chance to show them her letter before a uniformed doorman hustled her out onto the sidewalk again. She was gone so quickly Baylis didn't even see her leave.

The rain had stopped, but a gray pallor filled the sky, and everything seemed to be dripping. Wall Street looked ugly and cold, dirty puddles covering it like pockmarks. A trolley lumbered past, the big dray horse marked by deep girth galls and open sores. She could not only read the resigned misery in the horse's eyes, but at that moment she felt a deep affinity with the hopeless creature.

At first, so devastated and emotionally drained, she could manage no other reaction than to start dumbly walking. Her newfound freedom from Baylis should have been embraced, but she felt nothing except loneliness and despair. She headed northwest on Wall Street toward the spire of Trinity Church a few blocks ahead. With each lapsed second, however, she realized how completely her hopes had been dashed, how utterly common and foolish she had looked in that office. *Say, fellows! She has a letter.*

For far too long now she had borne so many troubles in silence, kept her heartfelt hopes and dreams to herself. But the miserable failure at Sheridan's office was the final straw, the death of her hopes. Right now she needed to share her misery with someone, anyone who might care. The one person, in fact, who knew all of it.

A cab discharged a fare just ahead of her, and Mystere called out to the driver, bidding him wait. It was only a few blocks around the corner on Broadway to her destination, but suddenly she didn't want to waste any time getting there. She hurried forward and took the driver's hand as he helped her into the passenger compartment beneath his high seat.

"Where to, ma'am?"

"The Astor House Hotel," she replied, a new tone of resolution in her voice.

She savored this new feeling of actually wanting Rafe's company for a change. Of course, she must not let desperate hope cloud her vision. But it seemed to her that he was her friend, though he wouldn't call himself that. It also appeared to her as if he was somewhat indecisive about his reckless plans, and she was secretly praying he would change his mind.

Despite her terrible setback at Sheridan's office, she had decided to remain hopeful that disaster was not imminent. Rafe could well be right about Paul—the Breaux letter may have served notice without forcing a crisis.

Ultimately, to be sure, it hardly mattered. She must flee New York before Rafe, friend or not, was forced into a dangerous marriage with her. And perhaps her disappearance, its subsequent shock to the Four Hundred, would accomplish all Rafe's plans for him—a fitting ironic end to this turbulent episode of her life.

Right now, however, as the cab turned in toward the curb in front of the hotel, Mystere found herself hoping Rafe was there, for she had neither desire nor courage to visit his corporate offices. The need to talk, to be held and kissed to the point of sweet oblivion, seemed to pulse in every cell of her being.

She paid the driver and turned toward the big revolving front door of the hotel. She was cold and wet and looked no better than a beggar from the streets, but somehow she prayed she could find him. Suddenly he seemed very much like a kind of salvation, and she desperately wanted to be saved.

She was perhaps ten paces from the door when Rafe suddenly emerged as if coughed out by the building. Their eyes locked in the next instant.

A hopeful smile pulled at her lips; a fractional second later, however, Antonia Butler spun out the door right behind him, linking her arm through Rafe's, and Mystere felt all the misery of her life suddenly pinpointed to that moment.

Chapter 32

Rafe watched the beginning of a smile part her expressive lips, watched the first gleam of joy in her eyes as Mystere recognized him. He was still looking moments later when she spotted Antonia. The smile wilted in a heartbeat, and Mystere turned abruptly away, recklessly dodging traffic as she crossed Broadway and escaped into City Hall Park.

Damnit, he thought, on the verge of chasing her. But already Antonia, who evidently hadn't seen Mystere, was trying to engage him in more of her tiresome, "clever," thinly veiled sexual banter. And why not, for he had just spent the past hour or so playing along with it himself.

He ignored it now, however, still watching Mystere's retreating figure. At first he had not been sure it was she, so wildly weather mussed was she, so frankly provocative in her damp clothing and literally unrestrained beauty. But those forget-me-not eyes had been unmistakable.

Of all the damned rotten luck, he cursed mentally. All his efforts to create a shocking impression, and look who took the brunt of it. And most irritating of all, the fact that he had found himself unexpectedly bound to Mystere's crushed feelings.

Antonia repeated something, her tone offended, and he realized she was waiting for his response.

"What?" he asked somewhat brusquely.

She stopped in her tracks, tugging him to an abrupt halt also.

" 'What?' " she mimicked his absent interrogative. "You haven't been listening to me at all, have you, Rafe Belloch?"

"Of course I have," he insisted with the rote conviction of a parrot.

"You have not, and it's as obvious as clown makeup," she accused. "Suddenly your unique sense of daring adventure seems more like a standard guilty conscience."

"That right?" he replied absently. He was so distracted that he added with unintended honesty, "You don't say anything anyway."

She frowned, and with good reason, for it was he who had initiated their insipid seduction ritual.

"I don't . . . ?" Antonia's flirtatious pique suddenly became real anger. Her pretty face had the tendency to distort itself into a vengeful mask when she was offended. *"You* called me, Rafe, remember? It was your idea to be 'boldly bohemian,' not mine."

"I'll never accuse you of ideas," Rafe promised, his tone so mild he only confused her more. He continued to ignore the woman at his side and everything else except Mystere, disappearing behind a tall hedgerow.

Sam Farrell had been right, Rafe thought, he could, indeed, wear Mrs. Astor's scorn as a badge of honor. But not, he was devastated to learn now, Mystere's.

He made up his mind and reached for his wallet, pulling a banknote out and tucking it into Antonia's hand.

"I'd loan you my carriage," he explained as he extracted his arm from hers, "but I may have need of it. You'll have no trouble finding a cab. Please excuse me, something's come up."

Antonia's jaw fell open in astonishment at his manners, but Rafe was off in the next moment, eliciting curses from drivers as he tore across Broadway with as little heed as Mystere had paid.

Rafe skidded round the hedgerow and caught up with a sodden Mystere just before she reached the Chambers Street exit.

"Mystere! Wait up a moment!"

Even swept up in the turmoil of her distraught emotions, she couldn't help realizing he had called her by her real name—something he usually did only for the benefit of others.

"You must have finished with Antonia," she flung at him as she quickened her step, "to part so suddenly now."

He was faster, sprinting in front of her to block a narrow gate in the iron fence surrounding the park.

"It's not what you think," he protested.

"I agree—it's what you *are*. Let me pass."

"No, not until you let me explain. We merely had coffee and dessert in the hotel restaurant. We did not go upstairs." He frowned and added, "Not that it's technically any of your damned business."

"I never said it was. Now let me pass, I said!"

"You little fool, I set all this up to cause a buzz of scandal, don't you see? To push Caroline, for I knew it would get back to her, which it will. Perhaps has already."

"And that makes it all acceptable?" she demanded, wide-eyed with outrage. Hot anger knotted her insides. "You know full well Lance Streeter and that blood-sucking pack of scandalmongers will make a public fuss over it. So what if our engagement is a sham; the public accepts it as real. And what you've done today will humiliate *me* more than anyone else. You swore you had no plan to destroy me."

He shook his head. "Wrong, you're all wrong. You speak

of the public, but to them a provincial morality has no place in the sinful city. It's Caroline who will seethe, for it shows that her tight reins are slipping."

"Oh, you make me ill, Rafe, do you know that? The masses this, Mrs. Astor that . . . you and Abbot really are alike. It's Mrs. Astor's closed world versus the steaming dung-heap, and you seem determined to show her the dung-heap is winning. But where's the victory in being right?"

Rafe was not used to being concilliatory. But neither could he deny that for the moment at least, she had him dead to rights.

"I see your side of it," he conceded, "and you're right, to a point. I've sunk to some base tactics, granted. But look at my side of it. For the price of high tea, and a couple hours of boredom with Antonia, I can outrage my enemy. With no actual transgression, I have upped the ante in my contest of wills with Caroline."

"Fine. Then, why are you here now, blocking my path, once again trapping me? Why aren't you still with Miss Horse Grin, creating your precious 'impression of sin'?"

"Because of that look you gave me a few minutes ago, that's why. It felt like I'd been knifed. The question really is—why were you coming to my hotel?"

A sudden blush was only part of her answer, but the best part, judging from his smile.

"I . . . I went to Sheridan's office this morning," she explained, rubbing the rain from her miserable sodden face.

"I thought you might. And . . . ?"

Her chin trembled for a moment before she got control of herself and replied, "It was a disaster. I did manage to protect my identity, I think, but they laughed to my face, and who could blame them?"

His eyes traveled the length of her, from sodden hair to well-turned ankles. Her limp, soaked dress only made her tangled hair seem even wilder. The dinted fabric of the thin cotton bodice clearly marked her nipples. "Beauty Unbound," he remarked with a smile through the rain.

"I look horrid," she retorted stubbornly.

"Wrong. You look uncivilized and insatiable . . . really quite fetching." He kissed her wet nose. "Tell me, what do we do now? Sit and play a harp?"

"Don't you already have Antonia to entertain?"

"Nope. I was rude with her, now it's your turn."

"Well, I'm used to your rudeness. But I'll tell you this much," she rallied in a burst of defiant indignation, "I'm *not* going into that hotel with you now. Not after you've just been there playing kissy-face with her."

"Fine by me. How's this for a plan? The sun's due back out. I'll take you by your place so you can change into some dry things. Then we'll both play hooky and go for a little cruise up the Hudson. How 'bout it?"

Actually, she thought, it was a wonderful idea. She needed a respite from the close, crowded, frenetic world of Manhattan. And even if it was only self-delusion, only his lust masquerading as affection, she also needed attention, comforting. . . .

"Only one stipulation," he added. "When you change— don't wear those damned binding cloths."

Her eyes fled from his, but she nodded. "If you think you can control yourself."

"Hell, I won't even try. But I'm sure you'll manage to do that."

Their eyes met and held.

Together they both laughed.

While Mystere changed into dry clothing and brushed out the wild, tangled thatch of her hair, Rafe telephoned his yacht crew at their Manhattan slip and told them to ready the *Courageous Kate* for cruising.

The steam turbines were at full capacity by the time Rafe and Mystere arrived, and within minutes the yacht was already tacking around the Battery, bearing north through City Harbor into the mouth of the Hudson, while Rafe gave her a quick tour of the sleek craft.

Mystere was especially impressed by the luxury and quality of the master stateroom, with its gold velvet curtains and compact stove with nickel trimmings. An onboard generator powered by the engines provided electric lights throughout the yacht.

They both finally settled near the bow, leaning against the gunnel to watch the city gradually dwindle into rural pastures as they steamed farther north. Grassy banks teeming with timothy and clover marked the New Jersey shore, from which fishermen idly waved at them. Simply by turning her back, Mystere could pretend there was no city at all. The sun was stuck high in the sky as if pegged there, and to her it felt good burning on her neck and shoulders, comforting to feel its weight.

As the smoky, clamorous city receded farther behind them, a kind of lazy peace settled over her. Rafe was in a different mood, too, and hadn't been sniping at her as usual but actually conversing with her.

"Who's the original Courageous Kate?" she asked him. "Some beauty you squired until she broke your heart?"

"No, but in a sense she is my sweetheart. She's a brave little girl out west who saved one of our trains after a trestle washed out. Crossed a raging river in pitch-black darkness to flag down the approaching train. Just fifteen years old when it happened and she's become a heroine to railroad men everywhere."

"A heroine," Mystere repeated with thoughtful softness. "So unlike the Lady Moonlight. The difference between fame and infamy."

He studied her in silence, seemingly transfixed by her in that moment. She had brushed out her long, coffee-colored hair but left it free to cascade down over her back and shoulders. Sunlight spun a golden crown on her head.

"That difference," he suggested, "is perhaps less clearly defined than we think."

She wasn't sure if the odd contortion of his mouth was meant as a smile. She only knew that she was drawn to him, suddenly kissing his harsh lips with a burning passion even hotter than the July sun.

"I admit it," she confessed in a voice just above a whisper. "Sometimes I dread thinking of the time when you won't be with me."

Stop now, an inner voice warned her. *Do not ruin this closeness, even if it's illusory, because even a temporary illusion is better than a cold, lonely, dangerous existence without comfort, without the intimate touch of this man.*

He kissed her, beginning with her mouth and then tasting the soft skin of her throat, his lips causing an electric response that made her shudder.

"We don't need to think about that now," he whispered close to her ear. "The day's waning now. Come back with me to Staten Island—for the night, I mean."

She remained silent for some time, watching the river part before the prow of the yacht in a white curl. The silent lull became painful, then excruciating.

As if to break it, or perhaps to remind her, he moved the hand that was resting on her left hip—moved it up to caress her breast.

"Rafe," she protested at his shocking frankness, but without any effort to pull away from him.

"Shall I tell Skeels to head back to Staten Island now?"

She looked up into his teal gaze, shading her eyes from the sun.

"Yes," she surrendered, tired of the battles and the threats, tired of fighting her attraction to him.

Soon she would have to flee from everything and everyone she knew, flee from the known and familiar into an un-

known future fraught with dangers. But tonight, at least, she
would seize a few hours of happiness in Rafe Belloch's bed,
knowing that in the morning, if she was smart, she would
take her chance to be free from Rillieux and disappear forever.

Chapter 33

The sun had burned down to dying embers on the western horizon by the time the *Courageous Kate* was moored in her Staten Island berth.

"Hungry?" Rafe asked her as the two of them walked, arm in arm, toward the massive gates of his Garden Cove estate.

"Famished," she admitted, realizing she had eaten nothing since breakfast, and then only coffee and a croissant. "Well, this does feel odd," she added, smiling up at him in the grainy twilight.

"What does?"

"You asking me such innocent questions, and look—for a change you aren't tugging me along like I'm a bad child. I'm actually walking beside you of my own volition."

"You sound disappointed. Would you prefer to be forced?"

His tone was playful, but the double entendre did not escape her.

"Force," she replied, "does relieve one of responsibility. But I prefer being the ruler of my own fate."

"'Choices,' some sage once said, 'are the hinges of destiny.'"

"Yes," she almost whispered, for Rafe had no idea how true his words sounded in her ears. Her own destiny had reached a fork in the road, and very soon now she had to make the hard decision which turn to take. Both directions were crowded with danger, but for tonight, she vowed, she would think no more about it. Even though Rafe did not love her, and probably never could, she would settle for lies. She wanted to stop worrying about everything, to feel pleasure and closeness and warmth, to feel wanted and needed instead of always being used, hunted, and afraid.

"It's just us, Jimmy," Rafe said as they reached the gate in near darkness. "After we're in, run round to Milly's quarters, will you, and ask her to prepare a light supper for two. She needn't cook."

"Will do, boss."

"Oh, and then run down to the wine cellar, would you, and bring up a bottle of . . . burgundy, I guess."

The heavy iron gates groaned as Jimmy swung them open, then shut again. Mystere felt his eyes taking her measure, and she blushed unseen, suddenly wondering how many times the handsome Rafe Belloch had brought home a wench to bed. But she mustered her newfound resolve and chased off such thoughts. *Never mind grim reality,* she thought. *Just for tonight you live in a fairy-tale world, and you'll write your own happy ending.*

While the cook prepared their meal, Rafe and Mystere sipped wine in the front parlor.

She wandered about the room, studying framed photographs from a happier time in Rafe's life. To augment the meager candlelight, he built a small fire. It glowed blood orange behind an embroidered fire screen, and he silently studied Mystere in the flattering light. She studied him right back.

"I see where you got your good looks," she commented, nodding toward a photo on the mantel. "Your parents were a handsome couple."

"I always thought so, too," he replied, his tone more wistful than bitter. "And although not publicly demonstrative, they were very much in love. The years never seemed to diminish that."

Despite her newfound resolve, his poignant words stabbed at her heart.

"Rafe?"

"Hmm?"

"What do you plan on doing about Caroline's ultimatum? The September wedding date, I mean?"

"Don't worry about September," he dismissed her in a matter-of-fact tone. "Things will come to a head before then."

That reply only raised more questions. But just then Milly appeared in the doorway to announce that their meal was already laid out in the dining room.

They both enjoyed a light repast of sandwiches, cheese, and fresh fruit, Mystere reveling in their peaceful, enjoyable conversation. She had never seen this side of Rafe, or realized he could be so personable and authentically charming. For a hard-hearted man of empire he certainly seemed well read in poetry and the classics, and spoke with enthusiasm about the novels of the expatriate American Henry James.

"But to hell with James," he said abruptly, watching her in a way that made her stomach flutter nervously. "Let's go upstairs. I want to show you something quite beautiful."

Carrying a three-branch candelabra to light their way, he led her up the magnificent central staircase with the turned balustrade. The master bedroom occupied a northeast-facing wing. He set the candelabra on a bureau near the door and led her by the hand across the big room to a wide expanse of full-length windows.

"This house sits on high ground," he explained as he tugged the sheer lace curtains and brocade overdrapery apart. "You can't fully appreciate the view until after dark."

Mystere very nearly gasped at the startling, magnificent beauty of Manhattan lit by gas and electricity after dark.

Lights glittered like millions of stars across the dark expanse of the Upper Bay.

Rafe drew back the latches and opened the casements, and she felt the balmy night wind caressing her face like exploring fingers.

He stood close behind her, arms encircling her, chin resting on her head as they gazed for some minutes in silence, absorbed in the vista spread out before them like some grand diorama.

"There's no ugliness or suffering in this view of it," she finally remarked softly. "I wish I could always see the city from here, like this."

"Then, time stops here, tonight," he replied, kissing the side of her neck, then turning her to face him and pulling her close to kiss her mouth.

"Yes," she agreed in bittersweet surrender. "And the only world we'll have is the world we'll make."

He led her across the room to a mahogany poster bed with an arched canopy. When she modestly stepped behind a two-panel dressing screen near the bed, Rafe protested.

"No. I want to watch you disrobe just as I did that night in the drawing room."

"Is it an order this time, too?"

"No. A request."

"Then, you shall have your wish."

He kicked off his shoes and removed his shirt and vest, now bare to the waist. She already knew he was strong, but the hard, sloping pectorals and flat-as-a-board stomach took her again by pleasant surprise. In the gaslight, muscle wrapped his shoulders like taut steel cables.

He sat at the foot of the bed, watching in rapt fascination as she left her clothing in a pile at her feet. This time, however, she did not feel a burning shame, only a mounting heat that felt very different from shame.

"Turn around slowly," he told her when she stood naked, studying her figure bathed in soft light.

She did, watching desire transform his face, his own excitment fueling hers. He stood up and lifted his arms, a silent beckoning that drew her closer with magnetic power. When her bare breasts met his muscular torso, a groan escaped both of them simultaneously.

The tenderness of his kiss quickly heated to a greedy, needful hunger. The fact that they were both worlds apart and at each other's throats over everything from a robbery to a forced marriage seemed trivial to Mystere now. They had spent too much time battling.

Time stops here.

The phrase reverberated through her mind like a poem.

Rafe picked her up easily in both arms and carried her to the bed, laying her down on the silk sheets and then kneeling beside the bed to kiss and tease her nipples. Mystere gasped as he took first one, then the other into his mouth, knowing just exactly how much light pressure with his teeth would stoke her desire even hotter.

He caressed her body until she felt like she was burning up from within.

"Be with me now," she urged in a breathless whisper, tugging at him.

He stood up and pulled off his trousers, and she thrilled at the forbidden sight of his arousal. As he lay beside her she murmured in his ear, "I want you inside me."

He slid one hand high up the inside of her thighs, and she moaned at the pleasurable contact as his fingers spread her open like the petals of a dewy flower.

Only for a few brief moments, as he first entered her, was she again aware of his size. But the pleasure far outweighed any pain, and once he had slowly, carefully penetrated her to his full length, she felt herself opening to him, adjusting; and a blessed cry of pleasure rose from her when he began moving harder, faster.

He surprised her again as a lover, forceful and commanding, yes, but also tender and passionate, as eager to give pleasure as he was to receive. Again and again he took her with him to peaks of ecstasy, her insatiable need matching his own. Behind them, beyond the open windows, the lights of Manhattan winked out as the night edged toward midnight and then far beyond.

She wasn't sure precisely when the words "I love you" began to rise from her throat to her lips, but somehow she managed to stifle them. Even though she now realized it was true—not just the passion of the moment—she also realized it mustn't be. Not only because he didn't love her, but because this night must be their last.

Finally, exhausted and depleted, they dozed off together in a sleepy tangle of naked limbs. Mystere dreamt she was a great lady riding in a coach bearing the Granville coat of arms, with Rafe seated on one side of her, a smiling Bram on the other.

But then everything turned all wrong. Bram's handsome features melted, metamorphosed into Paul's fox face, laughing savagely at her, and when she turned to Rafe for help, he had become a horned, Satanic version of Mrs. Astor, who shrieked at her with demonic joy: *What about bub 'n' sis now, you filthy little thief?*

It was the sound of birds celebrating sunup that woke Mystere from her fitful rest.

The windows still stood wide open, and a cool, steady wind blew in off the bay, making her shiver a little when she peeled the covers back. Rafe still slept deeply beside her, even more handsome in repose, for his features showed no sign of his usual scorn for the world at large. The bed was a shambles from the force of their passion, which had pulled the sheets loose and even tugged the feather mattress partway off the bed.

She felt a pleasant soreness between her legs when she carefully, silently disentangled her legs from his. She kissed him once on the lips, very gently, before she got out of bed and began gathering up her clothing.

She dressed before the open windows, the breeze making gooseflesh on her skin while she watched the eastern horizon begin to glow salmon pink with the new day's sunrise. Already she could see the first ferry loading below at the public slip, and she hurried so she could catch it.

When she turned and saw Rafe lying there, however, she almost lost her courage. It would be so easy to just deny and postpone, crawl back in that warm bed with him . . . but no, *no,* she commanded herself with a merciless sense of purpose. That was the easy way now, perhaps, but by staying she would only endure the pain of watching all of it be destroyed.

Caroline Astor and Paul both expected a wedding, for different reasons, and either one of them was potentially dangerous; Paul if the wedding did happen, Caroline if it didn't. And Rafe was the most troublesome of the three.

If he did by some unlucky chance marry her, it would be a loveless match against his wishes; or he might sabotage everything in his implacable vengeance quest. No matter what, her best chance to remain free and search for Bram lay in flight. Especially now that her disastrous visit to Sheridan's office had convinced her she and Bram had no logical connection to the house of Granville. It was pointless to remain in New York any longer, pointless and dangerous.

Yesterday, when Rafe took her home to change into a dress of light French muslin, Hush had given her Helzer's reply to her note. She was to meet with him later today about the ring. With luck, she would only need to hide in her room on Centre Street for a few days at most.

She finished dressing and quickly located paper, a steel nib, and a pot of ink in the console table by the door. She left a brief note for Rafe, casting one long look back at him from the doorway.

The room suddenly seemed to melt as tears sprang from

her eyes, and the constricting pain in her throat felt like a
nail had lodged there. *You must leave him,* her mind admonished. *This hurt now is nothing compared to what's in store if
you stay. Paul's desperation, Caroline's pride, Rafe's vengeful-
ness—all of it will crush you unless you disappear.*

Then, vowing never to look back again, she left the man
she now realized she loved and went forth to confront an un-
certain destiny.

"God*damn* it," Rafe muttered, doing a slow boil as he
read the short message Mystere had left on the bureau for
him. She had taken no time to blot it, and some of the letters
had smeared, but it was readable.

> *I've gone forever and I beg you not to search
> for me. It's far better this way. Thank you for last
> night. You made it easy for me to pretend you
> love me.*

And in a final show of rebellious spirit that brought a bitter twist to his lips, she had signed it, *Lady Moonlight.*

For a few minutes, as he hurriedly dressed, Rafe was almost wild with fury at her. He was a man accustomed to
calling the shots, to being in complete control, and when it
came to women, it was *he* who did the rejecting, not they.

But as his anger began to subside, a cold, gnawing worry
rushed in to take its place. Despite his claims, he had not
protected her secret from Mrs. Astor, and scared those inept
blackmailers away, simply to retain control of events. It wasn't
just a matter of control, of his bruised male pride—the woman
he had taken into his arms last night, that demure little beauty
who had become such a passionate firebrand, was the one
woman in all the world to match him. He knew he *must* find
her before she could get too far away.

It's your fault she couldn't sign her name Mystere, he thought with bitter honesty. *You hardly ever used her name. . . .*

The search for her wouldn't be easy, not with her survival knowledge of the streets. He would have to have help, but he would find the men he needed. He was, after all, the man who moved mountains. He would find her, even if it meant moving heaven and earth.

Chapter 34

"In summation, gentlemen, the decision to consolidate all of our Midwestern short lines is now final. This will entail a radical reorganization at the management level, and the current system with seventeen field managers will be revised into a system with three regional supervisors located in Detroit, Cincinnati, and Omaha."

Rafe's clear, steady, strong voice easily filled the big meeting room where almost thirty executives of Belloch Enterprises sat around a long, rectangular table of polished oak. It was just past ten A.M., and the meeting was nearing the end of its second hour.

Although concise and well organized, Rafe looked tired, seemed at times distracted. Sam Farrell, seated at one end of the table, saw his boss impatiently consulting his watch every few minutes.

Rafe started to speak again. But suddenly a commotion could be heard out in the anteroom, a woman's voice protesting with forceful authority.

"I don't care if Jesus Christ is in there with his disciples. I said I *will* see Rafe Belloch and I'll see him right now!"

The doors flew open to admit a glowering Caroline Astor,

Ward scuttling beside her like a general's aide-de-camp. He carried a beautiful rosewood case under one arm. Two of Belloch Enterprises' private guards trailed them, shrugging their apologies at Rafe.

"She said we'd have to shoot her to stop her," one of them offered, his tone embarrassed.

"You missed your chance, boys," Rafe muttered, aware that all the men now assembled were staring in open-mouthed astonishment. The few who didn't recognize this intrusive female were quickly informed it was *the* Mrs. Astor.

"Gentlemen," she called out in her most magisterial manner, "I must ask all of you to leave the room. I have some private words for Mr. Belloch, and they will not wait."

The room went as silent as a lecture hall after a call for volunteers. All eyes shifted from Mrs. Astor to their corporate chief. Never had Rafe so acutely felt the weight of leadership as he did now. But it was Sam's quick diplomacy that saved him.

"Fellows," Sam suggested, rising from his chair, "we could all use a break anyway. I, for one, have no doubt that Mrs. Astor must have urgent business, or she'd not be here now. So let's adjourn until further notice."

"Thank you, sir," she responded with formal politeness. "And would you remain behind?" she asked Sam.

He glanced at Rafe, who shrugged and nodded permission. The moment the room was empty except for the four of them, Caroline got right to the point Rafe was expecting.

"Have you *seen* the newspapers, you unprincipled scoundrel?" she demanded.

"No," he replied flatly. "I've been busy."

"Not too busy for your little performance with Antonia yesterday, though, were you?"

"Coffee and napoleons?" he protested. "Where's the scandal in that?"

"You *are* vile, Rafe. You are a Patriarch of the Four Hundred, formally engaged, and you knew perfectly well how your actions would be interpreted."

"Oh? Has there been some mention?" he asked with galling innocence.

"Mention?" she repeated, outrage deepening her already stern voice. "The gossip writers are all squealing with glee over your apparent rejection of propriety. And since I've 'championed' your engagement, they're calling it the revenge of Father Knickerbocker."

Despite her outrage, Rafe liked the dig and barely managed to keep his face sober.

"What would they be writing instead, Caroline," he asked her quietly, "if you had seduced me as you once planned to?"

Sam, who had remained standing because Mrs. Astor did, looked astounded, a rare reaction for him. Ward turned white, no doubt in fear as he anticipated Caroline's reaction.

For a moment her anger was so severe that she visibly trembled. But in seconds her iron will asserted itself again, and a cool sense of determination was clear in her voice. "Ward, bring me the case."

She looked at Rafe. "All right, you want to be blunt, do you? Then allow me to play along. You have accused me of killing your parents. If you truly believe that, then honor requires you to kill *me.*"

Caroline lifted the lid of the felt-lined case.

Rafe stared at two handsome dueling pistols with ornate ivory and silver inlays. The initials W. B. A. were inscribed on the butts.

"My husband's family heirlooms," she explained needlessly. "And no, he doesn't know I took them."

"Am I to murder you in cold blood?" Rafe inquired, keeping a straight face only with effort. "Or are you challenging me to a duel?"

"Why not a duel? I know the rules. I have my second, you have yours, so it'll be properly witnessed. We can easily take ten paces in this huge room. Isn't that how 'offended' gentlemen such as yourself settle serious matters?"

"Caroline, you're showing your age. Dueling is illegal; we let lawyers fight our battles these days."

"Illegal? Come now! So is aiding and abetting a thief, Mr. Belloch, but laws haven't stopped you from keeping Mystere's secret, have they?"

Rafe wanted to laugh, yet her intensity intimidated him. She removed one pistol and held it out to him, offering it butt first.

"Take it," she demanded. "I believe you'll find it's properly loaded and primed. I will not have my name constantly dragged through the mud because you nurture a grudge. *Take* it, Rafe. If I killed your father, then shoot me for it. Or I'll shoot you, whichever the outcome."

"Caroline, don't—"

"You can't scare me, Rafe, nor make me feel guilty for your father's cowardice. So shoot me—it's your only alternative."

Rafe took the pistol, but he also snatched the case away from Caroline. He put the gun away and handed the case to Sam.

"Ward, for heaven's sake," Caroline snapped, suddenly offering him support for he seemed on the verge of fainting.

"I'll be outside with the others," Sam excused himself, seeing that his services would not be required.

Rafe paced a little in silence, feeling Caroline's eyes on him the entire time. It was she who spoke first after she had helped Ward into a chair.

"You're going to stop this vicious little game you're playing, Rafe. And there *will* be a wedding by the end of September. One more trick like the one you played yesterday with Antonia, and I'll destroy you, Rafe Belloch, one way or another. Bullet or bankruptcy."

"That's nice, Caroline," he replied wearily, still too preoccupied with thoughts and images of Mystere to care much about anything else. But oddly, Caroline's melodrama with the pistols had somehow eliminated his desire to destroy the matron. For in the depths of her willful anger and offended dignity, he saw the same class fanaticism that had destroyed his own father.

I've not been up against any individual villain, he realized, *despite focusing all my resentment on Caroline—it's an outmoded way of life I'm up against, and it's already in its death throes.*

All these years he had lived to kill a chimera that existed only in the mind. And thanks to his myopic spite, the best thing that had ever happened to him was, even now, fleeing from his life forever.

"Actually, Caroline," he said after a minute, "you're partly right. My father did show a moment of cowardice at the end. No one murdered him, death was his choice, and to that extent I've harbored an illogical grudge. But you'll never convince me he wasn't wronged, after his death, by those who owed him better treatment. Yourself included."

Mrs. Astor softened a little at this image of him, so brilliant and virile and good-looking . . . and unattainable.

"Perhaps, after all, we did wrong you somewhat," she relented.

"Not I, my parents."

"Yes, well, the pronoun isn't important. My point is that you're a fool. You are obviously in love with Mystere or whoever she really is; and yet you've been prepared to destroy her just to vent a childish spite."

He took her words in silence, for she had him dead to rights.

Her voice became more reasonable. "The whole secret to survival, Rafe, is to simply deflect pain and move on. You *re*flect too much. Self-absorption in one's own misery is a prerogative of the middle classes only, not we who are their social betters. I was hoping Mystere would help you see that."

Mystere . . . Rafe knew that Mrs. Astor couldn't possibly have learned yet that she had run away, gone into hiding. If it was scandal Caroline dreaded, then the lid would definitely blow off when Mystere's absence was noticed. In fact, Rafe suddenly realized, suspicion would center on him, the last person to be with her.

"Oh, don't misunderstand me," Caroline added. "Of course it knocked me sick and silly when I finally surmised who, and what, she must be. Of course the public must not find out or we'll all become laughingstocks. But I don't care if she's the Whore of Babylon; I *like* the girl."

Rafe nodded. "I know that. You've always been fond of her."

"One cannot help it; she's compelling, Rafe, and vital. I can't put a name to it, but there's something in her eyes. She's searching for something. . . ."

"Transcendent?" he supplied.

"Yes, exactly. She may not find it, of course, but bless her heart for the search. Lord knows she's no angel, but I wish I could be like her. If you ever quote me on any of this, I'll call you a liar."

"Oh, Ward will back me," he said with absentminded cynicism. He knew damn well Ward would never contradict one word Mrs. Astor claimed, fearing his tongue would be torn out for blasphemy.

"Can we strike a truce, you and I?" Caroline asked him. Her voice had softened with feeling.

Rafe met her imploring gaze and saw how Mystere had been right all along. Only Mrs. Astor still stood, wounded but victorious, on the battleground where powerful wills had clashed.

"Truce," he conceded, for all he really wanted now was to find Mystere.

His surrender moved Caroline to a rare candor.

"I shan't be a total hypocrite now that Sam's gone. I, too, was willing to foolishly risk a great deal, Rafe, to be your lover. Even my self-respect if you used me once and then rejected me. You knew that, didn't you?"

"It crossed my mind," he said diplomatically.

"But in any case you won't do it now because you're in love," she added, placing slightly jealous emphasis on the last three words. "By the way, I've been unable to reach Mystere. Her . . . 'uncle' claims she did not come home last night. I assume she's staying with you?"

"Yes," he lied.

"For God's sake be discreet. And keep her away from your hotel. And ask her to call me," Caroline requested, adding, "Come along, Ward. Rafe must get back to his work."

But Rafe had no such intention.

"You close out the meeting," he ordered Sam the moment the latter poked his head inside the room. "I'm going to see Paul Rillieux. Jesus, I've made a hell of a mess of things."

"Perhaps you have," Sam replied. "But you'll set it all to rights, boss. Remember what you told your engineers when the Rock Island Line got bogged down at Walnut Creek? The subsoil wouldn't hold deep pylons, and everybody was ready to give up."

Rafe grinned. "Sure I remember. I said if we can't raise the bridge, then we must lower the river. And damn me if we didn't lower the river."

"I'll take care of things here," Sam assured him. "You go find Mystere."

Paul Rillieux seemed amused, and somewhat disdainful, at Rafe Belloch's manner and tone. Paul had been expecting this visit ever since he realized, some time late last night, that Mystere had finally run away.

"Where is she?" Rillieux repeated his visitor's question, placing his cane across his knees and leaning back in his chair. "She's working her way west, as we used to say of women traveling alone. Although I doubt she's selling her body, for she's a stubbornly high-minded—"

"I know what she's like, Rillieux," Rafe cut him off impatiently.

The fox face grinned at him. "I'm sure you must."

"Old man, you have fewer friends than you think. And age does not keep a man from prison, once convicted."

"Sir, you enter my home and threaten me?"

"*Your* home?" Rafe stood up and took a few steps across the parlor, advancing on Rillieux. "I asked you where Mystere is, and I expect an answer."

"Let's not be precipitate, Mr. Belloch." He banged the floor three times with the tip of his cane. Almost immediately a side door was flung open, and the burly "butler" Rafe knew only as Evan stepped into the room, a shotgun tucked under one arm.

"You best hark to your manners, you lily-livered mange pot," he advised Rafe in a surly tone, "or you'll get a load of Blue Whistlers in your belly."

Rafe had no choice but to back off. The homicidal glint in Evan's hostile eyes was unmistakable, and it only served as a reminder that Mystere's trespass was not so great, after all, in the scheme of things. It was Rillieux's evil that had controlled her so long in this den of thieves.

"When one pleads guilty," Rillieux told his visitor, "he skips the jury. I admit to everything you've accused me of, more or less. As to your inquiry about Mystere's whereabouts—I have every intention of cooperating with you. I am quite confident that she could not have left the city yet. But at the moment I do not know her precise location. I have several people working on that as we speak."

"I shouldn't wonder, for she's the key to the mint as far as you're concerned. *You* got rid of her brother, didn't you, Rillieux? Tipped off an impress gang to nab him because if there was any wealth to be inherited, you figured Mystere would be easier to control."

"I see she told you about her precious letter."

The topic didn't seem to bother Rillieux at all. Obviously having read the letter from the law firm in New Orleans, he would know there was no need to lie, no point for pretense with Belloch.

"So what if I did arrange the boy's abduction?" Rillieux countered. "Although I mean the question rhetorically. Remember, the mere fact that those children possessed a certain letter, and I knew about it, doesn't make that letter at all significant. I made some quiet inquiries over the years, but to no avail."

"And it doesn't matter to you any longer," Rafe supplied, "since your sights are fixed on my money now."

Paul made a deprecatory gesture with one hand. "You attribute too much power to a sick old man. However, since you've touched on the topic of money—my network has been alerted, and Mystere will not get out of this city undetected."

"This is an offer, I take it?"

Rillieux shrugged. "Right now you're neither up the well nor down. If you want to find Mystere, your best chance is with me. I'm in constant contact with my people."

"Yes, and so far you've come up with nothing."

"That will change, I assure you. And when it does, you will be the first person I contact."

Rafe nodded at this, for he was too desperate not to. But he had agreed to nothing so far as payment; let the old blackguard believe what he chose.

The moment Rafe had left the house, Rillieux began to fret. Belloch, too, had extensive resources at his command. There were really only two feasible ways Mystere could leave the city: by water or by rail. That meant watching the waterfront ticket offices and Grand Central Station. And

Belloch's men might spot her first—or the police if any of this went public.

Rillieux had reached a critical conclusion: Belloch had no intention whatsoever of surrendering his fortune to anyone, and Mystere was no longer the obedient little girl susceptible to suggestions. If Paul wanted to profit, he must do so now, not later, and then flee before Caroline could crush him.

"Put the word out on the street," he instructed Evan. "Three hundred dollars cash reward for whoever captures Mystere and brings her to me. Belloch is badly smitten— he'll pay a king's ransom to get her back in his arms again."

Chapter 35

Three days spent as a virtual prisoner in her room on Centre Street was sufficient to remind Mystere how spoiled and pampered she had become while posing as Rillieux's debutante niece. She also quickly realized what a blind fool she had been to think grabbing one night of pleasure and happiness could excise Rafe from her thoughts. Just the opposite: Torrid memories of him became sheer torture during the long, sleepless nights in her strange and uncomfortable bed with its lumpy mattress.

There had been a few fine old furnishings in the room when it was shown to her. But when she arrived on Tuesday, after fleeing from Rafe, the nice pieces had vanished; instead, she found a rustic rope bed and a crudely fashioned washstand of the type sold through catalogs.

She now shared a drabby, windowless water closet with three other tenants, all of whom seemed to resent her presence. And she was forced to a spartan diet of items that would not spoil quickly, for the room was always hot and she had neither icebox nor cooking stove. There were some clean restaurants nearby on Broadway or Sixth Avenue, but she feared being recognized and fared forth only when necessary.

Her landlady, Mrs. Cunningham, was humorless and petty, a stout, aging widow with folds of excess flesh ruining the interesting bone structure of her face. She was barely civil and seemed always resentful of something, but at least she wasn't a snoop and did not bother to interrogate Mystere.

The other tenants, however, had not shown such discretion. She coolly rebuffed their attempts at conversation, always polite but deliberately haughty, hoping such snobbery would seem familiar enough to keep her from appearing "different." It apparently worked, for yesterday morning a brief dialogue was staged outside her door. The mocking voices were raised deliberately so she would hear their new name for her:

"Shall we invite the new tenant to lunch, girls?"

"Oh, don't you know? The marchioness does not take her meals with commoners."

"No, for the marchioness would far rather gnaw on cold penny rolls all by her superior self."

Their laughter sounded coarse, somewhat forced, for they truly resented her.

Let them vent their petty spite, she thought. Anything to keep them from wondering about her. Soon, with luck, she would be gone and this place merely a fading memory.

She had concluded her business with Jerome Helzer, and now her escape from the city was at least funded if not assured. She still shuddered at the memory of Water Street, the tenements looming nearby amid their malodorous school-sink privies and the stink of rot and decay.

Helzer had treated her with professional courtesy, but at first feigned a crafty reluctance to buy, implying that the Butler emerald was too notorious, thus too risky. But no doubt he had his emery wheel and diamond-tip saw in motion before she even got back to her room, for she had heard no man was better at transforming a gem than he—or quicker to get rid of one. She hardly cared, for he had paid her one thousand dollars cash, no questions, and that was enough to allow her to relocate and survive awhile. With luck, long enough to find some means of gainful employment.

She had decided on Boston, for she knew of respectable areas where rooms were let at reasonable rates. She also knew she mustn't delay, for too many persons were after her. At least she felt somewhat lifted by the realization that it was in almost everyone's interest to suppress word of her escape. No one benefitted by the newspapers playing it up except the newspapers themselves. Nonetheless, word would get out, for there were too many informants among the domestic staffs of the Four Hundred.

So she devised the best plan she could, knowing that Grand Central Station and the shipping offices of Trans-Atlantic and the other passenger ship lines would be under close surveillance. There would probably be less attention paid to the rivers, and Mystere had already booked passage on the Hudson River Line to the town of Croton-on-Hudson. From there she would travel to Boston by rail.

Her boat was set to disembark from its West Street berth at nine A.M. today, and she had been awake since well before dawn, confronting the fear that by now had caused a piercing headache. She did not just dread the unknown, but also the fact that she was leaving Rafe's life forever. At one time she had prayed for this; now she secretly hoped he would somehow appear and stop her.

At eight A.M. she walked to the cab stand at Fourteenth Street and quickly arranged to have a second driver pick up her trunk and deliver it to the steamboat terminal.

Face obscured by the lace veil of her widow's bonnet, Mystere pressed well back into the seat of her cab, feeling naked and exposed, vulnerable to countless eyes. She thought again, with sinking dread, of the big, drab, frame terminal building, where anyone off the street could easily lurk among the ticketed passengers.

Preoccupied, at first, by such worries, it took her some time to realize the cab was heading toward the Lower East Side, not the City Harbor.

"Sir!" she called up to the driver, vexed. "You're going the wrong way to reach West Street!"

"I know 'zacly where I am, lady," he assured her, snapping his quirt across the horse's rump to quicken the pace, assuring that his passenger could not flee.

Only now did she realize she had no idea what happened to the cab that was hauling her trunk. Dread sickened her as the speeding hackney careened into a series of unpaved alleys along the docks.

Suddenly they halted beside a deserted loading dock, so abruptly she almost slid forward off the seat.

"I think I've nabbed that sly little piece you been looking for," the driver called out to someone she couldn't see. "Come glom her face."

She fought hard to control her breathing, fear seeming to paralyze her muscles. For a few seconds she debated leaping from the cab. Before she could do anything, however, a big, mean, unshaven face thrust around the canvas fender to look at her. The breath suddenly blasting her nostrils stank of rotgut whiskey.

"Let's have a better look at you, muffin," Sparky said, reaching up to grab her veil.

"Leave your hands off me!" she protested, pushing his hand away.

"You're a feisty little bitch, ain'tcher?" he demanded with approval. "P'raps I'd better check you for guns, anh?"

He reached toward her breasts, and quick as a snake striking, Mystere bit his hand hard. Sparky loosed a bray of rage and pain.

"You like to cut up rough, eh?" he goaded, his voice suddenly hoarse with excitment. "That's *my* game, too."

She saw him double up his right fist, but before she could protect herself, Sparky struck her so hard in her left temple

that the blow literally stunned her. She was helpless to interfere when he reached up and yanked her bonnet off.

A wide smile creased his big, moon face as he recognized
her. The cab rocked wildly when the big man heaved himself
up beside her, forced to push her out of his way.

"Good eye, Hiram, you've bagged our quail," he called
up to the driver. "Now let's head toward Great Jones Street
and collect the bounty."

"I'll take that," Paul told Rose, rising from his chair. He
hooked his cane over one forearm so he could take the tray
from her. "I told you when Mystere was first brought here
that you are to stay away from her. Is that clear?"

"But, Paul, I only—"

"Rose, you have grown too sympathetic to her."

"*Some*one has to," she bristled. "I saw that bruise on her, la!"

"Now, now, she's safe here and no one's going to hurt her.
I won't have you scheming with her, do you mark me? She
has become my—I mean our last chance to raise a bit of capital before we all must flee. Rafe Belloch can afford to pay
our needs out of his postage drawer."

The tray held a bowl of soup, bread and butter, a glass of
milk and some toiletries. Walking slowly, Paul took it downstairs into the gaslit basement room used as the servants'
dining hall. He removed a key from his pocket and unlocked
a door at the far end of the room, hidden by the big coal furnace.

It opened onto a small, windowless storage room cluttered with garden tools and food staples. Enough light
spilled in to reveal Mystere, lying on her side on a quilt pallet. Her wrists and ankles were bound with ropes.

Paul set the tray down on a nearby wooden crate. Then he
removed her cloth gag.

"Must you keep that in my mouth?" she protested. "I'm
not the screaming type."

"I know, but it's difficult to predict just who might pop by, and I'd rather not risk it. Here's some delicous beef-and-barley soup Rose has made," he added in a coaxing tone. "I'm sorry the boys are out right now, so I can't take the chance of untying your hands. It's come to this, that my little girl can now overpower me. You'll have to let me feed you."

"I'm not hungry," she tried to snap. But her voice sounded thick and sluggish; the words came to her slower than usual. She vaguely recalled her arrival, how Paul had forced some not-unpleasant-tasting liquid down her throat. Whatever it was, she had blacked out soon after.

"What time is it?" she asked him.

"About five P.M. You've been asleep all day."

"Asleep? Drugged, you mean."

Paul shrugged. "If it pounds nails, call it a hammer. Here, try a bite of this."

"No," she insisted, turning her head away. "If you make me taste it, I'll spit it on you."

Paul gave up with a sigh, setting the bowl aside again. He winced when he glanced at the big, grape-colored swelling over her temple. Even in the stingy light it was ugly.

"Sweet love, you were foolish to resist a pig like Sparky," he lectured her.

Mystere said nothing to this, although secretly she was glad she fought with him, for evidently it made him give up the idea of raping her. Sparky had gone no further.

"I don't want Belloch upset," Paul added. "It won't do to sell him damaged goods when the man's a hothead like you."

A sense of helpless frustration made her actually groan. "Paul, no, please reconsider what you're doing. Just let me go, please."

He shook his hoary head, lips pursed like a coldhearted accountant. "Out of the question, dear. Hush has already been sent to fetch him."

There must have been a telltale gleam of hope in her eyes at this, for he added wryly, "Don't expect the boy to rescue you like Tom Sawyer, for he doesn't know you're here. And don't look at me like that; I have no choice in the matter. I realize now that all my grand schemes are hopeless. I am a tattered old man who must save his breath to cool his porridge. I've lost control of you, and I'm losing the others, too. Most troubling of all, I suspect that Caroline is 'cooling out' toward me—that could signal real damage. But I still have one thing of value to Rafe Belloch: his fiancée."

"Paul, you've got it all wrong. Rafe has no intention of marrying me."

"No, you're the one who has it wrong. I've talked to the man, and he wants you the way they want ice water in hell. He's in love with you, and you with him. Don't deny it."

"I admit I love him, so what? He does *not* love me, and he will not marry me. How many times do I have to tell you that? He is a dangerous, unpredictable man, and you are a fool to think you can manipulate him just because you're desperate."

"I'm a fool, all right," he conceded sadly. "An old fool who played a fool's game far too long. But I have no intention of dying in prison, dear heart. Belloch will be here soon, I expect, and the bargaining will begin in earnest. Now, if you insist on not eating, I must tie this gag on you again."

"Oh, Paul," she protested, close to tears as she realized the game was finally, at long last, up. And she had come so close to freedom. So close to protecting the man she loved. The despair choked her like a noose. "I beg of you, please don't hurt him."

They were her last words before he tied the gag.

"Well then," he replied, "if we are all bound for hell, Mystere, at least *I'm* whipping the team."

Chapter 36

Darkness had begun to settle over the city by the time Hush returned with Rafe Belloch. Paul, Baylis, and Evan had all joined forces to wait in the parlor. The shotgun lay conspicuously across Evan's lap.

Hush didn't bother with the bellpull, using his own key to open the front door. Rafe stopped in the doorway of the parlor to stare at the trio for a moment.

"Ahh, Mr. Belloch," Paul greeted him smugly. "So glad you could stop by."

"So here's the cock of the dung-heap," Rafe replied. "A thief and grifter who expertly imitates Mrs. Astor's supercilious tone."

Evan scowled and patted the scattergun. "You're valiant as an Essex lion," he said scornfully. "You'll watch your mouth, you banker's pimp, or I'll let daylight into you."

Rafe ignored him, still staring at Rillieux. "All right, I'm here. Where is Mystere?"

"You'll *pay* me for that information, Mr. Belloch, and you'll pay handsomely."

"I'll see you bark in hell first. Where is she?"

Evan and Baylis exchanged sneering smiles. Evan pushed up out of his chair, leveling the shotgun on Rafe.

"Your robber-baron ways don't cut no ice here, Belloch," Evan snarled. "You're in *our* home now, and under law we can blow you away as an intruder."

"Hush," Rafe spoke quietly, for the lad stood just behind him in the hallway. "Step well aside. That's the lad. Boys, you're on."

Rafe took several steps into the room, making space for Jimmy and Skeels, who suddenly stepped in from the hallway where they had been waiting. Both men held pistols at the ready and took up positions well to either side of their boss.

Between his vest and his coat Rafe, too, wore a pistol in an armpit holster. In a moment it was out, and there was a muzzle trained on each of the three adversaries.

"You can probably kill me," Rafe told Evan in a cold, authoritative voice. "But that's a single-barrel gun with one shot. My life for all three of yours. Now either put down that shotgun or pull the trigger."

Evan, whose face had turned pale as fresh linen, did not wait for Paul's order. Not one of the three men confronting him looked in the least bit afraid. He set the gun down on the floor, and Jimmy came over to claim it.

"Now, let's take it from the top," Rafe told Rillieux. "Where are you keeping Mystere?"

"Rot in hell," Rillieux replied savagely. "I said you'll pay for that information."

Rafe stared from one to the other. "There's nothing wrong with you three that a can of blasting powder couldn't fix. Hush!"

"Sir?"

"Could Mystere be somewhere in the house?"

"I dunno, sir. I ain't seen her."

"Wasting your time," Rillieux assured Rafe. "She's nowhere near this house."

All the commotion had brought Rose from her quarters.

She poked her head into the room, then gasped when she saw all the drawn weapons.

"Rose?" Hush said. "Honest Injun now. Are they keeping Mystere here in the house?"

Rafe turned to stare at the redheaded servant. She paled, but only shook her head, too intimidated to even speak.

"You've got them all afraid of you, old man," he told Rillieux. "But you've a telephone in the hallway. Perhaps Inspector Byrnes would take some interest in this matter."

Rillieux calmly called the bluff. "Perhaps he would, at that. Particularly when he learns the identity of Lady Moonlight—and the fact that *you've* been protecting her to maintain your bedroom privileges."

Paul's mocking face seemed to ask Rafe if he was so God-almighty tough *now*. But it was Rose who finally broke the impasse.

"Sir?" she said hesitantly to Rafe. "I know where Mystere is."

"Damn you, Rose, put a sock in it!" Paul exploded, his angry eyes warning her. "I've told you before that disloyalty will—"

"Oh, shut up, Paul," she snapped. "I've kept quiet far too long while you've abused that poor girl. I'm sick of you and your bullying ways. Do what you want to me, I'll not play the good dog for you any longer."

"He'll do nothing to you," Rafe assured her. "I'll see to that. Is she here in the house, Rose?"

"Yessir. Down in the basement, I'll show you."

"Rillieux," Rafe ordered tersely, "you'll come with us. Jimmy, you and Skeels stay here and keep an eye on these two. If you have to shoot them, fine by me. It'll save the citizens the cost of feeding them in prison."

* * *

Absolutely nothing, Mystere realized with a sinking sensation of despair, *focuses the mind like captivity.*

In the darkness she had no idea how much time had passed. Her hands and feet had gone numb from being tied so long, and the air in the storeroom was heavy and close. The gag hurt her mouth and made it difficult to breathe. But it was her mind that tormented her even more than her body.

With so much time to ponder her stark situation, she had given up all hope of a positive outcome. Many things could happen, depending on Paul and on events she could not predict or control. But one terrible conclusion seemed inevitable: Rillieux would see her dead.

Never, in the bleakest depths of misery, had she felt such helpless loneliness. She cried until she had no more tears left. When the door was finally flung open, and she heard Rafe's angry curse, instead of joy she felt only a terrible dread.

"Damn you, Rillieux," Rafe muttered as he hurriedly untied her ropes. Rose held a candle to augment the dim light spilling in, and it clearly revealed Mystere's badly bruised left temple. "Were you planning on delivering a corpse as my bride?"

Terrified at Rafe's sudden fury, Rillieux began loudly protesting. "See here, Rafe, I did not—"

"Shut up, you ruthless old bastard." He began gently chafing Mystere's limbs, restoring her circulation. "You've drugged her, too. I see it in her pupils."

"Merely a good dose of Miss Pinkerton's to help her slee—"

"That stuff is pure laudanum; you might have killed her. Get out of my sight before I shoot you. Give me a hand, would you, Rose?"

Rose went to help him, but they were interrupted by Rillieux's cold announcement.

"She is not yours to save, Belloch."

Rafe's head snapped up. Mystere saw the glint of the

small ladies' muff pistol in Paul's hand. With utter despair, she realized her worst fears were coming true.

"No—I won't let you hurt him!" she cried out with all her strength.

"You protect him?" Paul spat. "When I am the one who took you from the streets—?"

"And kidnapped my brother!" she accused.

"If I could have ever gotten to Sheridan to see if that fortune was yours, it would have been worth it to both of us to have gotten rid of Bram," Rillieux spitefully confessed.

"What did you do to him?" Mystere was hysterical. Rafe's strong hands on her were almost not enough to keep her on the pallet.

"He went where every poor lad is doomed to go. To the sea. And by God, I hope he's rotted to fish food by now." Rillieux's face turned murderous. "He had the same traitorous spirit as you. And I'll see you die by my own hand before you'll profit from my machinations." He cocked the muff pistol and pressed it to her swollen temple.

A ferocious bellow seemed to come from the pits of hell. Before Mystere could even comprehend what was taking place, she realized Rafe was upon Rillieux, attacking him with the viciousness of a feral dog.

The old man Rillieux was no match for Rafe. If not for the gun.

A loud report sounded. Blue gunsmoke hung in the air as deadly testament.

Rafe doubled over.

Rose screamed.

In bilious rage Paul stood over Mystere, cocking and firing the now empty gun as if ignorant of its impotence. Footsteps thundered overhead as Rafe's men sounded the alarm and scuffled with Baylis and Evan.

"I'll have my vengeance on you yet, you turncoat bitch!" Rillieux screamed at Mystere. "You'll never be free of me! Every time you look across your shoulder, you'll fear it will be me at your back!" With that, he flung the useless muff pistol at Mystere's face and fled through the outside cellar stairs.

No doubt Baylis was already ahead of him with the waiting coach.

"Rafe! Rafe!" Mystere wept, nearly crawling to his doubled-over form.

"Go after him!" Rafe barked at his men when they appeared at the door. "Don't let him get away!"

"Rafe, you're hurt," Mystere cried, watching her hand that was on his side turn red.

Rafe straightened, his face tight with pain. "It would seem Ruth will have another wound to tend. But it's not too terrible. Went clean through my side."

Together they walked up the stairs to the parlor. Rose went to fetch bandages, and Rafe took a deep quaff of brandy. By the time the spirit was gone in the glass the color had returned to Rafe's face.

"Take her ladyship upstairs and draw her a bath. She looks paler than a ghost," Rafe proclaimed.

Refusing to leave his side, Mystere had to be nearly dragged upstairs with Rose's constant assurance that Rafe's wound was not lethal.

Rose quickly tended to her. Rafe waited anxiously in the upstairs hallway while Rose helped Mystere bathe and change into nightclothes.

While Rafe waited, Jimmy came upstairs. "Boss? The old man is missing. Him and his minions. Clean gone. We can't find them anywhere."

Rafe nodded, grim resignation on his face. "It's every man for himself and the devil take the hindmost. Tell Skeels to go wait for us on the yacht, all right? I want you to stay here."

Jimmy nodded and went back downstairs.

Moments later Rose emerged from Mystere's bedroom.

"She's resting now, God bless her," she reported to Rafe. "She's not very sleepy, though, and she's asked to see you. You needn't knock, she's waiting."

He nodded. As she turned to head downstairs, Rafe called after her: "Rose?"

She turned around. "Yes, sir?"

"I suppose Mystere being from Ireland was born Catholic, was she not?"

Rose looked startled. "Well, yes, sir."

"Then, I want you to send Hush for a priest." Rafe handed the startled woman some banknotes. "This should fetch one. Tell Hush to inquire at the rectory at Saint Patrick's."

"Oh, but, sir," Rose protested, "Mystere is not in any grave danger. She doesn't need Last—"

"Just go," he insisted.

Rose went downstairs, and Rafe let himself into the bedroom. He felt a sudden flood of relief when he saw Mystere resting comfortably in bed, her beautiful hair fanned out around her head on the pillows. Although her bruise was still puffy and dark, she felt good enough to greet him with a warm, if somewhat diffident, smile.

"So how are you feeling?" he asked.

"I should be asking that of you," she offered.

He ruefully grinned. "Believe it or not, I've had worse."

"I'm afraid I'm a miserable failure as a fugitive."

"You're certainly quite good at slipping out of a man's bed," he assured her, but with a smile.

"It wasn't easy. I was of a mind to crawl back in and kiss you awake."

Rafe sat down on the bed, gently pushing her hair aside to better examine the bruise. "Did Rillieux or his men do this?"

"No, it was Sparky."

Rafe nodded, saying nothing. But the man had been fairly warned, and now Rafe made a mental note to talk to Sam about it. Sparky's days of beating women would soon be over.

"Anyhow, I wish you *had* crawled back into bed," he assured her.

The covers were turned down, and Mystere's silk chemise clung flatteringly, emphasizing the fullness of her breasts. She saw his eyes lingering on her and self-consciously pulled the covers higher.

"What about Mrs. Astor?" she inquired, changing the topic. "Does she know I tried to run?"

"Caroline, I've learned over the years, generally knows much more than anyone suspects she knows. But it really doesn't matter."

"It certainly does, and you know it."

He shook his head. "For your information Caroline adores you. Do you know that she herself has started a rumor about how the Lady Moonlight has migrated to the West Coast?"

"But . . . why would she—?"

"Why, to take any suspicion off you so you can remain here in the city safely."

"Perhaps," Mystere suggested sadly, "she'll feel less charitable toward me after our wedding doesn't happen. Or when the vengeful Rafael Belloch completes his elaborate revenge scheme against her."

"As to your second point," Rafe insisted, "Caroline came to see me, even chased my top men out of our boardroom to have it out with me."

"And . . . ?"

Rafe smiled wryly at the memory. "Let's just say that she and I have settled accounts. Which is to say—she won and I accept it. As to your first point . . ."

He brought his face close to hers, gently kissing the tissue-thin skin of her eyelids. "You were right, Mrs. Belloch. Revenge is not a good enough reason for living."

Mrs. Belloch . . . his unexpected words made her heart race as new hope surged within her. But outwardly doubts clouded her eyes.

Rafe frowned, misunderstanding. "Unless," he corrected himself, pulling back from her a bit, "you are rejecting me?"

"I've tried so hard not to fall in love with you," she confessed miserably.

"Then, we have no problem. I'm making an honest woman out of you. I've sent for a priest. We'll be married right here in the house—tonight."

"Rafe. We can't."

"Can and will. You needn't worry about Rillieux, for the old goat has fled. Besides, for all I know you're pregnant. Are you?"

"It's too soon to know yet," she replied, blushing.

"Let's play it safe, then. And after all, it will quiet Caroline. She just wants a marriage, not a grand wedding. Unless it's you who—"

"I've had enough publicity for two lifetimes," she assured him. "I don't care about the grand wedding."

Her gaze fled from his.

"Then, why this strange reluctance?" he demanded. "You just said you're in love with me."

"Rafe, don't you see? That's my reason—love. It's the only reason I'd ever get married. You aren't the problem; it's your motives. Quieting Caroline, making an honest woman of me . . . if you can't—can't love me, I must find another man who will."

He bent close to her again, so close she felt the warmth radiating from him.

"That morning you left me," he told her, his voice enlivened by passion, "my first reaction was anger. But then . . . do you remember telling me how you felt when Bram was taken? As if half of your soul went with him?"

She nodded, fighting back tears of feeling.

"Well, that's how I felt when I feared you were out of my life forever. Mystere, the truth is your wounded soul matches mine in every way. The only way we can mend is to be together. I love you, my mystery girl, love you with all my heart. Please marry me?"

"I will," she whispered, her heart ripping away the bindings that had prevented her from hoping, from loving in return. Almost afraid to believe, she hesitated, but when she joyously felt his arms go around her, she began to hope again. Even when she thought the laudanum and her own mind were playing wretched tricks on her, she watched his expression fill with love for her and helplessly surrendered to his long and passionate kiss.

Only a timid knock broke them apart.

"Yes?" Mystere called out.

Hush and Rose stepped in.

"Hush brought a priest," Rose explained. The smile she couldn't quite suppress showed that she had guessed why Rafe sent for one. "A nice old gent named Father Perry. He's waiting downstairs."

"Send him up," Rafe said. "And you two come with him, for I believe two witnesses are required. By the way—would both of you be willing to come live with us at Garden Cove? There's to be no more stealing, just honest work for honest wages."

"Man alive!" Hush exclaimed, face brightening as he realized he would be with his beloved Mystere. "You bet, Mr. Belloch!"

"Now, sir, I'm warning you," Rafe added with mock solemnity, "I will *not* have you courting and sparking my wife behind my back. Gentleman's word?"

"Cross my heart," the youth promised, flushing with pride.

"Now you two men clear out of here," Rose fussed, her flurry of sudden activity meant to detract attention from her tears of joy. "There'll be no marriage in a bedroom. Go keep the priest company until Mystere is properly dressed and I bring her down. La, she shan't be married in her underclothing! What will Father Perry think of us?"

Within the hour Rafe's wound had been bandaged, and he and Mystere had exchanged nuptials. It was too late by then to bother returning to Staten Island, so the newly wed couple decided to spend their first night as man and wife at the Great Jones Street residence.

Baylis, Evan and Rillieux were long gone, but Jimmy spent the night downstairs just in case any of them were fool enough to return.

Later that evening, as Rafe unbuttoned the back of Mystere's dress, he murmured in her ear, "Well, you haven't found your brother, but at least you've found your true husband. Are you happy?"

Tears filmed her eyes, and she felt like bursting from the fullness of joy within her.

"One does not replace the other," she replied. "But yes, Mr. Belloch, I am exceedingly happy."

Both of them undressed in the glow of a small electric lamp on Mystere's chest of drawers. The moment she turned out the lamp, however, Rafe noticed shafts of bright moonlight streaming through the room's dormer windows.

"Walk over by the windows," he whispered in her ear just before they got into bed.

"But why?"

"Please, just for a moment."

Completely naked, Mystere crossed silently to the windows and slowly turned around. Silver-white moonlight bathed her in a luminous aura like stardust. In that moment, with Rafe's worshipful gaze upon her, she felt like a nocturnal goddess that had been carved from ivory and then brought to life by some divine spark.

He was silent for a long time.

"The Lady Moonlight," he finally said in a voice softened by love, deepened by desire. "So come to bed now, my lady," he added, raising his arms.

And as she crossed the room to join her husband, she did not seem to be walking at all, but rather gliding like moonbeams across a gentle sea.

Epilogue

Trevor Sheridan leaned forward in his upholstered walnut armchair, resting both forearms on the desk to read a neatly typed note lying on his blotter. It had turned up two days earlier in his inter-office correspondence. The author was one of his best clerks, a man who had started with the firm seven years ago as a messenger boy and had an exemplary work record.

> *Sir,*
>
> *A few months ago a young woman arrived at the offices to make inquiries about a possible connection between herself and the Sheridan or Granville ancestral line. I mention it at this late date only because, just recently, I saw a photograph of Rafe Belloch's new wife in the* Times. *I'd swear it's the same woman who came to your office.*
>
> *One or two others present in the office that day have remarked the same thing. I felt it my duty to men-*

tion this, sir, because she claimed to have a letter of some kind, and I thought you might like to see it.

Yrs. respectfully,
Nathan Winkler

Even as Sheridan finished reading and folded the note again, he heard footsteps in the hallway outside the open door of his second-story office in the Commerce Building. He looked up and saw Rafe and Mystere Belloch in the doorway.

"Come in, come in, please," he greeted them, rising to his feet as they entered. He indicated a pair of Louis XVI carved giltwood fauteuils in front of his desk. "Please have a seat. I'm glad you agreed to come."

His casual greeting struck Mystere as somewhat forced, as if civility was foreign to his nature. One side of Sheridan's mouth made what might have been the beginning of a smile. *Or just as likely,* she thought, *it's merely a growl.*

This was the first time she had actually met him, and she disliked Trevor Sheridan instantly. His grim intensity was even more noticeable at close range, and she decided the Predator was an apt name for him if first impressions could be trusted. But she reminded herself how she had also disliked her own husband at first, an aversion that had since turned to a passionate love.

"I must admit," she began somewhat nervously, "that I've been consumed with curiosity since your call, Mr. Sheridan."

"As have I, Mrs. Belloch, since only belatedly learning of your visit. Thankfully, a sharp employee brought your visit to my attention after realizing who you were."

Despite her burning curiosity, Mystere could not help an indignant frown at the memory of that rainy day. Or his implicit admission that only women with social rank deserved serious notice.

"The reception I was accorded by your office staff, Mr. Sheridan, was not deserved by even a murderer."

He raised his hands from the blotter and spread them in a helpless gesture. "Excuse us, Mrs. Belloch, if we've become a cynical fraternity around here. I am not, I confess, a good model of chivalry for my subordinates. Too, the stories we're told are all drearily similar, yours included, from what I've heard of it."

"Yes, well, all that's nothing to the matter," Rafe intervened impatiently, all business and used to taking charge. "Just look at the letter."

Hands trembling, Mystere opened the silver clasp of her bag, then the protective chamois pouch holding the letter. She removed the dog-eared sheet of stationery. Careful of the worn creases, she unfolded it.

"It's gotten wet and smeared the ink at some point long ago," she explained. "It becomes illegible toward the end, including the signature."

"Of all places," Sheridan observed, his cynical tone causing Rafe's fists to clench on the arms of his chair. But Mystere's imploring glance settled him down again, and Rafe couldn't help a little grin, probably realizing it was just the tone he might have used himself.

Sheridan accepted the letter and said nothing for perhaps the next two or three minutes, face turned downward to study the letter. He tilted the bronze Sinumbra lamp on his desk, its long-faceted prisms ringing, to throw more light on it. Mystere watched with growing anxiety, unconsciously perched on the edge of her chair.

Finally he looked up from the letter and scrutinized her face as if he had been ordered to sculpt its likeness. His hazel eyes were unusually dark, and even now wrathful.

"Of course you could always favor the female side," he remarked as if thinking outloud. "I never met Maureen or saw a likeness of her. Frankly you're a bit too classically wrought for a Sheridan. Mara proves we have our female beauties, but not of your kind."

"For a Sheridan?" she repeated uncertainly.

His tone became unexpectedly emotional. "I wrote this letter to my cousin Brendan, all right. More than twenty years ago when I first began to make my fortune."

"Then, my father was a Sheridan," she repeated, looking at Rafe, then off at the windows for a moment. "Oh, thank God, I know it at last," she added in a murmur, suddenly overcome with emotion. Shock, wonder, joy washed over her in a floodgate-opening tide. "I'm somebody. *Bram* is somebody," she wept, wishing with all her heart Bram was there by her side now, sharing in the happiness she now knew was hers.

"Brendan's mother was a Sheridan," he stipulated. "But of course her name changed with marriage. Mine did not as my father was a Sheridan. All you need do, to prove you are Brendan's girl, is tell me your surname."

"You know she cannot," Rafe interceded. "She told you that when you called her."

Sheridan nodded slowly. "I know she did. But I will assume nothing where kinship claims are concerned. You must prove to me that Cousin Brendan was, indeed, your father. If you can prove that, you will become a Sheridan with all the rights of our name."

"Now see here, Sheridan," Rafe remonstrated. "I understand such skepticism in other claims you've dealt with. But you just admitted you wrote this letter. Surely that is not part of the routine?"

"No, but so what? I have no idea whatsoever how this letter came into your wife's possession."

"Yes, you have," Rafe objected. "Her word that her mother gave it to her and her brother. But I suppose you're implying Mystere stole it, no doubt to sink her hooks into your vast fortune."

"You might sound less scornful," Sheridan reprimanded,

"if you knew the actual amount of that vast fortune, Mr. Belloch."

"Look, I'm duly impressed by you. Anybody who matters in this city knows that you own bulging warehouses on Pearl Street and that your fortune can buy entire nations. But let's be candid: So can mine. My wife has no need for two fortunes—just a family."

Sheridan made that one-sided smile again. "She may well be speaking the truth—so far as she knows it, that is. But I have no way of knowing who gave her this letter or how that party came to acquire it. If she could at least tell me her surname, I'd be far more convinced."

Sheridan fell silent a moment, studying Mystere's prosperous appearance in the generous illumination of the electrified lamp. She had already explained, during his questioning when he called her the day before yesterday, the rather remarkable claim that she did not know her own surname. She had implored him, reasoning that it was possible she did not know it, however, given her young age then.

"Perhaps life has played a scurvy trick on you in the past," he remarked. "Obviously your fortunes have been reversed."

"Both of you think like men," she upbraided the two of them. "You home in on 'fortunes' as if that's all I care about. You don't understand—money has never been the issue. I rate finding my brother Bram above all else. And next comes the desire to know, absolutely and unmistakably, our surname."

"Yes, of course. In your case it's not money at all, it's only love," Sheridan summarized, his sarcasm subtle but detectable.

Rafe's jaw muscles suddenly bunched tightly. "Don't step on me, Sheridan. I won't be so easy to crush as some others you've ruined."

"Oh, stop it, both of you," Mystere pleaded, in no mood to get embroiled in a clash of proud males.

"Look, I find Mrs. Belloch quite persuasive," Sheridan conceded. "But I must have a little more knowledge of your family back in Ireland. Come back here with some proof—your brother himself would be ideal, for he's older and must recall more—and we'll declare both of you legal Sheridans."

"I warned you he's a hard twist," Rafe declared the moment they had collected their overcoats from the porter downstairs and exited the Commerce Building. "But to hell with his scruples. You're his kin, God help you, I'd wager on it. His admitting he wrote the letter as good as warrants it."

He handed Mystere into the carriage and told Wilson to head down to the Battery.

"No, he's right," Mystere said. "I can't prove I have a right to own his letter. And I realize now that even if I could—he doesn't have any idea, either, where Bram might be. You've been right all along, I suppose."

"I? How do you mean?"

"My quest for Bram. I know you think it's a waste of time."

Tears threatened to overwhelm her. She glanced outside at the late-autumn evening, watching pedestrians with their chins tucked in against the chilly wind. Here and there she spotted trees already mulched for the coming freezes.

"You're wrong," Rafe assured her, cupping her chin with one hand and turning her face toward him. "The old veterans in my father's regiment always told me no man is truly dead until he's forgotten. You've kept your brother alive in your own way; I'll never fault you for that."

Rafe's words, meant to solace, instead sent hot tears quivering onto her long lashes. "It was Paul," she said, more convinced than ever. "It was he who was behind Bram's disappearance."

Rafe, after a moment's debate with himself, replied, "Last summer, when you were hiding, I questioned Rillieux about it. Technically, of course, he admitted nothing, the old weasel. But he as much as confessed he sold Bram to an impress gang, his motive being to have you in the line of inheritance in case a fortune turned up."

Cold, numbing despair hit her like an Arctic squall.

"All those years and all that money I spent," she lamented, "in a useless quest for Bram. Oh, Rafe, at least then I had *hope* to cling to. I'll never, ever be able to find him."

With her final word, her voice gave out in a great sob, and she collapsed against Rafe, weeping.

"Never mind now," he soothed gently in her ear. "All is not lost, Lady Moonlight."

She looked up at him from swollen, red-rimmed eyes. "I can think of nothing else."

"I turned the problem over to the best answer man I know," he assured her.

"Sam Farrell?"

He nodded.

"You don't mean—then Sam knows where—?"

"No, not Sam. But he has found the one person in this wide world who stands the best chance of finding Bram. And I have already arranged to take some time off from the office because I'm going to take you to this person myself. We're going to find your brother."

Mystere looked at him in awe and wonder. If she had ever doubted he loved her, she had no doubts now. Unable to help herself she flung her arms around him and hugged him in unspeakable joy.

"They should have warned me," Rafe murmured against her hair.

"About what?" she asked, her face beatific with happiness.

"That your talent lay in stealing hearts as well." He kissed her. "I love you, Lady Moonlight."

Always the
Last to Know

Kristan Higgins

BERKLEY
New York

BERKLEY
An imprint of Penguin Random House LLC
penguinrandomhouse.com

Copyright © 2020 by Kristan Higgins
Excerpt from *Pack Up the Moon* copyright © 2021 by Kristan Higgins
Penguin Random House supports copyright. Copyright fuels creativity, encourages
diverse voices, promotes free speech, and creates a vibrant culture. Thank you for buying
an authorized edition of this book and for complying with copyright laws by not
reproducing, scanning, or distributing any part of it in any form without permission.
You are supporting writers and allowing Penguin Random House to continue to
publish books for every reader.

BERKLEY and the BERKLEY & B colophon
are registered trademarks of Penguin Random House LLC.

ISBN: 9780451489470

Berkley hardcover edition / June 2020
Berkley trade paperback edition / June 2020
Berkley mass-market edition / April 2021

Printed in the United States of America
1 3 5 7 9 10 8 6 4 2

This book is dedicated to Huntley Fitzpatrick,
strong and kind, brilliant and fierce.
I am so very, very glad to be your friend.

Acknowledgments

At Berkley, my profound gratitude to my brilliant editor, Claire Zion, for her keen eye and big heart, and to the rest of the brilliant Berkley team: Ivan, Christine, Jeanne-Marie, Craig, Erin, Diana, Bridget, Jin, Angela, Anthony and every single person in art, sales and marketing.

To my agent, Maria Carvainis, who has shaped my career with dedication, enthusiasm and an unwavering eye on the future, thank you, Madame.

Thank you to Mel Jolly, for always remembering what I forget and knowing what I don't, and for being a lovely person in addition to all that. Thanks to my funny, smart, hardworking intern, Madison Terrill, for her innovation and insight these past two summers.

I had no idea what this book was about until I slipped off to Cape Cod in the cold winter and hid for a month, just me, my laptop and my good dog. Thanks to the owner who rented her beautiful house to me; to Luther, the most loyal and sweetest dog, who kept me company and got me outside for walks every day; to Ivan of the Red Sox hat and gold tooth, who helped save a dolphin with me that blustery, cold day, and to the marine wildlife rescuers who actually knew what they were doing, and again to Ivan for driving Luther and me home, even though I was sopping wet and covered in sand.

Thanks and love to my sister, Hilary Higgins Murray, who listens so well and showed me how to fix all the problems with one word—*amputate*. Who knew? She did!

To Laura Francis, my town's first selectman, for helping me understand just how much there is to do in a small town;

To the folks at Gaylord Specialty Hospital, for the information they provided on stroke and brain injury;

To Stacia Bjarnason, for her time, insight, friendship and laughter;

To Jackie Decker, sister of my heart, for her insider information about painting and art;

To Terence Keenan, the love of my life and my best friend, all in one rather adorable package;

To Flannery and Declan, who are such remarkable, wonderful people and fill my heart with love every single day;

And thank you, readers, for the gift of your time.

CHAPTER ONE

~

Sadie

"Y ou're engaged? Oh! Uh . . . huzzah!"

Yes. I had just said *huzzah*.

You know what? I couldn't blame myself. *Another* engagement among the teachers of St. Catherine's Catholic Elementary School in the Bronx. The fifth this year, and yes, I was counting.

I couldn't look away from the diamond blinding me from the finger of Bridget Ennis. The stone was the size of a bumblebee, and my hypnotized eyes followed her hand as she waved it in excitement, telling the rest of us teachers—six women, one man—about how *romantic*, how *unexpected*, how *thrilling* it had been.

I had nothing against Bridget. I even liked her. I'd mentored her, because this was her first year teaching. She was twenty-three as of last week; I was ancient at thirty-two (or so it felt in teacher years). It had been raining diamond rings, and despite my having had bubbly hopes on my own last birthday, the fourth finger of my left hand remained buck naked.

Bridget was talking about save-the-date magnets and paper quality and color schemes and flower arrangements and the seventy-nine dresses she was already torn between. Another woman falling victim to wedding insanity. Bridget was the only child of wealthy parents. This did not bode well for me, her sort-of friend. Was it too late to distance myself? *Please don't ask me to be a bridesmaid. Please. Please. I am way too old for this shit.*

"My daddy said whatever I want, and I want it to be perfect, you know?" Bridget looked at me, and I felt the cold trickle of dread. "Sadie, obviously I want you as a bridesmaid." Her pure green eyes filled with happy tears.

Oh, the fuckery of it all.

"Of course!" I said. "Thank you! What an honor!" My cheek began to twitch as I smiled.

"And you, Nina! And you, Vanessa! And of course, Jay's three sisters and my gals from Kappa Kappa Gamma. And my cousin, because she's like a sister to me. Do you like violet? Or cornflower? Off the shoulder, I was thinking, but I think *my* dress might be off the shoulder and . . ." I stopped listening as she began speaking in tongues intelligible only to those addicted to *Say Yes to the Dress*.

This was not my first time around the bridesmaid block. Bridget's would be my sixth stint, and I knew what was coming. Engagement party. Bridal shower. Dress shopping for Bridget. Dress shopping for me and the other eleventeen bridesmaids. A lingerie shower. A household goods shower. Meeting(s) of the families. Bachelorette weekend in some city that caters to large groups of drunken people—New Orleans or Vegas or Savannah, which meant a flight and hotel. Rehearsal dinner. The wedding itself. Brunch the next day. All with or without Alexander Mitchum, my boyfriend, who had not yet proposed, despite his references to a future together, his one-time question about if I'd think about changing my last name from Frost to Mitchum—"hypothetically," he'd added—and the deliberate slowing of my footsteps whenever we passed Cartier on Fifth Avenue.

"You don't have to say yes, idiot," came a low voice next to me. Carter Demming, my best friend at St. Catherine's.

"She's sweet," I murmured back.

"Oh, please. Let her sorority sisters be her bridesmaids. Show some dignity for your age."

"I'm thirty-two."

"Your most fertile years are behind you."

"Thanks, Carter."

"Miss Frost? I need you for a second," Carter said loudly. "Mazel tov, sweetheart," he added as Bridget brushed away more glittering tears.

We left Bridget's cheery classroom and went to the now-empty teachers' lounge, where we teachers discussed which kids we hated most and how to ruin their young lives (not really). Carter posted the occasional *Legalize Marijuana* sticker somewhere, just to torment our principal, the venerable and terrifying Sister Mary.

I was the art teacher here. No, I could not support myself on a teacher's salary at a Catholic school in New York City, but more on that later. I loved teaching, though it hadn't exactly been my dream. Just about every kid loved art. If I didn't have the same stature as the "regular" teachers, I made up for it by being adored.

"So you're thinking about marriage and why you're still single," said Carter, pulling out a chair and straddling it.

"Yep." I sat down, too, the normal way, like a human and not a cowboy.

"So propose already."

"What?"

"Propose marriage to your perfect boyfriend."

"Meh."

"Why should men have to do all the work? Do you know how hard it is to buy the perfect ring, pick the perfect moment and place, say the perfect words and still have it be a fucking surprise? It's very hard."

"You would know." Carter had been married several times, twice to women, once to a man.

"Listen to your uncle Carter."

"You're not my uncle, unfortunately."

"Some men need a shove toward the altar, honey. Shove him. Do you really want to go out into the Tinder world again?"

"Jesus, no."

"Don't become a statistic. Kids are getting married younger and younger these days. Your window is closing. Match and eHarmony worked fifteen years ago, but now they're filled with criminals. As you well know."

"He was a minor felon, and it wasn't exactly listed in his profile. But yes, I see your point."

Alexander (not a felon) and I *had* been dating for a couple of years. Ours had been the classic rom-com meet-cute. I turned around on a wine night with my friends and sloshed my cabernet onto his crisp white shirt. He laughed, asked for my number, and called a few days later. We'd been together ever since.

We had a marriage-worthy relationship by any measure. Maybe it was the distance factor—he was a traveling yacht salesman (someone had to do it)—so we weren't bothered by the slings and arrows of daily life together. He was constant—we saw each other almost every week-end. He brought me presents from his travels—a silk scarf printed with palmetto leaves from the Florida Keys, or honey from Savannah. He'd met my parents, charmed my mother (not an easy task), chatted with my father and wasn't in awe of my older sister, which was definitely a point in his favor. Alex had great stories about his clients, some of them celebrities, others just fabulously wealthy. He was, er . . . tidy, a quality that shouldn't be undersold.

Alexander lived on the Upper East Side, which I tried not to hold against him. His apartment was impressive but soulless. Every time I stayed over, I felt like I was staying in a model home—a place that was interesting and taste-ful, but not exactly homey. He'd bought it furnished. Some of his art came from HomeGoods, and since I'd been—correction, *was still*—an artist, that did make me wince.

Sex was great. He was good-looking—his hair a shade I called boarding school blond, which would get nearly white in the summer. His eyes were blue and already had the attractive crow's-feet you'd expect for a guy who sold boats. In a nutshell, he looked like he'd stepped out of a J. Crew catalog, and why he was dating me, I wasn't a hun-dred percent sure. "You have no idea how hard it is to find a nice girl," he said once, so I guess it was that.

But I wasn't really a girl anymore, not like Bridget. Already past my prime fertility years, according to Uncle Carter, who did tend to know everything.

"Hello?" he said, scratching his wrist. "Sadie. You're in vapor lock. Make a move."

Another fair point. I'd been at St. Cath's for eight years, painting on the side, living in a nine-hundred-square-foot apartment in Times Square, the armpit of Manhattan. "Yeah," I said. "Sure. I could do it. We're seeing each other tonight."

"See? Written in the stars." He winked at me. "Now, I have to go wash the grime from these little motherfuckers off me because I have a date. A sex date, I want you to know."

"I don't want to know."

"Josh Foreman," he said, referring to the security guard who worked at St. Cath's.

"Please stop."

"His hands are so soft. That smile. Plus, he screams like a wildcat in bed."

"And . . . scene." I brought my hands together, indicating *cut*. Carter grinned and left the teachers' lounge.

More evidence of Alexander's plans to marry me someday flashed through my head. Once he'd said, "Margaret's a nice name for a girl, don't you think? I wouldn't mind a daughter named Margaret." Another: "We should look at property on the Maine coast for a summer place. It's so beautiful up there. And Portland has a great art scene."

Maybe it *was* time for me to take action. Juliet, my sister, older by almost twelve years, enjoyed lecturing me on how I floated through life, in contrast to her color-coded, laminated lists for How to Be Perfect and Have Everything. (I jest, but not by much.)

It was just that when I pictured being married, it was never to Alexander.

The vision of a black-haired, dark-eyed boy standing

in the gusty breeze came to mind. My own version of Jon Snow, clad in Carhartt instead of wolfskin.

But Noah and I had tried. Tried and failed, more than once, and that was a long time ago.

Carter was right. Why wait? Alexander and I had been together long enough, we had a good thing going, we both wanted kids (sort of, maybe). We weren't getting any younger. I loved him, he loved me, we got along so well it was almost spooky.

Bridget's bumblebee ring flashed in my mind. Call me shallow, but I wanted a big diamond, too. My materialism ended there. (Or not . . . Was it too soon to picture buying a brownstone in the Village? Alexander was loaded, after all. As for a wedding, we could elope. No color schemes or Pinterest boards necessary.)

He was due in around four, depending on traffic. Where was a romantic place in New York in January? It was freakishly mild today—thanks, global warming!—so maybe down on the Hudson as the sun set? The High Line was pretty, and I could go to Chelsea Market and buy some nice cheese and wine. We could watch the sunset and I'd just say it: "I love you. Marry me and make me the happiest woman on earth." And the tourists and hipsters who frequented the High Line would applaud and take pictures and we'd probably go viral.

I imagined calling my dad tonight. He'd be *so* happy. Maybe we wouldn't elope, because I wanted my father to walk me down the aisle. Fine. A small wedding, then. I'd wear a white dress that Carter could help me pick out. Brianna and Sloane could be my flower girls, even if they were a little old for that. I was their only aunt, so may as well. Plus, it would make my prickly mom happy.

Yes. I'd propose tonight, and enter the next phase of my life, where I was sure Alexander and I would be very, very content.

As luck would have it, the temperature took a plunge, as weather in the Northeast is cruel and fickle. What had been sixty-two was the low forties by the time Alexander met me in front of the Standard, an odd-looking hotel that straddled the High Line. "God, it's freezing," he said as the wind blew through us. "I found a parking spot on Tenth, but I didn't know it would be this cold."

"Oh, it's not so bad!" I said. I had a plan, and I was sticking to it. "Just brisk! The sunset will be gorgeous." Or it wouldn't. There was only one other couple who seemed to be sightseeing, everyone else hunched against the weather and hurrying to wherever New Yorkers hurry.

"Christ. I didn't dress for this." Alexander wore a brown leather jacket over a blue oxford shirt and bulky sweater, khakis and expensive leather shoes. I'd dressed to be beautiful—pretty black knit dress, hair in a ponytail (now being undone by the wind), the necklace he'd given me for Christmas and a cute red leather jacket that did nothing to keep me warm. Should've worn pants. And a parka.

"Well, come on," I said. "We don't have to stay too long. It'll be fun."

He followed me down the sidewalk, past clumps of grass and dead flower bushes. Come spring, this most elegant of New York's parks would be filled with color and life, but as it was, it was a little, uh, barren.

Shit. Well, I'd make it quick. "Sunset's in ten minutes," I said.

"I'll be dead by then."

"I'll revive your cold, hard corpse. Or at least give it a really strong attempt, then go into the Standard and drown my sorrows at the bar."

He laughed, and my heart swelled a bit. He really was a good, kind person. Great husband material. Never too demanding, always cheerful . . . the opposite of Noah, which was probably no coincidence, and I shouldn't be thinking of Noah, I reminded myself. I glanced at the other couple. Would they film us when I got down on one knee? Also, *should* I get down on one knee? These were my only black tights.

"I cannot *believe* you're saying this!" Ah. They were fighting. Not a great sign.

I really wanted the light of the sunset to spill onto us, which it would in about six minutes. Being a painter who had once loved skyscapes, I was an expert on natural light. "How was your day, hon?" I asked, trying to kill time.

"Oh, fine," he said, putting his arm around me. "Pretty sure I nailed down a sale to a hedge fund guy. He wants it made from scratch, of course." He detailed the many requirements this guy had for his boat—private master deck, helipad, indoor garden, sauna, steam room and gym.

"So just a little wooden boat to paddle around in, then," I said.

He smiled. "It's a living. Are we about done, babe? I'm starving."

"I bought cheese." I pulled the block out of my bag. Shit. We'd have to bite right into it, since I didn't have a knife.

"Hon. It's forty degrees out here. Maybe thirty-five. It's supposed to snow tonight."

"It's not so bad. See? That other couple's brave. Plus, we're Yankees. This is practically summer."

He glanced at the other couple. "They have winter coats on."

They did, both dressed in those down coats with patches that announced them as explorers of Antarctica. The woman crossed her puffy arms. "Are you shitting me, Dallas?" she practically yelled.

"Oh," murmured Alexander. "Maybe this *will* be fun after all."

"I never said I wanted to be exclusive! That was all in your head!" the unfortunately named Dallas answered.

"How many women have you been seeing, you cheating bastard? Belinda? Are you seeing that whore again?"

"She's not a whore!"

"So that's a yes! Jesus! We're done, asshole. If I have an STD, I will slit your throat and burn your apartment to the ground."

She stomped past us, cutting us a look. "Hi," I said.

"Fuck you," she snapped.

Alexander laughed. The cheater skulked past us, arms folded, head down against the wind.

"Okay, so that was fun," Alexander said. "They do have the right idea about leaving, though. This cheese is almost frozen, and I don't really see eating it here. What do you say, babe? Shall we go? Grab a drink somewhere with heat?"

Do or die. "Right. Okay." Shit. We were sitting. I scrambled to my feet. "Um, can you stand up for a second?"

"About time. Do you want to go out for dinner?" The cold wind whipped his blond hair, and his ears were bright red.

"Just one thing first." I looked into his eyes, which were watering a little from the wind. Just then, the sun slipped behind a bank of clouds that had come out of nowhere. So much for fiery skies burnishing the moment.

It didn't matter. I loved him. He was rock solid, this guy, and we . . . we had such a good thing going. Before I changed my mind, I knelt down. Felt my tights catch on the rough surface of the walkway.

"You all right?" he asked.

"Alexander Mitchum, will you marry me and make me the happiest man—shit, I mean *woman*—alive?" The wind gusted again, blowing my hair into my face.

"Uh . . . what are you doing, Sadie?" His face was incredulous.

"I . . . I'm proposing." My heart felt like the sun, abruptly swallowed in clouds. *Do not make me go back on those dating websites, Alexander Mitchum.*

"I'm the one who's supposed to propose."

"Okay! Sure. Go for it." Thank *God*.

He laughed a little. "Well, babe . . . I'm not ready. There are things I need to have in place. A ring, for one."

"We can get one later. Cartier is open till seven. Probably. Not that I checked."

He laughed. "Well, I'd like to surprise you. When the time comes."

"I'm down on one knee here, Alexander."

"Get up, then! This is crazy." He pulled me to my feet. I felt my tights tear. "You nut. It's the man's job to propose."

Sexist, really. "It seemed like a good idea. I mean, we've been together two years. We're the right age." I forced a smile.

"What is the right age, really? Is there an age that's wrong?" he asked, but he kissed my forehead. "I'll do it when the time is right. Okay?"

Well, didn't I feel stupid. "Okay."

"I want the moment to be when we're not freezing our asses off in the dark. Don't worry. It'll be perfect."

My heart felt weird. Happy weird, or disappointed weird? "I mean, now that we're talking about it . . . you could just . . . ask."

"No. I want it to be really romantic. Not on a night so cold my balls are retracting."

"Got it."

In case there was any doubt that my plan sucked, those dark gray clouds opened and a cold rain started to fall.

"I'm gonna pass out if I don't eat soon. Want to grab something, then go back to my place and fool around so we can salvage this night?"

"Sure."

Feeling like a dolt, I followed him to the stairs that led to street level.

Alexander's phone chimed. He studied it, then looked up. "Shit, babe," he said. "I have to go up to Boston. That idiot Patriots player is pitching a fit over a painting of himself that was supposed to be hung on the ceiling over his bed, and the designer put it on the wall instead. What time is it? Damn. I'll have to drive up tonight." He looked at me. "Want to come? We could grab some fast food on the road and stay overnight. A suite at the Mandarin with some spa time tomorrow, maybe?"

That was the thing about Alexander. He was so thoughtful. But my feeling of ineptitude lingered.

"I think I'll just go home. I have a painting due Sunday."

"Gotcha." We stood there awkwardly. "Want me to drive you home?"

"Subway's faster," I said.

"Okay."

"Well. Drive safely."

"I will. Talk to you, babe." He kissed me quickly and strode off.

It really was cold. I started walking toward Eighth Avenue to catch the subway. Soon, I'd be home. Maybe I'd take a shower to warm up. Order Thai food and work on that blue-and-white "like Van Gogh except not as swirly" painting I'd been commissioned to do. Bitter sigh, followed by the reminder to be grateful that I had these gigs at all and wasn't living in a paper bag.

Just then, my phone rang. Juliet, who almost never called me. "Hi!" I said. "How are you?"

"Listen, Sadie," she said, her voice strange, and instinctively, I stopped walking, my free hand covering my ear so I could hear her better. "Dad had a stroke. He's in surgery at UConn, and it's pretty bad. Get here as soon as you can."

~

CHAPTER TWO

Barb

I was in a meeting with the head of the town crew, discussing his zealous use of salt so far this winter and the complaints about undercarriage rust I'd been fielding, when I got the call.

Yes, being first selectman of a small town in Connecticut was a nonstop thrill fest. I smiled at the thought. Truth was, I loved my job. Even moments like this.

It was my last appointment of the day, and I didn't have any committee meetings tonight. Maybe I'd head over to Caro's if John was already parked in front of whatever war documentary he was watching these days. If she didn't have plans, that was.

"Yeah, well, people always bitch and moan if they skid half an inch, so I can't win for losing here, Barb," Lou said.

"We're halfway through the salt budget, and we've only had two inches of snow so far. You know we'll have at least four or five more storms this year."

"Like I said, I'm the one who gets blamed!"

Lindsey, my secretary, opened the door.

"Barb?" she said, her voice almost a whisper. "I'm so sorry, but you need to take this call. Right away. Lou, out you go."

I picked up the phone. "This is Barb Frost, how can I help you?" I said in my warm, mayoral voice. Most people who called my office wanted to complain about something, and I found that being polite always shocked them a little. I grew up in Minnesota, where manners were drilled into us. This was New England.

"Mrs. Frost, it's George Macon." George was a paramedic in town, but I didn't think we had any issues with the first responders. I hoped he wasn't going to ask for new equipment. They just got a new ambulance last year.

"How can I help you, George?" I said.

"I'm really sorry to have to tell you this, Mrs. Frost. Your husband is on his way to the ER, and he's unresponsive and not breathing on his own. Seems like he took a bad fall off his bike. Can someone drive you to the hospital? Right now?"

Gosh. *Right now* sounded real ominous, all right. My mouth moved for a moment before the words came out. "Of course. Thank you." I hung up.

Mind you, I'd always been good in emergencies. My mind could prioritize needs and get things taken care of in near-perfect order. When Juliet was eight and sliced open her hand so deeply the blood was pulsing out of it with every beat of her heart, I wrapped it tightly, told her to keep it over her head, and put her in the car rather than calling 911, mentally doing the math on how long it would take the ambulance crew to get there versus how quickly I could take her to the hospital myself. At the same time,

I was wondering if I should tourniquet her arm, but I was thinking that might cut off her blood supply. I remembered my purse so I'd have our insurance card and grabbed her Pooh bear for comfort. Got a blanket to tuck around her in the car in case she was going into shock. We were at the hospital in under ten minutes, and I only went ten miles an hour over the speed limit, because I didn't want to drive like a crazy person and cause an accident. That wouldn't have helped anyone, for Pete's sake.

When Sadie was bitten by the neighbors' dog, same thing. Ice for her face, call to the police to secure the dog and get proof of rabies vaccination, call to Caro to ask her to pick up Juliet from school, call to the hospital to tell them we'd be needing the plastic surgeon, not some resident who wanted to practice stitching, thank you very much. Six months later, you could barely see the scar.

But now . . . with John in the ambulance already . . . I felt kind of . . . well . . . frozen.

Because tomorrow, I was planning to tell my husband that I'd be filing for divorce.

And even with that, and though I'd often pictured myself a happy widow . . .

I did not ever see this moment actually happening.

Unresponsive. Not breathing.

"Barb?"

I looked up. I was still at my desk. Lindsey, the dear girl, had her coat on. "Why don't I drive you?" she said. Guess she knew, then.

"That's—that's a good idea, Linds. Thank you, hon."

My hands were shaking as I grabbed my purse. Things seemed to be moving in slow motion. I should've been well on my way to the hospital right now, but instead, I wasn't quite sure what to do next.

"Don't forget your coat," she said, because I had.

Then time sped up, and we were on 95, and I had Juliet on the phone, and she would be on her way as soon as her sitter got there. I don't know what I said to her, to be honest.

"Do you want to call your other daughter?" Lindsey asked, and no, I didn't, because it didn't seem fair to Sadie, not if ten minutes from now I'd be telling her her dad was . . . was dead.

My throat was tight. I kept swallowing, but it didn't help.

The doctor was waiting for me in the hallway of Lawrence and Memorial, which I knew wasn't a good sign. I wondered if Westerly would've been a better choice. But maybe not. Maybe this place was better for unresponsive, not-breathing patients.

"Mrs. Frost, I'm Dr. Warren," she said. "We're going to have to chopper your husband to UConn, okay? He's getting a CAT scan now, but I'm pretty sure he's got a ruptured aneurysm with massive bleeding. His condition is grave, I'm sorry to say, and he'll need surgery as soon as possible to relieve the pressure. We need you to sign these forms."

Grave? Massive? Did she have to say *massive*? My breathing was loud enough that I could hear it.

"Just sign here, and here, and initial here."

Forms. Yes, God forbid we just treated him. God forbid I got to stand by my husband and hold his hand and reassure him.

An old man was wheeled in on a gurney into a stall. Because the ER *was* like a barn. There were barns nicer than this, frankly, with all this beeping and noise and chaos and people in different-colored scrubs. Barns were beautiful, peaceful places. Sadie had taken horseback riding lessons, and the barn had been so gosh-darn pretty, but she lost interest after—

"You can see him now," the doctor said.

Oh. The old man . . . the patient they'd just parked . . . that was John. I could barely see him amid all the people in there, the equipment. He was in a neck brace. Intubated, too. His face was bloody, his eyes shut. There were electrodes and wires and an IV, and he looked so unlike himself that I nearly told the doctor there'd been a mistake.

But those were his hands. Old man hands, but wearing the ring I'd put on it fifty years ago. He'd aged well, but his hands looked old now. Then again, they may have looked old for some time. I couldn't remember the last time I'd noticed. We weren't the hand-holding type.

People were talking, but I didn't listen to what they said. They weren't talking to me, anyway.

"He's very healthy," I said. "He's been taking real good care of himself. Swimming, running, riding his bike. He wants to do a triathlon in the spring. I told him, 'John, don't be crazy, you're seventy-five years old.'"

No one was listening. I didn't blame them. He was *massively bleeding*. They had important things to do.

I suddenly remembered one sunny Sunday morning in the winter, just weeks after our wedding. The sunlight had streamed into the bedroom, turning it buttery and warm, and his hair—he'd had such thick, glorious hair back then, light brown and all crazy if he didn't comb it down. I'd thought those freckles on his shoulders so endearing. We made love . . . maybe the first time when it wasn't awkward, because that's how inexperienced we'd both been. Both of us virgins on our wedding night, hardly typical for the crazy seventies. But I'd been brought up with old-fashioned values, and John had been, too.

Anyway, we were pretty happy with ourselves that morning, since we'd finally figured out this sex thing, and we spent the whole day in bed, eating toast and then left-over spaghetti, reading the Sunday *Times* until it got dark. Then we showered and dressed and went to the movies. Can't remember what we saw.

"Go ahead, Mrs. Frost, talk to him," someone said, putting a hand on my arm. A nurse. Gosh, she seemed so young. Beautiful skin. Her eyes were kind.

"John?" I said, looking down at him. I wanted to call him honey, or darling, but it had been so long since either of us used a term of endearment for the other. "John, don't worry. I'm here. You're being taken care of. Darling." I put my hand over his.

Please don't die.

The thought came as a shock, a lightning strike right to the heart. We could do better, couldn't we? It wasn't too late?

"Here are his things," someone said, thrusting a plastic bag at me.

"Mom! Oh, my God, Daddy!" Juliet was there, and started to hug her father, but he was too confined. She hugged me instead, her body shaking.

"I know, honey, I know," I said. "He's going to UConn, and they'll do everything they can for him. World-class medicine, don't you know."

"Mrs. Frost." It was the doctor again, with some papers in her hand. "He's ready to go. The CAT scan did show a significant bleed, but no head or neck fractures. The chopper is here. Are you okay to drive to Farmington?"

"We're fine," Juliet said, then looked at me. "Riley London's watching the girls and Oliver's on his way home. I'll drive. Do you have your car? Can someone drive it home?"

The details of emergencies. Who drove which car? Did Lindsey have my coat? Did I thank her for driving me? Would she cancel all my appointments for tomorrow? Oh, wait, it was Friday. Should we take Route 9 or Route 2? What was the traffic like? Did I need the ladies' room before we left? I did.

It's strange how your body keeps going when your life is falling apart. I needed to go to the bathroom—I was seventy years old, of course I did. I washed my hands, aware that I was in a hospital with a lot of sick people. It was flu season. It wouldn't help anyone if I got sick.

My husband might be dead right now.

Juliet had pulled her BMW to the entrance. I got in and buckled up. "I didn't text Sadie," she said. "I wasn't sure if you told her anything yet. I thought it might be better if we knew something first. When he's stable. Or . . . if he doesn't make it. I hope someone can drive her. She's gonna take this hard."

Exactly my thoughts. "Are *you* all right to drive, sweetheart?"

"I'm a rock, Mom." Her voice shook a little, but she was. She really was. She drove efficiently and safely, always using her turn signal.

We didn't talk much. But she reached over and took my hand and squeezed it. "Whatever happens," she said, "we'll get through it."

By the time we got to Farmington, John was already in surgery. He was still alive, the nurse told us, but it was a critical situation, given his age and the location of the aneurysm.

According to the paramedic report, John had been riding his bike. In January, down Canterbury Hill Road, and honestly, why? I mean, sure, he had to have his hobbies, and when he started that whole silly running/biking/ swimming thing last year, I was relieved that he'd found something to keep him occupied. But riding a bike in January? That's just foolish, even if today had been real nice.

"Based on his injuries, the doctor thinks he had the stroke first and then fell smack onto the pavement, which is why his face is banged up," the nurse said. "He didn't raise his hands to protect himself." She demonstrated how someone would instinctively cover their face. "He has a concussion on top of the stroke, and his nose is broken, but the bleeding is the big problem right now."

"Will he live?" Juliet asked. My strong girl, asking the hard questions.

"These things are hard to predict," she said. "Try to keep good thoughts. We'll tell you more as soon as we know." She put a hand on my arm. "I'm sorry. I know this is incredibly hard. I wish we had more information."

"Thank you. You're very kind."

"I'll call Sadie," Juliet said.

"Oh. Yes. Do you want me to?" I asked. "Maybe I should, don'tcha think?"

"No, Mommy. You sit down, okay? I'll be back in a few. I'll bring you a coffee and a snack. There's a Starbucks here. I'll be right back. Text me if there's any news." She smiled suddenly. "I can hear your Minnesota."

"Oh, can you, now?" I asked, exaggerating the accent as a joke, and we managed a little laugh. It was true; stress brought out the accent.

Off she went, and as ever, I was so grateful that she was mine, and here.

The family waiting room on this floor looked like an

airport lounge, sleek and cheerful. I found a chair and sat down, still in my winter coat. The chair was meant to look like a Morris chair, sturdy and reassuring. A good choice for this place.

When we first moved to Stoningham, I'd loved tag and estate sales and combed half the state looking for antiques that needed a little sanding, some repairs. John still worked in family law then, and we had to be smart about money, what with all the house costs we had—new kitchen, bathrooms, a leak in the roof, a new boiler. But we also had to furnish the place.

One day, I'd come across a beautiful wooden chair with leather cushions and clean lines. It cost ten dollars. I brought it home, cleaned and oiled the leather, polished the wood, and presented it to John when he came home that night. He'd been so pleased. So pleased. It was a vintage Morris chair, we learned, and John sat in it every night until he moved it to his study.

It was the best gift I'd ever given him.

I wondered when he moved it from the living room into the study.

The bag I'd forgotten I was holding gave a strange buzz. Right. John's things were in there, those slippery, strange clothes that were thin as paper but somehow kept you warm. Honest to Pete. He was too old to be an athlete. I'd tell him that if he lived. He could take up fly-fishing or something. My fingers closed on his phone and pulled it out.

It was his work. John still did some consulting here and there. Shoot. I should tell them, shouldn't I? He loved some of those folks. I typed in his code (0110, our anniversary), but it didn't work. He must've changed it after being hacked or something, not that he said anything to me. I typed in his birthday. That didn't work, either. Sadie's birthday. There.

His screen was lit up with texts. I put on my reading glasses.

After a second, I took off my reading glasses and put the phone down. Held down the little button so it would turn off. My face felt hot, my hands like ice. My heart felt sick and slow, flopping like a dying bird.

I glanced around. Could anyone tell? Were they looking at me? Did they know?

No. Everyone else was worried about their own people. I should worry about John. His brain was bleeding. Juliet would be back in a minute.

Shame. That's what I felt. Shame and humiliation, and fear that everyone would see on my face what I had just learned.

CHAPTER THREE

~

Juliet

On the day her father had his stroke, Juliet Elizabeth Frost was considering leaving her perfect life and becoming a smoke jumper in Montana—husband, children and job be damned.

The thing was, her life really *was* perfect. Excellent health, fabulous education, a career as an architect that earned her a ridiculous salary. She had a husband who loved her *and* was from London with a dead-sexy accent to boot. They had two healthy daughters and lived in a beautiful home overlooking Long Island Sound. Juliet drove a safe, fancy but not too pretentious German car. They brought their daughters on vacations to places like New Zealand and Provence. She spoke French and Italian. Her boobs had survived nursing two babies, and while they might not be perky anymore, they weren't saggy, either.

She knew a lot of successful, intelligent women,

though her mother was her true best friend. She tolerated her younger sister and was sometimes even fond of her. Her father, who had always been distracted where she was concerned, had recently morphed into a raging asshole . . . and Juliet was going to have to tell her mother about it. Soon.

None of this explained why she was currently sitting in her closet, having a panic attack, hoping she'd faint.

The girls were at school, thank God, and Oliver was at work, designing jet engines. It was lucky that Juliet was working from home today, because last week, when she had a panic attack at work, and the idea of her coworkers, her boss, and *Arwen* seeing her hyperventilating and crying and possibly fainting . . . no. She'd had to get down eight floors and rush into the Starbucks on Chapel Street, and thankfully, the restroom was free. The first time it hadn't been, and she'd slid to the floor and had to pretend she was having a sugar crash in order to keep the barista from calling the ambulance.

Today, the panic attack had just sneaked up on her right during the conference call with her team at DJK Architects, one of the best firms in the U.S. Seemingly out of nowhere, it came . . . that creeping, prickling terror that started in her feet and slithered up her legs, making her knees ache, her heart rate accelerate. *Keep your shit together*, she ordered herself. Her boss, Dave, was drawing out the goodbyes with his usual jargon . . . "So I think we all have our action points" and "we've really drilled down on the issue," all those stupid clichés. Would it kill him to just end the damn meeting?

Her heart was beating so hard, and she was trying not to blink too fast, but the sweat was breaking out on her body, chest first, then armpits and crotch, back of the legs, forehead. In another ten seconds, she'd start to hyperventilate.

"Arwen, e-mail me those numbers, okay?" she said. Her voice sounded strained and thin.

"Already done."

Of course it was. "Great! Talk soon, everyone!" Her voice was a croak. She clicked the End button, closed the computer just in case the feed was still live, and bolted for the closet.

Sometimes, the hyperventilation caused her to pass out, which was actually a lot easier than talking herself down, that forced slow breathing, the mantra of *you're fine, you're fine, you're fine, slow down, slow down, slow down.* Fainting was lovely. If she fainted, everything grayed out gently, giant spots eating up her vision, and it felt as if she were falling so slowly.

Then she'd wake up, normal breathing restored, on the carpeted floor of her expansive closet—because so far, four of the six panic attacks had been in the closet, conveniently—safe among her shoes and sweaters. Like a nap. Like anesthesia. Juliet loved anesthesia; last year, she'd had to have a uterine biopsy, and the IV sedation was the best feeling she'd had in ages. She wished she could've stayed in that state, that lovely, floating, almost unconscious state, for a long time. Totally understandable why people got hooked on those drugs.

The attack was passing. No pleasant fainting this time, apparently. She'd have to shower again, since she was damp with sweat, and change, and get her current outfit to the dry cleaner's. If Oliver noticed their dry-cleaning bill had seen a significant bump, he hadn't said anything. Then again, that was her job: pick up dry cleaning on the way home from the office.

None of these was the reason she was sitting hunched in her closet.

The problem was Arwen.

No. No, she wasn't the problem. Juliet hated women who blamed other women for their issues . . . or maybe their own lack of success.

But the problem was maybe Arwen. Arwen Alexander, Wunderkind.

Yes. Fuck it, Juliet's heart started racing again. *Come on, fainting! You can do it!* A laugh/sob popped out of her lips.

The panic grew. Fast. Like a mushroom. Like cancer. How had she been reduced to sitting in a fucking closet with the full-on shakes when she had a perfect life?

In the past few months, everything Juliet took for a fact seemed fluid. She'd always wanted to be an architect, but did she anymore? Somehow, inexplicably, it felt like she was living the wrong life. How could that be? Every detail had been planned, mapped out, worked for and achieved. Harvard, check. Yale, check. Oliver, check. Two healthy daughters, check and check and thank God. This house that she'd designed in the town she loved. Check. Parents who loved her and had a solid (ha!) marriage.

But suddenly it all felt wrong. Never before had Juliet questioned that she was on the right path . . . until now.

Was she a good mother? A good wife? She loved her girls, of course she did. She'd *die* for them. Kill anyone who threatened them with a song in her heart and a smile on her lips. She did everything she could for them, and from the outside, it probably looked like she was a good mother.

She just didn't *feel* like it these days. Brianna had grown sullen and withdrawn—she was twelve, so it wasn't the world's biggest surprise. But the thing was, Juliet hadn't done that with her mother. She *adored* her mother, every day, every year. Sloane was right behind Brianna at ten . . . Would she stop talking to her, too? Oliver had been a little . . . distant, maybe. And if there was one thing Juliet couldn't stand, it was distant. Her father had been that way (except with Sadie). And Dad had been *especially* distant with Mom.

Of course things stopped being hot and heavy after fifteen years of marriage. You couldn't keep that shit up, no matter how hard you tried, how many thongs you bought. Things became expected and comfortable, and that was *good*, wasn't it? Even if she tried really hard to be spontaneous and exciting, she and Ollie knew each other inside and out. Would she find herself walking her parents' path, barely speaking, being invisible to the other?

This seeping dread, this flight response . . . why did it feel so real? Was she a fake somehow, in both work and life? Why was Arwen so terrifying when she was perfectly . . . fine?

Shit, shit, shit. This was what happened. One little crack, and the whole building comes down.

Juliet stood. Her legs felt shaky, and her hair looked greasy. There were circles under her eyes.

That faint would've been welcome. A little nap.

Instead, she went to her computer and Googled "how to become a smoke jumper in Montana." Very conveniently, the U.S. Forest Service was hiring. So she would need a little experience fighting wildland fires. She'd get it. Juliet was in great shape. She liked heights and fires (though more of the bonfire/fireplace type). She was brave—always the first to jump in the water, or try waterskiing or leap off the platform while zip-lining. She was an adrenaline junkie who had just emerged from hiding in her closet.

The idea of being far, far away doing heroic things had such pull, such promise. Her sister Sadie would probably do it. Move to Montana, be handed a job, meet a cowboy who happened to also be a billionaire and spend the rest of her life traveling and getting massages on various beaches, because that's how life unfolded for Sadie. Juliet worked and planned for everything; Sadie skipped off to New York City, doing things in the most irresponsible, unplanned, carefree way possible. *No money? No problem. I can waitress! I can work in a tattoo parlor! I'm an artist, you see. Things are different for us, since we're pure and superior. No career? No worries! Something will come along. In the meantime, look at this hovel I'm living in after Mom and Dad remortgaged the house to put me through college!*

In typical Sadie fashion, she got a cute little job at a cute little school and somehow started earning money on paintings that allowed her to buy a cute little apartment and then found a cute wealthy boyfriend. Sadie never had to work for a thing. Juliet worked every fucking day, every fucking minute. Did people think Oliver just saw her and fell in love? Oh, no. She had to *work* for him. The guy was absolutely wonderful—handsome and charming and smart and kind and funny—and *everyone* had wanted him. Juliet had taken one look at him and thought, *Game on.* She'd had to *earn* him, which she had.

All work, all the time, every part of her life. Me time? Please. Juliet brought work with her on every weekend away, every vacation. She took a bubble bath for effect, only when Oliver had come home from a trip, and she'd run the bath and sprinkle flower petals in and light candles the way no one ever did in real life, and it was all for seduction, to say, "Sure, we've been married for fifteen years, but I'm still a voracious sex beast, you betcha!" Long walks on the weekends or after school were to incorporate health and outdoor time into the girls' lives, even if Juliet's brain was fogged with all the work she had to do to earn that fat salary, how late she'd have to work to make up the time spent walking, how to help Sloane catch up on reading and make gluten-free, peanut-free, dairy-free cupcakes for Sloane's class and later have sex with Oliver so he wouldn't forget he loved her, or take Mom out to dinner because she deserved it, or plant flowers in the front yard because Oliver's British mother loved gardens and had once said a house without a garden is a house without a soul, and then what about the mentorship thing she'd promised to do for Yale, and the workshop (not keynote) she was giving at the annual American Institute of Architects conference on risk management (not the sexy one Arwen was doing on "breaking boundaries") and right, their cleaning lady had moved and Juliet hadn't found another one yet so she had to clean the house because she liked things tidy and couldn't relax if things were messy.

"Shit," she said aloud. "Next time, faint, you idiot."

She left her closet, intending to take a shower, but there was her phone, buzzing on the desk of her study.

Mom. She always took calls from Mom.

"Sweetheart," her mother began, "I'm real sorry to have to tell you this, but your dad's been in an accident, and he's hurt. Real bad. I'm on my way to Lawrence and Memorial."

Her heart thudded hard, rolling in a sickening wave—once, twice, three times.

"I'm on my way," Juliet said, her voice firm. "Hang in there, Mom, I'll be there in twenty minutes."

Smoke jumper. She would make a great smoke jumper.

CHAPTER FOUR

~

Sadie

In the blur of terror that followed Juliet's call, I rented a car and drove through the snarl of traffic between Manhattan and Connecticut, doing eighty miles an hour when I could, slamming on the brakes when I saw taillights. Even though I'd tried calling Alexander as soon as I hung up with Jules, he wasn't answering. He had a habit of keeping the phone off while he drove, which was not at all convenient at this moment. After leaving six messages, I called Carter and told him instead, hiccuping with sobs.

"Oh, sweetheart," he said. "Good luck. I'm here for anything you need. If you want me to call Sister Mary or anything, if you need me to water your plants, let me know."

The whole way there, tears streaked down my cheeks and I had to fight not to break down. My dad had been my idol growing up—always encouraging, upbeat and fun . . . not to mention the parent who actually liked me. He taught me to play poker and swim and never said art school was a bad idea. He told me I was pretty and never criticized my clothes, even in my goth stage. He came to visit me once a month in the city, and still held my hand when we were crossing the street. He couldn't be dying. Not without me there.

All my life, there'd been a clear division in the family. Juliet "Perfection from Conception" was Mom's; I, the lesser child in just about every measurable aspect except artistic ability, was Dad's. He never seemed to think he got the short end of the stick.

"Please don't die, please don't die," I chanted under my breath. Who else would root for me the way he did? Who else would be so . . . so delighted at every turn of my life? It seemed that all my childhood, Mom had lectured on everything from posture to how to clean the bathroom to grades, and Dad had been right behind her, sweeping away the criticism with a grin or a wink and maybe a trip to the ice cream parlor. Everything he did let me know I was loved, whereas everything Mom did let me know I was wrong.

There was a reason I rarely came back to Stoningham, and when I did, it was only for a day. And there was a reason my father came to visit me in the city, sleeping on the pullout couch, thinking it was the best fun ever. Those were always like old times, when I was little and afraid of thunderstorms, and Dad would tell me stories about girl warriors who rode monsters they'd tamed into battle.

My chest felt like it was being crushed. Where the hell was Alexander? Why wasn't he calling me?

Finally, after an eternity, I pulled into the UConn Health Center's giant parking lot, threw my shitty little rental in park and ran to get inside, slipping and sliding, since the rain had frozen when the temperature dropped, and it was a good ten degrees colder up here.

An orderly directed me to the family waiting area, and I ran there, too.

Mom, Jules and Oliver were in the waiting room, Jules looking worried, Mom a thousand miles away.

"Is he—" I began, but my voice choked off.

"Unconscious but alive," Oliver said, getting up to hug me. "He made it through surgery. We're waiting for the doctor to tell us what we can expect."

My sister got up and we hugged awkwardly, too. She stepped on my foot, and my hair got tangled in her earring for a second.

"Hi, Mom," I said.

"Hello, Sadie." Her voice was expressionless. Shock, I guessed. She was clutching a plastic bag to her chest. I kissed her cheek, and she still didn't look at me. "Hello, Sadie," she repeated, and I felt a twinge of sympathy.

"Hi, Mom. You doing okay?" She was younger than Dad, and I'd heard that seventy was the new forty, but still.

"I'm fine," she said. My hands were shaking, but she seemed utterly calm.

"Can I see him?"

"He's resting."

"I'd like to see him."

"Sure, sure," said Jules. "Come on. We're only allowed a few minutes an hour, but come say . . . well." Her voice choked off, and she took a shaky breath.

We walked down a long, brightly lit hallway and went into a room.

Oh, God. Oh, Daddy.

He was on a ventilator, his face swollen, a cut on his

nose, a black eye. His head was shaved and bandaged. "Jesus," I whispered.

"They had to drill into his head to relieve the bleeding," Jules said.

He didn't look like himself, but it was him, all right. Those were his outrageous eyebrows. That was his wedding ring on his left hand, his class ring from Boston College on his right. The scar on his arm from when he had a bad break in college.

"It's a wait-and-see situation," Jules said, and her voice was uncharacteristically soft.

I didn't know where to touch my father; he looked so small in the hospital bed.

"Daddy?" I whispered, putting my hand on his chest, over his heart. "It's Sadie. I'm here. I love you so much, Daddy."

That was all I was allowed. A nurse told us he needed quiet, and Jules led me back to the waiting room.

"What happened?" I asked, and Oliver, the diplomat in the family, filled me in.

It was such a Dad move, deciding to go for a bike ride on a nice day, winter be damned. Apparently he had a stroke and fell, then lay there for an unknown amount of time before someone saw him and called 911. They missed the golden hour, that window after a stroke when intervention can make a huge difference. "A pity, really," Oliver said. The vast understatement of that word made me want to smack him.

My tears kept falling. My mother stared into space. Juliet checked in with the babysitter and sat next to Mom. They murmured to each other. Oliver smiled every time I looked at him. I kept checking my phone to see if Alexander had turned on his—Boston wasn't that far, and I'd texted, too. But he was one of those people who would forget his phone was off until hours later.

A few friends from St. Catherine's had texted; I guess Carter had put the word out. Even Sister Mary sent me a message, saying she'd pray for my family.

An hour ticked past. A couple of times, I had to get up and go to the window so I wouldn't sob in front of my family, in case Mom said something like, "There's no point in crying, Sadie. Save that for when he dies." Not that she would. But I kept imagining that kind of thing— Juliet sighing and rolling her eyes at me, or my annoyingly chipper brother-in-law saying something British, like, "Stiff upper lip, Sadie! No need to get all collywobbles!"

Where was Alexander? Where was the doctor? (He probably had a good excuse, like saving someone's life, but I was still irked.)

It started to snow, first just a few drifting flakes, then a near whiteout. The TV on the wall showed meteorologists peeing themselves with glee, standing at intersections where cars slid by to report that, yes, it was snowing. If one of those sliding cars hit them, it would be natural selection.

My father's condition had rendered me vicious, it seemed.

Finally, as I stared out the window at the "polar vortex" (because calling it *snow* was so yesterday), Alexander's name flashed on my phone. I told him the grim news.

"Babe, I'm so sorry. I'll be there as soon as I can," he said. "You know me and driving with the phone off. But I'll keep it on, and I'm getting right back in the car."

"Is it snowing there?" I asked.

He hesitated. "Yeah. Pretty hard."

"Here too. Why don't you call in the morning? Stay in Boston tonight. The forecast is eight to twelve inches."

"That's what she said."

My jaw clenched. "Not now, Alexander."

"Sorry. Just trying to make you laugh."

"I know." I paused. "I miss you."

"I miss you, too. I'm so sorry about this, babe. I know how much you love your dad."

The tears started again, stinging the now-raw skin under my eyes. "Thanks, honey," I said, my voice husky.

"Love you, Sadie."

"Love you, too."

I went back to rejoin the family. No one looked up.

"No word from the doctor?" I asked.

"Alas, no," said Oliver.

Alas? I tried not to be annoyed, but Oliver . . . he was perfectly nice. If he lacked substance in my opinion, I guess it didn't matter. He was a good father, a good husband, and a brilliant son-in-law, at least according to Mom.

I Googled "stroke with cerebral hemorrhage" on my phone, then decided it would only lead to terror. May as well hear from the doctor first. I sighed. Studied my family. I'd seen them at Christmas, just a few weeks ago, but that seemed like millennia now.

Jules looked frazzled, which was rare, but who could blame her? Her hair was perfectly straight, smooth and dark blond, shoulder length, but now it was tangled, as if she'd been sleeping. Her clothes were wrinkled, too. Usually, she was so put together—her personal style could be called understated hip. Always quality stuff, always a little boring unless you looked closely and saw that her shirt was asymmetrical or she was wearing a wicked cool silver ring. As ever, she was Mom's guard dog, sitting by her side, reminding her to drink some water, offering her a Life Saver.

She didn't offer me a Life Saver.

And then there was Oliver, terribly handsome as always, brown hair, green eyes, his teeth blindingly white and straight (he'd gotten braces when he and Juliet were engaged, succumbing to the pressures of American orthodontic standards). He was scrolling through his phone, and I wanted to rip it out of his hands and hit him on the head with it. Every time he caught me looking, he gave that knee-jerk smile. *Oliver,* I wanted to say, *my father might be dying and I realize I'm probably the only one who would really miss him, but could you stop flashing your perfect teeth at me?* He'd always been nice to me . . . and also had never made an effort to do more than exchange pleasantries. Then there was the way Juliet showed him off, like he was a prize cow at the state fair. "This is my *husband*, Oliver Smitherington." It was that last name, probably. How could you have sex with someone with such a silly last name?

And Mom. Right now, she was a frickin' statue, her blunt white bob perfectly in place, mascara unsmudged by tears. Why *would* she cry? She practically hated my father. Tolerated him at best, and while it didn't feel great to think of my mother as a user, she had sure used Dad. His name, his hard-earned money. She hadn't had her own job till last year.

That being said, she looked pale and alone right now. I'd expected Auntie Caro, Mom's closest friend, to be here, since they'd been besties since before I was born. But no. Mom just stared into the distance, probably planning a tag sale to get rid of Dad's things.

"How are you doing, Mom?" I said.

"Fine."

"This must be very hard for you."

She blinked. "What's that, Sadie?"

"This must be hard for you," I repeated more loudly, getting an evil look from Jules. "Having your husband of fifty years in a life-threatening situation. Brain bleed. Surgery."

"I don't need a summary, Sadie. Of course it's hard."

"Don't be a jerk," Juliet told me.

"Well, it's a little odd, all of you stone-faced here. Except you, Oliver." He smiled again. Jesus.

"Want some sackcloth and ashes?" she asked. "Sorry if we're keeping it together. You keep doing you, though."

Finally, the doctor appeared, a tall, handsome African American man wearing scrubs and a white doctor jacket with his name stitched over the pocket. *Daniel Evans, MD. Neurosurgery.*

God. Brain surgery. *Please make it, Daddy. Please don't die.*

"I'm so sorry," he said. "We had another emergency right after your . . . uh, Mr., uh . . ."

"Frost," Juliet and I said in unison.

"Yes, of course. So." He sat down. "Your father—and husband, Mrs. Frost—had a significant bleed, as we suspected. Right now, he's resting, as you know. We're keeping him on the ventilator to help his breathing, more as a precaution than anything else, since he had started breathing on his own again in the ambulance on the way here."

My insides started to quiver. It sounded so dire.

"I wish I could tell you what to expect. There *is* damage to the part of the brain that controls speech, we're sure of that. There's also bruising from the fall, which has caused some swelling. But he survived the surgery. It's going to be one step at a time. Now, I'm sure you have questions."

"Will he wake up?" I asked.

He tilted his head. "We don't know yet. Brain injuries are hard to predict. Every one is different. All I can say now is he's stable but critical. The next couple of days will tell us more. Where do you folks live?"

"Stoningham," Juliet answered. Mom still hadn't said a word.

He nodded. "Why don't you go home and get some rest? We'll call if his status changes."

"That's a good idea," Oliver said.

"No, it's not," I said. "He'll want us close by."

"We've been here for hours," Juliet said. "And we can't camp out in his room, Sadie. It's critical care."

"Well, I'm not going," I said. "If something . . . happens, I want to be here."

"We have the girls," Oliver said.

"I'm aware of that, Oliver. You guys go. The girls need you. I know that."

"Thanks, Dr. Evans," Jules said. "We appreciate your kindness."

He shook our hands, his face somber, and left.

"Too bad you're dating a yacht salesman," Juliet said.

I ignored that. "I can sleep right here if I have to, but I want to be close by."

"That's fine," Mom said. "But I'll go home with Juliet, I think. It's been quite a shock."

The obligatory hugs were doled out, and they left.

My mom might be a widow soon. For all her flaws as a wife, that had to be scary. They'd been married fifty years. God. Fifty years tomorrow.

I went to the nurses' station and asked to see my father again. He was in the same position, but then again, he'd been heavily sedated, I guessed.

He looked awful. It was hard to imagine he could survive—the bandage on his head, the tube coming out of his mouth, some stitches on his eyebrow, the bruising.

"I'm here, Daddy," I said. "I'm right here. You and me, just like always." I told the nurses where I'd be, and they were so nice, telling me to get some food. One of them gave me a blanket.

If my father died in the middle of the night, he wouldn't be alone. There'd be someone who loved him to hold his hand and thank him, and I was glad it was me, because honestly, I couldn't imagine Juliet or my mother doing it.

~

CHAPTER FIVE

Barb

I tried to remember when my marriage went from real good to fine to not bad to downright nonexistent, and could not pinpoint a time. No, I couldn't.

Once, John and I loved each other. I didn't have any doubt about that, no sir. It could be said that we didn't know each other real well in those early days, but we were happy.

It was the infertility that started the downward slide. John didn't try real hard to understand my pain, and being a second-generation Norwegian and daughter of a Minnesotan farmer, maybe I didn't know how to share the full heft of it. We Minnesotans don't like to complain.

But it didn't take a genius to understand that I *was* suffering. Looking back, I think John wanted to pretend I *didn't* suffer, because that would get him off the hook for a problem he couldn't fix.

Then, when we *were* blessed, of course my focus was

Juliet. Unfortunately, having a baby didn't bring us a heck of a lot closer, which was partly my fault. I can see that now.

But isn't that what good mothers do? I was a stay-at-home mom in an age (and a town) where most of us *did* stay home, or only worked part-time. I'd wanted more than anything to be a mother. I wasn't about to put my little baby in someone else's care. Absolutely not! She was my whole purpose in life, don't you know. I wouldn't have had it any other way.

But John didn't get it. He didn't see all that I did. It used to make me downright crazy when he would comment on her progress or abilities. "We had a lot of fun this afternoon," he said one Sunday in August when he'd taken her to the beach, practically giving himself the father of the year award. "Do you know what a great swimmer she is?"

"Who do you think taught her?" I snapped. "And did you forget the sunscreen? She looks mighty pink to me."

The same with reading. "Our four-year-old is reading chapter books!" he exclaimed, as if he was telling me something I didn't know. Me, who spent every day with her, who read to her for hours, who gave her her love of books. I wanted him to see that, to credit me, to honor those hours, those *years*, when everything I did was for the good of our daughter. I was a wonderful mother. I told Juliet I loved her all the time, and that was something I never heard growing up, no sir. I was generous and thoughtful and affectionate. I set boundaries so she got enough sleep, ate nutritious meals, respected others and herself, was brave but not foolish. She was my life's work.

And while John would give me a card on Mother's Day and make me a breakfast that used every pot and pan in the kitchen, and tell me to "take the day off from housework" (so I could do twice as much on Monday), he just didn't see it. Or he pretended not to. When he "babysat" Juliet so I could do exciting things like grocery shopping all by my lonesome, I'd come home to find him reading with her parked in front of the TV, watching something other than the shows I allowed (half an hour a day on weekends, nothing on school days). He didn't notice that the house was sparkling clean, even when she was a tiny baby, because the house had *always* been sparkling clean, and let me tell you, it wasn't because he knew his way around a scrub brush.

He thought Juliet had just come out a certain way, as if she raised herself.

Sometimes, I had to grit my teeth when people told us what a great kid she was, and John would glow with pride. He'd say things like, "Well, my mom loves poetry, too," forgetting that I read poetry to our daughter (and no one had ever read poetry to me, you can be sure about that). *He* sure didn't read poetry—and he was related to Robert Frost, maybe! He rarely made it home in time to read anything at all to Juliet.

The truth was, John didn't do a lot with our daughter except provide. And he *was* a good provider. I valued that. Of course I did, and I still tried to be a good wife, asking him how his day went, arranging our social life because he certainly didn't. I'd invite the partners of his firm over for dinner and make sure everything was delicious and beautiful, and he'd say, "That was nice, hon," and then try to put the moves on me, and ignore the fact that I had just made a dinner for twelve people and was darn tired. But I'd have sex with him, and when he was sound asleep, I'd go downstairs and clean up the mess from dinner.

His personal habits began to scrape my nerve endings raw. When we were new to Stoningham and I had nothing but the house and volunteering to occupy my time, it was absolutely fine if he left a towel on the bathroom floor or didn't rinse out the sink after he shaved. I was a housewife, so I didn't mind cleaning up after him, though it reminded me that when we both worked full-time, I still did ninety-five percent of the housework.

But now, raising our beautiful, wonderful daughter, that towel and sink told me he didn't think anything had changed. That he was too important to put his own dang towel on the rack or in the laundry basket, that three seconds of sink rinsing was beneath him because he was a lawyer and I was *just* a mother.

Again, in hindsight, I probably should've said something about this.

His own mother appreciated me, because she'd *been* me. When his parents came to visit, John and his father would play golf, while Eleanor and I admired Juliet, because really, isn't that what grandmothers do? She cooed and praised and held her granddaughter close. Once, when it was just the two of us, Juliet asleep in her arms, she said, "No one knows how much of your soul you give to your baby. They think it's just luck or chance that your baby sleeps through the night, or doesn't pitch a tantrum when you're leaving a store, or knows to say thank you. They think you were tapped by a fairy wand, and they ignore all the hours you put in, shaping them."

Gosh, it felt so good to be truly seen that way! Sad to say, Eleanor died when Sadie was three months old. I wondered if things would've been different if she'd lived. I bet she would've helped, and maybe recognized that I had postpartum depression, because she was a smart one, that Eleanor. She was always kind and wise. Much more so than my own mother, may she rest in peace.

But as it was, both John and I lost our mothers in the span of six months, and right smack in between those deaths, we had a newborn. Seemed like God was laughing at all those years of trying to have Juliet, and then, when Juliet was almost twelve, surprise!

John felt very heroic, taking care of Sadie, changing diapers and getting up in the middle of the night . . . something he'd almost never done with Juliet. He loved to tell me how much he did, as my breasts felt like they were being sliced by knives and turning hard as rocks. When my incision needed to be restitched because I'd had a coughing fit (don't the doctors just love to tell you how you were responsible for everything that goes wrong?), John told me how he'd brilliantly arranged for Caro to pick up Juliet for Girl Scouts. Not only that, he'd taken a casserole I'd made the month before out of the freezer, so dinner was all set. I'd been saving that casserole for when he went back to work and was traveling, when I'd be alone with our baby and adolescent, when all household and child-related responsibilities would be on me and me alone. "It's good, isn't it?" he said at dinner that night. "Who made this?"

He was just so . . . obtuse sometimes. Most times, to be honest.

Just as Juliet and I had our own little world, he had one with Sadie. Juliet loved her little sister, but their time together was limited; she had homework and projects, activities and friends. The sides were pretty clear—Sadie and John, Juliet and me. I couldn't help resenting his adoration of Sadie, because Juliet had gotten none of that.

Sometimes I'd see her face as she watched her father giving horsey rides to Sadie, or drawing with her for an hour after supper, and I knew she was hurt.

When Juliet left for college, things got worse in our marriage. He was critical of how I interacted with Sadie, telling me I was too strict, that Sadie was a free spirit, that I had to be more flexible. If I said, "No more cookies, Sadie," he'd inevitably sneak her one more. If I said it was bedtime, he'd give her fifteen minutes longer. He came home every night at six thirty and it seemed like all he did was pick at me regarding Sadie. Why was she in her room? So what if she'd told her teacher math was stupid and she wouldn't do her assignments? Everyone hated math. Were we having pork chops again? Didn't we just have them?

And he said these things in an amiable way, so if I were to say, "No, John, that was in April. I make a meal plan so we never have the same dinner twice in any month, and I've done that since the day we were married. Haven't you noticed?" he'd say, "Okay, okay, I'm sorry. My mistake. I didn't mean to offend you." Then he'd wink at Sadie, or sigh if she wasn't in the room, letting me know I was the bad guy here.

He always, always took her side. "She's not Juliet. She's her own person, Barb."

"I know that! But she needs more boundaries and focus, John! I spend all day with her, and you breeze in for two hours of fun after all the hard things are done."

"What's so hard about your life, Barb?" Again, said in a condescending way.

You can see there was no winning these arguments.

By the time Sadie finally left for school, I was fifty-eight years old, tired and awfully relieved. And this time, John was the one who cried on the trip home. I've got to admit, it felt a little bit like justice.

I did hope that once we were alone, things would improve between us . . . hoped that my constant irritation with him would fade and we could become close again. But there was always a disconnect. If I put my hand on his leg in bed, he'd say, "Oh. I'm sorry, hon. I'm exhausted." The next night, he'd be completely up for it if you get my meaning, and *I'd* be fighting to stay awake. If we did have sex, it was rare that we recaptured that old sunshiny feeling. Instead, it was just a box to be checked. Sex with husband. Done, thank heavens.

Men didn't understand how hard it was to get in the mood. I hated movies when one kiss was enough for the woman and three seconds later they were doing it. Men thought that was normal. They took it personally if you weren't like that, and please. I wasn't twenty-five anymore. Men didn't realize that we women had to talk ourselves into the mood a lot of the time, had to go through the motions until they were sincere, had to deal with the consequences of an aging reproductive system. Dryness. Hot flashes. Urinary tract infections. Less sensitivity. Cysts. All men had were penises that were or were not erect.

We started sleeping in different bedrooms during Sadie's sophomore year of college, when his snoring took a turn for the louder and my bladder got me up two times a night. When we watched TV together, he'd sit in the recliner, and I'd sit on the couch, and ten minutes later, he'd be asleep.

John worked. I volunteered. Though he was Sadie's favorite parent, I was the one who knew her college schedule.

I was the one who made her retake her math requirement at the community college so she could graduate. I asked Genevieve London, who lived here in Stoningham and was quite a force in fashion, if Sadie could have an internship in the design department, hoping her art degree could somehow support her. (Sadie turned that internship down, FYI.)

And yet, I was always the mean parent, always the odd man out. I wondered what it was like to be loved by Sadie, to be respected, to have her come up and put her arm around my waist. Must've been real nice, I thought. If I put my hand on her hair or tried to give her a hug, she'd act all surprised and give me a look that said, *What are you* doing?

It was just so . . . draining.

To fill myself up, I turned to the place where I felt most like myself: Juliet. And her family, of course. But Juliet especially. There, with them, I was the best, truest version of myself. Happy, funny, helpful, listening intently as Juliet told me something about work or her friends, offering advice when asked. "That's a great idea, Mom," she'd say, or "I knew you'd have the perfect words."

I volunteered, as I always had in Stoningham. I was on the school board, the historical society, the garden club, the Friends of the Library. There were hardly any year-rounders I didn't know by name. Shopkeepers greeted me gladly; teachers would come to me with problems; newcomers to town were steered to me for guidance on how to fit into our tight-knit little community. I knew the pastor, the priest and the rabbi. I recommended volunteer groups—trash pickup, the food pantry, adopt-a-grandparent, the after-school program.

John knew I did these things, but they didn't interest him. He played golf; he was on the fishing derby committee, which meant I wrote a check for $500 for the Scouts each spring, and John went and talked to the other dads.

And still I tried. It's the woman's job to steer the relationship, Caro told me (which didn't prevent her divorce, mind you). So over dinner, I'd ask John about his day and get the customary answer . . . "Nothing exciting. Just the usual." If I offered up what I did, his eyes would glaze over, and he'd say, "Hm?" in response. We took to reading instead of talking as we ate.

Holidays were generally wonderful, because of Juliet and the girls. I'd bake and decorate and play special music—all the things my childhood lacked out there in cold Minnesota. Juliet and her girls would help or admire, and Sadie would come home and sometimes even say something nice, like, "The house looks pretty, Mom" or "It smells so good in here."

Times like these, I'd look at my husband and smile, thinking, *Aren't we so lucky? Two healthy children. Two healthy grandchildren. A lovely son-in-law. A beautiful home.* Sometimes, I'd even say it. "Sure are," he'd answer, and that would be it.

It was hard, feeling nothing but irritation toward him. Harder and harder with every passing year. When he retired at sixty-eight, my heart sank, because after all those years, he would be here, every day, day after day, getting in the way, pretending to try to be helpful but gumming it up enough so I'd shoo him away. He'd clean up the kitchen, which to him meant putting the dishes in the dishwasher and running tepid water into the pans. He wouldn't wipe off the counters or empty the drain catch . . . The bits of food would just sit there until I took care of it. Inevitably, I couldn't take the mess, so I'd start cleaning the pots and pans, and John would say, "Oh, I meant to do that! I'll do it now."

But of course, he didn't. If he'd meant to do it, he *would've* done it. If he really and truly wanted to be helpful with the laundry, say, he wouldn't have poured bleach right into the washing machine—on darks, no less—three times in a row.

"For a smart man, you sure can be dumb," I said, trying to keep things light.

"It's not a big deal," he said. "There's a learning curve."

"And there's three hundred dollars' worth of clothes ruined because you didn't read the instructions or listen to me." The thrifty Norwegian in me was furious.

"I didn't like that shirt, anyway."

"Well, I liked mine a lot."

"Barb. It's not a big deal. Buy another one. You don't have to get so upset all the time."

"I'm not upset. I'm stating a fact."

"I'm *sorry*," he said in that condescending way that really meant, *I'm sorry you're being so petty, and I'm sorry I have to deal with this, and I'm sorry you don't realize I'm the most wonderful thing in the known world.*

I'm not sure when I started picturing widowhood as my happy alternative. John was healthy, but he was a man. He played golf. Weren't there lightning strikes on golf courses? He drove down to the city to see Sadie, and you know how those New York drivers are.

It wasn't that I wanted him to die. I just didn't want to be married anymore.

"I think there's something called divorce," Caro said one blissful night when John had decided to stay over in the city (on the pullout couch in Sadie's apartment, pretending to be twenty again, it seemed. We could afford a hotel room, after all).

I sighed. "We've been married for fifty years almost, don't you know. Do people get divorced after that long?"

"Yes, but between now and your death—let's say twenty-five more years—how do you want your life to be?" she said, taking a sip of her margarita. She had a point.

I thought for a moment. "Exactly the same, minus him."

I'd already done some research. We were comfortable because of John's work, but he never made partner. Too unambitious, too friendly to move up in the world. If we got a divorce, both of us would take a hit financially, which I told Caro. "I love this house and everything in it. I don't want to have to move in with Juliet or live in some three-family house in New London and worry about paying my bills." Caro had divorced long ago. But she had family money, and she'd gone back to school and become a public relations consultant and made a real good income. Real good.

She nodded slowly. "So . . . I guess we have to murder him." She flashed her beautiful smile. "Or . . . or what? Is there any chance you can make things better? It's not like he's a horrible man."

"No, he's not horrible."

"Trying to get along again would probably be better than murder or divorce."

"Probably." I smiled, but the thought made my shoulders sag. Another task for me to do. You could bet John's friends weren't telling him to be a more loving husband.

"As I tell my clients, fake it till you make it. You never

know. If you pretend to be in love, maybe you'll fall back in love again. So much of happiness is the habit of positivity." Another sunny smile.

"I'm very glad to have you as my best friend, Caro," I said, my voice a little husky.

"Oh, Barb! I'm glad to have you, too! I love you! And I love this margarita! Please tell me there's more."

We spent the rest of the night chatting, and she drank a bit too much and stayed over in the guest room, which she could do without a single phone call explaining her actions. She had two boys a little older than Juliet; one lived in Vermont, and the other in New York City, so just like that, we were having a sleepover. I couldn't remember the last time I'd had so much fun with anyone except Juliet. Next to my daughter, Caro was my best friend. She lived around the corner and had brought over a cake the very first day we moved in. We clicked right away.

I took her advice, even though my heart wasn't in it. I tried. I made a point of lining up things to do with John, or for the two of us and with other couples, like our newlywed days. Caro had a steady beau named Ted (she refused to use the word *boyfriend*), and the four of us took ballroom dancing lessons, though John was clumsy as an ox on the dance floor. Karen, the dance instructor, would laugh till she cried sometimes, making us laugh, too. When Caro ruptured her Achilles tendon on a hike, we dropped out. There was a bowling league we tried, but I had some arthritis in my wrist, and it was painful. We went on a wine-tasting tour of Connecticut. Booked a trip to Italy with a group, which John summarized as "on the bus, off the bus; on the bus, off the bus" for the girls. Sadie lectured us about how shallow those bus tours were, and how we should've asked her for recommendations instead, since she was an expert on all things Europe (in her own mind, at least).

I'd thought our trip was quite nice. I liked the ease of the coach, not having to wonder where we'd stay each night, knowing a fairly decent hotel was part of the package. No, we didn't explore and wander on our own, but we saw some beautiful churches and countryside. Why did John have to poke fun at it?

It was the same as always, somehow. If we had a good time, John always credited someone else. "That Caro is a spitfire" or "Ted has the funniest stories, doesn't he?" or "Boy, that museum had some amazing pieces!" There was never a "thanks for looking that up and buying the tickets and getting me out of my chair when I was whiny about going in the first place." He never called *me* a spitfire or complimented me on telling a good story, even though Caro and Ted laughed and laughed when I told them about my childhood war with that giant goat we'd had.

No, John just gave me a look. *Her one fun story from childhood. Here we go again.*

And in the entire time I was faking it, hoping to make it, John never reciprocated. He didn't bring me flowers. He didn't suggest we do something, go somewhere. He just showed up, sometimes after I had to pitch it to him, to win him over to the idea of seeing a darn movie.

Exhausting.

Sex, which had become rote during the infertility years, became something I just didn't want to bother with anymore. I knew I was supposed to care, but a person got tired of asking, don't you know. A person can feel real bad for having to ask. John didn't seem to notice. I stopped trying to do couple things. He didn't seem to care. We stopped talking almost completely. It was better than forcing a meaningless conversation.

So when I got the call that he was probably dying, the grief came as a real shock. Not as big a shock as the adultery, but that came an hour or so later.

~

CHAPTER SIX

Barb

WORK: Babe, I miss U so much! Last week seems like a thousand years ago. I can't stop thinking about how U make me feel. I have NEVER come that hard before. I swear I thought I was dying. U ARE EVERYTHING TO ME!

JOHN: SAME!!! You're amazing. I've never felt this way. All I think of is you, you, you. Us together. God! I feel like a new man!

WORK: That thing U did with your tongue has me on FIRE just thinking about it.

JOHN: You deserve to be worshipped. Your body is incredible. God, I wish I had more "golf" weekends!!! LOL!

WORK: You can put your iron in my hole anytime.

OMG, I can't believe I said that!

JOHN: Keep talking, sex kitten. You make me roar like a tiger!!!!

WORK: I want U. All the time, any time, every time. When can we meet again??? I'm dying for U.

JOHN: Soon. But never soon enough, my love!!!

WORK: The things I could do to U for an entire weekend . . . week . . . month . . . lifetime! My ♥ swells just thinking about it!!! Will we ever be that lucky?

JOHN: My heart is swelling too and not just my heart!!! LOL!!! We will make it happen!! I want to spend the rest of my life with you. You make me HAPPY.

WORK: I am so hot for U right now. If I saw U, I'd be all over you in SECONDS. I am so PROUD of U for taking your happiness into your own hands and not feeling guilty. LIFE IS TOO SHORT!

JOHN: IKR? I didn't know what happiness WAS before this. I get hard just thinking about you! Have to go now. I want to do some cycling for our TRIATHLON together! I can't even believe I'll be doing this. I am a new man because of you!!! Miss you miss you miss you!!!

A series of emojis followed John's last text. A red heart. A smiley face with heart eyes. A smiley face blowing a kiss. A purple heart. A smiley face with a tongue hanging out. Another red heart.

Then there was the abundance of exclamation points. The words in capital letters. The acronyms (I had had to look up IKR, which stood for "I know, right?"). The poor comma usage and use of the letter *U* instead of the onerous three-letter word. I might not have set the academic world on fire, but for Pete's sake.

Clearly, John had been going through a second puberty.

"My God," Caro said, handing the phone back. "I—I don't know what to say, except let's kill the bastard." Her cheeks got red the way they always did when she was mad.

"Well," I said. "The wife is always the last to know. Isn't that what they say?"

It was two days after John's accident. Caro stopped by after getting the message that John was in the hospital, and (unfortunately) still alive. The girls were at the hospital . . . Well, Sadie was. Hopefully Juliet was home right now, getting a little TLC from Oliver and the girls.

"Fuck him," Caro said, throwing up her hands. "How dare he have a mistress! Fuck him, Barb!"

"Apparently, 'WORK'"—I used air quotes—"is fucking him plenty." It felt strange to curse. Kind of good, too. I'd read an article that said people who cursed were more honest. All those years of saying *heck* and *gosh darn* . . . they were over now.

"Are you okay?" Caro asked. "You seem so . . . calm."

"Well, you know, he's most likely dying."

"I hope he does." Caro covered her mouth with her hand. "Sorry."

"I hope so, too."

We were quiet a minute.

Thank *God* for Caro, a friend for so long, privy to just about all the issues and troubles and joys I had ever had. She was the only one who knew how hard it had been for me to get pregnant with Juliet. She was the one I called in shock when I found out about my pregnancy with Sadie. The one who'd consoled me when I dropped Juliet off at Harvard, so proud and devastated at the same time. Caro had been my campaign manager for my run for first selectman—*Barb Frost for Stoningham: The Name You Trust.*

Caro was also the only one who knew I had been planning to file for divorce.

"So let's text her back," Caro said, taking a sip of the bourbon she'd brought over, good friend that she was.

"You think so?"

"Yeah. Why not?"

The last few texts were, obviously, from WORK, since John had been too busy having a hole drilled in his head. There was some joke in there, but I wasn't in the mood.

WORK: Babe, haven't heard from U. U OK? Love U and miss U!

Thinking of U and us and the way we are together. Miss U!

Starting to worry. Is it HER? Pls call me. ♥ ♥ ♥ x 10000000!!!

"'Is it her?'" I read. "That would be me, I'm guessing."

"Answer her. Just to buy time for when you can think of what you want to say."

"And say what? 'Hey there. This is John's wife. You can have him. By the way, he's brain damaged.'"

Caro snorted. "Sounds good to me."

I sighed and let my head rest against the back of the couch. "This would really hurt the girls. Sadie especially. She thinks her dad walks on water."

"So tell her. Take no prisoners."

"Would you tell the boys?"

"In a heartbeat." That was probably a lie. Caro and Rich, her ex, had divorced with grace and humor, and I still didn't understand how they'd pulled it off. Those two still had dinner together once a month. Caro went to his wedding, for heaven's sake!

That's what I'd been hoping for, if not expecting. An amicable divorce where we still saw each other on the holidays. If he wanted someone else, I wouldn't have cared, not once the divorce was final.

It was the deceit that had my panties in a twist, as the young people said. He'd cheated on me. Had there been other women? Was WORK the first time he'd had an affair?

I'd probably never know, would I?

I closed my eyes. The bourbon made a nice warm spot in my chest, and after two nights without sleep, I could use some relaxing. When I left the hospital earlier today, Sadie gave me the stink eye for saying I needed to go home. Juliet told me to take a long bath and make sure I ate a real dinner. Such was the difference between my two children. I'd only just walked in the door when Caro came in like an angel with bourbon, and a long, comforting hug to boot.

John had a mistress. He was young again. He had discovered what happiness was, did things with his tongue and was now in a medically induced coma.

"I want to find out who she is," I said suddenly. "I mean, Caro, who the hell would want that old windbag? She sounds like she's twenty-three. He's seventy-five years old, don't you know! And he's got that horrible nose! Thank God the girls took after me. That there's a blessing, you know what I'm saying?"

Caro laughed. "I love when you talk Minnesotan to me."

"It's because I'm a little drunk. I think I had a breakfast bar in the car this morning, so this is my dinner." I held up the glass. Caro always had the good stuff. Woodford. John was cheap when it came to liquor. He'd never bought a bottle of wine that cost more than ten dollars.

Caro squeezed my hand. "By the way, yes. Thank God

they both look like you. But some women will do anything for a man. Especially a married man." She stood up. "I'm gonna call for a pizza. I'd offer to cook you something, but I just don't love you that much."

I started laughing, the exhausted, wrung-out kind of laughter that was hard to stop.

A mistress! Who'da thunk it?

From the kitchen, I heard Caro calling Wood Fire. "It's a rush job, okay? A pizza emergency for the first selectman." Caro's voice was soothing and warm, and people just loved her. I sure did.

People loved me, too. They should. I loved being useful, loved helping out and being friendly. The only two people who didn't love me were my husband and Sadie. Well, Sadie probably loved me. She just didn't like me all that much.

"So why would someone want a married man?" I asked when Caro came back from the other room. "Especially an old married man?"

"Money, honey. For one, he's close to death. Whoops. Sorry. I meant figuratively. I bet she's some young slut who figures he'll leave you, marry her, and then she'll get all his money."

"You know, we're not exactly rolling in it. We did fine. We have enough for retirement. No one's going to inherit much other than this house."

"Which our trashy whore probably doesn't know," Caro said. "For two, he's already proven he's a keeper for someone. 'Married fifty years? Oh, he's a family man!' She never thinks, 'If he cheated *with* me, he'll cheat *on* me.' Because that could *never* happen. Her vagina is so special, it has unicorns in it."

I snorted again.

Caro took a sip of bourbon. "And for three, she gets a rush off the competition."

"How are you an expert on this?"

"I read articles on the Internet."

I smiled, but it died a quick death. "The thing is, Caro, I didn't know we were competing. I thought John was just . . . done. You know. In the bedroom. He never . . . you know. Made a move. Not that I minded. We were barely talking these past ten years."

"Fuck him. I'm going with smothering. It's the best way for everyone."

"I'm trying to feel angry here. I didn't want to stay married, and neither did he, apparently, but I'm not the one who snuck around. And now look! If she'd take him off my hands, I'd be grateful."

"Of course you would!" Caro said staunchly. "You were all set to ditch him. He didn't deserve you, Barb."

"I know." Another sip of bourbon.

And yet . . . and yet there was the embarrassment.

My husband was cheating on me. It was so ridiculous and cliché. WORK made him feel young again. Wow. Breaking news, people. Screwing around behind your wife's back is exciting. Dating a younger woman makes you feel like a stud.

It was *pathetic*. There was no other word for it. He was acting like every idiot man who'd ever cheated on his wife. And like teenagers discovering sex, he thought he invented all those feelings.

I had been planning to take the high road. Divorce him. Bury the corpse that was our marriage.

Cheating had never occurred to *me*. I took those vows seriously, you bet I did.

I'd worked so hard to make our home a lovely place,

and even harder raising our girls. If Sadie and I rubbed each other the wrong way sometimes, it didn't matter too much. They were fine girls. Good people. Juliet designed those amazing buildings, and Sadie taught little children to appreciate art. There was so much to be proud of.

But it had always been *me* who did the work. John was the provider, and I made it so he didn't have to lift a finger around the house. He liked it that way. Who wouldn't?

But when it came to the marriage, the nuts and bolts of it, the conversing, the staying close, the intimacy and the social life, I felt it should've been more mutual. He had done nothing. Those dance lessons, going to the annual scholarship auction, the bird-watching club, the bowling league . . . none of those things had been his idea. Women were responsible for what the couple did. It wasn't fair, but it was true. John agreed to do this and that, but he never suggested a damn thing.

Then, being turned down for a little love, some affection, well, that stung. Before I'd thrown up my hands regarding sex, his absentminded professor bit had hurt when he failed to notice a filmy nightgown or the fact that I'd sprayed the pillowcases with perfume, moisturized my skin like it was religion. I'd been a nice-looking woman. Still was. John, he had to be reminded to take a shower, for Pete's sake! He'd go for days without shaving, looking like a bum. That potbelly, his drooping man-breasts. He didn't care if I found him attractive. But WORK . . . oh, she inspired him to do a triathlon!

I had wondered about his sudden interest in the gym last fall. About those new clothes he'd bought with Sadie on one of his visits to the city—shirts with floral prints, like something a girl would wear, and pants that stopped an inch above his anklebone. He'd even taken to wearing a little porkpie hat, and I had to stop myself from rolling my eyes, he looked so dang ridiculous. He wasn't fooling anyone. He wasn't from Brooklyn, and he wasn't thirty years old.

But apparently, WORK found him just amazing.

A flash of hatred hit me like lightning. For him and WORK both.

"Okay, here goes," I said, sitting up abruptly. I took the phone and started texting. "'My darling, so so SO'—all caps—'sorry to not be able to answer you,' exclamation point, exclamation point, exclamation point. 'Family crisis going on here. Miss you and love you too. Will be in touch very soon. Longing to see you,' exclamation point, exclamation point, exclamation point." I looked at Caro. "How do you get those little happy faces and hearts?"

"Pass it over," Caro said. She tapped a few keys, and handed the phone back. "Are you going to send it?"

"Watch me." I hit the blue arrow, and a second later, we heard the swish of the text going out into the wide world.

"Cheers," Caro said, toasting me with a smile. "And the pizza's here, too. A good omen."

In between going back and forth to the hospital and taking care of the work that couldn't wait, I found that I was having an odd bit of . . . well, not *fun*. Satisfaction, that was it.

I'd texted WORK twice more, soothing her (his?) concerns about when they'd get together. Imitating my husband's idiot language was simple, and WORK suspected nothing. Just sent more drivel about sex and passion and fires and what they could do to each other at the earliest possible convenience.

If John was gay, that would make things a lot better.

Living in a straight marriage, yearning for a man . . . everyone could understand that. I'd be kind to his boyfriend, welcome him, even. Maybe we'd all be friends. Brianna and Sloane could have two grandfathers, since Oliver's dad had died when Oliver was twelve. John would finally admit that it was never me that was the problem; it was his fear of coming out, but now that he had, he would thank me for the most wonderful daughters in the world. We'd be a happy, loving, modern family, laughing and cooking elaborate dinners, and this new man (Evan, I thought, Evan was a nice name) . . . Evan would help me decorate at Christmas and bring the most delicious pies to Thanksgiving and compliment me on a turkey that was absolutely delicious, because I did do a great turkey.

On the third text exchange, however, WORK had referenced her breasts and how she loved when John worshipped them, so that was the end of the happy gay fantasy, which was a real shame, because I had been getting awfully fond of Evan there.

I wasn't crushed. I wasn't heartbroken.

I was *furious*.

John had made my life into a cliché. *My wife of fifty years doesn't understand me. Finally, I can talk to someone! Life had become so routine, so gray. I wasn't living . . . I was just existing. You, my beloved WORK, have changed all that.*

And meanwhile, John just wouldn't die. No sir. He kept on keeping on, leaving his daughters in misery, leaving me to stare at him as he slept in the hospital bed. For fifty years, I'd accepted his flaws. I knew I wasn't perfect. I knew I had to work at life, not one of those people like Sadie, who seemed to have people falling into her lap. Yes, I wanted to divorce him. I *deserved* a divorce.

John, on the other hand, had been sneaking around, becoming an athlete at seventy-five, having sex with another woman for God knew how long, all the while wearing me down with his neglect until I felt like a ghost in my own marriage.

How dare he find happiness with another woman? How dare he leave me in charge of him now, this brain-damaged old man with a catheter?

Honest to Pete, Caro was right. If I thought I could get away with it, I'd put a pillow over his face and smother the old fool.

CHAPTER SEVEN

John

Something is wrong with his wife's face. It's too soft. Saggy. Her eyes aren't gentle anymore.

He thinks she might be . . . not sick, that's not right, but something like that.

The years have rushed by in a river. There's an old man living in his room. John isn't sure who he is. His wife doesn't notice. It's not his grandfather, but he looks familiar. He'd ask his wife, but he can't make words come out.

She smells nice. Not the way she used to, but the smell makes him feel safe, and safe is the best feeling, even if she doesn't stay near him very long. Those ungentle eyes. Shark eyes, flat and cold when they should be . . . different. He wishes she would sit against him and put her head on his shoulder. He wishes she would let him hold her hand longer, but if he does manage to grab it, she gives it a firm pat and pulls away. If he had words, he would tell her he loves her, but words are gone now, and hearing comes and goes.

There is another woman who is here quite a lot. She talks and sits with him and sometimes gives him food. Her eyes are the same color as his wife's but not flat. He knows her, but he can't remember her. Some children come and go, but John doesn't know them. They make a lot of noise and fling themselves around, and they're scary . . . so fast and strong. Their mother is another someone he used to know. She talks to him in a brisk, kind way. Maybe she's someone he works with at the . . . the . . . the place you go in the day to make money.

There is a big man here, too. John doesn't know him, but the big man helps him and talks to him. John has been hurt somehow. He thinks it was a car accident. His legs must be broken, because walking is so hard, and his knees hurt.

John knows he's been . . . changed. He's not sure how.

Trying to figure these things out is too hard. If he thinks or listens too much, his head hurts, and he falls asleep. He just wants to be outside, working in the garden, but when he looks out the window, summer is gone. John doesn't know what month it is or what he's supposed to do today. The people who make him do things—the women, the big man, his wife—come and go. Maybe they tell him what to do, but he's not sure.

Other people come and go. A man with strange words that John can't understand, but who hugs him and smiles. Another person he should know. A woman with long hair twisted into ropes. She is not here for him, he knows, but she comes anyway because she is . . . she is that way of being when a person is kind for no reason. Her voice makes him happy and sleepy. Like warm rain.

There is the man who was a boy but isn't a boy anymore who comes, first to the place for sick people, then to the other place where his warm-rain friend was, and now to his grandfather's house. Sometimes, he brings a baby. He is a father, this boy who is grown up now. They have dark hair, father and son, and the young man lets John hold the baby, who laughs.

Images flash through his head too fast to make sense— a girl with blond hair and freckles with that dark-haired boy, and colors, and John once held her hand as they crossed a street in a place with many lights. Once she cried because of that dark-haired boy who's now a man.

Then, there's nothing. Nothing but emptiness and gray and the horrible feeling of loss. Time passes, swirling past him, knocking him down, pulling him out into the sea of puzzling memories, and there's nothing he can hold on to, so he falls asleep, and sleep is what he likes best.

His wife comes in. Her name is sure in his mind. Barbara. His Barb. He's not sure why they're not in the little red house anymore. She says words, and he looks at her, smelling her good smell, loving her, wishing she wasn't always leaving. But she is. She does.

Then it's later, or another day, and John can't remember where he is. But the boy is here again with his little one, and a toolbox—*toolbox* jumps right into his head, and he knows it's the right word. John reaches out and the man puts the baby into his arms and sits there a minute, his hand on the baby's head, making sure John knows how to hold him.

He does.

The baby looks up at him with dark eyes, then smiles. John feels his mouth move, and he looks at . . .

. . . the name is coming . . .

. . . *Ned. Neil. Nick . . .*

Noah!

And Noah smiles, then opens the toolbox and starts doing things. John is not sure what or why.

The baby makes noises, but John knows they are not words, and it's such a relief, letting the sounds just be sounds, and nice sounds at that. Happy sounds. Then the baby puts his head against John's shoulder, and John's eyes get wet, because he remembers this feeling. He had a baby once, too. Maybe more than one. He knows how to hold this baby, yes he does. One arm under the baby's bottom, one hand resting on his back, feeling the breath going up and down, up and down.

Then those thoughts are gone, and there's just the baby, and the smell of his head, and the feeling of his dark silky hair, and the soft, sweet warmth of his weight as the baby breathes. Up and down. Up and down.

CHAPTER EIGHT

Sadie

Moving back to Stoningham was not something I'd ever wanted to do.

But move back I did. Who else would take care of my father? Jules was too important and busy and had Brianna and Sloane and Oliver. Mom was first selectman, and the truth was, I think she stopped loving my father decades before. Maybe before I was born, aside from one obvious coupling.

I couldn't leave him alone. He stayed in the critical care unit at UConn for ten days, then was transferred to Gaylord, a specialized rehab center, where his healing would really begin.

It became apparent that Dad wasn't going to die, despite being seventy-five years old and all that had gone wrong. In addition to the stroke, he'd had a bad concussion. It was complicated, the handsome neurosurgeon told us. Only time would tell, which, you know, I'm glad Stanford and Johns Hopkins had taught him. Only time would tell, huh? Great. Try not to overwhelm us with complicated medical terms, Doc.

I mean, I understood. Of course I did. Words like *apraxia*, *aphasia*, *neuroplasticity*, *executive functioning* and *hemiparesis* became part of my daily vocabulary. Dad had all kinds of therapy at Gaylord—physical, speech, aqua, occupational, community reentry, where they'd take patients to the grocery store or a restaurant. There was a robotic suit of some kind that helped him relearn to walk. He was given an iPad, which he didn't understand, even when the therapists guided his fingers.

What I wouldn't give for an e-mail or message from him saying, "Don't worry, sugarplum. I'm in here. Just give me a little time. Love, Dad." Instead, he stared blankly, then turned his head to the window.

I came every day, driving back and forth from the city every night, practically living in my rental car, which was full of fast-food wrappers and half-drunk coffees from Dunkin'. Sometimes Alexander came with me, but it was generally easier if he didn't. He was one of those guys who didn't know what to do around a sick person. He was a peach, though, always ready to take me out to dinner or sending me flowers, checking in during his travels.

Dad started walking again, first with one of those belts and a walker, then with crutches, then on his own, though he tended to list to one side. He could almost dress himself. He could hold a fork, but not always on command— apraxia, the PA told me, where the messages between his brain and muscles got scrambled. He tried to talk a few times, but only managed strangled, labored noises, which broke my heart.

It was wrenching. There was no other word for it. My

father had always been so smart, so playful in his dry way, open for anything. All the times he'd come down to the city to see me over the years, doing anything I suggested, from going to a performance where the woman drenched herself in what she said was menstrual blood and Dad and I had to sneak out the back because we were laughing so hard, to taking the Staten Island Ferry back and forth for the view. We'd ridden bikes along the Hudson River Greenway, eaten street meat with gusto and gone to a scotch tasting that left us both tipsy and giggly. He'd even taken me for a carriage ride in Central Park. "You're my princess, after all," he'd said, and we snuggled under the blanket to the sounds of the horse's hooves.

He was my hero.

"He would hate this," Juliet said on a day when we happened to be visiting Gaylord at the same time. We were waiting for Dad to come back from the pool with one of his therapists, both of us itchy and tired. "Sometimes I think it would've been better if he—"

"Jules! That's our father! No, it wouldn't have been better if he'd died! He's getting better every day."

She sighed, sounding exactly like Mom. Speaking of Mom, she was down the hall making a phone call. Whenever she was here, she spent as little time near Dad as possible.

"Here he is, and he did great!" said Sheryl, wheeling Dad back into the room.

"How was the pool, Dad?" I asked. "The pool? Did you like it?" *Keep it simple* was one of the things we'd learned.

He didn't answer.

"Hey there," said a woman. Janet, the sister of another patient. "How's it going, John? Did you eat that chicken for lunch? It was pretty good, wasn't it? I liked the spinach. Nice touch. How you girls doing? You doing okay?"

I liked Janet. Her brother had had a traumatic brain injury and was a patient down the hall. She was devoted to him, visiting every day. But she also wandered up and down the hall when he was sleeping or in therapy. Janet dressed in overalls most of the time, granny glasses and big, clunky clogs. She chatted to my father like he was an old friend.

It was strange, the unwilling little community of family members, all of us here for shitty reasons. My mother spent most of her time talking with them, and Jules was fairly helpless. But I didn't mind the nitty-gritty of helping my father. While it broke my heart that he was struggling, I knew he'd get better. It would take time and work, but he was on his way. I had to believe that. A life without my dad—the old dad—was not something I was prepared to imagine.

"He seems to have plateaued."

"Well, shit," Jules said.

We were at a meeting with the team, the therapists and doctors and nurses, Mom, Jules and Oliver, me.

"So at this point," Dr. McIntyre continued, "because he's doing well with the tasks of daily living, we usually send the patient home. Often, that improves their mental capacity, being around familiar things and people."

"He can't come home," Mom said.

"Of course he can," I said. "Where else would he go?"

"Rose Hill has an adult wing now."

"No. He's not going into a home, Mom. You have to give him a chance."

"Rose Hill *is* an excellent facility," the team leader murmured.

"But he should be home! He deserves to be home. His odds of recovering are better there, just like you said."

"We can't predict anything, sadly," said the doctor. "I'm sorry, I realize it's incredibly frustrating, but it's best to focus on the amazing progress he's already made and set small goals for the future."

"Like what?" Jules asked.

"Maybe some intelligible words. Of course you want him to be the man you knew before, but right now, just saying 'hungry' or 'tired' would be a breakthrough. We have to manage expectations."

"Won't he need a caregiver?" Mom asked.

"Yes. He won't be able to be left alone until his cognition is significantly better."

Mom, Jules and I exchanged looks. "None of us has medical training," Mom said, and I felt a guilty flash of relief.

"No, of course not. We'll arrange for therapists and some nursing help. You're not alone in this."

"Thank God," Mom said.

"But there should be a point person, someone who lives with him or very close by. Mrs. Frost, since you—"

"No. It won't be me. I have a more-than-full-time job, and I'm seventy years old."

Wow. I mean, yes, her age was a factor, but boy, she couldn't get those words out fast enough.

"I also have a full-time job, plus two kids," Juliet said. She glanced at Oliver, who nodded and smiled, the asshole.

"I live in New York City," I said. They looked at me. "But yeah, I'll do it." I closed my eyes. "Of course I will. I'll . . . move home. It'll take me a week or two, but yeah." Shit. But of course I would.

"Good girl, Sadie," my mother said.

I shrugged. It wasn't like I wanted to, but who else would take care of Dad?

In the week that followed, I listed my apartment with Airbnb so it would earn me some money while Dad was recovering. Carter helped me touch it up with a new comforter and throw pillows and the like. I put my personal stuff in crates and brought them with me. Jules let me put some things in her basement.

Sister Mary gave me a leave from St. Catherine's, and all my friends there took me out the night before I left. I tried not to cry as Alexander drove me east to my hometown.

The first couple of weeks, I barely left the house, too busy learning things from the nurses, therapists and equipment people and trying not to kill my mother.

Old Barb seemed devoid of any midwestern capability where Dad was concerned. Instead, she did everything she could to distance herself from my father, becoming conveniently invisible when my dad needed a bath, or physical therapy, or just some damn company. Jules came by and sat next to his bed, but she checked her phone constantly.

"Do you have to do that?" I snapped.

"I'm working, okay? Insurance doesn't cover all of this, and I don't want Mom and Dad to drain their retirement. So I'm making up the difference, if it's all right with you."

I sat back, chastened. "Sorry," I muttered, ever the little sister.

"It's okay," she said. "We all do our part." Gaylord had provided the names of a few occupational and physical therapists, and (I guess with Juliet's help) we hired a physical therapist named LeVon Murphy to stay with Dad from eight until four five days a week to keep working on his improvement. LeVon was amazing, calm and funny, and all three of us Frost women loved him. He was also big and strong, so he could do things like lift Dad if necessary.

My part was the nitty-gritty, apparently. The sponge baths. The occasional change of linens when he wet the bed. "Look," I told him the first time, LeVon looking on to supervise. "We're both uncomfortable with this. But I love you, Dad, and you washed me when I was little, so now I'll take care of you. And when you're better, we can both get hypnotism to forget this." I thought he might have smiled. Well. His mouth moved, either in horror or humor or reflex. It was hard to say.

When he looked at me, I sensed he was striving to say something. "It's me, Dad. Sadie. Can you say my name?" He didn't. If he grew restless, I'd hold his hand and stay positive. "You're getting better every day. The brain is incredible. You just have to relearn things."

It was like a bad dream. Dad, unable to talk; me in my old room, which had been redone about half an hour after I left for college; Mom and me trying not to bicker over dinner. At least Caro would pop in, alleviating the tension. My nieces would come over, Brianna a little freaked out by seeing Grampy this way, Sloane oblivious and happy.

New York seemed far, far away.

After three weeks of living at home, I told my mother I needed to get out of the house.

"Well, I can't stay here alone with him, Sadie!" she said. "That's your job."

"LeVon isn't here today, and Dad is still your husband!" I snapped. "He just needs company. Is that so hard? Can you just sit with him for half a damn hour so I can get some fresh air?"

"Fine. Go," she said. "Be back before lunch, please." She hated watching him eat, which I admit wasn't the prettiest sight.

Shit. I so wished it had been her. In her case, a nursing home would've been more than enough.

I left the house. It was March now—eight weeks since Dad's stroke, and mud season for New England, but the air had the promise of spring. The sky was pale blue, the breeze brisk, blowing the fug off me and bathing me in the smell of salt air.

I walked away from town, toward the tidal river. When I came to the wooden footbridge that spanned it, I took a seat the way I had when I was a kid, my legs dangling, the river gurgling past below me, the long reeds along the bank golden in the sunlight. My dad and I used to play Poohsticks, dropping twigs in on one side, then looking over the other to see whose came out from under the bridge first.

In the distance, the Sound was empty; all the boats were still in dry dock.

I lay down, the boards warm and strong under my back, soothing the ache I didn't realize I had till now. I'd been doing a lot of heavy work, packing up my apartment, helping Dad get in and out of bed, moving furniture around their house to make it more accessible. Right now he was using a walker, and they had a lot of furniture that got in the way. My mother loved antiques, and it seemed like they all weighed three times what modern stuff did.

I hadn't been back in Stoningham for more than two days in a row in eons. The sound of the river, the distant slapping of the waves against the shore, the shrill cries of the gulls were comforting—sounds I hadn't realized I'd missed till now—and the sun was warm, even if the air was cool.

A few tears slipped out of my eyes and into my hair. I thought I'd cried myself out over my father's stroke, but apparently, I hadn't.

He'd get better. I had to believe that.

"Sadie?"

I jolted into a sitting position, my heart jackrabbiting.

Of course I'd known I'd run into him. Somehow, I just hadn't prepared myself for it.

"Noah." I blinked, then shielded my eyes from the sun. It took a minute to see him clearly.

He had a baby in one of those front-pack carriers.

A *baby*.

The fabric of the carrier blocked all but the baby's black hair on top, and tiny feet clad in little blue socks on the bottom.

A baby. A baby who, I imagined, looked a lot like the man carrying him. My speeding heart dropped to my stomach.

"I was really sorry to hear about your dad," Noah said.

"Yeah. Thanks." I tried to smile. "Thank you. Thanks for the card." He'd sent one when Dad was still at UConn.

"How's he doing?"

"Um . . . he's doing okay. Slow going." The little blue feet kicked, and I remembered to blink.

"Heard you're back to help out."

"Yeah." I paused. "Is that . . . your baby?"

I wanted him to laugh and say, "God, no, it's my sister's," but of course he didn't have a sister. He could've been babysitting for a friend, and—

"Yes. This is my son. Marcus." He looked down at the

little black head and smoothed the unruly hair with undeniable tenderness. "Sixteen weeks old."

Jesus God in heaven.

Now I was blinking too fast. *Do not cry, Sadie. Don't you dare cry.* "Um, wow! A son! Wow! Congratulations. I didn't . . . no one told me . . . Congratulations! Are you, uh, married?"

He leaned against the railing of the footbridge, his face losing expression. "No. Michaela Watkins is the mom. We're coparents."

"*Mickey* Watkins?"

"Yeah."

I swallowed. Okay. Mickey Watkins had been our classmate from third or fourth grade on. And she was gay.

"We both wanted to be parents, and nothing else seemed to be working out," he said.

I realized a response was required. "Wow. Um . . . congratulations."

"Yeah. Thanks." He stood stiffly, the wind ruffling his hair, and looked to the left of me. On the other hand, I couldn't stop staring at him. The unshaven face that never could grow a proper beard. His long lashes and slight scowl. His big hands, one on the baby's back, the other on his hip. He should've looked ridiculous—brooding hot dad with baby in carrier meets ex-lover.

He didn't look ridiculous at all.

I became aware of the fact that I should speak. And maybe close my mouth. "Mickey. How is she? That's . . . this is a big surprise."

"I'm sorry," he said, an edge in his voice. "Should I have consulted you? Asked if it was okay?"

"No!" I scrambled to my feet. "I just . . . I mean, I knew you'd been engaged, but I, uh . . . I didn't . . ."

"That didn't work out. Also, I thought you were never coming back to this godforsaken town, as you called it, and now I have a four-month-old and all of a sudden, you're living here again. If I'd known you were coming back, maybe I wouldn't have impregnated a lesbian."

"I'm here to take care of my father, Noah. Not have your babies."

"Oh, I know. Believe me, I know. Nothing else could've gotten you back here to this hellhole."

I was quite sure I'd never called Stoningham a hellhole. "Still bitter, are we?"

"Yes."

His hair, which had been short a couple of years ago (thank you, Facebook), had grown longer and wild again, and I was glad.

"Can I take a peek at your baby?" I said.

He scowled properly, then undid two clips and lifted out his son. I went over to them.

The baby was asleep, but I could tell he was Noah all over, tiny black eyebrows, the full cheeks, the perfect mouth. "Hey, little one," I whispered, and touched his cheek. It was as soft and perfect as a puppy's ear.

"Okay, that's enough," Noah said, repacking him. "Look. You're here. I'm really sorry about your dad and I hope he gets better. But you left a mark, Sadie. We're not gonna be friends. I can't do that. I'm not your backup plan."

Oh, the *ego*. "Was I humping your leg just now, Noah? Or begging you to marry me? Because I must've missed that part."

"I'm just being clear. You'll ruin me all over again, and I have a son to raise now. So if we run into each other, it's not old home week. Okay?"

I pursed my lips. "Got it. But before you go, I have to

point out that you were as stubborn as I was, Noah. We could've been together if you'd been open to anything but your own life plan. So you ruined me, too."

"Yeah, right. Heard about your rich boyfriend."

"And I heard about your event planner. So neither of us has been sitting around nursing a broken heart. Good for us."

"You did exactly what you wanted to, Sadie."

"And so did you, Noah!" I dropped my voice, remembering the baby. Noah glared at me, somehow still looking as hot as Jon Snow, even with a baby carrier on. Maybe *because* of the baby carrier.

"Hey! Sadie! How the hell are you, woman!"

It was Mickey Watkins, dressed in running gear.

"Hey," I said, recalibrating fast. "I just met your son! Wow! Congratulations!"

"Right? He's the cutest baby in the entire world, isn't he? Hi, Marcus! It's Mommy! Who shouldn't be running with two breasts full of milk!" She put her hands over her boobs, ever without a filter, just like I remembered, and I grinned. "God, this hurts! The second I see him, I'm leaking like a bad radiator. Look at this." She moved her hands, and yep, there were two big wet spots. She went to Noah and kissed her son's little head, and Noah smiled.

"You two okay?" Mickey asked.

"We were just yelling at each other," I said.

"We're fine," Noah said at the same time.

"Sorry about your dad," Mickey said.

"Thanks. He's doing okay."

"Glad to hear it. Hey, you should come by sometime. I'll let you sniff Marcus's head. It's good for the soul."

"Mickey," Noah muttered.

"What? Am I supposed to hate her because you loved

her once? Get over yourself, straight boy." She looked at me and winked. "Well, I can't run with these milk jug boobs. Noah, where's your car? I have to nurse this little guy or I'll explode. Sadie, great seeing you. I mean it about coming over. Noah and I share custody. Three nights with him, three with me. Have you ever seen a breast pump? Clearly invented by a man. It's a fucking torture device. Anyway, take care, hon! See you soon!"

Off they went, leaving me in a state of shock. After a minute or two, I started back toward home.

Noah had a child. With Mickey Watkins, one of the best people in our year, a funny, boisterous girl—woman now—who was always full of life and laughter. Good. Her genes would balance out the Prince of Gloom's over there.

Noah was a *father*.

It was a lot to take in.

"Hey," I said when I got to the house. Jules was there, eating lunch at the table with Mom. "Thanks for telling me Noah and Mickey Watkins had a baby together."

"So? You two have been done for ages," Mom said.

"Completely slipped my mind," Jules said.

I sighed. Reminded myself that I had a nice boyfriend and didn't care what Noah did. "Where's Dad?"

"Asleep," said Mom, taking a hostile bite of her sandwich.

I went to check on him; we'd turned the dining room into his room until he could handle the stairs. I fixed his blanket and sat in the chair. He wasn't sleeping, just staring ahead.

"Remember my boyfriend, Dad? Noah? He's a father," I told him. "He made a baby with Mickey Watkins from our class. It's a boy. Also, he's still mad at me."

Dad said nothing. *He could've had you*, I imagined Dad saying. *Inflexible, that one. Not a good quality in a spouse. I should know.*

For some reason, I had a lump in my throat. Even if I shouldn't. The heart wants what the heart wants, and the heart can be a real idiot.

CHAPTER NINE

Sadie

Ever since I could remember, I'd wanted to leave Stoningham, because even though I loved it, I hated it. It was so smug. So content. So adorable. So assured of itself. In a way, it was like my sister, never questioning its value. *Welcome to Stoningham. You're lucky we let you in,* the town seemed to say. *If you play your cards right, we might let you stay.*

The fact that my mother viewed Stoningham as an achievement, rather than a place, definitely colored my views as a teenager, when I felt it was my duty to think the opposite of everything she did. When I was little, it was paradise, of course—a rocky shore with a couple of sand beaches, huge stretches of marsh, land reserves, the gentle Sound always murmuring, that one part of the shore where the Atlantic roared in, unfettered by Long Island. There was Birch Lake, still so pristine and quiet, surrounded by old-growth forest with gentle paths for walking. We had the most beautiful skies, and they were my first paintings. Skyscapes in pastels or watercolors, those endless shades of blue, violently beautiful sunsets in the winter, summer skies smeared with colors.

But it was a small town. A tiny town, and so stuffy it was hard to breathe sometimes, especially if you were Juliet's not-as-smart-or-athletic sister, or the daughter of Barb Frost, Queen of Committees and Volunteerism, daughter of John Frost the lawyer, and yes, related to *that* Robert Frost.

Being average was difficult.

I had one talent, though, and I would use it to get away, distance myself from the smugness, the familiar, the "aren't you Barb's daughter?" of Stoningham.

Looking back, it's hard not to be a little embarrassed. Girl from tiny town in Connecticut goes to New York to become artist. Wears black and pierces nose. Fails to set the art world on fire. Becomes waitress, then teacher, then sells out. Eventually goes home to help ailing parent.

The thing was, I'd been sincere. At eighteen, my heart was pure, my determination boundless. I was talented . . . I'd won first prize in the annual Stoningham art show since I was fourteen and even sold three paintings at Coastal Beauty Art Gallery in Mystic. I'd placed third in the Young Artists of Connecticut Competition, Acrylics.

I couldn't remember a time when I didn't draw or paint. I loved it so much—the smells, the textures, the way a single flicker of a brush could take you on a journey, how the slightest color variation could make all the difference. I loved mixing paints, the sweet perfection of a new brush, like the smallest baby animal, so soft and innocent and full of potential. I loved seeing something come from nothing. And not just something, but an experience. Not just a picture, but *emotions*, an entire story in a frame. There was nothing else I wanted to do.

Of course I was going to New York to study art! What other city in America was there for art? (Aside from Austin, Denver, San Francisco, Chicago, etc., but I was young and ill-informed.) New York it would be.

Dad was encouraging—"Of course! Follow your dream, sugarplum!" Mom was baffled.

"An *art* major?" she cried, as if I'd said *assassin for drug cartel*. "What are you going to do with an art major? Your sister is an *architect*!" Just in case I'd forgotten what Perfection from Conception did for a living.

Speaking of Juliet, who was also sitting in judgment, she laughed. "You're adorable. Do you like living in cardboard boxes?"

"Have you ever been to a museum?" I asked in my oh-so-sophisticated way.

"I've *designed* museums, Sadie."

"Then you should remember that they're just places to hold art. Have you ever bought a painting? Seen a movie?" I raised an eyebrow at my mother in response to her snort of disapproval. "People who think art is a waste of time should have to live in a world without color."

"Have you ever been poor?" Jules asked. "Ever eaten at a soup kitchen?"

"This might come as a shock to you, Jules, but money and luxury aren't everything." She'd just built her house on the water, tearing down an old gray-shingled cottage to construct what was admittedly a fabulous home with views from every angle. "You're all very narrow-minded," I said. "Except you, Daddy."

"Well," he said. "If you can't follow your dreams now, baby, when can you?"

"See?" I said, hugging him.

"Oh, super, John," Mom said. "She needs to have something to fall back on. Something practical."

"What if she's the next Jackson Pollock?" Dad said.

"Then she'll kill herself in a car crash while drunk-driving," said my sister.

"Keith Haring, then," Dad said.

"AIDS."

"Vincent van—ah, shit. Georgia O'Keeffe, then."

"She lived to be ninety-eight," I said. "Guess art isn't *always* fatal. But I do appreciate the support."

My mother would not be convinced. She wore my dad down until he agreed that I should double major in studio art and art education. I had nothing against teaching. I pictured myself in a Tribeca studio, allowing worshipful artists in every Saturday for a master class. At least one of them would be named Lorenzo and be madly in love with me. So off to Pace University I went. (Columbia and the School of Visual Arts had rejected me, thanks to medio-cre grades, I told myself.) But hey. It was still New York, and I was going.

In doing so, I broke Noah Pelletier's heart, and he broke mine.

High school sweethearts. The only boyfriend I'd ever had. Wise beyond his years, stoic, hardworking, a fifth-generation townie and my first love. He was wrenchingly beautiful—eyes so dark they were nearly black, full lips that made him look a little grumpy unless he smiled, and wild, curly unkempt black hair that framed his face.

We'd been friends since before I could remember. When we were small, we'd go over to each other's houses to play once in a while, and as we grew older and play-dates stopped being a thing, he remained one of the nicer boys in school—quiet, good at sports, a mediocre student, like me. We sat next to each other in band during fourth and fifth grades, me on flute, him on clarinet, neither of us very good, though he practiced more. He always picked me to be on his team in gym class. Smiled at me during recess. Once, he got hit in the head with a baseball, and I walked him into the nurse's office, holding his arm to make sure he didn't fall. In junior high, we didn't see each other much, since he was busy being a guy and playing soccer, and an art teacher had told me I had "a real gift."

Then high school started. Something had happened to Noah over the summer. His voice dropped an octave and his hands were suddenly big and strong. He'd grown a few inches, and when he smiled at me, it felt . . . profound. I could practically feel my heart changing—a lifetime of good-natured affection suddenly turning into a pounding, beautiful ache.

In the front yard of my parents' house was a beautiful Japanese maple tree, and in the fall, it grew so red it glowed. That was the color of my heart when Noah looked at me, and all freshman year, my paintings were filled with red and black, the black of his hair and eyes, the pure Noah-red of my love. Noah Sebastian Pelletier, he of French Canadian descent, a boy who looked as if he would've been at home in the Canadian Rockies on his own, sitting by a fire, watching the stars, the wolves surrounding him in recognition of his wild beauty and soul.

Hey. I was a teenage girl. It was my job to think this way. I dared not draw him, afraid my mother would find the pictures and lecture me about sex. Or worse, tell me I could do better than a blue-collar boy—Mom was such a snob, and couldn't resist telling people that my sister had married a man who was somehow related to British nobility. My mother might call his mother and tell her we were too young to be in love, and that would be worst of all . . . because Noah was not in love with me.

Unfortunately. His gentle, "Hey, Sadie," in the halls of Stoningham High, the occasional scraps of conversation about assignments or, once in a while, an amused smile when he caught my eye when our peers were goofing around . . . same as he was with everyone. There was nothing special between us, and it made my heart hurt in the most pleasurable way, pulsing with that pure, glorious crimson. Once, we sat together at the mandatory holiday pageant, watching Gina Deluca, who was two years ahead of us, do an interpretive dance of Mary giving birth to Jesus, and we laughed silently till tears ran down our faces, Noah's hand covering his face as his shoulders shook, peeking at me through his fingers, both of us laughing harder in that wonderful, uncontrollable way. Oh, I relived that moment thousands of times. Thousands.

The summer between sophomore and junior years, I was fifteen, being on the younger side of my class, since Mom had kicked me into kindergarten when I was four. One sunny, perfect afternoon when the gulls drifted on air currents and red-winged blackbirds called to each other, I took my sketchbook down to the tidal river. The school fields were nearby, and I'd heard some sportsball type of yelling, but I was on another plane. When I was drawing or painting, I was adrift in the moment . . . It irritated my mom that she'd have to say my name over and over before I'd lift my head, but to me, it was the best, most beautiful way to be, alone in a world of my own making. I'd go for hours without eating or drinking. I could sit in the cafeteria at lunchtime and not hear a word . . . unless it was said by Noah.

This day, I was sketching with a new set of graphite pencils, a gift from my father, focused on the sway of the reeds and the curve of the piping plover's head as it darted along the muddy edge of the river. The sun was hot on my hair, the gentle gurgle of the tidal river was music, and the quick steps of the little bird were so cunning and sweet. All of it flowed from my pencil onto the paper, and I was in a state of utter bliss.

Then a black-and-white ball bounced down the hill, and instinctively, I stopped it with my foot before it hit the river and was carried out to sea. It took me a second to put the pieces together: soccer ball. Intruder. Sports. Boys.

Noah.

He stood there, hands on his hips, his legs already a man's legs, tan and muscled, appropriately hairy, which I suddenly found *extremely* attractive. Sweat dampened his T-shirt, and his cheeks were ruddy, his hair tangled and unruly and glorious.

"Hey, Sadie," he said with a half grin, and my stomach contracted with a strong, hot squeeze.

"Hi," I managed.

"Thanks for saving the ball."

"Sure."

He glanced at my sketchbook. "Wow. That's incredible."

The heat of pride (and lust) crept up from my chest, tickling my neck. "Thanks."

He sat down next to me, taking the ball under his arm, the smell of his sweat and grass from the soccer field enveloping me. "You having a good summer?"

"Mm-hm." My cheeks were hot, and I kept my eyes on the drawing to avoid melting into a puddle of lust. "Are you?"

"Sure."

I sneaked another look at him. Long lashes on top of that wild beauty. His face had taken on more definition in the past year, and I had to swallow. I wanted to draw that face. Heathcliff. He was Heathcliff of the moors, if I ignored the Ramones T-shirt and gym shorts.

"I should get back," he said.

"Oh, right. Sure." My conversation game was red-hot.

"All right if I kiss you?"

I may have twitched. "I . . . What did you say?"

He grinned and half shrugged, so I leaned toward this wild boy, and our lips met, a soft, gentle kiss. The deep scarlet in my heart flared with such heat and beauty, I already loved him.

When the kiss ended, he rested his forehead against mine, his eyes still closed. "Wanna be my girlfriend?" he whispered.

"Okay."

"You sure?"

"Yes."

And that was that.

My parents didn't mind too much; I was that age when kids started dating, and everyone knew the Pelletiers as a good, solid family. Besides, Juliet was pregnant, and our mother was obsessed with throwing her a ridiculous shower (as she'd been obsessed with the wedding two years before). Me having a boyfriend barely registered.

Noah's parents didn't mind, either. He was an only child; they loved him and welcomed me, seeing me as a nice girl for their boy, though his mom's forehead did pucker when I mentioned traveling and applying to schools in San Francisco and Barcelona.

Noah had a job on the weekends; his father was a general contractor, and a lot of his work was expanding houses for the summer people that populated Connecticut's long, gentle shoreline. He'd worked on Juliet's house, in fact. Noah would put in long hours most Saturdays and Sundays, not returning till late, when he would come to my house or, if it was super late, to my window, tossing pebbles against the screen until I came out. In these cases, *I* was Juliet. Juliet Capulet. Or Montague. I always forgot who had which last name.

"Hey, Special," he'd say softly, and that glowing red would pulse in every molecule of my being. You bet I'd sneak out to be with him . . . to the town green down the block, where we could lie on a blanket and kiss, or, in the off-season, to the dock of one of the summer "cottages," the waves lapping and lifting us as we fitted together, wrapped so tightly around each other it almost hurt.

In school, his black eyes would rest on me like I was the only person in the world. My friends were jealous; not only was I dating the cutest, nicest boy, but he *loved* me, and made no secret about it. He *loved* me. When we were together, everyone else fell to the wayside, and every spare minute was given to each other. It made my friends irritable, but I couldn't help it. I was smitten. Utterly, completely in love.

For our first Valentine's Day together, I gave him my first big canvas oil painting—a periwinkle-blue sky just before sunrise, golden clouds tipped with the same color of glowing, lush vermillion that lit up my heart. He hung it in his bedroom and took down all his movie posters and memorabilia so my painting was the only thing on that wall.

Oh, the kissing, the sweaty tangle of young limbs and heated murmurs that painting saw . . .

In our junior and senior years, Noah went to a vocational school part-time, taking a bus to New London on Thursdays and Fridays to learn carpentry, since he loved woodworking as much as I loved painting. I thought we were perfect for each other, both of us artists, though he'd laugh when I said that and say making door frames or coffee tables wasn't exactly art. Though I'd never thought of myself as unhappy before, being with Noah—so seen, so important . . . it taught me what happiness was.

He had one flaw: he wanted to stay put. He wanted life to be exactly like his parents' and grandparents'. He wanted to marry me in a few years and raise a bunch of kids, preferably five. (How many teenage boys say they want five kids?) I loved that he saw us together, because I did, too. Just . . . not here. I pictured us traveling, hiking on the moors or walking through the streets of Rome, on the Great Wall, in the spice markets of Mumbai. How we would fund this was unclear, but we were young. We could, er, backpack or however it was that people without rich parents traveled.

But as graduation drew closer, things got a little prickly. Noah had no problem with my plans for the next four years, but there was always a hint of condescension somewhere in there. Like once I'd gotten this "see the world/ live in the city" bug out of my system, I'd understand that Stoningham was the only place to be.

But there was no way on earth I wanted to live in the town I'd grown up in. A thousand year-round residents, thick with pretension because of the brushes with celebrity or true wealth—Genevieve London of the handbag empire; an Oscar-winning actress who spent all of two weeks a year in her six-thousand-square-foot house. I didn't want to run into the same people on the same streets in the same places I'd already been every day of my life. Staying here was an admission of fear of something greater . . . or a total lack of ambition. Only people like Juliet, with her Ivy League degrees and brilliant success, could come back to Stoningham without seeming like a loser. Or so it seemed to me.

I didn't want to be Barb and John's daughter and Juliet's not-as-amazing sister. I didn't even want to be called "Noah's girlfriend." I wanted to be myself . . . with Noah, still my parents' daughter, but I wanted to be Sadie Frost, yes, *that* Sadie Frost, the artist.

Change. The word was a siren call that filled me with an energy and thrill I couldn't describe. When you grow up in Connecticut, you're defined by the absence of things. We had hills but not mountains. A shoreline, but not really the ocean. Farms, but not exactly farmland. Cities, but either scarred by urban blight or too small to hold their own with Boston and New York just a train ride away.

New York. Oh, New York. All the songs were true. I wanted to be in the hard, glittering city, with its harsh reflections and sharp-toothed skyline, its roar and breath, to meet new people, to *not* have my family history ambling beside me, to be the only one who defined me. I was eighteen. I ached for it the same way I ached for Noah, with the same molten red longing.

The fact that he had none of this desire baffled me. I thought we were *supposed* to want these things. Noah did not. He was utterly happy with the idea of waiting me out.

I didn't hate Stoningham, but God, it was relentless in its familiarity. Every street, every inch of shoreline, every type of weather was something I'd lived over and over and over. The sameness was squeezing the life out of me.

We didn't make any promises about the future . . .

Each of us figured the other would see the light. Their light. I went off to New York, and the first thing I put up in my dorm room was a picture of Noah and me, our arms around each other on the town dock, both of us smiling. His curly hair whipped in the breeze, and my eyes looked more blue because of the sky and water behind us. Breaking up was not in my plans. Ever. We were meant to be. We could find a way where we were both happy and fulfilled. We were different from other high school couples. Our love, I was certain, would last forever.

I was wrong.

~

CHAPTER TEN

Barb

I never liked my name. I should've changed it when I was sixteen.

Barb. Barb Frost. Barbara Marie Johnson Frost. The most boring, unremarkable, midwestern name on every level. Oh, Frost was a fine last name, especially given that John was somehow related to Robert Frost. I'd been so excited by that when we first met. How thrilling, being related to the great poet! To have that gentle, insightful, famous blood running through your veins! Gosh!

"Well, I don't know about that," John had said, and maybe I should've taken more notice, because it was true. Turned out, there was nothing poetic about him.

At our wedding, his mother told me no one was quite sure how Robert Frost was connected to them . . . It was more of a rumor than anything that could be fact-checked at the time. Not that it mattered, but it seemed like John had been keeping that from me. *Maybe* related to Robert

Frost is different from *being* related to Robert Frost. As for the name John, well, it was the most common name in the English-speaking world, wasn't it? At least no one called him Jack. Jack Frost. Jeez Louise, that would've been horrible.

When I finally had a baby, I gave her the most poetic name in the world. Juliet Elizabeth Frost. A beautiful name for a beautiful girl. I only wanted one baby, I'd already decided; I had three sisters and three brothers, and it wasn't the way they show it in books. I remember reading *Cheaper by the Dozen* and feeling so cheated. We Johnson kids were no happy gang of seven romping and singing and helping each other, heck no. My oldest brother, fifteen years my senior, barely knew I was alive, and Elaine, older by sixteen months, picked on me endlessly. I was the fifth child, lost in the middle blur. My father never got my name right on the first try, and my mother was exhausted and exasperated all the time. I shared a room with my sisters, and all our clothes were hand-me-downs from our wealthier cousins, first to Nancy, then Elaine, then to me, then to Tina, who at least had the honor of being the baby of the family.

Seven children in nineteen years. Russell, Nancy, Henry, Elaine, me, Arthur and Tina. We weren't poor, but we weren't comfortable, either. We didn't go hungry, but that was because we had a small farm, and Dad could always slaughter a pig. No vacations except for one time when we piled into the gigantic station wagon and drove for ten hours to an aunt's rented house on a lake, where there was one bathroom for thirteen people. We kids slept on the floors of various rooms and porches, trying to make friends with cousins we had never met. The mosquitoes were relentless, and the lake water was murky and brown. Tina was still wetting the bed at night, which became my responsibility somehow. Every other summer was unbroken, just a stream of long days and hard work, endless laundry and cooking, loading hay, feeding the pigs, weeding our vast garden, crushing grubs between our fingers with no relief from the prairie sun. I hated it.

I was a not-bad student, not that anyone noticed. Solid Bs, the occasional A. I blamed my name. Barbara Marie Johnson. She doesn't sound much like a valedictorian, does she? Not someone who'd get a scholarship to St. Olaf or Columbia. My oldest brother went into the Army; Nancy went to secretarial school; Henry became a mechanic; Elaine got pregnant and married the summer after she graduated.

All I wanted was to get away. I took a few courses and became a legal secretary, then I applied for jobs up and down the East Coast. No way was I going to stay in Minnesota, no sir. When I got a job offer in Providence, Rhode Island, I took it sight unseen. I had just turned eighteen, since I'd skipped fourth grade, much to Elaine's annoyance. Without much fanfare, I moved to Rhode Island, so small and charming and eclectic compared to Minnesota!

I loved Providence. It was busy and cultured, with the colleges and the restaurants and such. I told people my name was Barb, which sounded a little more energetic than Barbara. Barbie was out. I couldn't go by my initials—B. M. or B. J. (A girlfriend told me what BJ stood for, and gosh, I was shocked.) Bobbi was too popular at the time. I tried BeBe, but it didn't take. Barb was the best I could do.

The law firm that had hired me was large and paid well. I shared a cute apartment with two other girls, and buckled down at being a grown-up, learning to drink a gin and tonic (my family was dry in every sense), painting old furniture I got at garage sales. I learned to accessorize and shop at thrift stores for good-quality clothes and tried to look professional and a little sassy at work. Sometimes people teased me about my accent, which I didn't even know I had, and I tried to tone it down.

I worked hard at my job, one of dozens of legal secretaries at the firm. I needed to stand out, so I was first in the department every day, last to leave. I learned my boss's preferences and rhythms, handing him the paper and a coffee just the way he liked it ("You don't have to do that, Barb!" he'd say every day, pleased that I did). In addition to making sure my work was absolutely immaculate, I put his wedding anniversary and kids' birthdays on my calendar to remind him. I offered to order flowers for his wife or call restaurants for reservations. I was friendly and respectful and didn't miss a day.

It worked. He recommended that I get promoted to paralegal, because this was back in the day when you didn't need to have a degree for that. You just had to be sharp. And I was.

Soon it felt natural, being perky and cheerful and making the most out of my ordinary looks with makeup and flattering hairstyles. Elaine was "the pretty one" in our family, Tina "the feisty one," Nancy "the smart one." I didn't have a title—once, my father called me "the angry one," and I burst into tears, scaring him. I'm not sure I ever forgave him for that. It should've been "the hardworking one."

I had to work just as hard socially. I didn't come from a close-knit, adoring family like Becky, one of my roommates. I wasn't beautiful, like Christine, one of the other secretaries, who made men fall silent and forget what they were saying. I was just Barb Johnson, cheerful, hardworking, helpful. So when it came to parties or dating, I studied the other girls and learned how to flirt, talk, walk with my hips swaying just enough. I was making the best of what I had. That was something I *had* learned from my parents.

I met John at a company cocktail party. I worked in Real Estate; he worked in Family (one of the lower-earning divisions). But he was nice-looking and had a gentle voice, and he seemed to like me quite a bit, laughing at my jokes, smiling as I spoke. We dated for six months before he proposed, saying he loved me. I loved him, too. I thought I did, anyway. He was a perfectly nice young man with good prospects. I liked kissing him. I liked his hands on me, but I kept things chaste, because who marries the cow if you get the milk for free, even if this was the wild seventies?

That makes me sound cold, doesn't it? Well, you have to know, there was no romance in my upbringing. My parents married each other because they were both immigrants, both Norwegian, both Lutheran, and my father had land.

John would be a good husband. There was nothing to dislike, no skeletons, no weird fetishes or unkindness. We wanted the same things—stability, family, comfort.

When my parents finally agreed to come to Rhode Island to meet him and his parents, my father opened by saying a big wedding wasn't in the budget and there was nothing wrong with city hall. John's parents exchanged a glance. His mother said, "Oh, please, let us throw the kids a wedding. John's our only child, and we love Barb like a daughter already!"

I felt so pathetically grateful. My own parents didn't

care, but Eleanor Frost did. Our wedding was small but tasteful—forty guests, a fancy lunch at the Hotel Adelade. I invited my siblings, but none of them came. Tina was in a snit because I didn't want her to be a bridesmaid, Nancy was pregnant and the rest of them didn't have the money or time or interest to come, frankly. Nancy sent a card and a casserole dish, which, given that she already had four kids, was truly thoughtful.

I stayed at the law firm, relishing both my job and our domesticity. John and I weren't setting the world on fire, but I read a few books about making a happy marriage, and we *were* happy, back then. We bought a real cute house on a lovely street in Cranston. On Friday nights, we had cocktails and a nice dinner, just us two, sometimes going out, sometimes me making a fuss and trying something from *Mastering the Art of French Cooking*, because the books said to make an effort and show your appreciation. On Saturday nights, we went out with friends—bowling or the movies, Mexican food. We had sex on Tuesdays and Fridays, and sometimes on Sunday mornings, too.

I loved being married. The rhythm of it, the safety. When I woke up in the middle of the night, I'd snuggle against John's back, so grateful to belong.

I loved being a wife. Loved doing little things to make him feel special—cranberry orange muffins on the weekends, or a note tucked into his briefcase.

Maybe more than him, I loved *us*. The unity of us. He'd roll his eyes in sympathy when I endured my mother's phone call each month, knowing that she peppered me with a litany of complaints and dissatisfactions. When *he* called his mother (every other day), I'd run my hand through his hair or give him a kiss on the cheek, glad he was a good son, a good man, then take the phone and update Eleanor on the girlier things in our life—how I'd planted tulips, could I have her recipe for those delicious potatoes with the rosemary and such.

When I was twenty-three, I decided it was time for a baby. Keep in mind I was a midwesterner, and twenty-three in Minnesota was a full-on grown-up, and we'd already been married for more than two years. John agreed. He'd be a wonderful dad, so solid and reliable, so unwavering, especially if our baby was a boy.

As I said, I only wanted one child. Growing up in a sloppy litter of children, I never wanted my child to feel unloved or pushed aside. Though John said he'd been a bit lonely without siblings, he'd also felt completely loved by both parents. He had no idea how lucky he was in that respect.

So it was settled. We had enough in the bank, we had this marriage thing down, and it was time. I repainted the empty bedroom pale yellow and started shopping at antiques stores on the weekends, buying a nice old mantel clock and some porcelain Winnie-the-Pooh figurines that would look so sweet on a bookcase. Threw myself into baking, dreamily imagined my little one running in from the school bus to eat a chocolate chip cookie warm from the oven, chattering about his or her day.

I got pregnant right away. Oh, gosh, we were so happy. We wanted to wait to tell folks, just in case something went wrong, but we celebrated, just the two of us. I think that's when I loved John the most, and he loved me the most, too. He worshipped my body, in awe, even if I wasn't showing. My tender breasts, the veins that were suddenly so visible through my pale skin. He'd bring me an Awful Awful from Newport Creamery—a milkshake that got its name from being awful big, awful good.

A miscarriage never crossed my mind, not until I felt the warm rush of blood, and helpless terror flooded through me.

By the time we got to the hospital, it was over. Ten weeks. Not uncommon, especially with first pregnancies. Nature's way of sensing a problem with the fetus.

I'd never thought of it as a fetus. That had been our baby. Our son. Though the doctor didn't say, I knew it was a boy.

I was *so* glad we hadn't told anyone, because I felt an awful sense of shame. I couldn't put it into words. On the one hand, I believed the doctor when he said it wasn't my fault. On the other, I hated my stupid, stupid body. My mother had seven children! My sister Nancy was on her sixth! Elaine had three!

John was kind. And sad. But you know, it felt like it was my fault, no matter what anyone said. I missed that baby. Gosh, I missed him.

All I wanted was to get pregnant again, and fast. As soon as I recovered, we started trying again. Figured since I got pregnant right away the first time, it'd be no problem the second.

We were wrong.

The weeks turned into months. That was fine, I told myself. I loved John, loved working as a paralegal, loved keeping our house perfectly tidy and appealing. If I lay awake in bed at night, tears slipping into my hair, well, of course I was taking it hard. Now that I'd had a taste of that kind of love, I needed another baby to heal my heart. I wanted to be a mother so much, I ached with it.

The second year I didn't get pregnant, we saw a doctor. Nothing was wrong with either of us, and I was still young. "You're not infertile," the doctor said, "because you *did* get pregnant. Keep trying." I cried in the parking lot, and John tried to console me.

I found myself growing brittle. It was harder to keep smiling, to stay perky. My mind drifted at work, and I made mistakes, too busy wondering if *this* month would be when nature deigned to let me have—and keep—what everyone else seemed to get so easily. John was sympathetic enough, but it was hard to put into words just how empty I felt. Like all the work and time I'd put into getting to this point in life meant nothing, not without a baby. What good was I if I couldn't be a mother? Oh, I knew it was harder for some women, of course I did. But when Tina called with the news that she was having twins, I hung up, then called back later, saying a storm had knocked out our phone lines.

Babies were everywhere but in my womb.

I went on Clomid, but had to go off it because of the blinding headaches it caused. "There's nothing medically wrong with either of you," the doctor said, and I quit his practice and found someone else.

The second year of trying turned into a third year.

It wasn't *fair*. Going out with other couples was harder now; once we'd all been in the same boat; now Ellen was having her second and was tired, and the Parsons couldn't get a babysitter, and Abby and Paul had exciting news, and I didn't want to see them anymore. Friday night dinners, which had been such fun and felt so grown-up, were now morose. Why us? When would it happen? What if something was really wrong? Should we be trying to adopt now? Could we afford a trip to Korea? Colombia? Russia? We were on three agencies' lists, and not once did we make it to the interview stage.

Then John's grandfather died, and much to his surprise, John inherited the old man's home in Stoningham, Connecticut. When we pulled up to the house, I sat there, stunned silent. Grandpa Theo had been living with his sister in Maine for years and years. I'd never even been to Stoningham. Didn't know this house existed.

It was absolutely beautiful. A Greek Revival that needed some work, but was elegant and large and so . . . so classy. As I wandered through, taking in the huge windows, the columns, the pilasters, friezes and cornices and other words whose meaning I didn't even know, I fell in love. A front hall with a curving, graceful staircase. Fireplaces. A front parlor, a study, a family room, a dining room, a sunny if dated kitchen. Five bedrooms upstairs. Five!

A far cry from our run-down farmhouse in Nowhere, Minnesota. Our house in Cranston was cute but humble, not a place where we could have more than two couples over because the rooms were so small. But *this* house . . . this was heaven! The town, the house, the small enclosed yard, the nearby library, the smell of salt in the air, the cheerfully painted businesses on Water Street . . . honest to Pete, I was in heaven.

Stoningham was what a person thought of when they heard the word Connecticut—a little village of Colonials and Victorians, old cemeteries, posh boutiques, several restaurants, the historical society, the garden society, Long Island Sound sparkling, dotted with the white sails of boats.

Suddenly, marriage seemed wonderful again, new lifeblood injected into our lives. We needed this, John and I. The change. The freshness. We moved, John commuting half an hour or so to Providence. I decided to quit my job and devote myself to the house, which hadn't been lived in for nearly a decade. *This* was where I was meant to be. This would be where my child would be born. We would belong here in a way I'd never belonged anywhere. I'd been the girl who lived on that cow farm outside of town, one of the many Johnson kids. I'd been Barb from Minnesota in Providence, and since I worked the whole time we lived in Cranston, we still hadn't met some of our neighbors.

But in Stoningham, I could be someone. I *wanted* to be someone here, to fit into Stoningham's effortless grace, to be known by name, to have our house on the tour of homes at Christmas, to be recognized by the society ladies, because this was a town that had society ladies. Being a Frost was suddenly relevant; while we may or may not have been related to the poet, the name Frost was carved in granite on three war memorials here—Silas, Obadiah and Nathaniel.

I wasn't a paralegal anymore; I was the wife of an attorney. He'd gone to Boston College and Northeastern, and suddenly, that mattered more. He had a pedigree (maybe), and I would reflect that in everything I did, starting with our home. And once that was done, maybe God would grace me with a pregnancy, because this was where my child should be raised.

I threw myself into the town and was received graciously. Welcomed, even. I met Caro from around the corner. She was married, had one infant son and was desperate for an adult to talk to. I joined the Friends of the Library and asked for advice about the restoration of our columns from the head of the historical society, who was pleased that I took the house's history so seriously. John bought a little sailboat and we joined the yacht club.

I still didn't get pregnant, though. Years passed. *Years*

of trying, that one brief pregnancy. Four different ob-gyns.
No diagnosis.

It was devastating. Everywhere I went, I felt judged. I
wasn't childless by choice. I was broken somehow. Everywhere I looked, there were pregnant women, children,
babies. In the summertime, when the population doubled,
there were so many beautiful children everywhere that I
would cry. "Don't worry, honey," John said one night.
"It'll happen, and if it doesn't, well, we're happy just the
way we are."

I wanted to punch him. Hard. I was *not* happy, not on
the inside! Couldn't he see that? I almost hated him, living the same life as always, staid and unruffled, driving
back and forth to Providence, reasonably successful but
ever complacent. How dare he be happy when I wanted to
drop to my knees and sob?

When a woman can't get pregnant, the world judges
her. The husband, gosh, he's just a great guy, releasing
millions of sperm for his wife's selfish, snobby egg to re-
ject. He's so patient, so understanding, so good-natured,
so supportive (of *her* problem). *That John*, I imagined
people thinking. *He sure is a saint.*

I was *barren*. That hateful word. I wanted to be lush,
fertile, inviting, warm, nurturing . . . and instead, my
uterus was an empty white room with sharp angles and
immaculate floors.

One of my former coworkers was Japanese, and she told
me once that women who couldn't have children were
called stone women. I felt like stone, all right. I went
through the motions, sex becoming only about procreation.
I snapped at John. My smile felt hard as I volunteered on
committees and worked in the garden. When Genevieve

London, the most influential and beloved of all Stoningham's residents, told me I'd done a "truly stellar" job on the fund-raiser for a new wing in the library, I almost broke down. *I don't care about that!* I imagined sobbing on her shoulder. *I just want to be a mother.*

I spoke with adoption agencies, longing for the Victorian days when you could just go to an orphanage and pick out a child. "This one's adorable! We'll take her!"

Caro was the only one I told. She'd just had her second boy, and I'd gone over with a hot dish. She let me hold him, and I must've looked sad, because she said, "Are you okay, honey?"

"Oh, sure," I said. "It's just . . . we've been having some trouble on the baby front." A few tears dropped onto her son's tiny, perfect head. "He's awfully precious, Caro."

She got me a tissue and gave me a hug. "If you ever want to talk about it, or borrow the boys, I'm here." And she let me hold that baby a long, long time.

And then, finally, when John had stopped asking if I was late, when I was speaking to adoption agencies in nine states and three countries, it happened. John and I had gone through the motions the night before, and when I woke up in the morning, I knew. I just knew.

Those first three months, I was so careful, holding myself together with all I had. I told God I was grateful and waited, waited for every day to pass, to bring me closer to my child. When I went to the doctor at fifteen weeks and she pronounced everything normal and healthy, I burst into tears. Only when I started to show did I confirm that yes, I was pregnant.

That beautiful, rich, sacred word. *Pregnant.* I called my family, and they answered in typical Minnesotan fashion. "Oh, that's nice, Barbara. Didja hear Tina's pregnant again, too?" I hadn't shared my difficulties with them, but their nonchalance infuriated me.

Caro was wonderful. She threw her arms around me and cried with happiness. Took me shopping for maternity clothes and understood that I was too superstitious to want a baby shower.

What a completely terrifying time those nine months were! "Enjoy," people would say, and I'd look at them like they were crazy. Enjoy? When I could hold my baby, I would enjoy. For now, I was wrapped in fear, walking a razor's edge, taking such good care of myself and yet held hostage every minute.

John figured we were "out of the woods" once I hit the fourth month, unaware that I prayed ferociously and almost constantly, begging and bribing and cajoling and threatening God to give me a healthy child, to spare me another miscarriage. I would be the best mother. I would love my baby so much. I already did. I would make God so proud of me. Please. Please. Please. With every roll and push of the baby, I was struck by wonder . . . and fear. Oh, I loved this baby so much. So much.

When I went into labor, I was the most ready person in the world. None of this "please, it hurts too much, I can't do it," not for me. Gosh no. And it didn't hurt—well, of course it did, but not nearly as much as they tell you it will.

I was ready, and my baby was ready, too—two hours after John and I got to the hospital, she was here.

A daughter. Oh, the joy that filled my heart when they told me! I'm sure I would've felt the same way if it had been a boy, but upon hearing, "It's a girl, Mrs. Frost!" my heart overflowed with gratitude and joy and sheer, utter bliss.

Juliet Elizabeth Frost. My precious, wonderful miracle. I knew, in that moment, I would never love anyone as much.

Not even my second daughter. I'm not proud of it, but there it is just the same.

~

CHAPTER ELEVEN

Juliet

One Wednesday in late October, months before her father's stroke, when the sky was deep, pure blue and the last of the spectacular foliage was still lighting up the Yale campus, Juliet sat at the Union League Cafe, waiting for Arwen to arrive for their mentorship lunch. She'd been warmly greeted by the maître d' and put at a lovely table by the window, where she watched Yalies nearly get killed as they attempted the difficult task of crossing the street. They might be among the smartest in the world, but they lacked life skills, which Juliet could say, since she was a graduate.

She looked at her watch. Ten after one.

When she'd started the mentorship program at DJK Architects, Juliet thought a monthly lunch would be a relaxed, informal way to discuss issues, goals, the company structure, projects . . . whatever the youngling needed. All her other protégés had loved these lunches, and not to brag or anything, but Juliet had a damn good reputation for supporting and nurturing young talent, at Yale, in the Association for Women in Architecture and Design (AWA+D had given her an award for that just last year, thank you) and especially at DJK. Not a single new hire there hadn't benefited from Juliet's guidance or support, especially the women.

And not a single one of her mentees had ever been late to a mentorship lunch. It would be highly disrespectful.

Arwen was late.

Juliet wanted to bring it up somehow—the fact that while Arwen was talented and hardworking, there was a pecking order to be acknowledged. A ladder to be climbed, even if Juliet herself had given Arwen the chance to skip a few rungs. That, at thirty-one, Arwen still had a lot to learn, and Juliet would very much love to teach her, so she should be a little bit more respectful and drop the attitude. And . . . and yet . . .

Maybe the attitude was just confidence. Would a man be told to check in with his mentor more often if he was doing perfectly fine work? Would a boss tell a man to be less confident in his abilities? Did women do things differently because they were women? Was this more about Juliet's ego than Arwen's? Did Juliet just wish she'd been that confident, that—

Holy shit.

There was her father. Her father and a . . . woman. A . . . girlfriend.

Until that moment, she didn't know he had a girlfriend.

She knew the woman was his girlfriend because he was kissing her.

Really kissing her. Right there on Chapel Street, making out like they were teenagers who'd just discovered tongues. People had to go around them, they were so locked in.

That couldn't be her dad. Sure, he looked exactly like him, but maybe . . . nope. It was her father. They broke apart, gazed at each other, smiling, laughing.

Gross. Grotesque, that's what it was.

The woman was tall, with dyed black hair and sharp, strong features. For a second, Juliet thought it might be a man and almost wished it was—Gay Dad would be so much better than Cheating Dad—but no, it was indeed a woman.

Dad had his hand on her ass now. God! Get a room, people! No, don't, she quickly amended. Shit! This couldn't be happening. Her father? Her mild father, whose exciting life consisted of reading John Grisham novels and doing the crossword puzzle, maybe taking a walk in the afternoon, followed by a nap? This couldn't be happening.

They kissed again, deeply—Juliet shuddered—and then, finally, kept going, down Chapel toward the green.

It was as if the scene had been staged for her benefit. What were the odds that her father would decide to make out with a woman on Chapel Street? Three blocks from where she worked? *Was* it staged? Was it a prank? Who would think this was funny? Did he do this so Juliet would tell Mom?

What the actual fuck?

She realized she was half standing, watching them.

"Can I help you, ma'am?" said the server.

"Uh . . . uh . . . I'll have a martini," she said. Her heart was pounding. "Dry, three olives. Chopin, please."

Her father was having an affair.

She sank back into her seat and pulled out her phone,

thinking she'd call her mom right away. No. No, not Mom. Oliver. He was calm. He'd know what to do.

"All right, darling?" he said, which was his customary greeting.

"I . . . I just saw my father kissing another woman."

There was a moment of silence. "You must be mistaken, love. John Frost, with a bit on the side? I rather doubt it."

"Oliver. I just saw him outside the restaurant where I'm having lunch."

There was a pause. "Was it a joke?"

"No!" she said, though she'd been thinking the same thing. "His tongue was down her throat! His hand was on her ass!" She glanced around apologetically, lowering her voice.

"That's . . . astonishing," he said.

"I know!"

"Deep breaths, my love," he said. "Christ, if this is true, I'm gobsmacked."

Arwen walked in the door, wearing a white dress that fit her perfectly, black stilettos, and a huge wonking single pearl on a gold strand. Bright red purse. Heads turned, as they always did for Arwen. "I have to go," she said to Oliver.

"Love you, darling. Ring me later."

"Juliet. So sorry I'm late." Arwen bent down and kissed Juliet on either cheek. Weird, since they'd seen each other in the office two hours ago. Probably some body language domination trick.

"No worries. It's fine. It's fine."

Arwen tipped her head. "You sure? You look upset."

There was that tremor of fear. "I'm great," Juliet said, adjusting her posture.

"Your martini, madam." The server set it down. "And for you, miss?"

"Perrier, please. Unless you feel uncomfortable drinking alone, Juliet. Alcohol makes me sleepy, so I never drink at lunch."

Fuck. Alcohol made Juliet sleepy, too. She'd already lost this pissing match. "No. I'm fine. I . . . " *I just saw my father snogging another woman*. "I'm good. It's nice to see you, especially since we had to miss last month's lunch."

"How long do they go on, these mentorship meetings?" Arwen asked. The implication was clear. She no longer needed or desired them.

"We never set a formal policy, but generally, three years," Juliet said, making it up on the spot. The truth was, all her previous hires *loved* going out with her, viewing it as special time with the likely next partner of DJK. "How are you? How are things?"

"Excellent." She took her nonalcoholic drink from the server and nodded thanks, looking both elegant and warm at the same time. Juliet could feel the sweat breaking out under her arms. Her face was still flushed. Arwen took a sip of water and tilted her head. "Pardon me for asking a personal question, Juliet, but are you having a hot flash?"

Fuck you. "No," Juliet said, trying to laugh. "I'm forty-three. A little young for that."

"My mom started when she was your age." A sympathetic smile.

"Well, *my* mom had a baby at my age."

"Really? Are you planning to have another?"

You'd love that, wouldn't you? Me on maternity leave. "No, no. Two is just fine. Wonderful. The best."

Her father was having an affair. Would her parents get a divorce? A sudden lump rose in her throat. She took a drink of the vodka, its burn welcome. "Tell me about the stadium project. Ian said there was some confusion on ADA compliance."

"No. He was mistaken." She smiled. "It's going beautifully, and even a little bit ahead of schedule. Now. What shall we order?"

When Juliet got home that night, she was exhausted and wired at the same time. Oliver had fed the girls already, and Sloane was in bed, Brianna doing homework (i.e., messaging her friends).

"I've got a lovely big martini ready when you are," he said. "Salmon, couscous and brussels sprouts, with a fat slab of chocolate cake I picked up at Sweetie Pies just for you."

"You're amazing," Juliet said. "I'll go say good night to the girls and be right back."

Sloane was already sleepy, her Patronus being an elderly cat who slept and liked to be petted. "How's my girl?" Juliet asked, sitting on the edge of her bed, stroking Sloane's silky hair.

"I'm good, Mommy. How are you?"

"I'm fine." There was that lump again. What would the girls say if their grandparents divorced? Oliver's mother lived in London, and while she was fabulous and descended with gifts once or twice a year, it wasn't the same. Oliver's dad had died when he was twelve.

Sloane and Brianna saw their Frost grandparents at least three times a week.

Shit.

"Do you want me to sing your good-night song?" she asked.

"No, Daddy already did. He makes up funny rhymes." She smiled sweetly. Yes. Oliver did everything better than she did.

"Okay. Sleep tight, little one," she said, kissing Sloane on the forehead, nose and lips. Soon, if she were like her sister, Sloane wouldn't want kisses anymore and would say things like, "Did you brush your teeth today?" and slice away at Juliet's heart, one translucent layer at a time.

But maternal love was required to be unconditional, so Jules went into Brianna's room, knocking once.

"What?" her oldest said.

"Hi, sweetheart," she said.

"Why did you work so long today?"

"It's Thursday. I always work till seven on Thursdays. You know that. That way I get to be home when you're done with school on Monday, Tuesday and—"

"*Okay.* Fine. I remember. Sorry." She widened her eyes as if Juliet had been screaming at her.

"How was school?"

"Fine."

"Any quizzes or tests or fun things?"

"No. It was boring. Um, I'm kind of busy, if you don't mind. Ackerly and I are doing math homework."

Ackerly was the most poisonous of Brianna's friends, and one of these days, she would take Brianna down. Juliet could see the handwriting on the wall. "What about Lena? She's good in math, too." Lena hadn't been over lately, and Brianna had stopped talking about her as much as she used to. The two had been friends since preschool.

"Mom. Ackerly is also good in math. If it's okay with you."

Juliet opened her mouth to say, *I don't trust her* or *Watch yourself with that one* or *Lose the attitude, Bri, or you're grounded.* "Watch your tone," she said, the best she could manage.

"Okay. Sorry. Good night."

"Good night. Love you, baby. Lights out in half an hour."

There was no response. Juliet closed the door and went down the stairs, pausing in front of a beautiful black-and-white photo of Brianna as a baby. Back when she loved her mother. God, those dimples! Her father's huge, smiling eyes, and Juliet's square chin, and those dimples.

When was the last time Brianna had smiled at her?

Juliet knew this was normal. Teenage girls were hormonal and beginning that process of pulling away from their mothers especially. Because how could you bear to leave if you didn't hate your mother a little bit? Except Juliet never had. She'd cried and cried when Mom had dropped her off at Harvard, and had to pretend to love it for six weeks before it became true. It was only because Barb was so diligent in checking in, coming to visit, sending care packages, that Juliet made it through her freshman year. She was her mother's favorite, she knew.

And Sloane was hers. Mothers shouldn't have favorites. She loved both girls the same. But she *liked* Sloane a lot more these days. If Brianna could give her something to work with, it would be easier.

Please, God, she thought, *don't let Sloane ever get to this point.*

Oliver was waiting, shaker in hand. He loved making

cocktails to a fault, trying the Tom Cruise moves from that terrible movie.

"All right, darling? Must've been a terrible shock, seeing your dad today."

"Yep."

"Sloanie-Pop still awake?"

"Just barely."

"And Brianna?"

"Doing homework." She sat down on the stool. Remembered she hadn't kissed him that day, and since she'd vowed never to be one of those wives who took her man for granted, got up and kissed him, then sat back down. "So."

"Right. I've been thinking about the situation," Oliver said, the ice clacking around in the shaker. "Thanksgiving is in three weeks. Perhaps wait till after to address all this muck? Your mum does love that holiday." He rattled the shaker dramatically over one shoulder, then poured her drink. "And her turkey *is* the stuff of legend."

Her second martini of the day. She'd had to drink hers at lunch, since Arwen had thrown down the gauntlet, and fought the afternoon sleepiness that it caused out of sheer will.

But if ever a day called for two martinis, it was today.

"Do you think she'll leave him?" Juliet said, her voice low.

"I would leave *you*, darling. And you'd have me murdered and thrown in the ocean in tiny bits and pieces."

"They've been married almost fifty years, Ollie." Her throat was tight. "How can you cheat on someone after fifty years?"

"Oh, my darling, there, there." He came around the counter and put his arms around her, and she clutched his shirt. "I've no idea. Your father's a twat."

"What do I do? Tell him I saw? Tell her? Order him to tell her or I will? Ignore it? I mean, it's not like they have the best marriage in the world. God. Maybe they have an open relationship."

"Well, darling, Barb has been incredibly busy this year, and—"

She jerked back. "And what? That gives my father permission to cheat on her?"

"No! Not at all. It's just that perhaps things on the home front have . . . I'm going to stop talking now. This is awkward, isn't it? Go on, love. What were you going to say?"

"Nothing. I have to let this sit a little while."

"Good plan. Maybe talk to a friend? Saanvi?"

Saanvi was one of their summertime neighbors. She worked in New Haven, too, at the hospital, and sometimes she and Juliet had lunch or, more rarely, a glass of wine after work. She couldn't see bringing up her parents' marriage, though. Too personal.

The truth was, Barb was Juliet's best friend. In any other circumstance, Barb was the one she'd go to.

Juliet wiped her eyes and let Oliver kiss her on the cheek. They ate dinner, and since it was late, went to bed, where they made love, tenderly and quietly, since Brianna had ears like a bat. "I love you, sweetheart," he whispered just before he fell asleep.

"I love you, too," she said, but the words almost made her cry.

Her father loved her mother, once. Now look.

Ten minutes later, Oliver sound asleep, Jules got out of bed, put on her bathrobe and went to her study. Googled "why do married men cheat?"

All the clichés were true. Boredom. Trying to reclaim

lost youth. Not getting enough at home. The thrill of the chase. Lack of communication.

The hard fact was, if someone wanted to cheat, they could. If someone wanted a divorce, he or she could just end things. *I don't want to be married anymore. Well, not to you.* And just like that, your carefully built life would crumble.

Juliet's mother had built a life *so* carefully. She had always put the family first, and Dad had reaped those benefits. The beautiful home, the respect of the community, Juliet and Sadie themselves, and now, by extension, Oliver, Brianna and Sloane. She saw how hard her mother tried—she'd always seen it. Cooking lovely meals, the house always a haven, trying to make conversation with topics such as "tell me the happiest thing that happened to you today" at dinnertime. She remembered her parents taking ballroom dancing classes, going to Scotland, learning about wine.

So if Barb couldn't pull it off, who could?

Oliver was perpetually happy, and not tremendously empathetic to people who weren't, always a little confused as to why they didn't just shrug off what they couldn't control and focus on the positive.

Which made it hard to talk to him about difficult, complicated matters like her parents. Or Arwen, since he said things like, "Sounds like you picked a winner in that one!" or "That's bloody fabulous for her!" missing the point entirely.

It was hard to talk about the fact that Brianna made her feel sad and tired these days, and not liking her own child made her feel small and mean. She couldn't say out loud that she liked Sloane better, and she couldn't discuss the fear that Brianna would be able to tell, the same way Sadie knew Juliet was the favorite, and this was karma getting Juliet back for being their mom's favorite.

And now, it would be hard to talk about the creeping terror that if her father could somehow justify cheating on her mother, Oliver would see his point.

CHAPTER TWELVE

Barb

I hadn't wanted another child. I was too old. My husband and I were *both* too old to have another child. It was absurd. We had one, and she was—forgive me—perfect.

Juliet had been that way since birth. Since conception, to be honest, because I hadn't had one day of nausea or swelling or heartburn. And my body was miraculous. I could do everything she needed—nurse her, soothe her, intuitively know when she was about to wake up at night, or when she was coming down with a cold.

She was a happy, healthy, beautiful baby, speaking in full sentences by her first birthday, smiling, a good sleeper. She began reading at three. She was a friend to all her classmates, especially those who seemed to need a little more—the boy who wet his pants every day in kindergarten, or the girl who had a speech impediment. Teacher after teacher told me she was exceptional.

She was Mommy's girl. John loved her, of course—who wouldn't?—but he worked more during her childhood. He switched from family law to regulatory compliance, which required him to travel out of state once or twice a week. Sometimes, he'd stay overnight or come home very late, and I loved those mother-daughter nights.

Juliet was the purpose that had been missing in my life, because marriage wasn't enough, and work had been a placeholder for me. Our house and my role in town were just to prepare the way for Juliet. I was born to be her mother, and we lived in a beautiful world built by the two of us. I made sure she got enough fresh air, taking her for walks every day, first in the pram, then holding her hand. We took our big canvas tote to the library and filled it with books, even when she was tiny, and I read to her for hours. I made nutritious meals and snacks, way ahead of the curve regarding organic, locally sourced food. I chose my words carefully, always explaining to her why she shouldn't touch something rather than just "because I said so." Even my voice changed, and my flat upper-midwestern accent morphed into the blander, more cultured Connecticut non-accent.

Every day was bliss. It truly was.

John faded into the background. I never hired a babysitter. Every few years, John's mother would visit from Seattle, where they'd retired, and spend a week with us. Eleanor would urge John and me to go out, and we would, but I was anxious, never able to relax the way I sensed I was supposed to. I only wanted to be home with my precious, wonderful daughter. The very word was magical. My mother-in-law deserved a little time alone with her, though, so I did it.

Home, our gracious, warm, inviting home, was made more perfect because of Juliet. Her artwork hung on the fridge, and I couldn't seem to take enough photos of her. Her room was a delightful chaos of books and stuffed animals and projects. I turned one of the extra bedrooms into her own library, filling it with books she had loved, did love, would love. Oh, the happy hours we spent there, reading together!

My parents visited only once (we bought them tickets, but even so, you'd think they were being sent to a work camp in Outer Mongolia). They'd never seen the house before, and all my mother had to say was, "Aren't you the fancy-pants now?" My father commented that I "fawned over" Juliet, and maybe I could send some money Elaine's way, since I liked to flash it around so much. Who needed a house with five bedrooms when you had one single kid?

We didn't invite them back. Still, I sent them a Christmas photo of Juliet each year; though they had more than twenty grandchildren by then, I felt they should see her utter perfection.

By the time she was nine, Juliet was doing algebra and reading at a twelfth-grade level. She took ballet and was wonderful, even dancing the part of little Clara in *The Nutcracker.* She was helpful and thoughtful and funny, doing her chores without being asked, taking on extra-credit projects or tutoring other kids just because she liked to.

In the evenings, when her homework was done, she'd snuggle up next to me on the couch and say, "What are you doing, Mommy?" The fact that she, this bright star, was interested in me . . . it touched my heart in a way I couldn't explain. Even though she was clearly smarter than I was, she never made me feel unneeded. She asked me to teach her needlework—her room was filled with pillows and sachets I'd embroidered, and her closet full of gorgeous sweaters knit by my own hand. She wanted to learn to knit, too, so we could do it together. I loved to bake, and she loved to help. We picked flowers and arranged them, and the house shimmered with our love.

Then, when Juliet was eleven, that magical age when she was starting to ask questions about the world, as we started to be able to really talk about life, and our relationship began to bloom with that added gift of friendship, my mother was diagnosed with stomach cancer. It had already spread to her intestines and liver, and she didn't have long to live.

It surprised me—that panicky sensation, the primal yearning for my mother, no matter how mediocre she'd been. I found myself crying uncharacteristically, and eating at all hours, something I'd never done. My mother was dying in slow agony, and when she was gone, I'd lose the chance to ever win her approval.

By the time I visited in March, the cancer had spread to her brain and bones, and she was thrashing around on the bed like a trapped animal. Oh, I cried and cried when I saw her—that poor skinny body, her skin bruised, face sallow. The hospice nurses said it could happen anytime, but that tough old bird just wouldn't die, as much as she wanted to. She lasted and lasted, in constant, grueling pain, and it was torture. There was just no other word for it.

I ate my emotions. My period was light, then stopped for a month or so, which I attributed to stress. It had happened to Caro when her husband was deployed. Then

Mom finally did die, and I went back for the funeral with John and Juliet.

So I didn't suspect pregnancy, not after all the trouble I'd had. I was old enough to start flirting with menopause. Nancy had hit it at thirty-nine, Elaine at forty-three. Besides, John and I had only had two very mediocre . . . couplings . . . this entire year.

Well, I *was* pregnant, turns out. No signs this time. No flash of knowing. I had no idea until I saw a chiropractor for back spasms.

"How many weeks are you?" she asked, and I actually laughed.

"I'm not pregnant," I said. "My mom died recently, and I stress-ate. I . . . oh."

Oh, no. The crying. The hunger. I hadn't been eating my emotions; I'd been eating for two. I went from the chiropractor to my regular doctor, and yep. I was pregnant. Almost halfway along.

Juliet was in sixth grade, high school and teenage years just around the corner, not a time I wanted to be distracted by an infant. My god, an infant! Middle-of-the-night feedings, spit-up, dragging around a diaper bag for two years, ever in need of a shower. What had been a privilege with Juliet now seemed like a terrible burden.

Surprisingly, John was thrilled. Even more so than when I was pregnant with Juliet. "It'll be a second chance," he said, and I snapped back with, "A second chance at what?"

"At family life," he answered, and I may have hissed at him.

Juliet, true to form, was happy, though she admitted that my pregnancy was "kind of gross and embarrassing."

I couldn't disagree. To know your parents were having sex when you're in junior high school (even if it had been practically an immaculate conception) *was* gross and embarrassing.

I hoped the baby would be a boy, because then I wouldn't have to compare him to Juliet. His name would be Nathaniel, I thought, after one of his ancestors who'd fought for the Union and died in the Civil War. A fine New England name. Nathaniel Robert Frost. Though the pregnancy was a shock, I loved the baby as it wriggled and writhed in me. It was the unknown that had me worried.

And God, I was tired. I wasn't quite forty, but I felt eighty. I'd nod off as I tried to read the paper, yawned constantly. My back hurt as if someone had hit me with a baseball bat, and my ankles were swollen. I had pregnancy-induced hypertension, and my cheeks were flushed and hot all the time. I couldn't sleep, and I had heartburn so horrible I had to keep a huge vat of antacids with me at all times. Even at night.

I went into labor early on a Tuesday morning. It was brutal. Maybe because I was older, but I felt like I actually might die. Hours and hours of contractions, fiery knives of pain shooting down my legs, my back clenching and spasming. I vomited and had diarrhea, and my throat burned with bile. How could I survive this? All through that day into the night, into the next morning, I suffered and labored and endured. With every contraction, I felt desperate, trying to claw my way away from the wrenching, twisting pain. Was this how my own mother had felt with cancer? How could she have endured it?

After fifty-four hours of labor and no progress, only

five centimeters dilated, they finally decided to take the baby via C-section because "mother failed to progress."

As always, my fault.

"The worst of both worlds," the nurse chuckled. I was too exhausted to answer. They took me to the operating room and stabbed my back with a needle that felt as big as a chopstick and then, when the epidural had taken effect, sliced me open.

It hurt. They say you'll feel nothing, and they lie. As the doctors yanked and pulled, elbows-deep in my body, tears slipped into my hair. Those were my insides they were jerking around! How would the baby be healthy after such a battle? How could I love the little thing when all I felt was failure and exhaustion, literally torn apart by the savagery of childbirth?

"It's a girl!" Dr. Haines said, holding her up for a glimpse. I saw a huge, whitish baby with dark hair before they whisked her off.

"Is she all right?" I asked.

"Looks perfect to me!" said the jolly nurse.

John was crying with joy. "Another girl!" he said. "Oh, honey, I'm so happy."

"Nine pounds, nine ounces! She's a bruiser! Apgars are all nines, too. Guess we know what your lucky number is, guys!"

Another daughter. I'd been so sure it was a boy. I closed my eyes, so wrung out that I started to fall asleep.

"Barb, look! Our little girl! Isn't she beautiful?"

I forced my eyes open.

She wasn't very pretty, her head tubular from all that time stuck in the birth canal. She seemed giant compared to how I remembered Juliet, who'd been seven pounds even. The baby's eyelids were bruised and her face looked swollen. Her little rosebud mouth moved, and she opened her eyes.

I loved her. Oh, thank God, I loved her.

"Hello, little one," I whispered. John kissed her forehead, and put her face against mine, and the softness of her cheek was so beautiful. "Hello, sweetheart."

Then she started to cry. She started to *scream*. I had to turn my head away, because she was right against my ear.

"Sounds perfect!" said the irritatingly cheerful nurse.

It was startling that a newborn could make that much noise. "There, there, little one," John said, holding her close, and just like that, the baby stopped crying.

"Aw. She loves her daddy," said Dr. Haines. "Barb, I'm stitching you up, but you can snuggle her in a few minutes, okay?"

John was crooning to the baby, telling her she was beautiful, Daddy's little angel, and I fell into a deep, black sleep, unable to wake up for her first two feedings.

Having a C-section is much worse than giving birth the other way. With every move, it felt as if my insides were going to spill out onto the floor. Flashes of white-hot pain seared through my abdomen. When they made me get out of bed, I fainted. They made me pedal my feet to avoid blood clots, but I got one anyway, which they said was because I didn't get out of bed soon enough (ignoring the fact that unconscious people do have trouble on that front). My leg throbbed and burned. I couldn't hold the baby by myself for the first two days, because I was too weak. All I wanted to do was sleep, but they kept waking me up to feed her. I had to have a pillow over my stomach to protect my incision.

She didn't want to nurse. She screamed and screamed, her body shaking with rage as I tried to offer my breast again and again. They brought in a special nurse who was an expert, and she wrestled the baby close to me. When she latched on, I gasped in pain. My entire body was drenched in sweat as my sutured uterus contracted.

Juliet came to the hospital to meet her new sister. That was the bright spot of my six days there. I got mastitis, the cure for which was nursing more. My incision got more sore, not less, but I couldn't take any effective pain medications because I was nursing. My nipples started to bleed. That was the last straw. She could be bottle-fed. It was fine.

John picked her name. Sadie. Like a factory worker in World War II. He suggested Barbara as a middle name, to which I said, "Don't curse her with that." I know it was meant to be a compliment. But honestly. Sadie Barbara Frost? How would that look on a diploma?

And so her middle name was Ruth, after his grandmother. It was fine. It would grow on me, hopefully. I didn't have any other suggestions.

Looking back, I realize I had postpartum depression. In those first few months, however, I just thought I was a failure.

When she was asleep, I loved her. When she was awake, it soon became clear that she didn't prefer me. She wanted John, and he took a partial leave so he could work from home to help. When Juliet was born, he'd taken all of two days off.

But for Sadie, he was here, and it *was* helpful. He'd make me lunch and feed the baby, walk the floor with her, take her for a ride or put her in the carriage and tell me to rest and bounce back.

I didn't bounce back.

I was exhausted but couldn't sleep. The surgery and its complications took a lot out of me, and I just didn't bond with the baby the way I wanted to. The way I had with Juliet. I had a coughing spell a few days after I came home and tore my stitches, so that fun event had to be repeated.

I started to resent Sadie, the way she wouldn't be comforted by me, the exhaustion from the moment I woke up, dreading the long day ahead. When John went back to work full-time, I held Sadie as she cried and fussed—colic, teething, always something—and I'd look at the clock and count the minutes until Juliet would get off the school bus. Then I'd feel that love. I'd find enough energy to make dinner and pretend I was fine, because when my older daughter was around, I did feel so much better, gosh, yes.

I waited for my second-born to love me the way Juliet had. She didn't. She didn't hate me, of course not, but we just didn't have that special connection. Sometimes I'd see her looking at me, and I swore she knew. What was it about me that she sensed? That I was a fake? That I hadn't wanted her as much as I'd wanted Juliet? Was I a terrible mother?

During this same time, Juliet and I became closer than ever. Whether she knew it or not, I think she saved me. The sweet girl would bring me a cup of tea without asking if I wanted one, or she'd pick me flowers from the garden, knowing I was too tired to do it myself. That Mother's Day, she gave me a card that said, "After intensive research and based on my own experiences, this fact cannot be denied: you are the best mother in the history of the world." That was also the day Sadie cried and cried; she was teething, so I rubbed her gums, and she bit down hard, slicing my finger with her razor blade of a new tooth. My finger bled a shocking amount, and it throbbed for the rest of the day.

That about summed things up. I kept trying to get my second-born to love me, and everything I did was wrong, whereas my first daughter continued to adore and *like* me. I tried. I really did. You can't compare your children, all the authorities said, and I tried not to. I wanted to make room for Sadie. I tried to. But John was her favorite, and my poor body was ravaged by the pregnancy and birth. While I had bounced back in weeks after Juliet, it took nearly a year before my incision stopped hurting, before I could pee normally again.

Decades later, when postpartum depression came into the social conversation, I recognized that I'd had it with Sadie. It didn't solve anything, but it was good to know. But once again, something in me had been wrong. Always, always my fault.

As Sadie grew, our relationship didn't change much. If she woke from a nightmare, she called out for Daddy, not Mommy. She wanted him to push her on the swing, him to take her to the library on Saturdays, him to make her macaroni and cheese. (They both thought Kraft was better than my homemade version, which I found ridiculous. If there's one thing a Minnesotan knows, it's how to make a baked dish with noodles in it, thank you.)

Juliet started high school when Sadie was two, and the dreaded countdown began for the time she would leave me. Every minute of those four years with her was precious, every drive, every morning when I made her breakfast, every weekend, every little moment we had together.

Sadie would go to bed at seven or seven thirty—the earlier the better, as far as I was concerned. I let John read to her at night, telling myself it was only fair, since he'd missed out on those times with Juliet. It also gave me more time with Juliet, who told me about her classmates, her papers, which teachers were better, who was going to the spring dance.

When she was at school, I'd try to play with Sadie, but neither of our hearts were in it. If I made her a fort, she'd want to be in it alone. She told me hide-and-seek was only fun with Daddy and "Jules." She didn't like to bake or knit or pick flowers. If I drew with her, she was lost in her own little world. I'd ask her what she thought of my picture, and she'd say, "It's nice. Will you make lunch now?"

But Juliet never let me down, was never sullen, didn't have sex as a teenager, managed to have a nice group of friends without too much drama. She went to Harvard, and I sobbed all the way back from Cambridge. After that, I visited her once a month, trying not to let on that I needed those visits, that they sustained me. At college, she'd introduce me all around, and she was *proud* of me. Of me. "This is my awesome mother," she'd say, putting her arm around me and resting her head on my shoulder. "My best friend." We'd go shopping and have lunch and stroll around campus, hand in hand. Yes. We still held hands. Sadie only let me hold hers if we were crossing a street, and only because I insisted.

Juliet was so . . . kind. So *generous*. I was more grateful than I could put into words. Meanwhile, Sadie didn't seem to notice me, didn't take my advice. I loved my second child, but she was her father's girl, lost in her head, dreamy, unaware of her surroundings, sloppy, heedless of my requests to put her dirty laundry in the basket or bring her plate to the counter. I tried to engage, to feel as close, but she wasn't interested. When I asked if she wanted me to read her a story, she'd say no, she could read herself, though she let John read *The Lord of the Rings* to her out loud, a story that so bored me, I couldn't stay in the room.

I told myself not to mind. I had Juliet, after all. Juliet who, after graduating with honors from Harvard, chose Yale to get her degree in architecture. She asked if I'd come down for lunch every Wednesday. She met Oliver, who was the loveliest young man in the world. A month after they graduated—Oliver from the School of Engineering, Juliet once again with honors—Oliver drove up from New York City to Stoningham and asked me if he could have my blessing to marry my girl. Me. Not John. Of course I said yes, and he asked me what kind of ring I thought Juliet would like. I pointed him in the right direction, and when she called me the next week, we cried with joy together. (And she *loved* the ring.)

Oliver started calling me Mum in a way that made me feel flushed and proud. His mother was wonderful, and when she visited to talk about the wedding, we got along so well! Oliver was an only child, and Helen adored Juliet (as she should have), and asked to pay for half the wedding so it could be as extravagant as possible.

"I adore them together, don't you?" she asked, and we bonded over our love of our offspring.

Juliet and I spent the most wonderful year talking about colors and flowers, church readings and dresses, without a single cross word or bridezilla moment. We went to New York to pick out her dress, just the two of us, because that was how she wanted it, and oh, yes, I cried when she came out, smiling . . . beaming, really. It seemed that just yesterday, we'd been playing in her room, or I was wrapping her up in a big towel after her bath, breathing in the smell of her clean skin, making her laugh.

My beautiful little girl.

Sadie was eleven when Juliet and Oliver got married, a tomboy with a sketchbook who said she didn't want to be a junior bridesmaid, "whatever that was." It was fine. It was better, really, without a sullen tween sighing dramatically and reading Sylvia Plath as the other bridesmaids laughed and chatted.

The wedding was every mother-of-the-bride's dream. Every detail was gorgeous, from the cream and apricot flower arrangements to the delicious hazelnut cake. At the reception, Juliet thanked me for being a perfect mother in front of 250 guests, and said she could only hope to be half as good a mom as I was.

When she and Oliver moved into their Chelsea apartment, she asked for my help decorating it, "since you have such great taste, Mom." There was a second bedroom painted in pale blue, my favorite color, and the bed had feather pillows on it, because Juliet knew I preferred them. My favorite tea was always in their cupboard, and Oliver was always wonderful when I visited for the occasional weekend, making us dinner the first night, then sending us out for some "lovely mum and daughter time." The theater, or shopping, or best of all, just a long, drawn-out dinner at a quiet restaurant with my favorite person in the world.

Meanwhile, Sadie embraced every cliché of a teenage girl. The weariness, the cynicism, the all-black clothing. She became obsessed with painting, giving minimal effort in her other classes, lecturing me on the importance of art over all else.

"Really?" I said. "Over medicine? Do you think art is more important than, gosh, I don't know, saving lives?"

"Life isn't worth living without art," she said airily. Spoken like someone who'd never been sick.

Honest to Pete. Did she think art would count for more than actual learning? We argued over her mediocre grades, but John always took her side. "As long as you're doing your best, sweetheart, we don't care about your marks." Which was a total lie. Juliet had had the highest GPA of any child from Stoningham in a generation! She got into all eight Ivy League schools! Sadie never even made the honor roll, and it wasn't because she wasn't smart. She just didn't try.

Then, that boyfriend. Did she think I was blind, the way she looked at Noah Pelletier? He was a nice enough young man, but I knew about teenage boys and what they were after. She only rolled her eyes when I talked about unwanted pregnancy, as if she already knew so much more than I did.

That was her attitude about anything. Whatever I said, she treated it as if she was vastly more intelligent than I was. If Juliet thought I was the best mother in the world, how dare Sadie dismiss and avoid me, or worst of all, simply *tolerate* me? Endure me, as if I was such a burden, such an embarrassment?

Art school. Honestly. It would've been one thing if she'd gotten into . . . wherever one goes if one is good enough. Rhode Island School of Design, or Savannah College of Art and Design, with a plan toward historic restoration or something like that. Instead, she went to Pace, a school I'd never heard of, so she could become an artist. Oh, she had talent, not that it meant anything in the cold, hard world.

Then Juliet got pregnant. Again, I was included in every detail. She brought me to a few appointments so I could hear my grandchild's heartbeat. I came down four days before her due date and pampered her, and when she went into labor, I went to the hospital with them, right into the labor room, so welcomed and included, so needed. I held her hand and told her she was strong and amazing and I loved her so much, and when the baby finally came out, Juliet clutched my hand, crying tears of joy.

A girl.

They named her Brianna. "After you," Juliet said. "I know you never loved your name, so we took letters from Barbara Marie Johnson and made Brianna. So she's your namesake in a special way, Mommy."

Was there ever a more perfect daughter?

And so, as Sadie drifted like a butterfly, living her New York dream of art, poverty and waitressing, my older daughter continued to be my pearl. When Brianna was one, they moved back to Stoningham. Juliet called me several times a day just to talk and invited John and me for dinner a few times each month, and came to our house most Sunday afternoons.

If Sadie had given me anything more than scraps from her heart, I could've done better, but the truth is, I got tired of trying. Sadie had her father; I had my Juliet, and Oliver, and Brianna, and a few years later, another beautiful granddaughter, Sloane.

John was a bit disappointing as a grandfather, frankly. He was fine when a child was deposited on his lap, but he wasn't all that enthusiastic. He still worked a few days a week and played golf (the most unimaginative hobby in the world). Twice a year, he went away for a golf weekend with his friends, and I loved being in the house without him. Sometimes he'd go to the city to see Sadie and take her out to dinner and spend the night in a hotel down there, or at her place, once she got an apartment of her own.

"You never did that when I lived there," Juliet said, a rare rebuke from our gentle girl.

"Didn't I?" was his response, and I felt the venom well up in my throat, like one of those dinosaurs that could spit acid. Still, I held my tongue.

I continued to be a contributing member of Stoningham, working on committees and serving on boards. I watched my granddaughters when asked—unlike me, Juliet and Oliver liked to go out, and it was a joy to be the one to care for the girls. I'd read to them, or bake cookies with them, or do crafts and let them take an extra-long bath, and when they were asleep, I'd fold some laundry or pick flowers. Juliet's house was beautiful, and she had a cleaning lady, but I still liked to fuss and tidy.

It was so nice to be wanted.

I thought about divorcing John. It had been so long since we'd done anything meaningful together, connected in any way. But there was that affordability thing. The thought of losing my house.

Then Bill Pritchard said he wouldn't run again for first selectman.

"You should run, Mom," Juliet said over dinner at her house when John was on a golfing weekend. The girls were in bed, and we were enjoying a glass of wine on the deck on the top of their house, which overlooked the Sound.

"Oh, absolutely," Oliver concurred. "Can you imagine how shipshape this town would be if you were in charge, Mum?"

"That community center project would be in the bag, that's for sure," Juliet said. She put her hand over mine. "You should do it. You'd be amazing."

"Honey, I'm almost seventy."

"And? You have more energy than I do. And organizational skills. And smarts. And everyone adores you."

The idea took root. I *was* good at organizing. I'd been on every committee there was. Being Juliet's mother still carried cachet in this town; everyone loved her (and Sadie, too, just not as much . . . she'd left Stoningham years before, after all, impatient to shake the small-town dust from her shoes).

I won in a landslide. John had the nerve to be surprised on election night. "Well, holy crap, Barb. Who could've called that?" he said right there in the school gym, loud enough to be overheard. I saw a few people give him a strange look. An angry flush crept up my chest. Where had he *been* all these years we'd lived in Stoningham? Didn't he know how hard I worked, how many people respected me, how much I'd given to this community? How dare he be surprised by my success?

Then he took to calling me Queen Bee at home. "Please stop," I said. "It's really not funny, and it's sexist besides."

"Oh, it's a little funny," he said. "And it's not sexist in the least. The queen bee is the most important—"

I stopped listening. He loved those nature documentaries that never ended, some British man extolling the virtues of ant colonies or monkey dexterity.

Divorce. I'd give it a year, and then we'd move on. Shouldn't your husband be the one who truly believed in you? We'd be fine financially, now that I was working, and I'd save every penny of my salary this year. I could probably get the house, and even if I didn't, well. I'd cross that bridge.

A year. I threw myself into the town. Applied for grants. Talked to almost every single year-round resident about their concerns. I *did* get the old school approved for a community center, and I didn't even have to raise taxes to do it, thanks to a hefty state grant and what Juliet called my velvet glove approach with the summer people, asking them to donate in a way they couldn't refuse.

Not only that, we bought Sheerwater, that magnificent old house on Bleak Point, after Genevieve London died, got it listed on the National Register of Historic Places and got the land approved as a park, the house available for weddings and reunions and other functions. I was on a roll. I worked with the chamber of commerce to increase our tourism outreach, catching some of the casino crowd on their way *to* the casinos, rather than on the way back, when they were broke. We got rid of the stoplight that wasn't needed and drove everyone crazy and wooed a salmon fishery to open on the old paper mill site. Clean energy, ecologically responsible and employing seventeen full-time people.

It was a brilliant year. Juliet was so proud of me, and I knew this because she told me. Often. When that first year was up, I decided to wait till after the holidays to tell John I wanted a divorce. Why punish the grandkids over Christmas? Because of course they'd be upset. Our fiftieth anniversary was January 10; I'd do it then, since the fact that we barely acknowledged the date would provide a perfect lead-in. I was tired of dragging the corpse of our marriage behind me. It was over.

On January 9, he had the stroke.

Four hours after I got the call from the paramedics, I found out my husband had a mistress.

~

CHAPTER THIRTEEN

Juliet

We're just so sorry to hear about your father," said Dave Kingston, one of the partners at DJK Architects, the *K* in the DJK. "If there's anything you need—extra time off, more flexibility to work from home—you just let us know."

"Thank you, Dave. I really appreciate it. And the flowers were beautiful. My mom really appreciated them." The fact that part of Juliet would rather see her father die than deal with his adultery . . . well, best not to go there right now. A wave of love for that same father washed over her, and she had to swallow the tears in her throat. *Not now. Not now.* It was becoming her mantra.

Juliet sat in the conference room of DJK with Dave; Dave's personal assistant, the ever-silent and slightly terrifying Laurie, who took notes at every meeting Dave ever had; and Arwen Alexander. That Arwen was here was . . . disturbing.

Dave had been Juliet's boss since he hired her out of Yale. He wasn't a bad boss, not by a long shot, but he had a way of letting her know how grateful she should be to work there. She hadn't missed the *extra* time off, the *more* flexibility.

She'd taken all of three days off, thank you. The firm's HR policy gave her three *weeks* of sick time, which included family illness. The last time Juliet had taken a sick day was four years ago, because, like their mother, the girls almost never got sick, having the immune systems of Greek deities. And when Juliet worked from home, she worked longer hours than if she were at the office, and she had the time sheets and productivity to prove it. But at the age of forty-three, she felt her worth to the company was something she shouldn't *have* to prove. She'd been here almost seventeen years and worked on many billion-dollar buildings, delighting clients, leading teams, dealing with crises and labor issues, managing projects on time and sometimes even under budget, which, in the world of large-scale construction, was akin to calling Lazarus forth from his tomb.

Her work spoke for itself. Or it used to. In the past six months, there'd been a tremor in the Force. Lots of tremors, actually.

"So," Dave said. He cleared his throat. "I think we'll use this as an opportunity to give Arwen a little more responsibility. I'm putting her on the lead for the Hermanos headquarters."

The tremor became a quake. The new home of a Fortune 500 company under Arwen's lead? Why? Juliet was completely capable of doing her job.

"Absolutely. Anything I can do to help," Arwen murmured.

"I appreciate that," Juliet said, keeping her voice low and pleasant. "But I'm really fine. Totally in the game. Thanks just the same, Dave."

"Let's see how it goes. Great. Good meeting. I feel reassured. Again, anything you need. Anything at all. Thanks, Arwen, that'll be all."

Arwen put her hand over Juliet's and gave it a quick squeeze. "I really am so sorry about your dad." She left, leaving a hint of jasmine in the air. Even her perfume was gorgeous.

When the door closed, Juliet fixed Dave with a firm look. "I do not need Arwen taking over my responsibilities, Dave. I'm the project manager. She has her plate full already."

"You know what? I think you're right, but we'll try this out just the same. It'll be good for you. Good talk. I like that we're thinking outside the box. Let's circle back and see if we can move the needle on this project. Great! Good! We're all on the same page. Give your mother my best." He stood up, and Silent Laurie closed her laptop and trailed after him, but not before she gave Juliet a look that seemed to say, "Watch your back, sister."

Juliet sat alone in the big room, Dave's cliché business-speak ringing in her ears and the too-familiar waves of dread lapping at her feet.

Two years ago, Juliet had recruited Arwen to join DJK Architects. It had seemed so innocuous at the time.

Recruitment was part of Juliet's job, unofficially . . . to

keep an eye out for young talent, especially female talent. Not that anyone made extra time for her to do this—the partners had never said, "Juliet, take two days a month and dedicate them to finding young female architects so we don't look so middle-aged white male around here, okay?"

It was just a given, since she was the highest-ranking woman at DJK, the only firm she'd ever worked for. The message was she was lucky to work here (and she was), so this would be paying it forward. Sure. She was happy to do it, frankly. There *weren't* enough women in architecture, and she could help solve that in her corner of the industry. The firm was international, with branches in seven states and sixteen countries. Bringing in new perspectives was only going to help everyone, from the partners to the clients to the world, who'd get to see beautiful buildings designed by people from all backgrounds.

Arwen came to her attention because of her work at another firm. She'd been Architect II—basically responsible for daily design—on a hospital wing in Denver, and it was gorgeous *and* ahead of schedule. Her name was mentioned in a small article about the building, and Juliet did a little poking. UCLA undergrad, master's at SCI-Arc, the Southern California Institute of Architecture. She had five years of experience on big projects.

Juliet did her thing: flew to San Diego, where the other firm was based, and took Arwen out to dinner while Oliver and the girls frolicked on the beaches and went to the botanical gardens. Arwen was sharp, good-natured and a little in awe of Juliet.

"I can't believe Juliet Frost is taking me out for dinner," she said the first night as they sat at Juniper & Ivy.

"You've designed some of my favorite buildings ever. That hotel in Dubai? And the hospital in Cincinnati? Next level."

But Arwen was happy at RennBore, she said. The weather in San Diego would be hard to beat. Why would she want to move to New Haven?

Game on. Juliet pitched her hard, extolling the loveliness of New Haven, the Yale School of Architecture, the proximity to New York and Boston, the beauty of the state with its many small towns and cities, the vibrant cultural scene (a bit of a stretch, but hey). Then it was onto salary and benefits packages, international opportunities, which would take Arwen years more at a huge firm like Renn-Bore. Arwen considered it, and Juliet took her out again the next night to field any questions.

She finally won Arwen over by offering her a position as Architect III, a jump that usually took a few more years for someone so young, and a step right below Juliet herself as Senior Architect/VP Design. It would be fine. Juliet would work with her closely, and Arwen was talented, smart and hardworking.

She joined DJK within a month. A press release had been sent out and picked up by every major architecture magazine. *Arwen Alexander Leaves RennBore for DJK/ Connecticut as AIII.* A few interviews came Arwen's way, in which she mentioned her heroes in architecture, including Juliet and Dave Kingston (smart girl, mentioning a partner, even if Dave spent most of his time golfing and drinking scotch). Arwen worked hard. Designed well, took critiques, adjusted her designs when needed, credited other team members. There was nothing—absolutely nothing—wrong with her work.

But here's the thing about architects. Every generation, there are two or three innovative, change-the-field-forever people. I. M. Pei, Frank Lloyd Wright, Mies van der Rohe, Zaha Hadid . . . architects who invented entire schools of design. They were the geniuses who created buildings the likes of which the world had never seen before. Sometimes that was a good thing (Frank Lloyd Wright's Fallingwater), and sometimes not (Frank Lloyd Wright's Guggenheim . . . can't win 'em all). But they were the geniuses, the innovators, the type who changed the landscape, literally and figuratively.

And then there's every other architect. Ninety-five percent of the best architects in the world designed buildings and interiors that were dazzling and beautiful, but built on the shoulders of those greats. Juliet felt she was in that category—creative, energetic, sometimes even brilliant—but not someone who was going to invent a new way of thinking.

Arwen, too, was a solid designer with a lovely portfolio. A little derivative, in that she clearly borrowed from her idols, but that was the way of the world, in everything from literature to fashion. Not everyone was Lin-Manuel Miranda, but that didn't make them a bad songwriter. Not everyone was Gianni Versace, but that didn't mean they didn't make beautiful clothing.

Juliet thought Arwen had some flair. With experience, Juliet thought, Arwen could rise to Juliet's own level, and sure, maybe surpass her . . . in a decade or so, after she'd learned more about the craft and worked with more senior architects. Hopefully, Arwen would become bolder and more confident, develop her own style and voice.

And then, six months into her employment at DJK,

abruptly and without explanation, Arwen became the It Girl of Architecture.

Suddenly, articles about feminism and sexism in the industry appeared, with Arwen giving quotes . . . something Juliet didn't know until the piece ran in the *Times*. It was nothing new, nothing that hadn't been said by dozens of female architects before, but it got buzz. Then *Architectural Digest* asked Arwen to comment on the booming architecture in China and its impact on the future of cities, even though she'd never been to China or designed a building there.

Juliet had. She'd been lead on a massive retail and office center in Hangzhou, and an apartment building in Chengdu.

The CEO of a Fortune 100 company that DJK had just landed said, "We'd like Arwen Alexander on the team." Dave and Juliet exchanged quick glances.

"Absolutely!" Dave boomed. "You got it! She's a keeper, that one!"

All fine. Juliet had been planning to put Arwen on this project anyway. But . . . why had he asked for her by name? Why all this attention? Had Arwen hired a really good PR firm? Was she connected in ways Juliet was unaware of? It wasn't that the girl—woman—was without talent. But she was a long way from superstar. Maybe someday, but those other greats, like Zaha Hadid, had been dazzling from day one. And Arwen, as solid and reliable as she was, was not dazzling.

That was a minority opinion, apparently.

Arwen was listed as the number one Forty Under Forty in *Architectural Review*, a "bolt of lightning with her stunning designs and razor-sharp outlook."

Juliet had turned forty just three months before that article ran. Not being included . . . it stung.

Arwen was quite attractive, which didn't hurt, but nonetheless, it was a shock for Juliet to see her photo on the front page of the style section in the *Los Angeles Times*. She was asked to give workshops and even a TED talk.

Apparently, her work was setting the world on fire . . . and Juliet, her boss, was scratching her head. It was great for the firm, this sudden outpouring of adoration, but Juliet was a little . . . baffled. Glad for her success and its echoes on DJK, and yet . . . why Arwen? Juliet had been an architect for more than a decade and a half. She knew brilliance when she saw it, and Arwen was good. She could be great. She was a far cry from brilliant.

Juliet was not the only one to think so.

"I just don't get it," muttered Kathy Walker, an interior architect who'd been Juliet's first female friend at DJK. "Do you?" She lowered her voice to a whisper. "We've had better. You're *way* more talented than she is."

"We work in a subjective field," Juliet said. Kathy was a friend, but also a gossip, and if Juliet said anything that showed the slightest flicker of faith in Arwen, word would spread. Juliet would die before she seemed jealous. Women in architecture had it hard enough without other women backstabbing or gossiping about them.

"Maybe all this adoration is because she's"—Kathy looked around—"young."

Oh, that word. That terrifying word. "Don't be catty. She's doing great stuff."

But of course it had crossed her mind. Juliet was only eleven years older than Arwen. But apparently, those were akin to dog years, and it sent a quiver of fear through her, a shameful fear she couldn't admit to anyone. She'd always been a solid presence in the architecture world, often asked for quotes or sound bytes, speeches, articles.

Then, just like that, she was yesterday's news.

After Arwen had been working at DJK for a year, Juliet went out for drinks with some of her closest architect friends, all of them women. They were in Chicago for a one-day design showcase, a PR kind of thing. Arwen was in Maui, checking the site of a hotel expansion, and Juliet suspected she'd been DJK's second choice as spokesperson for the Chicago gig.

Whatever. The drinks arrived, and within seconds, the issue Juliet knew was coming arrived. "Tell us about your whiz kid," said Yvette.

"She's doing very well," Juliet said. She couldn't be anything but positive, and she suspected the group knew it.

Silence dropped over the table. "What's said in Chi-Town stays in Chi-Town?" suggested Lynn. Everyone nodded, except Juliet.

"I'm sorry, Juliet," Yvette said, "but what's the big deal with her? She's not exactly special. Forgive me for saying so, but there it is. All of a sudden, it's like there's only one female architect in the world, while the rest of us have been slogging it out for decades."

"Maybe it's timing," Juliet said. "You know how it is. Sometimes you just get attention."

The other women murmured. A few looks were exchanged—disappointment, maybe, that Juliet wasn't going to throw her protégé under the bus.

"Do you ladies know I love opera?" Susan said. She

was the oldest of the group at sixty-five and, at one time or another, had been a mentor to every other woman at the table. "I even studied it in college, believe it or not. Music performance minor."

"You're so cool," Juliet said with a smile.

Susan smiled back, her face kind. "One time, my husband and I went to hear Pavarotti sing. And from the first note out of his mouth, my body just broke out in goose bumps. Everyone in that building *knew* we were hearing the greatest tenor in three generations." She took a sip of her martini. "Then, a few years later, we heard Andrea Bocelli. You know, the handsome one?"

"He's blind, you know," said Linda.

"Yes, dear, everyone knows that," said Susan. "So we went to the concert, and Bocelli was good. Very good. It was very entertaining. The crowd was in love." She paused. "But he's no Pavarotti. He's not even a great opera singer. He's a pop star who sings opera, Elvis Presley and Christmas carols. Which is not to take away from his talent, his spark. But if you love opera, if you *know* opera, he's a mediocre singer who gives a great performance."

"By which you're saying . . ." said Lynn.

"This young woman we're discussing is no Pavarotti."

Juliet was so relieved, she closed her eyes. It wasn't just her.

The week following the conference, Santiago Calatrava, one of the actual living legends of architecture, was quoted saying Arwen Alexander was the most exciting new voice out there.

Susan sent Juliet an e-mail. Guess I was wrong about Andrea Bocelli. What do I know?

A week later, Arwen was nominated for the AIA Young Architects Award and the Moira Gemmill Prize for Emerging Architecture.

No one at DJK had ever been so recognized. Juliet's friends, those women at the table in Chicago, went silent. Arwen was on the rise, and you didn't cast aspersions on a woman on the rise no matter what she did or did not bring to your field.

It was the elephant in the room. If there were any men who shared the opinion that Arwen was a Bocelli, not a Pavarotti, they didn't dare say it, especially after Santiago had praised her.

Arwen was no dummy. Without saying a word, the dynamic in the office changed. She stopped popping into Juliet's office to chat, or asking if she wanted to grab a glass of wine before heading home. Her clothes got better—she'd always had style, but now it was Armani and Christian Louboutin, Tom Ford and Prada. She bought a Tesla. She moved from a rental in downtown New Haven to an incredibly hip and spacious loft in a former manufacturing building and had a party for the entire staff plus spouses, and did all the cooking herself. Apparently, she'd developed a passion for Northern Indian cuisine when she spent a summer there during college. Oliver, who had lived in New Delhi for a few years as a teenager, said Arwen's samosas were the best he'd ever had. Traitor.

Architects were paid well. But not that well. Family money? A rich lover? Arwen never mentioned anyone, and she lived in the loft alone. As far as Juliet knew, she was single.

Juliet still offered input and guidance on Arwen's projects, because that was her job . . . but there was that tremor. Arwen seemed to tolerate her advice now, not seek it. Dave and the rarely seen Edward Decker, the *D* in DJK and the other living partner, stopped by Arwen's office to chat when Edward graced the New Haven office with his presence. Once, it had been Juliet he stopped by to see.

It was chilling. It was as if architecture were a river, and Juliet had been a white-water rafter for all these years. Suddenly she'd been turned into a rock, the water flowing around her, the raft way, way ahead.

Well. She was a rock sitting in a conference room who had better get to work while she still had a job. Her phone chimed, reminding her the girls had a half day. Oliver had taken off three days on Christmas break, so this was definitely her turn.

Leaving the office early had never felt like a liability before.

Snap out of it, she told herself. *You have a lovely marriage.* (Which reminded her, she should have sex with Oliver tonight, because it had been almost a week and he got grumpy if he went too long. He'd been so wonderful about Dad and deserved some attention.) *You have two healthy children. (Who haven't had a full week of school since mid-September; honest to God, who sets these school calendars?) You love your job. (Even if your star is sinking, you feel helpless and you're having panic attacks in your closet.) You were raised by parents who love you. (Take the girls to see Dad, and try to get Brianna not to sob when she sees him, and also check in with Mom and see how she is, because there's something she's not telling you.)*

That smoke-jumping job looked awfully great right about now. The mountains. A cabin. A good dog. Lots of books and a woodstove, and no one around who needed anything.

Juliet felt like crying. Like crying and eating an entire box full of Dunkin' Donuts Boston Kremes.

If she'd known how hard it was to have it all, she would've asked for less.

CHAPTER FOURTEEN

Barb

John had come home, and I wasn't feeling real thrilled.

Oh, go on, now. He'd been cheating on me for God knows how long with some floozy, and now he needed a full-time caregiver, and guess who won that prize?

The six weeks without him had been hard, of course—I visited him almost every day while still handling the myriad duties of first selectman, from going to the Winter Concert at the elementary school to commissioning a summer traffic study to getting more money for the library budget, because what was a town without a decent library?

But on those nights when I got home from Gaylord, which took a solid hour and fifteen minutes, or on those even better nights when I just couldn't find the energy to go, I'd pour myself a glass of wine and make a sandwich. Watch *Broadchurch* on Netflix—gosh, what a show!—or see if Caro wanted to come over and visit. In the mornings, I got up at seven; John liked to get up at five so he could go to the gym (and now I knew why), so the extra sleep was bliss. I'd make my coffee (I liked it stronger than John did, and always had to dump out his weak brew and wash the pot out, because God forbid he did that himself). I made oatmeal, one of the rare dishes from my childhood I had loved. John hated oatmeal. Said it gave him the dry heaves just looking at it.

I hadn't realized how much room he took up. How much space he demanded.

There was less laundry. Less noise, because John loved those punishing Russian composers. He often walked around in those silly clip shoes he wore to ride his bike. The house was immaculate again without his workout gear littering the place—the pants with the padded behind, his aerodynamic helmet, gloves, Day-Glo shirts, water bottles, running shoes. (I'd called them sneakers and been schooled in what may have been our last conversation.)

I had never lived alone. I'd gone from my parents' house to an apartment with roommates to marriage.

Living alone, I was finding, was rather wonderful. I just didn't want it *this* way, a husband trapped in a brain that no longer worked the way it used to. Almost every night, I'd wake up and think about him, not being able to speak, confused, needing help with everything from going to the bathroom to getting out of bed. Was he scared? Was he in pain? What was he thinking? Did he miss home? Did he miss WORK and all her texts and wonder why she hadn't visited him? Did he even know his children? Did he remember me?

Then the tears would slip out of my eyes, down my temples and into my hair. He was a liar and a cheater and hadn't been a good husband even without that. But no one deserved what he was going through. And I was going to have to suck up my hurt and stay with him and do my best to take care of him. And I would, because I'd meant those marriage vows, even if he'd forgotten his.

Sometimes, being an honorable person was quite the dang burden. Here I was, trapped in the in-between space of being a devoted wife and a wronged woman, a wife who'd wanted to leave my husband and was stuck with him forever now. And not even him. A husk of his former self.

He came home, requiring my dining room to be turned into his bedroom, the beautiful walnut table put in storage along with the chairs and the highboy that had been John's grandfather's. I packed it all up with Caro and Sadie one Sunday; Juliet had been in Chicago on a business trip. We made room for a hospital bed and a bureau, made sure he had ample space so he wouldn't trip and a cleared path to the downstairs bathroom, which luckily had a shower. He was brought home, and the next phase started, and I was so tired already.

Yes, I had help—LeVon Murphy was just wonderful, a cheerful, strong and handsome man who came at eight and left at four. He handled John's physical and occupational therapy, took him for walks, tried to engage him with puzzles and problem solving. Sometimes he stayed for dinner, and it was so nice, having a man who complimented me on my cooking and helped wash up. In addition to LeVon, a speech and language therapist came three times a week.

And Sadie was here, sleeping in her old room. I had to give her credit. She stepped up. She did the grocery shopping, the housework, took John to his doctors' appointments and kept a log of who said what and when. Filled his prescriptions and sat with him, talking, bringing her paints over, sometimes even bringing Brianna and Sloane to do art therapy, saying it was good for John to have the kids around. She wiped her father's face at dinner with a tenderness that made me almost jealous. Would she have done that for me? I doubted it.

Sadie and I picked at each other. I didn't mean to, and some of my comments were harmless enough—*Do you think you'll get a job?*—but Sadie always found a way to take offense. That calm sense of being alone faded with her there, tromping up and down the stairs, reading aloud to her dad, asking me question after question about his care.

Not that John seemed to notice she was here. He looked at everyone like a curious chickadee, head tilted. Or he'd fall asleep in the middle of a conversation.

Even in his current state, he could make me feel irrelevant. It wasn't a fair thought, but it came nevertheless.

One night, Sadie plunked herself down in the sitting room, where I was knitting a rainbow sweater for Sloane. John was in the dining room, and the TV we'd moved from his study was on. "Mom," she said, "I think I'm going to move out."

"Is that so?"

"Yes." There it was, the edge to her voice.

"Okay, then." Sometimes there was nothing to do but agree with my younger daughter. Truth be told, it was no picnic having her here.

"I'll come over every day after LeVon leaves and help out till Dad's bedtime."

I sighed. "I'm finding a home health aide to keep an eye on him when I'm not here."

"I just *said* I'll do it."

"And I just said no." My voice was sharp. "It's not your job to take care of your father. He'd hate that, and you know it. You've been real great, Sadie, and of course you can visit and spend as much time here as you like. But you should be living your own life. So go ahead. Move out. There's a real cute fixer-upper that just came on the market if you're looking to buy. Then again, I don't know how much you make with those paintings of yours, or if you've managed to save anything on a teacher's salary, or if that rich boyfriend of yours is ever going to propose, but let me know if I can help."

Sadie's jaw was like iron, because of course I said the wrong thing. I always did to her way of thinking. "I'll come over every day, Mom."

"Good. That'd be real nice for your father."

"Great." She stood up and left the room.

Always the two of us rubbing each other the wrong way, scraping and chafing like corduroy pants that were too tight.

John's phone chimed. I kept it with me at all times for obvious reasons.

Ah, WORK. She was a faithful correspondent, that was for sure.

> Baby, me so horny! LOL!!! But totally true, too! R U back from
> Cali? Hope U R not too sad!!!

Broken heart, red heart, smiley face blowing kisses, a cat with heart eyes, a lipstick imprint, a smiling devil, fire and, inexplicably, a chicken. Best not to know why that poor chicken was included.

So this was love? This was what John had wanted? A semiliterate lover who communicated through tiny cartoons?

I had been texting WORK for weeks now. John's mother, may she rest in peace having died before Sadie

was born, had once again gone on to her great reward . . .
at least, that's what I told WORK. Guess John and his
lover had never gotten around to talking about family, too
busy being new and happy and horny again.

The estate, I had told the other woman, was complicated with many valuable pieces of art and furniture to be
dealt with. Not to mention the house on the water in Santa
Barbara. The response had been immediate:

> OMG! I love SB! Babe, do U need company??? I can come help
> and we could spend some time together doing all sorts of dirty
> things! LOL!

An emoji of an eggplant had followed. Caro hooted
over that one. "You are too much, Barb! Hey. If WORK is
a moneygrubbing whore, she deserves what's coming."

I set my knitting aside and considered what to write. It
was probably time for John to come home from his poor
mother's second funeral. I put on my reading glasses,
glanced to make sure Sadie wasn't hovering, and typed.

> Baby, me so horny, too!!!! Not too sad, bc Mom was 105. I
> didn't know she was such an art collector! The Sotheby's guy
> went cray-cray.

John's IQ had dropped well before his accident, so I
felt no compunction about making him sound like an
idiot.

> WORK: Really??? Can't wait to hear!!!

"I bet you can't," I muttered.

> JOHN: So many wonderful surprises! Much to discuss. When
> can we meet??? I miss U!!!

> WORK: ANYTIME! Love you so much, tiger!!!

I sighed.

> JOHN: Will be in touch soon! Love you too, my sweet honey angel kitten!!!

Nothing appeared to be too nauseating with these two.

I then took a screenshot of the exchange and texted it to Caro.

> I'm going to meet the other woman. You in?

The answer was immediate.

Holy crap, yes.

Caro was worth her weight in diamonds.

After that, I read for a while. When it was time for me to go to bed, I got up first to check on John. Sadie was in there, just getting up from the chair next to his bed.

"I was reading to him, and he fell asleep," she said, her voice husky. "Just like he used to do for me."

"That's real nice of you, honey. I'm sure he appreciates it."

For once, there was no hostility or subtext. "Well. Good night, Mom," Sadie said. She went upstairs, the sixth stair creaking reliably, just like it had when she used to sneak out to meet Noah Pelletier.

I sat down next to John. "You used her birthday so you could text your mistress in secret," I whispered. "How do you think she'd feel about that, her perfect dad having an affair? I was in labor with her for two and a half days, John Frost. How dare you use her birthday?"

He didn't answer, as he was asleep. "You know, if you'd asked me for a divorce, I'd have burst into song, mister. I would've said yes so fast, it would've given you whiplash. But no. It was more fun to sneak around, I guess. Maybe you were never going to divorce me. After all, I'm a darn good housekeeper, aren't I?"

God! I couldn't bear it. I hated him, this man I once loved. Once, I'd felt so lucky that he'd married me. I'd taken such pride in the life we'd made. The old love, dusty from neglect, was still there, and yet, the knowledge of his affair was a corrosive acid, eating away at it.

"I'm going to meet your lover," I said. "I'll report back. Tiger."

I got up and then sat back down, fast and furious. "I tried, John. I made room for you right until you had the nerve to be surprised that I won that election. Not once did you say, 'Good job, Barb,' or 'I'm proud of you.' Not once in this entire year! Instead, you found an idiotic woman who can't even spell, because why, exactly? I wasn't good enough? Because I had the nerve to get older? Maybe this stroke is exactly what you deserved."

Tears spurted out of my eyes. Oh, the *fury*. Sometimes it felt exactly like grief.

~

CHAPTER FIFTEEN

Sadie

My mom, who thought she knew everything, was irritatingly correct about the little house for sale.

It had a leaking roof, one tiny bathroom on the first floor with a rusting iron tub and no shower, two bedrooms, one of which was too small to fit a twin bed (so they called it a bedroom because . . . ?) and floors that sloped so much, a marble would roll from one end of the house to the other. The kitchen was outfitted with harvest-gold appliances and Ikea's cheapest cabinets. One cupboard gaped open like a loose tooth. The kitchen was big enough for maybe four people, and the living room had stained beige carpeting and drafty windows. There was no garage, and the basement was made from stone and had a dirt floor and evidence of a recent squirrel rager, based on the litter and tiny little footprints in the dust on the workbench.

We went outside and walked around the . . . well, the

structure. It wasn't quite a house just yet. Juliet closed her eyes and shook her head.

"I'll take it," I told Ellen, the real estate agent.

"Seriously?" she said. "I mean, great! It's a . . . unique property."

It was.

"You're an idiot," Juliet said, tilting her head to squint at the house. It did look straighter that way. "Looks like it'll collapse in a strong wind."

"Ah, what do you know? You're just an *architect*. By the way, do you do any pro bono work?"

She smiled a little, which was nice to see. Jules hadn't smiled much since Dad's stroke. She did have a point about the building in front of us. But I was one of the few people in Connecticut who viewed an eleven-hundred-square-foot house as spacious, and if there was another house I could afford in Stoningham before I won Powerball, it was invisible, like Wonder Woman's plane.

"I'll draw up the papers," said Ellen, getting into her car before my sanity was restored.

"You can live with me, you know," Juliet said.

"We'd kill each other. It might scar the girls, seeing their mother and aunt lying in pools of blood."

"True. Well, you have a nice view, I'll give you that."

"That's why I bought it," I said, turning around to look out to sea, like the wife of a sea captain from long ago. Or like a regular person who enjoyed pleasant views. Because the view was *incredible*. The house, teetering though it may have been, was on what had become a nature preserve, which meant it couldn't be expanded or torn down for a rebuild (which is what would've happened in a heartbeat otherwise, and a grotesque "cottage" would sit here now). Ten years ago, a monster storm had devastated this area, and none but this house had survived. The owner died in the fall, and the market for tiny, decrepit houses was soft, so I was in luck.

"You haven't signed anything yet," Juliet said. "It's my professional opinion that you shouldn't. I happen to know a few things about buildings, Sadie. This is a money pit."

"I enjoyed us getting along for ten minutes," I said.

"Seriously. You'll regret this. I can loan you some money for a rental if you need it. A rental with a flushing toilet and everything."

"I'm only staying in Stoningham till Dad gets better, and I'm not working. I'll spruce this place up, slap on some paint and sell it at a profit."

"Stop watching HGTV. It's all make-believe." She sighed and looked at me critically, as our mother taught her. "Hard to believe you have enough money for anything more than a paper bag."

"Please. I can afford an entire refrigerator box."

"You're a teacher at a Catholic school."

"It's my art, Jules. Some people actually like what I do."

She got that constipated look I loved so well.

As an architect of super-fabulous buildings, my sister could have recommended me to some of her clients, or commissioned me to make lobby art for, say, that corporate headquarters she designed in San Fran a couple of years ago.

She did not. She wasn't in charge of artwork, she said, and besides, DJK usually went with . . . *other* artists.

By which she meant *important* artists. And hey. I got it. Plus, I didn't want to make it because my sister used nepotism and threw me a bone. Still, it would've been nice to be able to turn her down (and have her competitors start a bidding war for me, but so far, nada).

I put my hands on my hips. "Well, I have my work cut out for me. Want to drive me to Home Depot?"

"Will you let me make you a list, at least?"

"No thanks! I got this." I smiled.

Her jaw hardened. Oh, it would drive her crazy to have me buy laminate flooring, some fake plants and a couple of throw pillows to sex the place up, but that was exactly my plan. There was nothing wrong with Ikea chic. I should know. I'd been living with it since college. My apartment was currently drawing $175 a night on Airbnb, thanks in large part to my new throw pillows.

I'd make this house adorable, too, thank you. And, as my mother pointed out, I did have a rich boyfriend. If he wanted to help me out, that would be quite lovely, especially as I was ninety-five percent sure he was going to propose, now that Dad's crisis had stabilized and he was on the mend.

"Instead of having me chauffeur you around, why don't you borrow the Volvo while you're home? That little shitbox you're renting is a death trap. You get hit in that, you're dead."

Death trap, money pit, shitbox. So judgy. "Can I have your Porsche instead?"

"No."

"I had to try. Sure, I'll take the Volvo. Thank you so much, Jules." It *was* awfully nice of her.

She nodded. Pushed her hair back and sighed again, looking at my house.

"Everything okay, Jules?" I asked. "Aside from Dad?"

"Sure. Listen. About Dad. I think you better . . . prepare yourself. He might be like this for the rest of his life. Which could be really short."

"Jesus. Why don't you dig his grave while you're talking?"

"Just facing facts."

"The facts are, the brain is very elastic. People have come back from far worse. Clara, that nurse at Gaylord? She said they've had people in comas who—"

"I know," she snapped. "I was there, remember?"

"Well, don't you *want* him to get better?"

"Of course I do!"

"Then stop being so pessimistic! A caregiver's attitude can really affect—"

"Get in the car, okay? I have to help Brianna with a history project."

Two days later, it was official. I was a property owner.

My house—such nice words, *my house*!—did need a bit more work than perhaps I acknowledged, now that I was here. Alexander, who was in Sausalito at the moment, the poor bastard, had very sweetly covered the cost of moving my furniture from Juliet's to here, and the movers had just left after cursing and sweating and wrestling my bed up the narrow stairs, for which they received a generous tip. Otherwise, I had a couch, a table for two, a chair and some pots and pans and kitchen stuff. A couple of lamps. My books and pictures were still at Juliet's, but I wanted to sleep here tonight and get the feel of the place.

I also wanted to put some distance between my mother and me. Her disapproval of whatever I did, had done and would do seeped into every interaction we had. Even my care of Dad seemed to irk her, and her own lack of tenderness irked me right back. I had paintings to do, and she hated the smell. Even though their house was huge, there never seemed to be enough room for the two of us.

Hence, my purchase.

Perhaps not the best decision.

Did I mention I had no neighbors? Fifteen years in New York City had made me used to that safety in numbers thing. In the entire time I'd lived there, I'd never once been scared.

But I was kind of scared now. What if Connecticut had a serial killer? What if those giant coyotes that ate cats marked me as a slow runner?

I should get a dog. I *would* get a dog. I glanced at my watch. Shit. Six o'clock and already dark. Allegedly, my heat was on, but it was cold in here. I did have a fireplace, but Jules told me I'd burn to death if I tried to make a fire.

Maybe I'd go to my parents' house to sleep. Get the dog tomorrow, preferably a large, vicious, loyal-to-only-me type, and see if Alexander would be back from California and wanted to spend the weekend in scenic Connecticut doing a little house renovation. We'd be a team, like that irritating couple on the house-flipping show that I did indeed watch. Except that we'd be adorable. In fact, maybe we'd get our own show. I knew art and had great taste, and Alexander was rich and photogenic. What else did you need?

The knock on the door made me scream.

"Jesus!" yelled the person. I peeked out the window.

It was Noah.

No baby this time. Just him, looking irritable and beautiful.

"Hi," I said, opening the door.

He didn't answer.

"Hello, Noah," I said, enunciating.

"Your mother sent me."

I sucked in a breath of cold air. "Why? Is my dad okay?"

"He's fine. She wanted me to check your house." I

closed my eyes in relief. "But I can go if you want. Which would be my preference."

"You're so very sweet, Noah. Come on in. What little heat I have is racing out of here."

He came in, brushing past me.

Damn. He smelled so good—wood and polyurethane and laundry detergent. "How's your baby?" I asked.

He deigned to allow half his mouth to twitch in a smile. "He's great."

I nodded. "Good. Well. What do you think?"

"Money pit."

"That's what Jules said. I'm glad you let your hair grow again, by the way." *No, Sadie. Nope. Don't say that. Too late. You did.* "I saw your picture on Facebook. That's all. Nothing big. I wasn't stalking you." *Please stop.* "It was when you were engaged, that's all. All our classmates were talking about it." *Sigh.*

He just looked at me with those dark, dark eyes. As opposed to looking at me with his teeth, for example. God. I needed a drink.

You have a boyfriend, some distant part of my brain sang happily. *He's very nice to you! You almost always have an org—*

"I don't like the sound of that furnace," Noah said. "Okay if I go downstairs?"

"Sure! Yeah! It's super dark, though, because there's no light down there. Which is what happens in the absence of light. Darkness."

"Are you drunk?" he asked.

"I wish. I'm just feeding off all that brooding masculinity of yours." I snorted and regretted it deeply.

Noah sighed, took a flashlight out of his toolbox, which

I hadn't noticed before, and found the cellar door, which was easy, because it was right in front of him.

I took a few cleansing breaths. Texted Alexander that I missed him.

It would just take some getting used to, seeing Noah again. He was my first love. Of course I still had a soft spot for him. There would always be a place in my heart for—

"Sadie! Can you come down here and hold the flashlight, please?"

"Coming!" I groped my way down the stairs. Lightbulbs. I definitely needed to buy some lightbulbs. Shouldn't have dismissed Jules and her list quite so fast. Noah was at the hulking black thing (furnace, I assumed), doing something with his hands. Something manly and hard and dirty.

He handed me the flashlight, which I pointed in his eyes. "Sorry," I said, shining the light at his feet.

"Your filter is filthy."

"So are my . . . never mind. Filthy filter. Got it. Should I call someone? Or buy something?"

"You have someone." Oh, my heart! "I'll be right back."

"Are you—" Nope. He was already up the stairs. I heard my front door bang closed.

I had to get a grip. Yes, he was gorgeous. What did I expect? That he'd become Nick Nolte in my absence? And yes, that brooding Jon Snow act was doing things to my lady parts.

But he had a child, and I had a serious, long-term, almost engagement going on, and Noah didn't even want to be friends. I could respect that.

Except it seemed to trigger dirty thoughts that had the added benefit of irritating him, which, I had to admit, was kind of fun. Maybe I was just overtired. Maybe I needed something to distract me from Dad's condition, which made me cry if I thought about anything other than a full recovery. Every time I thought about him, lost in his own brain, panic slithered around my heart.

Whatever the case, I shouldn't mess with Noah.

But once, we'd been so happy together.

Noah came thumping down the stairs. "This is a furnace filter. You need to change it once a month on your model. Watch me so you can do it yourself next time."

I watched. It didn't seem difficult, not in those capable hands. That frickin' beautiful hair. His soft voice. I bet he was a great dad.

"All done."

"Okay. Thank you." Finally, a normal sentence. "Are you seeing anyone these days?"

"Not your business."

"Sorry."

We went upstairs—him in front, which gave me a perfect view of his ass, and I'm sorry, how could I miss it? The radiators were clicking with what I assumed was heat.

"I appreciate this, Noah."

"Don't do any construction on this house without checking with me, all right? I might not like you anymore, but I don't want you dying. Your mother would be crushed."

"Or relieved. But yes, I see your point."

He finally looked me in the eye, and his expression softened a little. "I really am sorry about your dad."

"He's getting better. You know, when it first happened, I was scared, but he's . . . he's good. He's improving."

"I brought Marcus over to see him the other day. You were at the grocery store, LeVon said. I hope that's all right. We, uh . . . we visited him at Gaylord, too. Figured it would be okay."

The image of my first love, bringing his beautiful baby to my father, punched me in the heart. "Thank you, Noah," I whispered. My eyes were suddenly wet. "It's really kind of you."

He nodded once. "Well. Enjoy your new place."

"Thanks. Have a nice night."

"Don't tell me what to do."

And there it was, that tug of a smile on his beautiful face. Then he was gone, and my house was warmer because of him. The quiet settled around me, bringing with it all the memories of how Noah and I had failed each other.

CHAPTER SIXTEEN

Sadie

I thought when Noah came to visit the city I was obsessed with, he'd understand. He'd never been to New York before, aside from the obligatory eighth-grade field trip. I wanted him to drink in the architecture, the life and pulse of the city. I thought he'd appreciate the glittering skyscrapers and gracious brownstones, the cobbled, uneven streets of SoHo, the thrum and rush of noise, the smells of street food and the variety, my God, the *newness* of every single block.

He came to visit for the first time on Columbus Day weekend of my freshman year. He didn't love a thing. In fact, he hated it. "How can you live here?" he asked the second night, rubbing his forehead. "You can't hear yourself think. How do you paint?"

My mouth dropped open. "I'm getting really good!"

"You were good already."

I made a disgusted noise. "Anyone can do a pretty landscape, Noah," I said patiently. Landscapes had been my forte in high school, and they won me those prizes at our town's art contest (which meant nothing, I had quickly learned). "I'm really growing as an artist. It's mind-blowing, what I don't know yet, and how good I could get."

I stopped in front of a gallery; we were in SoHo, and you couldn't swing a cat in this neighborhood without hitting a posh space staffed by black-clad beautiful people who spoke three languages. "*This* is art," I said, pointing to the sole oil painting in the window. "It's so much more than a pretty picture. This says something."

"Looks like blobs of black tar to me," he said.

"It's a statement on materialism and abstraction," I said. "There's a tension here, a grittiness and impact. It's a dissonant whole worldview about what's real and what we want to be real."

"It's black blobs, hon," he said. "That painting you did of the blood moon rising? Now *that's* beautiful."

I sighed. "Yeah, well, I'd kill to have been the one to come up with this. You know how much it goes for?" I knew, because my class had had a field trip here just last week (hence my knowledge of dissonance and such). "Three hundred *thousand* dollars, Noah."

His eyebrows jumped. "Jesus. But then you'd have to look at the goddamn thing. Whereas if someone bought one of your paintings, they could actually feel happy."

"Noah . . . knock it off." But I smiled, even if I felt somehow slighted by his compliment. Happiness because of a painting? How *plebeian*. Why not just frame a picture of your dog? (I mean, yes, I did have a picture of my dog, the late, great Pokey, who died when I was eleven.) But art was supposed to do more.

I went home for Christmas break, but only for ten days,

because I was going to Venice for the remainder. And oh, that beautiful city was everything I'd imagined. It spoke right to my heart, the crumbling buildings, the canals, the decrepit, genteel beauty, the patterns of bricks, the beauty imbued in everything, even the rainspouts. I loved the garbagemen who chatted animatedly with each other, smoking, but who paused to give me an appreciative glance with "*ciao, bellissima*." The riotous glory of stained glass in every church, the beautiful window boxes and brightly painted shutters. I took the water taxi to Murano and watched handsome men blowing glass, their arms brown and scarred. The beauty of the city, the foreignness of it, filled up parts of my soul I didn't even know I had.

When I got back to school, I signed up for a summer session in Barcelona and found a waitressing job so I could pay for it.

A quick trip home, travel on break, back to New York. It became my pattern. My painting changed; the gentle landscapes that had gotten me into Pace were cast aside. Now I did mixed-media and monochromatic paintings. I tried sculpting. I started wearing only black (I know, I know). I got my nose pierced.

Noah visited when he could, which wasn't often. He was apprenticing as a carpenter, working six days a week. When we were together, in bed, skin against skin, his light scruff gently scraping my cheek, our fingers intertwined, the red glow returned. But he kept asking about the next break, when I'd come home. When I did go back to Stoningham, I felt itchy—my mother, still the same but only on more committees; Juliet, securing her status as favorite by giving birth to a girl she and her perfect husband named after my mother.

And Noah. His love was so big and fierce it was like a dragon, waiting for me.

I could feel the resentment growing in him.

My return visits consisted of Noah and me sleeping together whenever and wherever possible, and seeing the two friends I'd kept in touch with from high school. My dad was the only one who asked me the questions I wanted to answer, who listened with real interest as I described the wonder of the Duomo di Milano's rooftop, the hundreds of different shades of green in Ireland, that moment when I stood at the very tip of South Africa, one foot in the Indian Ocean, one in the Atlantic, and compared the shades of blue. He was the only one who didn't ask when I was going to come home, the only one who believed I could succeed out in the world.

New York had its hooks in me, and I believed with all my heart that I would make it.

When you're a student in that city, all you see around you is what you could become. It is a city of wanting—wanting to live in that neighborhood, have that view, stride through that lobby every day. Wanting to show at this gallery, eat at this restaurant, be a regular at that bar. Wanting to shop at that boutique, wear those clothes, be invited to that person's parties. Wanting to know all the city's secrets.

I started bicycling all over the city, and the overriding emotion I felt was a combination of wonder and hunger. When I saw a woman who seemed to have it all, I wanted to be her—the confidence, the look, the way she belonged, the casual grace and comfort she exuded just walking down the street or sitting in a restaurant. Me, I'd almost killed myself gawking at a particularly beautiful building on the Upper East Side, and a cop yelled at me when I attempted to zip through the intersection on a yellow light, which apparently wasn't done in the Big Apple. Everywhere I went, I wondered, *Who are these people? How do they pull it off? How do they make it?*

I wanted to weave myself into the fiber of this city. I wanted to paint it, eat it, breathe it, own it. I wanted to be right without even wondering what right was. I wanted to live in a building with character and flair. I wanted to walk into an art exhibition and have people murmur—"Oh, my God, Sadie Frost is here." I would be that strangest anomaly—a warm, welcoming, super-successful New Yorker who knew everything and shared everything. The parties I would throw! The students I would mentor! The love and admiration of my peers and teachers! I would be celebrated, and I would give back.

Except I wasn't, and I didn't.

The thing about going to art school is that you're surrounded by talent. I might've been the best artist in my graduating high school class, but as I hit the end of my sophomore year of college, I started to see that I was . . . average. Skilled. We'd *all* started off as talented kids. All of us had different strengths. But while I'd been great at the technical aspects of art, now was the time where my professors were using words like *fragility*, *vision*, *articulation* . . . and they weren't using them on my pieces.

That was okay. I'd learn. I'd change. I could refine my voice and clarify my point of view. My travels had deepened and educated me—didn't I backpack through Europe with ten bucks in my pocket? Didn't I sleep under a tree in the Parc Municipal in Luxembourg? I bought breakfast for the old woman who begged for food outside Temple Expiatori del Sagrat Cor in Barcelona and talked to the heroin addicts of Manchester. Surely all those things made me a *real* artist. I would take it all and express it, beauty and darkness both, hope and despair, rage, loneliness, love . . .

"Sadie," my professor sighed during my senior year conference, "you have to stop trying to be what you're not." She pointed to the angry scribbles of charcoal. "This is what you *think* art should be."

I tried not to let my confusion show. Wasn't that the point?

She tilted her head. "Do you even know what you want to say with your art?"

"Of course I do," I said. "It's the melding of rage and darkness with the, um, the scope of architectural beauty and . . . uh, poverty. But hope, too. That things will change. For the better."

She grimaced.

"How is this worse than Zach's work?" I asked, because yes, my classmate had also done a series of black charcoal abstracts and gotten a show at Woodward Gallery in fucking SoHo.

My teacher folded her hands. "Zach's work shows a modernist fusion and battle of urban life and nature. It's a poem to the fragility and strength of humanity. The minimal quality of movement, the strength of message . . . if you don't see the difference, Sadie, I'm concerned."

I cried on the phone that night to Noah. "She's wrong," he said. "You're fantastic, Sadie. You are. You just have to . . . I don't know. Find your audience."

"You mean, paint pictures of sunsets and sell them to the summer people?"

"Well, yeah. What's wrong with that, Special?"

It was the wrong time to use that nickname, beloved though it had always been. I had just been told I was anything but special. "I want more, Noah! I don't want to be stuck in that stupid town, painting stupid pictures of stupid clouds!"

He answered with silence.

Right. I'd given him that painting of clouds, and he'd just hung it in the little apartment he'd rented over the hardware store. He'd sent me a picture of it there.

"I'm sorry," I said belatedly.

A few weeks later was the senior art show. Our school sent out invitations to art buyers and critics, gallery owners and collectors. Some students got a big break this way, and I was hopeful, anxious . . . and a little desperate.

Noah came, as well as my parents. "Your stuff is the best here," he said, ignoring the fact that everyone seemed clustered around Zach the charcoal boy and Aneni, a woman who painted strange animals with miraculous detail.

My work *wasn't* the best. I knew it, and so did everyone except Noah. Dad told me he was so proud of me and couldn't wait to see what was next . . . which, in my funk, I interpreted as "keep trying and maybe you'll get better someday." My mother bought one of Zach's paintings. "Imagine what this will be worth in ten years," she said, and I wanted to bite her.

I latched on to one woman who owned a gallery in Greenpoint, my voice high and fast as I tried to describe the references to Warhol and my love of Venice in my sculpture, only to find that her gallery had closed last month and she was going back to school to become a physician's assistant. The art critic from the *Village Voice* glanced at my display as she moved across the space and didn't even slow. My heart cracked.

I didn't sell a single piece, except to my dad.

My parents were staying at a hotel; Noah came back to my dorm room. My mind buzzed and fretted as I swallowed the sharp tears in my throat.

I hadn't been discovered. All those trips, the thousands of photos I'd taken, the open heart and mind I'd kept for four years had resulted in the *Village Voice* reviewer walking right past and my father pity-buying the Zach knockoff.

I'd have to keep working. Be more daring. Be different. It would be hard, but wasn't it better this way? Who cared if you were discovered at a school show, especially at Pace (which had been good enough until this moment but had now completely failed me as an institution).

No. A much better story would be of Sadie Frost who, believe it or not, was told she was unoriginal by her own art professor! I'd be in the same league as J. K. Rowling, who was rejected a zillion times, or Gisele Who Married Tom Brady, once told her nose was too big for modeling. Bill Gates. Oprah. I'd be in great company, goddamnit.

Then Noah got down on one knee.

"I know we're young," he said. "But I've loved you since I was fifteen years old, Special. Marry me. Come home. I promise we'll be happy."

The timing . . . it really sucked.

"Are you kidding me?" I asked, my voice squeaking with disbelief.

His dark eyes lost their light. "No."

"Noah. Honey. Come on. I haven't accomplished one thing I want to. I can't marry you! I can't quit before I even get started!"

He stood up. "I'm not *asking* you to quit. I just want us to be together. I love you. You love me. Why are we wasting time?"

"Because I have to be here!" I said. "Noah, I've never wanted to live in Stoningham. That's your dream. Mine is something different. You move *here*, and we'll see how it goes."

He wasn't going to move here. It was loud. Dirty. Crowded. The air smelled bad.

"I have to stay here," I said. "And you know what? I love it here. This is where I have to be right now. If I leave, I'll never prove I'm good enough." My voice broke.

"Sadie. You're more than good enough."

"You're the only one who thinks so, and Noah, I'm sorry, you just don't know that much about art."

"I do know about you, though."

Tears slid down my cheeks. "Then you know I have to stay."

"I've saved money so we can travel, and I'll build us a house where you can have a studio with the right light—"

"You're not listening to me. We're twenty-two, Noah. I'm not getting married this young. And I don't want to move back to Connecticut. Maybe ever."

He closed his eyes.

"So let's just keep going this way," I said, reaching for his hand. "Long-distance. We'll figure something out. Weekend lovers. It's not perfect, but it's enough."

"No. It's not."

The weight of those words seemed to squeeze all the air from the room. "Are you going to dump me because I have ambition, Noah?" I asked. My throat felt like I'd swallowed a razor blade.

"I'm just saying you can have ambition and work from anywhere in the world. I'm asking you to make a life with me. I thought it's what we both wanted. You can't raise a family if one parent doesn't live in the same state."

"Okay, it's way too early to be thinking about raising a family," I said. "You can work from anywhere, too, Noah. You could get a job here in a heartbeat. There's a housing boom, in case you didn't notice."

"I don't want to live here. I hate this city."

"Well, I hate Stoningham."

"No, you don't! You just think you have to because it's small and quiet. It's not part of the story you made up about how New York would fall over itself when you came to town."

Oh. His words sliced me right through the heart. They were so big and painful—and true—that I was frozen where I stood.

And then I said, "So you won't move for me, and I won't move for you. I guess we're at an impasse." I couldn't bring myself to say, *I guess we're breaking up.* Not to the wild boy who loved me. Whose pet name for me was Special. Who lit up my heart in such glorious, vibrant, pulsating color.

"All right, then." His eyes were shiny. I'd never seen him cry before, and I couldn't now. I looked away. "I'll wait for you, Sadie," he said, his voice rough. "But not forever."

"Same." The lump in my throat was strangling me. I still couldn't meet his eyes, and while I was staring out the window, he left.

At dinner that night, my mother asked, "Why isn't Noah here?"

"We're taking a break," I answered, the words wooden and hard in my mouth. I drained my martini, even though I hated martinis, but it was what Zach had ordered the last time we'd all gone out, and . . . and God, I was so fucking unoriginal.

My dad squeezed my hand. "These things happen," he said kindly. "Don't worry, sugarplum."

"Marriage is an outdated institution," Mom said. Dad sighed and let go of my hand.

I cried so much that for the next month, there were salt deposits in my eyelashes. It felt like Noah had slammed the door on my pulsing heart. Why did *I* have to move? Why wouldn't he even *try* living here? Why was there no compromise? What was this sexist bullshit?

And then I'd flip. *Should* I move home? What would happen to me if I did? Would I hate him for cutting my dreams short? How long was I going to try to be an artist in this vicious, competitive city? Was he right? Did I want five black-haired babies? The truth was, I wasn't sure. I didn't hate babies, but I didn't stare at them or fawn over them like some of my friends.

He would wait, he'd said. Apparently in silence, because we didn't talk to each other for a month.

Not many high school couples stay together, I rationalized. Not many twenty-two-year-old men really know what they want. Sure, I could marry Noah, and within a decade, we'd be stale and old and bitter, scratching to make ends meet in a town that catered to the wealthy. Our kids would grow up in the weighted gloom the way I had, tiptoeing around their parents' disappointment in each other. We'd inevitably divorce, and those five kids and I would resent him. Or worse, they'd love him better. Who wouldn't?

I'd picture his face, his wild beauty and curly hair, the rare smile with the power of the sun, and I'd cry again.

But I had to try. I'd always only wanted to be a painter, and I knew I had to give it my best shot. I had just graduated. It was too early to call myself a failure.

With a little help from my dad, I was able to rent a shared apartment in Hell's Kitchen, the only part of Manhattan that had resisted gentrification. It was a grubby, stuffy place with two roommates, not counting the cockroaches. Mala never left the apartment and barely spoke, just sat with her face practically touching her phone, thumbs twitching away. (I had no idea how she paid her bills, if she worked, if she had friends or family . . . She never offered anything.) Sarah was a violinist and only came home with her friends to cook giant vegan meals and leave all their dirty dishes in the tiny kitchen for days at a time.

Two months after my graduation, there was a knock on the door. I opened it to see Noah standing there with a duffel bag. I burst into tears and wrapped myself around him, sobbing with relief and love.

"I'll try it. Okay? I'll try." His eyes were shiny again, and we fell into bed without another word.

He got a job in construction—not finish construction, which was what he did back home—trim work and custom cabinets and, occasionally, a piece of furniture. Here, he worked with a company that built skyscrapers—Juliet had connections and got him the job. So every day, he went to work with metal and cement, thirty or more stories above the ground.

Noah was afraid of heights. I remembered the summer I got him to jump off a rock into the Sound, and how he'd been shaking, how it took half an hour of my talking him into it, and when he did and we surfaced in the briny water, he'd kissed me, and I pushed his wet curls off his face and loved him so, so much. I knew he was doing this for me, just as he had jumped for me, too.

I worked, too, waitressing at a sleek restaurant in

Tribeca (hoping my proximity to the heart of the art world would grant me a lucky break). I made a website featuring my artwork, dropping in the fact that I was (probably) a distant relative of Robert Frost . . . anything that would help. It didn't. During the days, I painted in the tiny living room, my easel on the couch because there wasn't enough floor space for me, the canvas, my paints and brushes, and Mala, staring at her phone, cackling occasionally.

Noah and I didn't have a lot of leisure time together, but at least we were here. When we could, we'd take walks, because that's the best thing to do in New York. We'd poke around St. Mark's Place, or get some street meat near Central Park. I told him about the city, the history, the art, the famous people who'd thrived here and loved it here.

He was trying. I could see that. And he was failing. To him, the city was too loud, too hard, too full of chaos. He didn't sleep well, and dark circles appeared under his eyes. He didn't smile as much as he used to. He had always been the quiet one in our relationship, but now, he was rivaling crazy Mala in silence.

As Heathcliff needed the moors, so my wild boy needed to go home. Stoningham was as lovely a town as there was, but I knew it wasn't the pretty streets and green that Noah loved. It was the birdsong, the tide, the sound of the wind in the marsh grass, the way a storm would roll up the coast and light up the horizon with lightning. The deep woods with their three-hundred-year-old oaks and maples, the farmland and stone walls that wandered through forest and field, marking out the history of the land. He missed working with wood; his job was now pouring cement. He missed his parents and knowing everyone he ran into.

One night, I woke up and looked at him. He was asleep, his lashes like a fanned sable brush on his cheeks, the scruffy beard that never seemed to fill out. He'd lost a little weight, and he didn't have it to lose. With his arm over his head, his ribs seemed too sharp.

My city was hurting him.

In the morning, I made him breakfast as Mala stood near the window with her goddamn phone. "Mala, could you give us a minute?" I asked. She shot me a dark look and stomped to her room.

"I've been thinking," I said to Noah, setting his eggs and toast down in front of him. "I think you should move back, honey. I know you hate it here."

He took a deep breath, the relief clear on his face. "Will you come, too?"

"No. I have to stay, and you have to leave."

"Are you breaking up with me?"

"No. I just can't stand seeing you so unhappy." My eyes filled. "I love you, after all."

He looked at his plate. "I love you, too. I want a life with you, with kids and everything, but I can't wait forever."

"Fair enough." Was it, though? Was it fair to ask someone to give up trying to get what they'd always, *always* wanted?

It was a wretched goodbye. I cried. A lot. My tiny bed seemed huge without him. And yet . . . and yet it was easier, too, without him looking like a beaten dog, without him silently judging my paintings, knowing he thought I should be drawing puffy clouds or dogs romping on the beach, rather than trying to stretch and grow. I missed him. I was glad he was gone. I loved being here, doing what I was. I hated being without him.

I tried to get an agent and absorbed their feedback— *nice color palette but the content is a bit too familiar . . . once you've honed your eye . . . not taking new clients at this time . . . have you considered taking an art class?* I had taken four *years* of art classes, for crying out loud! I could teach art classes! I had a double degree, thank you very much.

That was okay, though. Content too familiar . . . I could use that. Every failure, I told myself, was a step closer to success, even if it didn't feel that way.

I lugged my portfolio to the galleries who would see me, and sent countless e-mails to those who wouldn't. I was suckered into paying hundreds of dollars to be featured in a show for a week . . . the "gallery" a former garage that still stank of diesel, the promised opening consisting of cheap wine in plastic cups, with not even a dozen people attending. I entered contests, paying the fees with my hard-earned waitressing money, never once placing. But I tried to learn and absorb from every experience. New York was a harsh teacher, but the best teacher, too.

Months passed. A year. Noah came to visit twice, and I went home to Stoningham to see my parents and nieces from time to time. We were still together. We talked on the phone almost every day. Then less. Then a little less.

My art school friends started leaving the city . . . It was so expensive, so competitive. Only Aneni stayed—even Zach, my professor's favorite student, left for Cincinnati and a job at an advertising company. *So much for your wunderkind*, I wanted to say.

Aneni, she of the amazing and bizarre animal drawings, was our school's pride and joy. She was showing at all the hot places and guest lectured at the Art Students League. Every time she had an opening, I was invited, and she hugged me and introduced me around to her friends, gallery owners, critics. Once in a while, someone would say, "Send me your info" or "Stay in touch," but it never leveraged into anything.

Aneni . . . she had a true gift. You could see it a mile away, because her paintings were like nothing I'd ever seen before. I was so happy for her, because she was incredibly nice, but I couldn't lie. I was also jealous. Really, really jealous. How had she done it? Her viewpoint was so clear, her drawings incredibly precise, beautiful and odd. Was it because she was from Zimbabwe that she had such a different point of view? Why did I have to grow up in Connecticut, a state no one (except Noah—and my mother) took seriously?

Of course, I tried to figure out what my art was missing. I knew I could be better, clearer, more. As the months passed, I stayed resolutely openhearted. I took classes when I could afford them, listened to my teachers and tried, so hard, to be better. I pored over the great works at MoMA, the Guggenheim, the Met, the Frick, the Whitney. I went to galleries and studied the paint strokes, the textures, the voices.

I still loved painting with all my heart. It was more like painting didn't love me. Or the art world didn't. I'd stare into gallery windows and think, *Is that piece really so special, or did someone just anoint it?* And if it was anointed, how could I get some of that holy oil, hm?

Then one of my professors sent me a link to a teaching job at St. Catherine's, a small Catholic elementary school in the Bronx. I applied, and the rather terrifying nun, Sister Mary, seemed to like me. I was good with kids for the same reason I didn't seem to burn for them—to me, they were entertaining little aliens. Wanting kids never felt as real to me as painting did. I knew what I wanted there. Kids? They were . . . nice. Fun. Kinda cute.

At any rate, I took the job. I had a solid education, appreciated health care and didn't mind the tiny paycheck, since waitressing was pretty lucrative.

Carter, who taught third grade, took me under his wing, and suddenly, I had new friends, not in the art world. Normal people, many of whom had been at St. Cath's for decades and had children older than I was. There was a handful of us in our twenties and thirties.

The job was nice. The art room was bright and cheery, and I got hugged a lot.

Noah was furious. If I could teach in the Bronx, why not Stoningham? He saw it as a betrayal, and we stopped speaking for a while. Fine. The way he seemed to be watching and waiting for me to give up made me want to kick him, anyway. Then he sent me a card with a bluebird on the front. Inside, he'd written, "I still love you." Nothing else.

I made him a pastel, one of those easy skyscapes that virtually anyone could draw, and wrote on the back, "I still love you, too."

So we weren't quite apart, even if we weren't together.

When we saw each other the next time I went to Stoningham, we were practically strangers.

"How's teaching?" he asked as we sat in his mother's kitchen.

"It's really nice." It was so strange to feel awkward around him, of all people on earth. We seemed to be having trouble making eye contact.

"Painting going okay?" he asked.

"Yep." I didn't tell him about the galleries and rejections and meh feedback, not wanting to give him ammo in his argument for me to come back home. "How's carpentry going?"

"Good."

"Great."

We'd never been like this before. He drove me to New London to get the train, and when I got my ticket, he kissed me, hard and fierce and beautiful, and if we'd kissed like that when we first saw each other, maybe things would've been different.

I still waitressed downtown. I grew to hate Mala, who never even tried to be nice. I cleaned up after Sarah, who was a pig but pleasant. I painted and critiqued my own work and painted more, still not able to pinpoint what I was trying to accomplish with my work, other than make somebody see its value.

But something started to happen. Two years out of college, no longer shielded by my student status, I *was* becoming a New Yorker. I knew which subways to take, which street would be clogged with tourists, how to avoid the Yankees fans swarming to the stadium for a day game. I didn't worry about what to wear and knew which boutiques were cool and cheap. I painted all summer, and my work was getting better. I even sold a few pieces at those studio open houses where you paid to play.

Then one of the moms at St. Catherine's approached me. She was an interior decorator and wondered if I'd do pieces on commission to match the rooms she was doing. It was too hard, she said, to find art that matched exactly right. Maybe she could give me some paint colors and fabric swatches, and I could make something that would fit on the wall she had in mind?

I didn't hesitate in saying yes. Why the hell not? Would Aneni? Never.

My first piece for Janice, the decorator mom, was a ten-by-five-foot painting for over a couch. "Here's the couch fabric, and the throw pillows," she said, handing me swatches of fabric. "Make it with some texture in it, swirly, you know? Like that one with the stars in it by the dude who cut off his ear? Super! Oh, and sign it. My client will love having an original piece."

So I made it—an oil painting in sage, apricot and lavender with swirly brushstrokes (like Van Gogh, you betcha). Was it a complete sellout? Yes, it was. Did I earn five hundred bucks? Yes, I did.

Janice was thrilled. She came back to me again, and then again, and then it became part of her selling point: original artwork made *just for your house*. It gave me an idea, and I contacted half a dozen more decorators. Selling out, with the emphasis on sell. I was loyal to Janice and kept my prices low, but I asked for triple that with the other folks, and they didn't blink. Apparently, some artists were quite fussy about being told what to do and how to do it. Not me.

Later that year, I quit my waitressing job (which never did produce any contacts) and ditched the horrible little apartment in Hell's Kitchen, Mad Mala and Sloppy Sarah. Juliet alerted me to a "motivated seller" with a place in Times Square (the worst neighborhood in all five boroughs to any true New Yorker). But the apartment was affordable, and nicer than I could've gotten in any other neighborhood. Juliet loaned me the money for a down payment (we artists had no pride), and just like that, I had a one-bedroom place of my own, lit up at night by the garish lights of enormous, flashing advertisements.

I still tried to paint more than just the couch paintings, as I took to calling them. I still took the occasional class, still entered contests with influential judges, still sent e-mails to those galleries that could make a career. I was still young. But however mundane, I was also selling art . . . made, alas, to match comforters or bathroom tile. Between that and teaching the little darlings at St. Catherine's, I was making a living. At painting. Not a lot of people could say that. Not even Zach of Cincinnati.

Besides, it would make another great story, I told myself. Philip Glass had once been a cabdriver. Kurt Vonnegut had sold cars. David Sedaris had been an elf at Macy's. Oprah Winfrey had worked at a grocery store.

"This is an early Sadie Frost!" someone might brag someday of my couch paintings. That purple-and-blue horror I'd done to cover a sixty-inch flat-screen TV? It might sell for millions.

Noah still came to visit, but I could sense his heart hardening toward me. It almost felt like he wanted me to fail. He viewed my apartment as proof I didn't want to get married, but for crying out loud, we were twenty-four years old. I *didn't* want to get married! Not now! I was getting tired of his broody bullshit. He was an artist, too, though he hated when I said it. Only in bed did we recapture that beautiful, fierce glow and remember why we were together.

I settled into this new phase of my adulthood, one in which I could pay my bills and go out for dinner once in a while, get cable, if not HBO. Carter lived on the Upper West Side (family money) and he and I hung out a lot. One of Janice's clients asked to take me to coffee to thank me for her "stunning" watercolor, and we started going to yoga classes together. Alexa, the sixth-grade math teacher, and I both loved to wander through the New York Botanical Garden, which wasn't far from St. Catherine's.

I made good use of the city, believe me . . . I went to author readings at the 92nd Street Y and student recitals at Juilliard. My father came to visit, the only other person in our family who loved New York—not even Juliet, the architect, enjoyed being here. But Dad loved it. He thought my apartment was perfect, and loved walking as much as I did. We went out for dinner to my favorite little Italian place in the Village, and then meandered through Washington Square Park, where some kid from NYU was doing ballet while her friend played the violin. Sometimes, Dad would even stay over, insisting on sleeping on the pullout couch rather than taking my bed. "It's fun, sugarplum," he said, and we talked and talked.

He understood my ambition. "I wanted to be a writer," he told me once. "Law school was supposed to be temporary. But then, you know . . . we moved to Stoningham, and your mom loved it so much, and then Juliet came along. It never seemed like the right time to quit my job and try to write a novel."

"You could still do it, Dad!" I said. "There's no age limit. You're retired now! You should start tomorrow!"

"Well . . . I don't know about that. I think the urge is gone now. Besides, your mother thinks I'm enough of an annoyance without me talking about a crime novel."

"She'd probably love for you to have a hobby." And get out of her space, I thought. But she wasn't exactly the encouraging type (unless your name was Juliet Elizabeth Frost).

"Well. I'm very proud of you, Sadie. Not everyone is brave enough to go for it, and here you are. My fierce little girl, making it in the Big Apple."

No one else felt that way. No one had said they were proud of me in a long, long time. Noah used to, but not anymore, not if it meant me staying here. Our love for each other was becoming a clenched fist of frustration and uncertainty.

Love is not all you need. Don't believe that lie.

On my twenty-fifth birthday, Noah called. "I need to see you," he said, and it didn't sound promising. We weren't a couple, not really, not in his eyes, and yet we weren't not a couple. I gathered we were about to come to a conclusion.

When I saw him in Grand Central Station, my old love for him hit me like a wave, tumbling me in its force. I still loved him. I'd always love him. And when he saw me, his face softened just a little, an almost smile there on his lips. He never could grow a proper beard, but he looked sixteen if he shaved, and it was so . . . so endearing. My heart glowed that scarlet color that only Noah could bring.

"Hey, stranger," I said, and gave him a big hug. We hadn't seen each other in months, and he seemed bigger—broader shoulders, more muscle, and there was a sudden lump in my throat at the idea that my wild boy was now a man.

He wanted to go to a nearby restaurant and "get this out of the way."

"Sure thing," I said, nervousness and irritability fluttering in my stomach. I took him to a tourist-trap Irish pub just across the street, and we ordered beers and burgers. He could barely look at me.

So there was someone else, I guessed, and for a minute, I had to bend my head so I wouldn't cry.

"How've you been?" I asked, my voice a little rough.

"I want you to marry me," he said.

My head jerked back up. Not what I expected.

He was scowling.

"I want you to marry me and come home. I love you. I've never loved anyone but you, Sadie. But I'm not waiting anymore."

"This sounds vaguely like a threat, not a proposal," I said.

He didn't answer. The waitress brought us our beers and wisely slipped away.

"Sadie . . ." He looked away. "Do you still want to get married?"

I sat back in the red booth, choosing my words carefully. "I don't want to be with anyone but you, Noah. I love you. But I'm not sure I want the same life you do. You always had our future mapped out, and there doesn't seem to be any room for compromise."

"I did compromise! I lived here for four months."

"And you hated it, just like you promised you would."

"I can't help that. You're the one who sent me away." He glowered.

"I didn't send you away, Noah. I put you out of your misery."

The waitress brought us our burgers. "Enjoy," she said. We ignored her.

"Stoningham sucks the life out of some people," I said. "I know you're not one of them, but I am."

"That's ridiculous."

"Thank you for being so understanding."

He scowled.

I rolled my eyes.

"Are you happy, Sadie?" he asked.

"Yes. Mostly." Content, maybe. Climbing my way to happiness.

"Because from here, it looks like you're killing time. Being a teacher, doing those paintings you hate, listening to sirens and car horns all day, taking your life into your hands every time you cross the street. You gave it a shot. It didn't work. Come home and be with me."

My jaw clenched. "Wow. So now that I've failed—at least the way you define it—I should come home and marry you and get pregnant."

He leaned forward. "I *love* you. Doesn't that matter at all? Because to me, that's everything."

"It doesn't sound like everything. It sounds like everything *you* want, with no room for me. Why can't we be together, me in the city, you in Stoningham? Lots of people have long-distance relationships."

"You can't raise a family that way!"

"So that's it? Your way, or nothing?"

"What would I tell our kids? Mommy doesn't love you enough to live with you?"

"I don't see me having kids anytime soon, Noah. And certainly not because you bullied me into it."

We glared at each other over our cooling burgers.

"So you're saying no, is that it?" he asked. "Because I'd like an answer. The waiting period is over, and I'm not gonna chase after you all my life."

"This is a very hostile marriage proposal."

"Don't make jokes, Sadie. Give me an answer. Will you marry me?"

There was no right answer I could give.

"I'm so sorry, Noah," I whispered. "I love you with all my heart, but I don't want that life right now."

His face didn't change. He just looked at me with those dark, dark eyes, then glanced away and swallowed. Twice. He pulled out his wallet and put two twenties on the table. Then he left me at the table with our untouched burgers and unfinished beers.

Sitting there in that pub, I think I knew. A love like that didn't come along every day. No other man was going to light my heart up in shades of red so beautiful it hurt. I loved Noah, loved his gentleness and kind heart, how hard he worked. I loved his smile, his mouth, the way he looked on the water with the wind blowing in his tangled hair. I knew that being with someone who thought you were the most wonderful, precious thing in the world didn't happen very often, and maybe would never happen again.

But I wasn't going to marry a man who'd proposed via ultimatum.

Three years after I'd turned Noah down in that stupid Irish pub, he got engaged.

My sister told me about it. We were having a perfectly nice, perfectly bland chat about her perfect life when she said, "Hey, by the way, Noah's getting married. Gillian something. You guys were pretty hot and heavy, weren't you?"

I didn't answer.

Noah was getting married. To someone who was not me. *Married.* As in living together. Sleeping together, waking up together, eating together, and probably having kids together.

My sister's words sat in my stomach like stones. "That's nice," I said belatedly, but Jules was already talking about the perfect vacation she'd be taking.

I'd managed to avoid imagining Noah with someone else. It was much more romantic to think of him staring out at the horizon, wind whipping his hair, arms crossed, his heart still mine. Occasionally, he showed up in my dreams, at times happy, sometimes angry and, worst of all, sad.

You can try to talk yourself out of loving someone. You can pitch it all the right ways, ways that make sense. *We wanted different things. It was beautiful while it lasted. Not every relationship is meant to be forever. I'll always have a soft spot for him. You never forget your first love.* And all that makes sense . . . in your head, if not your heart. I still loved Noah, and sometimes I'd find myself walking down a street and letting out a growl of frustration. Why couldn't he have at least tried to love my city, to open his heart to it? Why did he view Stoningham, that beautiful, pretentious, infuriating, lovely little town, as the be-all and end-all for our lives?

And who the hell was this Gillian person he was marrying?

A quick Facebook search brought me to her page. Gillian Epstein, the future Mrs. Noah Pelletier. She was an event planner—Epstein Events, not a very creative name.

Neither was she subtle about their engagement; her profile picture was her hand on a man's chest. Noah's chest. On her finger was a very pretty solitaire. Other photos showed the two of them at McMillan Orchards, in what was obviously their engagement photo shoot. I knew this because her page wasn't private, and there were thirty-seven pictures captioned *Engagement Photo Shoot!!!* A lot of Stoningham people had weighed in on how beautiful they were, how happy they looked, couldn't wait for the wedding, a year and a half away, for the love of God. If you were going to do it, just do it.

I didn't like the look of her. She was pretty, but very done. Those too-perfect eyebrows. Eyelash extensions (or very blessed). She looked . . . smug. Oh, she was nice-looking, of course. Quite pretty.

But it was Noah's face I really studied. His hair was cut

short. Why on earth would he cut that beautiful, curly black hair? He looked—he was—older. I blew up the picture to see if he was really smiling, if his dark eyes crinkled and sparkled in that special way I remembered, and shit, yes, he did look happy.

My wild boy.

Tears spilled out of my eyes, surprising me. Obviously, I could've been his wife. I'd said no for all good reasons. He was uncompromising, and that wasn't a good sign for a marriage. We didn't want the same things, no matter how much we loved each other. So of course he was moving on. He deserved happiness, and I felt a hot, fast burn of shame that I hadn't been able to give it to him. No. I'd broken his heart instead.

Then again, he'd broken mine, too. It was a mutual devastation.

So I would be glad for him. I took my unjustified sense of betrayal and stuffed it down deep. Before I could talk myself out of it, I took out my pastels and drew him a little card with a heart-shaped cloud on it and wrote, *Congratulations on your engagement. I'm happy for you, Noah.* I didn't sign it. I didn't have to.

He didn't answer, nor did I expect him to. I just wanted him to know I wasn't resentful or furious or sobbing on my desk . . . even if I'd sobbed a little.

In a way, his engagement freed me. I didn't have to justify or prove myself, because Noah wasn't out there, watching and waiting and judging anymore. I relaxed, not knowing my heart had been clenched with tension until it loosened. Something softened in me. Now when I saw that New York confidence, when I read about Aneni's latest show, I felt the familiar sense of wonder, but it was no longer infected by envy. Maybe I'd never be them, those brilliant, sharp-edged, confident New Yorkers, but it was okay. I was doing just fine.

I got a couple of raises at St. Catherine's—Sister Mary seemed to like me. Teaching was more fun than I'd expected, introducing the kids to Picasso and Seurat, Jackson Pollock and Georgia O'Keeffe. I was told I was loved multiple times throughout the day, and was the beneficiary of many hugs. At least once a month, a kindergartener or first grader would propose. It was good for the ego, all those bright eyes and happy faces, and it was nice to leave them, too, and return to my lovely apartment in the armpit of the city.

Though I was embarrassed by their utter vapidity, the couch paintings were profitable. I could bang out one of those in a couple of hours, depending on the medium and size. If it looked like something you'd buy at Target, so be it. I still got to sign my name and deposit a sizable check. I took down my website, since nothing I was doing needed to be immortalized in cyberspace.

I saw friends often and enjoyed the nights when I was alone, despite the urge to machete my way through Times Square on the way home every night. (Tourists taking pictures of neon signs should be thrown in jail. There. I *was* a true New Yorker.) I even dated a little. A slurry of first dates, one regrettable hookup, then a nice person named Sam. We dated for a few months—he was a funny guy who did something with the wastewater of New York City. I liked him very much. We never had a bad time together. One night, when we'd been together long enough that we didn't wonder if we were going to spend the weekend together, he said (in bed, no less), "I think I'm falling in love with you, Sadie."

I replied with, "Oh, wow, that's so . . . flattering."

Thus ended Sam and me. I was grateful he broke it off before we got more entangled in each other's lives. Breaking another heart was not something I could handle. And besides . . . *I think I'm falling in love with you*? Kind of tepid. I'd never had to ponder that with Noah. It was, to quote the great Stevie Wonder, signed, sealed, delivered. Done.

Once in a while, I'd check Gillian's Facebook page. She was the kind of bride who gave me a rash—obsessed with the *me*-ness of the upcoming day. "Which bouquet do you like best?" she'd ask. Sure, sure, she was an event planner, but come on. She had Pinterest boards of dresses, bouquets, centerpieces, bridesmaid dresses. She had a bachelorette weekend with her twelve closest friends in Miami (those poor women . . . I imagined it cost them *thousands*), and every photo showed Gillian's blinding white teeth in a near-feral smile. She wore a tiara that said *BRIDE*, in case we were unclear.

In short, she was milking every drop of attention she could possibly get, and while I tried not to hate her, I failed. She had a countdown to the wedding on all her pages. Every frickin' day, she mentioned something wedding related, even posting a picture of the white corsety thing she'd be wearing under her gown. For Pete's sake, as my mother would say.

Then, four months before the "Big Day," there came a cyber-silence (not that I was stalking her or anything). Five days later, she posted that she appreciated all the concern and kindness, but she and Noah were going their separate ways. No one was to blame, and they'd stay friends. He was wonderful, and she wished him only the best.

I clicked off immediately, shoving aside the shameful

rush of satisfaction. Their breakup was too personal for me to read about, even if she'd posted it for all to see. Noah didn't have a Facebook page, except for his business: Noah Pelletier Fine Carpentry, on which he posted pictures of kitchen cabinets and decks and, in one case, a rather magical tree house made for one of the summer people.

I didn't send a card this time. Somehow, some way, even though we hadn't spoken for years now, I felt responsible for his heartache.

CHAPTER SEVENTEEN

John

Here are the things he knows.

The old man in the house . . . it's him. He finally understands how the mirror works, and that old man is *him*. He's gotten much older. He looks like his father.

The big man who helps him is named LeVon. He is a friend, but not really, because he works for John. But John thinks of him as his friend and would like to talk to him, but talking isn't happening.

He has had something called a stroke and a BLT. Or not a BLT, but something like that. A BLT is a sandwich with bacon, and John likes bacon. But the thing he has means his brain has been hurt. His little daughter tells him not to worry about this because he'll be better soon. His big daughter says less. She is less happy than his little daughter, even though she has very pretty little girls herself. This means she is a mother now. John doesn't remember that, or the little pretty girls, and that makes his eyes wet and sloppy.

When the little pretty girls are here, he likes it. Their voices are like birds, chirping and fast. He can't understand most of the words they say, but sometimes it clicks. *Grampy. Nana. Upstairs. Cookies.* These he knows. They run to him and kiss him and are gone, like the . . . the . . . the flower-bugs that float and drift. Flutter-bugs. Flutter-byes. Something like that. He knows he is close with the word, and also wrong with the word.

John also knows his wife doesn't love him anymore. She is important in some way, and she doesn't like him very much, but she isn't unkind. John tries to remember why she doesn't love him, but he can't remember or understand why that would be.

Barb. Barb. He wants to talk to his Barb. When he tries to make his mouth say her name, he only hears a wheezy old man—his now-self—making horrible sounds, so he stops trying. A bossy lady comes to see him and tries to get him to talk, but those sounds are too awful. Sometimes, if he moves his mouth too much, he drools, and this makes him feel small and stupid.

Barb.

Barb.

She looked so pretty on their wedding day, back in the long-ago.

They lived in a little red house in the long-ago. Not this house. Things were better there, but then there was something very sad, and she was different. Closed and locked. Case closed.

Case closed. Those words mean something to him, but he's not sure why.

Barb lives here now. In his grandfather's house. It's her house now, not his. Not theirs.

Barb wanted something very much in the long-ago. Was it this house? No. But something to do with this house. A boat? No, but almost a boat, with the same starting sound, that's what the bossy lady says when she tries to make him talk. The starting sound. Boat. Bank. Baby.

Baby. She wanted a baby. So did he. Lots of them. He wanted four, because four was a nice number, many but not too many. But they couldn't find the baby. No, not *find.* Get the baby. No, not that, either. They couldn't buy the baby?

Have the baby. They couldn't have a baby, and Barb was pretending to be happy, but she wasn't. She would have people over and make meals and light candles and pretend-smile, and he hated it. The . . . *untruth* of it. She would do those things and then he'd hear her crying in the bathroom, but she wouldn't talk to him. *Fine. Fine.* That was a word he knew was a lie when Barb said it.

She had . . . pretended, pretended happiness, and did things with people John barely knew, and filled their days with people and work and . . . and . . . and there were always *things* in the way, *her* things, her projects and papers, and he just wanted it to be the two of them, like the time in the little red house, when home was home, not a place to do so much. Always, there were the new people who thought Barb was fine, fine.

One night in the long-ago, he heard that noise, that horrible again-noise of Barb crying in the bathroom, the slight echo, how hard she tried to be quiet, how she'd run the water so he wouldn't know. He wanted to go in and tell her not to cry, that he would . . . find . . . no, not find, but do *something* to help. But she didn't want him to know she was crying, which was why she had the water turned on.

He almost went in. He put his hand on the . . . the . . . that thing you turn to open a door, but then the water went off, and John jumped back. He walked silently down the hall to pretend he hadn't heard her, didn't know, hadn't almost come in.

He *should* have gone in, he realizes now. Maybe she would still love him if he had gone in. He's sorry he didn't go into the bathroom. If he could do it over, he would have gone in and not let her pretend to be fine. He would've let her be not-fine. They could've been not-fine together.

But too much time passed, blurry time that John doesn't remember. Then Barb was happy because of the baby, the girl baby, and he was the one who was alone. He was alone and no one listened to him, and he wasn't sure what to say, anyway. He wanted four children, but there was only one and she was Barb's, until a long time later, another one came, and this time, it was his baby. This time, he wasn't shut away. He got to be needed again.

Sadie. Sadie!

He smiles because he remembered her name. Sadie. Such a pretty, happy name.

He tries to say it, but no sound comes out. His mouth is moving, but not the part that makes sound.

He wishes he could tell his daughter he remembers her name. He wishes he could say, *Hi, Sadie*, and make her smile and hug him. But he can't, and this makes his eyes water, and so he tilts his head back and escapes to sleep once more.

CHAPTER EIGHTEEN

Juliet

It wasn't anything to be ashamed of. Juliet knew this. That being said, she wouldn't mind a paper bag to put over her head right now. Or no, a silk bag. They could afford it, that was for sure. That way, no one would have to look at each other and pass judgment.

Park Avenue Aesthetics.

Yep.

There were four of them, three women, including Juliet, and one man. One woman had that freakish, ageless look that didn't say youth, but did say that plastic surgery was a legit addiction. Her skin was so tight it seemed like her whole face would crack if she blinked, which she seemed unable to do. Another woman was stunningly beautiful and, honestly, why was she here? Could she be a day over thirty? *Don't buy into the patriarchy, sweet-heart! You're perfect!* Then again, what if she'd been *made* perfect here? If so, could Juliet have what she was having? The man was a normal-looking guy who had a pleasant face and fit-enough physique. What did he want to change? Why?

Go home, people, she wanted to say, hypocrite that she was.

Clearly, business was booming, because the office occupied two floors of a Park Avenue building and had a waterfall in the lobby. She'd been offered a bottle of mineral water when she came in, and the chairs were luxuriously comfy. Harp music interwoven with whale song was playing from discreetly placed speakers. There were many brochures on the table, but Juliet couldn't bring herself to look at them.

Oliver would not be happy about this. Hopefully, he would never know. Juliet had taken out a separate credit card to hide the cost. Not that he would deny her anything (and not that she needed his approval to spend her hard-earned money) . . . she just didn't want him to know she was here. That fear—if she pointed out an imperfection, he'd say, "You know what? You're right."

He, of course, was aging perfectly, as had his grandfather, who died at the age of 104 and looked about sixty. Helen, Oliver's mother, could be a model, and she was seventy-five. That peachy British skin.

But Juliet was American, and ageism was a real issue.

Last week, Kathy Walker, who was six years older than Juliet, had come into the office with shocking red hair. Prior to this, Kathy had worn her prematurely white hair in a very elegant French twist, saying she couldn't be bothered to color it. Now, it was cherry red and short—quite a lot like Arwen's cut, gosh golly, big coincidence there.

Kathy had also taken to wearing stilettos with red

soles . . . Christian Louboutins, which cost a small fortune. Juliet could afford them, too, but it felt morally wrong, paying two grand for a pair of painful shoes. Kathy had been swinging by Arwen's office more and more, and Juliet's less and less. When Juliet texted her, asking if she wanted to grab a drink, Kathy responded that it was a nice idea and she'd get back to her. That was three weeks ago.

Back when Juliet had been new, she and Kathy were the only women in the New Haven office of DJK, and they'd supported each other, eventually becoming friends. They'd had dinners together, sometimes with their husbands. Juliet and Oliver had gone to Kathy's son's wedding last year. Before Arwen got hired, Kathy and she speculated about when a new partner would be named, since they were both on track to be tapped.

The past few months, Kathy had cooled considerably.

It didn't matter, Juliet told herself. She'd keep her head down and do her job. Her work had always spoken for itself. Sadie was the fun one, the kind of person who made a new friend every fifteen minutes, or had people telling her their life stories after ten seconds in her presence. Juliet was the worker. Organized, determined, a big-picture thinker with a list of details. Clear eyes, full heart, can't lose, as *Friday Night Lights* told her. That slogan had always spoken to her. Her heart had always been full, because she truly felt blessed in life, with a mother who encouraged and guided her, a stellar education, a wonderful husband, healthy children, a job she loved.

Clear eyes meant seeing what needed to be done. Oliver often marveled at her organizational skills. She had a monthly meal plan she put together so grocery shopping and dinner prep would go smoothly. Chore charts for the girls. She maintained the family calendar, juggled her and Oliver's work schedules so at least one parent would be present at every school or sport event. She researched their vacation destinations, booked flights, found hotels or rentals. Scheduled the dentist, the doctor, took the girls shopping for clothes (by the way, Brianna probably needed a bra, and she'd try to make that a bonding experience, the way her mom had done for her).

It was the *can't lose* part of the phrase that was coming into question. When Dave had appointed Arwen as the lead of the Hermanos building, Juliet had lost project management to a woman far less experienced than she was. She may have lost Kathy as well.

"Juliet Smith?" A strikingly beautiful woman with dark, dark skin and a shaved head stood in the doorway. "Ms. Smith?"

That was her. She'd given a fake name. "Hi," she said, standing up.

"Right this way," said the woman, smiling gently. "You're new to us?"

"I am."

"Welcome." She was shown into an exam room, and the woman smiled and left.

God. Juliet was sweating now. Why was she here? She'd never thought of herself as beautiful, but she liked her face. She looked a lot like her father, she knew, and had what Oliver's mother called a sporty face. Strong bone structure, symmetrical enough, not particularly girly-pretty, in that she didn't have full lips or doe-like eyes.

That was fine. She was attractive. With some makeup, she could look quite nice. She had good skin, in that it was clear and even-toned, more or less. She'd always thought she was aging well. Sure, she had crow's-feet, which she rather liked. And yes, her throat was starting to get crepey. And her hands looked like a crone's if she didn't drink enough water. And there was a wrinkle on her cheek when she smiled that hadn't been there last year.

But look at Helen Mirren. Meryl Streep. Don't even get started on Angela Bassett. They were older than she was and had never been more beautiful.

And yet, here Juliet was, at a posh New York plastic surgeon's office because she was terrified. She was forty-three, and Arwen was thirty-one, and maybe—gah—looking a little younger would remind the partners and perhaps the world that she was still a young(ish) woman, but really, why would you *want* a young architect? Wouldn't you want someone with experience and maturity? They made buildings! Experience was a good thing if you didn't want things crashing down on your head!

And yet she'd been passed over for the Forty Under Forty. *Vanity Fair* was doing a profile on Arwen. *Vanity fucking Fair.* "Women Who Are Changing the World." After being lead designer on three entire projects.

Three.

So yeah. That's why Juliet was here. It went against everything she believed in, and here she was. Not a proud moment, but she wasn't racing for the door, either.

The door opened. "Hello! I'm Dr. Brian. How are you? Juliet . . . Smith! What a pretty name."

He was about sixty and wore a white doctor's coat over jeans and a button-down shirt. And he was no supermodel himself. Should she trust a plastic surgeon with a nose that size? Why hadn't he gotten anything tweaked? Look at those wrinkles! *And* he was balding. "Hi," she said.

"What are you thinking of today, Juliet?"

Juliet took a deep breath, noticing that her hands were shaking. "I'd like to look . . . a little younger. Not different, just . . . rejuvenated." She closed her eyes at the overused word.

"Face? Body? Labia and vagina?"

"Jesus, no." She paused. "What's that? The vagina thing?"

He smiled pleasantly. "We can plump up your labia, maybe trim them, since they can get stretched out—"

Her knees locked together. "Trim my labia? Are you kidding?"

"No, not at all. We can get a very nice effect. We can also tighten your vagina. It says on your form you've had two children?"

"Mm-hm."

"Which can stretch you out, obviously. A few well-placed stitches, and—"

"Okay, no. I'm not comfortable talking about this." Did *men* do this? Was there any male at DJK who was being told his sac should be a little tighter and higher?

"I just want something quick and easy and very subtle," Juliet said. "I don't want to look frozen. I don't want to look weird or different or carved up . . . I just want to look like me, five or ten years ago. No scalpels." Her hands were tingling. A panic attack was lurking.

"Got it. Let's have a look." Another pleasant smile. "Listen, Juliet, it's normal to be nervous. I promise not to slice and dice when you're not looking." He laughed, and she felt a little better. He tilted her head, pushed her hair back, lifted her eyebrow, tapped on the underside of her chin. "What brings you in at this point in your life? Big birthday coming up, or anything like that?"

What the hell. "There's a woman at work who's

younger than I am by about ten years. She's getting a lot of plum assignments and kind of leaping up the food chain, and I can't help but think it's because she's so attractive. At least in part. The new kid on the block, you know?"

"What kind of work do you do?"

"I'm an . . . uh . . . uh, a magazine writer?" *I'm a world-class architect. You've probably seen my work. You may have been in one of my buildings.*

"Neat! What magazine?"

"It's . . . an online thing."

"Okay," he said. "Here's what I'd recommend. You're already a beautiful woman, and we can make you even more beautiful. You have some puffiness above your eyelids, which is very normal for a woman your age, and your jawline is starting to soften, which gives the appearance of jowls and definitely makes you look older. We'd cut some tiny holes, insert a laser—"

"A laser?"

"That's right! The heat will cause contracting and stimulate collagen growth. Or, for something more dramatic, a neck lift would give you great results, along with a lower face lift."

"No. No cutting."

"Fine, fine. You could go for an eye lift, since your lids are looking a tiny bit heavy, but you said something quick. Some lip plumping would definitely add to a more youthful appearance. Subtle. You, but five years ago." He smiled, trying to reassure her, which was nice of him, since she felt like puking on his shoes. "We can do some Botox injections to lift the brow. Some filler between your eyes to get rid of that." He touched between her eyebrows where, yes, she did have a crease. "There are also some more superficial things I'd recommend. Lash extensions, teeth whitening. A sassy haircut, even. You know we have an aesthetician wing here."

Juliet touched her hair. It was all one length, cut (rather well, she thought) straight across with a razor every two months or so. Not one bit of body to it, so it was reliably straight day in and day out. She could wear it in a ponytail or a bun, or just down, which was what she did most days.

Oliver loved her hair. Plus, Arwen had a sassy haircut, and Kathy had just gotten one as well, and Juliet didn't want to look like a follower.

"Um . . . okay, but not a haircut."

"Trust me?"

"I just met you."

He smiled. "Well, I'm a board-certified plastic surgeon. Dartmouth, Johns Hopkins, NYU residency. I've been practicing for twenty-two years."

Just not on yourself, apparently. She clenched her fists. "Okay. Let's do this. I'll be able to go home looking normal, right?"

"Of course."

"Not a lot of Botox. I don't want to look like those freaky Real Housewives."

"Two of them are my patients," he said. "But I hear you. Just a sprinkling. You'll look like you came back from a wonderfully restful vacation."

A wonderfully restful vacation where she fell asleep in the sun for eight hours, apparently.

"Am I bweeding?" she said, looking closer.

Her lips were swollen, which would subside, Dr. Brian said. He'd better not be lying. And for God's sake, she could hardly see through the forest on her upper lids.

"There are a few little dots, yes, but that's normal." He blotted her forehead, and the gauze showed blood.

"I—I can't go home wike this." Her glowing white teeth flashed against her red, red skin and swollen lips.

"It will just take a day or two."

"You said an hour!" She was blinking, the lash extensions so long they hit her cheeks (and possibly her eyebrows, but she couldn't feel those). She looked like Bambi trying to flirt. An evil, demonic Bambi. She tried to draw her eyebrows together, but they were no longer functioning eyebrows. She could lift them maybe a millimeter.

The redness. Jesus. Her face was the color of boiled lobster.

And those eyelashes. That was a mistake. "I thought it would wook more natural."

Dr. Brian smiled. "You look *beautiful*. The redness and swelling will go down, and the lashes will come off in a couple of weeks, so you may want to schedule a fill appointment now."

She cringed. "It wooks wike I have a small animal sitting on my eyewids."

A jolly chuckle. "No! You look amazing. Just make sure to brush them out when they get wet, or they clump together."

Great. Add that to her list of things to do every morning. "Can you twim them, at weast?" She sounded like the priest in *The Princess Bride*.

"Why don't you just sit with them a little while and get used to them. I'm telling you, you look wonderful. I can tell. This is my job. When that redness fades, you'll be very happy, I'm confident. You wanted to look younger, and you will."

She studied her reflection in the mirror. Maybe he was

right. The redness was distracting, and the eyelashes were . . . long. And fanned out, like a peacock tail. Her lips were sore from the injections, and her gums throbbed from that thing they'd stuck in her mouth while whitening her teeth.

She wouldn't want her girls to do this. Ever.

I'm sorry I put you through this, Face, she thought.

"Here's the numbing cream," Dr. Brian said. "In case the pain gets worse."

The pain got worse. Juliet called her office from I-95, said she had a migraine and went home. Thank God she'd taken the first available appointment of the day; the girls weren't home yet, and she could have some time to ice her face. If they saw her like this, Brianna would give her that disgusted look she'd mastered this past year, and Sloane might cry.

Juliet's face was still bright red. Some blood had crusted around her nose in tiny droplets. Not a great look. Frozen eyebrows. Her lips were throbbing and not noticeably fuller. Those ridiculous lashes. No one on earth would think they were natural.

There was only one person to call. She got into the house, tossed her bag on the table and took out her phone. "Mom? I'm having kind of a . . . cwisis here. Can you come over?"

"What's wrong, sweetheart? Are the girls okay?"

"It's nothing, except I need a wittle help. You'll see when you get here."

"Sure thing, hon. Give me fifteen minutes. I have to cancel a conference call."

Juliet's guilt was drowned out by gratitude. "Thanks, Mom."

When her mom got there, her eyebrows shot up (lucky thing). "Oh, sweetheart. What did you do? One of those facial peels?"

"Something with needles."

"I don't think those false eyelashes are doing you any favors, hon."

"They're extensions. Can you twim them for me?"

Mom put down her coat and purse. "You betcha. Let's get some ice on that face. It looks hot and painful."

"It is." She felt like crying. "I went to a pwastic surgeon. It's so humiwiating. I just thought I needed a wittle . . . fweshening."

"Why, honey? You're beautiful just the way God made you." Her mom smiled and kissed her forehead. "Let's get you into bed. Go on now. Change into your jammies and I'll get some stuff together down here."

Juliet went upstairs and did as she was told. She had friends whose mothers were, to put it bluntly, ass pains. Kathy's mother called her every day to complain that Kathy never called her. Jen's mother had a gambling problem and constantly begged for money so she could buy scratch offs. Iris's mother was cold and disapproving.

And Barb Frost was perfect. Oh, maybe not perfect, but damn near close. Who else would understand this ridiculous problem and help her fix it without judgment?

Mom came in with an ice pack wrapped in a dishcloth, and a cup of tea. She went into the bathroom and ran the water, then came out with a facecloth.

"Let's get that blood off your face, okay?"

The cloth was warm, and Mom dabbed carefully. It felt so nice, being taken care of after putting herself through the torture of this morning, that a few tears did slip out.

"Everything okay with you and Oliver?" Mom asked.

"Yes. He's wonderful. But I don't want him to know I did this."

"What exactly was it that you did, honey?"

"Micwoneedwing, eyewash extensions, wip injections, Botox and teeth whitening. I wook wike an idiot, and I feel worse."

"Why did you do all that, hm?"

If Juliet told her the truth, Mom would worry. She had enough on her plate these days. Plus, Barb hated when she couldn't help, and there was no helping here. She'd be distressed to hear that Juliet was aging out, that there was that tremor in the Force that had become a constant rumble, that someone else was now the favorite child. She'd given everything to Juliet, and it would distress her no end to hear her daughter was struggling.

And so she said, "Kathy wecommended it, and she wooked gweat, so I gave it a shot."

"Well, Kathy *needs* it, hon. You can tell she was a sun worshipper. Skin like leather. You don't need anything. Okay. Let's take a look at these silly lashes." She smiled. "You girls. So beautiful, and always trying new things when you don't need to. Hold still and I'll trim these a little."

"Thanks, Mama."

Yes. Forty-three years old and still calling her mother mama. Sometimes, Juliet thought her mom was the only person with whom she could be one hundred percent herself.

It was such a relief.

An hour later, the redness had faded. Her lips were less numb (though hardly at all fuller). Her lashes looked thick but not fake. "Looks like you had a little allergic reaction," Mom said, and there it was, the perfect lie, the thing she could tell her husband and children.

"I love you, Mom." Looked like she had her *l*'s back.

"I love you, too, sweetheart. So much. Oh! I'm having a little dinner party this weekend. You and Oliver are invited, of course. I'm inviting the event planner who's helping with the town's anniversary, she's just been wonderful. And she's single, and Sadie's bringing her single teacher friend from New York. And you know, Sadie has no friends here, so I figured I'd get a little business done and help Sadie, too. Caro and Ted are coming, and I thought maybe it would do your father some good, having folks around. Can you make it? Friday night around seven."

"I'll call Riley and see if she can babysit," Juliet said. "Thanks, Mom. Let me know what I can bring."

"I have to get back to work now," she said. "You just take a nap, all right? The girls will be home in an hour, so you just rest, honey. Everyone needs a break once in a while."

Mom kissed her on the forehead, smoothed back her hair, and before she'd even left, Juliet was asleep.

~

CHAPTER NINETEEN

Barb

Two days after Juliet needed me (the thought still gave me a warm feeling), Caro and I walked into a little café in Middle Haddam, which was far enough from Stoningham that we weren't likely to run into anyone we knew.

We were meeting WORK.

"Cute place," Caro said. "And clearly she's not here yet. Let me get us something. You want a tea, I already know. Any cake or cookies?"

"I'm good, Caro. Thanks." I wasn't good. I was nervous. And still angry. And sad. And humiliated. And gosh-darn tired, too. I got up every night at three a.m. to give John his medication, and I wasn't a young woman anymore. It often took me an hour or more to fall back asleep.

John had been home now for weeks. LeVon had become a fixture in our house, and that was a real blessing, I'll tell you.

Sometimes, it felt like he was the son I'd never had.

That first pregnancy of mine . . . I'd always thought the baby was a boy, and . . . well, sometimes I liked to picture what life would be like if that baby had lived. He'd be about LeVon's age—late forties. Maybe John and I wouldn't have grown apart if I hadn't struggled with infertility. Maybe Juliet would have relaxed a little more with a big brother to tease her, and Sadie would look up to him and be a little more responsible with him as a role model.

Most days, LeVon stayed a little late, joining me in a cup of tea before he left. It felt so comforting. Like he was protecting me, in some inexplicable way. He said he'd be with us until John's recovery was mostly done, and gosh, that was a relief. I'd adopt him if I could, but he had a wife and three kids, and his parents lived next door to him, so I guess that was out.

"Okay," Caro said, sitting down. "Any idea what she looks like?"

"Your guess is as good as mine."

"So they didn't text pictures."

"No. Thank God they didn't do that, you know? I'd hate to have to see a dick pic."

"The first selectman of Stoningham just said 'dick pic'!" Caro said.

It wasn't funny. It was awful. But it felt so good to laugh.

We settled down. I sipped my tea. Caro had already put in the sugar. She was drinking some monstrous thing with whipped cream. She also had a slab of coconut cake. "Go on, take a bite," she said, sliding into the booth next to me. "You know you're going to."

I did. Oh, it was good. I needed to bake a cake. Maybe LeVon could bring half of it home to his family. Maybe John would like it, since his swallowing had improved and he could eat almost anything now.

"Is John getting any better, do they think?" Caro asked. "Mentally?"

"In little ways. He seems more alert from time to time. His walking is better, but he still needs help getting in and out of bed. He makes some sounds, but talking isn't going so well. LeVon gave him a pen and paper, but he didn't seem to know what to do with it."

"Jesus, Barb. I don't know how you do it."

"In sickness and in health."

"Yeah, and forsaking all others. Let's not forget why we're here, after all."

The door opened, and a young couple came in with their baby. "How's your grandbaby doing, by the way?" I asked, and Carol pulled out her phone to show me the latest pictures of Garrett, her second grandson. "Beautiful. Looks like you, Caro."

She flashed me that gorgeous smile that lit up her whole face. "I thought so, too," she said.

Then the door opened, and a woman came in, late fifties, maybe.

"Hey," Caro said. "We know her. It's . . . uh . . . oh, shit, I can't remember."

"It's Karen, the teacher from ballroom dancing, remember?" I had great facial recall, which helped in my job. Also, we took those lessons for a few months, in those days when I'd still been trying to work on my marriage, making sure John had enough fun, trying to feel something other than irritation toward him.

"Right!" Caro said. "Hi, Karen! How are you?"

Karen looked over, then flinched.

The penny dropped, as the saying goes.

Seems we had just met WORK.

"Come on over!" Caro called. "Remember us? We took dance classes from you. We were all terrible."

Karen came over, her arms crossed tightly in front of her.

Caro went on blithely. "This is Barb Frost, and I'm Caro, and . . . oh. Oh, shit. It's you, isn't it?"

Yep. Her eyes darted between us.

"Here to meet my husband?" I asked, oddly numb.

"Um . . . uh . . ." She closed her eyes. "I think I might faint."

"Great. A drama queen," Caro said. "Well, faint away. We'll throw a bucket of water on you. You're not leaving till you've answered some questions."

"It's just that I only had a kale smoothie for breakfast, and—"

"We don't care," I said. "Sit down, you . . . adulteress."

"Oh, Barb," Caro said. "Call her what she is. Sit down, slut."

"Where's John?" she asked, holding her giant fabric bag in front of her.

"We'll get to that," I said.

Karen. Karen something boring. Sanders or Saunders.

She sat across from Caro and me, and I took a long look at her. Her face was flushing a dull red, and she looked at the table. Dyed black hair, a dull, drab color that came from a drugstore, not a salon. *I* was a natural blond, and over the years my hair had gradually become streaked with silver. Never colored it a day in my life. *She* was dressed like a twenty-year-old bohemian—long full skirt, a low-cut leotard showing off her speckled, bony chest. Hard features, small eyes, but cunning, like a . . . like a rhino. A beaky nose, thin lips.

Well, he wasn't with her because of her looks.

"So I guess you know," she said, swallowing.

"I sure do, Karen. Or should I call you angel kitten?"

"Barb's been texting you for almost two months. You didn't even know it wasn't your tiger," Caro said.

"How dare you?" she said, and Caro and I both laughed.

"Barb," Caro said, "the slut is mad because you pretended to be John."

"Caro," I said, "I'm mad because the slut was sleeping with my husband."

"It wasn't like that!" Karen said.

"Oh, please," Caro said.

She twisted one of her silver bracelets. "I . . . we love each other. And you didn't understand him," she said. "He said your marriage had been over for years."

"Jeesh," I said. "The oldest line in the book, kitten. Did you fall for that? He gave me a beautiful ruby pendant for Christmas." Juliet had picked it out, of course, but technically, it was from him. "Did he mention how much fun we had with our *children* and *grandchildren*?"

She glanced away. "Does he know you're meeting me?"

"I'll ask the questions, kitten," I said. "Let me guess. He and I had grown apart. He wasn't happy anymore. You made him feel young. He didn't know what love was until he found you, and if only he'd met you first, gosh golly, life would've been super great. He'd leave me, but the children. Or the . . . what, Caro?"

"Or the fact that a divorce would cost him every dime he ever made," she supplied.

"That's true, now, isn't it? Hm."

Karen's little eyes darted between us, and she fiddled with her ugly bag. "He *was* going to leave you. He probably still is."

Caro laughed.

"Is that what you want? Would you marry him, kitten?" I asked.

"Please stop calling me that," she said. "And yes. I love him."

"Oh. How touching," Caro said. "She loves him, Barb."

"My heart." This was oddly fun. "Well, you can have him, Karen. In sickness and in health." I took a bite of Caro's cake. "Tell me, what makes a woman go after a married man? Don't you have any morals?"

"I am a good Christian woman," she said, huffing.

Caro and I looked at each other and laughed. "Isn't there a tiny commandment about adultery?" Caro asked.

"You know, Caro, I think there is. I'm sure of it."

"This is different," Karen said.

"How so, dear?" I asked.

She glanced around. That hair was not only unnatural in color, it didn't move a bit when she turned her head. Helmet hair, my girls would call it. "Look. I'm sorry he doesn't love you anymore. But we didn't plan this. It just happened."

"So . . . you fell into a deep sleep and when you woke up, you were screwing another woman's husband?" Caro asked.

"No! We . . . we ran into each other at a treadmill class last spring."

I rolled my eyes. Just when you thought it couldn't get worse. "You had to take a class to learn how to walk on a treadmill?"

"It's more complicated than that."

"And then what happened, angel kitten?"

"We remembered each other. We got a carrot juice at the juice bar. We just . . . clicked. We ended up talking for hours. It was amazing."

"No, it wasn't," I said. "It was inappropriate and dishonest. He's married. Which you well knew. What God has put together, let no one put asunder, good Christian woman."

"I'm telling you, it wasn't like we planned to have an affair. It was just juice at first. But I started to look forward to it. He's so . . . wonderful. A brilliant man." Caro snorted. "The chemistry was undeniable. And *you* didn't even notice." She straightened her shoulders a bit, and her sternum bones showed even more.

She did have a point. I hadn't noticed. Last spring, Sloane had appendicitis, and I stayed with Juliet for four nights and played board games with Brianna and cooked for the family. I'd also been doing the job Stoningham's residents had elected me to do.

"How long did it take for these juice dates to lead to adultery?" I asked.

"About a week." She smirked, obviously proud of herself.

The words hit me in the heart like a hammer shattering glass.

A week. That's how much time and consideration he gave our marriage. Our vows. Our *five* decades together.

One goddamn week.

"The attraction was just so strong," she said, raising her penciled eyebrows at me. "I'm not that type of girl—"

"You haven't been a girl in sixty years," Caro said.

"—and I've *never* done anything like that before. But I believe God put us in each other's path, and life is too short. The past isn't a compass for the future. You have to give yourself permission to chart a new course."

"Been reading Snapple caps?" Caro asked.

"I won't apologize for loving someone with all my heart." Her little rhino eyes teared up. "I take it you gave him an ultimatum. What are you holding over his head, Barb? Is this why he hasn't been in touch? He said you were controlling and had anger issues, but this is beyond the pale."

"Oh, hush," I said. "I'm not holding anything over his head. He had a stroke." She sucked in a breath, her sharp nostrils flaring. "I found out about *you* when I was at the hospital. While my husband was having brain surgery to save his life, I got to read his idiotic, juvenile sexting with you."

"He had an operation? How is he now?"

For some reason, it was hard to say the words. "You tell her, Caro."

"Well, funny you should ask, kitten," Caro said. "He has the IQ of a celery stalk."

Karen jerked back. "What do you mean?"

"He's nonverbal and needs a full-time caregiver," I said. "Good thing you love him so very, very much. This must be why God put him in your path."

"Barb," Caro said, putting her hand on my shoulder, "I'm so glad you won't be shackled to him anymore, now that Sex Kitten will take over. You know, since their love is more special and so different from any love the world has ever seen."

"The house is in my name," I said. "And I have power of attorney over our finances. But I'm sure you're not materialistic. Good thing, too, since you won't be getting a fucking cent."

Her eyelids fluttered.

"I love that you said fucking," Caro said.

"It felt good."

Karen started to stand, then sat back down. "So he won't get better?"

"You'd have to ask God about that, Karen, since you and He are on such close terms. John can't talk, and he can't write, but he did learn to toilet himself, so he only wets the bed once in a while."

"What would Jesus do?" Caro asked. "I bet Jesus would comfort the sick, don't you, kitten? Small price to pay for ruining a marriage."

"I . . . I have to go," Karen said.

"Yes. You do." My voice was hard.

She got up and wobbled over to the door, and then she was gone.

"Well, we've seen the last of her," Caro said. "Good riddance to bad rubbish."

"Yep. That's true."

Caro looked at me with her kind, dark eyes and gave a sad smile, and that was it. The tears came hard and fast, and I cried in gulping sobs that made the other folks in the café look at me, but I couldn't seem to stop.

Caro put her arm around me, and we sat there for a long, long time, and a thought came to me. I didn't have a great husband, and maybe I never had.

But I sure had a wonderful friend.

CHAPTER TWENTY

Sadie

I got a dog. I *needed* a dog, for several reasons: company, of course; and snuggles; protection from murderers, since I didn't live close enough to anyone and my screams would go unnoticed during said murder; and to run for help if my house fell in on top of me, as it seemed intent on doing.

Stoningham's animal shelter had only three doggies—a wee little purse dog, who, though tempting, would not protect me (not very well, anyway) should a serial killer come knocking. Then there was a wheezing, balding sheepdog who was blind and deaf but also spoken for (God bless *that* person). And finally, Pepper.

Pepper was a mutt of House Mutt, proud descendant of mutts. Shepherd-bloodhound-rottweiler-something-something else, we'd never know. She was reddish-brown with some black markings, about thirty pounds and grow-ing, and when I came to her little kennel, she wagged her tail so hard she fell down. Her ears were silky soft, and the top of her snout was velvety and plush. If she wasn't going to defend me, at least I'd have a sweet, wagging pup as the last thing I saw as I slipped this mortal coil.

Her talents seemed to be licking people and pouncing on leaves. And cuddling. She was great at cuddling. Also, barking at such threats as wind, rain, the coffeepot and my cowboy boots.

I'd had her a week and now couldn't imagine life without her. I talked to her a lot—"Do you think this bucket is big enough to catch the leaks?" I'd ask, or "Should I have fish for dinner, or popcorn?"

The truth was, I was lonelier than I'd anticipated. The temporary loss of my dad made me realize how much and how often we talked and texted. Sometimes, it was just silly things—a photo of that grimy Elmo in Times Square, or a pigeon sitting on the shoulder of a sleeping man in Central Park. Sometimes it was an article . . . I'd send him links to writing workshops, hoping he'd still give it a shot, or events that he might want to come down for. He'd send me cartoons or make Dad jokes, teasing me for not drinking more, saying I was sullying his legacy.

Sometimes he'd just call me to say he loved me and was thinking of me and wondering what I was looking at.

Juliet was a good-enough sister, though we didn't have much in common. I loved her daughters and always had fun with them, but less was more in that respect. You couldn't be the cool auntie if you were around all the time. My mother was very . . . competent. But I had never met my Minnesotan relatives; Mom didn't get on with anyone except Aunt Nancy, and Dad was an only child. So as family went, Dad was kind of it for me. Dad, and Alexander, and I missed them both so much. Missed my life in New York fiercely.

But Alexander was coming to visit this weekend, thank God, and Carter had broken his vow never to leave the five boroughs and was coming up tonight for Mom's dinner party, though he'd booked an Airbnb after I Face-Timed him from my house.

It was so quiet here. Quieter in this little house than my parents', where there was always some kind of noise—cars, neighbors, the distant thump of music from the restaurants on Water Street, just two blocks away. Stoningham always had some event on the weekends—the library fund-raiser, a Presidents' Day trivia contest at the library, storytelling night and open mic night at the local bar. To its credit, Stoningham tried very hard not to be a summertime-only seaside town.

I hadn't realized how much my mother did. When she had run for first selectman, I thought it was cute, and pictured her sitting on a panel, fielding questions from disgruntled residents. Now I knew she worked with the state government, figured out how any federal and state budget cuts would affect Stoningham, built partnerships with the business community, tried to woo the kind of industry to town that would be green, clean and employ locals . . . and yes, handled complaints from disgruntled residents.

I felt a little bad that Dad and I had made some jokes about her being the queen of Stoningham.

And now she was having a dinner party, to which I was invited. The first time I'd be my mother's guest at something other than a family event. It felt kind of strange. Alexander was due in this afternoon . . . March was a busy time for him—all those rich folks getting itchy for summers on the Vineyard or Penobscot Bay or in San Diego. Many yachts to sell. We'd only seen each other three times since I moved back here—two quick runs back to the city for me, and once, dinner in New Haven. But he was coming tonight, staying all weekend, and I couldn't wait.

To show how strange life had become, I found myself looking forward to going to Mom's. It was the highlight of my social life since coming home.

Stoningham hadn't exactly welcomed me back with open arms. I was a local who'd let it be known I couldn't *wait* to leave my posh and pretty hometown behind, eager to be a New Yorker. Some of my classmates had never left, and I understood. It was a beautiful area. Others left to go to URI or UConn, came back and settled in, happy as clams. Mickey, Noah's baby mama, had done that—she was the music teacher at the elementary school and taught piano and violin on the side. Some kids, like Juliet, left and came back wreathed in glory, the local success stories, living in the best neighborhoods.

And then there were the blue-collar folks of any place like this . . . those who worked for the submarine plant in Groton or for the wealthier residents through skilled or unskilled labor. The townies who had struggled to make their peace with a fishing village turned summer retreat for the wealthy. Noah was one of those; his dad remembered when most of Stoningham was dairy farms with a few gracious houses on the water.

And then there was me. I'd run into a few old classmates since coming home, and they seemed confused to see me. Wasn't I in New York? Art, right? Still painting? Anything good? Oh. Private collections? (It sounded better than couch paintings.) What was I doing back? Was I staying? No kids? Oh. Still not married? This last one was always said with a little meanness, as if getting married would have proven my worth in a way that the other parts of my life could not.

I was a stranger in my hometown, in some respects. I knew the names of the people I'd grown up with—Mrs. Churchill from the library and her four grown sons, or Caroline DeAngelo, who taught me to double Dutch in sixth grade. There were the kids I used to babysit, now grown, and their parents, who still recognized me. There were the middle-aged women who used to babysit *me*.

So I knew people, but I didn't have any friends here. Jules let me come over and hang with the girls, and Oliver smiled and smiled. My New York pals felt far away, and the truth was, I didn't have a lot to say to them on the phone. *My dad is still recovering. I'm painting a little. I, uh . . . got a dog. No, I can't have guests just yet, it's kind of tiny here, and the roof leaks . . .*

There were nights when I was alone in my little house, wishing someone would text me or drop by, feeling a little afraid to reach out in case I'd be rejected. (You'd think a woman in her thirties wouldn't have those feelings. You'd be wrong.) I worked on the house every morning, learning what wood rot was, finding mouse droppings in my insulation, realizing that one outlet downstairs was probably not enough. In the evenings, I painted for my interior decorators—they'd send me a swatch of fabric or take pictures of a throw pillow and instruct me on what the homeowner wanted—those "little dot paintings" (Seurat, I assumed) or "swirly" (Van Gogh) or "messy" (Pollock) or "those weird stick figures where the person only has one eye" (Picasso). My favorite was "little bitty brushstrokes so up close you can't tell what it is but from far away, you can, like those Magic Eye puzzles" (Monet. So sorry, Claude).

The only time I felt like my old self was when I was with my dad. He'd made some real progress from those terrifying first days in January. He wasn't talking or otherwise communicating yet . . . I'd been trying some sign language with him, since I knew a little from St. Catherine's, where it was taught one day a week. LeVon was trying that, too, but we'd yet to have an Anne Sullivan/ Helen Keller breakthrough. Not yet. He was right on the cusp, it seemed. I could sense it.

He smelled different, my father. It was one of those things you didn't know would affect you until you were crying in the bathroom.

Mom and Juliet were there, and I was sure they missed him, too, but they hid it well. I had the feeling Mom wished he had just died.

But he *was* getting better. "It's tempting to read into every little thing," LeVon had warned me. "If he's having a breakthrough, we'll know, but it'll be harder if you attribute every reflex to meaningful interaction." He put a big hand on my shoulder. "But I agree with you. He's making progress."

We all fricking loved LeVon.

Meanwhile, something was happening to me.

It was the view. My house might be a decrepit pile of mold and decaying wood, but damn, that view. Because my house was on a little hill, I could watch both the sunrise and the sunset. Every morning, I woke up to the sun streaming in my room at the literal crack of dawn. I'd take Pepper out and let her romp and chase the dead leaves, and we'd watch the sun come out from behind the clouds, beams of light stretching out their arms. I'd sit on the porch with my coffee, listening to the birds. Each week they got more vocal—the chickadees, red-winged black-birds, blue jays, ducks and geese. A blue heron hung out at the bend of the river, just past the bridge.

At night, if I was home from my parents' house in time, I'd watch the sun set over the water, and it was even more startling in its beauty than the sunrise. Sometimes, the sun would glitter over the ocean, not a cloud in the sky, and after it sank below the horizon, a band of yellow and gold would linger for an hour as the stars came out. Other times, the clouds would catch and throw the light in all the shades of color I knew and then some—dianthus pink, iridescent pale gold, French blue, Montserrat orange. This past week had been milder, and Pepper and I stayed out till the last bird sang, and the smell of earth was strong as the sky deepened bit by bit.

I'd sit there and watch and listen, and all the yoga classes in all the world didn't make me feel this way. Still. Awed. I hadn't come back to Stoningham for Noah—I couldn't, not the way he'd demanded it of me, not under the weight of his expectations. But even though it was temporary, I was glad I was here now. The town was less insipid than I'd painted it as a teenager; the people were more layered than I'd imagined them to be. Maybe it had been a necessary exercise to prepare for the New York phase of my life. Maybe I'd had to minimize what home meant to me so I could leave it behind.

I loved my New York life. But I loved this, too. I was . . . happy.

Happy. Even though I was here for a terrible reason,

the happiness, the peace, snuck in. Right now, there was nowhere else I should be, could be or wanted to be.

The dinner party did not get off to a great start.

For one, Alexander was running late. "Babe. I'm so sorry, but this traffic is horrible."

"Well, what time did you leave?" I asked.

"At four."

"That's way too late! I told you to get out of the city by two thirty!" I groaned. "Honey. We haven't seen each other in weeks. I wanted to get you in bed before this party. Now you'll have to come straight to my mother's."

"I know. I'm so sorry. I had all this paperwork to file, and time just got away from me. I'll be there as soon as I can. I've missed you so much."

I sighed. "It's okay. Just . . . drive carefully. I love you."

"Love you, too." He clicked off.

I got ready, which meant showering downstairs (I'd installed a makeshift showerhead) and being licked by Pepper as I got out (she loved the taste of my soap). I got dressed in a skirt and shirt, then ditched it for a flowered dress and little sweater. Couldn't find my blue pumps so I wore the cowboy boots that made Pepper bark, and so I left the house with a dog who simultaneously loved me and feared my footwear. Getting her into the car took some effort, torn as she was. Right as I pulled up to Mom's, I realized I'd offered to bring wine, so I had to run to the package store and buy some that would pass the snob test. Jules and Oliver had a wine cellar *and* a wine fridge.

Finally, I got to the house. Pepper liked my dad, and he seemed to be interested in her. She bolted for the dining room the minute we got in. From the sound of it, people were already here.

"There you are," Mom said. "I said six o'clock. It's almost seven. Your friend Carter made it on time from New York. You had two miles, Sadie."

"I know, and Alexander will be late, too, I'm afraid. Here." I handed her the wine. "Hi, Mom. You look pretty."

She sighed and took the two wine bottles into the kitchen. I checked on my dad before going into the family room, where everyone else seemed to be. Sure enough, Pepper was already curled up on his bed.

"You're Pepper's favorite, Daddy," I said.

He didn't look at me. He was just looking ahead, but his hand was on Pepper's bony little head.

"You like her, Dad? Do you like the dog?"

He looked at me then, and my heart leaped. "You do, right? You like Pepper?"

She licked his hand, and he smiled.

Oh, my God, he smiled! "Good job, Daddy," I whispered around the immediate lump in my throat.

"Hey. I didn't know you were here." It was Jules. "Where's your boy toy? Also, did you know your friend Carter is gay?"

"Why, yes, I did, since I've known him for years and years. Jules, Dad just smiled at me! Because of Pepper!"

"Right. You got a dog."

"Juliet. Our father just *smiled*."

"Good. Great job, Dad." She took a sip of her wine. "You coming to join the rest of us? Also, you should've told Mom your friend is gay. She's trying to fix him up with one of her guests. A woman."

"Oh, shit."

"Also, Sadie, remember what the doctor said. Smiling could just be a reflex, you know?"

"No, Jules, it wasn't. I asked him if he liked Pepper,

and she licked his hand, and he smiled. That's significant."

"Sure."

"What is *with* you? Did he beat you or lock you in the cellar before I was born? Why aren't you more excited?"

"He's asleep now. You gonna join us or what?"

I closed my eyes briefly, then looked at my father. He *was* asleep, Pepper's head on his leg. I covered them both with a soft throw and followed my sister into the back. "You look good, by the way," I told her.

"Are you making fun of me?" She jerked to a stop in the hallway and turned to glare at me.

"No! Why? Should I have said you look like shit? You just look . . . pretty. I'm sorry. Was that a wrong thing to say? No. It's not. I revoke my apology."

"Can you do me one favor? Be nice to Mom."

"I . . . okay. Check."

Carter saw me first and gave me a big bear hug. "I've missed you so desperately! How are you, precious?" He lowered his voice to a whisper. "Why does your mother think I'm straight? Will she stone me if I tell her I like boys?"

"She's very accepting, if obtuse. I'm so sorry. I missed you, too!" I kissed him on the cheek. "We're still on for tomorrow morning, right?"

"What's tomorrow morning?"

"I show you my house, you wave your magical *Queer Eye* wand and boom! It's beautiful, and we go out for brunch with Alexander."

"Oh, honey, I'm sorry. I'm going to the casino tomorrow with Josh. He loves the craps table."

"You brought Josh?"

"He's coming tomorrow." Carter paused for effect. "It's

official. He's my boyfriend, and we're getting matching tattoos. Now come. Mingle, and break the news to your mother that I won't be dating that nice girl in the corner."

The family room was two steps down, and there were more people here than I'd expected. Oliver (smiling, ever smiling, which shouldn't irritate me as much as it did), Caro and her boo, Ted or Theo or Tim, I could never remember, and . . .

Oh, crap. Noah. And (not crap) Mickey and their baby. Little Marcus was being cooed over by my mother at the moment.

That could've been her grandchild. The thought came unbidden. But yeah. Once, I thought I'd be the mother of Noah's children, long before I'd asked myself if I wanted to be a mother at all.

Shit. Where was Alexander?

I turned, then froze. Sweet baby Jesus. Though I hadn't ever seen her in person, I knew her right away. Gillian Epstein. Noah's ex-fiancée.

What the *what*?

She looked up at me, and she obviously recognized me, too, because she flinched the teeniest bit. "Hi," she said after a beat. "I'm Gillian Epstein." Ah. A hard *G*, not the *J* sound. I hadn't expected that.

"I'm Sadie. Barb's daughter."

"Believe me, I know who you are." She forced a smile. "I was engaged to Noah a few years back."

"Right. I knew that. From Facebook, that is. You know. We have mutual friends, I mean, of course we do, we grew up together, Noah and I that is, not you and me"— *stop yourself, Sadie*—"and I guess one of my friends commented on your picture, and you'd tagged Noah, so I . . . well. I knew he was engaged."

She looked to the left, hoping for someone to save her, no doubt. I, too, cast about for a savior. Where had Carter gone? And why, *why* did Alexander have to be late today?

Gillian—I kind of hated the hard *G*—was even prettier in person. Olive skin, green eyes, really good lashes (natural, damn her). Perfect body, nice clothes. She even smelled nice, like oranges.

"So you and Noah stayed friends, I guess?" I said.

"No. It's kind of hard to stay friends with the person who broke your heart and embarrassed you by calling off your wedding."

Youch. "Yeah, that would be . . . tricky." I felt sweat prickling in my armpits. "You're very honest."

"Are *you* and Noah still friends?" she asked.

"Oh, uh . . . yes? Sort of? Not really, no. I mean, it's different, since he and I have known each other since kindergarten. Maybe before that. And we were never, um, engaged."

She cocked a well-groomed eyebrow, as if doubting me.

"Gillian, uh . . . you mind if I ask why you're here?"

"Your mother invited me. I'm an event planner, and I'm handling the town's three hundred and fiftieth anniversary weekend. I wasn't aware Noah and his . . . partner . . . would be here."

"Mickey." I lowered my voice. "She's gay. They're just coparents. It's not romantic."

"I *know* that."

"Cool. Great. Information is good to have. That's great." I needed a drink. Gillian probably needed more to drink. Or a Xanax.

Ah. My mother was handing the baby off to Mickey. "Mom! Let me help you with dinner!" I said. "Excuse me, Gillian. So nice to meet you."

I dragged my mom into the kitchen. "What are you doing?" I hissed.

"As usual, Sadie, I have no idea what you're talking about."

"Gillian Epstein and Noah used to be engaged."

"Oh. Oh, dear. I didn't think of that." She blinked at me. She looked tired, I suddenly noticed. Of course she did, living with Dad, doing her part in his care.

"Also . . . I used to date Noah, remember? It's awkward to have to schmooze with his ex. And it might be awkward for him, too, don't you think? And, not to put too fine a point on it, awkward for me to be with both of them."

"I just told you, Sadie, I forgot! I invited her because she'd mentioned how hard it was to meet a nice man, and I thought maybe your friend and she would hit it off."

"My friend is gay. And thirty years older than Gillian."

"Do you have to jump down my throat with a houseful of guests here? Hm? Do you? Noah's been very kind to your father. And you, missy. Didn't he fix your furnace?"

"Yes. But—"

"Gillian is handling the town's anniversary, and who knows? Maybe Noah will realize he made a big mistake."

I blinked. "I don't think you should try to get them back together."

"You have a boyfriend, Sadie. It's not really your business, is it?"

Ouch. "I don't. I mean . . . I just think it's weird to try to fix up your daughter's ex-boyfriend with his ex-fiancée."

Caro popped her head in. "Need help, Barb? Hi, Sadie, sweetheart."

"Hi, Caro. You look beautiful, as always."

"I know, and thank you, angel. Barb, what can I do?"

"We'll be eating in a few minutes, so if you could start herding everyone in here, that'd be great."

Caro flashed her dimples at me and popped back out.

"So. You won't try to push Gillian and Noah together," I said, just to be clear.

"Whatever happens with them happens, Sadie. She does a lot of events in town and she knows everyone. Maybe she can help you find a job while you're here, who knows? You could run errands for her."

Nice. "I have a job," I said.

"Is that right."

"I paint."

"Of course. Now, would you mind getting your father so we can eat?" She went back into the family room, all smiles for everyone but me.

It would be nice to like my mother as much as other people did. Then again, they didn't get the side of her I did—the slightly irritated, impatient, better-things-to-do mother who already had a perfect daughter and couldn't be bothered with me. She had a knack for peeing on everything I liked or did in ways both subtle and obvious and then wondered why I didn't seek her out the way Juliet did. It was exhausting.

I took a deep breath and went back to the dining room. I bet my dad missed being in a proper bedroom. Pepper was still curled at his side, looking like a giant cinnamon bun, snoring gently. My father's eyes were open. "Hey, Dad," I said. "Mom's driving me crazy, but what else is new, right?"

He glanced at me, looking blank, and my eyes filled. "It's me, Dad. Sadie. You know who I am, right?"

I thought his expression softened a little. "Of course you do. I'm your daughter, and I love you." Pepper's tail wagged, beating on the bed. "And my little doggy loves you, too. Right, Pepper?"

"Do you need help?"

Noah. I wiped my eyes before turning. "Sure. Thanks." He came closer, and his hair was extra curly. Must've just washed it. Not that I was thinking about Noah in the shower or anything. I cleared my throat. "Hey, I'm sorry my mom invited your . . . um, Gillian."

"Why?"

"Because it might be awkward for you."

"It's not. She's a good person." There was already an edge in his voice.

"I'm sure she is."

"Is it awkward for you?"

"Of course not! Why would it be? I'm great! How's the baby, by the way? And Mickey's still nursing? Is it going well?"

He gave me a pained look. "Why don't you ask her?"

"I will do so." Blathering like an idiot yet again, and over my father's balding head. "Come on, Dad. Time for dinner." Noah took one of his arms, and I took the other.

"Whose dog is this?" Noah asked.

"Mine. Pepper, meet Noah. Noah, this is my puppy, Pepper."

She licked his face, and he laughed.

Oh, that laugh. That sooty, low scraping laugh. A hundred memories of Noah laughing flashed through my head—hearing it in high school, turning to see him smiling at me, the two of us walking to get coffee, his big, strong hand holding mine, or best of all, in bed, his skin warm against mine, that soft, tangled black hair framing his face.

Yep.

Pepper was going to town on him, lucky thing, and he picked her up and set her on the floor. "Okay, Mr. Frost, one, two, three. There you go."

Together, we helped Dad get his walker and come into the kitchen.

It was really, really unfortunate that my boyfriend was stuck in traffic. I could use an ally to fight these memories before I fell in love with Noah Pelletier all over again.

CHAPTER TWENTY-ONE

Juliet

Juliet Frost had seduction on her mind, which was hard enough since she was in her mother's house with her brain-damaged father, her yappy sister and about six other people.

But sex with Oliver was on her list of things to do tonight, and she owed him some sparkly time. She sipped the wine she'd brought and smiled hard.

Knowing that her father had had an affair had shaken her to the roots. That her father—her *father*, that steadiest of men, married for *fifty* years—could have an affair made her feel that every second Oliver was not in view, he, too, could be screwing some other woman, or thinking about it, or flirting or looking or . . . or smelling some other woman.

Perhaps she should lay off the wine.

Which wouldn't calm her fears. Oliver had never once indicated anything but happiness in their marriage, but it happened. Half of marriages ended in divorce! Half! Why were she and Ollie any better than anyone else? She'd spent half her workday Googling "why do men have affairs?" It happens even in the best marriages, the literature said darkly.

So it *could* happen to them. Had she and Oliver fought? Of course. About stupid things, like . . . well, like the time she had to leave vacation early because of a work crisis a few years ago. The time he broke her favorite mug, because even though she told him it was fragile and special to her, he handled dishes as if he didn't have opposable thumbs. The way he let Brianna get away with things when Juliet tried to lay down the law. But they'd never spoken about unhappiness or a lack of love. Never. They'd never raised their voices to each other. Never.

Mom and Dad had never fought, either.

So reminding Oliver that she was a desirable woman who loved sex and was spontaneous and adventuresome, especially after she hadn't been able to kiss him for the past three days, thanks to those stupid injections . . . that was on her list. As was coming to this party, because Mom was utterly heroic, doing all this, trying to get people around Dad. (God. If she only knew.)

Juliet had dressed up for this evening, which Mom always appreciated, and wore a stretchy white dress that required a serious bra, which currently seemed to be intent on embedding itself in her rib cage. Three-inch red suede heels she hadn't worn in years. A thong for the planned seduction. A thong that may or may not have worked itself into her lower intestine.

Sparkly. Sparkly. She had to be sparkly. She'd talked to everyone here tonight—the event planner Mom thought so highly of, Noah, Mickey Watkins, Ted, Caro, Sadie's friend from the city, who was very nice. She'd held little Marcus. Endured Sadie's predictions of a full recovery for their father. If only *Sadie* knew. God. That would kill her, knowing their dad had had an affair. The two of them had always been so close. Dad had never paid too much interest in Juliet. Not that she resented it. Much. Anymore.

She finished her glass of wine and got another before everyone sat down. Sadie had been in charge of the wine tonight, and Juliet had brought a couple of additional bottles, correctly anticipating that her sister wouldn't bring enough. Not that she was cheap; she just wouldn't think too hard about how many people were coming.

"How's the house, Sadie?" she asked brightly as everyone sat down to dinner. "Fallen in the Sound yet?"

"Not yet," Sadie said. "A few shingles blew off the roof last night, but I plan on getting up there and fixing all that."

"Please don't," Noah said. "Hire someone."

"I think I'm very handy, actually," she said. "But thanks for your concern."

"You're handy?" Carter asked. Yes, Carter, that was his name. The friendly friend from the city. "Remember when you broke the sink in the teachers' bathroom because you forgot which way the knobs turned?"

"I have no recollection of that event, no," Sadie said, grinning. Always getting away with being a ditz and thinking it was charm. Maybe it was. Maybe Juliet should try it.

"Does anyone mind if I breastfeed?" asked Mickey, and, not waiting, pulled up her shirt and attached the baby. "No one is scared of boobs, right? Although I have to say, they do look a little scary these days. No one told me I'd become Joan from *Mad Men* after popping out this little bruiser. I was a 34-B before Noah knocked me up."

She glanced at Gillian, who looked green. "Sorry. Shit, Gillian, I'm really sorry. You too, Sadie."

Right. Right. The event planner had been engaged to Noah. The baby was making smacking sounds.

Sadie's teacher friend smiled. "I love watching a woman breastfeed," he said. "So natural."

"Thanks, dude," Mickey said. "You're okay."

Dad, too, was staring at Mickey's breast. It was hard to miss, but was he looking at it lustfully? And if so, doubly gross, because (a) it belonged to a woman not his wife and (b) it was feeding a baby, so lusting was just icky.

She *really* had to tell her mother about that other woman. Or she really shouldn't *ever* tell her mother. God! How could her father be such an asshole? She hated him . . . except seeing him wobbly and silent and staring at a strange woman's boob made her both want to curl into a ball and sob or kick him and also have him just die already and let her mother be free.

"Barb, this asparagus is wonderful," said the event planner. Gillian.

"It is," Oliver agreed. "You're a smashing cook, Mum."

The nicest man in the world was her husband. Time for a little seduction. She slid off her shoe (blessed relief) and reached her foot out to slide up his pant leg. Nothing . . . nothing . . . Could a foot grope? If so, her foot was groping into emptiness. There.

She hooked her toe in his pants and slid it up.

Mickey jumped. Oliver didn't. Shit. Wrong leg. Mickey gave her a reproachful look over her baby's head.

"Sorry," Juliet murmured. "I thought you were my husband."

"That's what they all say."

Okay, so no foot sex or whatever that move was called. More wine was a good idea.

Caro and Ted seemed to be fighting in whispers. Gillian looked wretched. "My mom says you're amazing at what you do, Gillian," Juliet said. "How did you get started?"

"Oh, funny story," Gillian said. "So, it was my mom and dad's thirty-fifth anniversary, and I thought, why not throw them a big party? And I got the bug! I just love organizing."

Juliet waited for the funny part, but apparently Gillian was done.

"That *is* funny. Ha. Ha ha." Yes. She was a little drunk. Dad was looking at Gillian now. Maybe he was interested in her in his foggy, befuddled state. Like the woman he'd been kissing, Gillian had dark hair.

How many women wished their fathers were dead after seeing them cheating on their moms? CNN should do a poll.

A knock came on the kitchen door.

"Who could that be?" Barb asked, getting up to answer it.

"Elijah the prophet?" Oliver suggested. It was his go-to joke when someone interrupted dinner, and it always made her laugh. No one else got it, apparently, and her laugh sounded too loud in the vacuum.

"Can I help you?" Barb said. "Oh! Hello there!"

It was Janet, the woman from Gaylord whose brother had been down the hall from Dad. She'd been really nice, Juliet remembered, if fashion challenged. Her hair was in two long, gray braids, and she wore overalls over a flannel shirt. "Oh, shit," she said. "You're having a party. I'm so sorry. I was in the neighborhood. Thought I'd drop in."

"No, no, come in. Please. Girls, do you remember Janet?

How's your brother, Janet? Have a seat. Would you like some wine?"

"No, thanks. I don't drink. Hey, Juliet. Sadie. Everyone else." Her eyes stopped on Dad's face. "Hey, John. How's it going, buddy?"

Dad's mouth hung open for a second, then he burst into a big smile. "You!" he said. "You."

There was a moment of silence.

"That's *right*, Dad," said Sadie, her voice breathless. "You know her!"

"You sure do," Janet said, going closer. "How's my old pal?"

Dad grabbed her hand and kissed it. Jesus. How nice for Mom. Had he slept with Janet while at Gaylord? Probably not, but still. Cheating asshole.

"You," he repeated.

His first word since the stroke, and it wasn't even directed at a family member, the bastard. Why put family first when he'd had his tongue down some other woman's throat? When he didn't even have the decency to divorce Mom before cheating on her? That slut should be the one stuck with him now.

Forty-three years old, and feeling like Brianna, sullen and judgmental and wishing she could kick a sick old man. Not a proud moment. She poured herself more wine and drank it, grateful that tomorrow was the weekend.

An hour later, Sadie was still happily snuffling her tears of joy. Mom had called LeVon, who said this was a very good sign, and Caro had gotten Janet a plate and heated it up in the microwave. Janet was talking about her brother's progress at Rose Hill, a care facility north of Stoningham. Noah was holding his sleeping baby, Mickey was in the bathroom, Gillian was subtly texting someone for help, no doubt, and Juliet was drunk.

That was when the vacuous waste of space known as her sister's boyfriend walked in.

"Our yacht salesman is here! The man of the people has arrived!" Juliet announced.

"Hon," Oliver said in a low voice, "I think you should tone it down a little."

"Why? He's three hours late."

Sadie got up and hugged him, but not before shooting a look at Noah. "Honey! You made it. Guess what? My father spoke tonight! He recognized Janet!"

"And who's Janet?" he said. "Mrs. Frost, I'm so sorry I'm late."

"Don't worry about it, dear," she said. "Do you know everyone? This is Janet, our friend from Gaylord, and Noah and Mickey and their little boy, and this is Gillian, a friend of mine."

"Hello. Nice to meet you," Alexander said, smiling blandly.

"We've met, actually," Gillian said. "I organized the yacht christening in Clinton last fall. The Parkers?"

"Oh, right!" he said, clearly not recognizing her. "Small world."

Mickey came in, still buckling her pants. "How long did it take for your period to get back to normal after you had babies, Juliet?" she asked.

"Nope. Not gonna talk periods at a dinner party," she answered.

"Thank you!" said Alexander, and Juliet rolled her eyes.

Bad idea. The room was starting to spin a little. "Let's go home and get naked," she whispered to Oliver. He gave her a look that did not say *great idea*.

Perhaps she had been a little loud.

Gillian stood up. "I should go. This has been . . . yes! Thank you, Barb. I'll be in touch. So good to see everyone."

Poor thing. "Sorry!" Juliet called. "We're usually better company than this."

"I'm taking you home," Oliver murmured.

"I should stay and clean up."

"No, you should come home and sleep it off. Come on. Mum, thank you. We have to get going." They muttered a minute, talking about her, no doubt.

As soon as they were in the car, Oliver said, "What on earth is going on with you?" His voice was sharp.

"Um . . . nothing?"

"You were *really* off tonight."

"Why?"

"You're pissed, for one."

"You know what, Oliver? It's kind of hard to see my father like this. Then he recognizes that woman? Not me, not Sadie, and God forbid, not Mom. Some woman he barely knows."

"So that makes it all right for you to get drunk at your mum's party? Does that make it easier on anyone?"

"Yes, Oliver. It makes it easier on me." She looked at him. "Don't be mad. I'm just a little"—*past my prime at work and hiding a horrible secret about my father and considering a job as a smoke jumper and not sure our older child loves me anymore and a little terrified that you'll leave me someday*—"stressed. Take me home and ravish me."

"I don't think so," Oliver said. "I don't ravish drunk women."

"Even your wife, who just asked you to?"

"When you've sobered up, I'd really like us to have a meaningful conversation."

Shit. Panic threaded through her foggy brain. "About what?"

"Darling. You're drunk. You had at least three glasses of wine."

"In England, that would be called a good start."

"You haven't been yourself lately, and it's not just your dad, though of course that's hard. But something's off, and it has been for months."

"Pull over."

"What?"

"I'm gonna puke."

And so her evening ended, barfing in front of the Mc-Masterons' house, her husband sighing and holding back her hair.

So much for seduction.

CHAPTER TWENTY-TWO

Barb

LeVon was leaving us.

I knew the day would come, but I cried just the same. He was going to Rose Hill Rehabilitation and Care Center a half an hour north, the place Genevieve London had endowed before her death. LeVon would be director of patient services, and of course I couldn't begrudge him the change. He said it was his dream job.

"We'll stay friends," he said over tea, kindly covering my hand with his. "And I can recommend some great caregivers and therapists."

I nodded. "You're irreplaceable, LeVon." I had to wipe my eyes on a napkin.

"I think you're pretty amazing yourself, Barb. A lot of people fall apart when something like this happens."

"They must not be from Minnesota." He laughed, those kind eyes and ready smile. I squeezed his hand. "If I'd ever had a son, I hope he would've been like you, LeVon."

It was his turn to get teary. "That means a lot to me. I'll be here till the end of the month, so don't you worry. I'm not abandoning this ship."

"Will he get better, LeVon? I know you're not supposed to guess, but what do you think?"

He took a deep breath and let it out slowly. "Technically, you're right. I can't guess, and patients surprise us all the time. But I don't think he'll ever recover completely, no. Most of the patients I've seen with hemorrhagic stroke and traumatic brain injuries . . . at his age, no, I don't think he'll ever go back to being the guy you used to know."

I nodded, my heart sinking even though I'd kinda known that already. "Well. Thank you."

Sadie wasn't coming today; she had to do something with that little pile of sticks she called a house, so I'd left work early. I had to e-mail Gillian about the town's birthday (and apologize for that wretched dinner party) and call Juliet (who had been a bit tipsy, which wasn't like her). I had a speech to write for the Small Town Coalition and a few e-mails to return. A phone call to Lucille Dworkin, who had been pestering Lindsey to see if we would arrest her neighbor for using his leaf blower before eight a.m. on a Saturday.

I looked in on John, who was asleep in his chair, and took the soft cashmere throw I'd splurged on last year, tucking it around him in case he was cold. Regulating his body temperature was one of his medical issues these days. His hair was sticking up on one side, and I smoothed it down. He didn't stir. I hadn't shaved him today, because it made him agitated, and he had a fuzz of white stubble on his face.

He looked so old.

A knock came on the door, and it was a relief to answer it.

Janet Hubb, who had crashed our dinner party and inspired John to say his first intelligible, post-stroke word, stood there, smiling.

"Hey, Barb," she said. "On my way to see my brother, thought I'd pop by."

"Hello, Janet. Come on in."

I wasn't sure why I liked Janet, but I did. She was the type of woman who didn't care about postmenopausal facial hair—I had to force my eyes not to study her lip—and she only seemed to wear overalls and those awful gardening clogs. I liked her hair, her granny glasses, her bulky, hand-knit sweaters (although perhaps I'd knit her something with a little less hay in it, fewer dropped stitches).

"How you doing today, friend?" she asked, taking a seat at the kitchen table. "How's our John?"

Our John. "He's resting."

"Yeah. So it's none of my business, but I picked up some weird vibes last weekend, and I just wanted to check on you."

"Ah. Yes."

"How are you feeling? I mean, you've been through the wringer. Your kids, too. The drunk one? I thought she might stab me with her fork."

"Oh, Juliet is lovely. She would never stab anyone with a fork. Or any instrument." I sat down, too. "Tell me, Janet. You obviously like John for some reason."

"Yeah. He's cool."

"Why would you say that?"

"I don't know. He listens really well."

"He has no choice, does he?"

She smiled. "Good point. I feel like he hears me, though."

"I feel like he hears you, too. He always brightened up when you came into his room at Gaylord, and the fact that he spoke when he saw you . . . that was a real breakthrough."

"Has he started talking more?"

"No." Just those three *you*s when he saw Janet. Apparently, the women who inspired John were not in his family. I wondered what he'd do or say if Karen visited, but she wouldn't, would she? Theirs was a love that was more than a love only when she thought he was wealthy. She wasn't the type who would wipe drool from a man's face.

As Janet had last weekend, after the hand kissing.

"This is a really pretty house, by the way," Janet said.

"John cheated on me," I said. "I only found out after his stroke."

"Well . . . fuck."

"Yes. My daughters don't know."

"So you're all alone with this?"

"My best friend knows. Would you like some coffee? I baked cookies with my granddaughters yesterday, too."

"I love cookies. Sure, I'll take a coffee. Thanks, Barb."

For the next hour, we talked. Janet told me about her brother and his progress. They only had each other, she said; their parents died when they were teenagers, and Janet had become Frank's legal guardian at the age of eighteen to his twelve. They'd had no other relatives for most of their lives, and they were so close they lived on the same street before his accident.

I thought about my six siblings. Nancy had sent a card when I told her about John via e-mail, but otherwise, I hadn't heard from anyone.

"Have you thought about putting John in Rose Hill?" Janet asked. "It's fab. They have a saltwater pool, and the food is great."

For a second, I imagined the freedom of having John in a facility. Those weeks when he was at Gaylord and I was alone in the house, and how . . . peaceful they had been. I was so tired these days.

Then I pictured myself in his situation, away from home, surrounded by strangers.

"I don't know that he meets the criteria," I said. Rose Hill was for the profoundly disabled, so far as I knew, and John could walk and do some of the tasks of daily living. "My girls and I can take care of him, anyway."

"You're good people, Barb."

"Thank you. You too."

"Okay if I visit with the old man?"

"Absolutely. He's in the living room, sleeping in the recliner."

She popped the last cookie in her mouth, waggled her impressive eyebrows and left the room.

It was strange, how many people had come to visit John. Caro's Ted came fairly often, even though the men had never been particularly close outside of our couple nights. Noah brought his baby over at least once a week, and seeing John hold sweet little Marcus made me happy and brokenhearted and angry. If Sadie ever had a baby, would John know it was hers? Would it break Sadie's heart, knowing her father could never be the type of grandfather who'd give piggyback rides and read stories? Not that he'd done that with Sloane or Brianna, mind you. Always with one foot out of the room, John.

Juliet and Oliver came, too, often bringing the girls.

And Sadie was here every day. She was so devoted. Had it been me in that recliner, I wondered if she would've moved back.

Well. Apparently John had a way with people. Just not with me. Our window had closed long before his stroke, and maybe long before I decided to divorce him.

It takes two to make a good marriage, and only one to ruin it. But in the past several weeks, I'd been spending a lot of time awake at night, thinking about my role as a wife. I had stopped making John a priority a long time ago. When Juliet came into this world, she had outshone everything, and I resented his half attention to her, the way he didn't seem to adore her as much as I did. He became superfluous to our life. If I hadn't had Sadie, I wondered if we might have divorced years ago.

I had tried, yes. Those dance classes (ugh), the forced conversations, the date nights, all that. But maybe it had been too little, too late. Maybe John had been waiting for *me* all those years when I gave him my half attention, my irritation, the unpleasant but honest feeling that he was in the way. I wanted to love him, and I'd thought I might again . . . but the truth was, I'd cast him in the role of inept and irritating husband long ago.

Not that it excused his affair, not at all. I'd been ready to divorce him; he'd gone the cheap and easy way of cheating.

Sometimes, though, I'd remember the way his eyes lit up when I came into the room in our little red house in Cranston. I'd had that, and yet somewhere during the in-between spaces of our lives, I let it slip away. Infertility had eaten away at me, and I'd tried to drown my sorrow by becoming part of Stoningham, and then, when motherhood did come, we stopped being a real couple. Maybe we would've faded away no matter what, but I didn't try real hard, either.

So maybe I owed John more than I wanted to admit. To love, honor and cherish . . . maybe I'd broken my vows, too.

CHAPTER TWENTY-THREE

Sadie

It was so, so good to spend the weekend with Alexander. He reminded me of who I was outside of my family, something more than the "other" daughter, the one who wasn't as smart, accomplished or wealthy, or married and a mom.

With Alexander, I was fun, smart, hot, interesting—a person he wanted to be with. Same as my dad (minus the hot part, obviously). We drove up to the casino for dinner with Carter and Josh. Carter, ever on my side, made a few little hints about marriage—"Can't wait to be your man of honor"—okay, pretty big hints. Alexander put his arm around me and kissed my temple. He picked up the tab with great flourish, and we all left fatter and happy and full of laughter and friendship. I felt loved again. I really did.

I felt better than I had since Dad's stroke. The way he'd recognized Janet was astonishing, and I'd been over every day, trying to get him to say another word (my name, can you blame me?). The speech therapist and I talked for two hours, and I went to the house when she was there. He might've said *dog* when Pepper jumped on his lap. *Duh* . . . It was close to *dog*, right? He was getting there.

But today, I told Mom I had to spend some time on my house and had already painted the upstairs bedroom pale gray. If Dad improved enough, I could go back to the city in the fall, so this little hovel had to be on the market for summer. Hours on the Internet had taught me everything I needed to know. Ikea was my friend, and yes, I could wield the sledgehammer taken from my parents' shed.

My plan was to knock down the wall separating the kitchen and living room, put in white cabinets and a couple of rough wooden shelves (so on trend), and make or buy a butcher block island for the middle. Small, yes, but also smart. Buff out those old floors, stain them dark walnut, spring for a new couch, and hang a Sadie Frost original abstract on the wall. Throw pillows. Rocking chair from my old room. A coffee table made from some cool wood. Bamboo and rice-paper blinds so the serial killers couldn't see in. Sand the rust out of the bathtub, bleach the shit out of the tile floor, buy some bright blue towels, and voilà. A summertime jewel.

You'd think with an architect sister, I might get some help. You'd be wrong. Juliet was weird lately. Jumpy. I invited her over one night, hoping for some advice and (cough) sisterly bonding, but she said she had to spend time working on Sloane's reading skills. Fair enough.

Time to take down that wall. "Okay, Pepper Puppy, stand back," I said, and she cocked her head at me, pricking her silky ears. "Maybe you should go outside," I said, remembering that people usually wore respirators for this kind of thing. I let her out; she never ran away, good doggy that she was. Then I tied a dishcloth over my face, cranked up Prince for company—"I Would Die 4 U"—and got a-swingin'.

Boom! Ohh. Therapy *and* home improvement rolled into one. Boom! Swinging a sledgehammer was fun!

And honestly, it didn't take that long, probably because the house was older than dirt, the Sheetrock crumbly with years of humidity and mold. Even the two-by-fours came down easily enough, crooked old nails and bits of other types of wood testifying that the house had been built by someone without a license.

Twenty minutes later, I stood in a much bigger area, a pile of rubble at my feet. "Take that, Jules," I said, and texted her a picture of my destroyed wall.

DIY, baby!

Then I turned off the music, went outside to get the dust out of my lungs. My dishcloth was covered in nastiness, which I hopefully hadn't inhaled.

Pepper lay on the lawn, gnawing on a stick, which I pried out of her mouth and threw.

"Fetch!" I said, and she raced after it, picked it up and lay down again. "Bring it here, Pepper! Here! Come! Come on!"

Nothing. Well, we all had our talents. I sat on the front steps of the porch and felt the stillness settle over me, seep into my bones.

The air was heavy with the smell of brackish water. The tide was coming in, the river rushing along the reed-filled banks, and the sunset was setting up to be glorious.

If I were to paint the scene, I'd use my palest blue for the sky, and slate gray for the clouds, edging them with tangerine and apricot, and a hint of gold. Every minute, the color changed, deepening, sliding from one shade to the next. The tidal river picked up some reflected color—red, salmon, pink—and the gold of the grasses seemed to glow. The red-winged blackbirds chuckled, and somewhere far away a wood thrush sang, rich and full.

This porch was perfect for sunset viewing. A little wicker couch, or two Adirondack chairs and a little table to hold your wineglass.

An osprey flew over me, its white belly and striped tail feathers picking up the gold of the setting sun. That would be in my painting, too. I glanced over my shoulder and saw someone driving over the bridge now, a pickup truck, its headlights sweeping the increasing dusk.

Yes. This would be my painting. This moment, right here, right now. *Homecoming*, I'd call it.

Not that I did that kind of thing anymore.

But suddenly, I wanted to.

I hadn't painted a skyscape in years and years. Not since I left for school and found out the art world didn't want pretty pictures of pretty places.

Fuck the art world. I headed inside for my camera to capture the colors, the moment, the scope and feeling.

Just as I went into the house, a pickup truck came into my driveway at top speed. I paused.

It was Noah, practically leaping out of his truck. "Sadie! Get out of the house!" Pepper ran to him, wagging her tail so hard it looked like it was going in circles as she yipped with joy.

"Hi!" I said. "What are you doing here?"

He ran up onto the porch, grabbed my arm and dragged me back into the yard. "Your sister texted me. You just knocked down a load-bearing wall."

"Is that bad?" I asked.

"Honey, get away from the house, okay?" He held my arms as if he wanted to plant me in place. "Let me see if I can get something up before the second floor falls in."

Honey. He called me honey.

Le sigh.

Then I blinked. "What? Shit! Let me help you. What's a load-bearing wall?"

"The kind that holds up the second floor." He cut me a look. "You need to stop being handy." He opened the door. "Jesus. You're lucky you're not buried right now. Come on. I have support beams in my truck. And a step-ladder. Quick."

I helped him haul the materials in.

Support beams, I quickly learned, were the kind that hold up second stories after people who watched too much HGTV did idiotic things. Noah quickly made two inverted Vs of fresh two-by-fours to hold up the second floor, securing them so they were jammed tight between floor and ceiling.

When he stood on the ladder to nail them in, his T-shirt pulled out of his jeans, exposing a strip of his lean belly, a trail of hair running from his navel into his waistband. I swallowed.

He knew what he was doing, this guy. Nail gun, drill, a few swear words, big, thick, strong arms, that beautiful head of hair . . . everything you'd want in a carpenter.

"You can't sleep here tonight," he said. "I'll come back tomorrow and put in a permanent beam, but this should hold it for now. Can you stop watching HGTV?"

"That's exactly what Jules said."

"She might know something, don't you think?"

"Yeah. Okay. I'm . . . I . . . thank you, Noah. You saved

me. And Pepper." At the sound of her name, my dog collapsed on his work boots, rolling over to expose her belly should he be so moved as to rub it.

He obeyed her silent command. "Just leave the carpentry to the carpenters."

"Yes, Mr. Pelletier."

He almost smiled at that. "You know," he said, jerking his chin at the front of my house, "I'd get rid of this picture window here and put in three floor-to-ceiling windows. The view is the only thing this house has going for it. Might as well make the most of it."

"Do you know any carpenters who might be available?"

"Finlay Construction. They're the best."

"I was broadly hinting that you might do this for me, Noah. I'll pay you, of course."

"I don't really do construction. I'm a finish carpenter. I work for Finlay on a lot of jobs. Furniture, doorframes, trim work."

"But you *could* do it. You are capable of doing it."

He looked at me assessingly. "I'm expensive."

"I just won Powerball. I can afford you."

"Good, because I'll charge you an irritation fee." He folded up the stepladder and grabbed his nail gun or screw gun or whatever the yellow thingy was called. "Don't go upstairs for anything. Your mom or Juliet will have a toothbrush and clothes you can borrow."

True enough. "Want a beer?" I asked. "We can drink it on the porch. Or in the back of your pickup." Well, didn't that sound like a proposition. "Or on the porch. If it's safe."

He hesitated before answering. "Sure."

As Noah put his stuff back in the truck, I got two IPAs

from my fridge, uncapped them (gently, in case the noise caused my bedroom to fall on me), and went out to the porch. Noah came and sat next to me, keeping a couple of feet between us. From somewhere behind us, the peepers were singing. It was full dark now, but the moon was rising.

"Full moon," I said.

Pepper lay down between us, and Noah petted her idly.

"Almost full. Tomorrow. The pink moon." He took a swig of beer.

"How do you know it'll be pink?"

"That's what the full moon in April is called."

"They have names?" I asked. What a cute idea.

"Yep."

"What's March's full moon called?"

"The worm moon."

"Really? Poor March. What about May?"

"Flower moon." He glanced at me.

"Are you making this up?"

He grinned. "Nope. Just a *Farmers' Almanac* geek."

I took a sip of beer, too. The peepers were so shrill and sweet. I'd forgotten that sound. "How are you, Noah? Are you happy?"

"Sure."

"Did fatherhood do that for you?"

"Mm-hm."

"It's nice, seeing you with a baby. You look like a natural."

He didn't answer for a minute. "I always thought we'd have kids together."

There it was.

"Me too," I whispered, then cleared my throat. "Yeah. Me too. Life is funny that way."

"Are *you* happy, Sadie?"

Earlier that evening, I had been. But right now, sitting next to my first love, the song of the little frogs in the background, the gurgle of the tidal river and the almost-full moon rising, all I felt was the sorrow of what could have been. The fullness and heft of it.

My eyes were wet, and I was grateful for the relative darkness. I took a drink of my beer, and Noah let my lack of an answer go. Pepper spied a leaf and bolted off the porch to pounce on it, then rolled in the grass.

"Cute dog," he said.

"She is."

We watched her antics another minute.

"Hey, Noah? You know how you told me we weren't going to be friends?"

He nodded, not looking at me.

"I was wondering if you might reconsider."

He closed his eyes a second, then put his arm around me, pulling me a little closer. "Sure."

He was warm and solid, and his good Noah smell and the tickle of his hair made me want to go back to that pub across from Grand Central Station and figure out a way that I could have said yes. I would've told those two stubborn, stupid kids to wrap themselves around each other, to look into each other's eyes, to kiss with all the love and passion in their souls, and instead of talking about all the reasons why it wouldn't work, just say yes, goddamnit. Yes, yes, we'll find a way, because a love like this doesn't come around twice.

"I should go," Noah said, putting down his half-empty beer bottle and standing up. "I'll come by tomorrow if the wind hasn't knocked this place down."

"I wish people would stop saying that." I couldn't look

at him, so I let Pepper lick my hands instead. "You're the best, Noah. Thank you."

He started to say something, then stopped. "Good night, Sadie."

I watched him drive off, the earlier image of home-coming in reverse. His headlights cut through the night, then disappeared, and the sky seemed cold and lonely.

I opted to sleep over at Juliet's and spent the rest of the evening playing Apples to Apples with Sloane, then lying on Brianna's bed as she stroked Pepper's ears. My niece told me about her friends and why they weren't really her friends, and how she wanted them back but didn't actually like them anymore and wished she could go to boarding school. "This town is so stupid," she said.

"It is, and it isn't," I said. "It's a good place to grow up."

"You couldn't wait to get out of here."

"And here I am, back again."

"Only because of Grampy." She rolled onto her belly and propped herself up with her elbows, my sister's little miniature. "Is he going to die, Sadie?"

"Nope," I said. "I mean, what happened was scary, and it *was* life-threatening, but he's out of the woods now." I tapped her little nose. "You don't have to worry about that."

"Then why does Mommy cry in her closet?"

Juliet? Cry? "Uh . . . well, it's stressful, you know?" Shit. "I mean, Grampy's getting better, but he's not his old self, and I'm sure she misses that. I do. Do you?"

She shrugged. "I guess so. I like Nana better, to be honest. She's the fun one."

"What does she do that's fun?" As ever, that image stung—my mother, a completely different person when I wasn't around. I listened as Brianna detailed things like planting seeds to grow flowers for the garden, baking, taking her clothes shopping, going to the movies just the two of them, getting matching pedicures.

Sounded damn nice. I hadn't known my grandmothers.

"Bedtime!" Juliet called, lurching to a stop as she saw me on her daughter's bed. "Sadie, the guest room's all made up." Pepper leaped off the bed, ready for the next adventure.

"Thanks," I said. "Good night, Princess Brianna. I love you!"

"Love you too, Sadie," she said with a smile. "Good night, Pepper."

A little while later, Jules stopped in my room. I had already thanked her profusely for sending Noah over, admitted my inadequacies as a home renovator and sworn to listen better and be nicer to Mom.

"Got everything you need?" she asked.

"Yes. Thank you again." Humility was the price I had to pay. "Hey, Jules. Brianna said . . ."

"What? Is she cutting herself?"

"No! Jesus. Is she?"

"I just asked you!"

"Well, not that I know of or saw. She was wearing shorty pajamas, and her skin is perfect." My sister's shoulders relaxed a few inches. "No, but she said she heard you crying? In your closet."

Jules grimaced. "Oh."

"You're okay, right?"

"Yeah. A work thing. Plus Dad and Mom."

"Do you want to talk about it?"

She sighed. Glanced down the hallway and came in,

shutting the door behind her. "There's this woman at work. She's great. Very talented. I hired her, and I have nothing but good things to say about her, but . . ." She stopped. "Don't tell Oliver. Or Mom. Do not tell Mom."

"Okay." Wow. I didn't know that Jules and I had ever had a secret, especially one we kept from our mother. "So what about her?"

"She's been . . . anointed. I don't know how or why, but suddenly, I seem to be yesterday's news."

I started to answer, then stopped. This was the closest Perfection from Conception had ever come to asking for advice or sharing anything except perfect nuggets from her perfect life. My answer had to be good.

"I can't imagine that someone with your talent and work ethic, with all the beautiful buildings you've designed, could ever be yesterday's news." I paused, curling my toes, and pulled out one of my best lines for my little students when they confided in me. "But that must be very hard."

Jules looked at me a second, and I wondered if maybe I blew it. Then she gave me a fast, hard hug, and left. "Sleep well," she said.

Then she was back. "And thanks for being so great with Brianna. She worships you."

She was gone again.

Well, well, well. "Pepper," I said to my dog, who was already asleep in the middle of my bed, "I think I've just had a bonding moment with my sister."

I got into bed, content with the world. Noah . . . well, we were friends again, at least. Dad was getting better. Juliet had said something nice to me. I loved my nieces.

And I had a very good dog.

If Sister Mary could've heard my thoughts, she would've said, "Count your blessings before the shit hits the fan."

A wise woman, that.

By the time I got back to my house the next day, Noah had been there and left, and there was a new and very sturdy-looking beam where the wall had once been. *Safe to go upstairs* said the note taped to it. *I'll be back later. Clean up the rubble in the meantime.*

So bossy. But it gave me a warm feeling, knowing Noah had been here. I'd have to sell a few more couch paintings to afford paying him. Maybe more than a few. Maybe I'd have to take out a bank loan.

Whatever it cost, I didn't care.

Alexander texted me, asking if I could come to the city tonight for dinner and stay over. I was just about to turn him down, since I had homeownery things to do, when a car pulled into my little driveway. An Audi.

It was Gillian Epstein of Epstein Events.

Pepper, faithless cur that she was, bounded over to her. I wish I could report that Gillian was the type to shriek and be afraid and fuss over any fur on her clothes, but instead she bent down and rubbed Pepper's neck and spoke to her, my dog's tail beating the air so fast it was a blur.

Then she straightened up. "Got a minute?"

"You betcha!" I said. Sometimes my mother's Minnesotan accent just popped out of me.

Gillian was dressed in a red pencil skirt, a pretty white peasant blouse and a brown suede jacket I wanted to marry. I was dressed in yesterday's jeans and a shirt I swiped from Oliver. She had that walk that some women have . . . the swaying, the grace, the somewhat arrogant stride that said, "Yes, I'm really this pretty."

"My house is under construction, so it's probably best if we sit out here. Um, hang on, I'll grab a chair."

I only had one, so I graciously gave it to her, then leaned tentatively against my decrepit railing, hoping it would hold me. It did. "Uh . . . that dinner party the other night . . . I hope it wasn't too horrible."

"Oh, it was," she said. "Your mother is wonderful, though. Such an impressive woman. I don't think she remembered Noah and I were . . . together once. It's fine."

"Mickey's pretty great, though, don't you think?" I asked. "I love her. Breast is best for baby, right? Funny that both you and I probably once thought we . . . Mickey, though, huh? She's so open and fun and . . ." My hands flailed for something. "Yeah. Just great. Sense of humor. She's very honest." *Stop talking. Stop talking.*

Gillian stared at me. She took a breath, then exhaled through her nostrils in a very evil-Disney-villain kind of way. "I don't know if I should tell you this, but my therapist recommended it."

Fuck. I had been discussed in therapy. That was never a good sign. "Okay. Fire away."

"I obviously have . . . *feelings* . . . regarding you, since Noah . . . well. That's neither here nor there."

Since Noah *what*? "Mm-hm." Traitorous Pepper put her head on Gillian's lap and gazed at her adoringly.

"So. I'm going to tell you this only because I feel it's the right thing to do. Not because I'm trying to make trouble or because I'm jealous of you. I have a very strong working relationship with your mother and the entire board of selectmen, and I don't want that to jeopardize—"

"Just spit it out, Gillian. It's fine. Go ahead."

Another breath. "You're dating Alexander Mitchum, correct?"

"Yep."

"Your mother told me you'd been seeing each other a couple of years."

"Correct."

"I mentioned at the dinner party that he and I had met last spring at a yacht christening."

I suddenly had a bad feeling about this. "Uh-huh."

She looked at me, her red-painted lips tight. "He made a pretty hard pass at me."

"Oh." My eyelids seemed to be blinking too fast. "Uh . . . are you sure?"

"Yes."

"Last . . . last spring."

"Yes. May seventeenth. I checked my planner."

"And by 'hard pass,' what are we talking about? Because he's nice to everyone, and you know, schmoozing is part of his—"

"He pressed me against a wall, kissed my neck and asked me if I wanted to spend the night at the Madison Beach Hotel with him."

Oh, the fuckery.

"That is a pass. Okay. Yep. You're right." I felt a little dizzy.

"And when I said no, he told me I didn't know what I was missing. He gave me his room key and told me I should change my mind so he could rock my world."

"Dick move." I swallowed.

"I thought so."

My legs felt weak, so I sat down, my knees wobbling like a newborn foal's. My breathing sounded funny. Too loud.

Rock your world. He'd said that to me on more than one occasion. *Want to come back to my place so I can rock your world?* I thought he meant it to be funny, and I always laughed.

And last May—I remembered it was May because of the lilacs—he'd called me and told me to take the train up to Madison. Spur of the moment, he said, because it had been late in the day on Saturday. We'd have fun. And I did, and we did, and I'd been his second choice. At *least* his second choice, because who knows if he'd made that offer to someone else at the yacht christening party?

"Look," Gillian said, and her voice was gentler now. "I'm sorry to tell you this. I know it must seem like I'm trying to get revenge because of Noah, but I'm not. I just thought I'd want to know if my boyfriend made a pass at someone else."

"No, I appreciate it," I whispered.

"Do you want a glass of water?"

"No, thanks." Pepper left Gillian and came over to me and tried to sit on my lap.

"Do you want to call someone, maybe? Your sister? Mom?"

I blinked. Put my chin on Pepper's head, getting my ear licked as thanks. "I'm okay, Gillian. I . . . I appreciate you telling me this."

She stood up, smoothed her skirt and walked past me on the steps. "I love your jacket," I whispered.

She put her hand on my shoulder. "In another world, we'd probably be friends."

Would we? "Drive safely. Bye."

She strode to her car, hips swaying the perfect amount, got in and gave me a little finger wave.

Just then, my phone beeped. I took it out. Another text from my loving boyfriend.

Please come, babe. I miss you!

Did he now?

On my way, I typed.

~

CHAPTER TWENTY-FOUR

John

There was another woman. In the not-so long-ago, he had been with another woman.

John remembers her hard face, which he had thought was not pretty when they met. (A party? There was dancing.) But the face became prettier as she said things he liked, things Barb didn't say anymore. He knows now he should have been smarter. That these were the things all bored old men want to hear. He thought he deserved those things. He was a man, and men should be told those things.

Handsome. Smart. Funny. Strong. Those were some of the feelings or words she had said.

He said things to that woman, and most of them were lies. He lied about Barb. He lied about his unhappiness being her fault when she had always worked so hard. He remembers how hard Barb tried to fit in, to be not so different, because she thought being from Minnesota made her less . . . something . . . than other women. He told that other woman about that, and they *laughed*. The hard-faced woman laughed at his *wife*, and John had been *glad* and it makes no sense now.

Now he remembers the meals Barb made, the cookbooks she bought, the vegetables she grew. How pretty their house was, how nice it always smelled. He remembers how loving she was with Juliet, how delighted Juliet made her.

Juliet. John knows he could have been a better father to her. He should have tried more. She is an important person in the world somehow. People know her. She is impressive.

That other woman, whose name he doesn't remember, doesn't want to remember, was like . . . like . . . like that plant that grows up a tree and chokes it. That invader. Invasive species, that's it. Kudzu. The word flies into his brain. She was kudzu, taking over, blotting out the view, tangling, and he let her.

Words are flying back into his head. Unfaithful. Cheater. Liar.

Cliché.

When his friend came, the new friend with the hair like pieces of rope, he was so happy. *She* didn't know him when he was wrong, when he was a liar and stupid. She only knows him the way he is now, and there is no disappointment or hope in her eyes, no expectation that he will be anything other than what he is. She talks to him and talks to him, and laughs. She is not pretty, not like his girls or Barb or even the other woman, but Janet—yes, her name is Janet—makes him feel at peace.

A fear seeps through him, its tentacles cold and coiling. That he has done something terrible by being sick, and that his family needs him to be the father again, the husband, and that he will never be able to do this. That he has to fix something or his wife and daughters will never get . . . never be . . . never know . . .

The thought is gone.

Shame. Another word he knows now. He is ashamed of himself, for lying to Barb, about Barb. For telling the invasive species his wife was cold and self-absorbed. That she didn't care about him anymore, didn't want to talk to him, when he knows that he should've turned that knob and opened the door to the bathroom that day in the long-ago, held her close and cried with her. He knows in doing so, he could have changed the course of their lives.

That is the thought that won't go away. He hears her crying in the bathroom as he sleeps, and when he wakes up, he is so sad.

There is something about a flower he has to tell Barb. Something important. Something that will fix things, but the flower floats away. It has to come back. He has to make it come back. He has to tell her about the flower, but LeVon makes him exercise and the bossy woman asks him to make sounds, and now he is trying, trying hard, because he has something important to say.

CHAPTER TWENTY-FIVE

Sadie

I chose the restaurant in which I planned to dump Alexander, and I made sure it was as expensive as I could find, which was really saying something in New York City.

He was there already, handsome, charming . . . shithead.

"You look beautiful, as always," he said, leaning in for a kiss. I gave him my cheek. The maître d' showed us to our table, which was in a corner, because Alexander always asked for a great table. The restaurant was everything I hoped it would be—sleekly decorated, Michelin starred, quiet, with well-dressed people murmuring and drinking.

I didn't plan on murmuring, but first, I did want to order pretty much everything on the menu. Alexander, my soon-to-be ex-boyfriend, wasn't getting out of here without bleeding money.

The waiter came over. "Hello!" I said, as was my way. "How are you tonight?"

"I'm quite well, *signorina*. My name is Luciano, and it is my pleasure to serve you tonight."

"What a beautiful name," I said. "Please tell your mom she chose well! Luciano, I'll have the Fiorentino, please." I pointed to the drink that cost, yes, forty-nine dollars. Only in New York, folks.

"I thought you didn't like brandy," Alexander said.

"I've grown and changed." I smiled brightly. "What are you having, hon?" The endearment felt like poison on my lips.

"I'll have the Dante," he said.

"Very good, *signore*," Luciano said.

"Oh, and we'll have a bottle of Cristal with dinner, okay?" I said, smiling my sparkliest smile.

"Excellent! Which year?"

"Surprise us. It's a special night." I'd studied the champagne list after picking this place. The cheapest bottle of Cristal cost six hundred dollars, and the most expensive was well over a thousand.

"Babe," Alexander said, "uh, that's kind of expensive."

"Oh! We can call him back, then, babe." I raised my hand, knowing he would stop me. It would look like he couldn't afford it, and he would hate that, especially here.

As predicted . . . "No, no, it's fine. A special night, like you said. How are you, babe? How was your week?"

"So good, Alexander. So good."

He smiled, not picking up on the venom in my voice. "Well, it's great to see you. I hope you can stay a few nights. I'll be in town for four days. We could have a lot of fun. The Guggenheim has a new show, and—"

I stopped listening.

He had made a pass at another woman. He wanted to sleep with her in the hotel where we'd had sex. That image of him kissing her on the neck . . . it was kind of a specialty of his.

I wished Gillian had kicked him in the nutsack.

When the waiter came back, I was ready. "I'm starving!" I announced cheerfully to both men. "It's been a tough couple of weeks, Luciano, and I haven't been in the city in ages, and I think I want a bite of everything! How about the sea urchin with pickled fennel, the Chinese caviar, maybe . . . hmm . . . the red prawn antipasto, and the garden salad, and oh! That lobster risotto sounds great! And for my main course, the sirloin, please. With the roasted potatoes, please. And heck, throw in those wild mushrooms, too."

Luciano was in love with me now. "Excellent choices, *signorina*. For the *signore*?"

Alexander looked incredulous. "Are you sure you can eat all that, babe?"

"I'm super hungry, babe." Sparkle sparkle. "Plus, you know how these Michelin-star places are. Every plate is basically two bites of food."

Luciano chuckled warmly. "*Signorina*, you are correct. Just enough to whet the appetite for the next course, *si*?"

"*Si*," I said, beaming.

"*Signore?* For you?"

"I'll have the sea bass," he said.

"Oh, come on!" I said. "You can't let me sit here and eat all those courses and just have one! This is an Italian restaurant! To eat is to love, right, Luciano?"

"*Si, signorina*. The beautiful lady is correct, of course."

I winked at him. Alexander had flaws, but being a shitty tipper was not among them, and Luciano would leave here with hundreds of dollars from our meal alone.

Alexander ordered a pasta course and the grilled octopus. I would also be ordering dessert. Possibly a dessert martini. Carter had already been notified about my romantic drama as I drove to the New Haven train station, and had ordered me to sleep over tonight, bless him.

I drank the cocktail, wincing a little at the taste but appreciating the warmth.

How could Alexander *do* this to me? Why? Wasn't I the easiest, most laid-back girlfriend in the world? Had I ever complained about his travel schedule? Ever insisted he come to a school event or birthday party? Before my father's stroke, he'd only visited Stoningham once. I was always cheerful and upbeat around him because I *was* those things, goddamnit.

Luciano brought our courses. I ate, laughed, murmured in the appropriate places. The food was amazing. At least there was that. Also, the champagne, my God. So good. I might even order a second bottle.

As I watched Alexander, I saw it. The performance. The need for validation. He was working hard to make sure we were The Couple to Be at this swanky, sophisticated restaurant. When I fake laughed, he'd glance around to make sure people saw that he had the power to bring humor. He smiled a lot, and where my dorky brother-in-law also smiled a lot, Oliver was . . . sincere. He loved my sister and his daughters. He adored my parents. He even loved me, not that I'd given him much reason to.

We ordered dessert (though I was going to go into a coma soon if I ate much more).

"Babe," Alexander said now, "I know this has been a rough couple of months for you."

"You, sir, are absolutely right." I was tipsy and enjoying it. It was fueling my rage.

"So I wanted to give this to you, and hope it will make things a little happier."

He reached into his breast pocket and pulled out a little velvet box.

Shit. If there was an engagement ring in there, I knew it would be big, and I'd want it, and I wouldn't be able to have it, and everyone in here would feel bad for the poor guy who proposed and got shot down. Cringing internally, I waited for him to get down on one knee.

Thank God, no. He just passed it across the many plates and smiled.

"Aw. So sweet of you!" I opened it and, shit, it was a beautiful necklace. A chunky bezel-set diamond surrounded by pink gold with a matching chain. "I love it." I did, damn it. I'd keep it, too. I could sell it and pay for something in my house. "Thank you. How much did it cost?"

"Oh, babe. Whatever it cost, you're worth ten times that much."

"So . . . what are we talking? A thousand dollars?"

He grinned. "More. Significantly more. Here, let me put it on you."

Ass. I allowed it. He sat back down, smug and pleased (glancing around to see if everyone had noticed).

"It's beautiful," said the woman from the next table.

"Thank you," Alexander and I said in unison.

"Hey, Alexander, I have a quick question for you, babe."

"Sure, babe."

"When you came to my mom's dinner party, did you remember Gillian?"

"Uh . . . the one with the baby?"

"No. That's Mickey. The very pretty woman?"

"Other than you, babe?"

"The one you made a pass at last May. At the yacht christening party she mentioned."

He blinked. "I think she . . . no. I've never met her."

"She said you pressed her against a wall, kissed her neck, gave her your room key to the Madison Beach Hotel. Where we then spent the night after she turned you down."

His neck was getting red. "She must have me confused with someone else."

"You said you'd 'rock her world.'"

He didn't answer.

Luciano came with our desserts. "The bomboloni for *signorina*, the cheesecake for *signore*."

"Thank you so much," I said sweetly. He left. "Anything to say, Alexander? You made a pass at a woman and then called me as your B-list fuck. Why would you *do* that? You were going to cheat on me!" My voice may have risen a teeny bit.

"Look," he said, glancing around, his hands up in the universal male sign for *don't make this a big deal, you hysterical female*. "We never said we were exclusive."

"What? We *were* exclusive! We've been dating for two years! We spend holidays together!"

"Calm down," he said.

"How dare you tell me to calm down!" But yes, people were staring.

"I never said we were exclusive," he repeated through gritted teeth.

"What does that mean? You get to sleep with other women?"

"Yes."

The bald-faced admission was like a bucket of ice water. "Do I need to get tested?" I hissed. Thank God we'd always used condoms *and* the Pill. But I did. I'd need to get tested. Good God!

"Look." He glanced around. "It's not like I'm promiscuous, okay? I'm not on Tinder. But yes, I have two other relationships."

"What?" There was the screeching again. Luciano was huddled with the maître d' in the front, casting us concerned looks, so I lowered my voice. "Explain yourself."

He looked at the restaurant ceiling, clearly aggrieved. "There's Toni in San Diego and Paige in North Carolina. I've been seeing Toni for four years, Paige for three."

"And me for two."

"Yes."

"So *I'm* the other woman?"

"No, no. Well . . . yes, I guess so. I don't see it that way."

"How do *they* see it?"

"They don't know about you. Why would I tell them, right? When I'm in San Diego, I see Toni. When I'm down south, I see Paige. But mostly, there's you, babe."

"Do not call me babe. Ever again."

"Listen, Sadie. You're my favorite," he said, leaning forward with a smile.

"I *proposed* to you," I hissed.

"And when I get married, you'll probably be my first choice. You know. When I'm ready."

Jesus. I stood up and threw my napkin on the table. "I'll send you the bill for my STD panel," I said loudly. "Make sure you leave Luciano a thirty percent tip. And I'm keeping this necklace." I looked down at the table. "And these little donuts."

Luciano patted my hand and waited for the cab with me, as I was busy crying (and eating the bomboloni), the shock of what I'd learned settling in.

Shit. It was so obvious now. The three days in San Diego turning into five. The many times North Carolina had thunderstorms that shut down the airport (not that I bothered to check the Weather Channel, because I was trusting and an idiot). The "turned-off" phone. All those yacht emergencies. How tired he could be after coming home from schmoozing and screwing his other girlfriends. The holiday weekends when he was traveling, or visiting his "mother." The truth was, he was probably taking Paige or Toni on lovely weekend getaways, same as he'd done for me.

I'd have to find them through his Facebook page or Instagram and tell them.

Shit. Shit, shit, shit.

I went to Carter's apartment and spilled. He made the appropriate noises, cursed occasionally, ate my remaining donuts and made me drink water.

"I know it's too soon to say this, honey, but you're better off without him," he said as I hiccuped and clutched his aging, obese cat to my chest. "Now go to bed. Uncle Carter's giving you some Motrin and water, and don't even think about puking in the guest room. Janice just redid it. I'll make you a nice big breakfast in the morning, okay?"

"How's Josh?" I asked, remembering that my friend was happy, and we talked about how Sister Mary had invited the guys over for dinner and told them to get married and not live together first.

Good. There was love in the world, even if I was a jerk.

I got in my pajamas, washed my face and brushed my teeth, avoiding my reflection in the mirror, and got into the wonderfully soft bed.

As I lay there, slightly drunk, tears leaking into the pillow, feeling as dumb as I'd ever felt, I had two overwhelming thoughts.

The first was that I missed my dad so, so much. That he would've known more than anyone how to make me feel better about this—less ridiculous, less like the younger, stupid Frost daughter.

The second was that Noah wouldn't have cheated on me with a gun to the back of his head.

CHAPTER TWENTY-SIX

Juliet

On Wednesday, Kathy stopped by Juliet's office, her gossip face on—eyes sliding from the left to the right, eyebrow raised (lucky . . . Juliet's were still frozen). She came in and closed the door. "Guess who was just named project manager on the school Beyoncé is building in Houston?"

"What Beyoncé school?" This was the first Juliet had heard of it.

Kathy sat down, looking too pleased with herself. "Yeah. Her."

"Arwen?"

"Who else?"

Anyone else, that's who. Matt, who was nine years senior to Arwen. Elena, who was six. Brett and Christopher, four.

"Are you going to talk to Dave?" Kathy asked, running a hand through her bright red hair.

"Are you?"

"No. Of course not. It's not like I could be PM, though I'm definitely hoping to be on the interior team. Maybe meet Queen Bey."

Juliet was very sure Kathy was too old and white to be using that nickname. She glanced out the window, her stomach clenching with nerves. "Did you know we were pitching Beyoncé?"

"Arwen mentioned it. It's really Beyoncé's foundation. Her PR team asked us to keep it a secret till ground is broken."

Beyoncé. Jesus. And Kathy knew, but hadn't said a word till now.

"Well. I have work to do, Kathy."

"I'm sure you do."

What did that mean? She and Kathy used to be friends, but Kathy had always been the office gossip. Juliet felt she'd been immune to that.

Now it was hard to trust her, with that Arwen haircut and the way Kathy brayed laughter from Arwen's office at least twice a day. Kathy was here to gather intel, that's what she was doing. To plant seeds and make trouble.

It worked.

A few hours later, so it wouldn't be so obvious, she went down the hall to Dave's office with the excuse of showing him the plans on a house for a former senator. She liked doing residences once in a while—she'd done her own house, obviously, and occasionally offered to do one at work, though it was small potatoes for her. She'd volunteered to do this one because it was fun and had a limitless budget, which was always pleasant.

"Is he available?" she asked the side-eying Laurie (who may have been casting a spell on her).

Laurie shrugged and jerked her chin, indicating that it was okay for Juliet to go in. Her boss had his feet up on the desk and was gazing out the window. Hard to believe he'd been a force in architecture once, since he mostly napped and went out for lunch these days.

"Hey, Dave, I've got the elevations on that house in Maryland. Want to have a look?"

"Sure." She sat down and watched as he gave them a glance. "Nice job, Juliet."

"Thanks. It's a beautiful site."

"That it is."

"So, Dave . . . I heard a rumor. You made Arwen the PM on a school for Beyoncé's foundation?"

He avoided looking at her, studying the house plans as if he'd just realized they'd come down from Mount Sinai in the hands of Moses. "Mm," he offered.

Be careful, a voice in her head warned her. But screw that. She'd earned her place here. "Since when does such a green architect get that kind of high-profile job? I thought the firm had a system. A ladder." One that she'd climbed, step-by-step, never skipping a single rung.

Dave sighed. Still didn't look up. "Arwen is very talented."

"I'm aware of that, Dave. But she's only thirty-one. She still needs supervision."

"Or does she? She's quite ambitious. People respond to her."

"There are a lot of ambitious people here who outrank her. Matt. Elena. Brett." She paused. "Me. I'm a little shocked that I wasn't informed we were pitching this job, frankly. I'm the senior project manager at this firm."

"Look, Juliet," he said, finally looking at her. Her chin, to be exact. "You've done some remarkable work for us."

"I *am* doing remarkable work for you, Dave." Her voice was firm but she made sure not to be too angry, because God forbid her boss had to deal with an angry female. "I realize Arwen is the shiny new thing, but my record speaks for itself, doesn't it?"

"I'm a fan of yours, Juliet. Don't get hostile."

Oh, the *fuckery*. "I'm not being hostile. I'm pointing out facts."

"Maybe if you smiled more, people would—"

"Dave. Do not finish that sentence."

"I'm just saying, Arwen is a really positive person. *She* smiles all the time."

"Are you giving her a promotion because she *smiles*?" she asked.

"There's that hostility." He smiled ruefully.

"It's disbelief, not hostility."

"Juliet, you're very serious."

"About my work, absolutely. You could say that's a positive attribute in an architect."

He put his hands behind his head. "Listen. You're right. Arwen is new and exciting, and the world seems to love her."

Time to be dead honest. "But her work isn't particularly special, and you must know that."

"Be careful, Juliet. You're sounding very jealous and competitive."

Hostile, serious, jealous and competitive. All code for bitch, or worse. If she were a man, it would be *fiery, dedicated, strategic* and *ambitious*.

But here she was, in a male-owned, male-run firm. So she lowered her voice to a tone Dave could tolerate. "I've always put the firm's best interests first and foremost,

Dave. I'm your senior architect. I've never let you down, have I?"

He tilted his head. "Nothing is coming to mind, no."

"Because it's never happened."

"What's your point, Juliet?" He glanced at his phone.

You could lose me. I might quit. I could sue you for ageism and discrimination.

Except Kathy was older and wasn't saying boo. And it would be hard to prove discrimination on the basis of gender, given that Arwen was a woman, too. A gay woman, for that matter, something Juliet had only found out a few weeks ago when she and Saanvi had had drinks at the same bar where Arwen had been with a woman, and they'd kissed once or twice. Arwen hadn't seen Juliet, and Juliet hadn't gone over, not wanting to intrude.

Now Juliet glanced out the window, then back at her boss. "Just be thoughtful, Dave. A green architect on a high-profile client's project could be risky."

"Fortune favors the bold," he said. "And you know how we like to think outside the box at DJK. Thanks for bringing me your concerns. I think we've cleared the air. And I'll see you at your party this weekend, right?"

Dismissed. "Yes. Thanks for hearing me out." She left his office, past the silent Laurie, the plans for the senator's house clenched in her hands.

Today was one of the days she left early and worked from home. She grabbed her stuff, fake smiled at her colleagues and got out of there as soon as possible. In her car, she sat for a minute, gripping the steering wheel, stymied, frustrated and . . . scared.

She could leave the firm and start her own. The thought had crossed her mind from time to time, but DJK had always been the best of both worlds—creativity within an established, respected firm. Starting her own would be twice the workload, and the girls still needed her. She could put out some feelers at other firms, but the truth was, if she left now . . . well. It would look exactly like what it was. She was leaving because another architect was taking over.

Was it possible she had peaked? Were her best days behind her? She was forty-three, and she hadn't recycled an idea yet. Maybe this was just a normal phase of a career, being established and therefore slightly less exciting.

But the thought of aging out struck a nerve. Arwen was so beautiful . . . That had to be a factor, even if it wasn't ever going to be acknowledged. Juliet looked in the rear-view mirror. She was still attractive. Of course she was! She had decades of youth in front of her! She was in her prime. Look at Meryl Streep! Look at . . . um . . . Sofía Vergara! And JLo! She'd just spent three grand on looking even younger, goddamnit.

She was too serious, was she? She should smile more? How dare her boss imply that she was . . . was stale and boring! She was absolutely not those things. Oliver still adored her. Even if they'd settled into a routine, it was a good routine.

Sort of like Mom and Dad.

Shit.

She flew up 95 to Stoningham. Oliver was working from home today with a slight cold and being an utter infant about it. He was about to have his mind blown. Time to be shiny, spontaneous and bold.

Oliver was in the laundry room, putting sheets in the dryer because Juliet still hadn't hired a new cleaning lady, goddamnit.

"All right, love?" he said as she came in.

"I want you," she said.

He side-eyed her. "Darling, I have a man-cold. I'm hovering at the precipice of death." He coughed to prove it, a meaty, phlegmy sound.

"I don't care. I'm so . . ." Shit. She should've paid more attention to the three pornos she'd seen in her entire lifetime. "I'm so . . . wet." Ick. It sounded like she'd peed her pants.

"I wouldn't wish this cold on my worst enemy, my darling girl."

"I won't kiss you on the mouth, then."

She dropped to her knees and started to untie his sweatpants.

"It's a lovely thought, darling," Oliver said, putting his hand on her head. His voice was thick with the cold. "Perhaps a rain check."

"No. I need you now. Here. Like this."

"Darling. I feel wretched."

He'd change his mind. She pulled down his pants. "It's so, um, big." Gah. It wasn't, not at the moment. She screwed her eyes shut and gathered her courage.

He stopped her, thank God, and pulled his pants back up. "Juliet, what are you *doing*?"

"Trying to give you a BJ." Men were supposed to love this shit.

"The girls will be home in five minutes."

Right. "Then I'll be quick."

"I swear that I'm thrilled about this theoretically, but seriously, darling, can we reschedule?"

"No."

"Juliet." He pulled her to her feet. "What's got into you?"

"I'm trying to be fun and spontaneous and . . . not so serious."

"Darling, we're married with two children. Spontaneous happens only when we put it on the calendar."

Well. She just couldn't fucking win, could she? Everything Oliver said was true, and he looked like vomit warmed over, but it didn't do much for her battered ego.

At that moment, the door banged open. "Daddy! Mommy!" yelled Sloane. "Guess what? Brianna got her period!"

"I rest my case," Oliver murmured.

"Shut up, Sloane! I hate you!" Brianna said.

Juliet opened the laundry room door as Brianna flew by, her eyes red.

"She's a woman now," Sloane said solemnly. "She could have a baby."

"Sloanie-Pop, this is a personal matter," Oliver said. "Let's get you a snack while Mummy talks to your sister, right?"

Sure. Give the hard child to me, Juliet thought. But yes. This was a mother's job.

She went to Brianna's room and knocked once. There was no answer, so she went in. Brianna was lying on the bed, sobbing.

Juliet didn't know what to say, so she just put her hand on her daughter's hair. "Hello, baby," she said.

"It was horrible! It was in math class, and I felt this stickiness, and then George Tanner said, 'Don't mess with Brianna, she's on her period,' and everyone laughed. The blood was on my jeans, Mom! You knew I had cramps last night! Why didn't you tell me to wear a pad?"

Yes. Why hadn't Juliet been more psychic? The fact

that Brianna had been claiming to have cramps every time she wanted to get out of a chore for two solid years was probably not what she wanted to hear.

"I'm sorry, honey. If it's any consolation, I've gotten blood on my pants, too. So has Sadie, and just about every female I know." Except Arwen. It probably hadn't happened to her.

Brianna gave her a sullen look. "I thought it would be different," she said, tears still dripping down her face. "I thought it would be cool and I'd feel sophisticated and in some kind of older girls club, but it's just gross and my stomach hurts and my legs do, too."

"I'll get you some Motrin," Juliet said. "And a hot-water bottle. It'll feel good against your tummy."

She went into her own bathroom and got the necessary items. A pad, just in case, and a tampon, too. She'd bought Brianna her own supplies last year, as well as a book about periods, but nothing ever did prepare you, did it?

She went back into Brianna's room and gave her the Motrin and a glass of water. Put the hot-water bottle against her daughter's abdomen and nodded at the tampons and pads. "In case you need it."

"I have my own," Brianna muttered. She rolled away from Juliet. "You can go now, Mom. Thanks."

Once again, dismissed. What would Barb, the perfect mother, do? "You'll always be my little girl. No matter how old you get."

"Thanks. Could you go? I just want to sleep."

"Right. Sleep tight."

By the time Juliet had made dinner and cleaned up, even though it was Oliver's turn (but he was suffering greatly), and checked on Brianna and helped Sloane with her reading and took a shower and got into bed, Oliver was asleep. He rolled over and put his arm around her, then started gently snoring in her ear.

So much for being the spontaneous, sexy, positive lover.

CHAPTER TWENTY-SEVEN

Barb

LeVon had gone to his new job, and John had recovered enough that he could handle the stairs. We moved him back into his bedroom, and the dining room furniture was returned. A home health aide named Kit came to keep him company and make his meals, but she was sullen and didn't talk much, and was no replacement for LeVon. Sadie also came over every day, always optimistic, always talking up John's mental progress (which I sure couldn't see, though having him go up the stairs was great, don't get me wrong). The speech therapist continued to come three times a week, and while John did seem to be trying to say words from time to time, the only clear thing he'd said was *you* the first day Janet came over.

Janet still visited once or twice a week, and I was grateful, if a bit mystified at her motives. If I was home when she visited, we'd have coffee and talk; if I was at work, she'd leave me a nice little note and, once, a pot of pansies. She worked at a nursery. I took to making sure there was some baked good in the house, cake or cookies, and always texted her to help herself.

Juliet was working like crazy these days. Caro, too. Sadie would move back to the city eventually; those paintings she did were fine as a side job, but I knew she wasn't exactly fulfilled (as I had predicted all those years ago, but who listened?). She seemed to like teaching in New York, and sooner or later, she'd get restless and leave again.

So this was what the rest of my life would be like. Alone, but a caregiver. Married, but to a man I'd wanted to leave, a man who'd found someone else and had been stepping out on me for God knew how long.

On a soft, gentle evening in April, I herded John onto the slate patio. Sloane and Brianna and I had planted pansies in the window boxes out here, and the birds were singing, and it was real nice. I settled John in a chaise longue, covered him with a blanket and got myself a glass of wine, then came back out and sat down next to him. Gosh, I was tired. I had a dozen things to do, but technically, I didn't have to work sixteen-hour days.

Everything could wait. My back twinged as I leaned back, and I wished I had a pillow, or someone who would bring a pillow to me. It was fine. The twinge stopped after a minute, and John was silent and still.

I loved this patio. We used to eat out here when the weather was nice, the whole family. I'd combed the countryside for antiques to decorate the space—a granite horse head sculpture sitting on the gatepost to the backyard, an old millstone, the iron planters.

The wine tasted so good—a fat, buttery chardonnay that John had hated, being the kind of wine snob who only drank reds, or port as an after-dinner drink. He'd made fun of me in that wine-tasting class. *Barb's the type who thinks there's nothing wrong with ice cubes in her pinot grigio.* The teacher had winced before recovering.

"Guess I got the last laugh," I said now, even though he couldn't know what I was talking about. "No more alcohol for you, John. I bet you miss it."

He was listening. Sometimes he just stared off into the middle distance, but tonight, he seemed a little more present.

"Juliet's party is this Saturday," I said. "I'm sorry I'm not bringing you. It's just that I need a little break. A few hours with people who like me, don't you know?" Another sip of the glorious chardonnay. "I've been wondering when you stopped, by the way. We were happy once. We were solid for a long time, I thought. Not exactly setting the bedroom on fire, but I liked our life. Thought you liked us, too. We had the girls and then the grandbabies. That was enough for me."

Except it hadn't been. Not really, if I was going to be honest.

"I'll tell you something, John. I was planning on divorcing you. I was going to tell you on our anniversary, for effect. 'Hey, we've been married for fifty years and I'd like a divorce. Happy anniversary.' I didn't know you were cheating. I was just done with you. It was how little you thought of me, John. I wonder how often I crossed your mind, even living in the same house."

"Dig," he said, startling me. I looked at him, and he scowled.

"That's good, John. Keep trying. You're doing real good." Or was he just making noise, poor thing?

"Horse."

"That's right. The horse head. You never liked it."

These word bursts were a good sign. *Dig* could be because of the gardening, but maybe that was a stretch.

His mouth worked.

"Got anything else to say there, John?" I asked.

He scowled again and pulled the blanket up to his chin, sulking much like Brianna did these days. Well, maybe he liked me talking to him as if he could understand. Maybe he could, who knew?

"I met a friend of yours." I poured a second glass of wine, glad I'd brought the bottle with me. "Karen. Your girlfriend. WORK, as she was listed in your phone. Gotta say, I was surprised when I saw her. Then again, I don't really know your type, except that I'm not it. She didn't seem like the brightest bulb in the box, but I suppose IQ isn't high up there on the list of things an old man looks for in a mistress."

He was still scowling.

"Caro and I met her for coffee. I told her about your stroke and whatnot."

His face changed, the scowl sliding down into old-man sadness.

I reached over and patted his hand. "I'd like to tell you she sent a card or stopped by or texted you, but she hasn't. I'm sorry about that."

Listen to me, apologizing that Karen didn't give a good gosh darn about him. Must've been the wine.

"Hello? Anyone home?"

"We're on the patio, Caro!" I said, letting go of John's hand. "Grab a wineglass. The bottle's out here." I heard the cupboard open, and a second later, there she was, looking so stylish and pretty.

"You two look cozy," she said, pouring herself some wine and taking a seat across from us.

"I've just been telling John about our meeting with Karen."

"Oh, that slut." She looked at John. "You do not deserve Barb, John. You hear me? You don't deserve to clean her toilet."

"Hush now," I said. "He's my husband. Not a great one, mind you, John, but my husband just the same."

"You're too good, Barb."

"You betcha," I said, and we laughed, Caro and I, and maybe, just maybe, John smiled a little bit, too. I closed my eyes, listening to the birds.

If this was my life now, I guess I'd have to take it. Aside from a cheating husband, I'd been real blessed. My girls, my friend, my home, this town . . .

"Go to bed, Barb," Caro said. "You must be exhausted."

"I'm pretty tired, I'll give you that."

"I'll get this old bastard settled, and I'll hardly kick him at all. How's that, John?"

"Oh, Caro. You're all talk. Don't listen to her, John. She'll take real good care of you."

And I did go to bed, not even brushing my teeth first. My clothes felt as heavy as lead.

Would John live a long time? Would I be able to keep this up?

Thank God for Caro. I lay down, comforted by the sound of my best friend's voice as she talked to my husband. I was asleep almost before my head hit the pillow.

~

CHAPTER TWENTY-EIGHT

Sadie

For the first time in years and years, Noah and I were in a car together.

It brought back a lot. Sure, we were driving down I-95 to Brooklyn, but memories of steamy windows, hands under shirts, lush kissing, panting breath, the way he knew exactly how I—

"You okay?" he asked.

"Yes! Why? Jeesh."

"You just squeaked."

"Did I? I don't think so. Must've been the truck."

This was going to be a long ride.

Why were we going to New York together, you ask?

I was delivering a painting to Janice, the interior decorator. This one was a "huge painting with those big flowers that look like vaginas. It's a lesbian couple, so don't hold back."

When I called her to ask about the delivery, Janice had

been more frantic than her usual self. "Can you come down and hang it yourself? This whole job is going to shit. It's a brownstone, and it needs custom work, and the guy who was supposed to make the window seat on the staircase landing just bailed, and I'm telling you, no one is available unless you book a year in advance these days, and they discontinued the wallpaper the owners loved and I'm pulling my hair out."

"Sure, I'll come," I said. Janice had probably forgotten that I was here in Connecticut with my dad, but I could use a day in the city. I hadn't spent any time there except to dump Alexander a few weeks ago, and I'd been in a state, obviously. It would be good for the soul, as it always was. There was nothing like a spring day in Brooklyn.

An idea popped into my head. "Hey, Janice, I might know someone who can make a window seat."

"Really? Oh, Sadie. That would be *miraculous*."

"I'll call you back." I hung up, then looked at my dog. "Don't judge," I said. "It's only business." She wagged kindly, her eyes suggesting I wasn't fooling anyone.

Noah had put in the beam so my house was no longer in danger of falling in on itself. He'd also put in the picture windows, and it was amazing how it changed the look of the house, both from the outside and the inside. Sure, it was still a bit crooked, but Noah said if I put on a new roof, it could be fixed. The thing about house renovation, I was learning, was that the more you did, the more you wanted to do. The huge vagina flower painting (sorry, Georgia O'Keeffe) would put some money in the bank.

A big butcher block island with stools would let you eat while staring out at the salt marsh. Maybe Noah could put in a spiral staircase, like Juliet's. Maybe he could make the entire northern wall a bookcase.

Maybe I just wanted to spend more time with Noah.

I was still recovering from Alexander's cheating and lying, granted. I had loved him, or the him I thought he was. Then there were the feelings of stupidity and humiliation, of being less than, because he needed *three* girlfriends, not just me. I'd thought I found a man who loved me without that sense of . . . expectation Noah always had. Like, until I lived life the way Noah wanted me to—that was, move to Stoningham and start popping out babies—I was a disappointment.

Alexander had taken me exactly as I was. He'd been generous, fun, not unintelligent, easygoing. All he needed was two other women to make his life complete.

Oh, the fuckery of it all.

At any rate, I'd called Noah, told him two wealthy brownstone owners needed a window seat pronto, did he want a quick job in the city? Much to my surprise, he said yes.

When I arrived at his house this morning, he'd been passing off Marcus to Mickey in the front yard, daffodils blooming, sun shining on his hair.

"Girlfriend!" sang Mickey. "How you doing? Damn, you're so stinkin' cute. I could be gay for you."

"You *are* gay, you tease. Hi, Marcus." The baby smiled at me, and my ovaries spontaneously frothed over with eggs.

"Want to hold him?"

"We need to get on the road," Noah said at the same moment I said, "God, yes."

Mickey smiled and passed me her son. The warm, wriggly weight of him, his sturdy little legs kicking, and yes, people, the smell of his head . . . God. "Hello, gorgeous," I said. His lashes were so long and silky, and his cheeks were fat and pink and delicious.

"Dwah!" he said, taking a fistful of my hair and tugging. "Baba!"

"He's a genius!" I said to the parents.

Noah was smiling. Just a little, and probably at his son.

"Please, please, let's get together," Mickey said. "I want to see your goofy little house and drink wine."

"Done," said I.

"You're nursing," Noah said.

"Oh, am I, Noah? I forgot that my breasts are as big as watermelons and my nipples look like saucers and milk spurts out of me every time this baby smiles." She rolled her eyes. "Mansplainer. Shame on you! I'll pump that night and chuck it. Jeez. The nursing police here, Sadie."

"He's horrible. I'm sorry for all you endure." She grinned. I liked her so much.

"We do need to go, Sadie," Noah said.

I kissed the baby's head—oh! The soft spot! So dear!—and handed him back to Mickey. "I'll call you."

"You better. Bye, Noah! Marcus, wave bye to Daddy!" She held up his fat fist and jiggled it.

Noah leaned in and kissed his child. "I love you," he said, and my ovaries frothed again. "See you tomorrow, sweetheart."

Which brought us to my current horndog state, sitting in Noah's truck, his tools and some walnut planks in the back, the smell of wood and coffee the best foreplay I could think of. "I brought pastries from Sweetie Pies," I said. "Want something?"

"Sure."

I handed him a chocolate croissant and watched as he

ate it, his jaw moving hypnotically. Would it be inappropriate to brush the crumbs out of his lap?

"Who's watching your dog today?" he asked.

"What? Nothing! Oh. My nieces." I took a calming breath and chose a cheese and raspberry Danish to get my mind off Noah's lap.

"How are they?"

"They're good. Brianna got her period and is officially a horrible adolescent, and Sloane is a little behind in school, but they're awesome."

He smiled, and I had to look out the window to avoid wrapping myself around him like an octopus.

When we got to the brownstone, all was chaos, as it tended to be with Janice. Movers were bringing in furniture, painters were finishing up, and she pounced on me, despite the fact that I was carrying the huge wonkin' vagina flower painting wrapped in brown paper.

"Let me see it! Let's get it inside. Up those stairs, second door on the right."

Noah followed with his toolbox.

"You must be Noah, thank you for coming, you're an angel, you really are, I hope you're good enough to do this right because I don't really have a choice right now. Unwrap the painting, Sadie, let's have a look!"

I glanced at Noah with a smile. Hopefully Janice hadn't offended him with her run-on sentences and half praise. He smiled back.

Unwrapping the painting carefully, I leaned it against the bed. "What do you think?"

"Oh, Sadie! It's beautiful! You signed it, right?"

"Mm-hm."

"*Look* how it matches the comforter!"

I suppressed a sigh. This was my bread and butter, after all.

The painting was a close-up of lilies, that most vaginal of all flowers, and sweet peas (labia), and I was rather proud of it. The lesbian couple could go to town under that painting. Unlike the "swirly" or "scribbly" paintings I often did, this one had taken more work and time. Sure, it was an O'Keeffe knockoff, but it was beautiful, and not just an imitation. Oil this time, with more texture and detail than the great Georgia. Her style with a tiny bit of my own.

"It's really pretty, Sadie," Noah said, staring at the painting, his head tilted the slightest bit. "Very . . . detailed." Then his dark eyes cut to me with a slight smile, and I felt my skin prickle with a blush. There was a bed right behind me. Just sayin'.

"Okay, hang it up, and Noah? It's Noah, right? Let's get you started on the window seat. You got the pictures I sent you, right? Can you match that? Did you bring wood?"

Yes, Noah, did you bring wood? God. I was ridiculous.

I hung the painting, chatted with the movers, wandered through the brownstone. What a lucky couple! I'd always been a Manhattanite, Brooklyn being too hip for me, but damn. The building was a block off Prospect Park on a street with fully leafed-out maples. All the windows were open, and the sun shone through the stained glass window on the landing, making it appear that Noah worked in a church.

He did look like an angel. Or maybe Joseph, Jesus's dad. The carpenter dad, not the God dad. Or with that black, unruly hair, scruffy beard and olive skin, maybe Jesus himself.

"Stop looking at me," he said without looking at me.

"Need a helper?" I asked.

"Sure. Sit there and don't touch or do anything." He cut me a look, and I felt it in my stomach. He had a black elastic on his wrist and, in a practiced movement I remembered well, pulled his hair back into a short ponytail to keep it out of his eyes as he worked. A few curls escaped.

Heathcliff hair. Jon Snow hair. Darcy hair. *Damn you, Noah*, I thought. *You've only gotten better.* Watching him work, his movements sure and confident, it hit me again that my wild boy was a man. A father, and who could be a better father than Noah?

"How's your dad?" he asked, picking up on paternal vibes.

"He's doing well," I said. "He's trying to talk, and write. I mean, he held a pen the other day, but he didn't write anything. Still, he held it the right way. Mom said he said 'horse' the other day. And maybe 'dog.' He definitely responds to Pepper."

"Good. He likes Marcus, too."

"Everyone loves that baby."

No response. He ran his hand over the walnut panel, which he'd already varnished. Lucky panel. "Pass me the hollow ground planer blade."

"I heard the words, but they mean nothing to me."

A flash of a smile. "Maybe you can walk around the block a couple times, hm?"

"Are you saying I'm in the way?"

"Yes. You're in the way, Sadie." His eyes met mine. "Take a walk, Special."

Time stopped. That name. It sliced into my heart like a burning arrow.

"How's it going here?" Janice said, racing up the stairs, her arms full of pillows. "Will you be finished by three, do you think? They're having a housewarming party! To-night! It's just crazy! I have to stage the whole house, get fresh flowers and make all the beds and hang the towels and put this damn cow statue somewhere, what was I thinking when I ordered it, oh, and guess who doesn't like fake orchids? My lesbians, that's who!"

Good for the lesbians. "Can I help?" I asked. "I'm just in Noah's way, and I'm great at making beds and such."

"You're an angel, Sadie! An angel! Noah, three o'clock?"

"No problem," he said, looking back down at his work.

By three o'clock, the house was more or less in order, Noah was finished, Janice was thrilled with the window seat and now on her phone, yelling at someone. She handed us two envelopes, mouthed, *Angels!* and waved goodbye.

We walked out of the brownstone, despite the fact that I'd sort of been hoping to meet the owners and be invited to the party and end up snogging Noah on a pile of coats somewhere.

Noah opened his envelope. "Holy shit," he said. "This is twenty percent more than my estimate."

"She pays a rush fee. She's a little crazy, but she's kind of wonderful, too."

"I should work here more often."

Words I would've killed to hear once upon a time. I let it go, but the casual way he said it scraped my heart. "Well, now that she's seen your work, she may well call you again."

"Thanks for the referral, Sadie."

"Of course."

"You gonna see your boyfriend tonight?" he asked as we walked toward the truck.

"Oh. No. We broke up. He had a girl in every port, as the old saying goes. Or two ports, anyway."

Noah stopped in his tracks. "Shit."

"Yeah."

"You heartbroken?"

For someone with the kind of verbal diarrhea I had, it was oddly hard to talk about this. Because it was him. Noah, the real breaker of hearts. "A little bit. I feel pretty dumb."

"Because you didn't know?"

"Yeah." Naive, dopey, innocent Sadie.

"Because you trusted him to be honest."

"Yep."

"That's not dumb, Sadie. That's just . . . you. You believe in people."

The wind rustled the maple leaves, which were so green and fresh they glowed. "Thanks, Noah."

"You want me to beat him up for you?"

I laughed. "Nah. He's a soft yacht salesman. You're a badass carpenter. It would hardly be fair."

The corner of his mouth tugged up. "Well, then. You wanna eat? I'm starving."

"You mean here? In this horrible city you hate?"

"I don't hate Brooklyn. Brooklyn's nice."

"Jump on the bandwagon, why don't you? Sure, let's go eat some street meat. It smells incredible."

And so we got a couple gyros on Seventh Avenue and took them up to Prospect Park to eat while we sat on a bench overlooking the grassy field. When we were done, I said, "Come on, wild boy. Let me show you the botanical gardens. You think you like Brooklyn now, just wait. It's the perfect day for it."

And it was. Late April, the cherry trees so fat and fluffy with pink blossoms, a few drifting down into Noah's hair, which I left for effect. What the lad didn't know wouldn't hurt him. Thousands upon thousands of flowers were in bloom, and Canada geese strutted about, their little goslings following in quick, darting movements. The constant noise of traffic and music that defined the city was silent here, and the smell of grass and flowers combined in the perfect perfume. Ahead of us was a guide dog, a Golden retriever, and I thought of Pepper. Would she like the city? Probably not at all, given what she was used to, romping on the shores of the tidal river, going for swims in the Sound, rolling in dead seagull whenever possible. Maybe she'd transition to pigeons. The thought made me wince. The pavement in New York could get so hot that . . .

Okay, no. I wasn't going to worry about that right now. My father was getting better, and I'd be in Stoningham till the end of summer, and it wasn't even May. People had dogs in New York. Pepper would be fine.

And I was with Noah, whose hair had escaped the elastic. Women looked at him, and so did a few men—he was cooler than cool because he wasn't trying at all. Levi's and work boots that actually saw work, a worn flannel shirt over a dark green T-shirt devoid of ironic sayings or rock band names. He was authentic, and that was something rare in this part of Brooklyn, especially among men our age.

"This is so beautiful," Noah said as we walked under an archway of entwined cherry blossoms. "I can see why you love this part of the city. There's a lot more to it than cement and noise."

My heart hurt. "True," I whispered.

"I'm glad we're friends again."

"Me too, Noah. I missed you." There it was, my heart on a plate, waiting for him.

He nodded. "Same."

A man of few words. We looked at each other a long minute. "Okay," he said briskly. "What's in that glass place there?"

"A whole lotta fun, that's what," I said, a little relieved. "Off we go!"

The conservatory *was* fun, a creative array of biospheres to explore. I tucked the hurt away, not saying anything about how things could've been if only he'd been a little more open-minded back then, and just . . . relaxed.

But Noah knew me. He could practically read my mind, and I could read his. We weren't going to have a summer romance. At the end of the day, I'd be coming back here, and he had a child and a full life in Stoningham, and if we broke each other's hearts again, it would be unbearable.

For just this day, we'd be friends again, like we'd been before we ever started dating, when just being together and talking was as uncomplicated and easy and as natural as breathing. For this day, I'd pretend not to be in love with him, because there was simply nowhere to go with that without leading to hurt. I'd cut off my hand before I hurt Noah Sebastian Pelletier again.

We ended up eating dinner at a little Italian restaurant and drove home late. I fell asleep at some point and woke up as we pulled off the highway to Stoningham.

"Sorry," I said.

"No need to be sorry."

"This was a great day."

"It was."

I guess the chatty part of it had ended, though. Noah didn't say anything else as we drove through town, past the now-closed shops and restaurants. I thought about asking him to drop me off at my parents' so I could check on my dad, but it was almost eleven.

Pepper had been returned, and as soon as we pulled into my driveway, I heard her happy barking. Noah got out, too, and a warm tingle began low in my stomach, spreading to my arms and legs.

If he kissed me, if he wanted to stay, I'd be helpless to say no, given the lust factor, the love, the everything he was.

He walked me up to the porch. "How's the roof?" he asked.

"Still leaking in a hard rain."

"I'll try to come over one day this week. There's a storm due about Wednesday."

"That's okay. I'll get to it."

"Why does the image of you on a ladder make me think of ambulances? Save your mother the worry. Let me do it."

Pepper was going crazy inside, so I opened the door and let her out. She waggled at me, licking my hands, and I bent down to pet her. She repeated the action on Noah with a little leg hump attempt. Like owner, like dog. "Off you go, girl," he said, sending her down the steps with a gentle shove.

"Want . . . coffee? Or water? I have water."

"I'm good." The wind blew then, and he pushed my hair back, his fingers sliding against my scalp. I closed my eyes for just a second. Then I was in his arms, and he was hugging me . . . not kissing, but a full-on, all-enveloping hug that made me feel so good, so safe and so . . . loved. I could feel his heart slamming against my chest. He smelled like home. Felt so perfect. I hugged him back for all I was worth, feeling his solid muscle, his collarbone against my cheek.

"I better go," he whispered.

"Okay." Neither of us let go. For a second, he hugged me that much closer, and every inch of me wanted him.

Then he stepped back, took a shaky breath and said, "Okay. Bye."

And that was that. A second later, he started up his truck and backed out, and I stood there, watching him leave.

Story of my life.

~

CHAPTER TWENTY-NINE

Juliet

Juliet hated throwing parties. This was unfortunate, given that she was doing just that.

Even having her small book club over caused her a great deal of agita—what drinks should she serve? If she made cocktails, would everyone be okay to drive? Was wine boring? Should she have baked something? Why had she chosen a nonfiction book? Was popcorn an acceptable snack?

This party was ten times the size of her book club. Had she had a couple of horse tranquilizers, she would happily take them. At least she had help for this one, but the stress level was even higher, given the work week she'd had.

But it was May first, and this was their tradition, hers and Oliver's. When they first moved to Stoningham, bought the old house that had once stood here, torn it down and created this gorgeous structure of wood and glass, they'd had a housewarming party on the first of

May. It became a tradition. Cocktails served by a bartender, caterers with trays of food, fairy lights strung in the trees, the house filled with bouquets of lilacs, and the rooftop deck shaded by the retractable awning. Square cement planters burst with ornamental grasses, and every table had a centerpiece—pots of live moss and ferns, very Brooklyn, very cool. The food was all farm-to-table, and four high school girls were earning twenty-five dollars an hour to serve and clear.

Juliet knew her house was extraordinary—a slender, four-story structure of dark wood and glass. It was an upside-down house—The ground floor had a beautiful entryway, a mudroom, a family room, a game or craft room, depending on the girls' interests, and Oliver's study. The second floor held the bedrooms—four of them, three full baths, as well as a cozy reading room with couches where she and Oliver read to the girls at night, or where they now read to themselves. The third floor held the huge kitchen, dining room and Juliet's spacious office, complete with antique drafting table and a huge desk for her computer monitors.

And the fourth story was what Brianna, then age four, had dubbed the sky room. One giant room on the entire floor. The view was so vast that on a clear day, you could see the very tip of Long Island. It was a gorgeous place to watch storms, the lightning crackling from sky to ocean, or the snow blowing against the windows, making you feel as safe and charmed as the heroine in a fairy tale. The pièce de résistance was a rooftop deck with cable railings and a retractable awning, couches and lounge chairs, a small bar and outdoor kitchen, and planters bursting with whatever annuals struck Juliet's fancy that year.

It was clearly an architect's house, meant both to impress visitors and shelter and nurture the family. This party was intended to remind people that the Frost-Smitherington family was here, that they cared about the neighborhood and community. That she was a Frost of the Stoningham Frosts. Barb's daughter.

It should've been nice. It usually was, hostess nerves aside.

But this year, Juliet wasn't feeling it. She stood in the sky room, feeling awkward and alone and hoping it didn't show. Oliver was laughing with some of his work friends—one woman was standing awfully close and tossing her hair. Should she go over and make a claim, slide her arm around his waist and say, "Back off, bitch"? Was that how her father's affair had started, with someone from work? Who *was* that practically drooling on Oliver? Had Juliet ever met her? Oh, now she was laying her hand on Oliver's arm, and was he doing a damn thing about it? No.

"Juliet, what a lovely party, as always!" Saanvi Talwar, their neighbor and Juliet's almost friend, smiled as she hugged her. "Now that Genevieve is gone, you're taking over as Stoningham's most beloved hostess."

Shit, I hope not. "So glad to see you, Saanvi. How are things at the hospital?"

"Oh, God, the insurance companies are killing medicine as we know it, but we soldier on!"

"Well, I'm sure you're doing great work. Did you try the dumplings? Make sure you do. I think you'll love them."

"Let's get together sometime, just us two," Saanvi said. "We should make a monthly wine date."

"I would love that." She would. But when? Was Saanvi just being her kind self? Would it be rude to whip out her phone and force her to commit?

"Oh, there's Ellen. I haven't see her in ages! Thank you again for having us, Juliet. This house is such a show-place." Saanvi smiled and walked away, effortless in her social grace. Juliet had to fake it.

She should've become a doctor, like Saanvi and her husband. Doctors didn't get upstaged by younglings, did they? They just got better and more esteemed.

Speaking of upstart younglings, here came Arwen. She drifted gracefully over to Juliet, almost floating as heads turned. "Thank you for inviting me, Juliet. What a lovely home you have!" The European air-kiss on each cheek.

"So glad you could make it. Hello, hello!" God.

Arwen wore a long white dress and simple sandals, looking like a Greek goddess with a badass haircut. Sandals, a toe ring, and a brown leather bracelet set with a single turquoise stone. One gold ring on her index finger, just above the second knuckle. She held a glass of rosé that seemed to complement her skin tone and outfit, her graceful fingers cupping the stemless glass.

Juliet felt immediately outclassed and overdressed. The formfitting black cocktail dress was meant to show that yes, she ran six miles on the treadmill every single day. No stockings, black kitten heels that had cost a fortune but suddenly felt a bit old-school.

"Oliver!" she called. "You remember Arwen!" She waved at her husband, who finally left the hair-tossing hand-layer and ambled over, drink in hand.

"Hello, Arwen. So nice to see you again. Did you bring a friend?"

"I did. Cecille, come meet our wonderful hosts." Arwen waved to a very tall woman with a beautiful Afro. "Cecille, this is my colleague, Juliet Frost, and her husband, Oliver."

Colleague? She was Arwen's boss.

"So nice to meet you," Cecille said. "What a gorgeous view. Did you guys build this house, Mrs. Frost?"

Mrs. Frost. Gah. "Call me Juliet. And yes, we did." She described the tear-down in quick terms, glancing at Arwen's face as she did so. Unimpressed. Bored, even.

"My wife is a genius," Oliver said, putting his arm around Juliet. "Every detail was her idea." He kissed her temple. "I'm so lucky to be married to an architect. I'd be living in a shoebox if not for her. No taste whatsoever. This is all her."

Juliet smiled gratefully.

"Oh, are you an architect, too?" Cecille asked. "I thought you were . . . in administration?"

Juliet made sure not to look at Arwen and arranged her face in what she hoped was a pleasant expression. "I'm an architect, first and foremost, but I also manage projects." Arwen hadn't mentioned what she did? Who she was? She didn't say, *My boss is having a party and we have to go*? "I'm Arwen's boss," she continued. "I oversee all her work, and the work of four other architects at DJK." She smiled (hopefully) and tipped her head against Oliver's shoulder. "Please enjoy yourselves, ladies. There's a deck on the roof. That spiral staircase in the corner will take you right up, and the view is gorgeous."

They went off, hand in hand. Juliet thought she heard the words *so nineties*, but she couldn't be sure.

"They're rather nice," Oliver said.

Her head snapped around to look at him. "Nice?"

"Aren't they?"

Of course she couldn't tell him. Not here, not now. Maybe not ever. "I need a drink."

"Sure thing. What would you like? And just a word of caution, love . . ." He lowered his voice. "Try not to overdo it tonight."

"Jesus, Oliver."

"Just putting it out there. I'll get it for you. Chardonnay?"

"I'll get it myself." She loved chardonnay. She loved cosmos, too, but they were so cliché now, so middle-aged. She even liked appletinis, goddamnit. She went out onto the deck, where one of the two bars was set up. "I'll have a glass of rosé," she told the bartender, hating herself. But she didn't dare look any more outdated than she already felt.

"Sweetheart!" Her mother extricated herself from a knot of people and came over, patting her cheek. "What a triumph this is! You've outdone yourself, and I know I say that every year, but that's because every year, it's true."

Finally, a true ally. "Hi, Mommy. Hi, Caro. Did you bring Ted?"

"Ted and I are on the rocks," Caro said, grinning. "You can see I'm really broken up about it."

"Oh! Um . . . well, I'm glad you could make it."

"Wouldn't miss it!"

Riley London, Genevieve's great-granddaughter and Juliet's favorite babysitter for the girls, ran past, chasing Sloane and a little girl with wild hair. The Finlay kid, maybe? "Hi, Ms. Frost!" Riley said over her shoulder. She was with Rav Talwar, Saanvi's son. Juliet had hired her to keep an eye on some of the younger kids, a move appreciated by the guests who had youngsters. Brianna could've done it, too, but she wasn't that kind of twelve-year-old, and besides, twelve was a little young . . . or was Juliet just making excuses for her? Should she have forced Brianna into service? What if she became one of those horrible, entitled kids, or was she already? Had Juliet failed her? Should she make Brianna volunteer at more than the town arts festival? Maybe bring her to a nursing home and—

"Everything all right, darling?" Mom asked.

"Just fine. Great! How are you? Remember, you're a guest here. Don't let everyone talk your ear off. I want you to relax. Did you have something to drink? The food is great, too. Go! Enjoy."

"Mrs. Frost, could I have a second of your time?" asked a woman whose name Juliet could never remember. "It's an issue involving some water runoff in my yard, and we left a voice mail with your office last night, but we haven't heard from you."

"Probably because it's Saturday, and even the first selectman gets a day off," Juliet said, smiling to soften the words. "My mom is officially off duty."

"No, it's fine. What's going on?" Mom said, ever gracious, and Juliet wondered if anyone had any idea how much work she did.

Juliet texted Brianna—ridiculous, yes, but she had sixty people here, and didn't have the time to go up and down four flights, looking for her eldest, who was doubtlessly hiding.

Nana and Auntie Caro could use some company and a bodyguard. Would you mind hanging out with them?

Sure, came the answer.

Good. That was nice. Maybe Brianna wasn't beyond salvaging. Now Juliet would know where her daughter was and that Mom was with one of her favorite people.

A burst of laughter came from a group in the corner—Emma London, who was Riley the babysitter's mom, Jamilah Finlay, whom Juliet knew from the Stoningham Women's Association, and Beth, who worked as the manager at Harvest, where she and Oliver ate from time to time. This reminded her that they hadn't gone on a date in ages. The women were all younger than she was—more like Arwen's age. Evelyn from her book club was here, as well as Lucia and Emiko, all women Juliet knew and liked. The folks from Oliver's work.

A lot of people she knew, but not a lot who were close friends. This was the toll of having a career that took her all over the world, of trying to be there for the girls at least ninety percent of the time, of having a marriage that wasn't lying neglected in some ditch of her life.

She didn't have friends. Not really. Not like the closeness Mom and Caro had.

Juliet suddenly felt like crying.

"Hey." It was Sadie. "How's it going?"

"Shitty. I hate parties."

"You hide it very well, then. The house looks gorgeous, and everyone seems to be having a great time."

"How are you?" Juliet asked. "Is Alexander here?"

"Ah, no. We broke up."

Juliet blinked. "Oh! Are you . . . are you okay?"

"You were right. He's an asshole. Feel good about yourself? Oh, hey, person with the tray, stop right there." Sadie grabbed three shrimp wrapped in bacon and popped one in her mouth, then looked back at Juliet. "You look stressed."

"Thanks. What do I say to that?"

"I don't know! I'm your sister. I'm supposed to worry about you. Everything okay?"

"Yes. Are you, though? You and Doofus were serious, weren't you?"

"I thought so. His two other girlfriends might disagree."

Juliet's jaw dropped. "Oh, that entitled little penis scum. Shit. Did you—" She lowered her voice. "Did you get checked by a doctor?"

"Yeah. I'm fine, thank God. I also found his other girlfriends on Facebook and told them. They seemed really nice. One was really broken up."

"Let me know if you want a building to fall on him."

Sadie grinned. "You're okay, Jules, you know that?" She looked around, eating the other shrimp. "Anyone I know here other than Mom and Caro?"

"Probably not. Come on, let me introduce you to some folks." She led her sister to the younger women of Stoningham and introduced them. Sadie mentioned to Emma London that she'd almost taken an internship with her grandmother's company one summer, and before Juliet knew it, Sadie was one of the gang, laughing, asking personal questions without restraint, getting answers. No doubt she'd be having them over for margaritas before the week was done, because that's how things always worked for Sadie.

Juliet went up the (not-anywhere-near-the-nineties) staircase to the rooftop, a feature so impressive that even the late great tastemaker Genevieve London had admired it. She took a deep breath and tried to shed the anxiety building in her.

But no.

"Juliet," came a voice, and it was Dave Kingston. And shit, Edward Decker was there, too. Both partners from DJK. Edward rarely spoke, and while he nodded during her yearly review and approved her raises, Juliet never knew exactly where she stood with him.

"So glad you could make it," she lied, air-kissing them as Arwen had air-kissed her. "Are you having a nice time?"

"Very nice," Dave said. "Listen, Juliet." Her heart curled in on itself. "We're a team at DJK, as I'm sure you know."

"Of course!"

"So this . . . chain of command thing. It's not necessary, is it?"

"I'm not sure what you're talking about."

"Arwen mentioned you 'put her in her place,'" Edward said, using air quotes and looking ridiculous doing it.

Shit. If Edward spoke, it was dire. "I did what, exactly?"

"Said you made it clear you outranked her in front of her . . . partner."

"Uh . . . no. Her friend asked if I was an architect, and I . . . I just explained that I was both a project manager and—"

"It doesn't matter," Dave said. "Titles are so misleading, anyway, don't you think? We like to color outside the lines at DJK, and we're a meritocracy. The optics aren't great if you're . . . well. You know."

"No, Dave, I don't," she said, starch in her voice. "Arwen *does* work for me. I have eleven years more experience than she does, and it would be irresponsible for us not to provide her with oversight and mentorship."

"Still, there's no need to throw her under the bus," Dave said.

"How did I—"

Edward interrupted. "The attention she's brought to

the firm is in everyone's best interest, Juliet. Let's make sure she stays happy, shall we?"

The prickling panic had started in her feet. "Of course. Understood."

"Good."

Juliet glanced over at Arwen, who was pointing out something on the Sound to Cecille. *She told on you*, Juliet's brain informed her. *You spoke up for yourself, and she tattled, and the bosses are on her side.*

"Excuse me," she said. "I need to check on something. Please enjoy the party." She forced her cheek muscles to retract in what might pass for a smile. The panic was in her knees now, and breathing had become a problem.

Down the staircase into the sky room, down the next staircase, *hello, hello, are you enjoying yourself, good, wonderful, make sure you try the cream puffs, they're so delicious, you're welcome, nice to see you.* Down the next staircase, take a left, here come the tears, but it was okay, here was her bedroom, close the door, check to make sure no one was in here, and they better not be, this was her *bedroom*, into the closet, close the door, safe, safe, safe.

She was crying. *Faint*, she ordered herself. Faint. *Go to the hospital, even, and make everyone feel fucking horrible for taking Arwen's side.* Maybe Juliet had some tragic wasting disease that would excuse her from everything except sitting in the sky room and coloring with Sloane, and Brianna would love her again, and the disease would last until the girls were grown and then she could just slip away, looking at the clouds over the ocean, and wouldn't that be fan-fucking-tastic.

Or maybe she'd just quit her job, pack her suitcase and head for Montana. Dedicate her life to saving others as a smoke jumper. The girls would miss her, but they could visit. If she died, at least it would be for a good cause. Oliver would be fine without her. He'd remarry in a matter of weeks. The thought made her sob.

Maybe she needed a therapist. That would be an hour a week she just didn't have. Other than Mom, there was no one she could talk to, and Mom had enough on her plate. Sure, people accepted her invitation to the party and made small talk and hugged her, but when was the last time someone asked her how she was and really listened?

She hated entertaining. Hated it. Hated trying to be friends with people who didn't reciprocate (okay, yes, Saanvi had invited her over once, but Juliet had to go to Dubai for two nights, and other than the very occasional glass of wine in New Haven, which was always at Juliet's initiation, Saanvi never asked again, except for maybe suggesting something vague earlier). Juliet shouldn't have thrown this party. She should've spent the night sitting in the hot tub and watching a movie. Which she never did anymore, but still.

Breathe in, breathe out. Breathe in love, exhale insecurity, as her meditation app told her to do. Another thing she'd let slide.

What was *happening*? She'd followed all the rules, but here she was, in her closet, and there was nowhere else she'd rather be.

But the partners were here, and Arwen was here, and Kathy, too, somewhere, and she had to put on a strong, confident front and show them that she was one hundred percent together. She was going to have to push for partner at DJK. Until the past six months, that had been almost a given. No other architect there had as many successful projects under their belts. No one had brought in as many clients. Partnership would guarantee her income for life. No one would be able to touch her. Even if Arwen eventually got on the partnership track, that would be fine. That would be fantastic, because two women partners would mean equal representation.

If she didn't make partner, though . . .

Not a tolerable thought.

She stood up, went into the bathroom, cleaned up her makeup, put on some bright red lipstick, and changed into a flowing black jumpsuit and the fat diamond earrings Oliver had given her for their tenth anniversary.

"You are a successful, confident woman," she said, ignoring the tremor in her hands. "This is your party. Your beautiful home. Your wonderful husband. Your healthy children. You made this all happen. You belong here."

She went back to the party and pretended not to mind that Arwen was making Dave and Edward laugh uproariously, pretended not to see the woman who'd been close-talking with Oliver was at his side again, pretended not to care that Sadie was having a great time with people Juliet had met first but didn't really know. She endured. For the next four hours, she sucked it up, buttercup. That's what her life was about these days. Making it through the day until it was acceptable to go to bed.

When the party was finally, finally over and the high school girls had done their best to clean up, and Sloane and Brianna were sound asleep, Oliver poured her a glass of chardonnay (thank God, because the rosé had been utterly insipid). They sat down in the sky room, since the mosquitoes were out in force on the deck.

"Great party, hon," she lied.

"I didn't think so." His voice was uncharacteristically tight.

"What? Why?"

"Where the hell did you go? You were missing for at least a half hour! Kathy was looking for you, and I had no idea where you were. Saanvi and Vikram had to leave without saying goodbye, and I had no cash to pay Riley, and the entire time, I couldn't find you. What is going on, Juliet?"

If she were a porcupine, all her quills would be up and ready.

"I had to change," she said.

"Why?"

"I . . . spilled something on my dress."

"And it took you all that time? You're lying. Why are you *lying* to me?"

She pressed her lips together.

Oliver crossed his arms. "For months, you've been at bits and pieces, Juliet. Before your father's stroke, before Sadie came back. You're hardly here anymore even when you're sitting right in front of us. You're constantly distracted, and believe me, I've noticed. So have the girls."

Whatever had been holding her together snapped, and it felt huge and delicious and black. She jolted to her feet, sloshing her wine.

"How dare you, Oliver? How fucking *dare* you? You're damn right I'm distracted. I'm fucking terrified. I've given everything to everyone, and my everything is a lot, not to blow my own horn. But somehow, that's never enough."

He started to speak, but she cut him off. "Do you know how hard I try, Oliver? Do you? You think it's easy to have my job and work full-time and still be here for the girls and still bake those fucking gluten-free vegan cupcakes and take Brianna to lacrosse and Sloane to violin and work on Sloane's reading and make sure we have downtime and organize the meal calendar and serve on committees and have sex with you at least twice a week? I have to be at a hundred percent all the time on every front, and it's fucking hard!"

His mouth hung open. "Darling," he began.

"And you, Oliver, *you* get to be the nice parent, the perfect husband with all the women just waiting for a crack in our marriage so they can slide in, and you think I didn't notice that slut hanging all over you tonight? Who is she?"

"What? Who? No one was—"

"Oh, sure. You're so fucking clueless. Next thing you know, you'll be cheating. Just like my father." Tears were streaming down her face, and the breath was ripping in and out of her.

"Cheating? Me?"

"I'm tired, Oliver! I can't do this anymore! I can't be perfect and work and shower and pretend to like salmon so the girls will eat it. I hate salmon! I got a warning tonight to pretend I'm not Arwen's boss because it offends her, and she gives good press! My father's a lump, my sister lives in her own little world, and I'm watching my mother fade away. What am I going to do if she dies? I have no friends! Brianna hates me, Sloane's behind in school, and I'm outranked at work by someone eleven years younger than me! I feel like I'm screaming and no one can hear!"

"Darling," he said, going to her, but she didn't want him to touch her, because she felt so brittle, she was afraid she'd shatter.

She stood up, avoiding his open arms. "I'm going to my mother's for a few days. I just . . . Tell the girls she needs extra help with my father."

"Please don't," he said. "Let's talk, sweetheart. You've just said so much, I can barely process it."

"No. I never want to talk again. I hate everything I just said."

"Juliet. Sweetheart."

"I'll see you in a few days."

With that, she went back to her closet, her safe space, threw some clothes into her carry-on and left.

CHAPTER THIRTY

Sadie

Pepper and I went over to my parents' house the day after Juliet's party and found my sister crying at the kitchen table, Mom patting her hand.

"What happened?" I said. "Where's Dad?" Panic speared my heart.

"He's fine. He's watching *SpongeBob*," Mom said.

"What's wrong, Jules?"

"Nothing," she wept. Pepper tried to crawl on her lap, whining. "I'm fine."

"Okay, liar. First, I'm going to change the channel. *SpongeBob*? Is there something wrong with National Geographic? Then I'm coming back in here for the truth."

"You can't handle the truth," Mom said.

"Mom! Did you make a joke? A Tom Cruise joke? What is this weird parallel universe I'm living in? Be right back."

My father was smiling at the TV. "Hi, Dad," I said.

He looked up at me. "Say."

My heart leaped. "Yes! Sadie! That's right! Great job, Dad!" He smiled at me and looked back at the TV. I kissed his head. "Got anything else for me? Can you say 'hi'?"

Nothing. Well. That was okay. He'd almost said my name. "I'll be back in a bit," I told him. "Juliet's having a crisis, and since this has never happened before, I want a front-row seat."

He didn't respond or look at me. I left *SpongeBob* on and returned to the kitchen. "I think Dad just said my name."

"Good for you," Mom said.

My sister looked like hell, despite the fact that Pepper was now licking away her tears. "What's wrong, sis?" I asked.

"My life is falling apart."

"Oh, that." My mom cut me a look. "Sorry. Is it really, Jules? You have the world's best husband, two healthy girls, that incredible job, a house, health care, money . . ."

She started crying again, and I felt evil. But come on. First-world problems, people!

"She's overwhelmed," Mom said. "She's allowed to be overwhelmed, Sadie. Your sister has done more with her life than anyone I know."

"Point taken. You have, Jules. You're amazing and impressive and sometimes even likable."

"Sadie!" Mom snapped, but my sister snorted a little, then blew her nose.

"Here's an idea," I said. "Mom, no offense, but you look wrung out. As much as we all enjoy my role as flaky little sister, why don't you let me take over for a couple days? You two go to . . . I don't know. Go to the city. Go to Boston. I'll stay with Dad, and if your girls need anything, I can handle it if Oliver's at work."

"Sadie. The town's anniversary is less than a month away," Mom started. "I have a thousand things to do."

"I think you're allowed to have a day or two off, even if you run the universe, Mother. Especially after the winter you've had."

"She's right," Juliet said, her voice thick, tears still dripping. "You need some time to recharge."

"You're going, too, Juliet. The two of you are best friends, and don't bother denying it. I'm Dad's favorite, at least. Oh! I know. That shithead Alexander took me to this great place last year. If he was good at anything, it was self-indulgence." I pulled out my phone and typed a few words. "The Mandarin Oriental in Boston. Amazing spa." Expensive spa. "I'll treat. I just sold a big painting."

"I'll pay," Jules said.

"Let me be the rich one this time," I said, tapping away. "Okay? Okay. That's settled. Ta-da! I just booked you a room for two nights with a couple hours at the spa. You go, girls. Throw some stuff into a bag, order room service, shop, eat, go on a duck boat. Enjoy. Relax. It's an order."

They looked at each other. "I will if you will," Jules said, and Mom smiled and went upstairs to pack

A half hour later, they were gone, and I had to admit, it was kind of nice, being all bossy and in charge, like my mother.

I went into the living room. "Crisis averted, or at least delayed," I told my father. "So now it's just you and me, Dad." My doggy was creeping into the chair next to him, trying to be tiny. "And Pepper, of course."

"Dog."

"Yes! High five, Dad!" I held up my hand, but he didn't respond. "You're really getting better. I'm so proud of you. Can you say that again? Dog? Dog?"

He didn't. The words were infrequent, but they were words. That brain elasticity was coming back.

For the rest of the day, we hung out. Took a slow walk around the town green, saying hi to some people we knew, stopping in the library to breathe in the good smell. I took out a book about real-life dog rescues and brought it home, made lunch and read to him. We went out onto the patio, and I deadheaded the flowers Mom had planted and made myself useful while narrating everything I was doing. Mom didn't seem to talk much to him, and Juliet didn't either. I made up for that.

Dad didn't try any more words, and his expression didn't change much. Those little flashes were few and far between, but at least they were progress.

Jules texted me a picture of her and Mom in big white robes, both of them looking a lot happier, and I texted back hearts and make sure you get the aromatherapy facial. Yes, it would be expensive, and no, I didn't care. It felt nice to be the generous one. I didn't even mind that the two of them were bonding (yet again) without me.

When Dad started to yawn, I brought him back inside, where he settled back into his recliner and promptly fell asleep, Pepper curled at his side, pressing herself against him. It was three thirty.

I wandered through the house. I didn't have a lot of downtime when I was here, since I tried to keep moving forward with the work LeVon did, making sure we took walks now that the weather was nice, did art therapy, worked on motor skills and all that. It felt like a long time since I'd really seen the house.

Mom had done a lot of work here. Every picture, every piece of furniture and art was thoughtful and well chosen. She even had a small acrylic I'd done in college (hanging in the downstairs bathroom, since it matched the wallpaper). Pictures of the family were framed and placed at even intervals up the stairs.

It was a lovely house. Sunny and classic, homey and elegant. Not my style, but really pretty. I should tell my mother that. She'd like hearing it.

My room had been remade into the guest room before I'd even graduated from college, and that was fine, too. Still, it was a little strange . . . nothing of me remained anymore. The horse figurines I collected in middle school had been given away, the bulletin board that had been plastered with pictures of my high school friends (and Noah) gone. The room was painted pale yellow now; when it was mine, two walls had been black, two purple. Couldn't fault Mom there.

I lay back on the bed. Ah, there was something familiar. The ceiling. That fuzzy-looking paint they used to use. I'd always liked that—it looked like a snowfield, and when I was little, I'd imagine tiny people crossing it, upside-down nomads huddling down for the night, coming to sleep under my pillow if it got too cold.

One time when I was about nine, I'd been really, really sick with strep throat, the bane of my elementary school years. This time was extra fierce, though. My throat had hurt so much I had to drool into a towel, completely unable to talk, let alone swallow medicine. I was limp with dehydration, and the doctor told me to push fluids when I couldn't even swallow spit, or I'd have to get IV hydration.

Mom made me a vanilla milkshake and told me to drink it down. "It'll numb your throat, and you have to drink something, or you'll end up in the hospital." I glared at her, sulky and sick, wishing she was more sympathetic, more worried and less . . . resigned. Maybe I *should* go to the hospital. Then everyone would feel sorry for me.

"Drink, Sadie." Her voice had been firm, and she was right; the milkshake was so cold, it took the hurt away. When I had finished, she told me there were two raw eggs in there as well as my antibiotics and Motrin, masked by the taste of the extra vanilla extract she'd added. Then she tucked me in and pulled the shades, and I remembered falling asleep to the sounds of the other kids walking home from school and my mother in the kitchen.

I knew I'd never have the same relationship Juliet had with our mom. Truth was, I didn't really deserve it. I had been Daddy's girl from the start. But she'd always taken care of me just the same. She always knew what to do, even if she . . . no. She always knew what to do. Full stop. It was time for Barb Frost to get some respect from her younger child.

I called the Mandarin Oriental and ordered flowers and a bottle of champagne sent to their room. Yes, yes, it cost the earth. So what? I didn't have children. I could afford it. "And for the card," I asked the hotel clerk, "would you write, 'To the best mother and sister in the world. Relax and enjoy. You deserve it. Love, Sadie.' Thank you so much!"

The warm fuzzies I got were only slightly more fun than picturing their shock that I was so damn wonderful.

That night, after I'd made mac and cheese for Dad (it was easy for him to spear with his fork), Dad watched a documentary on the wolves of Yellowstone that made Pepper tremble with the call of the wild (or terror, but I was going with the former). I set up my easel in the little glass bump-out that abutted the living room, having made a run home for some things while Kit, the rather bitchy home health aide, was here earlier. She was efficient, but she wasn't very nice. I'd have to help Mom find someone better.

But for now, all was well. Call me sentimental, but I was drawing a picture of my dad in charcoal. I wanted to capture him in one of his alert moments, with Pepper against him. His shirt was buttoned wrong, but in my picture, I'd fixed that, as well as the tuft of hair that just wouldn't sit flat on the left side of his head, where he'd had his surgery.

Sometimes, a picture took on a life of its own, almost against the artist's will. This was such a time. I mean, sure, I knew how to draw a human. I was nothing if not technically proficient, as a wretched professor had once told me. But the Dad in my drawing looked too sad, and lonely, and nothing I did was fixing that. Every line I added just seemed to emphasize the feeling of being lost.

Sometimes, the picture told the artist the truth.

A knock came on the door, and I answered it, expecting Caro.

It was Noah. And Mickey, holding the baby. "Hey!" I said.

"Yay!" said Mickey. "We came to see your dad, but we get you, too! Bonus points!"

"Come on in," I said. Stepping aside, I glanced at Noah, feeling shy and blushy. His eyes. That hug. Curly hair. Et cetera.

"Hi, Mr. Frost," Mickey said. "Oh, hi, doggy! Look, Marcus! A doggy! Woof woof!"

"Dog," my father said.

"He's talking so much," I told them, giving Dad's shoulder a squeeze.

Mickey deposited the baby on my father's lap, and Dad held him. He smiled, even. There. Not lost or sad or lonely. My drawing was wrong.

"I hope it's okay that we're here," Noah said.

"Yes, of course. It's really nice of you." My cheeks were hot.

"Your mom is the bomb," Mickey said. "She really helped me last year when I was pregnant. My own mom died a few years ago."

"Shit, Mickey. I didn't know that. I'm so sorry."

"No worries. But it was hard. Pancreatic fucking cancer. She and Barb were friends, and we got close. Plus, Noah here has always had a soft spot for your family."

"Is this true?" I asked.

He shrugged amiably. "Sure."

Marcus was babbling cheerfully and fascinated with my dad's ear. I would need to trim some ear hair soon. Such was the life of a loving daughter. Maybe he'd like to go to the real barber in town, like he used to, every four weeks.

"You guys want something to drink?" I asked.

"I'll have a beer," Mickey said. "Half a beer. It's good for nursing mothers. Don't stink-eye me, Noah Pelletier. Split a brewski with me."

"Okay." He smiled at her, and my heart pulled a little.

They were a couple. A family. Not a romantic couple, but families came in all shapes and sizes, didn't they? The ease between them, the affection, the way they were both so natural with their son . . . it was really lovely.

I was jealous. The certainty between Mickey and Noah was not something I'd ever had. Not with Noah, because we'd been too young, of course, and later because we'd wanted different things. And not with anyone else. The past few weeks since dumping Alexander, I'd come to realize that I'd filled in a lot of his blanks with answers I'd wanted, always making the best assumptions about him, never once wondering if he was lying to me.

Stupid.

I got the beer, and one for myself, poured them in glasses, because we were civilized and all that, and went back into the living room, doling out the sad little half beers to Noah and Mickey and feeling very grown-up with my full glass. Mickey took the baby, who was starting to fuss, and clucked at him, making him utterly delighted.

"Do you want kids, Sadie?" Mickey asked.

"I see we're going straight for the deeply personal questions," Noah said, rolling his eyes.

"You don't have to answer," Mickey said. "Sorry. Too personal? Is he right?"

"No! No. Um . . . you know, maybe?" I answered, trying not to look at the man who'd once told me he wanted me to bear five children. "I love kids. I'm a teacher. An auntie. I just never was . . . I don't know. In the position of really having one."

"Squatting, you mean? Or feet in stirrups?" Mickey grinned.

"Please tell me your birthing story," I said, smiling back (and relieved not to have to dissect my thoughts on being a mother). "You know you want to."

"I do!" she said. "Because I was fucking heroic, right, Noah?"

"You were. Are. Every day."

"Spoken like a well-trained man." She hiked up her

shirt, whipped out a boob and started feeding Marcus. "Okay. So there I was, driving down the fucking highway."

"Marcus's first word is going to be 'fuck,'" Noah said.

"And suddenly I'm sitting in a puddle, and I think, shit, did I just pee myself? But no! My water broke!"

Like every woman on the face of the earth, Mickey thought her labor was the most special thing that ever happened. And, like every woman, she was right. She walked me through the details of contractions and transition, the pain, the pushing, her fear of pooping herself. I glanced at my dad, but he seemed content, his hand on Pepper's head.

"And then they put the mirror up so I can see his little furry head coming out, and I'm thinking, 'Is that even me? It looks like the surface of fucking Mars or something!' You ever see your parts stretched out like that, Sadie?"

"Sadly, no, but I can't wait after hearing this."

"So anyway, I'm half-horrified, half-fascinated, half in love with myself because my fucking body is producing a *human child*, and Noah is crying—"

"Were you?" I asked.

"Manly tears. Yes." He smiled, that fast, flashing smile that was like a bucket of lust splashed over me.

"And then the baby's head pops out, and there's this gross little spurt of blood because of the *tearing*—"

"Oh, sweet Jesus," I said, my stomach rolling.

"—but it's a baby, right? A baby!"

"As opposed to the hippo we'd been praying for," Noah said.

"And then one more push, and there he was, all gross

and slimy and fucking beautiful." Her eyes were full of tears. "Best day of my life."

"Mine, too," Noah said, and he got up, kissed her head and sat down next to her, an arm around her shoulders.

"Well," I said, "that was disgusting, but I'm glad you went through it, because I'm rather fond of this little guy."

"Here's my advice. Don't have kids if you're not dying to. They're adorable, tiny terrorists, that's what they are, holding you hostage till the day you die." She slid her little finger into the baby's mouth, and he popped off, treating me to a graphic view of Mickey's nipple. Then she passed the baby to Noah, who put him on his shoulder and patted his back.

Noah Sebastian Pelletier was so . . . perfect. My face felt soft and gooey with adoration, same as when I saw pictures of Chris Hemsworth holding his children.

"What's the prognosis on your dad?" Noah asked. "Any updates?"

"What? Oh. No updates, but he's getting a lot better. Right, Dad? He said my name today. He's a lot more attentive, too. Doing great."

"No," said my father, and we all froze.

"What's that, Daddy?" I said.

"No."

"Are you . . . Do you need something? Are you okay?" Keep it simple, LeVon had said over and over. "Dad. Are you in pain?"

"No."

"Do you need something?"

"No." His eyes, once the same seaglass blue as mine with a burst of gold around the iris, seemed faded and tired, but his gaze was steady on me.

My heart was pounding. He was trying to tell me something. Not just a word, but something important.

"Do you want us to leave, Mr. Frost?" Noah asked.

"No."

"Um . . . are you worried about something, Dad?"

His face muscles worked as he tried to get the word out. "Bahr."

"Barb? You worried about Mom?"

He didn't say no. My shoulders relaxed. "Mom and Jules are in Boston. They're having a little girl time. Here." I pulled my phone from my pocket and showed him the picture. "See? They're at a spa. Don't they look happy? But I'm here. I'll take care of you."

He sat for a minute, looking peeved. Then he got up out of his chair, struggling a bit, and Noah passed the baby to Mickey and was by his side in a flash. "Where are we headed, Mr. Frost?"

Dad walked to the stairs, listing a little.

"I guess he wants to go to bed," I said. "I'll take care of this. You guys stay put and relax. I'll be right down."

Dad was halfway up the stairs, and I ran to catch up. He went to his old room, the one he'd shared with Mom. I steered him to Juliet's old room, where he'd slept for years because his snoring kept mom awake. The bed there had rails for him to grab, and to keep him from falling out.

"You're doing great, Daddy," I said. "I'm so proud of you. I know you're trying really hard, and you're getting there." There was a sick feeling in my stomach, though, and I didn't know why.

I helped him get into his pajamas and put toothpaste on his brush. He knew how to brush his teeth. When he first had the stroke, he couldn't even breathe on his own. Of course he was getting better.

He got into bed, and I secured the railing, then bent over and kissed his forehead. "I'm here for you, Dad. I know you're in there, and I want you to know that however long it takes, I'll be here. I love you."

He closed his eyes.

Maybe he was just tired. That was probably it. Mom got him ready for bed most nights. He'd probably been trying to say he was done with visiting and wanted Mom to help him. That made the most sense.

I washed my hands in the bathroom across the hall and looked at myself for a minute. I hadn't had a haircut in a while, and the longer it got, the worse it looked. I thought of the salon I went to in the Bronx, wondered if Robert, my stylist, missed me or wondered why I hadn't been in. It seemed like a long time ago, that New York life.

When I got downstairs, Mickey and the baby were gone, and Noah was standing at my easel.

"Shit," I said. "I'm sorry they left."

"Marcus has a window of time where he needs to get to sleep or he'll be up all night," Noah said. "Is your dad okay?"

"Worn out. I mean, he spoke more today than he has since the stroke, at least on my watch. So it was a great day. I think he was just tired."

He looked at me a minute. "You're a good daughter, Sadie."

"He was a great dad. *Is* a great dad."

"And Juliet and your mom? How come they got to go to Boston and you didn't?"

I sat down on the couch and smiled. "I sent them away

like a benevolent overlord. Jules is stressed about something at work, and Mom is exhausted."

"You must be, too."

"Nah. I'm fine."

"Mickey really likes you."

"She's great, Noah. You couldn't have found a better baby mama." Whoops. He let it slide. "I mean, she's really fun. And open. Just . . . seems like a great person."

"She is."

He nodded at my drawing. "This is really . . . touching."

"Oh, that. I was just . . . goofing around."

"It's beautiful."

"Thanks. Um, do you want another beer? A whole beer, just for you?"

"I'm good. Thank you."

So. We were going to sit and look at each other and exchange pleasantries? Nah. That would be boring. "Noah, can I ask you a personal question?"

"No."

"Why didn't you—oh. Sorry."

He laughed, that low, dirty sound. "Go ahead, Sadie. You know you can't stop yourself."

I pulled a face. He was right. "Why didn't you wait to find someone to marry if you wanted kids?"

"I told you. I tried that. Twice."

"By which you mean me and Gillian?"

"Yes, Sadie. You and Gillian."

"I'm not wild about the hard 'G' on that. I like the other way better. Jillian. Much nicer."

"I'll be sure to tell her."

"So why have a baby with Mickey? You're not that old."

He looked at his glass. "I'll take that beer after all." He got up and helped himself, then came back and sat down in the easy chair. "I wanted to be a dad. Always have. Gillian and I didn't work out, and I wasn't . . . I didn't find anyone else. One day Mickey and I ran into each other at Frankie's, and we had a drink, and we started talking. She got pregnant two months later."

"And how was that? Sex with a lesbian?"

"You're incredibly rude and nosy."

"And yet you feel compelled to answer." I grinned at him, knowing he'd spill.

"Let's just say we were both thinking of someone else."

"Heidi Klum? For both of you?"

Another laugh. "Something like that."

"How many times did you—"

"Once, okay?"

"Wow. She's fertile. Lucky."

He smiled at his beer, shaking his head.

"And what about Gillian?" I said. "Why not her? I saw your . . . ah, shit, I might as well come clean. I stalked her Facebook page and saw your pictures. You looked really happy, Noah."

"Yeah. We were happy for a while." I waited. He didn't say any more.

"Did she cheat on you?" I asked, wanting to kick her if the answer was yes. How could you cheat on Noah? Noah! Was it because he was a blue-collar guy and she was—

"No, no. Nothing like that. She . . . she's got a lot of really great qualities."

"You're making her sound like a monster."

His mouth pulled up. "She's not. She was a little crazy with the wedding planning, but it goes with the territory, right? That was fine. Things were . . . nice. We'd even put an offer on a house."

"Wow." I already knew this, thanks to her Facebook posts, but hearing it from Noah, the news had more of a resonance. That would have been huge for him, buying a house with someone.

"Yeah. So we . . . disagreed on decorating." He looked at his beer.

"Ah, yes, I can see how that would split you right down the middle. 'Blue? I hate blue! It's over!'" He smiled a little. "So what really happened, Noah?"

He was staring into that beer real hard. "She wanted me to get rid of something that meant a lot to me."

"Was it your hair? She was Delilah to your Sampson?"

"No, not my hair, idiot."

"Your first tooth? The family Bible? What?"

He didn't answer for a beat or two. Kept staring into that beer. "A painting some girl gave me a long time ago."

He looked up then, and I felt the full force of his dark eyes like a rogue wave, knocking my heart over with its power.

"You broke up over a painting?"

"More or less."

"My painting? The clouds? You kept that?"

"Of course I kept it."

I couldn't believe it. If it had been me, I would've burned anything related to me after I'd turned down his marriage proposal. Proposals, plural. "That goofy sunrise painting?"

"Don't sound so surprised. And don't call my painting goofy." His voice was low, and there was a . . . a light in his eyes, and that half grin of his was . . . affecting me. Do not underestimate the power of a crooked smile, ladies and gentlemen.

He and Gillian broke up because he wouldn't get rid of my painting.

Man, oh man alive.

"You . . . you . . . you wanna make out?" I croaked.

Such eloquence. It did the trick, though. Noah stood up, which was good, because my knees were already useless and weak and tingling. He came across the room and slowly, so slowly, knelt in front of me, held my face in his big, warm, manly hands and kissed me.

It had been so long.

Our kissing was slow and hot, and yet I was desperate for him. I'd missed him so much, my wild boy. One of my hands clenched in his hair, and the other was against his neck, feeling the fast, hard thud of his pulse. He tasted so good, felt so good, so right, it was like coming home. I couldn't think of anything except him, his mouth, his hands. Us. The two of us.

When he stopped kissing me, he wiped under my eyes with his thumbs, because I guess I was crying a little. "Oh, Special," he said, "you'll be the end of me."

Then we were kissing again. I slid to the floor, my bones useless, and we tangled into each other as if no time had ever passed and also like we'd never so much as touched. Every brush of his fingers, every time he kissed my lips, my neck, my hand, jolts of liquid electricity surged and hummed in my veins. I wrapped my arms around his neck and held him so tight, and it still wasn't close enough.

When his hand worked its way under my shirt, I managed to remember—with great difficulty—that my father was upstairs and prone to wandering the house at night. "My dad," I whispered.

"Got it. Just like old times," Noah murmured against my mouth, and I felt him smiling.

Old and new. He felt different now, bigger, stronger, heavier, but he was Noah, *my* Noah, and let's be honest. He'd had my heart since before I knew what love was.

~

CHAPTER THIRTY-ONE

Barb

You could've knocked me over with a feather when Sadie took charge like that. I'll admit I had no idea she could afford to pay for a weekend at this real nice hotel, no sir.

Gosh, I couldn't remember when I'd felt so relaxed. I'd have to tell Caro all about this, and we could come here the two of us sometime. But for now, it was so special, being here with my sweet little girl. Of course, she was forty-three. I knew that. When she turned up at my door Saturday night, crying, it had felt like she was little again. I made her a hot toddy, listened as she talked tangles about work and Oliver and Brianna, then tucked her into bed. Being Juliet's mother was the one place where I always knew what I was doing.

Being sent to this fancy-pants hotel with Sadie all cheerful and efficient . . . that was just extra.

Juliet and I had been scrubbed and massaged and had breathed in all sorts of lovely aromatherapy mists and whatnot. The sauna, the Jacuzzi, the steam room, a bowl of fruit, and glasses of delicious cucumber water. I felt warm and smooth and smelled like oranges.

Then we got back to the room, and there were flowers and champagne from Sadie!

It was a real nice surprise, don't you know. Real nice.

"Sadie is my absolute favorite sister," Juliet said, then giggled. My favorite sound in the world was my girls laughing, and boy, Juliet needed it.

"She's my favorite second child," I said, and we laughed together. "I hope she won't have to sell her apartment to afford this."

"Oh, I'll pay her back."

"No, you won't, Juliet Elizabeth. You let your sister do this nice thing for you. Don't take that away from her."

"You're right, Mom. As usual."

We were both wearing fluffy white robes and comfy slippers, sitting under the covers in the enormous king-size bed. That champagne went down nicely.

"So what's going on, honey?" I asked, turning to look at her. "You weren't making a whole lot of sense last night."

"I don't know, Mom. That's the problem. I have no idea. It's like all the rules have changed, and no one told me. I was playing one game, and I was winning, and now I'm not."

"Do you mean work?"

"Yes. There's this associate named Arwen—you met her at the party, and that time you came to the office last fall?" I nodded. "She's . . . there's absolutely nothing wrong with her. She's a good architect. She's good with people. She's ambitious and smart. But you'd think she was the first woman architect ever. *Vanity Fair* is doing a profile on her. She's up for the Moira Gemmill Prize, Mom!"

I gathered that was something real prestigious, and made a sympathetic noise.

"And I just don't see it," Juliet went on. "She's good. She's not great, but the partners *love* her, and clients are asking for her by name, and that leaves me pedaling in the air." She sighed and finished her champagne.

"That sounds awfully hard," I said.

"I'm a little bit afraid that my career is coming to an end. Maybe a lot afraid."

"Oh, honey. Don't be silly." She cut me a look. "'In the past decade, Juliet Frost has designed some of the most impressive buildings in North America.' You know who said that? The *New York Times*, that's who."

"Oh, yeah. They did, didn't they?"

"Four years ago."

"See, that's the thing. Four years ago. Today, I'm old news. It's not Arwen so much, Mom. It's that feeling that I did everything right, and I got screwed anyway."

I was quiet for a moment, then took her hand. "I know that feeling, hon. I'm sorry. All you can do is the right thing. You're talented and hardworking and ethical. No one can take that away from you."

Her eyes filled. "Thanks, Mama. I was afraid you'd be disappointed in me."

"That will never happen, Juliet. You're my pride and joy, and you know it."

She hugged me a long, long time, and I petted her silky

hair while she cried. Oh, it felt so wonderful to be needed by my little girl, even if she was a mother herself. There was nothing like it, this moment, the two of us.

I said a silent thanks to Sadie, then added a quick apology.

Juliet took a deep, shuddering breath, the sign that she was done crying. She got up, blew her nose, and then poured us more champagne. "Did I mention I love Sadie? To Sadie."

"To Sadie," I echoed. "I should check in."

"No, Mom, not yet. You said you knew that feeling of doing everything right and getting the short end of the stick. Is that . . . is that at work?"

I took a deep breath. "No. Not there. I love my job. I guess I meant, well . . . being married. I love your dad, of course"—that wasn't exactly the truth—"but we drifted apart. You know that."

"Yeah. I do." Her voice was odd, and I glanced at her, but she was staring straight ahead.

"We just didn't have a lot to say to each other, even before his stroke. I felt like I tried, but I could never seem to do the right things. I didn't know what they were."

Juliet burst into fresh tears. "Mom," she sobbed, "I'm so sorry to have to tell you this, but you can't blame yourself. Dad . . . Dad was having an affair."

"Oh, yeah, I know, honey."

That stopped her. "What?"

"I do know that."

"When?"

"I found out when he was in the hospital."

"Holy shit, Mom."

"Watch your mouth, honey. But yes. Holy shit." I snort-laughed, and she did, too. "How did *you* know, sweet-heart?"

"I saw him with another woman in New Haven this past fall. They were making out on the sidewalk outside the restaurant where I was having lunch. It was disgusting."

"You've known longer than I have, then. Oh, honey. I'm so sorry."

She started to cry again. "I should've told you, but it was just a couple weeks before Thanksgiving, and then Christmas, and then your fiftieth . . . I'm so sorry, Mom. I wanted to, and I dreaded it, too."

"No, no, honey. Your father is the one who did some-thing wrong. Not you. You were between a rock and a hard place, that's all. Don't cry, sweetheart."

My words made her cry even harder. "You know what I wish? I wish Dad had died. That makes me a horrible daughter, but then you'd be free, Mom. I know he's been a pretty good dad and all that, but he ignored you for so long." She grabbed a tissue and blew her nose. "You de-serve someone better."

"That might be the nicest thing anyone's ever said to me," I said. "You know, I always felt like people looked at us and thought the opposite. Like *he* could've done better. I'm just a girl from Nowhere, Minnesota, who took some legal secretary courses. He married down. He's a Frost from Stoningham."

Juliet huffed, then blew her nose again. "No, Mom. *You* built this family. You made our home. We're the Frosts of Stoningham because of *you*. It's not his last name; it's ev-erything you've done for the past forty-plus years. You think people don't know that? Of course they do."

I guessed it was my turn to get all teary-eyed. "Thank

you, honey." I toyed with the ends of my bathrobe sash. "Are you worried about anything in your marriage, honey?"

She closed her eyes. "No. Yes. I mean, part of me thinks if Dad could cheat on you, then Oliver could cheat on me." Her lips trembled a little, just as they had when she was little. "Ollie's so wonderful, Mommy. He's kind of perfect, and I have this stupid fear that he's going to wake up and think, 'Oh, my God, I could do so much better than her.'"

"There is no one better than you, Juliet," I said firmly. "Trust me. That man adores you. He lights up when you come into a room, and I can tell you, your dad sure never did that with me. Well. Not after the first couple of years, anyway. Oliver's different."

She swallowed. "You think so?"

"No. I know it. Plus, I'd stab him in the soft parts if he so much as looked at another woman. But he won't. You two are the real deal."

She put her head back on my shoulder. "You're the best mother ever."

"Mm. Tell that to Sadie."

"I do. And she doesn't have to be me, Mom. All the love you gave her isn't wasted. It just doesn't show up the same way."

"You're a wise woman, honeybun." I stroked her silky hair and kissed her head. "Don't tell her about your dad, okay? It would break her heart."

"I won't," said Juliet. "She's been great this whole time. And look at her, sending us off, taking charge. She sent us flowers, even!"

"And we smell so good, too. I might never shower again."

We started laughing, and then we couldn't stop, that wonderful, unstoppable laughter that made me run for the gorgeous bathroom, which made us both laugh harder.

Maybe it was the champagne. But I didn't think so. I think it was relief, and a little exhaustion, and most of all, love.

CHAPTER THIRTY-TWO

Juliet

Sadie knew a thing or two. The two nights in Boston had been heaven.

Juliet hadn't cried so much . . . well, ever. But they were the good kind of tears, the kind that washed away the dirt from your soul. Mom was magical. She could make every situation better just by her pragmatism, her dry sense of humor, her conviction. If the woman Juliet most admired in the world thought Juliet was the bomb, who was Juliet to disagree?

Even so, she felt nervous when she got home. Oliver could well be furious with her. When she texted to say she was going away for a couple of nights with her mom, his response had been, "Have fun."

That was it.

He was home when she got back . . . His car was in the garage, at least. Sloane swarmed her at the door, full of questions, wondering what presents she was about to receive. Juliet gathered her up and smooched her cheeks before doling out the gifts—a fake Boston Police Department badge, since Sloane wanted to be a cop, and a T-shirt that said *Chowdahead*. For Brianna, she'd bought a replica of the statue that showed Mrs. Mallard leading her ducklings through Boston Common.

"I loved this book when I was little," Brianna said.

"I know."

Brianna looked at her. "I'm not little anymore. Here, Sloane. You can have it."

"Yay!" Sloane said.

"I got you a T-shirt, too," Juliet said, holding it up. *Wicked Smaaht*.

"Thanks anyway."

Okeydokey, then. "Where's Daddy?"

"Daddy!" Sloane bellowed. "Mommy's back! She brought presents!"

He came up the stairs. "Hello, darling."

"Hi."

"Did you have a good time?"

"Yes. Definitely."

"Brilliant." His voice was tight. "Girls, would you mind going to your rooms?"

"Are you fighting?" Brianna asked.

"Not at all," Oliver said. But his eyes were not happy. "Darling, shall we go up to the deck?"

"Sure!" Too enthusiastic. Shit.

It was a gorgeous day, full-on May glory, the lilacs blooming below, their scent heavy in the air, the wind gentle off the water. She still felt like throwing up.

"Right. Well. You said some things the other night," Oliver began.

"Listen, I—"

"No, no. My turn. It's only fair, isn't it?"

She nodded. Sat down on the sofa and tried not to cry. Oliver took out a piece of paper.

"Do you want to sit down?" she asked.

"No. Please. Just let me read this." He cleared his throat. "Dear Juliet, you told me you were tired of trying to be perfect and that you were afraid I would cheat on you if you were anything less than one hundred percent. Please allow me to share the following with you." He glanced at her, frowning, and her toes curled in her shoes.

"The first time I saw you at Yale, you were standing in the rain at the corner of York and Elm, and I stopped in my tracks because I knew the world had just changed. Then, rather unfortunately, a cabbie blew past you, soaking you, and I felt it would be ungentlemanly to approach you."

Oh, God. She remembered that. She'd been drenched to the skin with filthy gray water, and the driver hadn't so much as tapped his brakes.

"The second time I saw you, you were buying tampons at the CVS just off the green, and again, the time didn't seem right to engage in witty conversation with you, because, knowing me, I'd have said something less than clever, such as 'Oh! I see you're menstruating! How wonderful!' and you rightly would've dismissed me as a wanker."

She felt a smile start in her heart.

"The third time I saw you, you were going into a party in Saybrook, and I begged my former flat mate to get me in so I could be in the same room as you, and when I saw you, my heart was pounding so hard, I thought I might vomit, and I was terrified you'd turn away and talk to your extremely good-looking and fit boyfriend, who would no doubt go on to become president of the United States or cure cancer. But you didn't turn away, and you didn't have a boyfriend, and you graciously said yes when I asked you out after forty-five agonizing minutes of mindless chatter, the subject of which I still have no recollection."

His eyes were tearing up. "You are the most beautiful woman I've ever seen, never more so than after you had our daughters, or when you're folding laundry, or in the car, or at your desk. You never have to eat salmon again. I will henceforth take on all the baking of the fucking gluten-free vegan cupcakes, and I can assure you that our firstborn doesn't hate you at all, she is merely blinded by the horrors of adolescence and will once again become your darling girl."

He folded the paper and put it in his back pocket. "I love you. It's pathetic, really. I worship you. You at twenty percent is more than every other woman in the world at one hundred, and you at one hundred is nothing short of a magnificent tornado, but if you need help, darling, please, ask for it. That's my job. To take care of you."

She was crying again, but the tears felt wonderful this time. "Why haven't you told me this before? I always . . . I never . . . I never knew you watched me buy tampons."

"Darling, I'm British. Free expression of emotion is forbidden by the Crown." He looked down. "I just assumed you knew."

"I love you."

"Thank God, because I'm nothing without you, Juliet Frost."

They were in each other's arms then, holding on tight, kissing with relief and love and blessed familiarity. His darling bald spot and strong arms, the smell of his soap, how they were the perfect height for each other.

"They're kissing," came Sloane's voice.

"Gross," said Brianna, and Juliet smiled against her husband's mouth.

What a joy, what a blessing to know that after all this time, love could grow and flourish like the lilacs below, growing stronger and intertwining, becoming more beautiful with each passing year.

The next day, almost purring from the lack of sleep and an abundance of sex, Juliet went into DJK and buckled down to work. A phone conference with a client, design tweaks on the senator's house, a long meeting with Brett on an airport addition. Nothing bothered her. Work was finally as it used to be.

To her surprise, Arwen stopped in her office around five. "Would you like to have a drink after work?" she said.

"Oh! Sure. Where did you have in mind?"

"Barcelona at six?"

"Sounds good."

And so, at six on the dot, she opened the heavy wooden door of the restaurant and went in. Arwen was already there at a high top. "Just a Perrier for me," Juliet said to the server.

"Same," Arwen said. "And privacy, please." She smiled at the server to soften the words. "How was your time off, Juliet?"

One day off. One day. "Lovely," Juliet said. "My mom and I went to Boston."

"Fun."

"Are you close with your mother?"

"Sure. Of course." She offered no further details, and Juliet realized she really didn't know Arwen at all.

The server brought their water and slipped away. "What's up?" Juliet asked.

"I'll get right to it. I'm leaving DJK and starting my own firm."

"My goodness." That was fast. Not entirely unexpected, and not terribly unwelcome news. "Are you sure you're ready?"

"Positive. It'll be called Arwen Alexander Architecture."

"Triple A."

"Exactly. I've already had a logo designed."

Juliet opted not to point out the car association. "Why are you telling me this?"

"I want you to be part of it."

Okay, now that was surprising. "That's very flattering. Thank you."

"You know I've gotten a lot of attention recently, and it'd be foolish not to seize on it and make a move now."

Smart woman. "There will be the usual noncompete issues, of course."

"Of course. I'm not worried. Are you interested?"

"What's the offer? I assume I'd be a partner."

Arwen sipped her water, maintaining steady eye contact, then set her glass down. "Actually, no. I'd like you to come on as senior associate."

The *nerve*. Eleven years her junior, and she wanted Juliet to be subordinate. "Who are the partners, then?"

"Just myself and Kathy."

Kathy? That was . . . wow. Kathy. "Well, good luck." DJK would go back to the way it was. No more It Girl, no more fawning over the shiny new thing. Good.

"Juliet," Arwen said, "please think about it. You're very reliable, you multitask well, and you're . . . well, steady."

"Gosh golly. Thank you so much, Arwen."

Arwen twisted her straw into a knot. "DJK just offered me a partnership. So you might be thinking it'll be nice not to have me around, but you'll still know that I leap-frogged over you. If—*if* they offer you a partnership—and I think it's odd they haven't yet—you'll have to live with the fact that you're their second choice. After you put in more than fifteen years with them, they offered it to me."

Well, shit. She was right. Juliet straightened her cocktail napkin. "Can I share something with you, Arwen?"

"Of course."

"I was you. Ten years ago, I was pretty much exactly where you are."

"Were you, though?"

"No, you're right. You've gotten much more attention than I ever did. But I got my fair share. I also listened to architects who were better than I was. I put in the work and the time, and I became a better architect, because I knew I had to, and I wanted to."

"So is this the 'I paved the way for you' speech?"

"No. It's me telling you you're not as good as you think you are. But you *could* be great. Someday. And you *won't* be great if you believe all the buzz around you. If your name had been Lorna Kapinski and you weren't quite so photogenic, I doubt you'd be getting all this attention. I, on the other hand, picked you for your potential as an architect. Nothing more, nothing less."

"I'm taking this as a no," Arwen said. "Thank you for your time, Juliet."

"Thank you for your offer."

With that, Juliet slid off the stool, pushed her hair behind her ears, and grabbed her bag. "Good luck, Arwen."

Arwen wasn't at work the next day, and her office was empty. Kathy, too, was gone, not so much as an e-mail of goodbye after all this time. That hurt, since Juliet thought they'd been friends. But Barb Frost hadn't raised any fools. Juliet had always been wary of Kathy.

Meanwhile, the rumor mill was churning out stories, and Edward and Dave were in a huddle in Edward's office. Juliet closed her door and did her work.

It was no surprise when Dave and Edward called her into the conference room at five.

"Juliet!" Dave said as if he hadn't seen her seventeen times today. "You look amazing! That week off did you some good, did it?"

"One day, Dave. One day off. And yes, it did."

Edward was staring at his iPad. "Let's get to it, shall we? We'd like to make you a partner, Juliet. Your excellent contributions here have not gone unnoticed or unappreciated."

"So true! We're a meritocracy, and you have merit, all right," Dave chuckled.

She listened as the men wooed her with phrases like *percentage of profits*, *principal ownership*, *staff management*, *increased vacation time*. When they were done, she folded her hands neatly in front of her.

"Arwen turned you down, I take it?"

The men exchanged glances. "Uh . . . well, she's decided to pursue other opportunities," Dave said.

"I know. She asked me to join her firm." They flinched in unison.

"Well, we know you're a team player, Juliet," Dave said. "Loyal. We gave you your start, after all."

"When I got my license, I had offers from nine firms, Dave," she said.

"But you came here, and I think we've treated you very well."

She could do it. Sure, they offered Arwen the spot first, but business was business, and Juliet wouldn't take it personally.

It was the recent memory of the two of them lecturing her in her own home just a few days ago that did them in.

"No thanks," she said. "I hereby tender my resignation. All the best to you, gentlemen."

She called Oliver from the car, and he congratulated her and said they'd talk more when she got home, but he was very proud.

Her righteous badassery lasted the entire drive home and up to dinner (which was not salmon, but a delicious roast chicken. Juliet's favorite. Oliver had served it with a flourish and a kiss).

"I quit my job today," she announced as the girls bickered. That did silence them.

"Hear, hear, darling," Oliver said, toasting her.

"Seriously?" Brianna said. "You *quit*? That's just great. Are we still going to Hawaii this summer? Has it occurred to you that you make more than Dad and maybe quitting isn't a great idea?"

The little . . . brat. "You know what, Brianna? Maybe we'll go to Hawaii, and maybe not. Maybe, if you don't lose the attitude, we three will go and you can stay with Nana and help with Grampy, because you're not . . . how should I put this? You're not bringing much to the table these days. I mean, we love you, but you're a real pain in the ass lately, and I'm not sure you deserve a vacation at all."

Brianna's mouth dropped open.

"Sorry, sweetheart," Oliver said, putting his hand over Juliet's. "But Mum's got a point."

"Am *I* a pain in the ass?" Sloane asked.

"Not yet, honey, and hopefully not ever," Juliet said.

"Brianna, you need to try harder. Okay? Great. Also, I'll be taking your phone for the rest of the school year. I don't think it's good for you, being attached to it as much as you are."

If looks could kill . . . There was no love in that glare, that was for sure.

Shit. The panic attack was coming. She'd quit her *job*. She'd turned down frickin' *partner* and was currently unemployed for the first time in her *life* and her daughter hated her and they might *not* go to Hawaii, and she had really, really been looking forward to it, and—"Excuse me."

Down the stairs, down the hall, into the closet. *Breathebreathebreathe*, nope not working. She lay down, legs weak, and wished she'd thought to bring a paper bag. Her vision grayed, but this time she didn't want to faint. She just wanted . . . she just wanted nothing.

The truth was, she had everything.

She'd find a job. She could start her own firm. She'd be fine. Oliver made a decent enough living. They could switch their health care to his work, even if it was a worse plan, and . . .

"Mommy?" Brianna sounded like a little girl again, scared from a bad dream. Shit. Had she done that?

"Yes, honey?" Juliet said, sitting up.

"Are you really that mad at me?"

"No! No. Just tired of the . . . bitchiness."

"You still like me, though, right?"

"Of course!" A lie, but really. Parenthood was ninety percent forgiveness, ten percent lies and a hundred percent love.

"Why are you in the closet?"

"Oh, I guess I'm . . . hiding from life. Sometimes I feel scared about things."

"Like what?"

"Like, am I a good mother? Have I been helpful and kind today? Will everyone I love be okay? Can I be doing more?"

"That's a lot." Brianna sat down next to her and picked up one of Juliet's shoes, fiddling with the strap.

"It is."

"Is being a grown-up hard?"

"Sometimes."

Brianna started to cry, her sweet little face crumpling. "I don't want to grow up, Mom. I hate all this, the periods and zits and boobs and boys and the drama. I want to be eight again. Eight was really fun." Her voice squeaked on the last word, and Juliet gathered her up against her, every molecule in her body wanting to wrap around her child and protect her from every hurt, every bad feeling.

"I understand, honey. I do. I remember how hard it is." She kissed Brianna's hair. "But you know what? You're going to like your body pretty soon. It's so weird, but you will. This is the hardest time. You'll get through it. Daddy and I are with you every step of the way."

"Is there *anything* good about being a grown-up?"

Juliet laughed. "Sure. You can pick someone really great, like your dad, to be your best friend, and you get to live with each other. You can find a job that you love doing."

"I don't know what I want to do. I hate when grown-ups ask me that."

"You're not supposed to know. Tell them that. Say, 'Hey, I'm twelve. Give me some room here.'"

Brianna laughed a little.

"You know what the best part of being a grown-up is?" Juliet asked.

"No."

"You get to be a mommy if you want."

"I thought I was a pain in the ass," Brianna muttered.

"You are. But you're *my* pain in the ass. I wouldn't trade you for anything."

Brianna didn't answer, didn't hug her any tighter, didn't say, *I love you so much*, or *You always make me feel better*, as Juliet would have said to her own mom.

Brianna didn't have to. Juliet already knew.

A few hours later, when the girls were in bed, and Oliver was "thoroughly shagged" and sound asleep, Juliet went to her computer and typed an e-mail.

To: arwenalexander@gmail.com
Subject: job offer
    The firm's name will be Frost/Alexander. I'll get 33% ownership, the tie-breaking vote if one is needed, head of design. Take it or leave it.
    Juliet

A few minutes later, the one-word answer came.

Done.

CHAPTER THIRTY-THREE

~

John

Dog. *Daw.* Baby. *Bay . . . bee.* Barb. *Baahr.* Juliet. *Zhool.* Sadie. *Say.* Tired. *Tahr.*

No. *No.* He has this one down.

These are the words he can say now, though the effort makes him feel foolish and old. Most times, words come out of his mouth wrong, sounding huge and shapeless, or like other words. He can look at a tree and think *tree*, but the word that comes out is *roo,* which means *root.* Sometimes he's understood, most times he's not. His mouth muscles are tired, and the bossy lady doesn't care.

Sadie does, though. She can understand his connections. Not always, but sometimes.

He wants to say, *I'm sorry, Barb.* Because she knows about the hard-faced woman who has never been to see him. He knows this. Barb told him, and Barb doesn't lie. He wants to talk about the flower, but he can't, and he doesn't remember why it's so important, but it is, and he tries to pull it close.

Ted still comes to visit, and John is glad. Noah comes, too, sometimes to fix something for Barb, and sometimes to let him see the baby, who is solid and warm and harder to hold now because he is growing. His daughters come. Juliet doesn't look at him much, which is better than Sadie with the hope in her eyes. John doesn't know which is harder to see, the mad or the hope.

Janet comes, too. She knows about the flower. Sometimes she brings him flowers that she grows. She works in a place that grows plants or babies, but the word is long and hard for his mind to remember. She talks and talks, gentle words falling around him like warm rain.

He loves her. Not the way he loved Barb, or the hard-faced woman, but in a new way. She is the only one who wants nothing from him. She has no hope or sadness or disappointment or . . . what is the word? Tired. She has no tired on her face.

He is not getting better. John understands this. The words he says are so hard and the trying is so heavy that he won't be able to do more. He wants to stop trying. The way he talked long ago, the way other people have the words tumble out of their mouths is not for him anymore. The doctor says words, and Sadie with hope in her eyes . . . no. He can feel it. He knows. He isn't trapped inside his body. This *is* himself. He will be this way always. His now-self, not his old self.

With Janet, his now-self is fine.

What he has to do is make his wife understand. He has to be the husband again, just for a little while. The father.

Images flutter from the long-ago. John would come

home from the place where he did the work. The office. He would drive the car into the driveway and go into the house. Sadie was little in the long-ago, and Juliet was bigger, and Sadie would run to him, and he would pick her up and smile, and Juliet would wait in the kitchen doorway, and he would remember to give her a hug, too.

Then he would kiss Barb on the cheek, not really listening as she talked, but smelling the good smells of the kitchen, feeling like a husband, a father. A man.

He needs to get to that place again, to be that man. It is like crawling through a snowstorm, up a mountain in a snowstorm on the darkest night. But he will get there. He will find the flower. He will be husband and father again for a moment, and then he can go back to being the now-self, who listens to the birds and the little baby and the warm rain voice, the now-self who likes to have the dog close to him, who can go to sleep whenever he wants.

~

CHAPTER THIRTY-FOUR

Sadie

The storm was full of bluster and drenching rain, a nice old-fashioned nor'easter, raging all day long. My little house sang and shook in the wind, creaking and groaning, sounds I decided to like, rather than worry that the roof was going to blow off. The rain slapped against the windows in sheets, and I couldn't have been cozier. I'd ventured into my attic the day before and nailed up some tarp until I could really fix the roof, and so far, I only needed one bucket for the leaks. The sound of the dripping was strangely companionable. Pepper was asleep on the couch, curled into her little cinnamon bun position, snoring gently.

Me, I was painting. Painting something because I wanted to, not because it matched a comforter or a couch.

Without a lot of forethought, I'd gotten out my paints, set up my easel, taken a canvas, prepped it and, before I could talk myself out of it, squeezed out the delicious, shiny blobs of oil paint onto my palette—cadmium red, cerulean blue, burnt umber, titanium white, Naples yellow, magenta, black—and put paint on canvas as fast as I could.

The sky.

I was painting the sky, lost in the smell of the oil paint, the bite of turpentine, the swirl of colors, the gentle, wet whisper of the brush against the canvas. The sun, the clouds, the sea.

A sunset, the most painted scene in the world, and I didn't care. I was lost in colors—and the infinite possibilities of mixing shades that created turquoise, lavender, purple, rose. Pushing the paint, dragging it, twisting it, dabbing, brushing, watching in an almost out-of-body experience as the sky began to form.

This wasn't a couch painting. This was an impulse. Instinct. For weeks, I'd been wanting to paint the sky, and I'd found all sorts of reasons not to start.

Today was different. Now that I'd started, I couldn't stop. Lightening the red here, bringing up the blue, adding more black and purple to the water and the clouds. Time was marked by the dripping in the bucket and the shifting gray afternoon light, and that was all.

I had nowhere to go. A branch had fallen just behind the car this morning (thank God it hadn't fallen *on* the car, since it was Juliet's). It was big enough that I couldn't drag it out of the way; I'd need a chainsaw to cut it and move it. I'd called Mom and Juliet and let them know I was stuck for the day, and an hour later, the storm knocked out the power. I had a battery lantern on in the kitchen, and the gray, watery light poured through the new windows Noah had put in.

So I was stuck, and I could do nothing outside, and I had

to release some of the energy and electricity that had been building since my marathon make-out session with Noah.

Somewhere around one a.m. that night, he'd said, "I better go," and we disentangled from each other. I was barely able to stand, so turned on I felt like I could float, but also like my legs wouldn't hold me. Noah was in no better shape.

"Time for a swim in the Sound," he said. "Hope the water's cold enough."

"I wish I could come with you," I said, and we were kissing again. It took him fifteen minutes to get from the living room to the door, because we just couldn't stop kissing, touching, winding ourselves around each other, our hands stopping to admire, caress, feel.

Finally, he caught both my hands in his and kissed them. Then he just looked at me, his hair tangled and wild, his eyes so dark and happy, and he smiled, and finally left the house, leaving me to collapse on the couch in a pile of raging pheromones.

Joy. That's what it was. It was joy. Whatever our future was, it was best to stay right here, right now, and let the joy fill me and lift me, because Noah and I were something. I didn't know what, but we were something to each other, and something important.

For now, that was enough. I didn't let myself think past that.

And it clearly had an effect on my mood. My house was immaculate, Pepper and I had gone for a five-mile run last night, knowing the storm would keep us inside. I sanded the butcher-block island I'd bought on Etsy, oiled it and then made spaghetti sauce from scratch.

Today, when the branch fell and the power went out, I busted out the paints.

It was time. All that joy, that floating, buoyant emotion, needed to come out on a canvas.

God, I'd missed this. It felt so good to see the painting bloom as my brush danced and bustled. All these weeks I'd been in this house staring west in the evenings, watching the sunset, the moon rise, the rain blow the reeds of the salt marsh. For the first time in years, painting once again felt like my destiny. For the first time since I could remember, I felt like myself again.

The painting was nearly finished—half of art was knowing when to stop—when Pepper jumped up and started to tremble and whine, pressing her nose against the front window. She did this when a fox or coyote was in the area, or a deer, or a mouse, or a worm. Often, I couldn't see what she saw, but I always took a look, because who wanted to miss out on seeing a little red fox, right?

I set my palette down, rested the brush on the easel lip and went to see.

Nothing. "Is one of your friends out there?" I asked. She started moaning, trembling violently now. I took my phone in case it was something cute and I could snap a picture for Carter, who loved hearing about wildlife, New Yorker that he was.

"Okay. Let's get your leash on, Pepper Puppy," I said, and she wagged gratefully, still pressing her nose against the glass. I got my slicker and her shoulder harness, since she was a puller.

The wind battered us the second we stepped out the door, but Pepper leaped and tugged me down toward the river. The tide was going out, so the river was getting more and more shallow, and the rain-soaked, salty mud made walking hard.

"Easy, girl, easy!" I said. The rain had already soaked my face and the front of my jeans, but my good old L.L.Bean boots kept my feet dry. A gust of wind made me stagger back a couple of steps, my foot nearly coming out of the boot, but Pepper was on fire to get to the water.

"Pepper!" I yelled. "Stay with me!"

Then I saw what she'd seen.

It was a beached dolphin. And it was alive! Holy crap. The storm must've pushed it up here, and it didn't have enough water to swim. Oh, it was tragic, flapping and struggling there. Pepper was crooning at it, her tail wagging madly, and the dolphin blew hard out of its blowhole in a whooshing sound.

Thank God I had my phone. I dragged Pepper a few yards away and tied her leash to a scrubby bush. She wanted to play with the dolphin, dropping her shoulders down, barking and wagging.

"It doesn't know what you are, Pepper," I said. "Settle down. But yes! This is very exciting!"

I pulled out my phone. One bar. I dialed 911, but the call dropped before it connected. I tried again. Same result. My one bar went away, and the dreaded words *No Service* appeared.

I texted Noah, Mickey, Mom and Juliet—in a nutshell, every capable person I knew. Dolphin stuck in tidal river by my house, please call someone, I have no service.

My phone told me the message was not delivered. "Shit!" I said.

I went closer to the dolphin—it may have been dying. Sometimes they stranded themselves, right? She (I thought it was a girl for some reason) struggled a little more and made a squeaking sound, and the noise hit me right in the heart.

"Okay. Hang on, honey. Help is on the way. I'll be right back."

I went back to the bush, untied my dog, had to practically drag her back to the house and shoved her inside. "Sorry, baby, you're not going to be much help here." I checked my phone—still no service, which had happened a few times since I moved here. That was okay. I'd get in my car and drive to Mom's or Noah's—

Right. My car was blocked by the tree branch.

I took a deep breath and thought. Google would be real handy right about now, but I had no power, and therefore no Wi-Fi.

Looked like I was about to become a dolphin rescuer. I grabbed a bucket, so I could pour water on her (because maybe she needed that?), and a shovel. I could dig the muck and maybe make a trench for her, and then as the tide came back in, maybe she could swim? Or I could carry her to deeper water, maybe? Oh, yes, a tarp. I could get her on it and drag her to deeper water.

"You were right, Mom," I said aloud. "I should've gone to college for something more practical. Marine biology, in this case."

Well, there was a little dolphin out there and she'd squeaked at me, and I wasn't going to leave her alone to die. I grabbed my New York Yankees cap to keep the rain off my face and set off with my makeshift dolphin rescue kit.

She was still there. Maybe not flipping her tail as much. I knelt down next to her. "Hi, honey. I'm going to try to help you." I stuck out my hand, in case she wanted to sniff it, like a dog, and she lifted her head up a little bit, and I swore to God she looked at me and knew I was one of the good guys. You could touch dolphins and not hurt them, right? Of course. They let you swim with them at those resort places in Florida. I touched her just south of her blowhole, and she was cold and firm and smooth. "I'll do my best, honey. Stay with me."

She flapped again, utterly helpless on the sand. I ran down the river to where the water was deeper and got a bucketful to pour over her. She did seem to like that, flipping and wriggling with more energy. Then I started digging the trench, which filled up with water immediately. Maybe if I could position her toward the river, she could sort of flop her way down . . .

"I'm going to touch you now, honey," I said. "Okay? I'm going to try to turn you."

She was, as best I knew, a bottlenose dolphin, and a little one. Maybe half-grown? I loved nature documentaries, but I was just guessing here. I knew dolphins were smart, maybe smarter than humans. And they traveled in groups—pods?—so maybe her family was waiting for her in the deeper water. Stoningham was the only town in Connecticut that had a little bit of oceanfront; most of the town hugged the very end of Long Island Sound. But out here, where I was, it was possible (if you were a dolphin, for example) to swim straight from the Atlantic, past Fishers Island to the east, and right here to the tidal river.

Taking a deep breath, I put my hands on either side of her and moved her so she faced the trench. She flapped her tail up and down, seeming to know that she had to do her part. A foot. Two feet. I dug some more, moved her a few inches in the inch or two of water, dug some more. I tried to pick her up, then abandoned the plan, afraid I would drop her. She was awkward and heavy, maybe seventy-five or a hundred pounds.

The tidal river was just too shallow, and getting more so every minute. Honey—I'd named her now—seemed to be getting tired. Her breathing wasn't as loud or frequent, and her efforts weren't as strong. The tide was going out too fast for my plan.

"Okay," I said after maybe an hour had passed. I was panting myself, my jeans wet and sandy, making my skin feel raw. I got another bucket of water and dumped it over Honey, then considered the tarp. If I could roll her onto it without hurting her, I could drag her closer to the Sound. It was better than nothing. I didn't know if the rain was hurting her skin, or if it was good for her, or if she was hungry and I should've brought that envelope of tuna in my cupboard to feed her.

I spread out the tarp next to her and knelt, putting my hands on her. If I rolled her, would it hurt her fin? I tucked it against her and looked in her eye. "I hope this won't hurt you, Honey," I said. "I just want to get you back to your family, okay? Okay. So on three, we'll roll. One, two . . . three."

She was heavy, but she rolled over pretty easily onto her back, and I managed to tuck her other fin so it wouldn't get hurt, and rolled her the rest of the way. She lay on her stomach, but now on the tarp. "You okay, Honey?"

She didn't answer, just blew hard. No more squeaks.

I went to the front of the tarp and started dragging it. God! She was heavy! I had to walk backward, and after a few steps, I tripped and landed flat on my ass in the wet sand. Got up and started trying again. She wasn't even trying to flap her tail fin anymore. "Please don't die, Honey," I said. "I'm giving it my best here."

I had never been this soaked. Even my raincoat was soaked through, and I was sweaty and clammy and shaking with exhaustion, but we'd come this far, Honey and I. I wasn't going to leave her now.

"Sadie! Hey!" Noah, his hair whipping across his face, was standing on the hill my house perched on.

"Oh, thank God," I said.

He ran toward me. "What are you doing?"

"Just saving a dolphin. You know."

"Did you call anyone?"

"I tried. No cell service out here, and my car's blocked in."

"Yeah, I saw. No service in town, either. I tried calling you to see if you were okay, then came out to check." He bent down to look at my new friend. "Have you named her?"

He knew me well. He really did.

"Honey."

"Yes, dear?"

"No, that's *her* name." I smiled at him. Noah, flirting with me over a baby dolphin. God! The feels! "Think we can pull her to the water? She's getting tired, and the tide is going out."

"Let's go."

It was a good quarter mile to the Sound. I talked almost nonstop to my little dolphin friend, telling her to be brave, be strong, relax and enjoy the ride. It was tough going, and Noah and I both fell once or twice more (fine, I fell twice, and he stumbled). By the time we reached the ocean, I could barely stand, I was so tired.

"Okay, Honey, let's go," Noah said.

We pulled her into the water, and my faithful L.L.Bean boots filled up immediately, the fleece lining acting like a sponge. The water was bitingly cold and stung my raw skin.

Honey didn't seem to rouse much. Flapped a little, but didn't make it off the tarp.

"Let's take her in a little deeper," I said. I put my hand

on Honey's back. "Come on, sweetie. You can do it." We were knee-deep now, then thigh deep. She flapped once, and the tarp slid out from under her.

She sank.

"No! Come on, Honey! Up you go!" I reached in and pulled her up so she could breathe. "Here, baby. Just sit a minute. Get your bearings."

"She might be sick, Sadie," Noah said.

"She's not." Stupid of me to say, but I didn't want her to be. My throat tightened with tears. All this to watch my little friend drown? No.

I took her out a few more feet, now waist deep in the ocean, the waves slapping me, sliding over Honey's blowhole, soaking my sweater. "Maybe you can run back to your truck and drive into town and get some help," I said, my teeth starting to chatter.

"I'm not leaving you in the ocean by yourself. With a dolphin. It's not even fifty degrees today, Special."

"Well . . . maybe if we swim her out a little more, she'll catch on."

Noah looked dubious.

"Please?" I added. "You're a father. She's a baby. Doesn't this inspire your paternal instincts?"

He shook his head, smiling a little. "Sure. Okay." We took her out a little more, and her tail moved. I was up to my shoulders now. She wasn't sinking, but we were holding her up, and let me tell you, a baby dolphin is not a tiny thing.

"Any other ideas?" Noah asked. A wave slapped me in the face, and I choked. "Pretty soon we'll be dead, so think of something."

I couldn't help a sputtering laugh.

And then, like magic, like proof of God, a full-grown

dolphin leaped out of the water *right* in front of us, and I screamed a little as it splashed down. Honey began squeaking and wriggling, and then, just like that, she gave a flip of her powerful tail and swam toward her mother (I thought it was her mother, anyway). She was a dark shape in the water, and then she was gone.

"Yes! Way to go, Honey!" Noah said.

But I felt suddenly . . . bereft. That was it? After two hours together?

It wasn't. In a glorious whoosh of water that pulled around my legs, Honey and her mama circled us, once, then twice, and for one beautiful second, we could hear their clicking and squeaking.

Then they were ten feet away, surfacing for air side by side, then twenty, and then they disappeared, indiscernible from the choppy waves in the darkening sea.

"They thanked you," Noah said, wonder in his voice. "Now that doesn't happen every day."

I was crying with the beauty of it. Wrapped my arms around Noah and sobbed, then kissed him full on the mouth, tasting the salt of my tears and the ocean.

"Okay, dolphin girl," he said, pushing my wet hair off my face. "Let's get you home."

Because God obviously approved of my efforts, the power came on five minutes after we got back to the house. Pepper greeted us ecstatically, and I bent down to kiss her. "We did it! She's back with her mommy! All because you saw her, Pepper!" I swear she knew what I meant, because she did a victory lap around the downstairs, found her squeaky possum toy and started the musical portion of our evening.

"Go take a hot shower before you get hypothermia,"

Noah said, scrubbing a hand through his wet hair. "Your lips are blue."

"*You* go take a hot shower before *you* get hypothermia," I said. "You were just a Good Samaritan, whereas Pepper and I have trained for this all our lives."

He rolled his eyes (fondly, I thought). "Don't be dumb, Sadie. You were out there a lot longer than I was."

"Warmed by my love of marine mammals, though."

"Get in the shower."

"I have to see if my phone will dry out."

"Forget your phone."

"I have to post something on social media so the world knows of my greatness."

"Damn you, Sadie," he growled, and then—finally—he was on me, mouth on mine, arms around me, tongue against mine. He lifted me up on the butcher block, muttering, "I could've made something a lot better than this piece of crap," before yanking open my jacket, pushing it down my arms so I was pinned. He kissed me like he was drowning, dying, and I was the only one who could save him.

And you know, saving *was* kind of my thing that day, so I wrapped my legs around him and kissed him back, freeing one arm so I could grip his wet hair.

"I have eight minutes of hot water in that tank," I said, gasping a little. "Let's make them count."

He still knew how to undress a woman with great efficiency. He could still carry me. He still had that look of intense concentration when he worked, and he still smiled during a kiss, hot water running over us, soap sliding between us. He still knew every place I loved to be touched, where I was ticklish, how to make my knees buckle.

But he was new as well. He turned off the water when it started to cool, stepped out and wrapped me in a towel.

Dried himself off fast, his six-pack rippling, his shoulders smooth and hypnotic with muscle. Then he kissed me and kissed me, sliding his hands under my ass, picked me up and carried me upstairs.

"I'm on the Pill and passed my STD panel with flying colors," I said as he dumped me on the bed.

"I see your dirty talk hasn't improved," he said.

"I just want you to know, I'd never take any chances with you, Noah." I was abruptly serious. "Even if we . . . I mean, if we're about to do this, I just wanted you to . . . feel safe."

He lay down on top of me, his skin so smooth and warm, still damp, his wet curls hanging around his face. "Special," he whispered, "the last thing I feel with you is safe."

I didn't know why the words were so romantic, why they wrapped around my heart and pulled.

But they did, and when we were finally making love, finally, finally together again, I knew I was home.

CHAPTER THIRTY-FIVE

Barb

The morning after the big storm, I had to take John back to Gaylord for an assessment with his team. He'd had another MRI, and they were going to go over the results with us and talk about future therapy and all that.

Driving the hour plus to Wallingford was almost peaceful. John didn't talk, though he'd been making more noise lately, trying to say words. And I tried to understand them, but it was tough. Sadie thought it meant a full recovery was just around the corner, but I wasn't so sure. He seemed to check out a lot, and those words . . . I knew he wanted to tell me *something*, but his speech was so unclear, and the effort exhausted him.

Poor John. I wondered if he'd have been so bad off if he hadn't been riding his bike that day. If someone had been there and saw him fall, gotten to him sooner. If he hadn't banged his head in addition to having the stroke. In other words, if he hadn't been having an affair and training for a triathlon in January, maybe the stroke wouldn't have been so bad.

But the anger and humiliation I felt had seeped away. It's real hard to be upset with a man who can't cut his own food.

I'd been awfully busy yesterday, fielding calls from people reporting power outages and downed trees, and sent the fire department out to help the Patrick family get their generator started, since Violet had a condition where she couldn't regulate her body temperature, and if their house got cold, she'd get so cold she'd have to check into the hospital. The Fieldings lost their cat, so once the fire department was done at the Patricks', they headed over there, and I went, too, since Juliet came over and said she'd watch her dad. I loved cats. Always wanted to get one, but John was severely allergic. We did find the sweet little thing, crouched under the car, scared of the wind.

Aside from storm issues, there was the impending town-wide celebration for the 350th anniversary of our founding. The garden club needed more volunteers, the auction that would raise money for college scholarships needed more donations, and half the people who'd answered the e-mail about hosting open houses hadn't filled in their forms.

I guess you could say I had a lot on my mind, plus John's future. Gosh, it made me tired.

"All right, John, we're here," I said, getting out of the car. I had to unbuckle him, because he couldn't seem to grasp that one. I wished LeVon was still with Gaylord. He'd come by last week to check in and, after John had fallen asleep, stayed for a cup of tea with me. It had been so nice, talking to him again.

It was slow going to the conference room, since John

seemed to wander to the left, and I had to half tow him down the long hallway. The whole team was there—Betsy, the speech therapist; Evan, the head of physical and occupational therapy; Dr. McIntyre, the head of outpatient rehabilitation; two physiatrists. They all had iPads and folders, and I suddenly had a bad feeling in my stomach.

"Lovely to see you again," Dr. McIntyre said. She'd been wonderful this whole time, sometimes even calling me on the weekend to check in. We all sat around the table, and my heart started jumping like a scared rabbit.

"So," Dr. McIntyre said. "I'm afraid the news isn't great, which doesn't mean it's horrible. John seems to have had at least two smaller strokes since the big one. That explains why his left side seems weaker than before, and why he's struggling with mobility more than he was a month ago."

I put my hand over John's, not sure what he understood. He seemed calm and unchanged. Sleepy, even. "Oh," I said, my voice small.

"He *has* made a little progress with speech," Betsy said. "But that seems to have plateaued. He can say a few words, but he's not putting them together in a meaningful way."

"Yes, I . . . I thought so, too." Oh, gosh. This was going to hit Sadie real hard. It was hitting me, hard, too. "Um . . . the strokes. Does that mean he'll have more?"

Dr. McIntyre looked kind. "We're adjusting his medications, but it's definitely possible."

John was asleep now, his chin on his chest. Good. I didn't want him to have to hear this. Know this. Oh, he looked so old, so sad!

"He's probably safer using the walker all the time," Evan said. "A wheelchair for when he's tired. You may want to look into hiring a full-time caregiver. We can give you referrals, of course."

"Gotcha. I . . . So he's not . . . going to improve." No one said anything. "Do you have any guesses on how long he'll . . . be with us?"

"It's always so hard to predict," the doctor said.

So they weren't going to say the words outright. "Can I have a sec?" I asked.

"Of course," Dr. McIntyre said. "Use the room next door."

I practically ran to it, closed the door and started to shake.

So this was it, then. My husband, the once intelligent, wry attorney, was gone. He'd never talk to his grandchildren again. Sadie and Juliet wouldn't get him back. We'd never have another night where talking was even a possibility, and suddenly, those silent nights of him watching television and me answering e-mails felt awfully precious.

I shouldn't have let them operate on him that day in January. I should've let him go, but gosh, I don't even remember that being presented as an option.

This was his life now. He'd just slip away, inch by inch, confused and scared and exhausted until he died. And not to put too fine a point on it, I'd be his caregiver for the rest of his life, or the rest of mine. Almost without knowing it, I pulled out my phone.

"Caro?" I said.

"What's wrong, honey?" The concern in her voice brought me to tears.

"He's not going to get better. He's had a couple of little strokes, and . . . and he's not getting better." I started to cry.

"Oh, shit, Barb. I'm so sorry. Are you at Gaylord now?"

"Yes. I didn't want the girls to come, because I suspected there would be bad news. I just didn't know it would be so . . . definite."

"Barb, why didn't you call me? I would've come! We're best friends, for God's sake!"

"I should have."

"Okay, here's what we'll do. You come home, I'll bring dinner tonight, and wine and lots of it, and we can talk to the girls and go from there. Don't worry, hon. We've got this."

We. A person forgot what a beautiful word that was when it had been *you* for so long.

~

CHAPTER THIRTY-SIX

Sadie

Noah left before dawn, kissing me gently on the lips, whispering that he wanted to see Marcus before he went to work. I spent a blissful half hour dozing, Pepper by my side, before getting up to take her for a walk. There was no evidence of our dolphin rescue; the tide had erased any tracks, and the birds were nearly deafening. I felt as happy as I'd ever felt in my life.

Grateful . . . a word made sappy by a million tacky wooden signs, yet a feeling that was so powerful. I felt as if sunbeams were shining from my skin. My dad was getting better. Noah loved me. We'd saved a baby dolphin! I had a dog! I'd painted a sunset yesterday, and the coffee was on.

I took in a few deep breaths of the salt-kissed air, the sun warm on my face. Noticed that Noah had moved the branch that had fallen behind the car. Of course he had.

God, I *loved* him. Alexander was barely a memory, though the other two women were my Facebook friends now, and we'd all shared our Alexander Breakup stories. I'd always known he was a pale shadow compared with Noah. I just hadn't wanted to dwell on it, feeling that *good enough* was about all I could expect.

Noah was amazing. He was so kind and decent and trustworthy and good in bed that he was a unicorn among men. I said a prayer of thanks that we were getting this second chance. If yesterday had shown me anything other than the fact that I loved baby dolphins, it was that I loved Noah more.

The coffee was extra delicious this morning. I took my mug and laptop onto the porch, sat on the step and let Pepper frolic on the lawn. Checked my e-mails.

Then I jolted upright so fast, my coffee sloshed.

To: SadieFrost1335@gmail.com
From: hasan@HasanSadikSoho.com
Re: your painting at Harriet White/Darcy Cummings house

Dear Ms. Frost,

I was recently at a housewarming party hosted by Harriet and Darcy in Brooklyn. They showed me your incredible painting, knowing I have a special interest in emerging artists. I was able to obtain your e-mail from their interior decorator.

I would be very interested in talking with you about showing in my SoHo gallery this coming fall and perhaps, if you'd be so kind, having the chance to see your portfolio. Is there any possibility you are available to meet? I am desperately hoping you don't have exclusive contracts elsewhere.

The very best to you,

Hasan

Hasan Sadik SoHo

29 Walker Street, New York, NY 10013

I reread the e-mail four times.

I'd *been* to that gallery. It was one of *those* galleries. The "I can make your career in one show" galleries. Aneni had had a show there, during which time a curator for the Guggenheim had bought one of her paintings. The Guggenheim!

In fact, Hasan Sadik SoHo was the gallery where I'd tried to explain to Noah why my skyscape paintings were touristy drivel and not true art.

And now the owner—Hasan Sadik himself—was desperately hoping I was free to show at his place. Just like that, a chance came out of the clear blue sky.

This could make my career. Every dream I'd ever had about art reared up and hugged me tight.

All I had to do was bang out some more Georgia O'Keeffe–type work, using the same kinds of touches I'd used on the vagina painting to make it clear that it wasn't just a knockoff and . . . and . . .

Shit. I'd be established. I'd be *that* New York artist, discovered after teaching Catholic school for years and years and making paintings that matched upholstery. It *was* a great story!

I needed to get to work. Mom had Dad at Gaylord today, so my schedule was clear.

I took a few deep breaths and, hands shaking, wrote back to Hasan Sadik, saying I'd love to meet with him and was a great admirer of his gallery. Kept it short and sweet, and nearly fainted when he wrote back *immediately*, offering to send a car to pick me up, and perhaps we could also have lunch? And did I have an agent he should be including in these e-mails?

I'll be in touch in the next day or two, I wrote, too overwhelmed at the moment, and afraid I'd say something stupid. Thank you so much for your interest.

Thank God I'd taken down my website years ago so he couldn't see all my previous attempts to be artistic and unique (or read my idiotic bio where I mentioned Robert Frost). I pulled up some images of Georgia O'Keeffe's work and printed out a couple for inspiration. Somewhere in one of my unpacked boxes was a juicy coffee table book on her flower paintings. Which box was it, dang it?

Listen. All work was derivative. It wasn't like I was doing anything that hadn't been done a million times before. I found the book, flipped through it and settled on a white rose, the oriental poppies and an iris.

A chance like this did not come around very often. I'd be an idiot to turn it aside. "Mommy's going to be a famous artist," I told Pepper, who nuzzled my hand encouragingly. "Let's get to work, shall we?" I set aside my sunset painting from yesterday, got a couple of canvases out of the closet, and started working, ignoring the little voice in the back of my head that was telling me to slow down.

I painted all day. Noah texted, asking me if I wanted to come to his house that evening, and I told him yes, I had some really exciting news and couldn't wait to see him, but had to have dinner at my mom's first to talk about Dad's progress.

I've been thinking about you all day, he wrote, and my heart melted.

Same here, I texted. Debated saying, *I love you*, even

though he knew already, and kept on painting, with a little more depth, deeper color.

Noah was good for my art. He always had been. I hoped I was good for him. I made him laugh. I knew him in a way that started in the very center of my heart. I had always believed in him, his goodness, his kindness, his talent at what he did. Also, I gave him the chance to save me from a collapsing house *and* the opportunity to save a dolphin.

I loved him. I loved him. I loved him so much. Small wonder that I was singing as I painted.

"So, girls," Mom said. "Sit down."

Jules and I had been cleaning up after dinner. We'd eaten Caro's delicious chicken and salsa verde casserole, and Dad had been settled in front of the TV with Pepper.

We sat, exchanging glances. Juliet looked spiffy as always in her chic, tailored clothes. I had paint on the back of my hand and wore stained leggings and a T-shirt with Bill Murray's face on it. The fact that Oliver and the girls weren't here struck me as ominous all of a sudden. So did the fact that Caro had stayed.

Shit.

"The news isn't good," Mom said. "I'm sorry."

"What news? Dad's news?" I asked. "How could it not be good? He's been doing great!"

"Could you let her talk?" Juliet snapped.

"Yes! Fine! I'm just . . . Go ahead, Mom."

She glanced at Caro, who gave her a little smile. "Well, girls, your dad's not progressing, I'm sorry to say," Mom said. "He's had two more smaller strokes, and he's likely to have more."

I jerked back. "Okay, first of all, when were these other

strokes?" I asked. "I think we'd notice. And secondly, he's *talking* now! How can they say he's not progressing?"

Caro covered my hand. "This is hard news, I know, honey."

"No, it's not! It's just wrong news."

"Calm down, Sadie," Juliet muttered, and I wanted to bite her.

"He can say a few words, but there's more weakness on his left side," Mom went on. Juliet scootched her chair closer and put her arm around her. "So he'll keep needing care. That's the long and short of it. Our insurance will cover an aide for when I'm at work, and we'll figure the rest out as we go along."

"I think we should look into a nursing home," Juliet said.

"No! Absolutely not!" I said.

"Mom does eighty-five percent of the work, Sadie. She's seventy years old."

"I'm not exactly dead yet," Mom said.

"You're getting worn out, Mom."

"I just sent you two to a spa for a rest!" I said, knowing it was ridiculous.

"Two nights isn't going to be enough, unless it's two nights a week, Sadie," Jules said. She looked at our mother. "I'm worried about you. Insurance would cover—"

"Would cover a shithole, Juliet!"

"Keep your voice down," she said. "Oliver and I can help."

"Juliet, you're starting your own firm, honey. You keep your money. Sadie's right. This is my responsibility, and with a little help from the visiting nurses and such, your father and I will be okay."

I glared at my sister. She'd put Dad in a kennel if I let her.

"What?" she snapped. "I don't see *you* making plans to stay here permanently. You want Dad cared for, maybe you have to do more than come over and paint and let your dog watch TV with him."

"That's not fair. I've done everything I can for him. God forbid you interrupt your perfect life—"

"That's enough, girls," Caro and Mom said in unison, then smiled at each other. I pressed my lips together and tried not to cry.

"The truth is, you're both right," Mom said. "I can't see putting him into a nursing home when all he needs is . . . well, a keeper. And yes, I'm tired. It hasn't been easy."

"In sickness and in health," I said.

"Exactly," Mom said.

"Fuck you, Sadie," Juliet said.

"Wow! Angry much, Jules? You *know* he'd take care of her if the situation were reversed."

"You're an idiot. And you don't know the half of it."

"Well, this has been wonderful," Mom said. "Now, both of you get home. You're upsetting me."

"I'm sorry, Mom," Jules said. "But if she knew . . ."

"If I knew what?"

"How hard it is for our mother," Jules ground out. "Getting him in and out of bed, showered, shaved, dressed, making sure there's enough food in the house, paying the bills, working more than a full-time job, checking in on him on her lunch hour or on the app—"

"Mom," I interrupted. "I know how devoted you are. And I admire you for it. I really do."

"Well, thanks, now, hon. It's still time for you both to

get on home. Sadie, your dog is curled up with your dad, why don't you just leave her here tonight? Juliet, honey, I'll see you for lunch tomorrow. Caro, want to stay for a glass of wine?"

My sister and I were dismissed. We went outside, giving each other plenty of space.

"How's my car, by the way?" she asked.

"Oh, Jesus. It's fine. Thank you for being so benevolent and generous, thou perfect human."

"Good. You can keep it as long as you're here. And if you wanted to move back forever and be Dad's caregiver twenty-four seven, I'd give it to you."

"Okay, I'm leaving now."

"As you do."

I sucked in a sharp breath. "Juliet, what do you expect me to say? I have a job and an apartment in the city. I have a second career as a painter, as much as you like to laugh at it. I know you're used to being the important one in the family, but that doesn't mean I can magically become a nurse and leave the life I built in the city. Dad and Mom are married. This is part of the territory. Would you want Oliver to stick you in a nursing home?"

"Yes! If it made his life better, you're damn right I would."

"And would you stick *him* in one?"

Ha. I had her there. She looked away, conceding defeat, and I got into the car and backed out of the driveway, heading for Noah's.

Those doctors were wrong. Dad was clearly getting better. They didn't spend as much time with him as I did. I mean, seriously. When was the last time they'd even seen him?

I was crying, and crying while driving was not safe. I

pulled over and let myself bawl a little. Two more strokes? When? Yes, he'd been a little . . . wandery lately, listing off to the left, but . . . but . . . the idea that I'd never have the old Dad back was intolerable.

Deep breaths. Deep breaths. My father *was* getting better, and . . . and I didn't know what else, but that had to be true. It had to be.

I hadn't been to Noah's house since I came back. I knew the address well, though; it was his parents' old house—Mom had told me years ago that the elder Pelletiers had moved to Ottawa, where Noah's grandmother lived.

The Pelletier home was in one of Stoningham's quiet little areas, the houses shaded by big maples whose branches wove together above the street as if the trees were holding hands. The sidewalk was pleasantly uneven from their roots.

I ran a hand through my hair and looked at my face in the rearview mirror. Red eyes, blotchy face. Another deep breath. Seeing Noah would make me feel better. He'd put things in perspective.

As you might expect, since both he and his father were carpenters, Noah's house was lovely. It was white, with a wide front porch, two stories. It had changed quite a bit since I was here: bigger windows, a new front door, the garage resembling a barn now. There was a baby swing hanging from a branch in the crab apple tree in the front yard.

It was a house for a family, that was for sure. Not like my crooked little place.

I knocked on the door, wishing I'd thought to bring something.

Mickey answered. "Hey! Heard you two got it on last night."

I couldn't help a smile. "Wow. He spilled, did he?"

"Well, we agreed that if one of us was in a relationship, the other should know. Well done. He looks very happy. Come on in. He's giving Marcus a bath."

The house was beautiful—different from when I was here last, when Noah and I were still hanging on to the threads of our relationship. Back in the day, Mrs. Pelletier would pop out of her study—she'd been a science editor for a news organization—and tell me to help myself to whatever was in the fridge. The floor plan was now open and bright, wide oak planks having replaced the beige carpeting. Ridiculously tidy, with sturdy furniture, and all the beautiful touches you'd expect from a carpenter. Cabinets with glass panes, a beautiful mantelpiece, built-in bookcases.

I followed Mickey toward the kitchen, then jolted to a stop.

There, on the stair landing, was the painting I'd made for him when I was sixteen years old. The one he'd refused to give up for Gillian.

Just a blue sky with soft, golden clouds.

No. There was nothing "just" about it. I hadn't seen that painting in years, and it hit me. The sky was cerulean, the clouds lit with gold and edged with Noah-red. The sun had been just about to rise that day, and I'd painted the sky from memory, not a photo. I could almost see the clouds drifting past on the soft breeze and hear the birds, feel the damp air of the early morning and smell the muffins baking at Sweetie Pies. I'd ridden my bike out to watch, to the bridge near where I now lived, in fact, and with all that young love in my heart, made this painting for Noah.

It was so beautiful.

"In here," Mickey called.

I snapped myself out of my reverie and went into the kitchen, which was cobalt blue and white. "Did the photographers just leave?" I asked. "Seriously. What man has a white kitchen?"

"I know. I can't wait till Marcus starts walking and his grubby little hands turn everything gray. I'll feel less inferior then. I'm not quite the housekeeper Noah is. When are you going to come over to my place, by the way? Tonight would work, since it's Noah's night with the little prince. Hang on, you probably want to nail the carpenter, right? See what I did there?" She laughed. "Don't scar my kid. Then again, Marcus *does* sleep through everything. Even that storm yesterday. So if you two *were* going to fool around—"

"Yeah, okay, let's change the subject. Speaking of the storm, did Noah tell you about the dolphin?"

"Is that a euphemism for penis or something? Want a beer or some wine or whatever he has?"

"Yes to wine, and no, a real dolphin." I sat at the kitchen table and told her the story.

"My God! You rock, kid," she said. "You both do. A fricking dolphin!"

"Thanks. In this case, I'd have to agree with you." I took a sip of wine. "Where do you live, Mickey?"

"Right next door."

"Oh, my gosh, how perfect."

"Yeah. No point in making life harder on the kid, right? So if you two are gonna get married, we should probably have a serious talk, don't you think?"

"Marriage is not currently being discussed."

"But you're gonna get there eventually, right?"

"Uh . . . how long do baths usually take?"

"As long as the baby wants," Noah said, and there he was, his son in his arms. He smiled at me; my face grew hot. Other parts, too.

"Hi, Marcus," I mumbled.

"Abwee!" he answered.

"Want to hold him?" Noah said. "He smells good. Now. That was definitely not true half an hour ago."

"Poop explosion!" Mickey said cheerfully.

I took the little guy. Oh, wow. He did smell good. He was a sturdy baby, and his black hair stood straight up. Dark eyes, like his father.

"How old is he now?" I asked.

"Six months," the proud parents answered in unison. Like Mom and Caro.

Had my parents ever been like that, so in sync that they finished each other's sentences? I couldn't remember.

Marcus yanked my hair. "You're pretty cute, kid," I said, untangling the strand from his chubby little fist. "Pretty cute indeed."

"Well, I'm feeling very third wheel here," Mickey said. "Should I go?"

"No! No, stay," I said. "Um, I got an exciting e-mail today. I think I might be having a gallery show in New York. Noah, remember that painting I did for the brownstone people? One of their friends owns a gallery, and he wants to feature me."

"Holy shit! That's great!" Mickey said.

"Yeah. It's funny, it's actually a gallery you've seen, Noah. Way back when."

"Really."

It wasn't a happy and excited word, not the way he used it. "Yep. So I'll be wicked busy for the next week or so. Painting. More of the same stuff, you know? Those flowers?" For some reason, I was glad to be holding the baby.

Noah took him from me, reading my mind as he usually did. "Mickey, would you mind taking Marcus next door? I'll come back for him in a little bit."

"Sure! Glad to. I need to nurse anyway." She shot me a look. "Maybe see you later? But not if you two are fighting, because I'm on his side. It's a coparenting loyalty thing."

"We're not fighting!" Shit. We were about to fight, weren't we?

Mickey left, Marcus babbling away.

"So," Noah said, sitting down across the table from me. "A gallery show. Wow."

"Yeah. Hasan Sadik. Very, very prestigious."

"For that flowery porn painting."

"Well, yeah. I mean, that's one way of putting it, sure. I think the interior designer called it a huge vagina painting. So I have to make more of the same. That's what I was doing most of today."

"How are you gonna work that?"

"Uh . . . what do you mean?"

"Are you moving back to the city?"

"Um . . . I don't know. I mean, eventually. I have a job there. Teaching. So yeah. I guess so. But the problem is, my father isn't—"

He threw up his hands. "Are you kidding me?"

"No. Why?"

"Jesus, Sadie! We slept together!"

"I know! I was there! And I'm really happy about that."

"Are you? Because I'm feeling used all of a sudden."

I tried a smile. "I think it was a mutual using, pal."

"I *love* you, Sadie."

"I love y—"

"I never stopped. So we spend more than a decade apart, and then you come home and we get back together, and now you're leaving again? For that same New York bullshit?"

"Okay, for one, it's not—"

"Your sister is right. You're unreliable."

"—bullshit. Noah. It's what I've worked for all my life. And when did Juliet say I was unreliable?"

"Once your father's situation is settled, you're done, aren't you? You'll go back to the city and maybe come out here to visit a couple times a year."

"And for two, my father's situation is a long way from settled." My eyes filled again at the thought of Dad, but I refused to cry right now.

Noah clenched his jaw and looked out the window. "I have a son now. A family. You can't pop in and out of our life whenever you feel like it. You have to make a plan, Sadie, and it's clear I'm not in it, and Jesus Christ, I can't believe I fell for this again."

"I think you missed the part where I said I loved you."

"And what exactly does that mean?"

"It means exactly what I said! I love you, Noah!"

"Are you gonna stay here? Are you going to marry me?"

"This is hauntingly familiar, you giving me ultimatums and telling me how life should be."

"Are you going to stay?"

"I don't *know*!" I shouted. "Should I? What's even here for me anymore? Maybe you, if I meet all your criteria? The father who loved me is gone, and according to my mother, he's not getting better. *You* have a family without me and you're just fine with that, you've made that clear. My sister and mother are in a club I was never asked to join. I was recently told by my boyfriend that out of all his girlfriends, he was almost sure I was his favorite. I teach school and earn just above the poverty rate and I'm making these fucking couch paintings and somewhere along the line, I seem to have lost my soul, and then I *finally* get a huge, life-changing chance to show at a dream gallery, and yesterday we sleep together and you tell me you love me, but today you don't want me. What the hell am I *supposed* to do?"

I sat back, panting, then drained my wine.

"You're still with your boyfriend?"

"No! I'm leaving. I'm furious and upset, Noah. Maybe I'll see you soon, and maybe you'll be sticking pins in a voodoo doll of me. I have no idea and I don't care right now. I'm going home to paint."

"Sadie." He stood up. "One thing. Your flower painting, the one you did for the brownstone ladies. That's not you. That's you pretending to be someone else. *That's* a couch painting."

"Fuck off, Noah." I slammed the door on my way out. You know. Just in case he missed the point.

CHAPTER THIRTY-SEVEN

Sadie

It was here. The biggest moment of my professional life.

Hasan Sadik had greeted me, kissing me on both cheeks, told his silent and beautiful assistant to get me an espresso (I hated espresso). He had me place my paintings on the waiting easels and now was looking at them, walking slowly past each one, pausing, tilting his head, waiting for them to "talk to me and tell me their story."

This required silence. The assistant was barefoot, lest her footfalls interrupt Hasan's conversation with my work. I sat, pressing my knees together, pretending to sip the bitter coffee, and tried to exude confidence.

Juliet had loaned me an outfit and jewelry (she had her flaws as a sister, but staying mad wasn't one of them). I was dressed better than I'd ever been—black tuxedo pants, red patent leather pumps with a chunky heel, a sleeveless ivory top with a slightly draped neckline, and a gray "jardigan" (new term for me, but Brianna had told me it was very on trend). Dangly gold earrings, one plain gold ring on my right forefinger.

It was how I thought a successful artist should look. Cool, simple, wealthy (thanks, Jules) and sophisticated.

Hasan, tastemaker of the New York art world, broker of some of the most lucrative deals for artists today, wore Levi's, a white T-shirt and Converse sneakers and somehow outclassed me by a thousand points. I owned the same outfit many times over. Should've worn it so we could bond over our matching look.

In the week since he'd e-mailed, I'd worked twenty hours a day, making seven more flower paintings. Iris, rose, peony, carnation, tulip, poppy and maple leaves (to show my range). At six this morning, I'd finished drying the last one with my blow-dryer, put them in my portfolio, left Brianna a note about Pepper's new propensity to eat worms, and drove down here two hours early, killing the remainder of time by sitting in my car, sweating with nerves and pressing tissues into my armpits.

I'd never been at this kind of meeting. Never been that chic woman who had something New York wanted to see. This was it. I was, as they say, having a moment.

If only my father could see me now. The thought made my throat tighten with emotion.

He wasn't getting better. I pressed my lips together, hard. I'd think about that later. He'd *want* me present, to soak it all in. I wanted that, too, but somehow, I felt hollow. Maybe because he wasn't quite here to share it. Juliet had wished me the best and hugged me, and Mom said she thought the paintings were "real pretty," but the hollow, fake feeling remained.

After all, I wasn't even wearing my own clothes.

I should've come in wearing one of my teacher dresses,

which were invariably flowered or striped, because my students were little kids, after all, and loved bright colors.

I missed them. I missed St. Catherine's and Sister Mary and Carter and the gang, but it seemed more and more that my New York life was a light post on the highway that I could only see in the rearview mirror. A life left behind.

I missed Noah.

Last night, he'd knocked on my door at ten o'clock, stood there awkwardly as Pepper pounced on his shoes.

"Listen," he said the second I opened the door. "I'm really sorry for what I said. I know how much this means to you, and I'm pulling for you. Okay?"

"Thank you," I whispered.

He nodded. "Knock 'em dead tomorrow."

"Did Mickey send you?"

He laughed at that, but his eyes were sad. "No," he said. "All my idea."

"Thank you, Noah," I said. "It means a lot."

He nodded once, then left before either of us made things more complicated.

So here I was, lunch planned with Hasan afterward.

He made another turn, another stroll, little humming noises coming from his throat. I kept my mouth shut to maintain an air of mystery and also not babble like an idiot, which was, of course, my way.

I glanced out the window, and there I was, looking in. Not me, not really, but some kid—God, so young, probably not even twenty. He wore black jeans and a black T-shirt and had dyed, messy black hair, a bull nose ring and pierced eyebrow. Yep. Me, fifteen years ago. I smiled a little. He gave me a nod, then kept going.

I remembered that feeling. That outside-looking-in feeling. The someday-that-will-be-me feeling. I had it right now, even though I was literally on the inside.

The paintings . . . well, they were frickin' beautiful, no doubt. How could they not be? They were flowers. The colors were rich and deep, the technique well executed. All week long, I'd painted with every damn emotion in the world—fear about my father, anger and love for Noah, ambition, hope, peace, contentment, joy, terror, uncertainty.

But looking at them here, where they might well sell for tens of thousands of bucks apiece, I had to admit it. Noah was right.

They were couch paintings, and they weren't me. They were the me of college, trying to be something I was not. I'd been telling myself I stumbled onto something with the vagina flower painting, but I hadn't. I'd done an O'Keeffe and added a few squiggles, and it was a cheap trick. These seven at least, had been done with some passion and energy. But they still weren't me.

That stupid sunset was. The one I'd practically flung off the easel to make these porn flowers.

"It's . . . interesting," Hasan finally said, looking at me. "When I saw the painting at the party, I was struck by its intensity and authenticity. These . . . I just don't think they have the same impact, and I'm trying to figure out why."

Well, shit. "Hm."

"There's something missing in these, whereas the lilies and sweet pea painting had such a stark disparity, such a contrast between the lush sensuality and the void of emotional despair. It was a battle between chastity and vulgarity." He shook his head. "I'm just not feeling that same emotional upheaval here."

Oh, the fuckery. "Interesting." It seemed like a safe word. Chastity and vulgarity? The void of emotional despair? Words that had never once entered my brain as I made the brownstone painting. These seven? The entire tornado of human emotions.

"Tell me about the lily painting, Sadie," Hasan said. "What was in your heart when you painted it? How can we capture that mood again? Because that painting was special, and I think, if you can tap into that darkness, that fury and sexuality once again, we would be onto something here. Perhaps you know I consider myself not just a collector, but a mentor as well. Someone who nurtures the expression of passion and emotion."

Jesus. Had this kind of talk always sounded so ridiculous?

"What was in your heart, Sadie Frost?" he asked again, putting his hand against his chin.

I nodded. "My heart. Yes. Well, Hasan, to be honest, money was in my heart, because I was getting six grand for that painting. Also, copying was in my heart, because anyone could see it was a Georgia O'Keeffe knockoff. I just played with some texture in the oils to make it a little different. Aside from that, I didn't have much in my heart at all."

"Oh. That's . . . that's disappointing."

"Hasan. I'm a hack. I painted those lilies to match the owners' comforter. These . . ." I gestured to the paintings in front of us. "These are me trying to please you. Maybe I should've used some fabric swatches as inspiration."

He frowned. "You clearly have talent. Did you bring anything else?"

I hesitated. Why not? My dad would want me to. *I* wanted me to. At least I could show this guy something that was authentically mine. "Yes, as a matter of fact, I did."

In the last pocket in my portfolio was the sunset picture, the one I'd painted the day of the storm. To me, it was the best thing I'd painted. Ever.

Except for Noah's clouds.

I pulled it out and watched him take it in. And I took it in as well. I could almost feel the calm of that day, hear the birds, the distant shush of the ocean, feel the damp salt air of springtime.

"Eh," he said. "Any art student could do that. That's not the kind of thing my clients are looking for."

"I didn't think so. Thank you for the opportunity." I started gathering up my sexy-beast flowers.

"I'm sorry, Sadie," he said. "I've wasted your day."

"It's okay. Really. These aren't me, these flowers. That sunset is, and I understand SoHo is not the place for sunset pictures."

"Would you still like to have lunch? Perhaps I could give you some guidance about where the market is these days."

"I think I'll get back to Connecticut. But thank you." I shook his hand, and left.

It was official. I was never going to be that artist.

But I'd had the chance. The big break. I'd been considered by a major gallery owner who had loved something I did. That was more than most artists got, regardless of their talent and training and outlook.

So I'd done it. I'd made it through the doors, and that—much to my surprise—was enough. There was a spring in my step as I lugged the paintings down the street. I wasn't going to make it, but I hadn't sold my soul, either.

I'd give the flower paintings as presents, maybe even

keep one or two. Maybe send one to the lesbians, since they were so nice to play a part in getting me today's chance.

But right now, I wanted to go home. I wanted to go home and play with my dog and sit on my battered front porch and watch another sunset.

CHAPTER THIRTY-EIGHT

John

He knows what is happening. Barb is going to take care of him forever now.

He is sliding away, not toward, and he still has not said the right words. The flower word that will save his wife. The other words he wants to say. He needs his girls to be here, and Barb, and when that happens, he has to be ready. He has to be *here*.

But the world is grainy and blank, and the feelings come without words. He keeps trying, but he is slipping down the mountain he was trying so hard to climb. The snow is too heavy, and he is so tired. Days pass, and he is unaware. Sometimes everyone is here, sometimes he seems alone, sometimes he is asleep and sometimes in the snow. He has to say the words. He has to tell his Barb about the long-ago.

And then one day, he wakes up on the patio, in the

chair that lets his legs stick out straight. It is warm and his daughters and wife and his friend with the warm rain voice are all here.

This is his chance, he knows. It will not come again. He knows that, too.

He grabs the arm of the person closest to him. Juliet, his oldest, his perfect girl, and she jumps. "You!" he says. He forces his mouth and his brain to work together. "Poor," comes out, the word tortured and heavy.

The women look at each other, confused.

"Pour?" Sadie asks "You want a drink?"

"No!" He looks at Juliet again. "Prow. Prow."

There is a silence, and the word slips away, Juliet's word, and John's eyes are wet because she didn't understand, and now the word is gone.

"Proud," Barb says. "He's proud of you."

She *knows*. She knows! John nods and takes Juliet's hand and kisses it.

"Oh, Dad," she says, and her eyes are raining, which is not the right word, but he has made her happy and sad. It was her word, and he gave it to her, at last.

Sadie kneels in front of him and says words, but they're blurring and tumbling in his head.

"Joy," he says, touching her face.

"Joy," she repeats, nodding. "Yes. Joy."

His heart is so full, and his eyes are raining, too.

Just a little more now. The snow has held off, but the clouds are heavy with it. "Bar," he says, and his wife comes closer. Sits on the chair next to him. She waits for her word, too.

Bathroom. The closed door. Crying. Sorry. I should have gone in and I didn't.

But the words are too many and too hard.

"Rose," he says. "Rose." The flower word! He said it at last.

"That's real nice, John," she says, patting his hand, but she doesn't know that this is the word that will set her free.

"No! Rose . . . Heel."

Everyone freezes. The snow is coming, and is this why no one is moving? Just a little longer, that's all he needs.

"Rose Hill?" says his friend, and he nods again, his head wobbling on his neck. He is an old man now. He closes his eyes just for a second.

"What do you mean, Dad?" Juliet asks. "You want to live at Rose Hill?"

He nods again.

"And not live here anymore." She is clarifying, his older girl, and he knows that is her way.

He nods. Oh, he is tired now, but he forces his eyes to open.

Sadie's face is crumpled and sad. Juliet is crying, yes, that is the word. Janet is smiling her nice smile, her rope-hair so tidy and twisty.

But there is one more word Barb needs to hear. One more word for John to tell her before the snow comes, because he knows the snow won't stop this time.

"Barb," he says, looking at her. He takes her hand, bringing it against his face. "Barb."

Sorry. Forgive. Love.

"Divorce," he says, and it is the right word.

They talk then, and he can hear their voices but not understand their words.

It doesn't matter. He knows he made it. He said the words they needed, and they understand.

The snow comes, but it is warm and light, and he falls into it, knowing he has once again been a father . . . knowing that, for the first time in a long time, and for the last time ever, he was a good husband.

CHAPTER THIRTY-NINE

Barb

John was going to Rose Hill. There was room for him, and the facility took every kind of insurance and made up the rest of the cost, thanks to its endowment.

He wanted a *divorce*. Now, after all these years, when he needed me more than ever, he was divorcing me. I wasn't sure I could go through with it, but . . . well, my eyes teared up every time I thought of it.

That thing men say when they're cheating . . . that their wives don't understand them. The real problem is, we do. And I did. John had said *divorce* to give me the last thing I wanted from him. When he'd taken my hand and said the words, something happened. He knew we'd failed at marriage, and he was letting me go.

Closure. They say you can never really have it, but here it was.

I wasn't sure if I was going to file the papers, but my

attorney had said we should discuss it. Financial reasons, that kind of thing.

Even if we did get divorced, I'd still look after him, of course. I wasn't the kind of person who'd turn her back on a sick man after fifty years, no matter what he'd done.

We visited Rose Hill, and John hadn't wanted to leave. It was a beautiful facility, and when I saw LeVon, I started to cry.

"I'm so glad he's coming here," LeVon said, hugging me. "I'll get to see you all the time." Gosh, what a comfort that was!

Janet was there, too, since she visited her brother four or five times a week. John's face lit up when he saw her, and I had to shake my head. Leave it to that old dog to find another woman, even in his current state.

But I was grateful. I didn't have someone else, of course, and I didn't even know if I would ever want that. But for the first time in decades, I felt like my husband had really seen me and understood me.

LeVon had suggested easing John into life at Rose Hill, so one night, just before Memorial Day weekend and the big town anniversary, I drove John up there and got him settled, then left. It was harder than I expected, coming back to my quiet, lovely house.

I went out on the patio and thought maybe I'd call the girls, but then decided against it. Juliet had her own family, and I'd just seen her two nights ago at her place. Besides, this is what the future would look like. Quiet and peaceful, maybe a little bit lonely. But beautiful, too, out here on the patio, a glass of wine in my hand.

"You home?" came Caro's voice.

"On the patio," I called.

"I brought wine."

"I already have some, but grab yourself a glass, hon."

She came out a minute later and sat next to me. "How are you? Did it go all right at Rose Hill?"

"Oh, sure. He seems to like it there a lot."

"But how are you, Barb?"

I smiled, feeling tears prick my eyes just a little bit. "Doing good. How about you? I feel like we haven't talked about you in ages."

She sighed and settled back. "Ted and I are done for good now."

"Is that right? What happened?"

She shrugged. "Is it callous of me to say I don't know and don't care enough to analyze it? We didn't have anything to say to each other these past few years, and I thought, why am I bothering? It's not like we're married."

"Is he sad?"

"No. He's dating a forty-eight-year-old."

"Oh, that's just gross, now."

"Tell me about it." She sighed. "I might get a condo, Barb. The house seems so big these days."

"Move in with me."

She smiled. "That'd be so much fun, wouldn't it?"

I sat up straighter. "Caro. Move in with me."

She shifted to face me. "Don't you want to be alone?" she asked. "After all this time? Date somebody, maybe? Join Tinder? Get laid?"

I laughed. "Does that sound like me?" I thought a minute. "I've been thinking a lot about marriage these days, Caro. What it means, what love is, commitment, all that."

"Sure you have. It's been a rough few months."

"The thing is . . . well, I'm not a lesbian, you know? I don't think so, anyway. No, I'm not. You're beautiful, of course, don't take it personally."

She threw back her head and laughed.

My throat grew tight. I always loved her laugh, her smile, those dimples and the way her eyes crinkled, making her look forty years younger. "Caro, I think you're the love of my life. No one's been there for me like you have. You're the best friend I ever had, the person I can really talk to. You can make me laugh at everything, even my husband cheating on me." I reached over and took her hand. "I can't think of anything nicer than us sharing a house."

"I *have* always loved your house more than mine," she said. "You know what? I'll think about it. We could do it on a trial basis, maybe. Let me run it past my boys and see what they think."

"That sounds great."

We kept holding hands, listening to the birds as they sang their evening songs, sipping our wine.

"The love of your life, huh?" she said.

"Well, it's sure not John."

She laughed. "Then I guess you're the love of mine, too."

"Girl power, as the kids say," I said.

"Friends till the end."

"I do love you."

She squeezed my hand. "I love you, too." She clinked her glass against mine. "Here's to housemates. Who cares what the boys think? I'm bringing my purple chair, though."

"You better. I love that chair."

We chatted until it grew dark and the mosquitoes found us, and then moved inside.

Life partner. Longtime companion. Cherished friend. Such beautiful words.

Love didn't have to be romantic to encircle you in its arms. It didn't have to make your heart race or your toes curl. Love could be just this, the sound of laughter on a warm night, the absolute comfort of being exactly who you were with the person who knew you inside and out.

~

CHAPTER FORTY

Juliet

She'd thought she would hate being the one in charge of the details, the legalities, the administration. She was wrong. It was completely different when it was a thing of your own.

Frost/Alexander opened three weeks after Juliet quit, the week before Memorial Day. Arwen and Juliet might never be friends, but they were a good team—Arwen giving the firm some buzz, Juliet backing that up with her reputation. They hired three other architects on a trial basis and already had six clients. Smaller projects than airport wings and Dubai skyscrapers, but they were just getting started.

The offices were in Mystic, so Juliet could be closer to home. DJK Architects had been housed in a sleek and stark building; Frost/Alexander occupied a four-story Victorian with stained glass and beautiful bookcases. She hired Noah to put in new windows and fix the front porch, but they were already working there. Arwen was moving from her loft in New Haven, and Juliet had recommended a real estate agent. Kathy was spending two weeks in Napa before starting.

"Kathy is a little miffed that you're senior partner," Arwen had told her over dinner. "But so be it. We needed your experience. And I have to be honest. You have balls, telling me your name goes first." She raised an eyebrow. "I respect that."

"Good," Juliet said. "I respect you, too, Arwen, striking out on your own so young. You're a very impressive person."

"Let's order a bottle of champagne," Arwen said. "To celebrate ourselves and each other."

"Maybe we should wait for when Kathy can join us."

"We can order it then, too," Arwen said. She waved the waiter over. "Bring us a bottle of your best champagne," she said.

"Mind the budget," Juliet murmured.

"Bring us a bottle of your cheapest champagne," Arwen amended, and they laughed. And cheap champagne . . . hey. It's not awful.

A few days later, Kathy showed up at Juliet's house around dinnertime. "I need to talk to you," she said tightly.

"Sure. Come on in and say hi to Oliver and the girls." She led Kathy up to the kitchen.

"Hi, Kathy," Sloane said, the friendlier child. So much like Sadie.

"Hi, Kathy," Brianna echoed, barely looking up from her math homework. *Just like I used to be*, she thought, smiling.

"Kathy!" Oliver said. "How lovely to see you! Shall I fix you a drink, then?"

Dear Oliver. So oblivious sometimes. Kathy's face was

already blotchy with anger, and she ignored him. Instead, she jammed her hands on her hips and glared at Juliet. *Here we go*, Juliet thought. *Women tearing other women down.* She tilted her head, waiting.

"How *dare* you move in on my company?" Kathy said, ignoring the fact that the girls were at the table and now gawping at her. "This was mine! *I* was supposed to be Arwen's partner! What did you tell her? How did you weasel your way in?"

"She asked me," Juliet said, her voice calm.

"To *work* for us. Not to be one of us! Senior partner? That's ridiculous! I didn't agree to that!"

Juliet raised her eyebrow (she could again, thank God, since the Botox had worn off). "That will be a problem, then, since Arwen and I can outvote you."

"You *bitch*. You've always had to be the star," Kathy said. "You think your shit doesn't stink, and you—"

"Shut up!" Brianna barked. "How dare you talk to my mother like that! She's one of the best architects in the country, for one, and for two, this is our house. You should leave now."

"Yeah," Sloane added. "Get out. You're mean. And quite rude."

Oh, that *feeling*. That feeling! Pride and warmth and love and surprise. Her girls, defending her from a bully. "Thank you, my darlings."

"My daughters have a completely valid point, Kathy," Oliver said. "I'll walk you out."

"I'll do it, honey," she said, but Kathy was already striding out on her own, hissing like an old radiator. Juliet caught up to her on the driveway as Kathy yanked open the door of her little MINI Cooper.

"Kathy, wait. Why are you upset? We've worked so well together all these years."

Kathy stopped and turned, jamming her fists on her hips. "Jesus, Juliet. I wanted to get away from *you*. You think you've struggled with Arwen being the golden girl for the past two years? Oh, you're too superior to admit it, but I knew. Well, try that for fifteen years."

Juliet blinked. "We do entirely different things, Kathy."

"Really? I had no idea. Please, lecture me."

"I honestly don't understand the problem."

"Well, it's not my job to educate you. Just think about this. I've worked with Arwen since she got here. I coached her and whispered in her ear about how good she was and got her half of those interviews so that she'd do exactly what she did. Leave and take me with her. But instead, you just step in at the last second and somehow get your name on the door. It was supposed to be Alexander Walker."

"Not according to Arwen." She looked at Kathy, who suddenly seemed a little pathetic with her cherry-red hair and painful high heels. "I think you underestimated her. Maybe she worked you a little bit, too."

"You both went behind my back."

"No, Kathy. If you can't hold your own, don't blame someone else. I gave Arwen my terms, and she accepted them. Clearly, she was in the position to make those decisions. Now. If your tantrum is over, I'd like you to stay with us. If it's not, we'll have to part ways." And get a new partner, probably. Brett, maybe. Or Elena.

"I've already talked to Dave about coming back."

"Then I wish you the best." All those lunches together, all those conversations, watching each other's kids grow up . . . it had meant something to Juliet. Quite a lot. But not to Kathy, apparently, because she just snorted and got into her car. Juliet watched as she sped down the street.

"I never really liked her," Oliver said as she came back into the kitchen. He sensed her lingering sadness and put his arm around her.

"I never liked her, neither," said Sloane.

"Me neither," echoed Brianna. "She was always jealous of you, Mom."

Out of the mouths of tweens came wisdom . . . sometimes, at least. Juliet smiled at her oldest, and, a little miraculously, Brianna smiled back.

"I think we should go out for ice cream tonight," Juliet said, earning a cheer from both her girls.

Life was good. She and Oliver were better than ever, and that was saying something. The girls were wonderful, even if Brianna was still sulky and hormonal, and Sloane would probably go through that, too. Mom was going to have an easier life when Dad went to Rose Hill, and Dad . . . well, she hadn't forgiven her father. Maybe she never would. Maybe some things shouldn't be forgiven.

But being angry was too great a burden to carry, and Juliet felt it slip away, there in the warm sunshine of the May evening. She owned her own business. She and Arwen would find a new partner. She loved her husband and daughters, mother and sister. There would be grief and loss and conflict ahead, and she'd get through it all.

She was her mother's girl, after all.

CHAPTER FORTY-ONE

Sadie

Joy. That was the word my father had given me, pulled with such effort from the depths of his heart and mind. I knew it was his way of telling me I'd brought him joy, and yet, I'd been thinking it might have been more, too.

Maybe . . . maybe it was advice.

Ever since I left Stoningham at eighteen, I'd been looking for that moment when everything in my life came together the way I dreamed it would. It never had, though, had it? I liked teaching quite a bit, loved my little students, St. Catherine's, loved New York with all its treasures, felt a bit of pride that my couch paintings paid the bills. I'd created a good-enough life in New York. A solid life, a happy life.

But joy was a different animal, wasn't it?

Joy was a quiet night watching the sunset, stroking Pepper's silky ears, laughing at her antics. Joy was painting those damn skies. Talking with my nieces. Taking care of my dad. Sending my mom and sister to Boston. Joy was that moment when the dolphin and her mama had swum around my legs before speeding out to sea. Joy was walking through the streets of New York looking up, always up, at the beautiful architecture, the sky, breathing in the smell of the city, listening to the constant song of traffic and languages and feeling that surge of life, all that life, swirling around me.

Joy was being with Noah, from the first time I'd seen him with that beautiful baby strapped to his chest, to irritating him as he fixed my furnace, to walking through a shower of cherry blossoms with him, to finally kissing him again.

But as much as I loved Noah Pelletier, the fact remained that I didn't want the life he did. I didn't really know what life I *did* want, even now. A little of everything, whereas Noah wanted a lot of one thing. He wanted home, a partner who was always there, more kids, and who could blame him? Those were nice, good things to want.

I was pretty sure I didn't want those things. Oh, I loved my nieces, loved little Marcus even, loved hearing Mickey talk about the horrors and wonders of motherhood. But in my heart of hearts, I wasn't sure it was for me. My mother had once called me a butterfly, flitting to whatever bright thing caught my attention, and she wasn't wrong.

I just wasn't sure how to make a life around being a butterfly. I mean, those things didn't live real long, did they?

A few days after my meeting in New York, I went to the hardware store for some more plastic to patch up another hole in my roof. I turned down the aisle and there was Noah, studying a drill bit. He did a quick double take when he saw me.

"Hey," he said.

"Hi." My insides flooded with heat, my heart pulsing with that beautiful scarlet red only he could incite.

"How was New York?"

"Oh . . . it was . . . it didn't work out. My stuff wasn't what he was looking for."

"Then he's an idiot."

I snorted a little. "An idiot with a lot of influence."

He just looked at me a minute. "I'm sorry, Sadie."

"No, it's fine. It's nothing I haven't heard a hundred times before. Two hundred. Five, maybe. Anyway. How are you?"

"Good."

That seemed to be all. "Well," I said. "Nice to see you. Love you." *Shit.* "I do. I mean, you know that. Anyway. Have a good day."

I left before I made things worse, and went to see my dad.

He hadn't spoken again since that day. It was awfully hard, finally admitting he was the man in front of me, in a place I couldn't reach or see. Maybe he'd have another breakthrough, but I had a feeling he was done.

Rose Hill had space for him in their new wing. It was only a half hour away. Still, the tears slid down my face. I'd visit a lot.

"I'm thinking about staying in Stoningham, Dad," I said. His expression didn't change. "Maybe I can get a teaching job up here. Keep doing my couch paintings, pop down to the city once in a while, keep the apartment on Airbnb. I don't know. Maybe not Stoningham, since it would be hard to see Noah, you know? Maybe Mystic or Old Lyme."

I sighed. Even talking to myself, I couldn't make up my mind.

Hasan had told me what I'd always known. Those sky-scapes weren't all that special. Not to the New York art world. Any first-year art student could do them. They weren't even that hard, technically speaking.

"I'm not that good as an artist, Dad," I told him, and tears filled my eyes. He didn't answer, but I wedged my-self in the chair against him and put my head on his shoul-der. His arm came around me, just like old times, but for once—for the first time since his stroke—I didn't look for more. Sometimes an arm around you is all you need.

"Thanks, Daddy," I whispered, and there it was again. Joy, soft and quiet this time. My father loved me. It was May. I had a good dog and options in front of me. Joy would be the key to my life. Be in the places that made my heart sing, do the things that made me feel whole and fulfilled, spend time with the people who did the same. No more phoning it in, no more *good enough for now*. I would find a way to make a life based on joy, because re-ally. What if you fell off your bicycle one day and injured your brain?

"Thanks for the pep talk, Dad," I said, and maybe it was my imagination, but I thought he held me a little closer.

On Memorial Day weekend, Stoningham celebrated its 350th birthday. I had to hand it to Gillian, my mother and the scores of volunteers. It was beautiful.

We started the day with a parade. I brought Pepper, since she loved people, and she wagged joyfully at every person she saw. At the last minute, I'd found myself one of the volunteers—the person in charge of the nursery school float had had a meltdown over the responsibility of it all, and my mom recommended me to step in. It was right up my alley, after all. Kids. Art. Last-minute accomplishments.

There's something so tender about a small-town parade. The handful of Stoningham veterans, some of them so old, so noble, riding in a convertible, waving with a gnarled hand as the townspeople cheered and teared up. The National Guard volunteers, somber in their uniforms. My mom, looking beautiful in a blue pantsuit with a red scarf, and the other two selectmen. The town clergy—Rabbi Fierstein, whose daughter had been my bus buddy in grammar school; Reverend Bateman, who used to read *The Giving Tree* on Easter Sunday; the handsome Catholic priest.

Then came the kids. The 4-H club, the sailing club, the school music bands (including Brianna on trumpet). The Brownies, Sloane looking so stinking cute in her uniform, saying, "Hi, Auntie!" like she hadn't just seen me that morning.

Then came my float, bright as a garden, decorated in hundreds and hundreds of crepe paper flowers (not the vaginal kind), all the little kids wearing (or taking off) the beaks and wings I'd made out of papier-mâché. Damn cute. *Fly, Little Birds, Fly!* I'd written across the banner, making the letters out of their handprints. As I said, it was my groove.

I saw Noah, Mickey and Marcus across the street. Mickey waved, nudged Noah, and he waved, too.

We hadn't spoken since the hardware store run-in. I understood. His son needed stability. Noah needed stability, and I wasn't exactly that. Love was not all you needed. You needed to match, to fit, to want the same things. I had never wanted five kids. I wasn't sure I wanted any. I'd never really known what I wanted, except to be a painter.

But my heart hurt just the same, looking at him. I loved him, and I didn't make him happy, and that was an awful ache I didn't know how to fix. I petted Pepper to remind myself I wasn't alone in the world.

After the parade, the shops and businesses of Water Street hosted a sidewalk stroll, serving snacks and drinks, putting bowls of water out for doggies. Sheerwater, that splendid house the town now owned, was open all day, the garden club giving tours and hosting a high tea. There was a small regatta (we were Connecticut, after all). In the evening, there'd be the auction to raise money for scholarships.

I hung out with my nieces, letting Oliver and Jules go to the high tea so my brother-in-law could get his Brit fix. When the girls got hot and tired, we went to my parents' house for a little rest, and I parked them in my old room and put cool cloths on their heads, like my mom used to do for me when I was little.

"Rest, little ones," I said, and they both smiled, even though they were pretty big. Dad was asleep downstairs, back from his overnight at Rose Hill, Pepper curled up next to him, good pup that she was.

My father had never been a great husband. It didn't take a rocket scientist to know that. These past few weeks, I'd seen some looks exchanged between Mom and Jules, and overheard a few whispers.

It was dawning on me that my father may have had an affair. Honestly, I didn't want to know. It was a moot point now. He was still our dad. He'd released my mom from her duties, something she would never have done for herself.

I looked at him now, the old man who needed his eyebrows trimmed. "You're a good guy, Daddy," I said.

Maybe not the perfect man I'd once thought, but good enough. I could still love him, and he deserved that love.

Then I got the scissors and took care of those eyebrows.

That evening, Brianna, Sloane and I walked to the green for the auction, which was the crowning event of the weekend. Gillian was there, zipping around like a gerbil on speed, flitting to my mom every thirty seconds. I chatted with some of the women I'd met at Juliet's party— Emma London, Beth, Jamilah Finlay with the cute little boys. There were Jules and Oliver, holding hands. They had such a good thing going, those two. I was glad for my sister. Ollie got on my nerves from time to time, but honestly, if his greatest flaw was smiling too much, then he was pretty damn great. The girls cantered over to them.

"Hang out with us," Jules said.

"Nah. I'm feeling melancholy and want to brood," I said.

"You're so weird," Brianna said.

"Takes one to know one," I said, and she grinned. "See you guys later."

I found a spot under a tree where I could watch the auction. Some of the big-ticket items were grotesque, thanks to Stoningham's summer people trying to outdo each other. It was a good cause—college scholarships for low-income families—so God bless, but even so. *A week at our ten-bedroom house in Jackson Hole, butler included! Starting bid $2,500. Dinner with Lin-Manuel Miranda after a* Hamilton *show! Starting bid $5,000.* (I would totally bid on that one, had I any money to spare, but I really wanted a new roof.) *Design for an addition on your house, courtesy of Frost/Alexander Architecture, starting bid $7,500.*

I hadn't been asked to donate anything. The truth was, it would be embarrassing to offer up a painting that my sister would pity-buy.

"Hey, Sadie! Do you teach painting?" came a voice. It was Emma London.

"I do," I said. "You interested?"

"Oh, God, no. I mean, I've been kicked out of those paint and drink nights, you know? Stick figures is the best I can do." She smiled. "I was thinking of lessons for a little friend of mine. She's four and a little wild."

"Sure. I could do that. I used to teach elementary school art."

"Cool! Thanks, Sadie. Hey, there's my guy. The father of your potential student, Miller Finlay. Do you know him?"

Of course I did. Miller owned Finlay Construction, and Noah had done an internship with him in high school. We did the two degrees of separation Stoningham thrived on, and then they wandered off. Nice couple.

Bidding was pretty hot and heavy. Dinner with Lin-Manuel went for sixteen grand. Jeez.

Then I saw Noah. He was carrying a painting.

My painting.

The clouds I'd given him for Valentine's Day so long ago.

He set it on an easel and stepped back, and my chest felt sliced open.

The auctioneer looked at his notes. "Next up, folks, something that's not listed in your program. A Sadie Frost original oil painting. Very pretty. Sadie's the daughter of our first selectman, I believe. She works as a . . . a teacher, is that right? An art teacher! Great. Let's start the bidding at . . . a hundred dollars? A hundred dollars, can I have a hundred dollars, thank you, sir. A hundred and fifty, fifty, can I see a hundred and fifty, thank you, ma'am, two hundred, two hundred."

Noah was selling my painting. No. He was giving it away. He was tossing it. He was . . . shit, he was ditching it, because what was that phrase? It didn't spark joy.

He'd kept it all these years. He'd broken up with his fiancée over it, and now he was essentially throwing it in the junk pile, for a couple of hundred dollars, no less.

I got up to leave, tears blurring my vision. Jesus. Why not just burn down my house or stab me in the throat? At least that would've been a little less public.

"Three hundred, three hundred, thank you, can I have four? Four, please?"

"Where are you going?" Mom asked, suddenly at my side.

"I'm . . . gonna see Dad."

"That's your painting, honey!"

"I know."

"You have to stay. Don't be silly, flouncing off." She took my hand, anchoring me to the spot.

"Four fifty, four hundred and fifty, thank you, ma'am."

Noah was still standing at the front, just off to the side of my painting, staring right at me.

Something was happening. I wasn't a hundred percent sure what, but that red flare was burning in my heart, and his dark eyes didn't leave me.

"One thousand, please, one thousand," the auctioneer said. "Thank you, sir, very nice, can I have fifteen hundred?"

"I wish I could bid on it, sweetheart. It's so pretty," Mom said.

"That's okay, Mom," I said. But it was a nice thought.

Maybe the first time she'd sincerely praised my work without telling me how impractical it was.

"Two thousand, two thousand to the gentleman in the blue shirt. Do I hear three, three thousand, three, thank you, going to four now . . ."

People—strangers, even—were bidding on my painting. Bidding quite a lot. I didn't know whether to laugh or cry. That was Noah's painting. Noah's.

"This is so cool!" Juliet had come over to Mom and me. "Can you believe it, Sadie?"

"Ten thousand dollars, thank you, sir, can I have eleven, eleven thousand for a Sadie Frost original oil, thank you, ma'am, do I hear twelve?"

Holy crap. That was double my most expensive couch painting.

Something was happening, all right.

Noah left the stage and came walking through the crowd, his eyes never leaving my face.

"Fifteen thousand, fifteen, thank you, sir, can I get seventeen, seventeen thousand . . ."

He was here, right in front of me. "You're giving away my painting," I whispered.

He nodded. "I wanted you to see how beautiful it is. That guy in New York doesn't know anything."

"But it's yours." My lips trembled a little.

"So you'll make me another." He slipped behind me and whispered in my ear. "Look at this, Sadie. Look at that painting and how many people want it. It's beautiful. It makes people happy. *You* do that, Special."

"It's for a good cause," I murmured, hypnotized by the auction.

"Eh," Juliet said. "Dinner with Lin-Manuel went for less than that."

"Gosh, this is exciting," Mom said. "Oh, the Stanleys just bid twenty grand, Sadie! Honey! I'm so proud of you!"

I started to cry.

"Maybe we should subtly drift away, Mom," Juliet said.

"Why? Do you . . . Oh, okay. Not too far, though. You okay, hon?" she asked me.

I nodded, wiping my eyes.

"Going once for twenty-two thousand . . . going twice . . . last chance to bid on this magnificent Sadie Frost original . . . sold to the man in the blue shirt!"

The crowd burst into applause.

Noah turned me around and kept his hands on my shoulders. His big, warm, manly hands. "Sadie, I've looked at that painting every day since you gave it to me. It's part of me."

"Then why'd you put it up for sale?"

"Because I wanted to show what you do. How beautiful your paintings are. I'm not the only one who sees it."

"But you won't have it anymore." A little sob popped out, and I covered my mouth.

"That's okay. That was the old us. That painting has tortured me for years now, reminding me that I've only ever loved you."

"Well, you're quite a masochist then, hanging it in your house. You could've just burned it."

"Absolutely not. Being mad at you was better than not having you at all. It was a way to see you every day. But, Special, I can't do that anymore. I can't keep you, and I can't let go of you again. I love you. I love that you're a painter. What you do is important and beautiful and . . . and magic. You just saw that. If you need to be in New

York, I understand. We can make it work. I want to make it work. I've been in love with you since I was fifteen. I'm not gonna wreck that again."

I seemed to be crying. Nope. Definitely crying. My mother and sister watched, smiling.

"I don't want five children," I said. "I don't know if I want any."

"I already have the world's greatest kid, and he has the world's greatest mother."

"I live in a crooked house that hasn't passed inspection."

"I can fix that. Or you can marry me and live in my house."

"I have a place in New York." I dashed a hand across my eyes.

"You can spend as much time there as you want. I'll even come visit when you want."

"Did you . . . did you just propose?"

"Yes. For the third time, I might add."

He was smiling.

"Are you sure, Noah?" I whispered.

He dropped down on one knee, and the folks around us cooed. A few people whipped out their phones. "Home is where you are, Sadie. I shouldn't have tried to make everything fit how I wanted it. Marry me. Be my son's stepmother. Be my wife. Go to New York if you need to, but come home to me, Sadie Frost. I love you with everything I have."

I looked down into his dark, dark eyes. They were full of love and happiness and . . . certainty.

"Third time's the charm, then," I said. "Yes, Noah Pelletier, I will marry you."

I kissed him then, threading my fingers through his

curly hair, feeling so much love, so much joy. My father's word to me was the key to everything.

Home had never been a place. Noah, my wild boy, *was* my home, my heart, my joy. Part of me had always known it, and now I would stake my claim and build from here.

Barb

Two years after he moved into Rose Hill, John died. In bed. With Janet.

They hadn't had a sexual relationship, she told me. They just liked sleeping together. I believed her. It was nice to think that he died next to a woman he loved, who loved him as he was, and had never known him any other way.

So I was a widow now. I never had divorced him. Just couldn't bring myself to sign the final papers. I had Caro, who'd moved in almost as soon as I asked her to. I hadn't known life could be so happy and fun, so free. I didn't need a divorce, wasn't interested in dating. I'd won another term as first selectman, and so I had at least two years more of working, and that was wonderful.

Juliet and Oliver were better than ever, and Brianna and Sloane were the lights of my life. I still saw them a few times a week, but . . . well, things had changed a little bit. Juliet was still my darling girl, but she had come into her own. She was more relaxed now, and I had to admit, she didn't need me as much as she used to. That was just fine. That was wonderful, in fact. The girls were putting them through their paces, and she was handling it like a real champ. Her firm was going gangbusters, and gosh, I was proud.

Noah and Sadie had gotten married about a month after the art auction. Just a little backyard affair here, at my house, with Caro officiating, since she was a justice of the peace. Brianna and Sloane were her bridesmaids, and Noah's parents came down from Ottawa. Nice people. Even Sadie's little dog got to come, and ate some cake before it was time, but we just cut it from the other side.

Now, too, I had little Marcus, who called me Nana and often came running into the town hall to give me a hug when Noah was there, filing paperwork with the building department. Mickey was a hoot and a holler, and she was a regular at our family gatherings. She loved to tease Caro and me about being lesbian wannabes, and we'd laugh so much at her comments.

Sadie had made good on her promise to flip that little house of hers. Granted, her sister was an architect and her husband was a carpenter, but she did most of the work herself, and it was quite the little charmer when it was finished. Her friend Carter and his husband bought it and called it their country house and often had lovely parties there. Caro and I were always invited.

Sadie had started an art gallery here in Stoningham. The Frost Gallery. It had her own pieces and some sculptures and photos by other artists, too. The summer folks gobbled it up. Another way our name was growing. Frost/ Alexander, now the Frost Gallery. Sadie lived with Noah most of the time, though she'd flit off to the city for a few days here, a week there. She was a little bird, my daughter, always flying somewhere, but always coming back. Sometimes Noah would go to New York with her, and Caro and I would petition to take Marcus for a night or two, letting him stay in the bathtub till his fingers were pruney, then cuddling him and reading to him, kissing his dark curls.

The garden club had proposed an area at Sheerwater to be named after me. The garden would have all the types of flowers that bloomed when the weather was still cold—the Frost Garden. It was quite an honor, and I was so proud of my girls, and myself, and our name—we Frost women were an impressive lot.

When John died, I was sadder than I expected to be. I knew it was coming; those little strokes had chipped away at him, but now that he was really gone, I kept remembering snippets of our marriage that I'd forgotten.

There was one morning during the infertility years after I'd had an awful night. Cried in the little bathroom in the Cranston house and ran the tap so John wouldn't hear me, since there was nothing he could do. I'd been embarrassed about being so sad over something I couldn't control. Sad again, sad every month, and I knew it had to wear at him, the feeling of helplessness, so I kept it to myself as best I could.

But the next morning, he'd made me French toast with powdered sugar, my favorite. We'd had it on our honeymoon—the first time in my life I'd had French toast, and I was so delighted with the powdered sugar and the sliced-up strawberries, John had laughed at my happiness.

And then there it was, on a regular morning when we both had to go to work. French toast and warm maple syrup, powdered sugar and sliced strawberries.

I hadn't thought of that since it happened, but now, those kinds of memories were slipping in.

Love isn't always the thing that fills up the room, or your heart. Sometimes, it's what sneaks into the in-between spaces. I never thought the love of my life would be my best friend. I never expected to get to the point where I found Sadie's butterfly life to be so enjoyable to watch. I never knew I'd get to have a grandson who wasn't technically mine, or that my family would grow to include the lesbian baby mama of my son-in-law, or the woman who was in bed with my husband when he died.

But here we all are.

I wouldn't have it any other way.

Always the
Last to Know

Kristan Higgins

Questions for Discussion

1. Relationships take a lot of compromise, and we can see Noah demonstrating this when he tries to live in New York for Sadie. Sadie also compromises, telling him to go back home when it's clear he's unhappy in the city she loves. For the sake of their relationship, do you think Sadie should have compromised the lifestyle she always wanted, or do you agree that they were too young at that point to make such large sacrifices?

2. What is the right time to adjust your dreams for someone else? The author makes no secret that Sadie and Noah love each other, but neither feels at home in the other's world. Do you think one of them should have bent a little more, or do you think they made the right choices? (Also, how unromantic were Noah's marriage proposals?)

3. Were you surprised with Barb's decision in the end, despite everything that happened and went wrong in her and John's marriage? Why do you think she chose what she did? What do you think about her view on marriage as opposed to what John's actions told us about his?

4. Juliet has a memorable visit to a plastic surgeon. We've all felt the pressure to look or act a certain way because of our age or what society deems appropriate or good. Can you think of a particular circumstance in which this happened? How did you handle it?

5. Have you ever felt the way Juliet did: that the window was closing on your chances, or that you'd aged out of an opportunity? What did you think of Arwen? Is she arrogant or just confident? Juliet is careful never to stoop to gossiping or complaining about Arwen, yet her confusion is obvious. Have you been in a similar situation?

6. How could both John and Barb have done things differently to understand each other and keep their marriage happy? They're not happy for a long time, but do you think they're just accustomed to the status quo? Do you know any long-married couples who seem to be getting things right? What are some keys to a long, happy relationship, or is that a myth?

7. One of the many types of relationships we see in this novel is the coparenting relationship between Noah and Mickey. Though they aren't romantically involved, their relationship is one of the most functional partnerships in the book. How do you think they make it work? Do you think this kind of relationship could work for you?

8. The theme of not being good enough is prevalent in this book, including feelings of not being a good

mom, partner or artist. Can you relate to any of the insecurities that the characters feel? Do you tackle these insecurities head-on or ignore them and hope better days are ahead? Everyone feels insecure or inadequate at some point in their lives. What are some positive ways to deal with that?

9. Caro and Barb have such a close, loving and unconditional friendship that truly makes them soul mates. How does it differ from Barb's relationship with John? What do you think are the key factors that brought Caro and Barb together and make their relationship work? How are the women different, and how are they the same? Who is your oldest or closest friend? What makes your friendship special?

10. Do you think reading John's perspective throughout the book made you a little more forgiving toward him? How might you have felt had the author decided to include only the Frost women's points of view?

11. In what ways do Juliet and her daughters' relationships reflect her own mother's relationships with Juliet and Sadie? What do you think of Juliet and Barb as mothers? If you're a mother yourself, have you struggled with one child more than another?

12. The Frost women are quite different from one another. To whom do you relate the most? Can you see yourself in all of them?

Keep reading for an excerpt from
Kristan Higgins's next novel . . .

Pack Up the Moon

Available Summer 2021 from Berkley

Was it weird to look for your wife at her funeral?

But he was. He kept glancing around for Lauren, waiting for her to come in and tell him what to say to all these people, what to do during this service. Where to put his hands. How to hug back.

She would know. That was the problem. She *knew* all about these things—people, for example. How to act out in the world. At her wake last night, she would've told him what to say as her friends cried and held on to his hand and hugged him, making him uncomfortable and stiff and sweaty. Classic spectrum problem. He didn't like crowds. Didn't want to hug anyone except his wife. Who was dead.

She would've told him what to wear today. As it was, he was wearing the one suit he owned. The same one he'd worn to propose to her, the same one he wore to their wedding three years ago. Was it a horrible thing to wear your wedding suit to your wife's funeral? Should he have gone with a different tie? Was this suit bringing shit up for her mother and sister?

This pew was hard as granite. He hated wooden chairs. Pews. Whatever.

Donna, Lauren's mother, sobbed. The sound echoed through the church. Same church where Josh and Lauren had gotten married. If they'd had kids, would they have baptized them here? Josh was pretty much an atheist, but if Lauren had wanted church as a part of their life, he'd have gone along with it.

Except she was dead.

It had been four days. One hundred and twelve hours and twenty-three minutes since Lauren died, give or take some seconds. The longest time of his life, and also like five seconds ago.

Lauren's sister, Jen, was giving the eulogy. It was probably a good eulogy, because people laughed here, cried there. Josh himself couldn't quite make out the words. He stared at his hands. When Lauren had put his wedding ring on his finger at their wedding, he couldn't stop looking at it. His hand looked complete with that ring on. Just a plain gold band, but it said something about him. Something good and substantial. He wasn't just a man . . . he was a husband.

Rather, he *had been* a husband. Now he was a widower. Utterly useless.

So much for being a biomedical engineer with numerous degrees and a reputation in health care technology. He'd had two years and one month to find a cure for idiopathic pulmonary fibrosis, a disease that slowly filled the lungs with scar tissue, choking off the healthy parts for breathing. He had failed. Not that a cure was easy, or someone would've done it before. The only devices on the market were designed to push air into lungs, work chest muscles or clear mucus, and those weren't Lauren's problems.

He hadn't figured it out. He hadn't created something or found a drug trial that would kill off those fucking fibers and scars. Since the day of her diagnosis, he'd devoted himself to finding something that would save his wife. Not just slow the disease down—they had those meds; she'd been on them, plus two experimental drugs, plus the Chinese herbs and traditional medicine, plus an organic diet with no red meat.

No. Josh's job had been to find—or make—something that would *cure* her. Restore her. Keep her.

He had not done so.

A large picture of her was placed on the altar. It had been taken on their trip to Paris just before Christmas that first year they were married. Before they knew. Her red hair blew back from her face, and her smile was so full of fun and love and joy. He stared at that picture now, still stunned that he'd gotten to marry her. She was way out of his league.

The first time they'd met, he'd insulted her.

Thank *God* he'd gotten another chance. Not that God existed. Otherwise, she'd still be alive. Who the hell took someone like her at age twenty-eight? A merciful God? Fuck that.

It didn't seem possible that she was gone forever. No. It seemed like Lauren, who had enjoyed childlike tricks such as hiding in the shower and jumping out at him as he brushed his teeth, could pull off the biggest trick of all— jump out from behind the altar and say, "Boo! Just kidding, babe!" then laugh and hug him and tell him she had just been testing him these past few years. She'd never been sick at all.

Then again, she'd already been cremated.

Apparently, Jen was done, because she came down from the altar of the church and stood before him.

"Thank you, Jen," he said woodenly. His mother, sitting beside him, gave him a nudge, and he stood up and hugged his sister-in-law. Former sister-in-law? That didn't seem fair. He *liked* being related to Jen and her husband, Darius, not to mention their two kids. He even almost liked Donna, his mother-in-law who, after a shitty start, had been great at the end there. When Lauren was actively dying.

Now, his wife was ashes inside a baggie in a metal container. He was waiting for the special urn to arrive from California, at which point he would mix her with an organic soil mix. He'd plant a tree in the bamboo urn, and Lauren would become a dogwood tree. Cemeteries were unsustainable, if beautiful, she'd said. "Besides, who wouldn't want to be a tree? Better than compost."

He could almost hear her voice.

Everyone began filing out of the church. Josh waited, being at the front of the church. His mom slid her arm through his. "Hang in there, honey," she whispered. He nodded. They both watched as Ben and Sumi Kim, his mother's best friends and next-door neighbors, went to the altar and stood in front of Lauren's picture. Ben bowed from the waist, then knelt on the floor and pressed his forehead to the floor, then rose and bowed again while Sumi sobbed gently.

Josh had to cover his eyes for a minute at the reverence, the heartache in that gesture. Lauren had loved the Kims, who were essentially Josh's second parents. Ben was the closest thing to a father he'd ever had. Of course Lauren had loved them. She had loved most people, and they had all loved her right back.

The Kims came over, hugged him. Josh stood there with the three adults who'd raised him, all helpless now in the face of his loss.

No one could help him.

"You'll get through this, son," Ben said, looking him in the eye. "I know it seems like you won't, but you will."

Josh nodded. Ben wasn't the type to lie. Ben gripped his shoulders and nodded back. "You're not alone in this, Josh."

Well. That was a nice thought, but of course he was alone. His wife was dead.

"Shall we head out, then?" the older man asked. Like his mother, Ben was good at giving Josh the cues he often needed in social situations. Not as good as Lauren, though.

Panic flashed painfully through his joints. What was he going to do without her?

"Let's go, honey," his mom said.

Right. He hadn't answered. "Okay," he said. It felt wrong, somehow, leaving the church. Ending the funeral.

There was a lunch after the service. So many flowers, despite Lauren's wish that in lieu of, there'd be donations for the Hope Center, Lauren's favorite place in Providence, her hometown. Her workmates from Pearl Churchwell Harris, the architectural firm where she'd worked as a public space designer, were all here: Bruce, who'd been such a great boss to Lauren, crying as if he'd lost his own child. Santino and Louise, who'd gone on walks with Lauren to keep her lung capacity up. That shitty Lori Cantore, who'd asked if she could have Lauren's office *two years ago*. Such a vulture, coming to the funeral when she'd been a pill in real life. He imagined grabbing her scrawny arm and dragging her out, but he didn't want to make her the center of attention. This was Lauren's funeral, after all.

And there were so many of Lauren's friends—Asmaa from the community center; Sarah, her best friend from childhood; Mara from RISD; Creepy Charlotte, the single woman who lived on the first floor of their building, and, Josh was almost sure, had been making a play for him since they'd met, wife or no wife. People from Lauren's childhood, high school and college, teachers, classmates, the principal of Lauren's grammar school.

Some people even came for Josh, having read Lauren's obituary. Not exactly his friends . . . he didn't have many of those. Lauren had been his friend. His best friend. Her family had welcomed him, but he was really just a phantom limb at this point. An amputation without her.

A short, stout woman with steel-gray curls came up to him. "I'm sorry for your loss," she said. Her voice was familiar. He glanced at his mother, who gave a small shrug.

"Uh . . . how did you know Lauren?" he asked.

"I don't. I work for you. I'm Cookie Goldberg. Your virtual assistant."

"Oh! Hi. Uh . . . right." Cookie lived in New York. Long Island. They'd never met face-to-face, though he'd seen her on Zoom and Skype often enough.

"Yeah, well, I'm . . . shit. I'm so sorry for you, Joshua. My heart is breaking for you." Her raspy voice cracked, and she looked a little shocked at her own words. "Okay. I got a long drive home. Call me if you need anything."

She turned and left.

"She works for you, but you didn't recognize her? You only have one employee, Josh," his mother chided gently.

"She's out of context," he said, sitting back down.

He didn't eat, or maybe he did. Darius, Jen's husband, got him a glass of wine, forgetting that Josh didn't drink. Eventually, Josh got to hold Octavia. Was she still his niece? He was her dead aunt's widowed husband. Did he still get to claim her and Sebastian? Was he still Uncle Josh?

Sebastian, age four, wailed, inconsolable despite Darius's best efforts. The kid was just old enough to understand Auntie Lauren was never coming back. Josh envied him. No stiff upper lip there. He was crying the way Josh wanted to, unfettered, anguished, horrified.

"Call if you need anything," said Creepy Charlotte, her pale blue eyes eerie. She handed him a piece of paper. Her phone number, he assumed. As she moved in to hug him, Josh stuck out his hand at the same time. Awkward. Lauren would've fixed it so it would've been funny, but it stayed awkward. Charlotte lifted an eyebrow, but Josh wasn't sure how to interpret that. He took the paper and put it in his pocket, then sat back down, but the paper rankled. It felt like betrayal, so he wadded it up and tossed it under the table with a silent apology to the cleaning staff. *Those people*, he pictured them saying. *Throwing trash on the ground like animals.*

He bent over and looked for it. "What are you doing?" his mother hissed.

"Stephanie," he heard a woman say. "I'm *so* sorry! She was a lovely girl. Um . . . where's Joshua?"

The wad was just out of reach. He stretched, heard his chair fall over behind him, grabbed the paper and stood up. Righted the chair. "Hi," he said to his mother's friend.

"Joshua, you remember Nina, right? From the lab?"

His mother had worked at Rhode Island Hospital's lab

for thirty years. He didn't remember this woman. "Yes," he lied, shaking her hand.

She pulled him in for a hug, and he winced. "So sorry for your loss, honey," she said.

"Thank you." He stood there another minute, then turned and went to the bathroom to throw out the paper. He didn't want Creepy Charlotte's number, or anyone's number. He just wanted his wife not to be dead.

The face in the mirror was nearly unrecognizable. He lifted his hand to make sure he was really there. This had to be a dream, right? Groping under a table for a piece of paper, all these people he didn't quite know . . . next thing would be he wouldn't have any clothes on, and then he'd wake up next to his wife. He'd hold her close and breathe in the smell of her hair and she'd smile without opening her eyes.

But he was still in the bathroom, looking at the face in the mirror.

Sarah, Lauren's best friend, was waiting for him when he came out. "You okay?"

"No."

"Me neither." Her eyes were wet. She took his hand and squeezed it. "This is a fucking nightmare."

"Yep."

"Did you eat anything?"

"Yes," he said, though he couldn't remember.

Sarah walked him back to his table. People spoke to him. Some of them cried.

Josh stared at the table. He may have responded to the people who talked to him. It didn't really matter, though, did it?

Sometime later, Darius drove him home to the old mill

building turned condos. "Want me to come in, buddy?" he asked in the parking lot.

"No, no. I . . . I think I want to be alone."

"Got it. Listen, Josh, I'm here for you, okay? Anytime, night or day. We married sisters. We're family forever. Brothers."

Josh nodded. Darius was very tall and had rich chocolate-brown skin, so Josh doubted anyone would mistake them for brothers, but it was a nice thought. "Thanks, Darius."

"This really sucks, man." His voice broke. "I'm so sorry. She was . . . she was a peach."

"Yes."

"I'll text you tomorrow. Try to get some sleep, okay?"

"Yes. Thank you."

He went up the stairs, his legs heavy. For the past six days, he'd been staying at his mom's house, glad for the familiar comfort of his childhood home, the smells and furniture. Lauren, whose own mother was a bit of a drama queen, had welcomed his mother's calm ways, understood her devotion to her only child, admired Stephanie for raising him alone. Lauren was more than a daughter-in-law to his mom; she was the daughter Stephanie never had.

Had been. She had been.

Jesus. He had to change tenses now. He unlocked the apartment door and went inside. He hadn't been here since Lauren was hospitalized . . . when was that? Six days ago? Eight? A lifetime.

The island lights shone gently, and the lamp by the reading chair was on low. Someone had been here. The place was immaculate. The pillows were plumped on the couch, pillows Lauren had bought. A bouquet of yellow tulips sat on the kitchen island, smack in the middle, obscenely cheerful. The blankets that Lauren had used, since she was always cold, were folded, one draped over the back of the couch.

It was so quiet.

Pebbles, their goofy Australian shepherd mutt, had been staying with Jen since Lauren's hospitalization; Josh had forgotten to ask for her back. Well. Another day wouldn't matter.

Josh went into the bedroom. Lauren's medical stuff—her at-home oxygen, her percussion vest—was gone. Josh had agreed to that, he remembered vaguely. Donate the stuff to someone in need or something. The pill bottles that had sat on her night table, the Vicks VapoRub . . . those were gone, too.

Idiopathic pulmonary fibrosis. Twelve syllables of doom. A disease for which there was no cure. A disease that usually hit older people but, occasionally, chose a young person to invade. A disease that had a life expectancy of three to five years.

Lauren had gotten the shorter end of that.

Their bed was made perfectly, same as Lauren used to make it, before the small task took too much out of her. He always tried to make it as precisely as she did and never quite managed, something that made her smile. The cute, useless little flowered pillows were in place.

It was as if she'd just been here.

Josh grabbed some jeans and an MIT sweatshirt and changed into them. In the kitchen, he pulled the tulips out of their vase and threw them in the trash, then dumped the water and tossed the vase in the recycling bin. He gathered up his suit, shirt, socks, even his boxers, and carried them up to the rooftop garden that had come with this apartment. For once, he didn't think about how much he hated heights. The bite of cold, damp air was welcome.

A seagull sat on one of the posts of the iron railing that encircled the garden, watching him, its feathers ruffling in the breeze.

He turned on the gas grill, all burners, as high as they'd go.

Then he burned the clothes he'd worn to his wife's funeral, and stood there long after they were ash and the snow had begun to fall.